THE COLLECTED STORIES

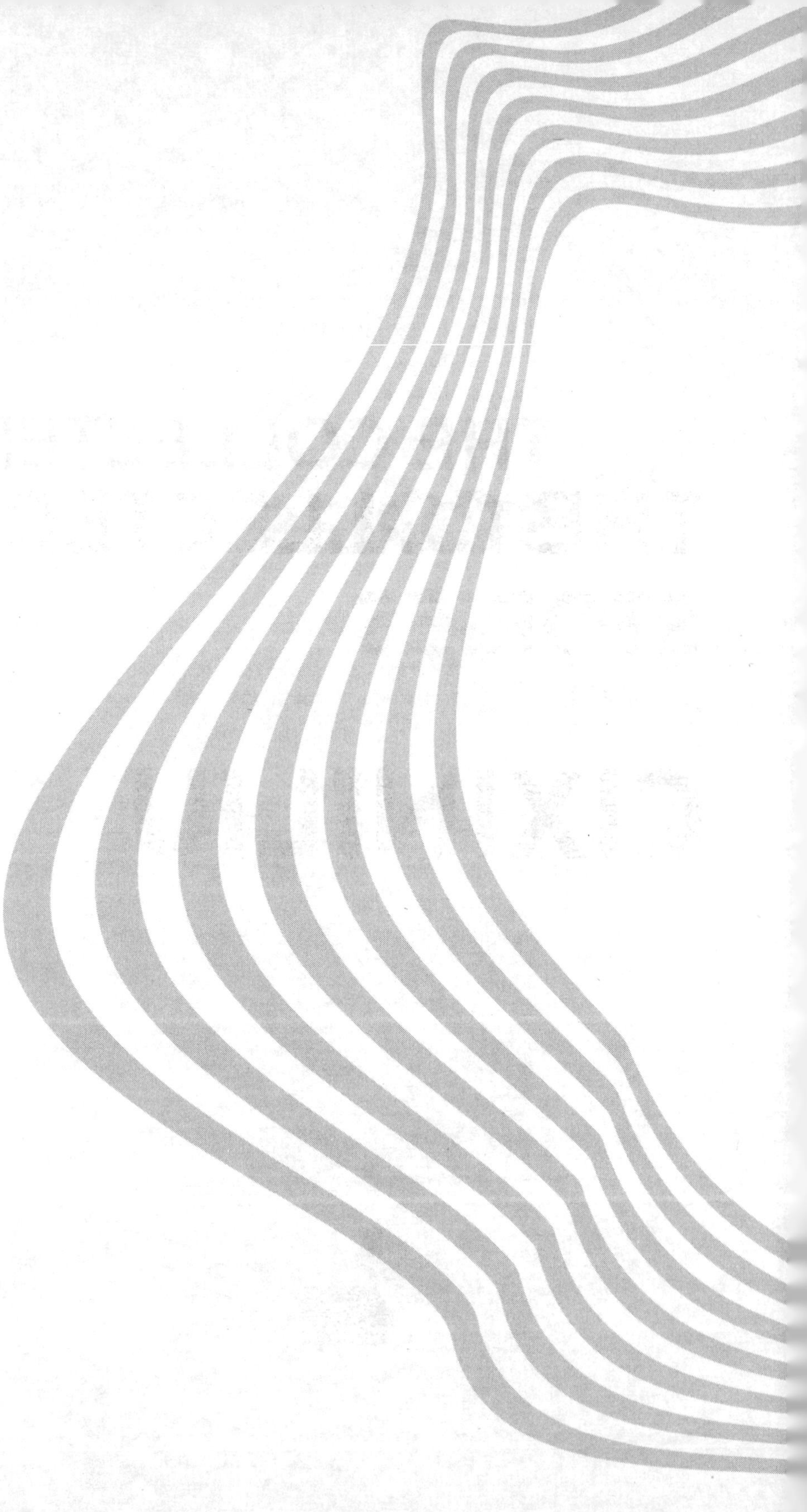

THE COLLECTED STORIES

CIXIN 刘慈欣 LIU

HEAD of ZEUS

An Ad Astra Book

First published in the UK in 2025 by Head of Zeus Ltd,
part of Bloomsbury Publishing Plc

9 7 5 3 1 2 4 6 8

A catalogue record for this book is available from the British Library.

ISBN (HB): 9781035903931
ISBN (EBOOK): 9781035903924

Cover design: Jessie Price
Typeset by Ed Pickford

Printed and bound in Great Britain by
CPI Group (UK) Ltd, Croydon CR0 4YY

MIX
Paper | Supporting
responsible forestry
FSC® C013604

Bloomsbury Publishing Plc
50 Bedford Square, London, WC1B 3DP, UK
Bloomsbury Publishing Ireland Limited,
29 Earlsfort Terrace, Dublin 2, D02 AY28, Ireland

HEAD OF ZEUS LTD
5–8 Hardwick Street
London EC1R 4RG

To find out more about our authors and books
visit www.headofzeus.com
For product safety related questions contact productsafety@bloomsbury.com

CONTENTS

WHALE SONG

Uncle Warner stood at the bow of the boat contemplating the Atlantic Ocean's tranquil surface. He rarely contemplated things, eschewing elaborate forethought in favor of following his instinct.

But now, the game had changed.

Uncle Warner wasn't the demon that the media made him out to be. In fact, he looked like Santa Claus. Incisive gaze aside, he always had a bold yet sweet smile on his face. He was never armed, except for the exquisite knife he carried in his breast pocket, which he used to peel fruit and to kill people.

He smiled doing both.

In addition to the eighty subordinates and two South American girls aboard, Uncle Warner also had twenty-five tons of pure heroin stashed in his three-thousand-ton megayacht – two years' worth of product from his refinery deep in the jungles of South America. A couple of months ago, the National Army of Colombia had surrounded the refinery to seize the shipment. His younger brother and more than thirty of his subordinates died in the struggle.

He badly needed the money he'd get from this shipment to construct a new refinery, perhaps in Bolivia this time, or even in Southeast Asia's Golden Triangle. He had to ensure the continued survival of the drug empire he'd worked so hard to build. But even after floating on the sea for a month, he still hadn't gotten a single gram of product onto US shores. Going through customs was completely out of the question. The instant a neutrino detector goes off, it becomes impossible to keep drugs hidden. A year ago, they tried casting heroin into the cores of steel bars to be imported, but they'd been found out all too easily.

Then, Uncle Warner thought up an ingenious plan: They'd load about 50 kg of product onto a light aircraft, usually a cheap Cessna, and fly in via Miami. Once they reached the shore, the pilot would strap the product onto their body and jump out with a parachute. Although it was a waste of an aircraft, the 50 kg of product still fetched a hefty profit. It was an invincible strategy for a while, but then the Americans used satellites and land-based radar to construct an aerial surveillance system capable of discovering and even tracking the parachuting pilots. Before Uncle Warner's brave lads could take the plunge, they'd find police already waiting for them on the ground.

Uncle Warner then attempted to use small boats to get product ashore, but the results were even more disastrous. The Coast Guard's speedboats had all been outfitted with neutrino detectors. As soon as one of Uncle Warner's boats came within three thousand meters of the patrol, a scan instantly revealed the drugs on board. Uncle Warner even considered using mini submarines, but the Americans had long since perfected their underwater monitoring network, first created during the Cold War. The submarine would be detected long before it reached the shore.

Uncle Warner was at his wits' end. He hated scientists – they were the ones who'd caused all this. Then again, scientists could also be of service to him here. He put his American-educated son to work on that front. Money wasn't an issue.

That morning, Warner Jr. disembarked from another boat and boarded the yacht, telling his father that he had found the person they were looking for.

'He's a genius, Dad. I met him at Caltech.'

Warner Sr. wrinkled his nose disdainfully. 'Hmph. You've wasted three years at Caltech and you're still no genius. Are they really that easy to come by?'

'He really *is* a genius, Dad!'

Warner Sr. turned and sat on a chair laid out on the forward deck. He took out his exquisite knife and began peeling a pineapple. The two South American girls stepped over to rub his meaty shoulders. The person Warner Jr. brought had kept far off to one side, looking out toward the ocean, but he came over now. He was shockingly thin. His neck was like a dowel – it was hard to believe that it could prop up such an unsurpassably huge head, rendering his appearance uncanny.

'This is Dave Hopkins. He holds a Ph.D. in marine biology,' Warner Jr. said, introducing the man.

'I heard you can help us out, sir.' Warner Sr. smiled his Santa smile.

'Yes, I can help you get the shipment ashore,' Hopkins said, expressionless.

'Using what?'

'Whales.'

Warner Jr. gestured for a couple of his people to carry over a strange object. It was a submersible made of some kind of clear plastic. A meter tall and two meters long, the submersible's streamlined cabin was about the same size as a small car's. There were two seats, a simple dashboard with a small screen, and a designated space behind the seats, clearly intended for storing the product.

'This submersible can carry two people and about a ton of product,' Hopkins said.

'And how is this thing supposed to go five hundred kilometers underwater to get to Miami's shore?'

'In a whale's mouth.'

Warner Sr. guffawed, the sound sharp at first before growing coarse. He used that laugh to express everything: amusement, fury, doubt, despair, fear, grief . . . every time he laughed, only he knew why.

'Clever kid! So how much do I have to pay the fish for it to take us to our destination?'

'Whales aren't fish. They're marine mammals with blowholes. You can give the money to me. I've already installed a bioorganic device in its brain, along with a computer that can receive incoming signals and convert them into the whale's brainwaves. You can control the whale's behavior with this.'

Hopkins retrieved a device from his pocket that resembled a television remote control.

Warner Sr.'s laughter became even more uproarious.

'Hahaha . . . This kid must've seen *Pinocchio*, haha . . . Ahaha . . .' He bent over double, wheezing, the pineapple in his hand tumbling to the ground. 'Haha . . . that puppet, ah, Pinocchio – with an old man, too, swallowed into the belly of a fish . . . haha . . .'

'Dad, just listen, his plan could really work!' Warner Jr. pleaded.

'. . . Ahahaha . . . Pinocchio and the old man were in that fish's belly for a while. Maybe they're still in there! Hahaha . . . still lighting candles . . . hahahaha . . .'

Warner Sr. stopped laughing then, his wild guffawing ceasing abruptly like a light going out, though his Santa smile remained. He asked one of the girls behind him, 'What happens when Pinocchio lies?'

'His nose grows,' the girl replied.

Warner Sr. stood, the knife he'd used to peel the pineapple in one hand, his other hand on Hopkins's chin, tilting his face up so he could observe his nose as the girls behind him watched mildly.

'Is his nose getting longer?' he asked the girls with a smile.

'It is, Uncle Warner!' the girls said in saccharine unison, as if seeing people meet their demise at his hands was a pleasure of theirs.

'Then let's help him out,' Warner Sr. said. His son wasn't quick enough to stop him. Warner Sr.'s quick knife sliced off the tip of Hopkins's nose. Blood gushed from the wound, but Hopkins was still as tranquil as ever. Even after Warner Sr. released his hold on Hopkins's chin, Hopkins continued to stand there with his arms hanging by his sides, letting the blood flow freely, as if his nose weren't even part of his face.

'Put this genius in that contraption and throw him into the ocean.' Warner Sr. waved a hand. The two girls shoved Hopkins into the clear submersible. Then, Warner Sr. picked up the remote and handed it to Hopkins through the door, as amiably as if he were Santa Claus handing a gift to a child.

'Take it. Summon your precious fish. Hahaha . . .'

He guffawed again. But as soon as the submersible hit the water with a huge splash, his smile disappeared, revealing a rare moment of solemnity.

'He'll die there sooner or later,' he said to his son.

The submersible sank into the ocean waves, as weak and helpless as a bubble.

Suddenly, the two girls screamed. A massive swell of water surged forth about two hundred meters away from the yacht. It moved astonishingly fast, soon splitting into two great waves as a black ridge broke the surface.

'It's a whale. Forty-eight meters long. Hopkins calls it Poseidon, after the Greek god of the ocean,' Warner Jr. said into his father's ear.

The ridge disappeared a dozen meters away from the submersible, its colossal fluke waving in its wake like a black sail. Then, the whale's enormous head appeared beside the submersible. It opened its massive maw and swallowed the submersible in one gulp, as if it were an ordinary fish eating bread crumbs. After that, the whale came back around to the megayacht. The living mountain approached solemnly, bombarding the yacht with breaking waves as it boomed out a rumbling call. Even a person as arrogant as Warner Sr. could be awed by such a sight. He was witnessing a god: an embodiment of the ocean's might, an incarnation of nature's power.

The whale completed its circle around the yacht. Then, it turned and stormed the ship, its massive head breaking the water's surface right beside it. The people aboard could clearly see the barnacles clinging to the whale's coarse, pebbled skin. It was only then that they truly realized how huge the whale was.

The whale opened its jaws and spit out the tiny submersible. The submersible arced over the side of the yacht in nearly a straight line before clattering onto the deck. The door opened. Hopkins emerged, the front of his shirt wet with blood from his nose, but he was otherwise unscathed.

'Hurry and call the doctor! Can't you see that Pinocchio's injured?!' Warner Sr. bellowed, as if Hopkins's injury had nothing to do with him.

'My name is Dave Hopkins,' Hopkins said severely.

'I'm calling you Pinocchio,' Warner said, once again donning his Santa Claus smile.

A few hours later, Warner and Hopkins wormed into the submersible, placing the ton of heroin wrapped in a waterproof bag behind the seats. Warner had decided to go himself. He needed to take risks to invigorate the sluggish blood in his veins, and this would be, without a doubt, the most invigorating trip he'd ever had. The sailors on the yacht lowered the submersible with thick cables to the ocean's surface, then cruised away.

Waves jolted the two passengers. The submersible bobbed on the water's surface, illuminated by the setting sun. Hopkins pressed a button on the remote to summon the whale. There was a low, muffled sound of something stirring far off in distant waters. The sound grew louder and louder until the whale's maw broke through the surface. It pressed on toward them, then sucked the submersible into a black abyss. The light retreated, narrowing into a thin gap before going out completely, plunging them into the dark. There was a loud *chomp*: the sound of the whale's titanic teeth crashing shut. Then, a zero-gravity feeling like plummeting in an elevator. The whale was diving into deeper, stealthier waters.

'How clever, Pinocchio! Hahaha . . .' Warner broke out into raucous laughter again in the dark, either expressing or masking his terror.

'Let's light some candles, sir,' Hopkins said, his voice happy and at ease. This was his domain. When Warner realized that, his terror deepened. A ceiling light came on in the cabin, bathing them in a dim ultramarine light.

The first thing Warner saw outside the submersible was a row of white pillars, each as tall as a person and tapered to a sharp point. The upper and lower pillars interlocked into a row of bars. He quickly realized that he was looking at the whale's teeth. The submersible seemed to be resting on a soft, wriggling mire. Above them was a vaulted ceiling supported by row after row of arched bone. The mire and roof beams all tilted toward an enormous black hole that kept changing shape. Warner's manic laughter started up again. The hole led to the whale's throat. Shrouded in a wet haze under the blue light's glow, the two of them seemed to be in a mythical grotto.

The display in the submersible showed a nautical chart of the Bahamas and the area around Miami. Hopkins used the remote to 'drive' the whale. A line tracing the ship's path appeared, mapping out a route to Warner's destination on Miami's shores.

'We've embarked on our journey. Poseidon is fast. We should arrive in about five hours,' Hopkins said.

'Won't we suffocate?' Warner asked, doing his best to hide his anxiety.

'Of course not. I told you, whales have blowholes. They breathe oxygen, too. We've got more than enough around us. Once it's been filtered, we can breathe like we normally do.'

'Pinocchio, you truly are the Devil! How did you come up with all this? For a start, how did you insert the controls and computer into this big fella's brain?'

'One person can't do it alone. To begin, the animal needs to be sedated with a five-hundred-kilogram dose of anesthesia. Poseidon is property of the US Navy; I oversaw the multibillion-dollar military research project that he was part of. He was used during the Cold War to transport spies and special forces to the shores of the Warsaw Pact countries. I oversaw other projects as well, such as implanting devices into the brains of dolphins and sharks so that they could be strapped with explosives and used as torpedoes. I did so much for my country, but, as soon as there were budget cuts, they kicked me to the curb. As I left the research lab, I took Poseidon with me. These past few years, we've swum the seven seas together . . .'

'Then Pinocchio, do you have any, hmm, ethical qualms about using your Poseidon for these kinds of activities? Of course, I'm sure me talking about ethics is laughable to you, but I had chemists and engineers working for me in my refinery who often had those kinds of misgivings.'

'I have no such thing, sir. Humanity recruiting innocent creatures into their vile wars is already the greatest sin. I devoted myself to my country and its military; I had the qualifications to get what I wanted. And since society denied me that, I might as well go take it myself.'

'Hahahaha. . . . Yes, best to take it yourself! Hahaha . . .' Warner laughed, then stopped suddenly. 'Listen – what's that sound?'

'It's the sound of Poseidon spouting water. He's breathing. The submersible is fitted with a sensitive sonar that can amplify the sounds outside. Listen . . .'

A droning sound mixed with the crashing of the waves, going from soft to loud, then loud to soft again, until it gradually faded out.

'It's a ten-thousand-ton oil tanker.'

Before them, the two rows of teeth yawned open. Seawater boomed as it surged in, drowning the submersible. Hopkins pressed a button. The nautical charts on the screen disappeared, replaced by a complicated waveform: Poseidon's brainwaves.

'Oh! Poseidon's discovered a school of fish. It's lunchtime.'

The whale bared its gullet, revealing the pitch-black of a deep ocean abyss. A school of fish surfaced and streamed into Poseidon's maw, banging against the submersible as they flooded past, dazzling and flashing silver in the submersible's light. Believing that they were swimming into a cave full of coral, the fish were unaware of their fate.

A crash pulsed through the flurry of fish. Barely visible beyond the wall of teeth coming together were the whale's still-parted lips. A howling torrent of water tumbled the fish backward until they were plastered against the pillars of teeth. The whale was expelling the seawater in its mouth, and the great pressure was also filtering out the tide that had come in with the school of fish. Astonished, Warner watched as water surged perpendicularly past the submersible. The whale soon emptied out the rest of the water, leaving the fish flopping wildly against each other in front of the pillars of teeth. The soft 'ground' beneath the submersible began to squirm, turning into a great, undulating wave that coaxed the fish backward. By the time Warner realized what was happening, terror had gripped him from head to toe.

'Don't worry. Poseidon won't swallow us,' Hopkins said, understanding the reason for Warner's terror. 'It can filter us out, just as we can separate the shell from the kernel while eating sunflower seeds. The submersible affects its eating, but it's used to it. Sometimes, when there's a large school of fish, it'll temporarily spit out the submersible before eating.'

Warner let out a relieved sigh. He wanted to laugh again, but he didn't have the strength to. He stared, dumbstruck, as the fish flopped past the absolutely stationary submersible to the black abyss behind them. Once the two or three tons of fish disappeared into the whale's gullet, there was a boom like a landslide.

The shock sank Warner into a long silence. Hopkins nudged him: 'Did you hear that?' As he spoke, he turned up the volume on the sonar's loudspeaker.

Warner heard a low rumble. Confused, he looked at Hopkins.

'Poseidon is singing. It's a whale song.'

Gradually, Warner picked a rhythm and even a melody out of the low, intermittent call. 'What is it doing? Looking for a mate?'

'Not entirely. Marine biologists have been researching the topic for a long time, but even now, the meaning of whale song isn't entirely clear.'

'Maybe it's meaningless.'

'Precisely the opposite. The meaning is too deep for humans to understand. Researchers believe it's a kind of musical language, but one that can express far more than any human language.'

Whale song is the soul of the ocean singing. In whale song, ancient lightning strikes the primordial sea, life glimmering in the chaos of the ocean; in whale song, life opens its curious and awestruck eyes, stepping out of the sea for the first time on scaled feet onto continents still alive with volcanoes; in whale song, a dinosaur empire goes extinct in a flash of cold – time slips by, and a world of changes passes in an instant, wisdom like blades of grass sprouting in the warmth left after a glacier's passage; in whale song, civilization rises like a specter on every continent, and Atlantis crumbles into the sea in a grand cataclysm . . . Naval war after naval war stains the ocean red with blood; countless empires rise and fall, each a wisp of smoke passing before one's eyes . . .

The whale drew from its ancient, unfathomable memory to sing the song of life, completely unaware of the tiny, insignificant evil in its mouth.

The whale reached Miami at midnight, stopping a couple of hundred meters from the shore so it wouldn't run aground. Everything went surprisingly smoothly. The moonlight that evening was good; Warner and Hopkins could clearly see the groves of palm trees on the shore and the eight runners wearing wetsuits waiting for them. They swiftly moved the ton of product ashore and readily paid the highest price Warner asked, even promising to buy however much product they had in the future. They were amazed that the little clear submersible could get past the strictly enforced maritime defense line; at first, they hadn't been sure if Warner and Hopkins were people or ghosts (Hopkins had already instructed Poseidon to swim far away).

Half an hour later, with the runners long gone, Hopkins once again summoned Poseidon. He hauled two briefcases of American bills as he and Warner boarded for their return journey.

'Excellent, Pinocchio!' Warner cheered. 'Today's profits are all yours. We'll split future profits. You're rich, Pinocchio! Hahaha . . . We'll still have to make another twenty-something runs to distribute the rest of the twenty-something tons.'

'We might not need to make that many trips. With a few changes, I think we can transport two or three tons at a time.'

'Hahahaha . . . Outstanding, Pinocchio!'

During the tranquil underwater journey, Warner fell asleep. After some time, Hopkins woke him. He glanced at the map and route on the small screen and realized that they'd already traveled two-thirds of their journey. Nothing seemed out of the ordinary.

'Listen.'

He heard a ferry on the surface. They had been a common sight on the last journey. Uncomprehending, he looked at Hopkins. But as he kept listening, he realized that the ferry didn't sound right. It was different from before. This time, the volume didn't change.

The boat was following the whale.

'How long has it been following us?' Warner asked.

'About half an hour. I've changed our route several times.'

'How can this be? The Coast Guard's patrol boat wouldn't detect a whale on a scan.'

'So what if they do a scan? The whale's not carrying any drugs right now.'

'Plus, if they wanted to take care of us, it would've been easier to do so in Miami. Why wait until now?' Baffled, Warner peered at the nautical map on the screen. They'd already passed through the Straits of Florida and were headed toward Cuba.

'Poseidon has to breathe. We have no choice but to surface – just a few seconds should be enough.' Hopkins picked up the remote. Warner nodded; Hopkins pressed the remote. A weight settled on them as the whale ascended. With a breaking wave, the whale surfaced.

The sonar made a sudden, muffled sound. The submersible shuddered. The sonar sounded again; the whale thrashed more wildly, tumbling the submersible around its mouth. The submersible slammed heavily into the whale's teeth a few times, landing with a *crack* that nearly knocked Warner and Hopkins unconscious.

'The ship's started firing at us!' Hopkins yelled in surprise. He did his best to calm the whale with the remote and send neural instructions, but the whale ignored the commands as it continued its aimless thrashing on the ocean's surface.

The whale's massive body was trembling – a tremble of pain.

'We have to get out, or else!' Warner shouted.

Hopkins issued the command to eject the submersible. This time, the whale obeyed. With shocking speed, the submersible burst out of its mouth and plunked onto the surface. The sun had already risen over the Atlantic, making them squint. But they quickly realized that they were sitting in water. The battering they'd taken in the whale's mouth had cracked the hull, and seawater was flooding in. The entire submersible was mangled; even with all their strength, they couldn't pull open the hatch to escape. They started to use whatever they could to plug up the holes, even using bundles of bills from the briefcases, but it was no use – the seawater continued to surge in, and soon, the water in the submersible was chest-deep.

Before the submersible sank, Hopkins saw the other boat. It was huge and had a strangely shaped cannon at its bow. With a flash, the cannon fired a harpoon into the struggling whale's back.

The whale beat against the waves with the last of its strength. Its blood had already stained the water red.

The submersible sank into the infinite billows of the whale's crimson blood.

'Who's responsible for our death?' Warner asked, the water up to his chin.

'The whaler,' Hopkins replied.

Warner guffawed for the last time.

'The international pledge completely banned whaling five years ago! These sons of bitches!' Hopkins said, letting loose a stream of obscenities.

Warner continued laughing. 'Hahaha . . . they're unscrupulous . . . hahahaha . . . society won't give it to them . . . hahaha . . . they'll get it themselves . . . haha . . . get it themselves . . .'

As the seawater filled the submersible, in their last moments of consciousness, Hopkins and Warner heard Poseidon sing its solemn whale song again. Life's last song carried through the bloody Atlantic, echoing, echoing, everlasting.

END OF THE MICROCOSMOS

Tonight, humanity attempts to split the quark.

The magnificent feat will occur at Lop Nor's eastern nuclear center. The center itself appears to be just an elegant white building in the desert. The enormous accelerator with a perimeter of 150 kilometers, however, is buried in a tunnel deep under the sand. Nearby, a custom-built, 1,000,000,000-watt nuclear power plant generates power for the accelerator. But today's experiment requires even more power, which the grid to the northwest will temporarily supply.

Today, the accelerator will speed particles up to 1020 gigaelectron volts, the same amount of energy released during the big bang, when all matter began. With such incredible power, the smallest particle known to humanity will be split, providing answers to the deepest mysteries of the physical world.

There are only a few people in the nuclear center's control room. Among them are two of the most illustrious theoretical physicists on Earth, representing two different approaches to research on the deep structure of matter. Herman Jones, an American, believes that the quark is the smallest particle and cannot be split any further. Meanwhile, Zhang Yi, from China, believes that matter can be infinitely split. Accompanying them are the chief engineer, who supervises operations, and a few journalists. The other workers are in dozens of control rooms deep underground; those in the main control room can see data only once it's been aggregated. The most surprising person present is an old Kazakh shepherd named Dilshat, whose village is located over the accelerator. The physicists tried some of his whole roast lamb yesterday and insisted that he be present today. Their thinking was that this is a moment of truth for physics, a moment of truth for all of humanity – so there should be someone present who has no understanding of physics at all.

The accelerator starts up. On a large monitor, the power curve climbs lazily like a newly awakened earthworm toward a red line showing the critical amount of energy needed to split the quark.

'Why aren't they broadcasting this?' Zhang Yi asks, pointing to a TV set in the corner showing a packed soccer match. Zhang Yi is still wearing the same blue work outfit he had on when he departed from Beijing. It's easy to mistake him for an ordinary handyman.

'Dr. Zhang, we are not the center of the world. If we can get even thirty seconds of airtime on the news after this experiment has concluded, I'd consider that good,' the chief engineer replies.

'Ignorant. Unbelievably ignorant,' Zhang Yi says, shaking his head.

'But it's a fact of life,' Jones says. His entire appearance is dispirited. His hair is long and shaggy, and, from time to time, he takes a flask from his pocket for a swig of alcohol. 'Unfortunately, I have the misfortune of not being ignorant. It's hard to live this way.' He flashes a sheet of paper to the others. 'Sirs, this is my suicide note.'

His words startle everyone present.

'After this experiment is over, the physical world will no longer have any mysteries to explore. Within an hour, the entire field of physics will come to an end! I'm here to welcome that time. Ah, physics, what a cruel mistress you are! Once you're exhausted, how can I keep on living?'

Zhang Yi objects.

'People said that back in Newton's day and Einstein's day as well, like Max Born and Stephen Hawking. But the field of physics didn't come to an end then, and it won't come to an end now. Soon you'll see that, once the quark is split, we'll reach another level on the ladder to nowhere. I'm here to welcome the birth of the world!'

'Dr. Zhang, you're simply restating what Mao Zedong believed. He brought up the idea of infinitely divisible matter in the 1950s,' Jones shoots back sarcastically.

'You two are too far in your own heads,' the chief engineer says, interrupting them. 'You can infer that the Earth is round from the differences in solar projections at wells in Egypt and Greece, and you can even calculate the Earth's diameter. But it wasn't until Magellan's trip that people felt inspired. Before, you physicists were all stuck at the bottom of a well. But today, we take a true voyage around the Earth through the microcosmos!'

The energy potential line continues to creep toward the red line. The world outside seems to detect the enormous amount of energy surging deep in the desert: a startled flock of birds takes flight from a grove of tamarisks and pulses through the night sky as distant wolves howl. Finally, the energy potential line crosses the red line. The particles in the accelerator have acquired the energy needed to split the quark, making them the most powerful particles in all of history. The computer leads the energized particles through a ring around the 150 km perimeter of the accelerator, then sends them into a feeder path, where they fly toward their target at close to the speed of light. Under this maximum-energy bombardment, the target bursts with a storm of atomic radiation. Countless sensors stare wide-eyed at the rainstorm. In an instant, they can distinguish the few raindrops that are of a slightly different color. From the combination of colors, the supercomputer can determine whether a quark has been hit, or even whether a quark has been split.

The energized particles continue to be produced and bombard their target. The probability of an accelerated particle hitting a quark is minuscule – no one in the anxious crowd knows how long they'll have to wait.

'Ah, friends from afar,' old Dilshat says, breaking the silence. 'I was here a dozen years ago when they began building all this. Back then, there were over ten thousand people at the construction site. There were mountains of steel and concrete, and there were hundreds of coils several stories tall. They told me that those were electromagnets. But what I don't understand is this: For the same amount of money, resources, and labor, you could irrigate the desert and fill it with grapes and hami melons. Yet you're doing something no one understands.'

'Sheikh Dilshat, we are investigating one of the mysteries of the physical world. This is far more important than anything else!' Zhang Yi says.

'I'm not very knowledgeable, but I do know that all of you with the greatest education in the world seem to be looking for the world's tiniest grain of sand.'

Everyone gathered is excited to hear the old Kazakh shepherd's clear description of particle physics.

'Excellent!' Jones shouts once the interpreter is done speaking. 'He believes,' he said, pointing to Zhang Yi, 'that the grain of sand can keep getting smaller. But I believe that nothing can be smaller than that grain of sand. No matter how hard you clobber it, it won't break. Who do you think is correct, sir?'

Old Dilshat shakes his head once the interpreter finishes translating. 'I don't know. You don't even know. How can an ordinary person make heads or tails of the outcome of all this?'

'So you remain agnostic?' Zhang Yi asks.

The old shepherd's timeworn eyes sink into deep contemplation.

'The world is truly incomprehensible. Ever since I was young, I've led flocks of sheep through the endless Gobi Desert to look for fresh pastures. There were many nights when I lay out in the wilderness with the sheep and gazed at a sky full of stars. The stars were so thickly dotted together, sparkling like gems, like the jewels in a woman's black hair. . . . When the night is young, the sands of the Gobi are still warm beneath you, and the wind sighs with the voice of the desert. In those moments, the world is alive, like a baby deep in slumber. You don't need ears. You simply have to listen with your heart, and you can hear a single sound filling the space between the sky and the earth. That's the sound of Allah. Only Allah can know what the outcome of all creation will be.'

At that moment, a buzzer pierces through the air: the signal that a quark has been hit. Everyone turns to the screen to face judgment day. A three-thousand-year-old question will soon be answered.

Data floods the screen. The two physicists immediately realize that something is wrong and shake their heads, perplexed.

The results don't definitively show that the quark has been split, but neither do they show that the quark has remained whole. The data from the experiment is incomprehensible.

Dilshat gives a sudden shout. Of all the people in the room, only he isn't paying attention to the data on the monitor. Instead, he is standing by the window.

'What in the world is going on outside?! Come look!'

'Sheikh Dilshat, please don't disturb us!' the chief engineer snaps, but Dilshat's next words make everyone turn around.

'What . . . what's wrong with the sky?!'

Light streams in through the window. The entire night sky has gone pure white. The people in the main control room rush outside, where, over the limitless Gobi, the once-blue dome of heaven now shines like a sea of milk with a soft white glow, as if the world is now cradled in an eggshell. Once their eyes adapt, the crowd discovers that there are black specks in the white sky. A close inspection of the position of those dots brings them to the brink of madness.

'Subhanallah, those black dots . . . are stars!' old Dilshat shouts, expressing what everyone sees but is too afraid to say: the universe's inverse.

Amid their shock, someone notices that the TV inside is still broadcasting a soccer match. The screen confirms that they're not dreaming: a thousand miles away, the soccer stadium is also shrouded in white light. The tens of thousands of spectators in the stands crane their heads to look up with alarm at the sky.

The chief engineer is the first person to calm down.

'When did this happen?' he asks.

'Just now, when that buzzer sounded,' Dilshat replies.

The people gathered fall silent again as they all turn to look at Jones and Zhang Yi, hoping that the two most renowned physicists on Earth since Einstein can make some sense of the nightmare they're in.

Meanwhile, the two physicists are no longer looking at the sky and both have their heads lowered in thought. Zhang Yi is the first to look back up at the blank white universe and let out a long sigh.

'We should have considered this way earlier.'

Jones also looks up, meeting Zhang Yi's gaze.

'Yes, this must be the meaning of the supersymmetry equation's variable!'

'What are you talking about?!' the chief engineer shouts.

'Chief Engineer, our voyage around the world is complete!' Zhang Yi declares, smiling.

'You're saying that the experiment caused all this?!'

'Yes indeed!' Jones proclaims as he takes another swig from his flask. 'Now Magellan knows that the Earth is round.'

'R . . . round?!' the others exclaim as they stare, bewildered, at the two physicists.

'The Earth is round. If you start at any point on its surface and keep going in a straight line, you will return to where you started,' Jones explains. 'Now, we know the shape of the universe. It's as if we've kept going straight into the microcosmos and reached the end – thus arriving at the macrocosmos. The accelerator pierced through the smallest building block of physics, and the energy impacted the largest building block, turning the entire universe inside out.'

'Dr. Jones, you still have something to live for. Physics hasn't come to an end,' Zhang Yi says, 'it's just begun, like how the field of geography only emerged once we figured out the shape of the Earth. We were all wrong. If I were to pick the analysis that came closest to what actually happened, it would be what Sheikh Dilshat said. Although I don't believe in Allah, the mysteries and secrets of the universe far surpass what we can comprehend.'

'I recall that an English science fiction author from the previous century, Arthur C. Clarke, once brought up the idea of the inverse of the universe in a story. Who would have thought that that really exists?'

'But now what do we do?' the chief engineer asks.

'This is good. I'm quite happy living in this inverse universe. It's just as beautiful as the obverse universe, don't you think?' Jones finishes off the rest of the alcohol in his flask. Tipsy, he throws open both arms to embrace the new universe.

'But, look . . .' The chief engineer points to the TV inside the control room. The crowd's agitation and panic is reaching a tipping point into mass hysteria. Surely the rest of the world has fallen into similar chaos.

'Keep bombarding the target,' Zhang Yi says to the chief engineer as the computer continues to analyze the results, its bombarding routine suspended.

'Are you crazy?! Who knows what will happen the second time there's a collision with a quark? Maybe it'll cause the collapse of the universe, or even a massive explosion!'

'It won't! What we've seen confirms the theory of supersymmetry. We know what will happen next,' Jones says.

The accelerator resumes bombarding the target with supercharged particles. The room waits for those few differently colored raindrops in an atomic storm to appear.

One minute . . . two minutes . . . ten minutes . . .

Curves and data roil through the screen.

Nothing happens.

On the TV, the sea of spectators loses control. Under the pure white sky, people stampede, trampling each other. The picture flickers as the TV's signal goes out, until all that's left is a field of fluttering snow. The universe's sudden change goes beyond all of humanity's understanding, beyond what humanity can bear. The world is on a path to madness.

The buzzer sounds for the second time, signaling a second collision with a quark.

Without warning, the universe returns to its usual state: a pitch-black sky glittering with stars.

'You're doing Allah's work!' old Dilshat says, standing along with everyone else under an intoxicating cosmos on the dunes of the Gobi.

'Yes, our relentless pursuit of the principles of physics has given us the power of God. This is beyond what any of us could have dreamed of,' Jones says.

'But we're still only human. Who knows what will happen in the future?' Zhang Yi says.

Slowly, old Dilshat kneels before the heavens.

'Mashallah . . .'

As the stars twinkle in the night sky, an inaudible melody fills the universe.

WITH HER EYES

PROLOGUE

Two months of nonstop work had left me exhausted. I asked my director for a two-day leave of absence so that I could go on a short trip and clear my mind. He agreed, but only on the condition that I take a pair of eyes along with me. I accepted, and he took me to pick them up from the Control Center.

The eyes were stored in a small room at the end of a corridor. I counted about a dozen pairs. The director gestured to the large screen in front of us as he handed me a pair and introduced me to the eyes' owner, a young woman who appeared to be fresh out of university. She was staring blankly at me. The woman's puffy spacesuit made her appear even more petite than she probably was. She looked miserable, to be honest. No doubt she had dreamt of the romance of space from the safety of her university library; now she faced the hellish reality of the infinite void.

'I'm really sorry for the inconvenience,' she said, bowing apologetically. Never in my life had I heard such a gentle voice. Her soft words seemed to float down from space like a gentle breeze, turning those crude and massive orbiting steel structures into silk.

'Not at all. I'm happy to have some company,' I replied sincerely. 'Where do you want to go?'

'Really? You still haven't decided where you're going?' She looked pleased. But as she spoke, my attention was drawn to two peculiarities.

Firstly, any transmission from space reaches its destination with some degree of delay. Even transmissions from the Moon have a lag of two seconds. The lag time is even longer with communications from the Asteroid belt. Yet somehow her answers seemed to arrive without any perceptible delay. This meant that she had to be in LEO: low-Earth orbit. With no need for a transfer mid-journey, returning to the surface from there would be cheap and quick. So why would she want me to carry her eyes on a vacation?

Her spacesuit was the other thing that seemed odd. I work as an astro-engineer specializing in personal equipment, and her suit struck me as odd for a couple of reasons. For one thing, it lacked any visible anti-radiation system, and the helmet hanging by her side appeared to lack an anti-glare shield on its visor. Her suit's thermal and cooling insulation also looked incredibly advanced.

'What station is she on?' I asked, looking over at my director.

'Don't ask.' His expression was glum.

'Leave it, please,' echoed the young woman on the screen, abjectly enough to tug at my heartstrings.

'You aren't in lockup, are you?' I joked.

The room displayed on the monitor looked exceedingly cramped. It was clearly some sort of cockpit. An array of complex navigation systems pulsed and blinked around her, yet I could see no windows, not even an observation monitor. The pencil spinning near her head was the only visible evidence that she was currently in space.

Both she and the director seemed to stiffen at my words. 'OK,' I continued hurriedly. 'I won't ask about things that aren't my concern. So where are we going? It's your choice.'

Coming to a decision appeared to be a genuine struggle for her. Gloved hands gripped in front of her chest, she shut her eyes. It was as though she were deciding between life and death, or as if she thought the planet would explode after our brief vacation. I couldn't help but chuckle.

'Oh, this isn't easy for me. Have you read the book by Helen Keller *Three Days to See*? If you have, you'll understand what I'm talking about!'

'We don't have three days, though. Just two. When it comes to time, modern-day folk are dirt-poor. Then again, we're lucky compared to Helen Keller: in three hours, I can take your eyes anywhere on Earth.'

'Then let's go to the last place I visited before leaving!'

She told me the name of the place. I set off, her eyes in my hand.

1

GRASSLAND

Tall mountains, plains, meadows and forest all converged at this one spot. I was more than two thousand kilometers from the space center where I worked; the journey by ionospheric jet had taken all of fifteen minutes. The Taklamakan lay before me. Generations of hard graft had transformed the former desert into grassland. Now, after decades of vigorous population control, it was once again devoid of human habitation.

The grassland stretched all the way to the horizon. Behind me, dark green forests covered the Tian Shan mountain range. The highest peaks were capped with silvery snow. I took out her eyes and put them on.

These 'eyes' were, in reality, a pair of multi-sensory glasses. When worn, every image seen by the wearer is transmitted via an ultra-high-frequency radio signal. This transmission can be received by another person wearing an identical set of multi-sensory glasses, letting them view everything that the first individual sees. It's as if the transmitter is wearing the recipient's eyes.

Millions of people worked year-round on the Moon and the Asteroid Belt. The cost of a vacation back on Earth was astronomical – pardon the pun – which is why the space bureau, in all their stinginess, designed this little gadget. Every astronaut living in space had a corresponding pair of glasses planet-side. Those on Earth lucky enough to go on a real-life vacation would wear these glasses, allowing a homesick space-worker to share the joy of their trip.

People had originally scoffed at these devices. But as those willing to wear them received significant subsidies for their travels they actually became quite popular. These artificial eyes grew increasingly refined through the constant use of the most cutting-edge technology. The current models even transmitted their wearers' senses of touch and smell by monitoring their brainwaves. Taking a pair of eyes on vacation became an act of public service among terrestrial workers in the space industry. Not everyone was willing take an extra pair of eyes with them on vacation, citing reasons such as invasion of privacy. As for me, I had no problem with them.

I sighed deeply at the vista before my eyes. From her eyes, however, came the gentle sound of sobs.

'I have dreamed of this place ever since my last trip. Now I'm back in my dreams.' came her soft voice, drifting out from her eyes. 'I feel like I am rising from the depths of the ocean, like I'm taking my first breath of air. I can't stand being closed in.'

I could actually hear her taking long, deep breaths.

'But you aren't closed in at all. Compared to the vastness of space around you, this grassland might as well be a closet.'

She fell silent. Even her breathing seemed to have stopped.

I continued, if only to break the silence.

'Of course, people in space are still closed in. It's like when Chuck Yeager described the *Mercury* astronauts as being—

'Spam in a can.' She finished the thought for me.

We both laughed. Suddenly she called out in surprise.

'Oh! Flowers! I see flowers! They weren't here last time!' Indeed, the broad grassland was adorned with countless small blooms. 'Can you look at the flowers next to you?'

I crouched and looked down.

'Oh, how beautiful! Can you smell her? No, don't pick her!'

Left with little choice, I had to lie almost flat on my belly to pick up the flower's light fragrance

'Ah, I can smell it too! It's like she's sending us a delicate sonata.'

I shook my head, laughing. In this age of ever-changing fads and wild pursuits, most young women were restless and impulsive. Girls as dainty as this particular specimen, who was practically moved to tears at the sight of a flower, were few and far between.

'Let's give this little flower a name, shall we? Hmm. . . . We'll call her Dreamy. How about that one? What should we call him? Umm, Raindrop sounds good. Now go to that one over there. Thanks. Her petals are light blue – her name should be Moonbeam.'

We went from flower to flower in this way, first looking, then smelling and finally naming them. Utterly entranced, she kept at it with no end in sight, all else forgotten. I, however, soon grew bored to death of this silly game, but by the time I insisted that we stop, we had already named over a hundred flowers.

Looking up, I realized we had wandered a good distance, so I went back to retrieve my backpack. As I bent down to pick it up, I heard a startled shout in my ear.

'Oh no! You crushed Snowflake!'

I gingerly propped the pale little wildflower back up. The whole scene suddenly felt comical. Covering a flower with both hands, I asked her, 'What are their names? What do they look like?'

'That one on the left is Crystal. She's white, too, and has three leaves on her stem. To the right we have Flame. He's pink, with four leaves. The top two leaves are separate, and the bottom two are joined.'

She got them all right. Actually, I felt somewhat moved.

'See? We all know each other. I'll think of them over and over again during the long days to come. It'll be like retelling a beautiful fairy tale. This world of yours is absolutely wonderful!'

'This world of mine? It's your world too! And if you keep acting like a temperamental child, those anal-retentive space psychologists will make sure you're grounded on it for the rest of your life.'

I began to roam aimlessly about the plains. It wasn't long before I came across a small brook concealed in the thick grass. I decided to forge ahead, but her voice called me back.

'I want to reach into that stream so much.'

Crouching, I put my hands into the water. A cool wave of refreshment flowed through my body. I knew she would feel it too, as the ultra-high-frequency waves carried the sensation into the far reaches of space. Again I heard her sigh.

'Is it hot where you are?' I was thinking of that cramped cockpit and her spacesuit's oddly advanced insulation system.

'Hot,' she replied. 'As hot as hell.' Her tone changed. 'Hey, what's that? The prairie wind?' I had taken my hands from the water, and the gentle wind was cool against my damp skin. 'No, don't move. This wind is heavenly!' I raised both hands to the breeze and held them there until they were dry. At her request, I dipped my hands back into the brook and then lifted them into the wind. Again it felt divine, and again we shared the experience. We idled away a long while like this.

I set out again, silently wandering for a while. I heard her murmur, 'This world of yours is truly magnificent.'

'I really wouldn't know. The grayness of my life has dulled it all.'

'How could you say that? This world has so many experiences and feelings to offer! Trying to describe them all would be like trying to count the drops of rain in a thunderstorm. Look at those clouds on the horizon, all silvery-white. Right now they look solid to me, like towering mountains of gleaming jade. The meadow below, on the other hand, looks wispy, as if all the grass decided to fly away from the earth and become a green sea of clouds. Look! Look at the clouds floating past the sun! Watch how majestically the light and shadows shift and twist over the grass! Do you honestly feel nothing when you see this?'

Wearing her eyes, I roamed the grassland for an entire day. I could hear the yearning in her voice as she looked at each and every flower, at every blade of grass, at every beam of sunlight leaping through the prairie and as she listened to all the different voices of the grassy plains. The sudden appearance of a stream, and of the tiny fish swimming within it, would send her into fits of excitement. An unexpected breeze, carrying with it the sweet fragrance of fresh grass, would bring her to tears. . . . Her feelings for this world were so rich that I wondered whether something was wrong with her state of mind.

Before sunset, I made my way to a lonely white cabin standing forlornly on the grassland. It had been set up as an inn for travelers, although I seemed to be its first guest in quite some time. Besides myself, the cabin's only other resident was the glitchy, obsolete android that looked after the entire inn. I was as hungry as I was tired, but before I had a chance to finish my dinner, my companion suggested that we go outside right away to watch the sun set.

'Watching the evening sky gradually lose its glow as night falls over the forest – it's like listening to the most beautiful symphony in the universe.'

Her voice swelled with rapture. I dragged my leaden feet outside, silently cursing my misfortune.

'You really do cherish these common things,' I told her on our way back to the cabin. Night had already fallen, and stars shone in the sky.

'Why don't you?' she asked. 'That's what it means to truly be alive.'

'I can't really find any satisfaction in those things. Nor can most other people. It's too easy to get what you want these days. I'm not just talking about material things. You can surround yourself with blue skies and crystal-clear waters just like that. If you want the peace and tranquility of the countryside or a remote island, you barely even need to snap your fingers. Even love. Think of how elusive that was for previous generations and how desperately they chased it, and now it can be experienced through virtual reality, at least for a few moments at a time.

'People don't cherish anything now. They see a platter of fruit an arm's length away, only to take a bite out of each piece before throwing the rest away.'

'But not everyone has such fruits within reach,' she said quietly.

I felt my words had caused her pain, but I wasn't sure why. The rest of the way back, we said nothing more.

I saw her in my dreams that night. She was in her spacesuit, confined to that tiny cockpit. There were tears in her eyes. She reached out to me, calling out, 'Take me outside! I don't want to be closed in!' I awoke with a start and realized that she really was calling me. I was looking up at the ceiling, still wearing her eyes.

'Please, will you take me outside? Let's go see the Moon. It should be up by now!'

My head seemed to be filled with sand as I reluctantly pulled myself out of bed. Once outside, I discovered the Moon had indeed just risen; the night mist lent it a reddish tinge. The vast wilderness below was sound asleep. Pinprick glows from countless fireflies floated through the hazy ocean of grass, as though Taklamakan's dreams were bleeding into reality.

Stretching, I spoke to the night sky. 'Hey, can you see where the Moon is shining from your position in orbit? What's your ship's position? Tell me, and I might even be able to see you. I'm positive your ship's in LEO.'

Instead of answering me, she began humming a song. She stopped after a few bars and said, 'That was Debussy's "Clair de Lune".'

She continued humming, seemingly forgetting that I was still listening on the other end – or that I even existed. From orbit, melody and moonlight descended upon the prairie in unison. I pictured that delicate girl in outer space: the silvery Moon shining from above, the blue Earth below. She flew between the two, smaller than a pinpoint, her song dissolving into moonlight . . .

When I returned to bed an hour later, she was still humming. I had no idea if it was still Debussy, but it made no difference. That delicate music fluttered through my dreams.

Some time later – I'm not sure how long – her humming turned into shouting. Her cries stirred me from sleep. She wanted to go outside again.

'Weren't you just looking at the Moon?' I was angry.

'But it's different now. Remember the clouds in the west? They might have floated over by now. The Moon will be darting in and out of the clouds; I want to see the light and shadows dance on the plains outside. How beautiful that must look. It's a different kind of music. Please, take my eyes outside!'

My head throbbed with anger, but I went out. The clouds had floated on, and the Moon was shining through them. Its light filtered hazily over the grassland. It was as though the Earth were pondering deep and ancient memories.

'You're like a sentimental eighteenth-century poet. Tragically unfit for these times. Even more so for an astronaut,' I said, peering into the night sky. I took off her eyes and hung them from a branch of a nearby salt cedar. 'If you want to look at the Moon, you can do it by yourself. I really need to sleep. Tomorrow I have to get back to the space center and continue my woefully prosaic life.'

That soft voice whispered from her eyes, but I could no longer hear what she was saying. I went back to the cabin without another word.

It was daytime when I awoke. Dark clouds covered the sky, shrouding the Taklamakan in a light drizzle. The eyes were still hanging from the tree, mist covering the lenses. I carefully wiped them clean and put them on. I assumed that after watching the Moon for an entire night she would be fast asleep by now. However, I heard her sobbing quietly. A wave of pity overwhelmed me.

'I'm really sorry. I was just too tired last night.'

'No, it isn't you,' she said between sobs. 'The sky grew overcast at half past three. And after five o'clock, it started to rain . . .'

'You didn't sleep at all?' I nearly shouted.

'It started raining, and I . . . I couldn't see the sun when it rose,' she choked out. 'I really wanted to see the sun rise over the plains. I wanted to see it more than anything . . .'

Something had melted my heart. Her tears flowed through my thoughts, and I pictured her small nose twitching as she sniveled. My eyes actually felt moist. I had to admit: she had taught me something over the past twenty-four hours, though I couldn't put my finger on exactly what. It was hazy, like the light and shadows moving over the grasslands. My eyes now saw a different world because of it.

'There'll always be another sunrise. I'll definitely take your eyes out again to see it. Or maybe I'll see it with you in person. How does that sound?'

Her sobbing stopped. Suddenly she whispered to me.

'Listen . . .'

I didn't hear anything, but I tensed.

'It's the first bird of the morning. There are birds out, even in the rain.' Her voice was solemn, as though she were listening to the peal of bells marking the end of an era.

2

SUNSET 6

My memories of this experience quickly faded once I had returned to my drab existence and busy job. When I remembered to wash the clothes I had worn during my trip – which was some time afterwards – I discovered a few grass seeds in the cuffs of my trousers. At the same time, a tiny seed also remained buried within the depths of my subconscious. In the lonely desert of my soul, that seed had already sprouted, though its shoots were so tiny they were barely perceptible. This may have happened unconsciously, but at the end of each grueling work day I could feel the natural poetry of the evening breeze stir against my face. Birdsong could catch my attention. I would even stand on the overpass at twilight and watch as night enveloped the city. . . . The world was still dreary to my eyes, but it was now sprinkled with specks of verdant green – specks that grew steadily in number. Once I began to perceive this change, I thought of her again.

She began to drift into my idle mind and even into my dreams. Over and over again, I would see that cramped cockpit, that strangely insulated spacesuit. . . . Later on, these things retreated from my consciousness. Only one thing protruded from the void: that pencil, drifting in zero gravity around her head. For some reason, I would see that pencil floating in front of me whenever I shut my eyes.

One day I was walking into the vast lobby of the space center when a giant mural, one that I had passed countless times before, suddenly caught my eye. The mural depicted Earth viewed from space; a gem of deepest blue. That pencil again floated before my mind's eye, but now it was superimposed over the mural. I heard her voice again.

I don't want to be closed in.

Realization flashed through my brain like lightning. Space wasn't the only place with zero gravity!

I ran upstairs like a madman and banged on the Director's door. He wasn't in. Guided by what felt like a premonition, I flew down to the small room where the eyes were stored. The director was there, gazing at the girl on the large monitor. She was still inside that sealed-off cockpit, still wearing that 'spacesuit'. The image was frozen; almost certainly a recording.

'You're here for her, I suppose,' he said, still looking at the monitor.

'Where is she?' My voice boomed inside the small room.

'You may have already guessed the truth. She's the navigator of *Sunset 6*.'

The strength drained from my muscles and I collapsed onto the carpet. It all made sense now.

The Sunset Project had originally planned to launch ten ships, from *Sunset 1* to *Sunset 10*. After the *Sunset 6* disaster, however, the project had been abandoned.

The project was an exploratory flight mission like many before it. It followed the same basic procedures as each of the space center's other flight missions. There was just one difference – the Sunset vessels were not headed to outer space. These ships were built to dive into the depths of the Earth.

One-and-a-half centuries after the first space flight, humanity began to probe in the opposite direction. The Sunset-series terracraft were its first attempt at this form of exploration.

Four years ago, I had watched the *Sunset 1* launch on television. It was late at night. A blinding fireball lit up the heart of the Turpan Depression so bright it caused the clouds in Xinjiang's night sky to glow with the gorgeous colors of dawn. By the time the fireball faded, *Sunset 1* was already underground. At the center of this circle of red-hot, scorched earth now churned a lake of molten magma. White-hot lava seethed and boiled, hurling bright molten columns into the air. . . . The tremors could be felt as far away as Urumqi as the terracraft burrowed through the planet's inner layers.

Each of the Sunset Project's first five missions successfully completed their subterranean voyages and returned safely to the Earth's surface. *Sunset 5* set a record for the furthest any human had traveled beneath the planet's surface: 3,100 kilometers. It was a record that *Sunset 6* did not intend to break, and with good reason. Modern geophysics had concluded that the boundary between the Earth's mantle and core lay between 3,400 and 3,500 kilometers underground; this convergence is referred to academically as the 'Gutenberg Discontinuity'. Breaching this boundary meant entering the planet's iron-nickel core. Upon entering the core, the density of the surrounding matter would abruptly and exponentially increase to levels that went beyond the *Sunset 6*'s design specifications to navigate.

Sunset 6's voyage began smoothly. It took the terracraft all of two hours to pass through the boundary between the Earth's surface and mantle, also known as the 'Moho'. After resting upon the sliding surface of the Eurasian plate for five hours, the ship began its slow three-thousand-plus kilometer journey through the mantle.

Space travel may be lonely, but at least astronauts can gaze at the infinity of the universe and the majesty of the stars. The terranauts voyaging through the planet, however, had nothing but the sensation of endlessly increasing density to guide them. All they could glean from peering into the terracraft's holographic rearview monitors was the blinding glare of the seething magma following in their ship's wake. As the craft plunged deeper, the magma would merge behind the aft section, instantly sealing the path that the ship had just forged.

A terranaut once described the experience. Whenever she and her fellow crew members shut their eyes, they would see the onrushing magma gather behind them, pressing down and sealing them in all over again. The image followed them like a phantom, and it made the voyagers aware of the massive and ever-increasing immensity of matter pressing against their ship. This sense of claustrophobia was difficult for those on the surface to comprehend, but it tortured each and every terranaut.

Sunset 6 completed each of its research tasks with flying colors. The craft traveled at approximately fifteen kilometers per hour; at this rate, it would require twenty hours to reach its target depth. Fifteen hours and forty minutes into their voyage, however, the crew received an alert. Subsurface radar had picked up a sudden increase of density in their vicinity, leaping from 6.3 grams per cubic centimeter to 9.5 grams. The surrounding matter was no longer silicate-based but primarily an iron-nickel alloy; it was also no longer solid but liquid. Despite having only achieved a depth of 2,500 kilometers, all signs currently indicated that *Sunset 6* and its crew had entered the planet's core.

The crew would later learn that they had chanced upon a fissure in the Earth's mantle – one that led directly to its core. The fissure was filled with a high-pressure liquid alloy of iron and nickel from the Earth's core. Thanks to this crack, the Gutenberg discontinuity had reached up one thousand kilometers closer to the *Sunset 6*'s flight path. The ship immediately took emergency measures to change course. It was during this attempt to escape that disaster truly struck.

The ship's neutron-laced hull was strong enough to withstand the massive and sudden pressure increase to 1,600 tons per cubic centimeter, but the terracraft itself was comprised of three parts: a fusion engine at the bow, a central cabin, and a rear-mounted drive engine. When it attempted to change direction, the section linking the fusion engine to the main cabin fractured due to the density and pressure of liquid iron-nickel alloy that far exceeded the ship's operating parameters. The images broadcast from *Sunset 6*'s neutrino communicator showed the forward engine splitting from the hull only to be instantly engulfed by the crimson glow of the liquid metal. A Sunset ship's fusion engine fired a super-heated jet that cut through the material in front of the vessel. Without it, the drive engine could barely push the *Sunset 6* an inch through the planet's solid inner layers.

The density of the Earth's core is startling, but the neutrons in the ship's hull were even denser. As the buoyancy created by the liquid iron-nickel alloy did not exceed the ship's deadweight, *Sunset 6* began to sink towards the Earth's core.

One-and-a-half centuries after landing on the Moon, humanity was finally capable of venturing to Mercury. It had been anticipated that we would travel from mantle to core in a similar time frame. Now a terracraft had accidentally entered the core, and, just like an Apollo-era vessel spinning off course and into the depths of space, the chance of a successful rescue was simply nonexistent.

Fortunately, the hull of the ship's main cabin was sturdy, and *Sunset 6*'s neutrino communications system maintained a solid connection with the control center on the surface. In the year that followed, the crew of the Sunset 6 persisted in their work, sending streams of valuable data gleaned from the core to the surface.

Encased as they were in thousands of kilometers of rock, air and survival were the least of their worries – what they lacked more than anything else was space. They were pummeled by temperatures of over five thousand degrees Celsius and surrounded by pressures that could crush carbon into diamonds within seconds. Only neutrinos could escape the incredible density of the material in which the *Sunset 6* was entombed. The ship was completely trapped in a giant furnace of molten metal. To the ship's crew, Dante's *Inferno* would depict a paradise. What could life mean in a world like this? Is there any word beyond 'fragile' that can describe it?

Immense psychological pressure shredded the nerves of the *Sunset 6*'s crew. One day, the ship's geological engineer woke, leapt from his cot and threw open the heat-insulation door protecting his cabin. Even though this was only the first of four such doors, the wave of incandescent heat that washed in through the remaining three layers instantly reduced him to charcoal. To prevent the ship's imminent destruction, the commander rushed to seal the open door. Although he was successful, he suffered severe burns in the process. The man died after making one last entry into the ship's log.

With one crew member remaining, *Sunset 6* continued its voyage through the planet's darkest depths.

By now, the interior of the vessel was entirely weightless. The ship had sunk to a depth of 6,800 kilometers – the planet's deepest point. The last remaining terranaut aboard the *Sunset 6* had become the first person to reach the Earth's core.

Her entire world had shrunk to the size of a cramped, stuffy cockpit. She had less than ten square meters to move around in. The ship's onboard pair of neutrino glasses allowed her a small measure of sensory contact with the planet's surface. However, this lifeline was doomed to be short-lived, as the craft's neutrino communications system was nearly out of power. By now, the power levels were already too low to support the super-high-speed data relay that these sensory glasses relied on. In fact, the system had lost contact three months ago, just as I was taking the plane back from my vacation in the plains. By that time, her eyes were already stored inside my travel bag.

That misty, sunless morning on the plains had been her final glimpse of the surface world.

From then on, *Sunset 6* could only maintain audio and data links with the surface. But late one night this connection had also ceased, sealing her permanently into the planet's lonely core.

Sunset 6's neutron shell was strong enough to withstand the core's massive pressure, and the craft's cyclical life support systems were fully capable of an additional fifty to eighty years of operation. So she would remain alive, at the center of the Earth, in a room so small she could traverse its area in less than a minute.

I hardly dared imagine her final farewell to the surface world. However, when the Director played the recording, I was shocked.

The neutrino beam to the surface was already weak when the message was sent, and her voice occasionally cut out, but she sounded calm.

'. . . have received your final advisement. I'll do all I can to follow the entire research plan in the days to come. Someday, maybe generations from now, another ship might find the *Sunset 6* and dock with it. If someone does enter here, I can only hope that the data I leave behind will be of use. Please rest assured; I have made a life for myself down here and adapted to these surroundings; I don't feel constrained or closed-in anymore. The entire world surrounds me. When I close my eyes, I see the great plains up there on the surface. I can still see every one of the flowers that I named.

'Goodbye.'

EPILOGUE

A TRANSPARENT WORLD

Many years have passed, and I have visited many places. Everywhere I go, I stretch out upon the Earth.

I have lain on the beaches of Hainan Island, on Alaskan snow, among Russia's white birches and on the scalding sands of the Sahara. And every time the world became transparent to my mind's eye. I saw the terracraft, anchored more than six thousand kilometers below me at the center of that translucent sphere, whose hull once bore the name *Sunset 6*; I felt her heartbeat echo up to me through thousands of kilometers. As I imagined the golden light of the sun and the silvery glow of the Moon shining down to the planet's core, I could hear her humming 'Clair de Lune', and her soft voice:

'. . . *How beautiful that must look. It's a different kind of music* . . .'

One thought comforted me: even if I traveled to the most distant corner of the Earth, I would never be any farther from her.

CONTRACTION

The contraction will start one hour, twenty-four minutes, seventeen seconds before sunrise.

It will be observed in the auditorium of the country's largest astronomical observatory. The auditorium will receive images sent back from a space telescope in geosynchronous orbit, then project them onto a gigantic screen about the size of a basketball court. Right now, the screen is still blank. There aren't many people here, but they are all authorities in theoretical physics, astrophysics, and cosmology, the few people in the world who can truly understand the implications of the moment to come. Waiting for that moment, they sit still, like Adam and Eve, having just been created from mud, waiting for the breath of life from God. The exception is the observatory head, impatiently pacing back and forth.

The gigantic screen isn't working and the engineer responsible for maintaining it hasn't shown up yet. If she doesn't show up in time, the image coming from the space telescope can be projected only on the small screen. The historic sense of the moment will be ruined.

Professor Ding Yi walks into the hall.

The scientists all come to life. They stand in unison. Aside from the universe itself, only he can hold them all in awe.

As usual, Ding Yi holds everyone beneath his notice. He doesn't greet anyone and he doesn't sit in the large, comfortable chair prepared for him. Instead, he strolls aimlessly until he reaches a corner of the auditorium, where there's a large glass cabinet. He admires the large clay plate, one of the observatory head's local treasures, propped up inside. It's a priceless relic of the Western

Zhou era. Carved onto its surface is a star atlas as seen by the naked eye on a summer night several thousand years ago. Having suffered the ravages of time, the star atlas is now faint and blurred. The starry sky outside the hall, though, is still bright and clear.

Ding Yi digs out a pipe and tobacco from his jacket pocket. Self-assured, he lights the pipe, then takes a puff. This surprises everyone, because he has severe tracheitis. He's never smoked before and no one has ever dared to smoke around him. Furthermore, smoking is strictly prohibited in the auditorium, and that pipe produces more smoke than ten cigarettes.

However, Professor Ding is entitled to do anything he wants. He founded the unified field theory, realizing Albert Einstein's dream. The series of predictions his theory has made about space over a vast scale have all been confirmed by actual observations. For three years, as many as a hundred supercomputers ran a mathematical model of the unified field theory nonstop and obtained a result that was hard to believe: The universe that had been expanding for about fourteen billion years would, in two years, start collapsing. Now, out of those two years, there's only one hour left.

White smoke lingers around his head. It forms a dreamlike pattern, as if his incredible ideas are floating out of his mind. . . .

Cautiously, the observatory head approaches Ding Yi. 'Professor Ding, the governor will be here. Persuading her to accept the invitation wasn't easy. Please, I beg you, use the influence you have so that she'll increase our funding. Originally, we weren't going to bother you with this, but the observatory is out of funds. The national government can't give us any more money this year. We can only ask the province. We are the main observatory for the country. You can see what we've been reduced to. We can't even afford the electric bill for our radio telescope. We're already trying now to figure out what to do about this.' The observatory head points to the ancient star atlas plate Ding Yi has been admiring. 'If selling antiquities weren't illegal, we would have sold it long ago.'

At that moment, the governor and her entourage of two enter the auditorium. The exhaustion on their faces drags a thread of the mundane into this otherworldly place.

'My apologies. Oh. Hello, Professor Ding. Everyone. So sorry for being late. This is the first time it hasn't been pouring outside in days.

We're still worried about flooding. The Yangtze River is close to its 1998 record high.'

Excitedly, the observatory head welcomes the governor and brings her to Ding Yi. 'Why don't we have Professor Ding introduce you to the idea of universal contraction. . . .' He winks at Ding Yi.

'Why don't I first explain what I understand, then Professor Ding and everyone else can correct me. First, Hubble discovered redshifts. I don't remember when. The electromagnetic radiation that we measure from a galaxy is shifted toward the red end of the spectrum. This means, according to the Doppler effect, galaxies are receding from us. From that, we can draw this conclusion: The universe is expanding. We can also draw another conclusion: About fourteen billion years ago, the big bang brought the universe into being. If the total mass of the universe is less than some value, the universe will continue to expand forever; if it is greater than that value, then gravity will gradually slow the expansion until it stops and, eventually, gravity will cause it to contract. Previous measurements of the amount of mass in the universe suggested the first alternative. Then we discovered that neutrinos have mass. Moreover, we discovered a vast amount of previously undetected dark matter in the universe. This greatly increased the amount of mass in the universe and people changed their minds in favor of the other alternative, that the universe will expand ever more slowly until it finally starts to contract. All the galaxies in the universe will begin to gather at the gravitational center. At the same time, due to the same Doppler effect, we will see a shift in stars' electromagnetic radiation toward the blue end of the spectrum, namely a blueshift. Now, Professor Ding's unified field theory has calculated the exact moment the universe will switch from expansion to contraction.'

'Brilliant!' The observatory head claps his hands a few times flatteringly. 'So few leaders have such an understanding of fundamental theory. I bet even Professor Ding thinks so.' He winks again at Ding Yi.

'What she said is basically correct.' Ding Yi slowly knocks the ash from his pipe onto the carpet.

'Right, right. If Professor Ding thinks so—' The observatory head beams with happiness.

'Just enough to show her superficiality.' Ding Yi digs more tobacco out of his coat pocket.

The observatory head freezes. The scientists around him titter.

The governor smiles tolerantly. 'I also majored in physics, but the last thirty years, I've forgotten practically all of it. Compared to you all here, my knowledge of physics and cosmology, I'm afraid, isn't even superficial. Hell, I only remember Newton's three laws.'

'But that's a long way from understanding it.' Ding Yi lights his newly filled pipe.

The observatory head shakes his head, not knowing whether to laugh or cry.

'Professor Ding, we live in two completely different worlds.' The governor sighs. 'My world is a practical one. No poetry. Bogged down with details. We spend our days bustling around like ants, and like ants, our view is just as limited. Sometimes, when I leave my office at night, I stop to look up at the stars. A luxury that's hard to come by. Your world is brimming with wonder and mystery. Your thoughts stretch across hundreds of light-years of space and billions of years of time. To you, the Earth is just a speck of dust in the universe. To you, this era is just an instant in time too short to measure. The entire universe seems to exist to satisfy your curiosity and fulfill your existence. To be frank, Professor Ding, I truly envy you. I dreamed of this when I was young, but to enter your world was too difficult.'

'But it's not too difficult tonight. You can at least stay in Professor Ding's world for a while. See the world's greatest moment together,' the observatory head says.

'I'm not so lucky. Everyone, I'm extremely sorry. The Yangtze dykes are ready to burst. I must go right away to make sure that doesn't happen. Before I go, though, I still have some questions I'd like to ask Professor Ding. You'll probably find these questions childish, but I've thought hard about them and I still don't understand. First question: The sign of contraction is the universe changing from redshift to blueshift. We will see light from all the galaxies shift toward blue at the same time. However, right now, the farthest galaxies we can observe are about fourteen billion light-years away. According to your calculations, the entire universe will contract at the same moment. If that's the case, it should be about fourteen billion years before we can see the blueshift from them. Even the closest star system, Alpha Centauri, should still need four years.'

Ding Yi slowly lets out a puff of smoke. It floats in the air like a shrinking spiral galaxy.

'Very good. You can understand a little. It makes you seem like a physics student, albeit still a superficial one. Yes, we will see all the stars in the universe blueshift at the same time, not one at a time from four years to fourteen billion years from now. This is due to quantum effects over a cosmic scale. Its mathematical model is extremely complex. It's the most difficult idea in physics and cosmology to explain. I have no hope of making you understand it. From this, though, you've already received the first revelation. It warns you that the effects produced from the universe contracting will be more complex than what people imagine. Do you still have questions? Oh, you don't have to go right away. What you have to take care of is not as urgent as you think.'

'Compared to your entire universe, the flooding of the Yangtze River is obviously not worth mentioning. But while the mysterious universe admittedly has its appeal, the real world still takes priority. I have other questions, but I really must go. Thank you, Professor Ding, for the physics lesson. I hope everyone sees what they want to see tonight.'

'You don't understand what I mean,' Ding Yi says. 'There must be many workers battling the flood right now.'

'I have my responsibilities, Professor Ding. I must go.'

'You still don't understand what I mean. I'm saying those workers must be extremely tired. You can let them go.'

Everyone is dumbstruck.

'What . . . let them go? To do what? Watch the universe contract?'

'If they aren't interested, they can go home and sleep.'

'Professor Ding, surely you're joking!'

'I'm serious. There's no point to what they're doing.'

'Why?'

'Because of the contraction.'

After a long silence, the governor points at the ancient star atlas plate displayed in the corner of the auditorium: 'Professor Ding, the universe has been expanding all along, but from ancient times until today, the universe that we can see hasn't changed much. Contracting is the same. The extent of humanity in space-time, compared to that of the universe, is negligible. Besides the importance to pure theory, I don't believe the contraction will have any effect on human life. In fact, after one hundred million years, we still won't observe even a tiny shift caused by contraction, assuming we're still around.'

'One and a half billion years,' Ding Yi says. 'Even with our most accurate instruments, it will be one and a half billion years before we can observe the shift. By then, the sun will already have gone out. We probably won't be around.'

'And the complete contraction of the universe needs about fourteen billion years. Humanity is a dewdrop on the great tree of the universe. During its brief life span, it absolutely cannot perceive the maturing of the great tree. You surely don't believe the ridiculous rumors from the internet that the contraction will squash the Earth flat!'

A young woman enters, her face pale and her gaze gloomy. She's the engineer responsible for the gigantic screen.

'Miss Zhang, this is inexcusable! Do you know what time it is?' The flustered observatory head rushes to her as he shouts.

'My father just died at the hospital.'

The observatory head's anger dissipates instantly. 'I'm so sorry. I didn't know. Can you take a look . . .'

The engineer doesn't say any more. She just walks silently over to the computer that controls the screen and sinks herself into diagnosing the problem. Ding Yi, biting his pipe, walks over to her slowly.

'If you truly understood the meaning of the universe contracting, your father's death wouldn't grieve you so much.'

Ding Yi's words infuriate everyone there. The engineer stands suddenly. Her face grows red with fury. Tears fill her eyes.

'You're not from this world! Perhaps compared to your universe, fathers aren't much, but mine's important to me. They're important to us ordinary people! And your contraction, that's just the frequency of light that can't possibly be weaker in the night sky changing a little. Without precise instruments to amplify it over ten thousand times, no one can see even the change, not to mention the light in the first place. What is the contraction? As far as ordinary people are concerned, it's nothing! The universe expanding or contracting, what's the difference? But fathers are important to us. Do you understand?'

When the engineer realizes who she lost her temper to, she masters herself, then turns back to her work.

Ding Yi sighs, shaking his head. He says to the governor, 'Yes, like you said, two worlds. Our world.' He waves his hand, drawing a circle around the physicists and cosmologists in the room, then points at the physicists. 'Small scale is ten-quadrillionths of a millimeter.' He points at the cosmologists. 'Large scale is ten billion light-years. This is a world that you can grasp only through imagination. Your world has the floods of the Yangtze River, tight budgets, dead and living fathers . . . a practical world. But what's lamentable is people always want to separate the two worlds.'

'But you can see that they're separate,' the governor says.

'No! Although elementary particles are tiny, we are made of them. Although the universe is vast, we are inside it. Every change in the microscopic and macroscopic world affects everything.'

'But what is the coming contraction going to affect?'

Ding Yi starts to laugh loudly. It's not a nervous laugh. It seems to embody something mystical. It scares the hell out of everyone.

'Okay, physics student. Please recite what you remember about the relationship between space-time and matter.'

The governor, like a pupil, recites: 'As proved by the theories of relativity and quantum physics that form modern physics, time and space cannot be separated from matter. They have no independent existence. There is no absolute space-time. Time, space, and the material world are all inextricably linked together.'

'Very good. But who truly understands this? You?' Ding Yi first asks the governor, then turns to the observatory head. 'You?' Then to the engineer buried in her work. 'You?' Then to the technicians in the auditorium. 'You?' Then, finally, to the scientists. 'Not even you? No, none of you understand. You still think of the universe in terms of absolute space-time as naturally as you stamp your feet on the ground. Absolute space-time is your ground. You have no way to leave it. Speaking of expansion and contraction, you believe that's just the stars in space scattering and gathering in absolute space-time.'

As he speaks, he strolls to the glass display case, opens its door, then takes out the irreplaceable star atlas plate. He runs a hand lightly over its surface, admiring it. The observatory head nervously holds his hands beneath the plate to protect it. This treasure has been here for over twenty years and no hand has dared to touch it until now. The observatory head waits anxiously for Ding Yi to put the star atlas plate back, but he doesn't. Instead, he flings the plate away.

The priceless ancient treasure lies on the carpet, smashed into too many pieces to count.

The air freezes. Everyone stares dumbstruck. Ding Yi continues his leisurely stroll, the only moving element in this deadlocked world. He continues to speak.

'Space-time and matter are not separable. The expansion and contraction of the universe comprises the whole of space-time. Yes, my friends, they comprise all of time and space!'

Another cracking sound rings through the room. It's a glass cup that fell out of a physicist's grasp. What shocks the physicists isn't what shocks everyone else. It isn't the star atlas plate. It's what Ding Yi's words imply.

'What you're saying . . .' A cosmologist fixes his gaze on Ding Yi. His words catch in his throat.

'Yes.' Ding Yi nods, then says to the governor, 'They understand now.'

'So, this is the meaning of the negative time parameter in the calculated result of the unified mathematical model?' a physicist blurts. Ding Yi nods.

'Why didn't you announce this to the world earlier? You have no sense of responsibility!' another physicist shouts.

'What would be the point? It could have only caused global chaos. What can we do about space-time?'

'What are you all talking about?' the governor asks, bewildered.

'The contraction . . .' the observatory head, also an astrophysicist, mumbles as if he were dreaming. 'The contraction of the universe will influence humanity?'

'Influence? No, it will change it completely.'

'What can it change?'

The scientists are scrambling to recalibrate their thoughts. No one answers him.

'Tell me, all of you, when the universe contracts or when the blueshift starts, what will happen?' the governor, now worried, asks.

'Time will play back,' Ding Yi answers.

'. . . Play back?' The governor looks at the observatory head, puzzled, then at Ding Yi.

'Time will flow backward,' the observatory head says.

The gigantic screen has been repaired. The magnificent universe appears on it. To better observe the contraction, computers process the image the space telescope returns to exaggerate the effect of the frequency shift in the visual range. Right now, the light all the stars and galaxies emit appears red on the screen to represent the redshift of the still-expanding universe. Once the contraction starts, they will all turn blue at once. A countdown appears on a corner of the screen: 150 seconds.

'Time has followed the expansion of the universe for about fourteen billion years, but now, there isn't even three minutes of expansion left. Afterward, time will follow the contraction of the universe. Time will flow backward.' Ding Yi walks over to the stupefied observatory head, pointing at the smashed star atlas plate. 'Don't worry about this relic. Not long after the blueshift, its shattered pieces will fuse back together like new. It will return to the display case. After many years, it will return to the ground where it was buried. After thousands of years, it will return to a burning kiln, then become a ball of moist clay in the hands of an ancient astronomer. . . .'

He walks to the young engineer. 'And you don't need to grieve your father. He will come back to life and you two will reunite soon. If your father is so important to you, then you should take comfort from this because, in the contracting universe, he will live longer than you. He will see you, his daughter, leave the world. Yes, we old folk will have all just started life's journey and you young folk will have already entered your declining years. Or maybe your childhood.'

He returns to the governor. 'If there is no past, the Yangtze River will never overflow its dykes during your term of office because there's only one hundred seconds left to this universe. The contracting universe's future is the expanding universe's past. The greatest danger won't occur until 1998. By then, though, you will be a child. It won't be your responsibility. There's still a minute. It doesn't matter what you do now. There won't be any consequences in the future. Everyone can do what they like and not worry about the future. There is no future now. As for me, I now just do what I wanted to do but couldn't because of my tracheitis.' He digs out a bowl of tobacco from a pocket with his pipe. He lights the pipe, then smokes contentedly.

The blueshift countdown: fifty seconds.

'This can't be!' the governor shouts. 'It's illogical. Time playing back? If everything will go in reverse, are you saying that we'll speak backward? That's inconceivable!'

'You'll get used to it.'

The blueshift countdown: forty seconds.

'In other words, afterward, everything will be repeated. History and life will become boring and predictable.'

'No, it won't. You will be in another time. The current past will become your future. We are now in the future of that time. You can't remember the future. Once the blueshift starts, your future will become blank. You won't remember any of it. You won't know any of it.'

The blueshift countdown: twenty seconds.

'This can't be!'

'As you will discover, going from old age to youth, from maturity to naïveté, is quite rational, quite natural. If anyone speaks about time going in another direction, you will think he's a fool. There's about ten seconds left. Soon, in about ten seconds, the universe will pass through a strange point. Time won't exist in that moment. After that, we will enter the contracting universe.'

The blueshift countdown: eight seconds.

'This can't be! This really can't be!!'

'No matter. You'll know soon.'

The blueshift countdown: five, four, three, two, one, zero.

The starlight in the universe changes from a troublesome red to an empty white . . .

. . . time reaches a strange point . . .

. . . starlight changes from white to a beautiful, tranquil blue. The blueshift has begun. The contraction has begun.

. . .

. . .

.nugeb sah noitcartnoc ehT .nugeb sah tfihseulb ehT .eulb liuqnart ,lufituaeb a ot etihw morf segnahc thgilrats . . .

. . . tniop egnarts a sehcaer emit . . .

. . . etihw ytpme na ot der emoselbuort a morf segnahc esrevinu eht ni thgilrats ehT

.orez ,eno ,owt ,eerht ,ruof ,evif :nwodtnuoc tfihseulb ehT

'.noos wonk ll'uoY .rettam oN'

'!!eb t'nac yllaer sihT !eb t'nac sihT'

.sdnoces thgie :nwodtnuoc tfihseulb ehT

'.esrevinu gnitcartnoc eht retne lliw ew ,taht retfA .tnemom taht ni tsixe t'now emiT .tniop egnarts a hguorht ssap lliw esrevinu eht ,sdnoces net tuoba ni ,nooS .tfel sdnoces net tuoba s'erehT .loof a s'eh kniht lliw uoy ,noitcerid rehtona ni gniog emit tuoba skaeps enoyna fI .larutan etiuq . . .

. . .

FIRE IN THE EARTH

Father had reached the end of his life. He breathed with difficulty, using far more effort than when he used to hoist hundred-kilo iron struts in the mine. His face was pale, his eyes bulged, and his lips were purple from lack of oxygen. An invisible rope seemed to be slowly tightening around his neck, drowning all of the simple hopes and dreams of his hard life in the all-consuming desire for air. But his father's lungs, like those of all miners with stage-three silicosis, were a tangle of dusty black chunks; reticular fibers that could no longer pull oxygen from the air he inhaled into his bloodstream. Bit by bit, through twenty-five years in the mine, his father had inhaled the coal dust that made up those chunks, a tiny part of a lifetime's worth of coal.

Liu Xin knelt by the bed, his heart torn by his father's labored breaths. Suddenly, he sensed another sound in the rasping, and realized his father was trying to speak.

'What is it, Dad? Are you trying to say something?'

His father's eyes locked on him. The noise came again, indecipherable through his father's scratchy gasps, but even more urgent-sounding this time.

Liu Xin repeated his question again, desperate to understand what his father was trying to say.

The noise stopped, and his father's breathing became a light wheeze, then halted altogether. Lifeless eyes stared back at Liu Xin, as if pleading with him to heed his father's last words.

Liu Xin felt frozen; he couldn't look away from his father's eyes. He didn't see his mother fainting at the bedside or the nurse removing the oxygen tube from his father's nose. All he heard, echoing in his brain, was that noise, every syllable engraved on his memory as if etched on a record. He remained in that trance for months, the noise tormenting him day after day, until at last it began to strangle him, too. If he wanted to breathe, to keep on living, he had to figure out what it meant. Then one day, his mother, in the midst of her own long illness, said to him, 'You're grown up. You need to support the family. Drop out of high school and take over your father's job at the mine.' Liu Xin absently picked up his father's lunch box and headed out through the winter of 1979 toward the mine – Shaft No. 2, where his father had been. The black opening of the pit gazed at him like an eye, its pupil the row of explosion-proof lights that stretched off into the depths. It was his father's eye. The noise replayed in his head, urgently, and in a flash he understood his father's dying words:

'Don't go into the pit . . .'

TWENTY YEARS LATER

The Mercedes was a little out of place, Liu Xin felt. Too conspicuous. A handful of tall buildings had been erected, and hotels and shops had multiplied along the road, but everything at the mine was still shrouded in dismal gray.

When he reached the Mine Bureau, he saw a throng of people in the square outside the main office. He felt even more out of place in his suit and dress shoes as he made his way through the work-issued coveralls and sweat-stained T-shirts. The crowd watched him silently as he passed. He felt himself blushing, and looked at the ground to avoid the gaze of so many eyes on his two-thousand-dollar suit.

Inside, on the stairs, he ran into Li Minsheng, a high school classmate of his who now worked as chief engineer in the geology department. Li Minsheng was still as wiry as he had been two decades before, though he now had worry lines on his face, and the rolls of paper he carried seemed like a huge weight in his hands.

After greeting him, Li Minsheng said, 'The mine hasn't paid salaries in ages. The workers are demonstrating.' As he spoke, he gestured at the crowd, and also looked Liu Xin over curiously.

'There hasn't been any improvement? Even with the Daqin Railway Company and two years of state coal restrictions?'

'There was for a time, but then things went bad again. I don't think anyone can do anything about this industry.' Li Minsheng gave a long sigh, looking anxious to move past Liu Xin. He seemed uncomfortable talking to him. But as the engineer turned to go, Liu Xin stopped him.

'Can you do me a favor?'

Li Minsheng forced a smile. 'In high school, you were always hungry,' he said, 'but you never accepted the ration tickets we snuck into your book bag. You're the last person who needs help from anyone these days.'

'No, I really do. Can you find me a small coal seam? Just a tiny one. No more than thirty thousand tons. It has to be independent though, that's key. The fewer connections to other seams, the better.'

'That . . . should be doable.'

'I need information on the seam and its surrounding geology. The more detailed the better.'

'That's fine, too.'

'Shall we talk over dinner?' Liu Xin asked. Li Minsheng shook his head and turned to leave, but Liu Xin caught him again. 'Don't you want to know what I'm planning?'

'I'm only interested in surviving, just like the rest,' he said, inclining his head toward the crowd. Then he left.

Taking the weathered stairs, Liu Xin looked at the high walls, the coal dust coated on them appearing for a moment like massive ink wash paintings of dark clouds over dark mountains. A huge painting, *Chairman Mao En Route to Anyuan,* still hung there, the painting itself free of dust but the frame and surface showing their age. When the solemn gaze of the figure in the painting fell upon him after an absence of more than ten years, Liu Xin finally felt at home.

On the second floor, the director's office was still where it had been two decades earlier. A leather covering had been applied to the doors, but it had since split. He pushed through and saw the director, graying head facing the door, bent over a large blueprint on the desk, which he realized was a mine-tunneling chart as he drew closer. The director seemed not to have noticed the crowd outside.

'You're in charge of that project from the ministry?'* the director asked, looking up only briefly before returning to the chart.

'Yes. It's a very long-term project.'

'I see. We'll do our best to cooperate. But you've noticed our current situation.' The director looked up and extended a hand. Liu Xin saw the same weariness he'd seen on Li Minsheng's face, and when he shook the director's hand, he felt two misshapen fingers, the result of an old mining injury.

'Go look up Deputy Director Zhang, who's in charge of scientific research, or Chief Engineer Zhao. I have no time. I'm very sorry. We can talk once you've got results.' The director returned his attention to the blueprint.

'You knew my father. You were a technician on his team,' Liu Xin said, then gave his father's name.

The director nodded. 'A fine worker. A good team leader.'

'What's your opinion of the mining industry now?' Liu Xin asked.

'Opinion about what?' the director asked without looking up. *The only way to get this man's attention is to be blunt,* Liu Xin thought, then said, 'Coal is a traditional, backward, and declining industry. It's labor-intensive, it has wretched work conditions and low production efficiency, and requires enormous transport capacity. . . . Coal used to be a backbone industry in the UK, but that country closed all of its mines a decade ago!'

'We can't shut down,' the director said, head still down.

'That's right. But we can change! A complete transformation of the industry's production methods! Otherwise, we'll never be free of those difficulties,' Liu Xin said, taking quick steps over to the window. He pointed outside. 'Mine workers, millions upon millions of them, with no chance of a fundamental change to their way of life. I've come today—'

The director cut him off. 'Have you been down below?'

'No.' After a moment, he added, 'Before he died, my father forbade me.'

'And you achieved that,' the director said. Bent over the chart as he was, his expression was unreadable, but Liu Xin felt color flooding his

*The Ministry of Coal Industries was abolished in 1998, some of its functions replaced by the State Administration for Coal Industries.

cheeks again. He felt hot. In this season, his suit and tie were appropriate only in air-conditioned rooms, but here there was no air-conditioning.

'Look. I've got a goal, a dream, one my father had before he died. I went to college to realize it, and I did a doctorate overseas. . . . I want to transform coal mining. Transform the lives of the mine workers.'

'Get to the point. I don't have time for childhood dreams and flights of fancy.' The director pointed behind him, but Liu Xin wasn't certain whether he was pointing at the crowd outside or not.

'I'll be as brief as I can. As it stands, the present state of coal production is: Under extremely poor conditions, coal is transported to its point of use, and then put into coal gas generators to produce coal gas, or into electric plants where it's pulverized and burnt . . .'

'I'm well aware of the coal production process.'

'Yes, of course.' Liu Xin faltered momentarily before continuing. 'Well, here's my idea: Turn the mine itself into a massive gas generator. Turn the coal into coal gas underground, in the seam, and then use petroleum or natural gas extraction techniques to extract the combustible gas, and then transport it to its points of use in dedicated pipes. Furnaces in power stations, the largest consumers of coal, can burn coal gas. Mines could disappear, and the coal industry could become a brand-new, totally modern industry, completely different from what it is today!'

'You think your idea is a new one?'

Liu Xin did not think his idea was new. He also knew that the director, who had been a talented student at the Mining Institute in the 1960s and was now one of the country's leading authorities on coal extraction, did not think it was new either. The director was certainly aware that subterranean gasification of coal had been studied throughout the world for decades, during which time no small number of gasification catalysts had been developed by countless labs and multinational companies. But it had remained a pipe dream for the better part of a century for one simple reason: The cost of the catalysts far outstripped the value of the coal gas they produced.

'Listen to this: I can achieve subterranean gasification of coal without using a catalyst!'

'And how would you do that?' the director said, pushing aside his blueprint and giving Liu Xin his full attention. An encouraging sign, Liu Xin thought, and revealed his plan:

'Ignite the coal.'

The director was silent for a moment, then lit a cigarette and motioned for Liu Xin to continue. But Liu Xin felt his enthusiasm drain as he realized the nature of the director's excitement: Here, after days of constant drudgery, he had at last found a brief opportunity to relax. A free performance by an idiot. But Liu Xin pressed stubbornly onward.

'Extraction is accomplished through a series of holes drilled from the surface to the seam, using existing oil drills. These holes have the following effects: First, they distribute a large number of sensors into the seam. Second, they ignite the subterranean coal. Third, they inject water or steam into the seam. Fourth, they introduce combustion air into the seam. Fifth, they remove the gasified coal.

'Once the coal is ignited and comes into contact with the steam, the following reactions occur: Carbon reacts with water to produce carbon monoxide and gaseous hydrogen, and carbon dioxide and hydrogen; then carbon and carbon dioxide react to form carbon monoxide; and carbon monoxide and water react to form more carbon dioxide and hydrogen. The ultimate result is a combustible gas akin to water gas, with a combustible portion consisting of fifty percent hydrogen and thirty percent carbon monoxide. This is the coal gas we will obtain.

'Sensors transmit burn and production conditions of all combustible gases at every point in the seam to the surface by ultrasound. These signals are aggregated by a computer to build a model of the coal-seam furnace, enabling us to control, through the holes, the scale and depth of the subterranean fire as well as the burn rate. Specifically, we can inject water into the holes to arrest the burn, or pressurized air or steam to intensify it. All of this proceeds automatically in response to changes in the computer's burn model so that the fire is kept at an optimum state of incompletely combusted water and coal, to ensure maximum production. You'd be most concerned, of course, with controlling the fire's range. We can drill a series of holes ahead of its advance and inject pressurized water to form a fire barrier. Where the burning is fierce, we can also employ a pressurized cement curtain, the kind used in dam building, to block the fire.' He trailed off. 'Are you listening to me?'

A noise outside had attracted the director's attention. Liu Xin knew that the image his plan evoked in the director's mind was different from his own vision. The director surely knew what igniting subterranean coal meant: right now, coal mines were burning all over the world, including several in China.

The previous year, Liu Xin had seen ground fire for the first time in Xinjiang. Not a stitch of grass on the ground or hillsides as far as the eye could see, and the air churned in hot waves of sulfur, shimmering his vision as if he were underwater or as if the entire world were roasting on a spit. At night, Liu Xin saw ribbons of ghostly red where light seeped through countless cracks in the earth. He had approached one to peer inside, and immediately gulped a nervous breath. It was like the entrance to hell. The light shone dimly from deep within, but he could still sense its ferocious heat. Looking out at the glowing lines beneath the night sky, he'd felt as if the Earth were a burning ember wrapped in a thin layer of crust. Aygul, the brawny Uighur man who had accompanied him, was the leader of China's sole coal-seam fire brigade, and Liu Xin's aim in making the trip there had been to recruit him for his lab.

'It'll be hard to pull myself away,' Aygul had said in accented Chinese. 'I grew up watching these ground fires, so to me they're an integral part of the world, like the sun or the stars.'

'You mean the fire started burning when you were born?'

'No, Dr. Liu. This fire has been burning since the Qing Dynasty.'

Liu Xin stood rooted in place and shivered as the heat waves rolled over him in the night.

Aygul had continued, 'I'd do better to stand in your way than agree to help you. Listen to me, Dr. Liu. This isn't a game. You're working with devilry!'

Now, in the director's office, the noise outside the window had grown louder. As the director stood up and went over to it, he said to Liu Xin, 'Young man, I really hope that the sixty million the bureau is investing in this project could be put to better use. You can see there's much that needs to be done. Until next time.'

Liu Xin followed the director out of the building, where the workers' sit-in protest had grown larger, and a leader was shouting something he couldn't make out to the crowd. His attention was drawn to a corner of the crowd, where he saw a group of people in wheelchairs. More were filing in, each one a miner who had lost a limb in a work accident.

Liu Xin felt like he couldn't breathe. He loosened his tie, lowered his head, and passed quickly through the crowd before ducking into his car. He drove aimlessly, his mind blank, and after a while slammed on the brakes at the top of a hill. He used to come here as a kid. From here, there was a bird's-eye view of the whole mine. He got out and stood motionless for a long time.

'What are you looking at?' a voice said. Liu Xin looked back and saw Li Minsheng, who had come up at some point to stand behind him.

'That's our school,' Liu Xin said, pointing off at a large mining school that housed both primary and secondary classes. The athletic field on the campus was conspicuously large. It was there they had lain to rest their childhood and youth.

'Do you think you remember everything?' Li Minsheng said tiredly as he sat down on a nearby rock.

'I do.'

'That afternoon in late autumn, when the sun was hazy. We were playing football on the field, when the building's loudspeaker came on . . . do you remember?'

'It was playing a dirge, and then Zhang Jianjun came running over barefoot to say that Chairman Mao had died . . .'

'We called him a counterrevolutionary, and walloped him, even as he was crying out that it was true, honest to Chairman Mao it was true. We didn't believe him, though, and dragged him off to the police . . .'

'But we slowed down at the school gate, since the dirge was playing outside too, as if that dark music was filling the whole world . . .'

'That dirge has been playing in my mind for more than two decades. These days, when the music plays it's Nietzsche who runs over barefoot and says, 'God is dead.'' Li Minsheng barked out a laugh. 'I believe it.'

Liu Xin stared at his childhood friend. 'When did you turn into this? I hardly even recognize you.'

Li Minsheng jumped up and glared back at him, jabbing a finger at the gray world at the foot of the hill. 'When did the mine turn into that? Do you still recognize it?' Then he sat down heavily again. 'Our fathers were such a proud group. Such a proud, grand group of miners. Take my dad. He was a level-eight worker* and earned a hundred and twenty yuan a month. A hundred and twenty yuan in the Chairman Mao era, no less.'

Liu Xin was silent for a moment, then tried to change the subject. 'How's your family? Your wife . . . uh, something Shan, is it?'

Li Minsheng smiled thinly. 'Last year she told me she was taking a work trip, told her work unit she was taking annual leave, and took our daughter and left me and vanished. Two months later she sent a letter, posted from Canada, in which she said she had no wish to waste her life with a dirty coalman.'

'You've got to be kidding. You're a senior engineer!'

'Same difference.' Li Minsheng swept his hand about them. 'To those who've never been below, it's all the same. We're all dirty coalmen. Do you remember how badly we wanted to become engineers?'

'Those were the days of record-chasing production,' Liu Xin said. 'We brought our fathers lunch. It was the first time we'd been down the shaft, and it was so dark down there. I asked my father and those standing near him, 'How do you know where the coal seam is? How do you know where to dig the tunnels? And how are you able to get two tunnels dug from different directions to meet so precisely so far down?' And your father answered, 'Child, no one knows except for the engineers.' And when we got to the surface, he pointed out a few men carrying hard hats and clipboards, and said, 'Look, those are engineers.' Do you remember that, Minsheng? Even we could see that they were different. The towels around their necks, at least, were a bit whiter. We've achieved that childhood dream now. Of course, it's not all that glorious, but we have to at least fulfill our duty and accomplish something. Otherwise, won't we be betraying ourselves?'

'That's enough,' Li Minsheng said, standing up with a sudden anger. 'I've been doing my duty this whole time. I've been accomplishing things. But you? You're living in a dream! Do you really believe you can bring miners up from the mines? Turn this mine into a gas field? Say all that theory is correct and your test succeeds. So what? Have you calculated the cost of the thing? Also, how are you going to lay

*The highest of eight working-class wage levels adopted nationwide in the 1950s.

tens of thousands of kilometers of pipe? You realize that we can't even pay rail shipping fees these days?'

'Can't you take the long view? In a few years, or a few decades . . .'

'The hell with the long view! The people here aren't certain about the next few days, much less the next few decades. I've said before that you live on dreams. You've always been that way. Sure, back in your quiet old institute headquarters in Beijing you can have that dream, but I can't. I live in the real world.'

Li Minsheng turned to leave, then added, 'Oh, I came to tell you that the director has arranged for us to cooperate with your experiment. Work is work, and I'll do it.' Then he set off down the hill without looking back.

Liu Xin silently surveyed the mine where he had been born and spent his childhood. Its towering headframes and their enormous top wheels spinning, lowering large cages down the shaft out of sight; rows of electric trams going in and out of the entrance to the shaft where his father had worked; a train outside the coal-separator building easing past more piles of coal than he could count; the cinema and soccer field where he had spent the best moments of his youth; the huge bathhouse – only miners had ones so large – where he had learned how to swim in water stained black from coal dust. Yes, he had learned to swim in a place so far from rivers and oceans.

Turning his gaze toward the distance, he saw the spoil tip, the accumulation of more than a century's worth of shale dug out of the mine. It seemed taller than the surrounding hills, with smoke rising where the sulfur heated the rain. . . . All of it black, blanketed over time in a layer of coal dust. It was the color of Liu Xin's childhood, the color of his life. He closed his eyes, and as he listened to the sounds of the mine below, time seemed to stop.

Dad's mine. My mine . . .

The valley was not far from the mine, whose smoke and steam were visible beyond the ridge during the day, whose glow projected into the sky at night, and whose steam whistles were always audible. Liu Xin, Li Minsheng, and Aygul stood in the center of the desolate valley. In the distance, a herder was driving a flock of scrawny goats slowly along the foot of the mountain. Beneath the valley lay the small isolated coal seam that Liu Xin wanted to use for his subterranean gasified coal extraction experiment, found by Li Minsheng and the engineers in the geology department after a month of combing through mountains of materials in the archives.

'We're pretty far from the main mining area, so we've got fewer geological details on it,' Li Minsheng said.

'I've read the materials, and from what we have now, the experimental seam is at least two hundred meters from the main seam. That's acceptable. We should get to work,' Liu Xin said excitedly.

'You're not an expert in mining geology, and you're even less familiar with the actual conditions here. I advise you to be more cautious. Think about it some more.'

'There's nothing to think about. The experiment can't proceed,' Aygul said. 'I've read the materials too. They're too sketchy. The separation between exploratory boreholes is too large, and they were made in the sixties. They need to be redone, to prove conclusively that the seam is independent, before the experiment can begin. Li and I have drawn up an exploratory plan.'

'How long until exploration is complete, according to your plan? And how much more investment is needed?'

Li Minsheng said, 'At the geology department's current capacity, at least a month. We didn't run the investment numbers. To estimate . . . at least two million or so.'

'We have neither the time nor the money for that!'

'Then put in a request to the ministry.'

'The ministry? A bunch of bastards in the ministry want to kill this project! The higher-ups are anxious for results, so I'm dooming the entire project if I go back and ask for more time and a bigger budget. Instinct tells me there won't be major problems, so why not take a little risk?'

'Instinct? Risk? Not on a project like this! Dr. Liu, do you realize where we're starting this fire? You call that a small risk?'

'I've made my decision!' Liu Xin cut him off with a wave of his hand and walked off alone.

'Engineer Li, why aren't you stopping that madman? The two of us are on the same side,' Aygul said.

'I'm going to do what I'm required to,' Li Minsheng said.

*

Three hundred men were at work in the valley. Besides physicists, chemists, geologists, and mining engineers, there were a few unexpected experts. Aygul led a coal-seam fire brigade of more than ten members, and there were two entire drilling squads from Renqiu Oil Field in Hebei Province, as well as a number of hydraulic-construction engineers and workers who would erect subterranean firebreaks. On the work site, in addition to tall rigs and piles of drilling poles, there were piles of cement bags and a mixer, a high-pressure slurry pump whining as it injected liquid cement into the ground, rows of high-pressure water and air pumps, and a spiderweb of crisscrossing multicolored pipes.

Work had been progressing for two months, and an underground cement curtain more than two thousand meters long had been constructed surrounding the seam. Liu Xin had thought of adapting hydraulic engineering technology used in waterproofing the foundation of dams to the subterranean firewall: high-pressure cement was injected underground, where it hardened into a tight fireproof barrier. Within the curtain, the drills had sunk nearly a hundred boreholes, each directly into the seam. The holes were connected by pipes that split into three prongs attached to different high-pressure pumps that could inject water, steam, or compressed air.

The final bit of work was the release of the 'ground rats,' as they called the fire sensors. The curious gizmos, Liu Xin's own design, resembled not rats but bombs. Each was twenty centimeters long with a bit at one end and a drive wheel at the other, and once released into the borehole, it could drill nearly a hundred meters farther into the seam and reach its designated location autonomously. Operable even under high temperatures and pressures, it would transmit the parameters at its location back to the master computer once the seam was ignited via seam-penetrating infrasound. More than a thousand of these ground rats had been released into the seam, half of which were positioned outside of the fire curtain to detect potential breaches.

Liu Xin stood in a large tent in front of a projection screen showing the fire curtain, with flashing lights that indicated the position of each ground rat according to the signals. They were densely distributed, giving the screen the look of an astronomical chart.

Everything was ready. Two bulky ignition electrodes had been lowered down a borehole at the center of the enclosure and were directly wired to a red button switch in the tent where Liu Xin was standing. All of the workers were in place and waiting.

'There's still time to change your mind, Dr. Liu,' Aygul said quietly. 'Or to take more time to think on it.'

'Aygul, that's enough. You've been spreading fear and uncertainty from day one, and you've complained about me all the way to the ministry. To be fair, you've contributed immensely to this project, and without your work this past year, I wouldn't be so quick to conduct the experiment.'

'Dr. Liu . . .' Aygul was pleading now. Liu Xin had never seen him like this. 'We don't have to do this. Don't release the demon from the depths!'

'You think we can quit now?' Liu Xin smiled and shook his head, then turned toward Li Minsheng.

Li Minsheng said, 'As you instructed, we reviewed all of the geological materials a sixth time. We found no problems. Last night we added an additional curtain layer to a few sensitive spots.' He pointed out several short lines on the screen, outside the enclosure.

Liu Xin went up to the ignition switch, and when his hand made contact with the red button he paused and closed his eyes as if in prayer. His lips moved, but only Li Minsheng, standing closest to him, heard the word he said—

'Dad . . .'

The button made no sound or flash. The valley remained the same as ever. But somewhere deep underground, a glittering high-temperature electric arc was created by more than ten thousand volts of electricity in the seam. On the screen, at the location of the electrodes, a small red dot appeared and quickly expanded like a blot of red ink on rice paper. Liu Xin moved the mouse, and the screen switched to a burn model produced from the data returned by the ground rats, a continuously growing, onion-like sphere, where each layer was an isotherm. High-pressure pumps roared, pouring combustion air into the seam through the boreholes, and the fire expanded like a blown-up balloon. . . . An hour later, when the control computer switched on the high-pressure water pumps, the fire onscreen twisted and distorted like a punctured balloon, although its volume remained the same.

Liu Xin exited the tent. The sun had set behind the hill, and the thunder of machines echoed in the darkening valley. More than three hundred people were assembled outside, surrounding a vertical jet the diameter of an oil barrel. They made way for him, and he approached the small platform at the foot of the jet. Two people were standing on the platform, one of whom twisted the knob when he saw Liu Xin coming; the other struck a lighter to light a torch, which he passed to Liu Xin. The turning of the knob produced a hiss of gas from the jet that rose dramatically in volume until it roared throughout the valley like a hoarse giant. On all sides, three hundred nervous faces watched in the faint torchlight. Liu Xin closed his eyes and spoke silently to himself again. Then he brought the torch to the mouth of the jet and ignited the world's first gasified coal well.

With a bang, a huge pillar of fire leapt into the air, shooting up almost twenty meters. Closest to the mouth of the jet, the column was a clear, pure blue, but just above that it turned a blinding yellow before gradually turning red. It whistled in the air, and those closest to it could feel its surge of heat. Its radiance lit the surrounding hills, and from a distance it would look as if a sky lantern were shining over the plateau.

A white-haired man, the director, emerged from the crowd and shook Liu Xin's hand. He said, 'Please accept the congratulations of a closed-minded relic. You've succeeded! But I hope you'll extinguish it as soon as possible.'

'Even now you don't trust me? It won't be extinguished. I want it to keep burning, for the whole country and the whole world to see.'

'They've already seen it.' The director pointed to the throng of TV reporters behind him. 'But as you well know, the test seam is no more than two hundred meters from the surrounding main seam at its closest point.'

'But we've laid three firebreaks at those spots. And we have high-speed drills on standby. There won't be any problems.'

'You're engineers from the ministry, so I have no authority to interfere. But there's potential danger in any new technology, no matter how successful it may seem. I've seen my share of dangers in my decades in coal. Maybe that's the reason for my rigid thinking. I'm truly worried. . . . However,' and the director again extended a hand to Liu Xin, 'I'd still like to thank you. You've shown me hope for the coal industry.' He gazed at the pillar of fire again. 'Your father would be pleased.'

Two more jets were ignited in the next two days, so there were now three pillars of fire. The production volume of the test seam, calculated at a standard supply pressure, had reached five hundred thousand cubic meters per hour, equivalent to more than a hundred large coal gas furnaces.

The underground coal fire was moderated entirely by computer, with the scale controlled to a stable-bounded area no larger than two-thirds of the total area within the curtain. At the mine's request, multiple fire-control tests had been conducted. On the computer, Liu Xin described a ring around the fire with the mouse, and then clicked to constrict it. The whining of the high-pressure pumps outside changed, and within an hour the fire had been contained within that ring. Meanwhile, two more fire curtains, each two hundred meters long, had been added in the risky direction of the main seam.

There was little for him to do. Most of his time he devoted to taking media interviews. Major companies inside and outside of China, including the likes of DuPont and Exxon, were swarming to propose investment and collaboration projects.

On the third day, a coal-seam firefighter came to Liu Xin to say that their chief was about to collapse from fatigue. Aygul had for the past two days led the firefighting squad in a mad series of subterranean firefighting exercises. He had also, on his own initiative, rented satellite time from the National Remote Sensing Center to survey the region's crust temperature. He hadn't slept in three days, spending his time instead doing rounds outside the curtain ring, each circuit taking all night.

When Liu Xin found Aygul, he saw that the stocky man had gotten much thinner, and his eyes were red. 'I can't sleep,' he said. 'The nightmares start as soon as I shut my eyes. I see those fire columns erupting all around me, like a forest of fire . . .'

'Renting a sensor satellite is a huge expense,' Liu Xin said gently. 'And although I don't see the need, you've done it and I respect your decision. I'll be needing you in the future, Aygul. I don't think your firefighting squad will have much to do, but even the safest place still needs a fire team. You're exhausted. Go back to Beijing for a few days' rest.'

'Leave now? You're insane!'

'You grew up above ground fire. That's why your fear of it goes so deep. Right now we may not be able to control a massive fire like the one in the Xinjiang mines, but we soon will be. I want to set up the first gasified coalfield for commercial use in Xinjiang. When that time comes, the underground fires will be under our control, and the land of your hometown will be covered in glorious vineyards.'

'Dr. Liu, I respect you. That's why I'm working with you. But you overestimate yourself. Where ground fire is concerned, you're still just a child.' Aygul smiled bitterly and walked away, shaking his head.

Disaster struck on the fifth day. The sun had just come up when Liu Xin was shaken awake by Aygul, who was out of breath, wild-eyed, and almost feverish. His trouser legs were soaked through with dew. He held a laser-printed photograph in front of Liu Xin's face, so close it blocked his vision entirely. It was a false-color infrared sensor image returned from the satellite, a vibrant abstract painting he couldn't understand, so he just stared in confusion. 'Come!' Aygul shouted, and dragged Liu Xin out of the tent by the hand.

Liu Xin followed him up a hill on the north side of the valley, his confusion growing all the while. First, this was the safest direction, separated from the main seam by more than a kilometer. Second, Aygul had led him nearly to the top of the hill, but the curtain ring was far, far beneath them. What was there to go wrong here? When they reached the top, Liu Xin was about to gasp out a question when Aygul pointed in a different direction, to a place even farther off. Liu Xin laughed in relief – there was no disaster. The mine was directly ahead of where Aygul pointed, and between that hill and the one beneath their feet was an even slope that led to a meadow at the bottom. That was Aygul's target. The mine and the meadow seemed peaceful at this distance, but after a longer look Liu Xin saw something strange about the meadow: in one circular spot, the grass appeared darker than the surrounding area, a difference only noticeable upon careful observation. He felt his heart seize, then he and Aygul raced down the hill to that patch of darker green.

When they got there, Liu Xin examined the round patch of grass, which had wilted to the ground as if it had been scalded. He put his hand on it and felt heat emanating from the ground. In the center of the circle a puff of steam rose in the light of the rising sun. . . .

After a morning of emergency drilling and the dispatch of another thousand-odd ground rats, Liu Xin confirmed the nightmarish fact: the main seam had caught fire. The scope of the fire was unknown for the time being, since the ground rats had a maximum below-ground speed of around ten meters per hour. However, with the fire so much deeper than the test seam, the fact that its heat was radiating above ground meant it had been burning for quite some time. It was a big fire.

The strange thing was that the thousand meters of earth and stone between the main seam and the test seam was whole and unbroken. The ground fire had ignited on either side of the thousand-meter buffer zone, leading someone to suggest that it was unrelated to the experiment. But that was no more than self-delusion; even the person who had said it didn't really believe the two weren't in some way connected. Deeper exploration cleared up the matter late that night.

Eight narrow coal belts extended from the test seam. Only half a meter at their narrowest point, they were hard to detect. Five of them were bisected by the fire curtain, but the other three led downward and just skirted the curtain's bottom edge. Two of these terminated, but the last one led directly to the main seam a kilometer away. All of them were actually ground fissures that had been filled up by coal; their connection to the surface provided them with an excellent supply of oxygen. The one linking the test seam and the main seam thus acted as a fuse.

None of the three was marked on the materials Li Minsheng had provided, and in fact, such long and narrow belts were extremely rare in the field of coal geology. Mother Nature had played a cruel joke.

'I had no choice. My kid's got uremia and needs continual dialysis. The money from this project was too important to me, so I didn't fight you as strongly as I could have. . . .' Li Minsheng's face was pale, and he avoided Liu Xin's eyes.

The three of them stood atop the hill between the two ground fires. It was another early morning. The entire meadow between the mine and the peak was now dark green, apart from the previous day's circular area, which was now a burnt yellow. Steam wafted from the ground, obscuring their view of the mine.

Aygul said to Liu Xin, 'My fire brigade from Xinjiang has landed in Taiyuan with equipment, and they'll be here soon. Teams from elsewhere in the country are headed here too. The fire looks to be spreading fast.'

Liu Xin looked silently at Aygul for a long moment before he asked in a low voice, 'Can you tame it?'

Aygul shook his head.

'Then tell me: How much hope is there? If we seal off the vents, or inject water to quell the fire . . .'

Again, Aygul shook his head. 'I've been doing this my whole life, but ground fire still consumed my hometown. I told you that where ground fire is concerned, you're still just a child. You don't know what it is. That far underground it's slipperier than a viper, wilier than a ghost. Mortals can't stop it from going where it wants. Under our feet is a huge quantity of high-quality anthracite, and this devil's been coveting it for millions of years. Now you've released it, and given it limitless energy and power. The ground fire here will be a hundred times worse than in Xinjiang.'

Liu Xin shook the Uighur man by the shoulders in desperation. 'Tell me how much hope we have! Tell me the truth, I beg you!'

'Zero,' Aygul said with a slow shake of his head. 'Dr. Liu, you can't atone for your sins in this lifetime.'

An emergency meeting was held in the main bureau building attended by the bureau leadership and the heads of the five mines, as well as a group of alarmed officials from the city government, including the mayor. The meeting's first act was to establish an emergency command center headed up by the director, with Liu Xin and Li Minsheng as members of the leading group.

'Engineer Li and I will do our utmost, but I'd like to remind you all that we're now criminals,' Liu Xin said, as Li Minsheng sat silently, head bowed.

'Now's not the time for recrimination,' the director said. 'Act, and think of nothing else. Do you know who said that? Your father. Once, back when I was a technician on his squad, I ignored his warning and enlarged the extraction range so I could meet production targets. As a result, a huge quantity of water entered the works, trapping more than twenty squad members in the corner of a passageway. Our lamps had gone out, and we didn't dare strike a lighter, afraid of gas on the one hand and of using up the oxygen on the other, since the water had sealed us off completely. You couldn't see your hand in front of your face, it was so dark. Then your father told me he remembered there was another passageway above us, and our ceiling was probably not all that thick. Next thing I heard was him scratching at the ceiling with a pick. The rest of us felt around for our picks and joined him, digging in the darkness. As the oxygen level dropped, we began to feel woozy and tight-chested. And on top of that there was the darkness, an absolute blackness no one on the surface is able to imagine, but for the glint of picks striking the ceiling. Staying alive was sheer torture, but it was your father who kept me going. Over and over he said to me in the darkness, 'Act, and think of nothing else.' I don't know how long we dug, but just when I was about to faint from lack of breath, a chunk of the ceiling fell in and the glare of the explosion-proof lamps from the overhead passageway shone through the hole. . . . Later your father told me that he had no idea how thick the roof was, but it was the only thing we could do: act, and think of nothing else. Your father's words have been etched ever deeper on my brain over the years, and now I pass them on to you.'

Experts who had rushed from all over the country to attend the meeting soon drafted a plan for fighting the fire. The options at hand were limited to just three. First, cut off the underground fire's oxygen. Second, use a grout curtain to cut the path of the fire. Third, inject massive quantities of water underground to quench the fire. These three techniques were to proceed simultaneously, but the first had been demonstrated ineffective long ago. Air vents supplying oxygen to the fire were difficult to pinpoint, and they would be hard to seal off even if located. The second method was effective only against shallow coal-seam fires and was much slower than the pace of the underground fire's advance. The third method was most promising.

News was still embargoed, and the firefighting proceeded quietly. High-power drilling rigs, emergency transfers from Renqiu Oil Field, passed through the mining city under the eyes of curious onlookers; the army entered the hills; whirling choppers appeared in the sky . . . a cloud of uncertainty descended over the mine, and rumors spread like wildfire.

The drills were lined up at the head of the subterranean fire, and once drilling was complete, more than a hundred high-pressure pumps began injecting water into the hot, smoking boreholes. The sheer quantity of water meant that the water supply to both the mine and the city was cut off, which only increased uncertainty and unrest among the public. But initial results were encouraging: On the big screen in the command center, dark spots appeared surrounding the position of the boreholes at the head of the red-colored fire, indicating that the water had dramatically dropped the fire temperature. If the line of dots connected, then there was hope for stopping the fire's spread.

But this slightly comforting situation did not last long. The leader of the oil field drilling crew found Liu Xin at the foot of the enormous rig.

'Dr. Liu, no more drilling can be done at two-thirds of the well positions!' he shouted over the roar of the drills and pumps.

'Are you joking? We've got to add more water-injection holes to the fire.'

'No. Well pressure at those positions is growing too quickly. Any more drilling and there'll be a blowout!'

'Bullshit. This isn't an oil field. There's no high-pressure gas reservoir. What's going to blow?'

'You know nothing! I'm shutting down the drills and pulling out.'

Enraged, Liu Xin grabbed his collar. 'You will not. I order you to continue drilling. There will not be a blowout. You hear me? There won't!'

Even before he finished speaking, they heard a loud crash from the direction of the rig, and they turned in time to witness the well's heavy seal fly off in two pieces as a yellowish-black mud spurted into the air together with pieces of broken drill pipe. Bystanders shouted in alarm, and the mud gradually lightened in color as its particulate content reduced. Then it turned snow-white, and they realized that the ground fire had heated the injected water into pressurized steam. High up on the rig they saw the body of the drill driver, suspended and twisting slowly in the roiling steam. There was no trace of the other three engineers who had been on the platform.

What happened next was even more terrifying. The head of the white dragon broke free from the ground and gradually took flight, until finally the white steam had risen above the rig like a white-haired demon in the sky. There was nothing in the space between the demon and the mouth of the well apart from the wreckage of the rig. Nothing but that terrifying hiss. A few young engineers, under the impression that the blowout had stopped, took hesitant steps forward, but Liu Xin grabbed two of them and shouted, 'That's suicide! It's superheated steam!'

They watched in terror as the damp headframe was blasted dry in the steam's heat, and the thick rubber pipes strung from it liquefied like wax. The infernal steam assaulted the frame with a hair-curling thunder. . . .

Further water injection was impossible, and even if it weren't, it would act more to combust than to quench the fire.

All emergency command center personnel assembled at the third mine, by Shaft No. 4, the nearest to the fire line.

'The fire is nearing the mine's extraction zone,' Aygul said. 'If it gets there, then the mine passages will supply it with oxygen and multiply its strength considerably. . . . That's the present situation.' He broke off, and glanced at the bureau director and the heads of the five mines uncomfortably, unwilling to violate the greatest taboo in mining.

'And conditions in the shafts?' the director asked without emotion.

'Excavation and extraction are proceeding as normal in eight shafts, primarily for stability's sake,' the head of one mine said.

'Shut down production altogether. Evacuate all staff in the shafts. Then . . .' The director paused and remained silent for a few seconds.

Those few seconds felt immeasurably long.

'Seal the shafts,' the director said at last, uttering the heartbreaking words.

'No! You can't!' The cry burst from Li Minsheng before he could stop himself. 'What I mean is . . .' He grasped for counterlogic to present the director. 'Sealing the shafts . . . sealing the shafts . . . will throw everything into chaos. And . . .'

'Enough,' the director said with a gentle wave of his hand. His expression said everything: *I know how you feel. I feel the same way. We all do.*

Li Minsheng crouched on the ground, head in hands, shoulders shaking with silent sobs. The mining leadership and engineers stood silently before the shaft. The cavernous entrance stared back at them like a giant eye, just as Shaft No. 2 had stared at Liu Xin two decades before.

They shared a moment of silence for the century-old mine.

After a while, the bureau's chief engineer broke the silence with a low voice: 'Let's take up as much equipment as we can from down below.'

'Then,' the mine chief said, 'we ought to get together demolition squads.'

The director nodded. 'Time is of the essence. You get to work. I'll file a request with the ministry.'

The bureau party secretary said, 'Can't we use military engineers? If we use miners for the demolition squad, and anything happens . . .'

'I've considered it,' said the director. 'But we only have one detachment of military engineers at the moment, far too few even for one shaft. Besides, they're not familiar with subterranean demolitions.'

Shaft No. 4, closest to the fire, was the first to shut down. When the tramloads of miners reached the entrance, they found a hundred-strong demolition squad waiting around a pile of drills. They inquired, but the demolition squad members didn't know what they were expected to do; their orders were only to assemble beside the drilling equipment. Suddenly, their attention was seized by a convoy heading toward the entrance. The first truck bristled with armed police, who jumped down to secure a perimeter around a parking area for the vehicles that followed. When the eleven trucks stopped, the canvas was pulled back to reveal neat stacks of yellow wooden crates. The miners were stunned. They knew what was in these crates.

Each crate held twenty-four kilos of ammonium nitrate fuel oil, fifty tons of it altogether in the ten trucks. The final, somewhat smaller truck carried a few bundles of bamboo strips for lashing the explosives together, and a pile of black plastic bags, which the miners knew held electronic detonators.

Liu Xin and Li Minsheng hopped down from the cab of one of the trucks and saw the newly appointed captain of the demolition squad, a muscular, bearded man, coming their way with a roll of charts.

'What are you making us do, Engineer Li?' the captain asked as he unrolled the paper.

Li Minsheng pointed to a spot on the chart, his finger trembling slightly. 'Three blast lines, each thirty-five meters long. Detailed positions are on the chart underneath. One-hundred-fifty-millimeter and seventy-five-millimeter boreholes, filled with twenty-eight kilos and fourteen kilos of explosives, respectively, at a density of . . .'

'I'm asking, what are you trying to make us do?'

Li Minsheng went silent and bowed his head under the captain's fiery stare.

The captain turned toward the crowd. 'Brothers, they want us to blow up the tunnels!' he shouted. There was a moment of commotion among the miners, but a wall of armed police came forward in a semicircle to block the crowd from reaching the trucks. But the police line distorted under the pressure of the surging black human sea, until it was at the breaking point. All of this took place in a heavy silence, with the scuffle of footsteps and clack of gun bolts the only sounds. At the last moment, the crowd ceased its tumult as the director and mine head stepped up onto the bed of one of the trucks.

'I started work in this mine when I was fifteen. Are you just going to destroy it?' shouted one old miner. The wrinkles carved into his face were visible even beneath the thick cover of coal dust.

'What are we going to live on after it's closed?'

'Why are you blowing it up?'

'Life in the mine was difficult enough without you all messing around.'

The crowd exploded, waves of anger surging ever fiercer over the sea of coal-blackened faces flashing white teeth. The director waited silently until the crowd's anger turned to restless movement, then, when it was just about to get out of control, he spoke.

'Take a look in that direction,' he said, pointing to a small rise near the mine entrance. His voice was not loud, but it quieted the angry storm, and everyone looked where he was pointing.

'We all call that the old coal column, but do you realize that when it was erected, it wasn't a column, but a huge cube of coal? That was in the Qing Dynasty, more than a hundred years ago, when Governor Zhang Zhidong erected it at the founding of the mine. A century of wind and rain have weathered it into a column. Our mine has weathered so much wind and rain during that century, so many difficulties and disasters, more than anyone can remember. That's more than a brief moment, comrades. That's four or five generations! If there's nothing else we've learned or remembered over the past century, then we must remember this—'

The director raised his hands toward the sea of faces.

'The sky won't fall!'

The crowd stood frozen. It seemed as if even their breathing had ceased.

'Out of all of China's industrial workers, all of its proletariat, none has a longer history than us. None has a history with more hardship and tumult than ours. Has the sky fallen for miners? No! That all of us can stand here and look at that old coal column is proof of that. Our sky won't fall. It never did, and it never will!

'Hardship? There's nothing new about that, comrades. When have we miners ever had it easy? From the time of our ancestors, when have miners ever had an easy day in their lives? Rack your brains: Of all the industries and all the professions in China and the rest of the world, are any of them harder than ours? None. None at all. What's new about hardship? If it were easy, now that would be surprising. We're holding up both the sky and the earth! If we feared hardship, we'd have died out long ago.

'But talented people have been thinking of solutions for us as society and science have advanced. Now we have a solution, one that has the hope of totally transforming our lives, bringing us out of the dark mines and into the sun to mine coal beneath blue skies! Miners will have the world's most enviable job. This hope has now arrived. Don't take my word for it, but look at the pillars of fire shooting skyward in the south valley. But these efforts have caused a catastrophe. We will explain all of this in detail later. Right now all you need to understand is that this may be the very last hardship for miners. This is the price for our wonderful tomorrow. So let's stand together and face it. As so many generations have before – again, the sky hasn't fallen!'

The crowd dispersed in silence. Liu Xin said to the director, 'I've known you and my father, and I can die without regret.'

'Act, and think of nothing else,' the director said, clapping Liu Xin on the shoulder, then gripped him in an embrace.

The day after demolition work commenced on Shaft No. 4, Liu Xin and Li Minsheng walked side by side through the main tunnel, their footsteps echoing emptily. They were passing the first blast area, and in the dim light of their headlamps, they could see the boreholes densely distributed in the high ceiling, and the colorful waterfall of detonation wires streaming toward a pile on the floor.

Li Minsheng said, 'I used to hate the mine. Hate it, because it consumed my youth. But now I realize that I've become one with it. Hate it or love it, it's what my youth was.'

'We shouldn't torture ourselves,' Liu Xin said. 'We've done something with our lives, at least. If we're not heroes, then at least we've gone down fighting.'

They fell silent, realizing that they were talking about death.

Then Aygul ran up, breathing hard. 'Engineer Li, look at that,' he said, pointing at the ceiling. A few thick canvas hoses, used for ventilating the mine, were now limp and slack.

Li Minsheng blanched. 'Shit! When was ventilation cut off?'

'Two hours ago.'

Li Minsheng barked into his radio, and soon the chief of ventilation and two ventilation engineers showed up.

'There's no way to restore ventilation, Engineer Li. All of the equipment from down below – blowers, motors, anti-explosion switches, and even some pipes – have been taken out!' the ventilation chief said.

'You fucking idiot! Who told you to take them out? Are you fucking suicidal?' Li Minsheng shouted, far past caring about decorum or professionalism.

'Engineer Li, watch your language. Do you know who told us? The director expressly said for us to take out as much equipment as possible before the shaft is sealed. We all were at the meeting. We've been working day and night for two days and have taken out more than a million yuan worth of equipment. And now you're cursing at us? What's the point of ventilation anyway when the shaft's going to be sealed?'

Li Minsheng let out a long sigh. The truth of the situation had still not been disclosed, leading to this kind of coordination issue.

'What's the problem?' Liu Xin asked after the ventilation staff had left. 'Shouldn't the ventilation be stopped? Won't that reduce the supply of oxygen to the mine?'

'Dr. Liu, you're a theoretical giant but a practical dwarf. You're clueless in the face of reality. Like Engineer Li said, you only know how to dream!' Aygul said. He had not spoken courteously to Liu Xin since the fire had started.

Li Minsheng explained, 'This coal seam has a high incidence of gas. Once ventilation is shut off, the gas will quickly accumulate at the bottom of the shaft, and when the fire gets here, it may touch off an explosion powerful enough to blow out the seal. At the very least it will blow out new channels for oxygen. There's no choice but to add another blast area.'

'But Engineer Li, the two areas above us are only half done, and the third hasn't even started. The fire is nearing the southern mining zone; there might not even be enough time to complete three zones.'

'I . . .' Liu Xin said carefully. 'I have an idea that may or may not work.'

'Ha!' Aygul laughed coldly. 'This is unprecedented. When has Dr. Liu ever been uncertain? When has Dr. Liu ever had to ask someone else before making a decision?'

'What I mean is that we've got a blast zone already set up at this deep point. Can we detonate it first? That way, if there's an explosion farther down the shaft, there will be one obstacle, at least.'

'If that worked we would have done it already,' Li Minsheng said. 'The blast will be large enough to fill the tunnels with toxic gas and dust that won't disperse for a long time, impeding further work in the tunnels.'

The ground fire's advance was faster than anticipated. The construction group decided to detonate with only two blast zones in place, and ordered all personnel evacuated from the shaft as quickly as possible. It was near dark. They were standing around a chart in a production building not far off from the entrance, considering how to detonate at the shortest possible distance using a spur tunnel, when Li Minsheng suddenly said, 'Listen!'

A deep rumble was coming from somewhere below ground, as if the earth were belching. A few seconds later they heard it again.

'Methane explosions. The fire has reached the mine,' Aygul said nervously.

'Wasn't it supposed to still be farther away?'

No one answered. Liu Xin's ground rats had been used up, and with the only sensing techniques now at their disposal it was difficult to precisely determine the fire's position and speed.

'Evacuate at once!'

Li Minsheng snatched up his radio, but no matter how he shouted, there was no answer.

'Before I came up, Chief Zhang was worried he'd smash a radio while working,' a miner from the demolition squad told him. 'So he put them with the detonation wires. There are a dozen drills working simultaneously down there. It's pretty loud!'

Li Minsheng jumped up and dashed out of the building without even grabbing a helmet. He called a tram, then headed down the shaft at top speed. The moment the tram vanished into the shaft entrance, Liu Xin could see Li Minsheng waving at him, and there was a smile on his face. It had been a long time since he'd smiled.

The ground belched a few more times, but then silence descended.

'Did that series of explosions consume all of the methane in the mine?' Liu Xin asked an engineer standing beside him, who looked back at him in wonder.

'Consume it all? You've got to be kidding. It will just release more methane from the seam.'

A sky-spitting thunder rolled, as if the Earth itself were exploding under their feet. The mouth of the mine was engulfed in flames. The blast lifted Liu Xin up into the air, and the world spun madly about him. A mess of stones and crossties were thrown by the blast, and he saw a tramcar hurtle out of the flames, spit out of the entrance like an apple core. He landed heavily on the ground as rock rained down on him, and it felt as if each was coated in blood. He heard more deep rumbles, the sound of the explosives detonating in the mine. Before he lost consciousness, he saw the fire at the entrance disappear, replaced by thick clouds of smoke. . . .

ONE YEAR LATER

He walked as if through hell. Clouds of black smoke covered the sky, rendering the sun a barely visible disk of dark red. Static electricity from dust friction meant the smoke flickered with lightning, which lit up the hills above the ground fire with a blue light, exposing the image indelibly onto Liu Xin's mind. Smoke issued from shaft openings that dotted the hills, the bottom of each column glowing a savage dark red from the ground fire before gradually blackening farther up the columns that swirled snakelike into the heavens.

The road was bumpy, and the blacktop surface was melted enough that with every few steps it almost peeled the soles off his shoes. Refugees and their vehicles packed the roadway, all of them in masks against the stifling sulfurous air and the snowflake-like ash that fell endlessly and turned their bodies white. Fully-armed soldiers kept order on the crowded road, and a helicopter cut through the smoke overhead, calling through a loudspeaker for no one to panic. . . . The exodus had begun in the winter and was initially planned to be completed in one year, but a sudden intensification of the ground fire meant they had to proceed more urgently. Chaos reigned. The court had repeatedly delayed Liu Xin's hearing, but this morning he had been left unguarded in the detention center and had made his way uncertainly outside.

The land around the road was parched and fractured into fissures filled with the same thick dust that billowed around him. A small pond steamed, its surface crammed with floating corpses of fish and frogs. It was the height of summer, but no stitch of green was visible. Grass was withered yellow and buried under dust. The trees were dead as well, and some were even smoking, their charcoal branches reaching toward the evening sky like grotesque hands. Smoke wafted from some of the windows of the empty buildings. He saw an astonishing number of rats, driven from their nests by the fire's heat, crossing the road in waves.

As he went farther into the hills, the heat became even more palpable, rising up around his ankles, and the air more choked and dirty.

Even through his mask it was hard to breathe. The fire's heat was not evenly distributed, and he instinctively skirted the most scorching places. It left him few paths. Where the fire was particularly fierce, the buildings had caught flame, and there were periodic crashes as structures collapsed.

He had reached the mine entrances. He walked past a vertical shaft, now more of a chimney, its enormous rig red-hot under the heat and emitting a sharp hiss that made his skin crawl. He had to detour around its surging heat. The separator building was enveloped in smoke, and the piles of coal behind it had been burning for days. They had melted into a single enormous chunk of glowing coal flickering with flames. . . .

There was no one here. The soles of his feet were burning, the sweat had almost dried off his body, his difficulty breathing pushed him to the edge of shock, but his mind was clear. With his last ounce of strength he walked toward his destination. The mouth of the shaft, glowing red from the fire within, beckoned to him. He had made it. He smiled.

He turned in the direction of the production building. The roof might be smoking but it was not on fire, at least. He walked through the open door and entered the long changing room. Light from the shaft fire shining through the window filled the room with a hazy red glow and caused everything to shimmer, including the line of lockers. He walked along the long row, inspecting the numbers until he found the one he wanted.

He remembered it from his childhood: His father had just been appointed head of extraction, the wildest team, well-known for being hard to handle. Those rough young workers had been dismissive of his father at first, because of the way he had timidly asked for a detached locker door to be nailed back in place before their first prework meeting. The crew had mostly ignored him, apart from a few insults, but his father had said only, 'Then give me some nails and I'll put it up myself.' Someone tossed him a few nails, and he said, 'And a hammer too.' This time they really ignored him. But then they suddenly fell quiet, and watched in awe as his father pressed the nails into the wood with a bare thumb. At once the atmosphere changed, and the workers lined up and listened respectfully to his father's prework talk. . . .

The locker wasn't locked, and upon opening it, Liu Xin found it still contained clothes. He smiled again, at the thought of the miners who had used his father's locker over the past two decades. He took out the clothes and put them on, first the thick work trousers, then the equally thick jacket. The uniform smeared with layers of mud and coal dust had a sharp odor of sweat and oil that was surprisingly familiar, and a sense of peace came over him.

He put on the boots, picked up the helmet, took the lantern out of the locker, wiped the dust off of it with his sleeve, and clipped it to the helmet. There were no batteries, so he looked in the next locker, which had one. He strapped the bulky lantern battery to his waist, then realized that it was drained: work had been halted for a year, after all. But he remembered where the lamp shop was, directly opposite the changing room, where in his youth female workers would spray the batteries with smoking sulfuric acid to charge them. That was impossible now; the lamp shop was shrouded in yellow sulfuric acid smoke. He solemnly put on the lamp-equipped helmet and walked over to a dust-covered mirror. There, in the flickering red light, he saw his father.

'Dad, I'll go down below in your place,' he said with a smile, then strode out toward the smoking mouth of the shaft.

A helicopter pilot recalled later that during a low-altitude flyby of Shaft No. 2, a final sweep of the area, he thought he saw someone near the opening, a black silhouette against the red glow of the ground fire. The figure seemed to be heading down the shaft, but in the next instant there was only red light, and nothing else.

120 YEARS LATER
(A MIDDLE-SCHOOL STUDENT'S JOURNAL)

People really were dumb in the past, and they really had a tough time.

Do you know how I know? Today we visited the Mining Museum. What impressed me the most was this:

They had solid coal!

First, we had to put on weird clothing: there was a helmet, which had a light on it, connected by a wire to a rectangular object that we hung at our waists. I thought it was a computer at first (even if it was a little large), but it turned out to be a battery for the light. A battery that big could power a racing car, but they used it for a tiny light. We also put on tall rain boots. The teacher told us this was the uniform that early coal miners used for going down the mines. Someone asked what 'down the mines' meant, and the teacher said we'd find out soon enough.

We boarded a metallic, small-gauge segmented vehicle, like an early train, only much smaller and powered by an overhead wire. The vehicle started up and soon we entered the black mouth of a cave. It was very dark inside, with only an occasional dim lamp above us. Our headlamps were weak as well, only enough to make out the faces right beside us. The wind was strong and whistled in our ears; it felt like we were dropping into an abyss.

'We're going down the mine now, students!' the teacher said.

After a long while, the vehicle stopped. We passed from this relatively wide tunnel into a considerably thinner and smaller spur, and if not for my helmet, I would have knocked a few lumps in my head. Our headlamps created small patches of light but we couldn't see anything clearly. Students shouted that they were scared.

After a while, the space opened up in front of us. Here the ceiling was supported by lots of columns. Opposite us, there were many points of light shining from lamps like the ones on our helmets. As we drew closer, I saw lots of people were at work, some of them making holes in the cave wall with a long-bore drill. The drills were powered by some sort of engine whose sound made my skin crawl. Other people with metal shovels were shoveling some sort of black material into railcars and leather satchels. Clouds of dust occasionally blocked them, and lanterns cast shafts of light through the dust.

'Students, we're now in what's called the ore zone. What you see is a scene of early mining work.'

A few miners came toward us. I knew they were holograms, so I didn't move out of the way. Some of them passed through me, so I could see them very clearly, and I was astonished.

'Did China hire black people to mine coal?'

'To answer that question,' the teacher said, 'we'll have a real experience of the air of the ore zone. Please take out your breathing masks from your bags.'

We put on our masks, and heard the teacher say, 'Please remember that this is real, not a hologram.'

A cloud of black dust came toward us. In the beams from our headlamps I was shocked to see the thick cloud of particles sparkling. Then someone started to scream, and like a chorus, a lot of other kids screamed as well. I turned to laugh at them, but I, too, yelped when I got a look: Everyone was completely black, apart from the portion the masks covered. Then I heard another shout that turned my hair on end: It was the teacher's voice!

'My god, Seya! You don't have your mask on!'

Seya hadn't put on his mask, and now he was as completely black as the holographic miners. 'You said over and over in history class that the key goal was to get a feel for the past. I wanted a real feel!' he said, his teeth flashing white on his black face.

An alarm sounded somewhere, and within a minute, a teardrop-shaped micro-hovercar stopped soundlessly in front of us, an unpleasant intrusion of something modern. Two doctors got out. By now, all of the real coal dust had been sucked away, leaving only the holographic dust floating around us, so their white coats stayed spotless as they passed through it. They pulled Seya off to the car.

'Child,' one doctor said, looking straight into his eyes. 'Your lungs have been seriously harmed. You'll have to be hospitalized for at least a week. We'll notify your parents.'

'Wait!' Seya shouted, his hands fumbling with the rebreather. 'Did miners a hundred years ago wear these?'

'Shut your mouth and go to the hospital,' the teacher said. 'Why can't you ever just follow the rules?'

'We're human, just like our ancestors. Why . . .'

Seya was shoved into the car before he could finish. 'This is the first time the museum has had this kind of accident,' a doctor said severely, pointing at the teacher and adding, before getting into the hovercar, 'This falls on you!' The hovercar left as silently as it had come.

We continued our tour. The chastened teacher said, 'Every kind of work in the mine was fraught with danger, and required enormous physical energy. For example, these iron supports had to be retrieved after extraction in this zone was completed, in a process called support removal.'

We saw a miner with an iron hammer striking an iron pin in one of the supports, buckling it in two. Then he carried it off. Me and a boy tried to pick up another support that was lying on the ground, but it was ridiculously heavy. 'Support removal was a dangerous job, since the roof overhead could collapse at any time . . .'

Above our heads came scraping sounds, and I looked up and saw, in the light of the mining lanterns, a fissure open up in the rock where the support had just been removed. Before I had time to react, it fell in, and huge chunks of holographic stone fell through me to the ground with a loud crash. Everything vanished in a cloud of dust.

'This accident is called a cave-in,' the teacher's voice sounded beside me. 'Be careful. Harmful stones don't always come from up above.'

Before she even finished, a section of rock wall next to us toppled over, falling a fair distance in a single piece, as if a giant hand from the ground had pushed it over, before finally breaking up and raining down as individual stones. We were buried under holographic rocks with a crash, and our headlamps went out. Through the darkness and screams, I heard the teacher's voice again.

'That was a methane outburst. Methane is a gas that builds to immense pressure when sealed in a coal seam. What we saw just now was what happens when the rock walls of the work zone can't hold back that pressure and are blown out.'

The lights came back on, and we all exhaled. Then I heard a strange sound, at times as loud as galloping horses, sometimes soft and deep, like giants whispering.

'Look out, children! A flood is coming!'

We were still processing what she said when a broad surge of water erupted from a tunnel not far away. It quickly swamped the entire work zone. The murky water reached our knees, and then was waist-high. It reflected the light of our headlamps to shine indistinct patterns on the rocky ceiling. Wooden beams stained black with coal dust floated by, and miners' helmets and lunch boxes. . . . When the water reached my chin, I instinctively held my breath. Then I was entirely underwater, and all I could see was a murky brown where my headlamp shone, and air bubbles that sometimes floated up.

'Mine floods have many causes. Whether it's groundwater, or if the mine has dug into a surface water source, it's far more life-threatening than a flood above ground,' the teacher said over the sound of the water.

The holographic water vanished and our surroundings returned to normal. Then I noticed an odd-looking object, like a big metal toad puffing out its stomach. It was huge and heavy. I pointed it out to the teacher.

'That's an anti-explosion switch. Since methane is a highly flammable gas, the switch suppresses the electric sparks that ordinary switches create. That's related to what we'll see next, the most terrifying mining danger of all . . .'

There was another loud crash, but unlike the previous two times, it seemed to come from within us, bursting through our eardrums to the outside, as huge waves contracted our every cell, and in the searing waves of heat, we were plunged into a red glow emitted from the air around us that filled every inch of space in the mine. Then the glow disappeared, and everything plunged into darkness.

'Few people have actually seen a methane explosion, since it's hard to survive one in the mines.' The teacher's disembodied voice echoed in the darkness.

'Why did people used to come to such a terrible place?' a student asked.

'For this,' the teacher said, holding a chunk of black rock into the light from our headlamps, where its innumerable facets sparkled. That was the first time I saw solid coal.

'Children, what we just saw was a mid-twentieth-century coal mine. There were a few new machines and technologies after that, such as hydraulic struts and huge shearers, which went into use in the last two decades of the century and improved conditions somewhat for the workers, but coal mines remained an incredibly dangerous, awful working environment. Until . . .'

It turned dull after that. The teacher lectured us on the history of gasified coal, which was put to use eighty years ago, when oil was nearly exhausted and major powers mobilized troops to seize the remaining oil fields. The Earth was on the brink of war, but it was gasified coal that saved the world. . . . We all knew this, so it was boring.

Then we toured a modern mine. Nothing special, just all those pipes we see every day, leading out from underground into the distance, although it was the first time I went inside a central control building and saw a hologram of the burn. It was huge. And we saw the neutrino sensors and gravity-wave radar monitoring the underground fire, and laser drills . . . all pretty boring, too.

The teacher recounted the history of the mine, and said that over a century ago, it had been destroyed in an uncontrolled fire that burned for eighteen years before going out. In those days our beautiful city was a wasteland where smoke blotted out the sky, and all the people had left. There were many stories of the cause of the fire; some people said it had been started by an underground weapons test, and others said it was connected to Greenpeace.

We don't have to be nostalgic for the so-called good old days. Life in those days was dangerous and confusing. But we shouldn't be depressed about today, either. Because today will one day be referred to as the good old days.

People really were stupid in the past, and they really had a tough time.

THE WANDERING EARTH

1

THE BRAKING ERA

I have never seen the night. I have never seen the stars. I have never seen spring, fall or winter. I was born as the Braking Era ended, just as the Earth stopped turning.

It had taken forty-two years to halt the Earth's rotation, three years longer than the Coalition had planned. My mother told me about the time our family watched the last sunset. The Sun sank very slowly, as if stuck on the horizon. It took three days and three nights to finally set. Of course, afterward there was no more 'day' or 'night'. The Eastern hemisphere was shrouded in perpetual dusk for a long time, maybe a decade or so. The Sun lay just below the horizon, its glow filling half the sky. During that endless sunset, I was born.

Dusk did not mean darkness. The Earth Engines brightly illuminated the whole Northern hemisphere. They had been installed all across Asia and North America – only the solid tectonic plate structure of these two continents could withstand the enormous thrust they exerted. In total, there were twelve thousand engines scattered across the Eurasian and North American plains.

From where I lived, I could see the bright plasma beams of hundreds of engines. Imagine an enormous palace, as big as the Parthenon on the Acropolis. Inside the palace, countless massive columns rise up to the vaulted ceiling, each one blazing with the blue-white light of a fluorescent tube. And you, you are just a microbe on the palace's floor. That was the world I lived in. Actually, that description was not totally accurate. It was the tangential thrust component generated by the engines that halted the Earth's rotation. Because of this, the engine jets needed to be set at a very precise angle, causing the massive beams to slant across the sky. It was like the grand palace that we lived in was teetering on the verge of collapse! When visitors from the Southern hemisphere were exposed to the spectacle, many of them suffered panic attacks.

But even more terrifying than the sight of the engines was the scorching heat they produced. Temperatures reached as high as seventy or eighty degrees Celsius, forcing us to don cooling suits before we stepped outside. The heat often raised torrential storms. When a plasma beam pierced the dark clouds, it was a nightmarish scene. The clouds would scatter the beam's blue-white light, throwing off frenetic, surging rainbow halos. The entire sky glowed as if covered in white-hot lava. My grandfather had grown senile in his old age. One time, tormented by the implacable heat, he was so overjoyed to see a downpour arrive that he stripped to the waist and ran out the door. We were too late to stop him. The raindrops outside had been heated to boiling point by the superheated plasma beams, and his skin was scalded so badly that it sloughed off in large sheets.

To my generation, born in the Northern hemisphere, all of this was perfectly natural, just as the Sun, stars, and Moon had been natural to the people who lived before the Braking Era. We called that period of human history the Ante-solar Era – and what a captivating golden age it had truly been!

When I started primary school, as part of the curriculum, our teachers led our class of thirty children on a trip around the world. By then, Earth had completely stopped turning. Except for maintaining this stationary state, the Earth Engines were only being used to make small adjustments to the planet's orientation. Because of this, during the three years from when I was three until I turned six, the plasma beams were less intensely luminous than when the engines were operating at full capacity. It was this period of relative inactivity that allowed us to take a trip to gain a better understanding of our world.

First, we visited an Earth Engine up close. The engine was located near Shijiazhuang, by the entrance to the railway tunnel that ran through the Taihang mountains. The great metallic mountain loomed over us, filling half the sky. To the west, the Taihang mountain range seemed like a series of gentle hills. Some children exclaimed that it must be as tall as Mount Everest. Our head teacher was a pretty young woman named Ms Stella. She laughed and told us that the engine was eleven thousand meters tall, two thousand meters taller than Mount Everest.

'People call it "God's Blowtorch",' she said. We stood in its massive shadow, feeling its tremors shake the earth.

There were two main types of Earth Engines. Larger engines were dubbed 'Mountains', while smaller ones were called 'Peaks'. We ascended North China Mountain 794. It took a lot longer to scale Mountains than Peaks. It was possible to ride a giant elevator straight to the top of a Peak, but the top of a Mountain could only be reached via a long drive along a serpentine road. Our bus joined an endless procession of vehicles creeping up the smooth steel road. To our left, there was only a blank face of azure metal; to our right, a bottomless chasm.

The traffic mostly consisted of massive, fifty-ton dump trucks, laden with rubble from the Taihang mountains. Our bus quickly reached five thousand meters. From that height, the ground below appeared blank and featureless, washed out by the bluish glare of the Earth Engine. Ms Stella instructed us to put on our oxygen masks. As we drew closer to the mouth of the plasma beam, the light and heat increased rapidly. Our masks grew shaded, and the micro-compressors in our cooling suits whirred to life. At six thousand meters, we saw the fuel intake port. Truckload after truckload of rocks tumbled into the dull red glow of the gaping pit, consumed without a sound. I asked Ms Stella how the Earth Engines turned stones into fuel.

'Heavy element fusion is a difficult field of study, too complex for me to explain it to you at this age,' she replied. 'All you need to know is that the Earth Engines are the largest machines ever built by humankind. For instance, North China Mountain 794 – where we are now – exerts fifteen billion tons of thrust upon the earth when operating at full capacity.'

Finally, our bus reached the summit. The mouth of the plasma beam was directly above us. The diameter of the beam was so immense that, when we raised our heads, all we could see was a glowing wall of blue plasma that stretched infinitely into the sky. At that moment, I suddenly recalled a riddle posed to us by our philosophy teacher.

'You are walking across a plain when you suddenly encounter a wall,' our haggard teacher had said. 'The wall is infinitely tall and extends infinitely deep underground. It stretches infinitely to the left and infinitely to the right. What is it?'

A cold shiver washed over me. I recited the riddle to Ms Stella, who sat next to me. She teased it over for a while, but finally shook her head in confusion. I leaned in close and whispered the riddle's dreadful answer in her ear.

Death.

She stared at me in silence for a few seconds, and then hugged me tightly against her. Resting my head on her shoulder, I gazed into the far distance. Gargantuan metal Peaks studded the hazy earth below, stretching all the way to the horizon. Each Peak spat forth a brilliant jet of plasma, like a tilted cosmic forest, piercing our teetering sky.

Soon after, we arrived at the seashore. We could see the spires of submerged skyscrapers protruding above the waves. As the tide ebbed, frothing seawater gushed from their countless windows, forming cascades of waterfalls. Even before the Braking Era ended, its effects upon the Earth had become horrifyingly apparent. The tides caused by the acceleration of the Earth Engines engulfed two-thirds of the Northern hemisphere's major cities. Then, the rise in global temperatures melted the polar ice caps, which turned the flooding into a catastrophe that spread to the Southern hemisphere. Thirty years ago, my grandfather witnessed giant hundred-meter waves inundating Shanghai. Even now, when he described the sight, he would stare off into space. In fact, our planet had already changed beyond recognition before it even set out on its voyage. Who knew what trials and tribulations awaited us on our endless travels through outer space?

We boarded something called an 'ocean liner' – an ancient mode of transportation – and departed the shore. Behind us, the plasma beams of the Earth Engines grew ever more distant. After a day's travel, they disappeared from view altogether. The sea was bathed in light from two different sources. To the west, the plasma beams still suffused the sky with an eerie bluish glow; to the east, rosy sunlight was creeping over the horizon. The competing rays split the sea in two, and our ship sailed right along the glittering seam where they met on the surface. It was a fantastic sight. But as the blue glow retreated, and the rosy glow strengthened, unease settled over the ship. My classmates and I were no longer to be seen above deck. We stayed hidden away in our cabins, blinds pulled tight across the portholes. A day later, the moment we most dreaded finally arrived. We all gathered in the large cabin that we used as a classroom to listen to Ms Stella's announcement.

'Children,' she said solemnly, 'we will now go to watch the Sun rise.'

No one moved. Every pair of eyes was fixed in a glassy stare, as if abruptly frozen to the spot. Ms Stella tried to urge us from the cabin, but everyone sat perfectly still. One of the other teachers remarked, 'I've mentioned it before, but we really ought to schedule the Global Experience trip before we teach them modern history. The students would adapt more readily.'

'It's not that simple,' Ms Stella replied. 'They pick it up from their surroundings long before we teach them modern history.' She turned to the class monitors. 'You children go first. Don't be afraid. When I was young, I was nervous about seeing my first sunrise, too. But once I saw it, I was just fine.'

Finally, we stood up and, one by one, trudged out through the cabin door. I suddenly felt a small clammy hand clasp my own, and looked back to see Linger.

'I'm scared . . .' she whimpered.

'We've seen the Sun on TV before. It's the same thing,' I assured her.

'How can it be? Is seeing a snake on TV the same as seeing a real live one?'

I did not know how to reply. '. . . Well, we have to go look anyway. Otherwise we'll be marked down!'

Linger and I gripped hands tightly as we gingerly made our way to the deck with the other children. Stepping outside, we prepared to face our first sunrise.

'In fact, we only began to fear the Sun three or four centuries ago. Before that, humans were not afraid of the Sun. It was just the opposite. In their eyes, the Sun was noble and majestic. The Earth still turned on its axis back then, and people saw the Sun rise and set every single day. They would rejoice at sunrise and praise the beauty of sunset.' Ms

Stella stood at the bow of the ship, the sea breeze playing with her long hair. Behind her, the first few rays of sunlight shot over the horizon, like breath expelled from the blowhole of some unimaginably colossal sea creature.

Finally, we glimpsed the soul-chilling flame. At first, it was just a point of light on the horizon, but it quickly grew into a blazing arc. I felt my throat close up in terror. It seemed as if the deck beneath my feet had suddenly vanished. I was falling into the blackness of the sea, falling. . . . Linger fell with me, her spindly frame quivering against mine. Our classmates, everyone else – the entire world, even – all fell into the abyss. Then I remembered the riddle. I had asked our philosophy teacher what color the wall was. He told me that it was black. I thought he was wrong. I always imagined the wall of death would be bright as fresh snow. That was why I had remembered it when I saw the wall of plasma. In this era, death was no longer black. It was the glare of a lightning flash, and when that final bolt struck, the world would be vaporized in an instant.

Over three centuries ago, astrophysicists discovered that the conversion rate of hydrogen to helium in the interior of the Sun was accelerating. They launched thousands of probes straight into the Sun to investigate, and eventually developed a precise mathematical model of the star.

Using this model, supercomputers calculated that the Sun had already evolved away from the main sequence on the Hertzsprung-Russell diagram. Helium would soon permeate the Sun's core, triggering a violent explosion called a helium flash. Afterward, the Sun would become a massive, cool-burning red giant, swelling until its diameter encompassed the Earth's orbit.

But our planet would have been vaporized in the preceding helium flash long before then.

All of this was projected to occur in the next four hundred years. Since then, three hundred and eighty years had passed.

This solar catastrophe would not only raze and consume every inhabitable terrestrial planet in the solar system – it would also completely transform the composition and orbits of the Jovian planets. After the first helium flash, as heavy elements re-accumulated in the Sun's core, further runaway nuclear explosions would occur repeatedly for a period of time. While this period represented only a brief phase of stellar evolution, it might last thousands of times longer than all of human history. As long as we remained in the solar system, humanity stood no chance of surviving such a catastrophe. Interstellar emigration was our only way out. Given the level of technology available to humanity at the time, the only viable target for this migration was Proxima Centauri. It was the star closest to our own, a mere 4.3 light-years away. Reaching a consensus on a destination was enough, the real controversy lay in how to get there.

In order to reinforce the lesson, our ship doubled back twice on the Pacific, giving us two sunrises. By then we were accustomed to the sight and no longer needed to be convinced that children born in the Southern hemisphere could actually survive daily exposure to the Sun. We sailed on into the dawn. As the Sun rose higher in the sky, the cool ocean air of the past few days retreated, and temperatures began to rise. I was drifting off to sleep in my cabin when I heard a commotion outside. My door opened and Linger stuck her head in.

'Hey, the Leavers and Takers are at it again!'

I could not have cared less. They had been fighting for the last four centuries. Even so, I got up to take a quick look. Outside, a group of several boys were fighting. One glance told me Tung was up to his usual tricks again. His father was a stubborn Leaver, and he was still serving a prison sentence for his part in an uprising against the Coalition. Tung was a chip off the old block.

With the help of several brawny crewmen, Ms Stella managed to pull the boys apart. Despite a bloody nose, Tung still raised a fist and shouted, 'Throw the Takers overboard!'

'I'm a Taker. Do you want to throw me overboard, too?' asked Ms Stella.

'I'll throw every single Taker overboard!' Tung refused to yield. Global support for the Takers had been rising of late, and they had grown unruly again.

'Why do you hate us so much?' asked Ms Stella. Several Leaver children immediately shouted in protest.

'We won't wait to die on Earth with you Taker fools!'

'We will build spaceships and depart! All hail spaceships!'

Ms Stella pressed the holographic projector on her wrist. An image immediately materialized in the air before us, arresting our attention. We quieted down for a moment. The hologram showed a crystal-clear glass sphere. The sphere was about ten centimeters in diameter and two-thirds full of water. It held a small shrimp, a branch of coral, and a bit of green algae. The shrimp swam languidly around the coral.

'This is a project Tung designed for his natural science class,' said Ms Stella. 'In addition to the things you can all see, the sphere also contains microscopic bacteria. Everything inside the sphere is mutually interdependent. The shrimp eats the algae and draws oxygen from the water, and then it discharges organic matter in its faeces and exhales carbon dioxide. The bacteria break down the shrimp's waste into inorganic matter. The algae then use the inorganic matter and carbon dioxide to carry out photosynthesis under an artificial light source. They create nutrients, grow and reproduce, and release oxygen for the shrimp to breathe. As long as there is a constant supply of sunlight, the ecological cycle in the glass sphere should be able to sustain itself in perpetuity. This is the best design by a student I have ever seen. I know that this sphere embodies Tung's dream and the dreams of all Leaver children. It is the spaceship you long after, in miniature! Tung told me he designed it according to the output of rigorous mathematical models. He modified the genes of every organism to ensure their metabolisms would be perfectly balanced. He firmly believed that the little world inside the sphere would survive until the shrimp reached the end of its natural life span. The teachers all adored this project. We placed it under an artificial light source at the required intensity. We were persuaded by Tung's predictions, and we silently wished the tiny world he had created would succeed. But now, less than two weeks later . . .'

Ms Stella carefully withdrew the real glass sphere from a small box. The shrimp floated lifelessly at the surface of the murky water. The decaying algae had lost any hint of green and had turned into a dead, woolly film that coated the coral.

'The little world is dead. Children, who can tell me why?' Ms Stella raised the lifeless sphere so that everyone could see it.

'It was too small!'

'Indeed, it was too small. Small ecosystems like this, no matter how precisely designed, cannot endure the passage of time. The spaceships of the Leavers are no exception.'

'We will build spaceships as large as Shanghai or New York City,' Tung objected, his voice much quieter than before.

'Yes, but anything larger is beyond the limits of human technology, and compared to Earth, those ecosystems would still be much too small.'

'Then we will find a new planet!'

'Even you Leavers don't really believe that,' replied Ms Stella. 'There are no suitable planets in orbit around Proxima Centauri. The nearest fixed star with inhabitable planets is eight hundred and fifty light-years away. At present, the fastest spaceship we can build can only travel at 0.5 per cent of the speed of light, which means it would take us one hundred and seventy thousand years to get there. A spaceship-sized ecosystem would not last for even one-tenth of the voyage. Children, only an ecosystem the size of Earth, with its unstoppable ecological cycle, could sustain us indefinitely! If humanity leaves Earth behind,' she proclaimed, 'then we would be as vulnerable as an infant separated from its mother in the middle of a desert!'

'But . . .' Tung paused. 'Ms Stella, it's too late for us and too late for Earth. The Sun will explode before we accelerate and get far enough away!'

'There is enough time,' she replied firmly. 'You must believe in the Coalition! How many times have I told you? Even if you don't believe, at the very least we can say, "Humanity dies with pride, for we have done everything that we could!"'

Humanity's escape was a five-step process. First, the Earth Engines would generate thrust in the opposite direction of the Earth's movement, halting its rotation. Second, operating at full capacity, the engines would accelerate the Earth until it reached escape velocity, flinging it from the solar system. Third, the Earth would continue to accelerate as it flew through outer space toward Proxima Centauri. Fourth, the engines would reverse direction, restarting the Earth's rotation and decelerating gradually. Fifth, the Earth would enter into orbit around Proxima Centauri, becoming its satellite. People called these five steps the 'Braking Era', the 'Deserting Era', the 'First Wandering Era' (during acceleration), the 'Second Wandering Era' (during deceleration), and the 'Neosolar Era'.

The entire migration process was projected to last 2,500 years, over one hundred generations.

The ocean liner continued its passage toward the part of the Earth shrouded in night. Neither sunlight nor the glow of the plasma beams could be seen here. As the chilly Atlantic breeze nipped at our faces, for the first time in our young lives we saw the stars in the night sky. God, it was a heartbreakingly beautiful sight! Ms Stella stood with one arm around Linger and I. 'Look, children,' she said, pointing to the stars with her other hand. 'There is Centaurus, and that is Proxima Centauri, our new home!' She began to cry, and we cried along with her. All around us, even the captain and the crew – hardened sailors all – began to well up. With tearful eyes, everyone gazed in the direction in which Ms Stella pointed, and the stars shimmered and danced. Only one star held steady; it was the beam of a distant lighthouse over dark and stormy seas, a flicker of fire beckoning to a lonely traveler freezing on the tundra. That star had taken the place of the Sun in our hearts. It was the only pillar of hope for one hundred future generations as they navigated a sea of troubles.

On our voyage home, I saw the first signal for Earth's departure. A giant comet appeared in the night sky – the Moon. Because we could not take the Moon with us, engines had been installed on the lunar surface to push it out of Earth's orbit, ensuring that there would be no collision during the acceleration period. The sweeping tail of the Lunar Engines bathed the sea in blue light, obscuring the stars. As it moved past, the Moon's gravitational pull raised towering breakers. We had to transfer to a plane to fly home to the Northern hemisphere.

The day of departure had finally arrived!

As soon as we disembarked, we were blinded by the glare of the Earth Engines. They blazed many times brighter than before, no longer slanted but pointing straight toward the sky. The engines were running at maximum power. The planet's acceleration created thunderous, hundred-meter waves that battered every continent. Blistering hurricanes howled through the towering columns of plasma, whipping up boiling froth and uprooting whole forests. . . . Our planet had become a gigantic comet, its blue tail piercing the darkness of space.

Earth was on its way; humanity was on its way.

My grandfather passed away just before departure, his burnt body ravaged by infection. In his final moments, he repeated one phrase over and over: 'Ah, Earth, my wandering Earth . . .'

2

THE DESERTING ERA

Our school was scheduled to relocate to an underground city, and we were among its first inhabitants. Our school bus entered a massive tunnel, which sloped gently downward into the earth. After driving for half an hour, we were told that we had entered the city, but nothing outside the bus windows resembled any city I had seen before. We whipped past a labyrinth of smaller side tunnels and countless sealed doors set back into cavities in the walls. Under the row of floodlights mounted to the tunnel ceiling, everything assumed a leaden blue tinge. We could not help but feel dejected at the realization that, for most of the remainder of our lives, this would be our world.

'Primitive humans lived in caves, and now so will we.' Linger said this quietly, but Ms Stella still caught her words.

'It can't be helped, children,' she sighed. 'The surface will soon become a terrible, terrible place. When it is cold, your spit will freeze before it hits the ground. When it is hot, it will evaporate even as it leaves your lips!'

'I know it'll be cold because Earth is traveling away from the Sun, but why will it get hot?' asked a little girl from one of the lower grades.

'Idiot, haven't you studied transfer orbits?' I snapped.

'No.'

Linger launched into a patient explanation, as if to dispel her sorrowful thoughts. 'It's like this: the Earth Engines aren't as powerful as you think. They can accelerate Earth a little bit, but they can't just push it out of its solar orbit straight away. Before Earth escapes the Sun, we still need to orbit it fifteen times! Through these fifteen orbits, Earth will gradually accelerate. Right now, Earth's orbit around the Sun is pretty much circular, but as it speeds up, it will become increasingly elliptical. The faster we move, the flatter the ellipse grows, and the more the Sun will be shifted toward one end of the orbit. So when Earth is furthest from the Sun, naturally it will be very cold—'

'But . . . that's still not right! It will be cold when Earth is far away from the Sun, but on the other end of the ellipse, its distance from the Sun will be. . . . Hmm, let me think.' The girl chewed on her lip. 'Orbital dynamics says Earth won't be any closer to the Sun than it is now, so why would it get hotter?'

She truly was a little genius. Genetic engineering had made this type of exceptional memory the new norm. Humanity was quite fortunate in this respect. Otherwise, unimaginable miracles like the Earth Engines could not have been realized in the span of four centuries.

'Don't forget about the Earth Engines, dummy,' I chimed in. 'Over ten thousand of those giant blowtorches are on full blast. Earth is basically just a ring to hold the rocket nozzles. Now be quiet. I'm getting annoyed.'

We began our new lives underground. Located five hundred meters below the surface, our city had space for over one million residents. Many others just like it were scattered across every continent. Here, I finished primary school and entered secondary school. My schooling concentrated on science and engineering. Art, philosophy, and other subjects deemed inessential had been minimized or removed from the curriculum. Humanity had no time for distractions. It was the busiest era in human history. Everyone had work to do, and the work was never finished. Interestingly, every world religion had vanished without a trace overnight. People finally realized that if God truly existed, he was a real bastard. We still studied history, but to us, the Ante-solar Era of human history seemed as mythical as the Garden of Eden.

My father served in the Air Force as an astronaut. He frequently flew low-Earth orbit missions and was rarely at home. I remember in the fifth year of orbital acceleration, when Earth was at aphelion, we took a family trip to the seashore. Aphelion Day was a holiday like New Year's Eve or Christmas. As Earth entered the part of its orbit furthest from the Sun, everyone basked in a false sense of security, though. We still needed to wear special thermal suits to go to surface. Instead of cooling suits, we donned sealed heating suits powered by nuclear batteries. Outside, we were nearly blinded by the Earth Engines' towering plasma beams. The harsh light eclipsed our view of the surface world, and it was difficult to tell if the landscape had changed at all. We had to fly for a long time in our car before we escaped the glare and we could actually see the shore. The Sun had shrunk to the size of a baseball. It hung motionless in the sky, surrounded by a faint, dawn-like halo. The sky was the deepest blue we had ever seen, and the stars were clearly visible. Looking around, I fleetingly wondered where the ocean had gone. There was now only a vast, white, icy plain stretching to the horizon. A large crowd of revelers had gathered atop the frozen sea. Fireworks whistled through the darkness. Everyone was carousing with unusual abandon. Drunken party-goers rolled across the ice, while others belted out the words to a dozen different songs, each trying to drown out the competing voices around them.

'Despite it all, everyone is living their own lives. No harm in that,' my father said approvingly. He paused, suddenly remembering something. 'Oh, I forgot to tell you – I've fallen in love with Stella Li. I want to move out to be with her.'

'Who is she?' my mother asked calmly.

'My primary school teacher,' I answered for him. I had started secondary school two years ago, and had no idea how my father knew Ms Stella. Maybe they had met at my graduation ceremony?

'Then go,' said my mother.

'I'm sure I'll grow tired of her soon enough. I'll come back then. Is that okay by you?'

'If you want to, certainly.' Her voice was as calm and even as the frozen sea. But a moment later, she bubbled with excitement. 'Oh, that one is beautiful! It must have a holographic diffractor inside!' She pointed to a firework blossoming in the night sky, genuinely moved by its beauty.

Movies and novels produced four centuries ago were baffling to modern audiences. It was incomprehensible to us why people in the Ante-solar Era invested so much emotion into matters that had nothing to do with survival. Watching the hero or heroine suffer or weep for love was bizarre beyond words. In this day and age, the threat of death and the desire to escape overrode everything else. Nothing but the most current updates on the solar state and position of Earth could hope to move us or even hold our attention. This hyper-focus gradually changed the essence of human psychology and spirituality. Humans paid scant attention to affairs of the heart, like a gambler taking a swig of water, unable to tear his eyes from the roulette wheel.

Two months later, my father returned from his jaunt with Ms Stella. My mother was neither happy nor unhappy to see him.

'Stella has a good impression of you,' my father told me. 'She said you were a very creative student.'

'Who said that?' My mother asked with a puzzled expression.

'My primary school teacher, Ms Stella,' I replied impatiently. 'Dad was living with her for the last two months!'

'Oh, I remember!' She shook her head and laughed. 'Not even forty yet, and my memory is already shot.'

She looked up at the holographic stars on the ceiling and the forest on the walls. 'It's good to have you home. Now you can switch up these images. Your son and I are sick of looking at them, but we don't know how to work the darn thing.'

By the time Earth began its fall back toward the Sun, we had all entirely forgotten the episode.

One day, the news reported that the ocean had begun to thaw, so we took another family trip to the seashore. Earth was just passing through Mars' orbit. The available sunlight should not have significantly raised temperatures, but the Earth Engines ensured the surface was warm enough to thaw the sea ice. It felt delightful to step outside without the encumbrance of a thermal suit. The Earth Engines still lit up the sky in our hemisphere, but on the other side of the planet people could really feel the Sun's approach. Their sky was clear and pure blue, and the Sun was as bright as it had been before departure. But from the air, we spotted no signs of a thaw. We saw only a white expanse of ice. Disappointed, we got out of our car. Just as we closed the doors, we heard an earthshaking rumble that seemed to rise from the very depths of the planet. It sounded like the Earth was about to explode.

'That's the sound of the ocean!' my father shouted over the noise. 'The sharp rise in temperatures is heating the thick ice unevenly – it's like an earthquake on land!'

Suddenly, a sharp noise like a thunderclap pierced the low rumble, eliciting cheers from the people watching the sea behind us. I saw a long crack appear, shooting across the frozen ocean like a black fork of lightning. The rumbling continued as more fissures appeared in the ice. Water gushed from the cracks, forming torrents that rushed across the icy plain.

On the way home, we looked out over the desolate land below and saw broad tracts of wild grass sprouting from the earth. All kinds of flowers had burst into full bloom, and withered forests were mantled in tender green leaves. Life was throwing itself into the business of rejuvenation as if there was no time to lose.

Every day the Earth drew closer to the Sun, dread knotted itself tighter in our stomachs. Fewer people made the trip to the surface to admire the spring scenery. Most of us retreated into the depths of the underground city, not to avoid the approaching heat, torrential rains, and hurricane-force winds, but to escape the creeping terror of the Sun. One night, after I had already gone to bed, I overheard my mother tell my father in hushed tones, 'Maybe it really is too late.'

'The same rumor was going around during the last four perihelions,' he replied.

'But this time it's true,' she insisted. 'I heard it from Dr Chandler. Her husband is an astronomer on the Navigation Commission. You all know him. He told her that they have observed accelerated rates of helium concentration.'

'Listen, my dear, we mustn't give up hope. Not because hope is real, but because we have to conduct ourselves nobly. In the Antesolar Era, nobility required wealth, power, or talent, but now one just needs hope. It is the gold and jewels of this age. No matter how long we live, we must hold on to it! Tomorrow, we'll tell our son the same thing.'

Like everyone else, I felt restless and uneasy as the perihelion approached. One day after school, I found myself in the city's central plaza. I stood by the round fountain in the middle of the plaza, looking down at the glittering water in the pool and then up at the ethereal ripples of light reflected on the domed ceiling. Just then I noticed Linger. She was holding a little bottle in one hand and a short length of tubing in the other. She was blowing soap bubbles, her eyes blankly following each string of bubbles as they drifted away. She watched them vanish one by one, only to blow another stream.

'You still like blowing bubbles at your age?' I asked, walking over.

Linger looked pleased to see me. 'Let's take a trip!'

'Take a trip? Where?'

'To the surface, of course!' She swept her hand through the air, using the computer on her wrist to project a hologram of a beach at sunset. A gentle breeze stirred the palm trees, and white surf lapped at the shore. Pairs of lovers dotted the yellow sand, black silhouettes against the gold-flecked sea. 'Mona and Dagang sent me this. They've been traveling all over the world. They said it's not too hot on the surface. It's so nice out. Let's go!'

'They were just expelled for cutting class,' I objected.

Linger sniffed. 'That's not what you're really afraid of. You're afraid of the Sun!'

'And you're not? You had to see a psychiatrist because of your heliophobia.'

'I'm a different person now. I've been inspired! Look,' said Linger, using the tube to blow another stream of soap bubbles. 'Watch closely.' She pointed to the bubbles.

I singled out a bubble, examining the waves of light and color surging across its surface, the iridescent patterns too complex and intricate for humans to process. It was as if the bubble knew it would lead a short life and was frantically broadcasting the myriad dreams and legends of its prodigious memory to the world. A moment later, the waves of light and color vanished in a silent explosion. For a half-second, a tiny wisp of vapor remained, but then that, too, was gone, as if the bubble had never existed at all.

'See? The Earth is a cosmic soap bubble. One pop, and it's gone. So what is there to be afraid of?'

'But it won't happen like that. It's been calculated that after the helium flash it will take one hundred hours before the Earth is completely vaporized.'

'That's exactly the scariest part!' Linger cried. 'Five hundred meters underground, we're like meat stuffing in a pasty. First we'll be slowly cooked through, and then we'll be vaporized!'

A cold shiver ran down my entire body.

'But it won't be like that on the surface. Everything will be vaporized in the blink of an eye. Anyone up there will be like soap bubbles: one pop and . . .' She trailed off. 'So I think it would be better to be on the surface when the flash hits.'

I couldn't say why, but I did not go with her. She went with Tung instead, and I never saw either of them again.

But the helium flash never happened. Earth swept past perihelion and climbed toward aphelion for the sixth time. Humanity breathed a collective sigh of relief. Because Earth no longer rotated, at this point in its orbit around the Sun the Earth Engines installed in Asia faced into the planet's direction of flight. As a result, the engines were completely powered down, save for occasional adjustments to the Earth's orientation. We sailed into a quiet, endless night. In North America, however, the engines were operating at full capacity, the continent securing the rocket nozzles to the planet. Because the Western hemisphere also faced the Sun, the heat there was devastating. Grass and trees alike went up in smoke.

Earth's gravity-assisted acceleration progressed like this year after year. When the planet began its ascent toward aphelion, we unwound proportionally to the Earth's distance from the Sun; at the new year, when the planet began its long fall toward the Sun, we grew tenser with each passing day. Each time Earth reached perihelion, rumors swirled that the helium flash was imminent. The rumors would persist until Earth climbed again toward aphelion. But even as people's fears subsided as the Sun shrank in the sky, the next wave of panic was already brewing. It was like humanity's morale was dangling from a cosmic trapeze. Or perhaps it was more accurate to say that we were playing Russian Roulette on a planetary scale: every journey from perihelion to aphelion and back was like turning the chamber, and passing the perihelion was like pulling the trigger! Each pull was more nerve-wracking than the last. My boyhood was spent alternating between terror and relaxation. Come to think of it, even at aphelion, Earth never left the danger zone of the helium flash. When the Sun exploded, Earth would be slowly liquefied, which was a fate considerably worse than being vaporized at perihelion.

In the Deserting Era, disaster followed disaster in quick succession.

The changes in velocity and trajectory generated by the Earth Engines disturbed the equilibrium of Earth's iron-nickel core. The turbulence passed through the Gutenberg discontinuity and spread to the mantle. As geothermal energy escaped to the surface, volcanic eruptions ravaged every continent, which posed a lethal threat to humanity's underground cities. Beginning in the sixth orbital period onward, catastrophic magma seepage events occurred all too frequently in cities around the world.

On the day it happened, I was on my way home from school when the sirens sounded. It was quickly followed by an emergency broadcast from city hall.

'Attention citizens of City F112! The city's northern barrier has been breached by crustal stress. Magma has entered the city! Magma has entered the city! Magma flows have already reached Block Four! Highway exits have been sealed off. All citizens should report to the central plaza and evacuate by lift. Please note that the evacuation will be conducted in accordance with Article Five of the Emergencies Act. I repeat, the evacuation will be conducted in accordance with Article Five of the Emergencies Act!'

Looking around the labyrinth of tunnels, our underground city seemed eerily normal. But I was aware of the immediate danger: of the two subterranean highways that led out of the city, one of those routes had been blocked off last year by necessary fortification work on the city's barriers. If the remaining route was also blocked, we could only escape through the vertical elevator shafts that led directly to the surface.

The carrying capacity of the lifts was very limited. It would take a long time to move all three hundred and sixty thousand residents to safety, but there was no need to scramble for a place on the lifts. The Coalition's Emergency Act had made all necessary arrangements for the evacuation.

Past generations once grappled with an ethical dilemma. A man is faced by rising floodwaters and can only save one other person. Should he save his father or his son? In this day and age, it was unbelievable that the question had ever been raised at all.

When I arrived in the plaza, I saw that people had already begun to arrange themselves in a long line according to age. At the front of the line, closest to the lifts, stood robotic nurses, each cradling an infant. Then came the kindergartners, followed by the primary school students. My place was in the middle of the line, still rather close to the front. My father was on duty in low-Earth orbit, leaving only my mother and myself in the city. Unable to see her, I began to run along the unending line of people but did not get far before I was stopped by soldiers. I knew she stood at the very back. Our city was primarily a university town, with only a few families, so she was grouped with the city's oldest residents.

The line inched forward at an excruciating pace. After three long hours it was finally my turn, but I felt no relief as I boarded the lift. There were still twenty thousand university students standing between my mother and survival, and I could already smell the strong odor of sulfur.

Two and a half hours after I made it to the surface, magma inundated the entire city five hundred meters beneath my feet. A knife twisted in my heart as I imagined my mother's final moments. Standing alongside eighteen thousand others who could not be evacuated in time, she would have watched magma surge into the plaza. The city's power supply would have failed, leaving only the dreadful crimson glow of the magma. The intense heat would have blackened the lofty white dome over the plaza. The victims likely never came into contact with the magma before the thousand-plus-degree temperatures proved fatal.

But life went on, and even in this harsh, terrifying reality, sparks of love still flew from time to time. During the twelfth climb toward aphelion, in an attempt to ease public tension, the Coalition unexpectedly revived the Olympic Games after a two-century hiatus. I competed at the Games in the snowmobile rally. Beginning in Shanghai, athletes raced their snowmobiles across the frozen surface of the Pacific to New York.

At the sound of the starting gun, more than a hundred snowmobiles shot off across the frozen ocean, blazing across the ice at two hundred kilometers per hour. At first, there was always a competitor in my sights. Two days later, however, having fallen behind or surged ahead, they had all disappeared over the horizon.

The glow of the Earth Engines was no longer visible behind me, and I sped into the darkest part of the planet. My world was the boundless starlit sky and the ice that stretched in all directions to the ends of the universe – or perhaps *this* was the end of the universe. And in this universe of infinite stars and endless ice, I was alone! As an avalanche of loneliness overwhelmed me, I wanted to cry. I drove as if my life depended on it. Whether or not I placed on the podium was beside the point: I needed to get rid of this terrible loneliness before it killed me. In my mind, the opposite shore no longer existed.

At that moment, I saw a figure silhouetted against the horizon. As I grew closer, I realized it was a woman. She was standing next to her snowmobile, her long hair fluttering in the icy wind. The moment our paths crossed, it was clear that the rest of our lives had been decided. Her name was Yamasaki Kayoko, and she was Japanese. The women's team had set off twelve hours before us, but her snowmobile had been caught in a crack in the ice, snapping one of the skis. As I helped her repair her sled, I shared with her the feeling that had gripped me earlier.

'I felt exactly the same way!' she exclaimed. 'It was like I was alone in the universe! You know, when I saw you appear in the distance, it was like watching the Sun rise.'

'Why didn't you call a rescue plane?' I asked.

She raised her small fist. 'This race embodies the human spirit,' she declared with the tenacity so characteristic of the Japanese. 'We must remember that Earth cannot call for help as it wanders through the cosmos!'

'Well, now we have to call. Neither of us has a spare runner, so your snowmobile is beyond repair.'

'Why don't I ride on the back of yours?' she suggested. 'If you don't care about placing, that is.'

I really did not care, so Kayoko and I made the rest of the long journey across the frozen Pacific together.

As we passed Hawaii, we saw a glimmer of light on the horizon. On this boundless expanse of ice, illuminated by the tiny Sun, we submitted an application for a marriage license to the Coalition Department of Civil Affairs.

By the time we reached New York City, the Olympic referees had grown tired of waiting and had packed their things and left. But an official from the municipal Bureau of Civil Affairs stood waiting for us. He congratulated us on our marriage and then began to perform his official duty. With a sweep of his hand, he summoned a hologram that was neatly lined with tens of thousands of dots. Each dot represented a couple that had registered for marriage with the Coalition in the last few days. In light of harsh environmental conditions, by law only one out of every three newly married couples was permitted to procreate. This right was awarded by lottery. Faced with thousands of dots, Kayoko hesitated for a long time before picking one in the middle.

When the dot turned green, she jumped for joy. I was not sure how I felt about the prospect of starting a family. If I brought a child into this era of suffering, would it be a blessing or a calamity? The official, at least, was over the moon. He told us it was always a happy occasion when a couple got their little green dot. He pulled out a bottle of vodka, and the three of us took turns drinking from it, toasting the continuation of the human race. Behind us, the faint light of the distant Sun gilded the Statue of Liberty. Before us, the long-abandoned skyscrapers of Manhattan cast long shadows over the quiet ice of New York Harbor. Feeling tipsy, I realized tears had begun to stream down my cheeks.

Earth, my wandering Earth!

Before we parted ways, the official handed us a set of keys and hiccupped, 'These are for your newly allotted house in Asia. Run along home, now. Run to your wonderful new home!'

'Just how wonderful is it?' I asked coldly. 'Asia's underground cities are fraught with danger – but of course you Westerners wouldn't know that.'

'We are about to face our own unique hazard,' he replied. 'Earth is about to pass through the asteroid belt, and the Western hemisphere is facing right toward it.'

'But we passed through the asteroid belt on the last few orbits. It's no big deal, is it?'

'We just swiped the edges of the asteroid belt. The Space Fleet could handle that, of course. They have lasers and nukes to clear small rocks from the Earth's path. But this time . . .' He paused. 'Haven't you seen the news? This time, Earth will pass straight through the middle of the belt! The fleet will deal with the small rocks, but the large ones . . .'

On the flight back to Asia, Kayoko turned to me and asked, 'Are those asteroids very big?'

My father was one of the Space Fleet officers tasked with asteroid diversion and destruction. Therefore, though the government had imposed the usual media blackout to prevent mass panic, I still had some idea of what was about to happen. I told Kayoko that some of the asteroids we faced were the size of mountains; even fifty-megaton thermonuclear bombs would only pockmark their surfaces.

'They'll have to use the most powerful weapon in the human arsenal,' I added mysteriously.

'You mean antimatter bombs?' she asked.

'What else could it be?'

'What is the fleet's cruising range?'

'Currently their strength is limited. My dad told me it extends out to about one and a half million kilometers,' I answered.

Kayoko gave a little squeal. 'Then we'll be able to see it!'

'Best not to look.'

But Kayoko did look, and she did so without protective glasses. The first flash of an antimatter bomb arrived from space shortly after we took off. At that exact moment, Kayoko had been admiring the starry sky outside the window. The flash blinded her for over an hour, and her eyes were red and watery for more than a month afterward. In the bloodcurdling moments that followed the flash, the antimatter shells continued to bombard the asteroid. Ruinous flashes pulsed across the pitch-black sky, as if a horde of colossal paparazzi had descended upon the planet and were frenziedly snapping away.

Half an hour later, we saw the meteors, dragging streaming tails of fire across the sky, mesmerizing in their terrible beauty. More and more meteors appeared, each streaking further into the atmosphere than the last. Suddenly, a deafening roar shook the plane, immediately followed by more rumbling and shaking. Thinking that a meteor had struck the plane, Kayoko screamed and threw herself into my arms. Just then, the captain's voice came on over the intercom.

'Ladies and gentlemen, please do not be alarmed. That was merely the sonic boom created by a meteor breaking the sound barrier. Please put on your headphones to avoid permanent hearing loss. Because the safety of the flight cannot be guaranteed, we will make an emergency landing in Hawaii.'

As the announcement ended, my eyes fastened on a meteor much larger than the others. I became convinced it would not burn up in the atmosphere like the ones before it. Sure enough, the fireball hurtled across the sky, shrinking as it fell, and smashed into the frozen ocean. Seen from ten thousand meters above, a small white spot appeared at the point of impact. The spot immediately spread into a white circle and rapidly expanded across the ocean's surface.

'Is that a wave?' asked Kayoko, her voice trembling.

'Yes, it's a wave over a hundred meters high. But the ocean is frozen solid. The ice will soon dampen it,' I replied, mostly to comfort myself. I did not look down again.

We landed in Honolulu not long after. The local government had arranged to take us to an underground city. The drive along the coast afforded us a clear view of the meteor-filled sky. It was as if a legion of fiery-haired demons had burst all at once from a single point in space.

We watched as a meteor struck the surface not far from the coast. There was no visible plume of water, but a white mushroom cloud of water vapor bloomed high overhead. Beneath the frozen surface, roiling seawater surged toward the shore. The thick layers of ice groaned as they splintered apart, rolling like waves, as if a school of giant, sinuous sea monsters was swimming beneath the surface.

'How big was that one?' I asked the official who had met us at the airport.

'Less than five kilograms, no bigger than your head. But I have just been informed that a twenty-ton meteor is splashing down eight hundred kilometers north of here.'

His wrist communicator began beeping. He glanced at it and immediately told the driver, 'We won't make it to Gate 204. Head for the nearest entrance!'

The van turned a corner and pulled to a stop in front of an entrance to the underground city. As we got out, we saw that several soldiers guarded the entrance. They stared unblinkingly into the distance, eyes filled with terror. We followed their gaze to the horizon and saw a black barrier. At first glance, it looked like a low bank of clouds, but its height was too uniform for clouds – it was more like a long wall stretching across the horizon. Closer inspection revealed that the wall was edged in white.

'What is that?' Kayoko asked an officer timidly. His answer made our hair stand on end.

'A wave.'

The tall steel gates to the subterranean city grated shut. Ten minutes later, we felt a deep rumble emanate from the ceiling, as if a titan were rolling about on the surface up there. We gazed at each other in speechless despair, for we knew at that moment hundred-meter waves were rolling over Hawaii and on toward the mainland. But the quakes that followed were even more terrifying. It was as if a giant fist were pummeling Earth from outer space. Underground, the assault was faint, but we felt each tremor keenly in our souls. It was the barrage of meteors against the surface.

The brutal bombardment of our planet continued on and off for a week. When we finally left the underground city, Kayoko cried, 'My God, what happened to the sky?'

The sky was a muddy gray. The upper atmosphere was filled with the dust that had been kicked up by the asteroid collisions. The Sun and stars were lost in this endless gray, as if the entire universe was blanketed in thick fog. On the ground, the seawater left in the wake of the monstrous waves had frozen solid. The surviving high-rises stood isolated above the ice, cascades of ice spilling down their sides. A layer of dust had settled on the ice, draining all color from the world except for that all-pervading gray.

Kayoko and I soon resumed our voyage back to Asia. As the plane crossed the International Date Line, which had long since ceased to matter, we witnessed humanity's darkest night. The plane seemed to cruise silently through the inky depths of the ocean. As we gazed through the windows, searching in vain for a glimmer of light in the gloom, our moods turned equally black.

'When will it end?' Kayoko murmured.

I did not know if she meant our journey or this lifetime of misery and suffering. I was beginning to think there was no end to either one. Indeed, even if Earth sailed beyond the blast radius of the helium flash, even if we escaped with our lives – then what? We stood on the bottom rung of an immeasurably tall ladder. In a hundred generations, when our descendants reached the top and glimpsed the promise of new life, our bones would have long turned to dust. I did not imagine the suffering and hardships yet to come, much less consider leading my lover and my child down that endless, muddy road. I was so tired, too tired to go on . . .

Just as sorrow and despair threatened to suffocate me, a woman's scream rang through the cabin: 'Ah! No! Darling, you can't!'

I turned and saw a woman wrest a gun from the hands of the man sitting next to her. He had just attempted to put the muzzle of the gun against his own temple. The man looked wan and emaciated, his eyes staring listlessly into the distance. The woman buried her head in his lap and broke into little chirping sobs.

'Be quiet,' the man said coldly.

The sobbing stopped, leaving only the low hum of the engines, like a steady funeral dirge. In my mind, the plane was stuck in the vast gloom, motionless. There was nothing else left in the entire universe except for the plane and the enveloping darkness. Kayoko pressed herself tightly into my embrace. Her entire body felt ice-cold.

Suddenly, there was a commotion at the front of the cabin and people began whispering excitedly. I looked out the window and saw a hazy light in front of the plane. The dust-filled night sky was uniformly suffused with a formless blue glow.

It was the light of the Earth Engines.

One-third of the Western hemisphere's engines had been destroyed by meteoroids, but Earth had sustained less damage than the calculations had projected before departure. The Earth Engines in the Eastern hemisphere, sheltered on the reverse side of the impact surface, had suffered no losses. In terms of power, Earth remained well equipped to make its escape.

When I laid eyes on the dim blue light ahead, I felt like a deep-sea diver finally seeing the sunlit surface after a long ascent from the abyss. I began to breathe steadily again.

From a few rows away, I heard the woman's voice. 'Darling, pain, fear – we can only feel these things while we are alive. When we die, there is nothing at all. Only darkness. It is better to live, don't you think?'

The emaciated man did not reply. He was staring at the blue light up ahead, tears rolling down his face. I knew he would live through this. Just as long as that hopeful blue light still shone, we would all live through this. I remembered my father's words of hope.

When we touched down, Kayoko and I did not go directly to our new underground home. Instead, we went to look for my father at the Space Fleet's base station on the surface. When we arrived at the station, however, I found only a medal of honor, posthumously awarded and ice-cold. The medal was presented to me by an air vice-marshal. He told me that my father had lost his life during the operation to clear the asteroids from the Earth's path. An antimatter explosion had blasted an asteroid fragment straight into his single-seater craft.

'When it happened, the rock was traveling at one hundred kilometers per second relative to his ship. The cabin was vaporized on impact. He felt no pain,' said the air marshal. 'I assure you, he felt no pain at all.'

When Earth began its fall back toward the Sun again, Kayoko and I traveled to the surface to see the spring scenery. We were sorely disappointed.

The world was still a monochromatic gray. Under the overcast sky, frozen lakes of residual seawater dotted the landscape. There was not a single sprig of green to be seen. The great pall of dust in the atmosphere blocked the light of the Sun, preventing temperatures from rising again. The oceans and continents did not thaw even at perihelion. The Sun remained a faint, dim presence, like a specter lurking behind the dust.

Three years later, as the dust in the atmosphere dissipated, humanity made its last pass through perihelion. As we reached it, those living in the Eastern hemisphere were privileged to witness the fastest sunrise and sunset in Earth's history. The Sun leapt up from the sea and streaked rapidly across the sky. Shadows changed directions so quickly that they looked like second hands sweeping across the faces of countless clocks. It was the shortest day Earth had ever seen, over in less than an hour.

When the Sun plunged below the horizon and darkness fell across the planet, I felt a twinge of grief. This fleeting day seemed like a brief summary of Earth's four-and-a-half-billion-year history in the solar system. Even until the end of the universe, Earth would never return.

'It's dark,' Kayoko said sadly.

'The longest night,' I replied. In the Eastern hemisphere, this night would last twenty-five hundred years. One hundred generations would pass before the light of Proxima Centauri illuminated this continent anew. The Western hemisphere was facing its longest day, but even so, it would last just a moment compared to our age-long night. On that side of the world, the Sun would quickly rise to its zenith, where it would remain motionless, steadily shrinking. Within half a century, it would be difficult to distinguish from any other star.

The Earth's intended trajectory called for a rendezvous with Jupiter. The Navigation Commission's plan was as follows: the Earth's fifteenth orbit around the Sun would be so elliptical that its aphelion would enter Jupiter's orbit. Earth would brush past Jupiter on a near-collision course. Harnessing the gas giant's enormous gravitational pull to assist its acceleration, Earth would finally attain escape velocity.

Two months after Earth passed perihelion, Jupiter became visible to the naked eye. At first, it appeared as a dim point of light, but it soon flattened and became disk-shaped. After another month, Jupiter had grown as large as the full Moon, reddish-brown with faintly visible banding. Then some of the Earth Engines' plasma beams, which had remained perpendicular for fifteen years, began to shift. Final adjustments were being made to Earth's orientation before the rendezvous. Jupiter sank slowly below the horizon, where it stayed for the next three months. We could not see it, but we knew the two planets were converging upon each other.

It almost came as a surprise when we heard that Jupiter was visible again in the Eastern hemisphere. Everyone thronged to the surface to take a look. When I passed through the airlock of the underground city, I saw that the Earth Engines, after running continuously for fifteen years, had been powered down. We could see the stars in the sky once again. Our final rendezvous with Jupiter was in progress.

Everyone peered nervously toward the western sky, where a dim red glow was beginning to show above the horizon. The glow swelled until it filled the entire skyline. I soon realized that the red expanse had formed a neat border against the stars; it was an arc so massive that it spanned from one end of the horizon to the other. As it slowly rose, the sky beneath it turned red, as if a velvet theater curtain were being drawn across the rest of the universe. I let out a gasp, reeling from the realization that the curtain was Jupiter. I knew that Jupiter was thirteen hundred times the size of Earth, but only when I saw its immense splendor did I truly take in its colossal size.

It was difficult to describe in words the fear and oppression that accompanied the behemoth as it reared above the horizon. One reporter later wrote, 'I did not know if I was in my own nightmare, or if the whole universe was just a nightmare in the enormous, twisted mind of that deity!' As Jupiter continued its terrible ascent, it gradually came to occupy half the sky. We then had an unobscured view of the storms raging in its cloud layers, which whipped the gasses in the atmosphere into chaotic, disorienting lines. I knew that beneath those thick decks of clouds lay seething oceans of liquid hydrogen and liquid helium. The famous Great Red Spot appeared, still raging across Jupiter's surface after hundreds of thousands of years. The maelstrom was large enough to swallow three Earths. Jupiter now filled the entire sky. Earth was like a balloon floating on Jupiter's boiling red sea of clouds. The Great Red Spot climbed to the middle of the sky and stared down upon our world like a cyclopean eye. The entire landscape was shrouded in its ghastly light. It was impossible to believe that our tiny planet could escape the gravitational field of this colossus. From the ground, it even seemed unimaginable that Earth might become a satellite of Jupiter – no, we would certainly plummet into the hell concealed beneath that unending ocean of clouds.

But the navigational engineers' calculations were faultless, and the bewildering ruddy sky continued to drift past us. After some time, a black crescent appeared on the western horizon and swiftly widened to reveal the twinkling stars. Earth was breaking free from Jupiter's gravitational clutches. Just then, sirens began to wail, announcing that the gravitational tide Jupiter had raised was rushing back inland. We were told later that giant waves, reaching over one hundred metres high, had again swept across the continents. As I ran toward the gates of the underground city, I stole one last glance at Jupiter, which still occupied half the sky. Distinct scoring marred the gas giant's cloud layer, which I later learned was the trail left by the gravitational pull of Earth on Jupiter's surface. Our planet, too, had left mountainous breakers of liquid helium and hydrogen in its wake. At that point, the Earth, accelerated by Jupiter's mighty gravity, was hurled into deep space.

As it departed Jupiter, Earth reached escape velocity. It no longer needed to return toward the Sun, where only death lurked. As it hurtled toward the open reaches of space, the endless Wandering Era began.

And under the dark red shadow of Jupiter, deep within the earth, my son was born.

3

REBELLION

After we left Jupiter behind, Asia's ten thousand Earth Engines roared to life again. They would operate at full capacity for the next five hundred years, constantly accelerating the planet. During those five hundred years, the engines would consume half of the mountains on the Asian continent as fuel.

Freed at last from the fear of death after four centuries, humanity breathed a collective sigh of relief. But the expected revelry never took place, and what happened next was beyond anyone's imagining.

After our subterranean city's celebratory rally concluded, I donned my thermal suit and ascended to the surface alone. The familiar mountains of my childhood had already been leveled by mega-excavators, leaving only bare rock and hard, frozen soil. The bleak emptiness was broken by patches of stark white covering the land as far as the eye could see: the salt marshes left behind by the great ocean tide. Before me, the city in which my father and grandfather had lived out their days – a city once home to ten million – lay in ruins. In the blue light of the Earth Engine's plasma beams, the exposed steel skeletons of skyscrapers dragged long shadows behind them, like the fossilized remains of prehistoric beasts. The chronic floods and meteor strikes had destroyed virtually everything on the surface. All that humankind and nature had wrought over millennia lay in ruins; our planet had been rendered as barren and desolate as Mars.

Around this time, Kayoko grew restless. She often left our son unsupervised while she took the car on long flights. When she returned, she would say only that she had gone to the Western hemisphere. Finally, one day she dragged me along with her.

We drove for two hours at Mach 4 before we caught a glimpse of the Sun. It had just risen above the Pacific Ocean. No bigger than a baseball, it cast a faint, cold light over the frozen surface.

At an elevation of five thousand meters, Kayoko shifted the car into hover. She then pulled a long package from the backseat. After she removed its cover, I saw that it was an astronomical telescope of the sort favored by hobbyists. Kayoko opened the car window, pointed the telescope at the Sun, and told me to look.

Through the tinted lens, I could see the Sun, magnified hundreds of times. I could even clearly see the light and dark sunspots slowly drifting across its surface and the faint prominences at the edges of the solar disk.

Kayoko linked the telescope to the onboard computer and captured an image of the Sun. She then pulled up a different solar image and said, 'This is from four centuries ago.' The computer proceeded to compare the two images.

'Do you see that?' Kayoko asked, pointing to the screen. 'Luminosity, pixel arrays, pixel probabilities, layer statistics – every parameter is exactly the same!'

'What does that prove? A toy telescope, a cheap image-processing program, and you, an uninformed amateur.' I shook my head. 'Pay no attention to those rumors.'

'You're an idiot,' she snapped, retracting the telescope and turning the car toward home. In the distance, I noticed a few other cars both above and below us. They hovered in the air just as we had, a telescope trained on the Sun through every car window.

Over the next few months, a terrible allegation swept like wildfire across the world. More and more people made it their business to observe the Sun with the assistance of larger, more sophisticated instruments. An NGO even launched an array of probes toward the Sun, which passed through their target three months later. The data transmitted by the probes finally confirmed the fact:

The Sun had not changed at all in the past four centuries.

On every continent, the situation in the underground cities was volatile, like bubbling volcanoes building toward eruption. One day, heeding a decree from the Coalition, Kayoko and I placed our son into a Foster Center. On the way home, we both sensed that the only tie that held us together was gone. As we neared the central plaza, we saw a man addressing a crowd. Others were distributing weapons to the citizens who had gathered around the speaker.

'Citizens! Earth has been betrayed! Humanity has been betrayed! Civilization has been betrayed! We are all the victims of a tremendous hoax! The sheer scale of this hoax would shock God himself! The Sun is entirely unchanged! It will not explode, not then, not now, not ever! It is the very symbol of eternity! What is explosive is the wild and insidious ambition of those in the Coalition! They fabricated all of it, just so they could establish their own tyrannical empire! They have destroyed Earth! They have destroyed human civilization! Citizens, citizens of conscience! Take up arms and rescue our planet! Rescue human civilization! We will overthrow the Coalition! We will seize control of the Earth Engines and steer our planet from the cold depths of outer space back to its original orbit! Back to the warm embrace of the Sun!'

Without a word, Kayoko stepped forward to accept an assault rifle from one of the people handing out weapons, joining the column of armed citizens. She did not look back as she disappeared into the haze of the underground city alongside the ranks of her neighbors. I just stood there. In my pocket, the medal for which my father had traded his life and loyalty was clenched in my hand, so tightly that its points drew blood.

Three days later, rebellion broke out on every continent.

Wherever the rebel army went, the people rallied to its call. Few citizens still doubted that they had been deceived. Even so, I still joined the Coalition army. It was not that I had any real faith in the government, but my family had served in the military for three generations. They had sown the seeds of loyalty deep in my heart, and to betray the Coalition was simply unthinkable, no matter the circumstances.

One after another, the Americas, Africa, Oceania, and Antarctica fell to the rebels as the Coalition army drew back to defensive lines around the Earth Engines in Eastern and Central Asia, ready to defend them to the death. The rebel army quickly surrounded these lines. Their forces overwhelmingly outnumbered the Coalition forces, but because of the close proximity of the engines the offensive made no progress for a long time. The rebel army had no desire to destroy the engines, and thus refrained from deploying heavy weapons, giving the Coalition a stay of execution. The two sides remained locked in a stalemate for three months. But after twelve field armies defected in succession, the Coalition defenses crumbled along all fronts. Two months later, with things looking bleak, the last hundred thousand government troops found themselves besieged on all sides at the Earth Engine control center on the coast.

I was a major in what remained of the army. The control center was the size of a mid-tier city, built around the Earth Navigation Bridge. A dead arm, seared by laser fire, had landed me in a cot in the combat casualty ward. It was there that I learned Kayoko had been killed in action in the Battle of Australia. Like the others in the ward, all day, every day, I would drink myself blind. We lost all track of the war raging outside, and we were indifferent to it. I do not know how much time had passed when I heard a voice bellow across the ward.

'You know why you have been reduced to this? You blame yourselves for standing against humanity in this war! So did I!'

As I turned my head to look, I saw that the speaker wore a general's star on his shoulder. 'No matter,' he continued. 'We have one last chance to save our souls. The Earth Navigation Bridge is only three blocks away. We will take it and hand it over to the sane humans outside! We have done our duty to the Coalition, and now we must do our duty to humanity!'

With my good arm, I drew my pistol and followed the frenzied mass of able-bodied and wounded soldiers surging through the steel corridors toward the bridge. To my surprise, we met almost no resistance along the way. In fact, more and more people emerged from the complex maze of passageways to join us. Finally, we arrived before a metal gate so tall that I could not see the top of it. It rumbled open and we charged into the Earth Navigation Bridge.

Even though we had seen it countless times on television, everyone was still floored by the bridge's grandeur. It was difficult to judge the size of the space, as its dimensions were hidden by the huge holographic simulation of the solar system that dominated the room. The entire image was essentially black space that stretched infinitely in all directions. As soon as we came in, we were suspended in this blackness. Because the simulation was designed to reflect the true scale of the solar system, the Sun and the planets were minuscule, like fireflies in the distance, but still distinguishable. A striking red spiral expanded out from the distant point of light that represented the Sun, spreading like concentric red ripples on the surface of a vast black ocean. This was the Earth's route. At a point on the outer edge of the spiral, the route turned bright green, indicating the distance Earth had yet to travel. The green line swept over our heads. We followed it with our eyes until it vanished into the depths of a brilliant sea of stars, its end beyond our sight. Numerous specks of glittering dust floated through the black expanse. As a few of these motes drifted closer, I realized they were virtual screens, filled with scrolling streams of digits and curves.

Then my gaze fell upon the Earth Navigation Platform, known to every human on the planet. It looked like a silvery white asteroid floating in the blackness. The sight made it even harder to grasp the size of the place – the Navigation Platform itself was a plaza. It was now densely packed with over five thousand people, including the leaders of the Coalition, most of the Interstellar Emigration Committee that was responsible for implementing the voyage plan, and the last remaining loyalists. The voice of the Chief Executive rang out in the darkness.

'We could fight to the last, but we might lose control of the Earth Engines. If that were to happen, the excess fissile material could burn through the entire planet or evaporate the oceans. Instead, we have decided to surrender. We understand the people. Humanity has endured forty generations of bitter struggle and must endure one hundred generations more. It is unrealistic to expect everyone to remain rational throughout it all. But we ask the people to remember that we, the five thousand who stand here, from the Chief Executive of the Coalition to the ordinary privates, kept our faith until the end. We know we will not see the day the truth is verified, but if humanity survives future generations will weep over our graves! This planet called Earth will be an everlasting monument to our memory!'

The massive gate of the control center rumbled open again, and the last five thousand Takers emerged. They were then herded to the shore by rebel forces. Both sides of the road were jammed with people. The onlookers spat at the prisoners and pelted them with ice and rocks. A few of the masks on their thermal suits were shattered, exposing the faces beneath to temperatures more than a hundred degrees below freezing. But even as they were numbed by terrible cold, they trudged on, fighting for every step. I saw a little girl pick up a chunk of ice and hurl it with all her might at an old man, the wild rage in her eyes searing through her mask.

When I heard that all five thousand of the prisoners had been sentenced to death, I felt it was too lenient. One death? Could one death repair the evil they had done? Could it make amends for the crime of perpetrating an insane hoax that destroyed both the Earth and human civilization? They should die ten thousand times over! I suddenly recalled the astrophysicists who had forecast the explosion of the Sun and the engineers who had designed and built the Earth Engines. They had passed away a century ago, but I truly wanted to dig up their graves and make them die the deaths they deserved.

I felt truly thankful that the executioners had found a suitable method for carrying out the sentence. First, they confiscated the nuclear batteries that powered the thermal suits of every person sentenced to death. Then, they deposited the prisoners on the frozen ocean and let the subzero conditions sap the life from their bodies.

The most insidious, most shameful criminals in the history of human civilization stood clustered together, a dark mass atop the ice. Over one hundred thousand people had gathered on the shore to watch. Over one hundred thousand jaws clenched in anger, over one hundred thousand pairs of eyes burned with the same rage I had witnessed on the face of that little girl.

By now, all the Earth Engines had been powered down, and the stars had blinked majestically into view over the ice. I could imagine the cold piercing their skin like daggers, the blood freezing in their veins, the life draining bit by bit from their bodies. A pleasant warmth ran through my body at the thought. As they watched the prisoners slowly succumb to the agonizing cold, the mood of the crowd on the shore began to lift and they began to sing a cheerful rendition of 'My Sun'.

As I sang along, I gazed in the direction of a star that was slightly larger than the rest, its tiny disk shining with yellow light – the Sun.

Oh, Sun, my Sun
Mother of life
Father of creation
Bright spirit, a god above!

Constant and eternal
We are but star dust in your orbit
and yet like fools
we dared dream your doom.

An hour passed. Out on the ice, those enemies of humanity still stood, but not one among them remained alive. Their blood had frozen in their veins.

All at once, I lost my sense of sight. Several seconds passed before my vision began to recover, and the ice, the shore, and the crowd of onlookers gradually sharpened into focus. Finally everything was clear again – even clearer than it had been before, in fact, because the world was enveloped in an intense white light. It was this abrupt glare that had blinded me a moment ago.

The stars, however, did not reappear, their radiance swallowed up, as if the cosmos had melted under the harsh light. The glare burst forth from a single point in space. That point had now become the center of the universe, and I had been staring right at it as it did so.

The helium flash had occurred.

The chorus of 'My Sun' froze mid-song. The crowd on the shore stood transfixed; like the five thousand corpses on the ice, they seemed frozen, as stiff and still as stone.

The Sun shed its light and heat upon the Earth for one last time. On the surface, the dry ice melted first, rising in plumes of white steam. Then the sea began to thaw, and the layers of ice began to creak and groan as they were heated unevenly. Gradually, the light softened and the sky took on a tinge of blue. Later, generated by the fierce solar winds, auroras appeared in the sky, great prismatic curtains of light fluttering across the heavens.

The last Takers stood firm atop the ice, five thousand statues thrown into clear relief by the sudden dazzling sunlight.

The solar explosion lasted only a short time. After two hours, the light rapidly weakened until it was extinguished altogether.

A dim red sphere had replaced the Sun. From our vantage point, it slowly swelled until it reached the size of the Sun of old, a strange memory from Earth's original orbit. It was so voluminous that its diameter exceeded the orbit of Mars. Mercury, Venus, Mars – Earth's constant companions – had been reduced to wisps of smoke by the intense thermal radiation.

But it was no longer our Sun. No longer emitting light and heat, it resembled a cold piece of red paper pasted onto the firmament, its muted glow merely a reflection of the surrounding starlight. This was the evolutionary fate common to all mid-sized stars: transformation into a red giant.

Five billion years of majestic life were now a fleeting dream. The Sun had died.

Fortunately, we still lived.

4

THE WANDERING ERA

As I recall all of this now, half a century has passed. Twenty years ago, Earth sailed past Pluto's orbit and out of the solar system, continuing its lonely voyage into the vast, cold reaches of space.

My last visit to the surface was a dozen or so years ago. I was accompanied by my son and my daughter-in-law, a blonde-haired, blue-eyed girl. She was pregnant at the time.

When we arrived on the surface, the first thing I noticed was that I could no longer see the Earth Engines' massive plasma beams, even though I knew the engines were still operating at full capacity. The Earth's atmosphere had vanished, leaving nothing to scatter the plasma's light. The ground was covered with strange translucent yellow-green crystals. They were made of solid oxygen and nitrogen, the remnants of our frozen atmosphere.

Interestingly, the atmosphere had not frozen evenly across the surface. Instead, it had formed irregular mounds, like hills. The frozen surface of the sea, once flat and smooth, now rose up into a fantastic crystalline landscape. Overhead, the Milky Way stretched motionless across the sky, as if it, too, had frozen. But the stars were bright, too bright to look at for long.

The Earth Engines would operate without interruption for the next five hundred years, accelerating the planet to 0.5 percent of light speed. Earth would cruise at this incredible speed for thirteen hundred years. After it had completed two-thirds of its voyage, we would reverse the direction of the Earth Engines and Earth would enter a five-hundred-year deceleration period. After twenty-four hundred years of travel, Earth would finally reach Proxima Centauri. In another hundred years' time, it would lock into stabilized orbit around the star, becoming one of its satellites.

I know I have been forgotten
This voyage wanders on and on
But call me when the time comes
When the East sees another dawn

I know I have been forgotten
Our departure is long past
But call me when the time comes
When men see blue skies at last

I know I have been forgotten
Our solar story is over now
But call me when the time comes
When blossoms hang from every bough

Every time I hear that song, warmth floods this stiff, aging body of mine, and these dry old eyes fill with tears. In my mind's eye, the three golden suns of Alpha Centauri rise above the horizon one after another, bathing everything in their warm light. The solid atmosphere has melted, and the sky is clear and blue again. Seeds planted two thousand years ago sprout from the thawed soil, breathing new life into the earth. I see my great-grandchildren, one hundred generations removed, playing and laughing on green grass. Clear streams flow through the meadows, filled with small silver fish. I see Kayoko, bounding toward me across the green earth. She is young and beautiful, like an angel . . .

Ah, Earth, my wandering Earth . . .

THE VILLAGE TEACHER

He knew he'd have to teach his final lesson early.

He felt another shot of pain in his liver, so strong he almost fainted. He didn't have the strength to get out of bed, and, with great difficulty, he pulled himself closer to the bedside window, whose paper panes glowed in the moonlight. The little window looked like a doorway leading into another world, one where everything shone with silver light, a diorama of silver and frostless snow. He shakily lifted his head and looked out through a hole in the paper window, and his fantasy of a silver world receded. He found himself looking into the distance, at the village where he had spent his life.

The village lay serenely in the moonlight, and it looked as if it had been abandoned for a hundred years. The small flat-roofed houses were almost indistinguishable from the mounds of soil surrounding them. In the muted colors of moonlight, it was as if the entire place had dissolved back into the hills. Only the old locust tree could be seen clearly, a few black crows' nests scattered among its withered branches, like stark drops of black ink on a silver page.

The village had its good times, like the harvest. When young men and women, who had left the village in droves to find work, came back, and the place was bustling and full of laughter. Ears of corn glistened on the rooftops, and children did somersaults in the piles of stalks on the floor of the threshing ground. The Spring Festival was another cheerful time, when the threshing ground was lit with gas lamps and decorated with red lanterns. The villagers gathered there to parade lucky paper boats and do lion dances. Now, only the clattering wooden frames of the lions' heads were left, stripped of paint. The village had no money to buy new trains for the heads, so they had been using bedsheets as the lions' bodies, which worked in a pinch. But as soon as the Spring Festival ended, all the youths of the village left again to look for work, and the place fell back into torpor.

At dusk every day, as thin wisps of smoke rose from the chimneys of the houses, one or two elderly villagers, their faces grooved like walnuts, would stand and gaze down the road that led beyond the mountains, until the last ray of gloaming light got caught in the locust tree and disappeared. People turned their lamps off and went to bed early in the village. Electricity was expensive, at ¥1.8 per kilowatt hour.

He could hear a dog softly whimpering somewhere in the village, whining in its sleep, perhaps. He looked out at the moonlit yellow soil surrounding the village, which suddenly seemed to him like a placid sheet of water. If only it *were* water – this year was the fifth consecutive year of drought, and they had had to carry water to the fields to irrigate them.

His gaze drifted into the distance, landing on the fields on the mountain, which looked in the moonlight like the footprints of a giant. Small, scattered plots were the only way to farm that rocky mountain, covered as it was with vines and brush. The terrain was too rough for agricultural equipment – even oxen would have had no good footing – so people were obliged to do all the labor by hand.

Last year, a manufacturer of agricultural machines had visited to sell a kind of miniature walking tractor, small enough to work those meager fields. It wasn't a bad little machine, but the villagers weren't having it. How much grain could those tiny plots produce? Planting them was detailed work, more like sewing than sowing, and a crop that could feed a man for a year was considered a success. In a year of drought, as it was, those fields might not even produce enough to recoup the cost of planting. A five-thousand-yuan tractor, and on top of that, diesel fuel at more than two yuan a liter – outsiders just didn't understand the difficulties of life in these mountains.

A few small silhouettes walked past the window. They formed a circle on a ridge between two fields and squatted down, inscrutable. He knew these were his students – as long as they were nearby, he could detect their presence even without seeing them. This intuition had developed in him over a lifetime, and it was particularly keen now that his life was drawing to a close.

He could even recognize the children in the moonlight. Liu Baozhu and Guo Cuihua were there. Those two were originally from the village and didn't have to live at school; nevertheless, he had taken them in.

Liu Baozhu's father had paid the dowry for a bride from Sichuan ten years before, and she had come and given birth to Baozhu. Five years after that, when Baozhu had grown a bit, his father began to neglect his wife, the small bit of closeness they'd had slipping away, and eventually she left him and returned to her family in Sichuan.

After that, Baozhu's father lost his way. He began gambling, just like the old bachelors of the village, and before long he had lost everything but four walls and a bed. Then he began drinking. Every night, he sold roasted sweet potatoes for eighty fen a kilogram and drank himself useless with the money. Useless and angry: he hit his son every day, and twice a week he hit him hard. One night the month before, he'd nearly beaten his son to death with a sweet potato skewer.

Guo Cuihua's home life was even worse. Her father had found a bride for himself through decent channels, a rare thing here, and he was proud. But good things seldom last, and right after the wedding, it became apparent that Cuihua's mother was unwell. No one could tell at the wedding – she'd likely been given a drug to calm her. Why would a respectable woman come to a village like this in the first place, so poor that even the birds wouldn't shit as they flew over? Nevertheless, Cuihua was born and grew up, and her mother got sicker and sicker. She attacked people with cooking knives in the daytime, and at night she would try to burn the house down. She spent most of her time laughing to herself like a ghoul, with a sound that would set your hair on end.

The rest of the children were from other villages, the closest of which was at least ten miles away on mountain roads, so they had to live at school. In a crude village school like this, they would spend the whole term there. The students brought their own bedding, and each hauled a sack of wheat or rice from home, which they cooked themselves on the school's big stove. As night fell in the winter, the children would gather around the stove and watch the cooking grain bubble and purl in the pot, their faces lit by straw-orange flames. It was the most tender sight he'd ever seen. He would take it with him into the next world.

On the ridge outside the window, within the ring of children, little stars of fire began to shine, bright in the moonlit night. They were burning incense and paper, and their faces were lit red in the firelight against the silver-gray night. He was reminded of the sight of the children by the stove. Another scene emerged from the pool of his memory. The electricity had gone out at school (due perhaps to a faulty circuit, or, as happened more often, a lack of funds) while he was teaching an evening class. He held a candle in his hand to illuminate the blackboard. 'Can you see it?' he'd asked, and the children answered, as they always did, 'Not yet!' It really was hard to read the blackboard with so little light, but they had a lot of material to cover, so night class was the only option. He lit a second candle and held them both up. 'It's still too dark!' yelled the children, so he lit a third candle. It was still too dark to read the board, but the children stopped yelling. They knew their teacher wouldn't light another candle no matter how much they yelled. He couldn't afford to. He looked down at their faces flickering in the candlelight, those kids, who had fought off darkness with every fiber of their beings.

The children and firelight, the children and firelight. It was always the children and firelight, always the children at night, in the firelight. The image was forever embedded in his mind, though he never understood what it meant.

He knew the children were burning incense and paper for him, as they had done so many times before, but this time he didn't have the strength to criticize them for being superstitious. He had spent his whole life trying to ignite the flame of science and culture in the children's hearts, but he knew that, compared to the fog of ignorance and superstition that enshrouded this remote mountain village, it was a feeble flame indeed, like the flame of his candles in the classroom that night. Six months earlier, a few villagers had come to the school to scavenge rafters from the roof of the already-dilapidated dorm, with which they meant to renovate the temple at the entrance to the village. He asked where the children would sleep if the dorm had no roof, and they said they could sleep in the classroom.

'In the classroom? The wind blows right through the walls. How can the children sleep there in the winter?'

'Who cares? They're not from here.'

He picked up a pole and fought them fiercely, and he wound up with two broken ribs. A kind villager propped him up and walked with him all the way to the nearest town hospital, fifteen miles or more on mountain roads.

While assessing his injuries, the doctor had discovered that he had esophageal cancer. There was a high incidence of this sort of cancer in the region, so it wasn't a rare diagnosis. The doctor congratulated him on his good fortune – he had come while the cancer was still in an early stage, before it had started to metastasize. It was curable with surgery; in fact, esophageal cancer was one of the types of cancer against which surgery was most effective. His broken ribs might well have saved his life.

After, he had gone to the province's main city, which had an oncology hospital, and asked a doctor there how much such a surgery would cost. The doctor told him that, considering his situation, he could stay in the hospital's welfare ward, and that his other expenses could also be reduced commensurately. The final amount wouldn't be too much – around twenty thousand yuan. Recalling that his patient came from such a remote place, the doctor proceeded to explain the details of hospitalization and surgery.

He listened silently and suddenly asked: 'If I don't get the surgery, how long do I have?'

The doctor regarded him blankly for a long moment and said, 'Maybe six months.'

The teacher heaved a long sigh, as if greatly relieved, and the doctor was nonplussed. At least he could see this graduating class off.

He really had no way to pay twenty thousand yuan. Over his life, he could have saved up some money. Community teachers may not make much, but he had worked for so many years, and he had never married, nor did he have other financial obligations. But he had spent it all on the children. He couldn't remember how many children's tuition he had paid, how many of their incidental expenses he had covered. Recently, there were Liu Baozhu and Guo Cuihua, but more often, he would see that the school's big cooking pot had no oil in it, so he would buy meat and lard for the children. All the money he had left would cover perhaps a tenth of the surgery.

After the appointment with the doctor, he had walked along the city's wide avenue toward the train station. It was already dark out, and neon lights had come on in a dazzling blur of stripes and dots, bewildering him. At night, the tall buildings of the city were like rows of enormous lamps extending into the clouds, and snippets of music, alternately frenetic and gentle, filled the air along his way.

In that strange world of the city, he reflected on his own short life. He was feeling philosophical, calmly considering that each person has their own path in life, and that he had chosen his own path twenty years prior, when he had graduated from middle school and decided to return to the village. In fact, his destiny had been given to him by another village teacher.

He had spent his own childhood at the school where he now taught. His father and mother had died early, and the school had been his home. His teacher had raised him as a son, and while his childhood might have been poor, it was not lacking in love. When school had gone on winter break one year, his teacher decided to take him home for the season.

His teacher's home was far away, and snow had lain deep on the mountain road. It was the middle of the night by the time they laid eyes on the lights of his teacher's village. Not far behind them, they saw four glints of green, the eyes of two wolves. There were many wolves in the mountains back then, and you could find piles of wolf shit all around the school. Once, as a prank, he had taken a gray-white pile of the stuff, lit it on fire, and thrown it into the classroom, which filled with acrid smoke, choking his classmates. His teacher was furious.

The two wolves in the forest had slowly approached them. While his teacher had snapped a thick branch off a tree and brandished it in the wolves' path, yelling loudly, he had run off toward the village, scared out of his wits, running with all his might. He worried the wolves would go around his teacher and come after him; he worried he would run into another wolf on his way. He ran heaving into the village. Several men assembled with hunting rifles, and he went back with them to look for his teacher. They found him lying in a pool of blood and slush, half of his leg and most of his arm bitten off. His teacher took his final breath on the way to the town hospital, and he saw his teacher's eyes in a ray of torchlight. A large chunk of his cheek had been bitten off and he was unable to speak, but his eyes expressed an urgent plea, one that he'd understood and remembered.

After he graduated from middle school, he had turned down a promising opportunity to work in the town's municipal government. Instead, despite having no family or friends there, he returned directly to the mountain village, to the village primary school that his teacher had pleaded with him to save. By the time he returned, the school was abandoned, having had no teacher for several years.

Not long before that, the Board of Education had begun enforcing a policy that replaced community teachers with state-supported teachers. Some community teachers were able to obtain state support by taking a test. He passed that test and got his teaching certificate, and when he found out he was a licensed, state-supported teacher, he was happy, but that was the extent of his reaction. Other members of his cohort had been elated. But he didn't care whether he was a community teacher or a state-supported teacher; he only cared about the classes of children who would graduate from his primary school and go out into the world. Regardless of whether they left the mountains or stayed, their lives would be different in some way from the lives of children who had never gone to school.

Those mountains were one of the most impoverished areas in the country. But worse than the poverty was the apathy of the people there toward their condition. He remembered how, many years ago, when agricultural output quotas were set for each household, the village had divided and distributed its fields, and then its possessions. The village had one tractor, and the villagers couldn't come to a consensus on how to pay for its fuel or allot time to use it. The only solution everyone could accept was to divide the tractor itself. They literally disassembled it – you get a wheel, he gets an axle. And two months ago, a factory had sent poverty relief in the form of a submersible pump, and, electricity being expensive, they also sent a diesel generator along with plenty of fuel to operate it. They had barely left the village before the villagers sold the machines, the pump and the generator together, for just two hundred and fifty yuan. Everyone ate two good meals, more than in most years.

Another time, a leather manufacturer had bought some land in the village on which to build a tannery – who knew how it got sold to them in the first place. Once the tannery was up, lye and niter flowed into the river and seeped into the well water. The people who drank it broke out in red boils all over their bodies – but no one cared! They were just happy the land sold for a good price. It was a village of old, hopeless bachelors who spent all day gambling and drinking, never planting. They had it figured out – as long as they stayed poor, the county would receive small amounts of poverty relief every year, more than they could make plowing their tiny fields of rocks and dust. They had come to accept this sort of life because they knew nothing else. The village's fruitless ground and poison water were dispiriting, but what could truly make you lose hope was the dull eyes of the villagers.

He had reflected on all these things as he had walked from the doctor's office through the province's main city. His diagnosis still didn't feel real; the doctor's words felt far away. This walking had tired him, though, so he sat down next to the sidewalk. In front of him was a large, glamorous restaurant. Its façade was a single, transparent window, through which the restaurant's chandeliers cast their light onto the street. The restaurant looked like a huge aquarium, and the customers inside, in their fancy clothes, looked like a school of colorful fish. A heavyset man sat at a table by the window. His hair and face were slicked with oil, making him look like a painted wax sculpture. Two tall young women sat next to him, one on each side. The man turned and said something to one of the women, which made her burst out in laughter, and he started laughing, too. Who knew women could get so tall, he thought. Xiuxiu would have only come up to their waists. He sighed – he was thinking about Xiuxiu again.

Xiuxiu had been the only girl in the village who hadn't married out of the mountains. Maybe she was afraid of the outside world because she, like most of the villagers, had never left. Maybe she had a different reason. Either way, the two of them had spent more than two years together, and it had seemed things might work out – her family had asked for a reasonable birth-pain price,* only fifteen hundred yuan. But soon, some villagers who had left to find work came back with a bit of money. One of them, about the same age as him, was a clever guy, though illiterate. He had left for the city, where

* A form of dowry payment in some rural areas of northwestern China, meant to compensate the bride's mother for the pain of having borne her.

he'd gone door-to-door, cleaning people's kitchen exhaust hoods, and in a year he had made a bundle.

This cleaner had spent a month in the village two years ago, and Xiuxiu had somehow wound up with him. Her family turned a blind eye. The rough walls of her family's home were covered in melon seeds and scratched tallies of her father's debts over the years. Xiuxiu hadn't gone to school, but she had an affinity for people who could read. He knew that was the main reason she had initially been attracted to him. But the village boy gave her bottles of perfume, gold-plated necklaces, and eventually won her over.

'Being able to read won't put food on the table,' she told him. He knew it could, but with his job, it wasn't *good* food, especially compared to what the cleaner could give her. So, he'd had no response. Xiuxiu had walked out the door and left only the smell of her perfume, which made him scrunch up his nose.

A year after marrying the village boy, Xiuxiu died in childbirth. He still remembered the midwife holding her rusty forceps over a flame for a second before poking them inside her. Xiuxiu's blood filled the copper basin beneath her. She died on the way to the town hospital. The village boy had spent thirty thousand yuan on the wedding, and it had been a spectacle like nothing the village had seen. Why wasn't he willing to part with a little more money so Xiuxiu could give birth in the hospital? He had asked around about the cost of delivering a child in the hospital. It was only two or three hundred yuan. But the village had its ways, and no villager had ever gone to the hospital to give birth. No one blamed the boy. They threw up their hands and said it was her fate. He heard later that compared to the cleaner's mother, Xiuxiu had been lucky. His mother had gone into obstructed labor. When the cleaner's father heard from the midwife that the child was a boy, he'd chosen to save the child. His mother was placed on the back of a donkey and driven around in circles, in order to spin the baby out. People who were there said that there was a ring of her blood in the dust.

The teacher took a deep breath and felt the ignorance and despair of the village sitting heavily on his chest. It was an ever-present sensation, and even here in the city he felt it just as strongly.

There was still hope for the children, he told himself, even as they sat in the freezing classroom in the winter and looked at the blackboard by candlelight. He was the candle. For as long as he could, with as much brightness as he could muster, he would burn, body and soul, for those children.

Eventually, he had risen from the city sidewalk and continued walking for a while, before stepping into a bookstore. The city was a good place – it even had bookstores that were open at night. There he spent all the money he had brought on books for the school's tiny library, saving for himself only enough to cover the fare home. In the middle of the night, clutching two heavy bundles of books, he had boarded the train.

In the center of the Milky Way, fifty thousand light-years from Earth, an interstellar war that had lasted for twenty thousand years was nearing its resolution.

A square-shaped, starless region was visible there, as distinctly as if it had been cut from the background of shining stars with a pair of scissors. Its sides were six thousand miles long, and its interior was blacker even than the blackness of space – a void within a void. Several objects began to emerge from within the square. They were of various shapes, but each was as large as Earth's moon, and their color was a dazzling silver. As more appeared, they took on a regular, cube-shaped formation. The cube of objects continued to emerge from the square, a mosaic set into the eternal wall of the universe itself, whose base was the complete, velvet blackness of the square and whose tiles were the luminescent silver objects. They were like a cosmic symphony given physical form. Slowly, the black square dissolved back into the stars, leaving only the cube-shaped array of silver objects floating ominously.

The interstellar fleet of the Galactic Federation of Carbon-Based Life had completed the first space-time warp of its journey.

The High Archon of the Carbon Federation looked out from the fleet's flagship onto a metallic, silver landscape. An intricate network of paths snaked across the land like circuits etched into an infinitely wide, silver circuit board. Teardrop-shaped craft appeared occasionally on the surface of the land; they shot at blinding speed along the paths, and after a few seconds, noiselessly disappeared into ports that suddenly opened in the surface to receive them. Cosmic dust had clung to the fleet during its warp travel; it formed clouds over the landscape that glowed faintly red as they ionized.

The High Archon was known for his cool demeanor. The endlessly tranquil, azure smart field that usually surrounded him was like a symbol of his personality. At this moment, however, traces of yellow light emerged from his smart field, as they did from the fields of the people around him.

'It's finally over.' The High Archon's smart field vibrated, transmitting his message to the senator and the fleet commander, who stood on either side of him.

'Yes, it's over. This war went on too long – so long that we have forgotten its beginning,' the senator replied.

The fleet began to cruise at sub-light speed. The ships' sub-light engines engaged simultaneously, and thousands of blue suns suddenly appeared around the flagship. The silver land below them reflected the engines' lights like an edgeless, infinite mirror, and each blue sun was doubled in the reflection.

The beginning of the war was a distant, ancient memory, and though it seemed to have been burned away in the fighting, no one had truly forgotten it. It was a memory that had passed through hundreds of generations, but to the trillion citizens of the Carbon Federation, it was still vivid, engraved into their hearts and minds.

Twenty thousand years earlier, the Silicon-Based Empire had launched a full-scale attack against the Carbon Federation from the periphery of the galaxy. The Empire's five million warships leapt from star to star along the ten-thousand-light-year-long battlefront. Each ship first drew power from its star to open a wormhole through space-time, then traveled through the wormhole to another star, which it likewise harnessed to create another wormhole and continue its travel.

Opening a wormhole depleted a large amount of a star's energy and shifted its light toward the red end of the spectrum. After the ship had jumped, the star's light would gradually return to its original state. The collective effect of millions of ships traveling in this way was terrifying. A band of red light ten thousand light-years long appeared at the edge of the galaxy and began moving toward its center, invisible to light-speed observations but clearly visible on hyperspace monitors. The band, created by the red-shifted light of stars, rushed toward the borders of Carbon Federation space, a tide of blood ten thousand light-years across.

The first Carbon Federation planet to be hit by the vanguard of the Silicon Empire forces was Greensea. It was a beautiful planet that orbited a pair of binary stars. Its surface was covered completely by ocean, on which floated great forests of soft, long, vine-like plants. These forests were home to the temperate, beautiful inhabitants of Greensea, who, swimming lithely among the plants with their crystal-clear bodies, had created an Edenic civilization. Tens of thousands of harsh beams of light suddenly pierced the sky of the planet – the lasers of the Silicon Empire fleet – and began evaporating the ocean. In a short time, Greensea's surface became a boiling cauldron, and all life on the planet, including its five billion inhabitants, died in agony in the boiling water. The ocean was completely evaporated in the end, and Greensea, which had once been so beautiful, was left a hellish, gray planet, shrouded in thick steam.

There was virtually nowhere in the galaxy untouched by the war. It was a ruinous fight for survival between carbon-based and silicon-based civilization. Yet neither side had expected the war to last twenty thousand galactic years!

Except for historians, no one remembers how many battles were waged between forces of a million or more ships. The largest-scale battle was the Battle of the Second Arm, which took place in the second spiral arm of the Milky Way Galaxy. In total, more than ten million warships from both fleets participated as combatants. Historical records tell that more than two thousand stars went supernova in the huge battle zone, like fireworks in the black void. They turned the whole spiral arm into an ocean of super-strong radiation, with groups of black holes floating like ghosts in its midst.

By the end of the battle, both sides had lost nearly their entire fleets. Fifteen thousand years had elapsed, and the story of the battle sounded like an ancient myth, except for the fact that the battle zone itself still existed. Ships rarely entered the zone. It was the most terrifying region of the galaxy, and not just because of the radiation and black holes.

During the battle, squadrons of ships from both unthinkably huge fleets made short-distance space-time jumps as a tactical maneuver. It was thought that in dogfights, some interstellar fighters made almost incredible jumps of a few miles at most! These jumps left space-time in the battle zone riddled with holes, more like rags than fabric. Any ship unfortunate enough to stray into the region risked hitting a patch of distorted space. A patch like that could twist a ship into a long, thin, metal pole, or press it into a sheet hundreds of millions of square miles in area and a few atoms thick, which the gale of radiation would immediately shred to pieces. More often, a ship that hit a patch of distorted space-time would regress into the pieces of steel it was made of, or immediately age into a broken husk, everything inside the ship decaying into ancient dust. Anyone aboard would revert in an instant to an embryonic state, or collapse into a pile of bones . . .

The war's decisive battle was not a myth. It took place a year ago. The Silicon Empire assembled its remaining forces, a fleet of 1.5 million warships, in the desolate space between the galaxy's first and second spiral arms. They set up an antimatter cloud barrier around their location, with a radius of one thousand light-years.

The first Carbon Federation squadron to attack jumped directly to the edge of the cloud and entered it. The cloud was very thin, but it was lethal against warships, and it turned those ships into brilliant fireballs. Dragging long tails of flame from their hulls, the ships bravely continued to advance on their target, streaks of fluorescence in their wakes. An array of thirty thousand or more shooting stars, rushing bravely forward – it was the most magnificent, tragic image from the Carbon-Silicon War.

But these shooting stars thinned out as they passed through the antimatter cloud, and at a location very close to the battle array of the Silicon Empire fleet, they disappeared. They had sacrificed themselves to open a tunnel through the cloud for the rest of the attack fleet. In the battle, the last fleet of the Silicon Empire was driven back to the most desolate region in the Milky Way: the tip of the first spiral arm.

Now, the Carbon Federation fleet was about to complete its final mission: constructing a five-hundred-light-year-wide isolation belt in the middle of the spiral arm. They would destroy most of the stars in the belt to prevent the Silicon Empire from making interstellar jumps. Interstellar jumps were the only way in the Milky Way system for large battleships to carry out fast, long-range attacks, and the greatest distance a ship could jump was two hundred light-years. Once the belt was built, the heavy warships of the Silicon Empire would have to cross five hundred light-years of space at sub-light speeds to get to the central region of the galaxy. In effect, the Silicon Empire would be imprisoned at the tip of the first spiral arm, unable to pose any serious threat to carbon-based civilization in the center of the galaxy.

The senator used his vibrating smart field to speak to the High Archon. 'The will of the Senate is as follows: We maintain our strong recommendation to conduct a life-level protective screening in the belt before commencing stellar destruction.'

'I understand the Senate's caution,' said the High Archon. 'In this long war, the blood of all forms of life has flowed, enough to fill the oceans of thousands of planets. Now that the war has ended, the most pressing concern for the galaxy is to reestablish respect for life – all forms of life, not only carbon-based life, but silicon-based life, as well. The Federation stopped short of completely annihilating silicon-based civilization on the basis of this ideal. Yet the Silicon Empire has no such qualms. They have an instinctual love for warfare and conquest. It has always been so, even before the Carbon-Silicon War. Now, these inclinations are embedded in each of their genes and in each line of their code. They are the ultimate goals of the Empire. Silicon-based life is far superior to us at storing and processing information. Even here, at the tip of the first spiral arm, their civilization will recover and develop quickly. It is therefore imperative that we construct a sufficiently wide isolation belt between the Federation and the Empire. Given the circumstances, a life scan on each of the hundred million stars in the belt is unrealistic. The first spiral arm may be the most barren region of the galaxy, but there are likely enough stars with inhabited planets to achieve leap density. Medium warships could use them to cross the belt, and just one Silicon Empire medium warship could cause immense damage if it managed to enter Federation space. We cannot conduct a life-level protective screening for each planet, only civilization-level. We must sacrifice the primitive life-forms in the belt, in order to save the advanced *and* primitive life-forms in the rest of the galaxy. I have explained this to the Senate.'

'The Senate recognizes this imperative, sir. You have explained it, as has the Federal Defense Committee. The Senate's statement is a recommendation, not a piece of legislation. However, stars in the belt with life-forms that have reached 3C-civilization status and above must be protected.'

'Rest assured,' said the High Archon, his smart field flashing a determined red. 'We will be extremely thorough in conducting civilization tests for each planetary system in the isolation belt!'

For the first time, the fleet commander's smart field emitted a message. 'I think you are worried over nothing. The first spiral arm is the most barren wasteland in the galaxy. There won't be any 3Cs or above.'

'I hope you are right,' said the High Archon and the senator simultaneously. Their smart fields vibrated in resonance and sent a solitary ripple of plasma into the sky above the metallic land below.

The fleet began its second space-time leap, traveling at near-infinite speed toward the first spiral arm of the galaxy.

It was late at night. The children had gathered by candlelight at the foot of their teacher's sickbed.

'Teacher, you should rest. You can teach us the lesson tomorrow,' said a boy.

The teacher managed a pained smile. 'Tomorrow we have tomorrow's lesson.'

If he could make it to tomorrow, then he would teach tomorrow's lesson. But his gut told him he wouldn't last the night.

He made a gesture, and one of the children placed a small blackboard on the sheet covering his chest. This was how he had been teaching them for a month. The children passed him a half-worn piece of chalk; he grabbed it weakly and put its tip to the blackboard with great effort. A sharp, strong pain shot through him. His hand trembled, knocking the chalk against the blackboard and leaving white dots.

He had not gone to the hospital since he returned from the city. His liver had begun to ache two months later – the cancer had spread.

The pain got worse with time until it overwhelmed everything. He groped under his pillow for a pain pill, the common, over-the-counter kind, packaged in plastic. They were completely ineffective at relieving the agony of late-stage cancer, but they had a bit of value as a placebo. Demerol wasn't expensive, but patients weren't allowed to take it out of the hospital, and even if they were, there was no one to administer the shot. As usual, he pushed two pills out of the plastic strip. He thought for a moment, then pushed out the remaining twelve pills and swallowed them all. He knew he would have no use for them later.

Again, he turned his attention to the blackboard and struggled to write out the lesson, but a cough overcame him. He turned his head to the side, where a child had rushed to hold up a bowl next to his mouth. He spit out a mouthful of red and black blood, then reclined on his pillow to catch his breath.

Several of the children stifled sobs.

He abandoned his effort to write on the blackboard. He waved his hand, and a child came over to remove it from his chest. In a small voice, almost a whisper, he began to speak.

'Like our lessons yesterday and the day before, today's lesson is meant for middle schoolers. It is not on your syllabus. Most of you will never have a chance to attend middle school, so I thought I would give you a taste of what it's like to study a subject in greater depth. Yesterday, we read Lu Xun's *Diary of a Madman*. You probably didn't understand much of it, but I want you to read it a few more times, or, better yet, learn to recite it from memory. You'll understand it when you're older. Lu Xun was a remarkable man. Every Chinese person should read his books. I know all of you will in the future.'

He stopped speaking to rest for a moment and catch his breath. He looked at the flickering candle flame. Another passage of Lu Xun came to him. It wasn't from *Diary of a Madman,* and it hadn't been in his textbook. He had encountered it many years before, in his own incomplete, thumbed-through set of Lu Xun's collected works. Since the first time he read it, he hadn't forgotten a single word.

> Imagine a windowless, iron room. Many people lie asleep inside. They will soon suffocate and die in their sleep. You shout, and a few hopeless sleepers awaken to a wretched fate that you are powerless to prevent. Have you done them a favor?
>
> Unless you wake them up, what hope do they have of escape?

With the last of his strength, he continued his lecture.

'Today's class is middle school physics. You may not have heard of physics before. It is the study of the principles of the physical world. It's an extremely rich, deep field of knowledge.

'We will learn about Newton's three laws. Newton was an important English scientist who lived a long time ago. He came up with three remarkable rules. These rules apply to everything in heaven and on Earth, from the sun and moon in the sky down to the water and air of our own planet. Nothing can escape Newton's three truths. With them, we can calculate to the second when solar eclipses – when the 'sun dog eats the sun,' as our village elders say – will happen. Humans can fly to the moon using Newton's three laws.

'The first law is as follows: A body at rest or moving in a straight line at a constant speed will maintain its velocity unless an outside force acts upon it.'

The children watched him silently in the candlelight. No one stirred.

'This means that if you took the grindstone from the mill and gave it a good push, it should keep rolling, all the way to the horizon. What are you laughing at, Baozhu? You're right, that wouldn't actually happen. That's because a force called friction will bring the stone to a halt. There is nowhere in the world without friction.'

That's right, nowhere in the world without friction – his life, especially. He didn't have the village surname,* so his words carried no weight. And he was so stubborn! Over the years he had offended practically everyone in the village in one way or another. He had gone door-to-door persuading each family to put their kids in school, and he had gotten some kids to stop following their parents to work by swearing he'd cover their tuition himself. None of this endeared him to the villagers. The plain truth was that his ideas about how to live were just too different from theirs. He talked all day about things that were meaningless to them, and it annoyed them.

Before he'd learned of his cancer, he had gone once to town and brought back some funds from the Education Bureau to repair the school. The villagers took a bit of the money to hire an opera troupe to perform for two days in an upcoming festival. This bothered the teacher deeply. He went to town again, and this time he brought back a vice county head, who made the villagers return the money. They had already built a stage for the singers. The school was repaired, but that was the end of what little goodwill there was for him in the village, and his life was even more difficult from then on.

First, the village electrician, the village head's nephew, cut off the school's electricity. Then they stopped giving the school cornstalks for heating and cooking, forcing him to abandon planting and spend

---

* In many Chinese villages, residents share a common, ancestral surname.

his time in the hills instead, looking for kindling. Then there was the incident with the rafters in the dorm. Friction was omnipresent, exhausting his body and soul, making him unable to move in a straight line at a constant speed. He had to come to a stop.

Maybe the place he was heading was a frictionless world where everything was smooth and lovely. But what was there for him in a place like that? His heart would still be in this world of dust and friction, in the primary school he had devoted his whole life to. After he left, the two remaining teachers would leave, too, and the school would grind to a halt, like the village millstone. He fell into a deep sorrow – in this world or the next, he had no hope of finding peace.

'Newton's second law is a little tricky, so we'll leave it for last. His third law is as follows: When a body exerts force on a second body, the second body will exert an equal force on the first body in the opposite direction.'

The children were silent for a long time.

'Do you understand? Who can explain it back to me?'

Zhao Labao, his best student, stood and spoke. 'I get the idea, but it doesn't make sense. This morning I got into a fight with Li Quangui and he hit me right in the face. It really hurt, and I've got a lump, right here. Those aren't equal forces!'

The teacher took a while to catch his breath, then explained, 'The reason you hurt is that your cheek is softer than Quangui's fist. They exerted equal forces against each other.'

He wanted to make a gesture to illustrate his point, but he couldn't lift his hand anymore. His limbs felt as heavy as iron, and soon his whole body felt heavy enough to collapse the bed and sink into the ground.

There wasn't much time.

```
Target Number: 1033715
Absolute Magnitude: 3.5
Evolutionary Stage: Upper Main Sequence
Two planets found, average orbital radii 1.3 and
4.7 Distance Units
Life discovered on Planet One
This is Vessel Red 69012 reporting
```

The hundred thousand warships of the Carbon Federation's interstellar fleet had spread out across a ten-thousand-light-year-long band of space to begin construction of the isolation belt. The first stage of the project was the trial destruction of five thousand stars. Only 137 of those star systems had planets; this was the first planet they had found with life.

'The first spiral arm is truly a barren place,' said the High Archon, sighing. His smart field vibrated, initiating a holographic projection that concealed the floor of the flagship and the stars overhead. The High Archon, the fleet commander, and the senator all appeared to be floating in a limitless void. Then, the High Archon switched the hologram feed to display the information sent back by the probe, and a glowing, blue fireball appeared in the middle of the void. The High Archon's smart field produced a white, square box; it adjusted its shape and moved to enclose the image of the star, plunging the space into near-darkness again. This time, however, a small point of yellow light remained. The focal length of the image adjusted rapidly, and in an instant, the yellow dot zoomed into the foreground, fully occupying half of the void. The three of them were bathed in its reflected, orange radiance.

It was a planet covered in a thick, tempestuous atmosphere, like an orange ocean. The motion of the gas produced an extremely complex, ever-changing lattice of lines. The image of the planet continued to grow until it seemed to occupy the whole universe, and they were swallowed by its orange, gaseous ocean. The probe took them through the thick clouds to a place where the fog was slightly thinner, enabling them to see the planet's life-forms.

In the upper part of the thick atmosphere floated a school of balloon-shaped animals. Their bodies were covered in kaleidoscopic patterns that changed from stripes to spots to all sorts of wonderful designs – perhaps a sort of visual language. Each balloon had a long tail whose tip occasionally produced a flash of light that traveled up the tail and into the balloon's body, where it became a diffuse fluorescence.

'Commence the four-dimensional scan!' said the pilot in command of Vessel Red 69012.

An extremely thin beam swept quickly across the balloons from top to bottom. Though the beam was only a few atoms thick, the interior of the beam had one more spatial dimension than normal space. It transmitted data from the scan back to the ship, and in the storage of the ship's main computer, the balloon creatures were cut into hundreds of billions of thin slices. Each slice was an atom-thick cross section that recorded everything with near-perfect accuracy, down to the state of each quark.

'Commence data mirror assembly!'

The ship's computer rearranged the hundreds of billions of cross-sectional images in its storage in their original order, superimposing them. Soon, a hollow balloon took shape – a perfect replica of the life-form they had found on the planet, re-created in the computer's vast digital universe.

'Commence 3C Civilization Test!'

The computer quickly identified the being's thinking organ, an elliptical structure that hung at the center of an intricate plexus of nerves. The computer analyzed the structure of the brain in an instant and established a direct, high-speed information interface with it, bypassing all of the creature's lower sensory organs.

The civilization test consisted of a set of questions selected at random from an enormous database. Three correct answers were considered a pass. If a life-form failed to answer the first three questions correctly, the tester had two options: He could end the test and declare a failure, or he could provide more questions. Three correct answers were considered a pass, regardless of how many questions the tester asked.

'3C Civilization Test, Question One: Please describe the smallest unit of matter you have discovered.'

'Dee-dee, doo-doo-doo, dee-dee-dee-dee,' answered the balloon.

'Incorrect. 3C Civilization Test, Question Two: According to your observations, in what direction does thermal energy flow through matter? Can its flow be reversed?'

'Doo-doo-doo, dee-dee, dee-dee-doo-doo,' answered the balloon.

'Incorrect. 3C Civilization Test, Question Three: What is the ratio of a circle's circumference to its diameter?'

'Dee-dee-dee-dee-doo-doo-doo-doo-doo,' answered the balloon.

'Incorrect. 3C Civilization Test, Question Four . . .'

'That's enough,' said the High Archon, after the tenth question. 'We don't have much time.' He turned and signaled to the fleet commander.

'Fire the singularity bomb!' ordered the commander.

Strictly speaking, a singularity bomb was a sizeless object, a point in space, infinitely smaller than an atom. It had mass, though: the largest singularity bombs were billions of tons, and the smallest were more than ten million tons. When the bomb slid out of the arsenal of Vessel Red 69012, it appeared as a sphere, several thousand feet in diameter, that glowed with a faint fluorescence – radiation generated as the miniature black hole consumed the space dust in its path.

Unlike black holes formed by the collapse of stars, these miniature black holes were formed at the beginning of the universe, tiny models of the universal singularity that preceded the big bang. Both the Carbon Federation and the Silicon Empire maintained fleets of ships that cruised the empty space beyond the galactic equator collecting these primordial black holes. Inhabitants of some marine planets called these fleets 'deep-sea trawlers.' The 'catches' that these fleets brought back were one of the most potent weapons in the galaxy, and the only weapon that could annihilate a star.

The singularity bomb left its guide rail and accelerated along a force-field beam from the ship toward its target star. It arrived in short order, a dusty black hole that quickly plunged into the star's fiery exterior. Stellar matter rushed from all directions in a turbulent arc toward the center of the black hole, where it disappeared. Copious radiation poured from the black hole, which appeared now as a blinding ball of light on the surface of the star, a diamond on the ring of the star's circumference.

As the black hole sank into the star's interior, the radiant orb grew dimmer, revealing the enormous, hundred-million-mile-wide vortex that encircled the orb. The rotating vortex scattered the orb's light in a kaleidoscopic display that looked, from the vantage of the ship, like a hideous, prismatic face. A moment later, the orb disappeared, as did the vortex, though more slowly; the star appeared to have returned to its original color and luminosity. This was the eye of the storm, the final moment of silence before annihilation.

The voracious black hole sank toward the dense center of the star, devouring everything in its path. In less than a second, it swallowed a mass of stellar material greater than the mass of a hundred medium-sized planets. Super-strong radiation spread out from the black hole toward the surface of the star. Some of it escaped, but most of it was blocked by stellar material, adding enough energy to the star to disrupt its convection and knock it out of equilibrium. The star's color began to shift, first from red to bright yellow, then to bright green, then to a deep, sapphire blue, and then to a forbidding violet. The radiation from the black hole by now was orders of magnitude more intense than the radiation from the star itself, and as more energy flowed out of the star in the form of nonvisible light, its violet color intensified – a spirit in agony, floating in the vastness of space. Within an hour, the star's billion-year journey had come to a close.

There was a flash of light that seemed to swallow the whole universe, then faded slowly away. Where the star had been, there was now a thin, spherical layer of material expanding rapidly, like a balloon being blown up. This was the surface of the star, swept outward in the explosion. As it expanded, it became transparent, and a second hollow sphere grew in its center, followed by a third. These waves of material were like exquisitely painted glass orbs, one inside another, and even the smallest of them had a surface area tens of thousands times larger than the original surface area of the star. The first wave vaporized the orange planet in an instant, though it was impossible to see its destruction against such a magnificent background. Compared to the size of the expanding stellar layer, the planet was a speck of dust, not even a dot on the surface of the orb.

The smart fields of the High Archon and the senator darkened. 'Do you find this work distressing?' asked the fleet commander.

'Another species gone, like dew in the sun.'

'Think of the Battle of the Second Arm, Your Excellency – more than two thousand supernovas detonated, one hundred and twenty thousand planets with life vaporized. We do not have the luxury to be sentimental.'

The senator ignored the fleet commander. He addressed the High Archon directly. 'Random planetary spot checks are unreliable. There may be signs of civilization elsewhere on a planet's surface. We should implement area scans, as well.'

The High Archon said, 'I have discussed that possibility with the Senate. We must destroy hundreds of millions of stars in the isolation belt. We estimate the belt contains ten million planetary systems and fifty million planets. Our time is limited; we will not be able to conduct a full area scan on each planet. All we can feasibly do is widen the detection beam to scan larger random samples . . . and pray the civilizations that might exist here have spread uniformly across their planets' surfaces.'

'Next, we'll learn Newton's second law.'

He spoke as quickly as he could, to teach the children as much as possible in the short time he had left.

'An object's acceleration is directly proportional to the force acting on it, and inversely proportional to its mass. To understand that, you need to know what acceleration is. Acceleration is the rate at which an object's speed changes over time. It's different from speed – an object that's moving fast isn't necessarily *accelerating* rapidly, and a quickly accelerating object may not be moving fast. For example, say there's an object moving at 110 meters per second. Two seconds later, it is moving at 120 meters per second. Its acceleration is 120 minus 110, divided by two . . . that's five meters per second – no, five meters per second squared. Another object is moving at ten meters per second, but two seconds later, it's moving at thirty meters per second. Its acceleration is thirty minus ten, divided by two – ten meters per second squared. The second object may not be as fast as the first, but its acceleration is greater! I mentioned squares – a square is just a number multiplied by itself . . .'

He was surprised that his thinking was suddenly so clear. He knew what this meant: If life is a candle, his had burned to its base, and its wick had fallen and ignited the last bit of wax there, with a flame ten times brighter than before. His pain was gone and his body no longer felt heavy; in fact, he was barely aware of his body at all. The life he had left seemed to be in his brain, which worked furiously to convey all its knowledge to the children gathered around him. Language was a bottleneck – he knew he didn't have enough time. He fantasized that the knowledge he had spent his life accumulating – not much, but dear to him – was lodged in his brain like small pearls, and that as he spoke, a crystal ax chopped the pearls out of his brain onto the floor, where the children scrambled to gather them like sweets at New Year's. It was a happy fantasy.

'Do you understand?' he asked restlessly. He could no longer see the children around him, but he could still hear them.

'We understand! Now please rest, teacher!'

He felt his flame begin to sputter. 'I know you don't understand, but memorize it anyway. Someday, it will make sense to you. *The acceleration of an object is directly proportional to the force acting on it, and inversely proportional to the object's mass.*'

'We really do understand, teacher! Please, please rest!'

With his last ounce of strength, he gave the children a command. 'Recite it!'

Through tears, the children began to chant. 'The acceleration of an object is directly proportional to the force acting on it, and inversely proportional to the object's mass. The acceleration of an object is directly proportional to the force acting on it, and inversely proportional to the object's mass . . .'

Hundreds of years ago, one of the world's great minds emerged in Europe, wrote down these words. Now, in the twentieth century, they filled the air of China's most remote mountain village, recited by a chorus of children in a thick, rural accent. In the sound of that sweet hymn, his candle burned out.

The children gathered around his body and wept.

```
Target Number: 500921473
Absolute Magnitude: 4.71
Evolutionary Stage: Middle Main Sequence
Nine planets found
This is Vessel Blue 84210 reporting
```

'What an exquisite planetary system,' the fleet commander exclaimed.

The High Archon agreed. 'Indeed. Its small, rocky planets and gas giants are spaced with wonderful harmony, and its asteroid belt is in a beautiful location, like a necklace. And its farthest planet, a little dwarf covered in methane ice, suggesting the end of one thing and the beginning of another, like the final note of a musical cadence . . .'

'This is Vessel Blue 84210. We are commencing a life scan on Planet One. This planet has no atmosphere, a slow rotation, and a huge temperature differential. Scan beam is firing. First random site: white. Second random site: white. . . . Tenth random site: white. Vessel Blue 84210 reports that this planet has no life.'

'You could smelt iron on the surface of that planet. We shouldn't waste time,' said the fleet commander.

'We are commencing a life scan on Planet Two. This planet has a thick atmosphere; a high, uniform temperature; and substantial acidic cloud cover. Scan beam is firing. First random site: white. Second random site: white. . . . Tenth random site: white. Vessel Blue 84210 reporting – this planet has no life.'

'I have a strong feeling that Planet Three harbors life. Scan thirty random sites,' said the High Archon, his message traveling instantly over the four-dimensional communicator to the duty officer of Vessel Blue 84210, over one thousand light-years away.

'Excellency, our schedule is very tight,' said the fleet commander.

'You have your orders,' said the High Archon resolutely.

'Yes, Your Excellency.'

'We are commencing a life scan on Planet Three. This planet has a medium-density atmosphere, and most of its surface is covered by ocean . . .'

The first shot of the life-scan beam struck a circle of land in Asia around three miles across. In the light of day, the effect of the beam would have been visible to the naked eye – it turned every nonliving object in its field transparent. The scan hit the mountains of northwest China; in daylight, an observer would have seen a spectacular sight as sunlight refracted through the mountain range and the ground under her feet seemed to disappear, revealing an abyss into the depths of the planet. Living things – people, trees, grass – remained opaque, and their forms would have stood out clearly against the crystal background. However, this effect only lasted for the half a second it took the beam to initialize, and onlookers would likely assume they had imagined it. Besides, it was nighttime.

In the direct center of the beam's field was the village school.

'First random site . . . we've got green! Vessel Blue 84210 reporting – we have discovered life on target number 500921473, Planet Three!'

The beam began automatically to sort the many life-forms it had hit, entering them into its database in order of complexity and according to an initial intelligence estimate. At the top of the list was a group of life-forms inside a square shelter. The beam narrowed and focused on the shelter.

The High Archon's smart field received an image transmission from Vessel Blue 84210. He projected it onto the black background, and in an instant, he was standing within a projection of the village school. The image-processing system had removed the shelter from view, but the life-forms inside were still hard to make out, as their bodies were so similar to the silicon-based planetary surface around them. The computer eliminated all nonliving objects in the image, including the larger, lifeless body the other beings encircled, and the beings now appeared suspended in a void. Even so, they were still dull and colorless, like a bunch of plants. This was clearly not a species with any remarkable phenotypic features.

Vessel Blue 84210 was an interstellar warship as large as Earth's moon, and in its position outside Jupiter's orbit, it was like an extra planet in the solar system. It fired a four-dimensional beam that moved through three-dimensional space nearly instantaneously. In a moment, the beam had arrived at Earth and pierced the roof of the village school's dorm. It scanned the eighteen children inside down to their elementary particles and transmitted the enormous amount of data back into space at an unimaginable rate. The main computer of Vessel Blue 84210 had a storage capacity larger than the universe itself; in an instant, digital copies of the children were constructed and stored there.

The eighteen children floated in an endless void whose color was indescribable. In fact, it didn't strictly have a color. It was a limitless field of perfect transparency. The children instinctively tried to grab hold of nearby classmates, but their hands passed through their bodies without resistance. They were terrified. The computer detected their fear and judged that they required some familiar objects for comfort, so it altered the color of the simulation's background to match their home planet's sky. Immediately, the children saw a cloudless, sunless, deep blue sky. There was no ground beneath them, just endless blue, the same as above, and they were the only things in it.

The computer reassessed the digital children and found they were still panicking. In a hundred-millionth of a second, it understood why: Whereas most life in the galaxy had no fear of floating, these creatures were different in that they lived on land. The computer added Earth-like gravity and a ground to the simulation. The children were astonished to find under their feet a pure white plain, extending into infinity in all directions and crossed by a neat, regular black grid, like a huge piece of writing paper. A few children crouched down to touch the ground, and it was the smoothest surface they had ever touched; they tried taking a few steps, but the ground was completely frictionless and didn't move beneath them. They wondered why they didn't fall down. One child took off a shoe and threw it level with the ground. It slid along at a regular speed, and the children watched it glide off into the distance, never decelerating.

They had seen Newton's first law.

A melodious, ethereal voice permeated the digital universe.

'Commencing 3C Civilization Test. Question One: Please describe the basic principles of biological evolution on your planet. Is it driven by natural selection or spontaneous mutations?'

The children had no idea. They stayed silent.

'3C Civilization Test, Question Two: Please briefly describe the source of a star's power.'

Silence.

. . .

'3C Civilization Test, Question Ten: Please describe the chemical composition of the liquid in your planet's oceans.'

The children still did not speak.

The shoe had slid off into the horizon, where it became a black point and disappeared.

'That's enough!' said the fleet commander to the High Archon, one thousand light-years distant. 'We won't be able to complete the first phase of the project on time if we keep on like this.'

The High Archon's smart field vibrated slightly, signaling his consent.

'Fire the singularity bomb!'

The beam containing the command shot through four-dimensional space and arrived immediately at Vessel Blue 84210, which was holding its position in the solar system. A faintly glowing ball left the long track at the front of the ship and accelerated along an invisible force field toward the sun.

The High Archon, the senator, and the fleet commander turned their attention to another region of the isolation belt, where several planetary systems with life had been discovered, the most advanced of which was a brainless, mud-dwelling worm. Exploding stars filled the region, like galactic fireworks. They all thought of the Battle of the Second Arm.

A while later, a small portion of the High Archon's smart field split off from the rest and turned its attention back to the solar system. He heard the captain of Vessel Blue 84210.

'Prepare to exit the blast radius. T minus thirty to warp. Commence countdown!'

'A moment, please. How long until the singularity bomb reaches its target?' asked the High Archon, attracting the attention of the fleet commander and the senator.

'It's passing the orbit of the system's first planet. Approximately ten minutes to impact.'

'We will take five minutes to continue the test.'

'Yes, Your Excellency.'

The duty officer of Vessel Blue 84210 continued administering the test. '3C Civilization Test, Question Eleven: What is the relationship between the three sides of a right triangle on a flat plane in three-dimensional space?'

Silence.

'3C Civilization Test, Question Twelve: Where is your planet's position relative to the other planets in your star system?'

Silence.

'This is pointless, Your Excellency,' said the fleet commander.

'3C Civilization Test, Question Thirteen: How does an object move when it is not subjected to any external forces?'

Beneath the endless blue sky of the simulated universe, the children recited, 'A body at rest or moving in a straight line at a constant speed will maintain its velocity unless an outside force acts upon it.'

'Correct! 3C Civilization Test, Question Fourteen . . .'

'Wait!' called out the senator, interrupting the duty officer administering the test. 'The next question is also about heuristics in low-speed mechanics. Doesn't that violate the test guidelines?' he asked the High Archon.

'Of course not, as long as the question is in the database,' interjected the fleet commander. He was shocked that these unassuming life-forms had answered a question correctly, and all his attention was now on them.

'3C Civilization Test, Question Fourteen: Please describe how two objects exerting force on each other interact.'

'When a body exerts force on a second body, the second body will exert an equal force on the first body in the opposite direction!' said the children.

'Correct! 3C Civilization Test, Question Fifteen: Please describe the relationship between an object's mass and acceleration when an external force acts upon it.'

In unison, the children said, 'The acceleration of an object is directly proportional to the force acting on it, and inversely proportional to the object's mass!'

'Correct! You have passed the Civilization Test! Confirming that there is a 3C-level civilization on Planet Three of Target Star 500921473.'

'Reverse the singularity bomb! Disengage!!' The High Archon's smart field flashed and vibrated frantically as he sent his order through hyperspace to Vessel Blue 84210.

The force-field beam began to bend. Its hundred-million-mile path through the solar system curved away from the sun, like a tree branch that had been weighed down. As the force-field engine on board Vessel Blue 84210 worked at maximum power, its enormous heat sink glowed, first dark red, then with a bright white incandescence. The beam's new thrust vector began to affect the trajectory of the singularity bomb, which curved away from its target. However, it was already inside the orbit of Mercury, very close to the sun, and no one was confident that the force-field engine could bend its course enough to prevent impact.

The whole galaxy watched over hyperspace as the fuzzy, dark ball veered and grew substantially brighter, a worrisome sign that it had already entered the particle-rich space around the sun. The captain's hand rested on the red hyperspace button, ready to leap away from the solar system the moment before impact.

In the end, the bomb shot by the very edge of the sun, only a few dozen miles from its surface, sucking in huge amounts of material from the sun's atmosphere as it brushed past. It glowed intensely with a blue-white light, and for a moment, the sun appeared to have a brighter twin star locked in close, binary orbit, a phenomenon that was to become an enduring mystery to the inhabitants of Earth. The sun's fiery surface darkened beneath the bomb, like the wake of a speedboat in calm water, and as the black hole swept past the solar surface, its gravity consumed the sun's light, scratching a dark, crescent scar into the sun's surface which grew to eclipse the whole solar hemisphere. As the bomb left the sun, it dragged an enormous solar prominence behind it, a beautiful string of flame one million miles long. The tip of the prominence flared violently outward, blossoming into a mass of whirling plasma vortices.

After the singularity bomb brushed past the sun, it grew dark again. Soon, it disappeared into the infinite night of space.

'We almost destroyed a carbon-based civilization,' said the senator, heaving a sigh of relief.

'A 3C-level civilization here, in this desert – unbelievable!' exclaimed the fleet commander.

'Yes. Neither the Carbon Federation nor the Silicon Empire has included this region in its plans for expansion and cultivation. If this civilization were to have evolved entirely on its own, that would be a rare thing indeed,' said the High Archon.

'Vessel Blue 84210, you are to hold your position in that star system and commence a full-surface civilization test on Planet Three. Another ship will take over your prior mission,' ordered the fleet commander.

The children in the village didn't notice anything amiss, unlike their digital replicas outside of Jupiter's orbit. They were still crying over their teacher's body in their candlelit dormitory. After a long time, they quieted down.

'We should go tell a grown-up,' said Guo Cuihua, stifling a sob.

'What for?' asked Liu Baozhu, his eyes on the floor. 'No one in this village cared about him when he was alive. I bet they won't even pay for a coffin!'

In the end, the children decided to bury their teacher themselves. With pickaxes and shovels, they dug a grave in a hill next to the school, and the brilliant stars above silently watched them work.

The senator watched Vessel Blue 84210's test results as they streamed instantly across a thousand light-years of space. 'The civilization on this planet isn't 3C – it's 5B!' he exclaimed, astonished.

The skyscrapers of human cities appeared as holograms aboard the flagship.

'They have already begun using nuclear energy, and they can fly into space using chemical propellants. They've even landed on their moon.'

'What are their basic features?' asked the fleet commander.

'You'll have to be more specific,' said the duty officer of Vessel Blue 84210.

'Well, how advanced is their heritable memory?'

'They don't inherit memories. They acquire all their memories during their lives.'

'What method do they use to communicate information to each other?'

'It's very primitive, and very rare. There is a thin organ in their bodies that vibrates, producing waves in their planet's atmosphere, which is primarily composed of nitrogen and oxygen. By modulating the vibrations, they encode information into the waves. They have separate organs – thin membranes – that receive the waves.'

'What's the transmission rate of that method?'

'Approximately one to ten bits per second.'

'What?!' Everyone on the flagship laughed out loud.

'It's true. We were incredulous at first, but it's been verified repeatedly.'

'Captain, this is lunacy!' yelled the fleet commander. 'You are telling us that an organism without *any* hereditary memory that transmits information using sound waves at *one to ten bits per second* can form a 5B-level civilization?! And that they developed this civilization entirely on their own, without any external assistance from an advanced civilization?!'

'Sir, that is the case.'

'If that's so, they have no way to pass knowledge between generations. Accumulated knowledge across generations is necessary for civilization to evolve!'

'There is a class of individuals, a certain proportion of the population spread evenly among their civilization. They act as mediums for the transmission of knowledge between generations.'

'That sounds like a myth.'

'It's not,' said the senator. 'Such a concept existed in the galaxy in prehistoric times, but even then, it was extremely rare. No one would know about it except historians of the evolution of civilization in the star systems where the idea had currency.'

'By 'concept,' you mean individuals that transmit knowledge between generations of a species?'

'Yes. They're called 'teachers.''

'Tea—cher?'

'An ancient word that was once in currency among a few long-lost civilizations. It's rare enough that it does not appear in most ancient vocabulary databases.'

The holographic feed from the solar system zoomed out to display the blue orb of Earth rotating slowly in space.

The High Archon said, 'A civilization evolving independently is rare enough, but I know of no other civilization in the Milky Way that has attained 5B level on its own, at least in the era of the Carbon Federation. We should let this civilization continue its evolution without interference, observing it as it does, not only to further our understanding of ancient civilizations, but also, perhaps, to gain insight into our broader galactic civilization.'

'I'll have Vessel Blue 84210 leave the star system immediately and designate a hundred-light-year no-fly zone around it,' said the fleet commander.

Insomniacs in the northern hemisphere might have seen a small group of stars begin to flutter slightly, then the stars around those, and so on across the whole sky, as if a finger had been dipped into the still water of the night sky.

The space-time shock wave caused by Vessel Blue 84210's hyperspace leap was considerably attenuated by the time it hit Earth. Every clock jumped three seconds ahead. Humans, confined as we are to three-dimensional space, were unaware of the disturbance.

'It's a pity,' said the High Archon. 'They'll be confined to sub-light speeds and three-dimensional space for another two thousand years without the intervention of a more advanced civilization. It will be at least a thousand years before they can harness the energy of matter-antimatter annihilation. Two thousand more years before they can transmit and receive multidimensional communications . . . and as for hyperspace galactic travel, that will take them at least five thousand years. It will be at least ten thousand years before they attain the minimum conditions for entry into the galactic family of carbon-based life-forms.'

The senator said, 'Independent evolution of this sort happened only in the prehistoric era of the galaxy. If our records of those times are correct, my distant ancestors lived in the deep ocean of a marine planet. They lived and died there in darkness, their governments rose and fell, and then, at some point, they felt adventurous. They launched a craft toward space – a buoyant, transparent ball that rose slowly to the surface of the ocean. It was the dead of night when they reached the surface. The people inside the craft were the first of my ancestors to see the stars. Can you imagine how they felt? Can you imagine how glorious and mysterious that sight was to them?'

The High Archon said, 'It was an era full of passion and yearning. A terrestrial planet was a complete, limitless world to our ancestors. From their home in a planet's green waters or on its purple grasslands, they looked up at the stars with awe. We have not known such a feeling for tens of millions of years.'

'I feel it now!' said the senator, pointing at the holographic image of Earth. It was a lustrous, blue ball, with white clouds floating above its surface, streaking and billowing. The senator felt as if he had found a pearl in the depths of his ancestors' ocean home. 'Such a small planet, populated by organisms living their lives, dreaming their dreams, completely oblivious to us and to the strife and destruction in their galaxy. To them, the universe must seem like a bottomless well of hopes and dreams. It's like an ancient song.'

And he began to sing. The smart fields of the three became as one, rippling with rose-colored waves. The song he sang was old, passed down from the forgotten beginnings of civilization itself. It sounded distant, mysterious, forlorn, and as it propagated through hyperspace to the hundreds of billions of stars in the galaxy, countless beings heard its sound and felt a long-forgotten kind of comfort and peace.

'The most incomprehensible thing about the universe is that it is comprehensible,'* said the High Archon.

'The most comprehensible thing about the universe is that it is incomprehensible,' said the senator.

There was light in the east by the time the children had finished digging the grave. They tore the door off the classroom and put their teacher's body on it, and they buried him with two boxes of chalk

* Albert Einstein, *Physics and Reality.*

and a used textbook. They stood a stone slab on top of the mound, and wrote on it in chalk: *Mister Li's Grave.*

The faint letters would wash off in the first rainfall, and not long after that, the grave and the person it contained would be forgotten completely.

The tip of the sun rose above the hills, casting a golden ray into the sleeping village. The grass of the valley was still in shadow, but its dew glowed with the light of dawn. A bird or two began timidly to sing.

The children walked along the narrow road back into the village. Their little shadows soon disappeared into the pale blue morning mist of the valley.

They were going to live their lives on that ancient, barren land, and though their harvests would be meager, they would always have hope.

FULL-SPECTRUM BARRAGE JAMMING

Dedicated with deep respect to the people of Russia, whose literature has influenced me all my life.

Liu Cixin (2000)

On the subject of selecting a method of electromagnetic jamming for the battlefield, this manual recommends the use of selective frequency-targeted jamming rather than engaging in barrage jamming over a wide range of simultaneous frequencies, as the latter will interfere with friendly electromagnetic communication and electronic support as well.

—U.S. Army Electronic Warfare Handbook

JANUARY 5TH, SMOLENSK FRONT LINE

The fallen city had already disappeared from view. The front line had retreated forty kilometers in the span of a single night.

Under the light of the early-morning sky, the snowy plain appeared a cold, dim blue. In the distance, black columns of smoke rose from destroyed targets. There was almost no wind; the smoke ascended straight and high, like thin strands of black gauze tying heaven to earth. As Kalina's gaze followed the smoke upward, she started: the brightening sky was clogged with a vast, dense bramble of white, as if a demented giant had covered the sky in agitated scrawls. They were the tangled fighter plane contrails left by the Russian and NATO air forces in their fierce night battle for control over the airspace.

The aerial and long-range precision strikes had continued throughout the night, too. To a casual observer, the bombardment wouldn't have seemed particularly concentrated. The explosions sounded seconds, even minutes apart. But Kalina knew that nearly every explosion had signified some important target hit, sparking punctuation marks in the black pages of the previous night. By dawn, Kalina wasn't sure how much strength was left in the defensive lines, or even whether the defensive lines had survived at all. It seemed as if she were the last one standing against the onslaught.

Major Kalina's electronic-resistance platoon had been hit by six laser-guided missiles around midnight. She'd survived by pure luck. The BMP-2 armored tank carrying the radio-jamming equipment was still burning; the other electronic-warfare vehicles in the battery were now piles of blackened metal scattered around her. Residual heat was dissipating from the bomb crater Kalina was in, leaving her feeling the cold. She pushed herself to a sitting position with her hands. Her right hand touched something sticky and clammy. Covered in black ash, it looked like a lump of mud. She suddenly realized it was a piece of flesh. She didn't know what body part it came from, much less whose. A first lieutenant, two second lieutenants, and eight privates had died in last night's attack. Kalina vomited, though nothing came out but stomach acid. She shoved her hands in the snow, trying to wipe away the blood, but the smears of blackish red quickly congealed in the cold, as stark as before.

The suffocating stillness of the last half hour signified that a new round of ground assault was about to begin. Kalina turned up the volume dial on the walkie-talkie strapped to her shoulder, but heard only static. Suddenly, a few blurry sentences emerged through the receiver, like birds flitting through thick fog.

'. . . Observation Station Six reporting! Position 1437 at twelve o'clock sees thirty-seven M1A2s averaging sixty meters apart, forty-one Bradley IFVs five hundred meters behind the M1A2s' vanguard; twenty-four M1A2s and eight Leclercs currently flanking Position 1633, already past the border of 1437. Positions 1437, 1633, and 1752, prepare to engage the enemy!'

Kalina forced back shivers from cold and fear, so that the horizon line steadied in her binoculars. She saw blurry masses of snow spray, edging the horizon with fuzzy trim.

That was when Kalina heard the rumble of engines behind her. A row of Russian tanks passed her position as they charged the enemy, more T-90 tanks leaving the highway behind them. Kalina heard a different rumble: enemy helicopters were appearing in the sky ahead in neat array, a black lattice in the ghastly white sky of dawn. The exhaust pipes of the tanks around Kalina kicked into action with low splutters, cloaking the battleground in white fog. Through its crevices she could also see Russian helicopters passing low overhead.

The tanks' 120 mm guns stormed and thundered, and the white fog became a wildly flashing pink light display. Almost simultaneously, the first enemy shells fell, the pink light replaced by the blue-white lightning of their explosion. Kalina, lying on her stomach at the bottom of the bomb crater, felt the ground reverberate with the intense percussion like a drumhead. Nearby dirt and rock flew into the air and landed all over her back. Amid the explosions, she could dimly hear the whinny of anti-tank missiles. Kalina felt as if her viscera were tearing apart in the cacophony, and all the universe, the pieces falling toward an endless abyss—

Just as her mind teetered on the breaking point, the tank battle ended. It had lasted only thirty seconds.

When the smoke cleared, Kalina saw that the snowy ground in front of her was scattered with destroyed Russian tanks, heaps of raging flames crowned with black smoke. She looked farther; even without binoculars, she could see a similar swath of destroyed NATO tanks in the distance, appearing as black smoking specks on the snow. But more enemy tanks were rushing past the wreckage, wreathed in the snow spray churned up by their treads. Now and then the Abramses' ferocious broad wedge heads emerged from the spray like snapping turtles launching themselves out of the waves, their smooth-bore muzzles flashing sporadically like eyes. Just above, the helicopters were still embroiled in their melee. Kalina saw an Apache explode in midair not far away. A Mi-28 wobbled low overhead, trailing fuel from a leak. It hit the ground a few dozen meters away and exploded into a fireball. Short-range air-to-air missiles slashed countless parallel white lines low in the air—

Kalina heard a bang behind her. She turned; not far away, a damaged and badly smoking T-90 dropped its rear hatch. No one got out, but she could see a hand hanging down from it. Kalina leapt from the bomb crater and rushed to the back of the tank. She grabbed hold of the hand and pulled. An explosion rumbled inside the tank. A blast of blazing air forced Kalina back several steps. Her hand held something soft and very hot: a piece of skin pulled loose from the tank crew member's hand, cooked through. Kalina raised her head and saw flames burst from the hatch. Through it, she could see that the tank interior was already an inferno in miniature. Among the flames, dimly red and transparent, she could clearly see the silhouette of the unmoving crewman, rippling as if in water.

She heard two new shrills. The artillery crew to her front and left fired its last two anti-tank missiles. The wire-guided Sagger missile successfully destroyed an Abrams; the other, radio-guided missile found its signal jammed and veered upward at an angle, missing its target. Meanwhile the six missile crewmen retreated from their bunker, running toward Kalina's bomb crater as a Comanche helicopter dove for them, its angular chassis resembling the profile of a savage alligator. Machine-gun bullets struck the ground in a long row, their impact abruptly standing snow and dirt up in a fence that just as quickly toppled. The fence crossed through the little squadron, felling four of them. Only a first lieutenant and a private made it over to the crater. There Kalina noticed that the lieutenant was wearing an antishock tank helmet, perhaps taken from a destroyed tank. The two of them held an RPG each.

The lieutenant jumped into the crater. He took a shot at the nearest enemy tank, hitting the M1A2 head-on, triggering its reactive armor, the sound of the rocket explosion and the armor explosion mingling peculiarly. The tank charged out of the cloud of smoke, scraps of reactive armor dangling from its front like a tattered shirt. The young private was still aiming, his RPG jittering with the tank's rise and fall, too uncertain to fire. Then the tank was just fifty, forty meters away, heading into a dip in the ground, and the private could only stand on the rim of the crater to aim downward.

His RPG and the Abrams's 120 mm gun sounded simultaneously.

The tank gunner had fired a nonexplosive depleted-uranium armor-piercing round in his desperation. With an initial velocity of eight hundred meters per second, it turned the soldier's upper body into a spray of gore upon impact. Kalina felt scraps of blood and meat strike her steel helmet, pitter-pattering. She opened her eyes. Just in front of her, at the edge of the crater, the private's legs were two black tree stumps, soundlessly rolling their way to the bottom of the crater next to her feet. The shattered remains of the rest of his body had spattered a radial pattern of red speckles in the snow.

The rocket had struck the Abrams, the focused jet of the explosion cutting through its armor. Thick smoke billowed from the chassis. But the steel monster was still charging toward them, trailing smoke. It was within twenty meters of them before an explosion from within stopped it in its tracks, hurling the top of its turret sky-high.

The NATO tank line went past them immediately after, the ground trembling under the heavy impact of treads, but these tanks took no interest in their bomb crater. Once the first wave of tanks was past, the lieutenant grabbed Kalina's hand and leapt from the crater, pulling her after him to the side of an already bullet-scarred jeep. Two hundred meters away, the second wave of armored assault was bearing down on them.

'Lie down and play dead!' the lieutenant said. So Kalina lay by the jeep's wheel and closed her eyes. 'It looks more realistic with your eyes open!' the lieutenant added, and smeared a handful of somebody's blood on her face. He lay down, too, forming a right angle with Kalina, his head pressing against hers. His helmet had rolled to one side, and his coarse hair pricked at Kalina's temple. She opened her eyes wide, looking at the sky almost swallowed by smoke.

Two or three minutes later, a half-track Bradley infantry fighting vehicle stopped ten or so meters from them. A few American soldiers in blue-and-white snowy terrain camouflage jumped from the convoy. The bulk of them leveled their guns and advanced in a skirmish line. Only one walked toward the jeep. Kalina saw two snow-speckled paratrooper boots step next to her face; she could clearly make out the insignia of the Eighty-second Airborne Division on the handle of the knife sheathed in his boot. The American crouched down to look at her. Their gazes met, and Kalina tried as hard as she could to make hers blank and lifeless across from that pair of startled blue eyes.

'*Oh, god!*' Kalina heard him exclaim. She didn't know if it was for the beauty of this woman with a major's star on her shoulder, or for the terrible sight of her bloody, dirty face; maybe it was both. He reached a hand to unfasten her collar. Goose bumps rose all over Kalina, and she nudged her hand a few centimeters closer to the pistol in her belt, but the American only tugged the dog tag from her neck.

They had to wait longer than expected. Enemy tanks and armored convoys thundered endlessly past them. Kalina could feel her body freezing almost solid on the snowy ground. It made her think of a couplet from an old army song, of all things. She'd read the words in an old book on Matrosov: 'A soldier lies on the snowy ground / like they lie on white swan down.' The day she received her Ph.D., she'd written the lines in her diary. That had been a snowy night, too. She'd stood in front of the window on the top floor of Moscow State University's Main Building; that night, the snow really did look like swan down, and through the haze of snow flickered the lights from the thousands of homes of the capital. She'd joined the army the next day.

A jeep stopped not far from them, three NATO officers smoking and conversing inside. But the area around Kalina and the lieutenant was clearing. The two finally rose. They jumped in their own jeep, the lieutenant turned the ignition, and they hurtled along the route planned out earlier. Submachine guns sounded behind them; bullets flew overhead, one shattering a rearview mirror. The jeep whipped into a turn, entering a burning residential area. The enemy hadn't pursued.

'Major, you have a doctorate, right?' the lieutenant said as he drove.

'Where do you know me from?'

'I've seen you with Marshal Levchenko's son.'

After a silence, the lieutenant said, 'Right now, his son is farther from the war than anyone else in the world.'

'What are you implying? You know that—'

'Nothing, I was just saying,' the lieutenant said neutrally. Neither of them had their mind on the conversation. They were still lingering on that last thread of hope.

Of the entire battlefront, this might be the only breach.

JANUARY 5TH, NEAR-SUN ORBIT,
ABOARD THE *VECHNYY BURAN*

Misha was experiencing the solitude of a lone inhabitant in an empty city.

The *Vechnyy Buran* really was the size of a small city. The modular space station had a volume equivalent to two supercarriers and could sustain five thousand residents in space at a time. When the complex was under centripetal force simulating gravity, it even contained a pool and a small flowing river. Compared to other space work environments of the day, it smacked of unparalleled extravagance. But in reality, the *Vechnyy Buran* was the product of the thrifty reasoning the Russian space program had demonstrated since Mir. The thinking behind its design went that, although combining all the functionality needed to explore the entire solar system into one structure might require a huge initial investment, it would prove absolutely economical in the long run. Western media jokingly called *Vechnyy Buran* the Swiss Army knife of space: It could serve as a space station orbiting at any height from Earth; it could relocate easily to moon orbit, or make exploratory flights to the other planets. *Vechnyy Buran* had already flown to Venus and Mars and probed the asteroid belt. With its huge capacity, it was like shipping an entire research center into space. In the field of space research, it had an advantage over the legion but dainty Western spaceships.

The war had broken out just as *Vechnyy Buran* was preparing for the three-year expedition to Jupiter. At that time, its over one hundred crew members, most of them air force officers, had left for Earth, leaving only Misha. The *Vechnyy Buran* had revealed a flaw: Militarily, it presented too big a target while possessing no defensive abilities. Failing to foresee the progressive militarization of space had been a mistake on the part of the designer.

Vechnyy Buran could only take avoidance measures. It couldn't depart for farther space, with numerous unmanned NATO satellites patrolling Jupiter's orbital path. They were small, but whether armed or unarmed, any one could pose a deadly threat to the *Vechnyy Buran*.

The only option was to draw near the sun. The automatic active-cooling heat-shielding system that was the pride of the *Vechnyy*

Buran allowed it to go closer to the sun than any other man-made object yet. Now the *Vechnyy Buran* had reached Mercury's orbital path, five million kilometers from the sun and one hundred million kilometers from Earth.

Most of the *Vechnyy Buran*'s hold had been closed off, but the area left to Misha was still astonishingly enormous. Through the broad, clear dome ceiling, the sun looked three times larger than it looked on Earth. He could clearly see the sunspots and the singularly beautiful solar prominences emerging from the purple corona; sometimes, he could even see the granules formed by convection in the surface. The serenity here was an illusion. Outside, the sun pitched a raging storm of particles and electromagnetic radiation, and the *Vechnyy Buran* was just a tiny seed in a turbulent ocean.

A gossamer-thin thread of EM waves connected Misha to the Earth, and brought the troubles of that distant world to him as well. He had just been informed that the command center near Moscow had been destroyed by a cruise missile, and that the *Vechnyy Buran*'s control had passed to the secondary command center at Samara. He received the latest news of the war from Earth at five-hour intervals; at those times, each time, he would think of his father.

JANUARY 5TH, RUSSIAN ARMY GENERAL STAFF HEADQUARTERS

Marshal Mikhail Semyonovich Levchenko felt as if he were face-to-face with a wall, though in reality, a holographic map of the Moscow theater of war lay in front of him. Conversely, when he turned toward the big paper map hanging on the wall, he could see breadth and depth, a sense of space.

No matter what, he preferred traditional maps. He didn't know how many times he'd sought a location on the very bottom of the map, forcing him and his strategists to get on hands and knees; the thought now made him smile a little. He also remembered spending the eve of military exercises in his battlefield tent, piecing together the newly received battle maps with clear tape. He always made a mess of it, but his son had done the taping neater than he ever did, that first time he came along to watch the exercises. . . .

Finding that his musings had returned to the subject of his son, the marshal vigilantly cut off his train of thought.

He and the commander of the Western Military District were the only people in the war room, the latter chain-smoking cigarettes as they watched the shifting clouds of smoke above the holographic map, their gaze as intent as if it were the grim battlefield itself.

The district commander said: 'NATO has seventy-five divisions along the Smolensk front now. The battlefront is a hundred kilometers long. They've breached the line at multiple points.'

'And the eastern front?' Marshal Levchenko asked.

'Most of our Eleventh Army defected to the Rightists too, as you know. The Rightist army is now twenty-four divisions strong, but their assaults on Yaroslavl remain exploratory in nature.'

The earth shook with the faint vibrations of some ground explosion. The lights hanging from the ceiling cast swaying shadows around the war room.

'There's talk now of retreating to Moscow and using the barricades and fortifications for a street-to-street battle, like seventy-odd years ago.'

'That's absurd! If we withdraw from the western front, NATO can swing north around us to join forces with the Rightists at Tver. Moscow would fall into panic without them lifting a finger. We have three options in our playbook right now: counterattack, counterattack, and counterattack.'

The district commander sighed, looking wordlessly at the map.

Marshal Levchenko continued, 'I know the western front isn't strong enough. I plan to relocate an army from the eastern front to strengthen it.'

'What? But it's already going to be a challenge to defend Yaroslavl.'

Marshal Levchenko chuckled. 'Nowadays, the problem with many commanders is their tendency to only consider a problem from the military angle. They can't see beyond the grim tactical situation. Looking at the current situation, do you think the Rightists lack the strength to take Yaroslavl?'

'I don't think so. The Fourteenth Army is an elite force with a high concentration of armored vehicles and low-altitude attack power. For them to advance less than fifteen kilometers a day while not having suffered serious setbacks seems like taking things slow on purpose.'

'That's right, they're watching and waiting. They're watching the western front! And if we can take back the initiative in the western front, they'll keep on watching and waiting. They might even independently negotiate a cease-fire.'

The district commander held his newest cigarette in his hand, but had forgotten all thoughts of lighting it.

'The defection of the armies on the eastern front really was a knife in our back, but some commanders have turned this into an excuse in their minds to steer us toward passive operational policies. That has to change! Of course, it must be said that our current strength in the Moscow region isn't enough for a total turnaround. Our hope lies in the relief forces from the Caucasus and Ural districts.'

'The closer Caucasus forces will need at least a week to assemble and advance into place. If we account for possession of the airspace, it might take even longer.'

JANUARY 5TH, MOSCOW

It was past three in the afternoon when Kalina and the first lieutenant entered the city in their jeep. The air raid alarm had just sounded, and the streets were empty.

'I miss my T-90 already, Major,' sighed the lieutenant. 'I finished armored-vehicle training right around the time I broke up with my girlfriend, but the moment I arrived at my unit and saw that tank, my heart soared right back up again. I put my hand on its armor, and it was smooth and warm, like touching a lover's hand. Ha, what was that relationship worth! Now I'd found a real love! But it took a Mistral missile this morning.' He sighed again. 'It might still be burning.'

At that time they heard dense explosions from the northwest, a savage area bombing rare in modern aerial warfare.

The lieutenant was still wallowing in the morning's engagement. 'Less than thirty seconds, and the whole tank company was gone.'

'The enemy losses were heavy, too,' Kalina said. 'I observed the aftermath. There were about the same number of destroyed vehicles on each side.'

'The ratio of destroyed tanks was about 1 to 1.2, I think. The helicopters were worse off, but it wouldn't have gone over 1 to 1.4.'

'In that case, the battlefield initiative should have stayed on our side. We have a sizable advantage in numbers. How did the battle end up like this?'

The lieutenant turned to eye Kalina. 'You're one of the electronic-warfare people. Don't you get it? All your toys – the fifth-generation C3I, the 3-D battle displays, the dynamic situation simulators, the attack-plan optimizer, whatever – looked great in the mock battles. But on the real battlefield, all the screen in front of me ever showed was 'COMMUNICATION ERROR' and 'COULD NOT LOG IN.' Take this morning, for example. I didn't have a clue what was happening in the front and flanks. I only got one order: 'Engage the enemy.' Ah, if we'd only had half our force again in reinforcements, the enemy wouldn't have broken through our position. It was probably the same way all down the line.'

Kalina knew that in the battle that had just ended, the two sides had sent perhaps over ten thousand tanks into battle along the front, and half as many armed helicopters.

At that point they arrived at Arbat Street. The popular pedestrian boulevard of yesteryear was empty now, sandbags walling off the entrances to the antiques shops and artisans' places.

'My steel darling gave as good as she got.' The lieutenant was still stuck on the morning's battle. 'I'm sure I hit a Challenger tank. But most of all, I'd wanted to take down an Abrams, you know? An Abrams . . .'

Kalina pointed to the entrance of the antiques store they had just passed. 'There. My grandfather died there.'

'But I don't remember any bombs getting dropped here.'

'I'm talking about twenty years ago – I was only four then. The winter that year was bitterly cold. The heating was cut off, and ice formed in the rooms. I wrapped myself around the TV for warmth, listening to the president promise the Russian people a gentle winter. I screamed and cried that I was cold, hungry.

'My grandfather looked at me silently, and finally he made up his mind. He took out his treasured military medal and took me here. This was a free market, where you could sell anything, from vodka to political views. An American wanted my grandfather's medal, but he was only willing to pay forty dollars. He said Order of the Red Star and Order of the Red Banner medals weren't worth anything, but he'd pay a hundred dollars for an Order of Bogdan Khmelnitsky, a hundred fifty for an Order of Glory, two hundred for an Order of Nakhimov, two hundred fifty for an Order of Ushakov. *Order of Victories are worth the most, but of course you wouldn't have one, those were only given to generals.* But Order of Suvorovs were worth a lot too, he'd pay four hundred fifty dollars for one.... My grandfather walked away then. We walked and walked along Arbat Street in the freezing cold. Then my grandfather couldn't walk anymore. The sky was almost dark. He sat heavily on the steps of that antiques store and told me to go home without him. The next day, they found him frozen to death there, his hand reaching into his jacket to clench the medal he'd earned with his own blood. His eyes were wide open, looking at the city he'd saved from Guderian's tanks fifty years ago . . .'

JANUARY 5TH, RUSSIAN ARMY GENERAL STAFF HEADQUARTERS

Marshal Levchenko left the underground war room for the first time in a week. He walked in the thick snowfall, searching for the sun, half set behind the snow-draped pinewoods. In his mind's eye, he saw a small black dot slowly moving against the orange setting sun: the *Vechnyy Buran,* with his son inside, farther than any other son from a father.

It had led to many ugly rumors within his homeland, and the enemy utilized it even more fully abroad. *The New York Times* had printed its headline in black type sized for shock: NO DESERTER HAS RUN FARTHER. Below was a photo of Misha, captioned 'At a time when the communist regime is agitating three hundred million Russians for a bloodbath defense against the 'invaders,' the son of their marshal has fled the war aboard the nation's only massive-scale spacecraft. Sixty million miles from the battlefield, he is safer than any other of his fellow citizens.'

But Marshal Levchenko didn't take it to heart. From secondary school to postgraduate studies, almost none of Misha's associates had known who his father was. The space program command center made its decision solely because Misha's field of study happened to be the mathematical modeling of stars. The *Vechnyy Buran* approaching the sun was a rare opportunity for his research, and the space complex couldn't be entirely piloted by remote control, requiring at least one person aboard. The general learned of Misha's background only later, from the Western news media.

On the other hand, whether Marshal Levchenko admitted it or not, deep down inside, he really did hope his son could stay away from the war. It wasn't solely a matter of blood ties; Marshal Levchenko had always felt that his son wasn't meant for war – perhaps he was the least meant for war of all the world's people. But he knew his notion was faulty: was anyone truly meant for war?

Besides, was Misha truly suited for the stars either? He liked stars, had devoted his life to their research, but he himself was the opposite of a star. He was more like Pluto, the silent and cold dwarf planet orbiting in its distant void, out of sight of the mortal realm. Misha was quiet and graceful. Solitude was his nourishment and air.

Misha was born in East Germany, and the day he was born was the darkest day in the marshal's life. He was only a major that evening in West Berlin, standing guard with his soldiers in front of the Soviet War Memorial in the Tiergarten, keeping vigil for the fallen for the last time in forty years. In front of them were a gaggle of grinning Western officers; and a few slovenly, shiftless German police officers trailing wolfhounds on leashes to replace them; and the skinhead neo-Nazis hollering 'Red Army Go Home.' Behind him were the tear-filled eyes of the senior company commander and soldiers. He couldn't help himself; he, too, let tears blur all this away.

He returned to the emptied barracks after dark. On this last night before he left for home, he was notified that Misha had been born, but that his wife had died of complications from childbirth.

His life after he returned was difficult, too. Like the 400,000 army men and 120,000 administrators withdrawn from Europe, he had no home to go to, and lived with Misha in a temporary shack of metal sheets, freezing in winter and broiling in summer. His old colleagues would do any work for a living, some becoming gun runners for the gangs, some reduced to strip dances at nightclubs.

But he stuck to his honest soldier's life, and Misha quietly grew up amid the hardship. He wasn't like the other children; he seemed to have been born with an innate ability to endure, because he had a world of his own.

As early as primary school, Misha would quietly spend the entire night alone in his small room. Levchenko had thought he was reading at first, but by chance he discovered that his son was standing in front of the window, unmoving, watching the stars.

'Papa, I like the stars. I want to look at them all my life,' he told his father.

On his eleventh birthday, Misha asked his father for a present for the first time: a telescope. He'd been using Levchenko's military binoculars to stargaze before then. Afterward, the telescope became Misha's only companion. He could stand on the balcony and watch the stars until the sky lightened in the east. A few times, father and son stargazed together. The marshal always turned the telescope toward the brightest-looking star, but his son would shake his head disapprovingly. 'That one's not interesting, Papa. That's Venus. Venus is a planet, but I only like stars.'

Misha didn't like any of the things that the other kids liked, either. The neighbor's boy, son of the old paratrooper chief of staff, snuck out his father's pistol to play with, and ended up shooting his own leg by accident. The general of the staff's children thought no reward better than their papa taking them to the company firing range and letting them take a shot. But that affinity seemed to have completely skipped over Misha.

Levchenko found his son's apathy for weapons unsettling, almost intolerable, to the point where he reacted in a way that embarrassed him to think of to this day: Once, he'd quietly set his Makarov semiautomatic on his son's writing desk. Not long after he returned from school, Misha came out of his room with the pistol. He held it like a child, his hand closed carefully around the barrel. He set the gun gently in front of his father and said, evenly, 'Papa, be careful where you put it next time.'

On the topic of Misha's future, the marshal was an understanding man. He wasn't like the other generals around him, determined that their sons and daughters would succeed them in the military. But Misha really was too distant from his father's work.

Marshal Levchenko wasn't a hot-tempered man, but as the commander in chief of the armies, he'd castigated more than one general in front of thousands of troops. He'd never lost his temper at Misha, though. Misha walked silently and steadily along his chosen path, giving his father little cause for concern. More importantly, Misha seemed to be born with an extraordinary aloofness from the world that at times elicited even Levchenko's reverence. It was as if he'd carelessly tossed a seed into a flowerpot only for a rare and exotic plant to sprout. He had watched this plant grow day by day, protecting it carefully, awaiting its flowering. His hopes had not fallen short. His son was now the most renowned astrophysicist in the world.

By this time, the sun had entirely set behind the pine forest, the white snow on the ground turning pale blue. Marshal Levchenko collected his thoughts and returned to the underground war room. All the personnel for the war meeting had arrived, including important commanders from the Western and Caucasus military districts.

Outnumbering them were the electronic-warfare commanders, all the ranks from captain to major general, most newly returned from the front. In the war room, a debate was raging between the Western Military District's ground- and electronic-warfare officers.

'We correctly determined the enemy assault's change in direction,' Major General Felitov of the Taman Division said. 'Our tanks and close air support had no problems with maneuverability. But the communications system was jammed beyond belief. The C3I system was almost paralyzed! We expanded the electronic-warfare unit from a battalion to a division, from a division to a corps, and invested more money in them these two years than we invested in all the regular equipment. And we get this?!'

One of the lieutenant generals commanding electronic warfare in the region glanced at Kalina. Like all the other officers newly returned from the front line, her camo uniform was stained and scorched, and traces of blood still stuck to her face. 'Major Kalina has done noteworthy work in electronic-warfare research, and was sent by the General Staff to observe the electronic battle. Perhaps her insights may better persuade you.' Young Ph.D. officers like Kalina tended to be fearlessly outspoken toward superiors. They were often used as mouthpieces for tough words, and this was no exception.

Kalina stood. 'General Felitov, that's hardly the case! Compared to NATO, the investment we've put into our C3I is nothing.'

'What about electronic countermeasures?' the major general asked. 'If the enemy can jam us, can't you jam them? Our C3I was useless, but NATO's worked like the wheels were greased. Just look at how quickly the enemy was able to change the direction of their attack this morning!'

Kalina gave a pained smile. 'Speaking of jamming the enemy, General Felitov, don't forget that in your sector, your people forced their own electronic-warfare unit to turn off their jammers at gunpoint!'

'What happened out there?' Marshal Levchenko asked. Only then did the others notice his arrival and stand to bow.

'It was like this,' the major general explained. 'Their jamming was worse for our own communication and command system than NATO's! We could still maintain some wireless transmission through NATO's jamming. But once our forces turned on their own jammers, we were completely smothered!'

'But don't forget, the enemy would have been completely smothered too!' Kalina said. 'Given our army's available electronic countermeasures, this was the only possible strategy. At this time, NATO has already widely adopted technologies like frequency hopping, direct-sequence spread spectrum, adaptive nulling systems, burst transmission, and frequency agility.* Our frequency-specific aimed jamming was completely useless. Full-spectrum barrage jamming was our only option.'

A colonel from the Fifth Army spoke up. 'Major, NATO exclusively

* A simplified explanation of the electronic battle vocabulary:
Frequency hopping: The transmitter switches carrier frequencies according to a pattern possessed by the receiver.
Direct-sequence spread spectrum: The signal is distributed across a wide range of frequencies to make eavesdropping and jamming difficult.
Adaptive nulling system: An antenna array that nulls out signals coming from the direction of enemy jamming, allowing it to communicate with ally antennae in other directions.
Burst transmission: Transmitting data at a high rate over a short period of time using a wider-than-average frequency range.
Frequency agility: The signal is capable of rapidly and continuously changing frequency to avoid jamming.

uses frequency-specific aimed jamming too, with a fairly narrow range of frequencies. And our C3I system widely incorporates the technologies you mentioned as well. Why would their jamming be so effective against us?'

'That's easy. What systems are our C3I built upon? Unix, Linux, even Windows 2010, and our CPUs are made by Intel and AMD! We're using the dogs they raised to guard our own gate! Under these circumstances, the enemy can quickly figure out, say, the frequency-hopping patterns used for our intelligence reports, while using more numerous and more effective software attacks to strengthen the effects of their jamming. The Main Command suggested the widespread adoption of a Russian-made operating system in the past, but met heavy opposition from the ranks. Your division was the most stubborn holdout of all—'

'Yes, yes, we're here today to resolve precisely that problem and conflict,' Marshal Levchenko interrupted. 'I call this meeting to order!'

Once everyone was seated in front of the digital battle simulator, Marshal Levchenko called over a staff officer. The young major was tall and skinny, his eyes squinted into slits, as if they had trouble adjusting to the war room's brightness. 'Let me introduce Major Bondarenko. His most obvious trait is his severe myopia. His glasses are different from other people's – their lenses rest inside the frame, while his stick out. Ha, they're as thick as the bottom of a teacup! This morning they got smashed when the major's jeep was hit in an airstrike, which is why we don't see them now. I think he lost his contacts too?'

'Marshal, it was five days ago at Minsk. My eyes only became like this in the last half year. If it happened earlier, I wouldn't have been admitted into Frunze Military Academy,' the major said stolidly.

No one knew why the marshal had chosen to introduce the major like this, though a few chuckled in the audience.

'Since the beginning of the war,' the marshal continued, 'events have shown that despite Russian losses on the battlefield, our aerial and ground weapons aren't far behind the enemy's. But in the field of electronic warfare, we've been unexpectedly left in the dust. Many events in the past contributed to this situation, but we're not here to point fingers. We're here to state this: In our situation, electronic warfare is the key to taking back the initiative in the war! We must first admit that the enemy has an advantage in this area, perhaps an overwhelming advantage. Then we must work within our army's hardware and software limitations to create an effective plan of battle. The goal of this plan is to even out our and NATO's electronic-warfare capabilities within a short period of time. Maybe you all think this is impossible – our military planning since the end of the last century has been based on the assumption of a limited-scope war. We really haven't done enough research for an invasion on all fronts by as powerful an enemy as the one we're facing right now. In our dire situation, we have to think in a completely new way. The central command's new electronic-warfare strategy, which I'm introducing next, will demonstrate the results of this mode of thinking.'

The lights went out, the computer screens and digital battle simulator dimmed, and the heavy anti-radiation doors shut tightly. The war room was plunged into total darkness.

'I had the lights turned off.' The marshal's voice came through the darkness.

A minute passed in dark and silence.

'How's everyone feeling?' Marshal Levchenko asked.

No one answered. The cloying darkness left the officers feeling as if they were at the bottom of a dark sea. It even felt hard to breathe.

'General Andreyev, tell it to us.'

'Like it felt on the battlefield these few days,' the commander of the Fifth Army said, eliciting a wave of quiet laughter from the darkness.

'Everyone else empathizes with him, I think,' said the marshal. 'Of course you do! Think of it – nothing but static in your headsets, solid white on your screens, not a clue as to your orders or the battlefield around you. That same feeling! The darkness presses down until you can't breathe!

'But not everyone feels like that. How are you, Major Bondarenko?' asked Marshal Levchenko.

Major Bondarenko's voice came from one corner of the room. 'It's not so bad for me. Everything was a blur around me anyway back when the lights were on.'

'Maybe you even feel an advantage?' asked Marshal Levchenko.

'Yes, sir. You may have heard the story of the New York blackout, where blind people led everyone out of the skyscrapers.'

'But General Andreyev's sentiments are understandable. He's eagle-eyed, a legendary marksman – when he drinks, he uses his revolver to take the caps off his bottles at ten-odd meters. Wouldn't it be interesting to picture him having a gun duel with Major Bondarenko at this moment?'

The darkened war room once again sank into silence as the officers considered this.

The lights turned on. Everyone narrowed their eyes, less because of the discomfort of the sudden brightness, and more for the shock of what the marshal had just implied.

Marshal Levchenko stood up. 'I think I've explained our army's new electronic-warfare strategy: large-scale, full-spectrum barrage jamming. With regard to EM communications, we're going to let both sides enjoy a blacked-out battlefield!'

'This will cause our own battlefield command system to completely break down!' someone said fearfully.

'NATO's will too! If we're going to be blind, let's both be blind. If we're going to be deaf, let's both be deaf. We can then reach equal footing with the enemy's electronic-warfare capabilities. This is the central tenet of our new strategy.'

'But what are we supposed to do now, send messengers on motorcycles to transmit orders?'

'If the roads are bad, they'll have to ride horses,' Marshal Levchenko said. 'Our rough prediction shows that this kind of full-spectrum barrage jamming will cover at least seventy percent of NATO's battlefield communication network, meaning that their C3I system will suffer a complete breakdown. Simultaneously, we'll be leaving fifty to sixty percent of the enemy's long-range weapons useless. The best example is with the Tomahawk satellite-guided missile. Missile guidance has changed a lot since last century. Before, it primarily navigated using onboard TERCOM with a small-scale radar altimeter, but now these methods are only used in end-stage guidance, while most of the launch process relies on a GPS system. General Dynamics and McDonnell Douglas Corporation thought this change was a big step forward, but the Americans trust their EM wave guidance from space too well. Once we disrupt the GPS transmission, the Tomahawk will be blind. The dependency on GPS exists in most of NATO's long-range weapons. Under the battlefield conditions we've planned, we'll force the enemy into a traditional battle, allowing us to fully utilize our strengths.'

'I'm still unsure about this,' the commander of the Twelfth Army sent from the eastern front said anxiously. 'Under these battlefield communication conditions, I'm not even sure my division can smoothly reach the western front from the east.'

'Of course it will!' said Marshal Levchenko. 'The distance was nothing even for Kutuzov, in Napoleon's time. I don't believe the Russian army needs wireless to do it today! The Americans should be the ones spoiled rotten by modern equipment, not us. I know that an EM blackout over all the battlefield will put fear in your hearts. But you have to remember, the enemy will feel ten times your fear!'

Watching Kalina disappear among the other camo-clad officers as they exited the war room, Marshal Levchenko felt apprehension rise in his heart. She was returning to the front, and her unit was stationed right in the middle of the enemy's most concentrated firepower. Yesterday, during his five minutes of communication with his son a hundred million miles away, the marshal had told him that Kalina was perfectly well. But she nearly hadn't come back from this morning's battle.

Misha and Kalina had met at one of the military exercises. The marshal had been eating dinner with his son one night, silently as usual, Misha's late mother looking on from her picture frame. Suddenly, Misha had said, 'Papa, I recall that tomorrow is your fifty-first birthday. I should give you a gift. I thought of it when I saw the telescope; that was a wonderful present.'

'How about you give me a few days of your time?'

Son quietly raised his head to look at father.

'You have your own work, and I'm happy for you. But surely it's not unreasonable for a father to want his son to understand his life's work! How about you come with me to observe the military exercises?'

Misha smiled and nodded. He smiled very rarely.

It had been the largest Russian war game of the century. Misha showed little interest in the torrent of steel-armored vehicles rumbling past them on the highway that night before it started; the moment he was off the helicopter, he ducked into the tent to assemble the newly arrived battle maps with clear tape in his father's stead. The next day, Misha didn't show the slightest interest through all the exercises. Marshal Levchenko had expected that. But one incident gave him all the reassurance he could ever want.

The exercise scheduled for the morning was a tank division assaulting high ground; Misha sat with some local officials on the north side of the observation station. The station was safely out of range, but in order to satisfy the curiosity of the local officials, it had been placed much closer to the action than before.

Tu-22 bombers soared in formation above, heavy aerial bombs fell like rain, and the hilltop exploded into an erupting volcano. Only then did the officials understand the difference between movies and a real battlefield. As the ground quaked and the hill shook, they pressed themselves flat against the table and covered their heads with their arms, some even crawling under the table with shrieks. But the marshal saw that Misha alone sat with his back straight, the same cool expression on his face, calmly watching the terrible volcano as the light of the explosions flashed across his sunglasses. Warmth flooded into Levchenko's heart then. In the end, son, you have a soldier's blood in your veins!

That night, father and son walked along the practice field. In the distance, the headlamps of armored vehicles densely sprinkled the valleys and plains with stars. The faint smell of gunpowder smoke still lingered in the air.

'How much did it cost?' Misha asked.

'The direct cost was about three hundred million rubles.'

Misha sighed. 'Our task group wanted a third-generation evolving star model to work with. We couldn't get a grant of three hundred fifty thousand for expenses.'

Marshal Levchenko at last said what he'd long wanted to tell his son. 'Our two worlds are too far apart. Your stars are all four light-years away at the least, yes? They don't have any bearing on the armies and wars on Earth. I can't claim to know much about what you do, though I'm very proud of you all the same. But as an army man, I just want my son to appreciate my own profession. What father wouldn't feel the greatest happiness telling his son about his campaigns? But you've never cared for my work, when really, it's the foundation and safeguard for your own. Without an army strong enough and big enough to keep the country safe, fundamental science research like yours would be impossible.'

'You've got it backward, Papa. If everyone were like us and spent all their life on exploring the universe, they'd understand its beauty, the beauty that lies behind its vastness and depth. And someone who truly understood the innate beauty of space and nature would never go to war.'

'That thinking's as childish as you can get. If appreciation of beauty could prevent war, we'd never be short of peace!'

'Do you think it's easy for humanity to understand this kind of beauty?' Misha pointed at the night sky, a sea of shining stars. 'Look at these stars. Everyone knows they're beautiful, but how many grasp the deepest nuances of their beauty? All these countless celestial bodies are so glorious in their metamorphosis from nebula to black hole, so vast and terrible in their explosive power. But do you know that a few elegant equations can accurately describe all of it? Mathematical models created from the equations can near perfectly predict everything a star does. Even mathematical models of our own planet's atmosphere are orders of magnitude less precise.'

Marshal Levchenko nodded. 'I can believe that. They say humanity knows more about the moon than the bottom of Earth's oceans. But the deeper beauty in space and nature you talk about still can't stop wars. No one could have understood that beauty more than Einstein, and didn't he advise the creation of the atomic bomb?'

'Einstein made little progress in his later research, largely because he became too involved in politics. I won't go down the same path as him. But, Papa, when it's necessary, I'll do my duty too.'

Misha observed the exercise for five days. The marshal didn't know when his son first met Kalina; the first time he saw them together, they were already conversing on familiar terms. They were talking about stars, about which Kalina knew a considerable amount. Seeing an untried youngster like Kalina already wearing a major's star for her Ph.D. left the marshal feeling a little offended, but other than that, she'd made a fine first impression.

The second time Marshal Levchenko saw Misha and Kalina together, he discovered there was already a deep sense of closeness between them. Their topic of conversation surprised him: electronic warfare. They were standing by a tank parked not far from the marshal's jeep. Due to their topic of conversation, they didn't seem concerned with privacy.

The marshal heard Misha say: 'Right now, your department has been focusing on only high-level pure software like the C3I, virus programs, the digital battlefield, and so on. But have you considered that this might leave you holding a wooden sword?' Seeing Kalina's surprise, Misha continued, 'Have you put thought into the foundation they're built upon? The physical layer at the bottom of the seven layers of protocol defined by the Open Systems Interconnection model? Civilian networks can use fiber optics, fixed lasers, and the like for media and communication. But the terminals in a military-use C3I network are fast-moving and unpredictably located, so only EM waves can keep them in communication. And you know how EM waves are as fragile as thin ice under jamming . . .'

The marshal was quite shocked. He'd never talked about these things with Misha, and his son would never have snuck a look at his classified documents, but here Misha had neatly and clearly laid out the same considerations that he'd come up with over the years!

Misha's words had an even greater impact on Kalina. She even shifted the direction of her own research to create an electromagnetic jamming unit code-named 'Flood.' It fit into an armored vehicle, and could simultaneously emit strong EM jamming waves ranging from three kilohertz to thirty gigahertz, drowning out all EM communication signals outside the millimeter radio range.

The first weapons test at one of the Siberian bases had sent a whole swarm of officials running over to protest. Flood had cut off all EM wave-based communication in the nearby city: cell phones found no reception, pagers fell silent, televisions and radios lost all signal. The impact on finance and stocks was disastrous; the local officials claimed astronomical losses.

Flood was inspired by a type of EMP bomb that utilized high explosives to create a powerful electromagnetic pulse within a one-use wire coil. As a result, Flood created shock waves like a rocket engine, shattering nearby windows in its trial. This meant that it could only be remotely operated, and its crew had to wear anti-microwave-radiation protective gear even though they were two or three kilometers away.

Flood had raised fierce debate in the armaments department and the electronic-warfare command. Many thought that it had no practical value; using it in a limited-scope battlefield would be like using a nuclear bomb in a street-to-street battle, devastating friend and foe alike. But under the marshal's insistence, two hundred Flood units had been mass-produced. Now, in the central command's new electronic-warfare strategy, it would take center stage.

That his son had fallen for a woman in the army had deeply surprised Marshal Levchenko. He assumed at the time that Misha's feelings for Kalina overlooked her occupation. But Misha later brought Kalina home on a few occasions. The first time, Kalina wore a pretty dress; when Marshal Levchenko walked close, he overheard Misha tell her, 'You don't have to dress up for us. Wear your uniform next time, I know you feel more comfortable in it.' That disproved the marshal's original theory. Now he understood that Misha fell for Kalina to some extent because she was a major in the army. He felt again what he felt that first morning of war training. The major's star on Kalina's shoulder now seemed incomparably beautiful.

JANUARY 6TH, MOSCOW THEATER OF OPERATIONS

Powerful electromagnetic waves gathered rapidly above the battlefield, at last becoming a mighty typhoon. After the war, people would reminisce: In the mountain villages far from the front line, they saw the animals fidget and stir, agitated; in the city with its enforced blackout, they saw induction trigger tiny sparks along the telephone wires.

As part of the Twelfth Army transferring from the eastern front to the west, the armored-car corps was advancing urgently. Their lieutenant general stood by his jeep parked at the roadside, watching his troops hasten through the snow and dust with satisfaction. The enemy's air raids had been far less intense than predicted, allowing his forces to travel by day.

Three Tomahawk missiles tore overhead, the low buzz of their jet engines crisp in the air. A moment later, three explosions sounded in the distance. The correspondent by the lieutenant general's side, his static-filled earpiece useless, turned to look in the direction of the explosion. He cried out in surprise. The general told him not to make a big deal out of nothing, but then a battalion commander beside him urged him to look, too. So he looked, and shook his head in confusion. Tomahawks weren't 100 percent accurate, but for three to land in an empty field, more than a kilometer from each other, really was a rare sight.

Two Su-27s flew five kilometers above the battlefield in an empty sky. They had belonged to a larger fighter squadron, but it had run into a skirmish with a NATO F-22 squadron above the sea, and the planes lost contact with the others in the turmoil of battle. Normally, regrouping would have been easy, but now the radio was down. The airspace that had seemed so small as to be cramped to a high-speed fighter plane now seemed as vast as outer space. Regrouping would be like finding a needle in a haystack. The lead pilot and his wingman were forced to fly wingtip-to-wingtip like stunt fliers to hear each other's wireless messages.

'Suspicious object to the upper left, azimuth 220, altitude 30!' the wingman reported. The lead pilot looked in that direction. The earlier snow had washed the winter sky clean and blue, and the visibility was excellent. The two planes ascended toward the target to investigate. It was flying in the same direction as them, but much slower, and it didn't take long to catch up.

Their first good look at the target was a bolt out of the blue.

That was a NATO E-4A early-warning aircraft. For a fighter-plane pilot to encounter one was like seeing the back of their own head. An E-4A could monitor up to one million square kilometers, completing a full sweep in just five seconds. It could locate targets two thousand kilometers from the defensive area, providing more than forty minutes of advance notice. It could separate out up to a thousand EM signals within one thousand to two thousand kilometers, and each scan could query and identify two thousand targets of any kind, land, sky, or sea. An early-warning aircraft didn't need the protection of escorts when its all-seeing eyes allowed it to easily avoid any threats.

That was why the lead pilot naturally assumed it was a trap. He and the wingman searched the surrounding sky carefully, but there was nothing in the cold, clear sky. The lead pilot decided to take a risk.

'Ball lightning, ball lightning, I'm going to attack. Guard azimuth 317, but be careful not to leave range of sight!'

Once his wingman flew in the direction he thought most likely for an ambush, he activated the afterburner and yanked at the controllers. Trailing black exhaust, the Su-27 lunged toward the early-warning aircraft above like a striking cobra. Now the E-4A discovered the approaching threat and turned to rush southeast in an escape maneuver. Magnesium heat pellets popped from its tail one after another to disrupt heat-seeking missiles, the trail of little fireballs looking like bits of its soul startled out of its mortal shell. An early-warning aircraft before a fighter plane was as helpless as a bicycle trying to outrun a motorbike. In that moment, the lead pilot decided that the order he'd given the wingman had turned out to be terribly selfish.

He followed the E-4A from above at a distance, admiring the prey he'd caught. The pale blue radar dome atop the E-4A was lovely in its curves, charming as a Christmas ornament; its broad white chassis was like a fat roast duck on its platter: so tempting, yet too lovely to violate with knife and fork. But instinct warned him not to drag this on any longer. He first fired a burst with the 20 mm cannon, shattering the radome, and watched scraps of the Westinghouse-made AN/ZPY-3 radar antenna scatter across the sky like silver Christmas confetti. He next severed a wing with the cannon, then at last lashed down the fatal blow with the 6,000 rpm double-barreled cannon, cutting the already tumbling and falling E-4A in two.

The Su-27 wheeled downward to follow the halves in their plunging descent. The pilot watched crew and equipment fall from the hold like chocolates from a box, a few parachutes blooming against the sky. He remembered the battle earlier, the sight of his comrade escaping from his hit plane: an F-22 had purposely flown low over the parachute, swooping past, three times, to knock it over. He'd watched as his comrade dropped like a stone, disappearing against the white backdrop of the ground.

He forced back the impulse to do something similar. Once he regrouped with his wingman, the pair abandoned the area at top speed.

They still suspected a trap.

*

The two weren't the only aircraft separated from their unit. A Comanche armed attack helicopter from the US Army First Cavalry Division flew with no target in sight, but its pilot, Lieutenant Walker, felt a rush of adrenaline all the same. He'd transferred from an Apache to the Comanche recently, and had yet to adjust to this sort of attack helicopter with troop-carrying capabilities, an innovation from the end of the previous century. He was unaccustomed to the Comanche's lack of foot pedals, and he thought the headset with its binocular helmet-mounted display wasn't as comfortable to use as the Apache's single sight. But most of all, he wasn't used to Captain Haney, the forward director sitting in front of him.

'You need to know your place, Lieutenant,' Haney had told him the first time they met. 'I'm the brain controlling this helicopter. You're a cogwheel in its machinery, and you're going to act like one!' And Walker hated nothing more than that.

He remembered the retired navy pilot who'd toured their base, a WWII vet pushing a hundred years old. He had shaken his head when he saw the Comanche's cockpit. 'Oh, you kids. My P-51 Mustang back in the day had a simpler control panel than a microwave today, and that was the finest control panel I ever used!' He patted Walker's ass. 'The difference between our generations of pilots is the difference between knights of the sky and computer operators.'

Walker had wanted to be a knight of the sky. Here was his opportunity. Under the Russians' berserk jamming, the helicopter's combat mission integration system, the target analysis system, the auxiliary target examination and classification system, the RealSight situation imager, the resource burst system, whatever, they were all fucking fried! All that was left was the two 1,000-horsepower T800 engines, still loyally churning away. Haney normally earned his spot with his electronic gewgaws, but now his incessant orders had gone silent with them.

Haney's voice came through the internal mic system. 'Attention, I've found a target. It seems to be to the left and front, maybe by that little hill. There's an armored-car unit that seems to be the enemy's. You . . . do what you can.'

Walker nearly laughed aloud. Ha, that bastard. What he would have said in the past was, 'I've found a target at azimuth 133. Seventeen 90-series tanks, twenty-one 89-series soldier convoys, moving toward azimuth 391 at an average speed of 43.5 klicks per hour and an average separation of 31.4 meters. Execute the AJ041 optimized attack plan and approach from azimuth 179 at a vertical angle of 37 degrees.' And now? 'It 'seems' to be an armored-car unit, 'maybe by' that little hill.' *Who the hell needed you to say that? I saw it ages ago! Leave it to me, because you're useless now, Haney. This is my battle, and I'm going to use my ass for an accelerometer and be a knight! This Comanche's gonna fight like its namesake in my hands.*

The Comanche charged toward its open target and launched all sixty-two 27.5-inch Hornet missiles. Walker watched rapt as his swarm of fire-stingered little bees buzzed happily toward their target, swamping the enemy in a sea of fire. But when he turned to fly over the results of the encounter, he realized that something was wrong. The soldiers on the ground hadn't tried to conceal themselves. Instead, they stood in the snow, pointing at him. They seemed to be cussing him out.

Walker flew closer and clearly saw the destroyed armored car's insignia for himself: three concentric circles, blue at the center, white in the middle, red on the outside. Walker felt as if he'd dropped into hell. He started cussing, too.

'You son of a bitch, are you blind?!'

But he still had the wisdom to fly away in case the enraged French returned fire. 'You son of a bitch, you're probably thinking of how to pin the blame on me in military court right this moment. I'm telling you here, you won't get away with this. You were the one in charge of identifying targets, are you clear?'

'Maybe . . . maybe we'll still have the chance to make up for our mistake,' Haney said timidly. 'I found another unit, right across—'

'Fuck you!' Walker said.

'They're definitely the enemy's this time! They're exchanging fire with the French!'

Walker perked up at that. He steered toward the new target and saw that the enemy force was primarily infantry without much armored-vehicle strength. This did support Haney's assessment. Walker launched his last four Hellfire missiles, then set his double-barreled Gatling gun to 1,500 rpm and started shooting. He felt the comfortable vibration of the machine gun through the chassis, watching as it scattered snow and powder like ground white pepper over the enemy skirmish line on the ground. But the intuition of a veteran armed helicopter pilot warned him of danger. He turned, only to see a soldier standing on a jeep fire a shoulder-mounted rocket launcher to his left. Walker frantically shot off magnesium heat pellets as lures and swung backward for evasive maneuvers, but too late. The missile, trailing cobwebs of white smoke, had punched into the Comanche right under the nose.

When Walker woke from his brief explosion-induced concussion, he found that the helicopter had crashed in the snow. Walker scrambled desperately from the smoke-filled interior, bracing himself against a tree that had been severed neatly at waist height by the propeller. When he looked back, he could see the remains of Captain Haney in the front seat, blasted into a pulp by the explosion. When he looked forward, he saw a band of soldiers running toward him with submachine guns raised, their Slavic features clear.

Shaking, Walker dug out his handgun and set it on the snow in front of him. He dug out his Russian phrase book and began to clumsily read out his surrender.

'Y-ya postavil svoye oruzhiye. Ya voyennoplennym. V Zhenevskoy konventsii—'

Walker took a gun butt to the back of his head, then a boot to his belly. But as he collapsed into the snow, he was laughing. They might beat him half to death, but only half. He'd seen the eagle insignia of the Polish army on the soldiers' collars.

JANUARY 7TH, MINSK,
NATO COMBAT OPERATIONS CENTER

'Get that goddamn doctor over here!' General Tony Baker roared.

The gangly military doctor ran over.

'What the hell went wrong?' Baker demanded. 'You've messed with my dentures twice and they're still buzzing!'

'I've never seen anything like it, General. Maybe it's your nervous system. How about I give you a shot of local anesthetic?'

'Give me the dentures, sir,' said a major on the staff, walking over. 'I know how to fix them.' Baker took out his dentures and set them on the major's proffered paper towel.

According to the media, the general lost his two front teeth when his tank was hit during the Gulf War. Only Baker himself knew that this wasn't true. That time he'd broken his lower jaw; he'd lost the teeth earlier.

It had been at Clark Air Base in the Philippines, during the Mount Pinatubo eruption, when the world around seemed to be volcanic ash and nothing else. The sky was ash, the ground was ash, the air was ash, too. Even the C-130 Hercules that he and the last of the base personnel were about to board was coated with a thick layer of white. The dim red of magma glimmered intermittently in the gray distance.

Elena, the Filipina office worker he had been sleeping with, tracked him down after all this. The base was gone, she said, and she'd lost her job. Her house was buried under ash. How were she and the child in her belly supposed to live? She pulled at his hand and begged him to take her to America. He told her it was impossible. So she took off a high-heeled shoe and whacked him in the face, knocking out two of his teeth.

Where are you now, my child? Baker wondered, gazing at the gray ocean. *Are you living out your days with your mother in the slums of Manila? In a way, your father is fighting for your sake. Once the democratic government takes over in Russia after the war, NATO's vanguard will be at China's borders, and Subic Bay and Clark will once again become America's Pacific naval and air bases, even more prosperous than they were last century. You'll find work there! But most importantly, under NATO's pressure, those Chinese just might give you folks what you've wanted for so long: those beautiful islands in the South China Sea. I've seen them from the air: snow-white coral surrounding the brown sand, like eyes in the blue sea. Child, those are your father's eyes . . .*

The major returned, cutting short the general's woolgathering. Baker accepted the dentures on the paper towel, put them in, and after a few seconds, looked at the major in astonishment. 'How did you do that?'

'Sir, your dentures were buzzing because of electromagnetic resonance.'

Baker stared at the major in clear disbelief.

'Sir, it's true! Maybe you've been exposed to strong EM waves before, for example near radar equipment, but the frequency of those waves must have been different from your dentures' resonant frequency. But now, the air is filled with powerful EM waves at all frequencies, which caused this condition. I've modified the dentures to make their resonant frequency much higher. They're still vibrating, but you can't feel it anymore.'

After the major left, General Baker's gaze fell onto the clock standing beside the digital battle map. Its base was a sculpture of Hannibal riding an elephant, engraved with the caption EVER VICTORIOUS. The clock had originally inhabited the Blue Room of the White House; when the president saw his gaze straying again and again in its direction, he'd personally picked up the clock from its century-old resting place and gifted it to him.

'God save America, General. You're God to us now!'

Baker pondered for a long time, then slowly said, 'Tell all forces to halt the offensive. Use all our available airpower to find and destroy the source of the Russian jamming.'

JANUARY 8TH, RUSSIAN ARMY GENERAL STAFF HEADQUARTERS

'The enemy has disengaged, but you don't seem happy,' Marshal Levchenko said to the commander of the Western Military District, newly returned from the front line.

'I don't have reason to be happy. NATO has concentrated all their airpower on destroying our jamming units. It's really proving an effective countertactic.'

'It's no more than we expected,' Marshal Levchenko said evenly. 'Our strategy would catch the enemy unprepared at first, but they'd come up with a way to counter eventually. Barrage-type jammers emitting strong EM waves at all frequencies wouldn't be hard to find and destroy. But fortunately, we've managed to stall for a considerable length of time. All our hopes now rest on the reinforcement armies' swift arrival.'

'The situation might be worse than we predicted,' said the district commander. 'We might not be able to give the Caucasus Army enough time to move into position before we lose the upper hand in the electronic battle.'

After the district commander had left, Marshal Levchenko turned to the digital map display of the frontline terrain and thought of

Kalina, right now under the enemy's massed fire, and as a result thought again of Misha.

That one day, Misha had returned home with his face bruised blue and purple. Marshal Levchenko had heard the gossip already: his son, the only anti-war factionist at the college, had been beaten up by students.

'I only said that we shouldn't speak of war lightly,' Misha explained to his father. 'Is it really impossible to reach a reasonable peace with the West?'

The marshal replied, his tone harsher than it had ever been toward his son, 'You know your position. You can choose to stay silent, but you will not say things like that in the future.'

Misha nodded.

Once they were through the door that night, Levchenko told Misha, 'The Russian Communist Party has taken office.'

Misha looked at his father. 'Let's eat,' he said, without inflection.

Later, the West declared the new Russian government unlawful. Tupolev assembled an extreme rightist alliance and instigated civil war. Marshal Levchenko didn't need to tell any of it to Misha. Every night, father and son silently ate dinner together as usual. Then one day, Misha received his order from the spaceflight base, packed his things, and left. Two days later, he boarded a spaceplane for the *Vechnyy Buran,* waiting in near-Earth orbit.

All-out war broke out a week later, an invasion by an unprecedentedly powerful enemy, from an unexpected direction, aiming to dismember Russia piece by piece.

JANUARY 9TH, NEAR-SUN ORBIT,
THE *VECHNYY BURAN* PASSES MERCURY

Due to the *Vechnyy Buran*'s high velocity, it couldn't settle into orbit around Mercury, only sweep past the sunward side. This was the first time humanity observed Mercury's surface at close range with the naked eye.

Misha saw cliffs two kilometers tall, winding hundreds of kilometers through plains covered with huge craters. He saw the Caloris Basin, too, thirteen hundred kilometers across, termed 'Weird

Terrain' by planetary geologists. The weird part came from the similar-sized basin exactly opposite it on the other side of Mercury. It was hypothesized that a huge meteor had struck Mercury, and that the powerful shock waves had passed right through the planet, simultaneously creating nearly identical basins in both hemispheres. Misha found new, thrilling things, too. The surface of Mercury was covered in shiny speckles, he saw. When he used the screen to zoom in, the realization took his breath away.

Those were lakes of mercury on Mercury, each with a surface area of thousands of square kilometers.

Misha imagined standing by the lake banks in the long Mercury days, in the 1,800-degree-Celsius heat: what a sight it would be. Even in a tempest, the mercury would lie calm and still. And Mercury didn't have an atmosphere, or wind. The surface of the lakes would be like mirrored plains, faithfully reflecting the light of the sun and Milky Way.

Once the *Vechnyy Buran* passed by Mercury, it was to continue approaching the sun until its insulation reached the absolute limit of what the fusion-powered active-cooling system could sustain. The sun's heat was its best protection; none of NATO's spacecraft could enter the inferno.

Gazing at the vastness of space, thinking of the war on his mother planet a hundred million kilometers away, Misha once again sighed at the shortsightedness of humanity.

JANUARY 10TH, SMOLENSK FRONT LINE

As she watched the gradual encroachment of the enemy's skirmish line, Kalina understood why her location alone had survived where the surrounding sources of jamming had been destroyed one by one. The enemy wanted to capture a Flood unit intact.

The helicopter squadron, three Comanches and four Blackhawks, had easily located this control unit. Due to Flood's massive EM radiation emissions, it could only be remotely operated via fiber-optic cable. The enemy had followed the cable to Kalina's control station three kilometers from the Flood unit, a lone abandoned storehouse.

The four Blackhawks, carrying more than forty enemy infantry, had landed less than two hundred meters from the storehouse. At the time they arrived, there had still been a captain and a staff sergeant in the station with Kalina. Hearing the sound of an engine, the sergeant had gone to open the door; a sniper aboard the helicopter immediately shot off the top of his skull. Enemy fire was careful and restrained after that, fearful of damaging the precious equipment inside the storehouse, allowing Kalina and the captain to hold their ground for a while.

Now, to Kalina's left, the captain's submachine gun that had sounded her only comfort went silent. She saw the captain's unmoving body behind the tree stump he'd used for cover, a circle of bright red blood blooming in the snow around him.

Kalina was in front of the storehouse, behind the crude cover of a few piled sandbags. Eight submachine-gun cartridge clips lay at her feet, and the hot gun barrel hissed in the snow atop the sandbags. Every time Kalina opened fire, the enemy opposite her would crouch down, the bullets splattering snow in front of them, while the enemy on the other side of the semicircular encirclement would spring up and push a little closer. Now Kalina only had three cartridge clips left. She began to fire single shots, but this tactic only announced to the enemy that she was running out of ammunition. They began to push forward more boldly. The next time Kalina reloaded, she heard a sharp squeaking sound from the thick snow on top of the sandbags. Something flew out and struck her on the right, hard. There wasn't any pain, just a rapidly spreading numbness, and the heat of blood running down her right flank. She endured, firing the remnants of this clip wildly. When she reached for the last clip on the sandbags, a bullet cut through her forearm. The clip fell to the ground. Her forearm, connected by a last strip of skin, dangled in the air. Kalina got up and went for the storehouse door, a thin trail of blood following her steps. When she pulled open the door, another bullet pierced her left shoulder.

Captain Rhett Donaldson's SEAL team approached the storehouse cautiously. Donaldson and two marines stepped over the Russian sergeant's body, kicked open the door, and rushed in. They found a single young officer inside.

She was sitting beside their target, Flood's remote control equipment. One broken forearm hung uselessly from the control desk, the other hand was clenched in her hair. Her blood dripped down steadily, forming little puddles at her feet. She smiled at the American intruders and the row of gun barrels pointing at her, a greeting of sorts.

Donaldson exhaled, but wouldn't get the chance to inhale: he saw her turn her good hand from her hair to a dark green ovoid object resting on the remote control equipment. She picked it up, dangling it in midair. Donaldson instantly recognized it as a gas bomb, sized small for use on armed helicopters. It was triggered by a laser proximity signal and would explode twice at half a meter aboveground, first to disperse a gaseous explosive, second to trigger the vapor. He couldn't escape its range now if he were an arrow in flight.

He extended a placating hand. 'Calm down, Major, calm down. Let's not get too hasty here.' He gestured around him, and the marines lowered their guns. 'Listen, things aren't as serious as you might think. You'll get the finest medical care. You'll be sent to the best hospitals in Germany and return in the first POW exchange.'

The major smiled at him again, which encouraged him somewhat. 'You don't have to do something so barbaric. This is a civilized war, you know. It would go like clockwork, I could tell already when we crossed the Russian border twenty days ago. Most of your firepower had been destroyed by then. That remaining little scatter of gunfire was just the perfect confetti to greet this glorious expedition. Everything will go like clockwork, you see? There's no need—'

'I know of an even more beautiful beginning,' the major said in unaccented English. Her soft voice could have come from heaven, could have made flames extinguish and iron yield. 'On a lovely beach, with palm trees, and welcome banners hanging overhead. There were beautiful girls with long, waist-length hair and silk trousers that rustled as they moved among the young soldiers and adorned them with red-and-pink leis, smiling shyly at the gawking boys. . . . Do you know of this landing?'

Donaldson shook his head, confused.

'March eighth, 1965, at nine A.M. It was the scene awaiting the first American marine forces landing at China Beach, the start of the Vietnam War.'

Donaldson felt as if he'd been plunged into ice. His momentary calm vanished; his breathing sped and his voice started to shake. 'No, Major, don't do this to us! We've hardly killed anyone, they're the ones who do all the killing,' he said, pointing out the window to the helicopters hovering in midair. 'Those pilots there, and the computer missile guidance gentlemen in the mother ships out in space. But they're all good people too. All their targets are just colored icons on their screen. They press a button or click a mouse, wait a bit, and the icon goes away. They're all civilized folks. They don't enjoy hurting people or anything, honest, they're not *evil* – are you listening?'

The major nodded, smiling. Who ever said that the god of death would be ugly and terrible?

'I have a girlfriend. She's working on her Ph.D. at the University of Maryland. She's beautiful like you, honest, and she attended the anti-war rally . . .' *I should have listened to her,* Donaldson thought. 'Are you listening to me? Say something! Please, say something.'

The major gave her foe one last radiant smile. 'Captain, I do my duty.'

A unit from the reinforcing Russian 104th Motorized Infantry Division was half a kilometer from the Flood operation station. They first heard a low explosion and saw the little storehouse in the broad, empty fields disappear in a cloud of white mist. Immediately after, a terrible cacophony a hundred times louder shook the ground. An enormous fireball emerged where the storehouse had been, the flames embroiled in black smoke rising high, transforming into a towering mushroom cloud, like a flower of lifeblood blooming in the expanse between heaven and earth.

JANUARY 11TH, RUSSIAN ARMY GENERAL STAFF HEADQUARTERS

'I know what you want. Don't waste words, spit it out!' Marshal Levchenko said to the commander of the Caucasus Army.

'I want the electromagnetic conditions on the battlefield for the last two days to last another four days.'

'Surely you're aware that seventy percent of our battlefield jamming teams have been destroyed? I can't even give you another four hours!'

'In that case, our army won't be able to arrive in position on time. NATO airstrikes have greatly slowed the rate at which our forces can assemble.'

'In that case, you might as well put a bullet in your head. The enemy is approaching Moscow. They've reached the position Guderian held seventy years ago.'

As he exited the war room, the commander of the Caucasus Army said in his heart, *Moscow, endure!*

JANUARY 12TH, MOSCOW DEFENSIVE LINE

Major General Felitov of the Taman Division was fully aware that his line could endure at most one more assault.

The enemy's airstrikes and long-range strikes were slowly growing in intensity, while the Russian air cover was diminishing. The division had few tanks and armed helicopters left; this last stand would be borne on blood and flesh and little else.

The major general, dragging a leg broken by shrapnel, came out of the shelter using a rifle as a crutch. He saw that the new trenches were still shallow, unsurprising given that the majority of the soldiers here had been wounded in some way. But to his astonishment, neat breastworks about a half meter tall stood in front of the trenches.

What material could they have used to build a breastwork so quickly? He saw that a few branch-like shapes stuck out from the snow-covered breastwork. He came closer. They were pale, frozen human arms.

Rage boiled through him. He seized a colonel by the collar. 'You bastard! Who told you to use the soldiers' corpses as building materials?'

'I did,' the divisional chief of staff said evenly behind him. 'We entered this new zone too quickly last night, and this is a crop field. We truly had nothing else to build with.'

They looked at each other silently. The chief of staff's face was covered in rivulets of frozen blood, leaked from the bandage on his forehead.

A time passed. The two of them began to walk slowly along the trenches, along the breastworks made from youth, vitality, life. The general's left hand held the rifle he used as a crutch; his right hand straightened his helmet, then saluted the breastworks. They were inspecting their troops for the last time.

They passed by a private with both legs blown off. The blood from his leg stumps had mixed with the snow and dirt into a reddish black mud, and the mud was now crusted over with ice. He lay with an anti-tank grenade in his arms. Raising his bloodless face, he grinned at the general. 'I'm gonna stuff this into an Abrams's treads.'

The cold winds stirred up gusts of snow mist, howling like an ancient battle paean.

'If I die first, please use me in this wall too. There's no better place for me to end, truly,' the general said.

'We won't be too long apart,' said the chief of staff, with his characteristic calm.

JANUARY 12TH, RUSSIAN ARMY GENERAL STAFF HEADQUARTERS

A staff officer came to inform Marshal Levchenko that the general director of the Russian Space Agency wanted to see him – the matter was urgent, involving Misha and the electronic battle.

Marshal Levchenko started at the sound of his son's name. He'd already heard that Kalina had been killed in action, but aside from that, he couldn't imagine what Misha had to do with the electronic battle a hundred million miles away. He couldn't imagine what Misha had to do with any part of Earth now.

The general director came in with his people behind him. Without preamble, he gave a three-inch laser disc to Marshal Levchenko. 'Marshal, this is the reply we received from the *Vechnyy Buran* an hour ago. He added afterward that this isn't a private message, and that he hopes you'll play it in front of all relevant personnel.'

Everyone in the war room heard the voice from a hundred million kilometers distant. 'I've learned from the war news updates that if the electromagnetic jamming fails to last for another three to four days, we may lose the war. If this is true, Papa, I can give you that time.

'Before, you always thought that the stars I studied had nothing to do with the ways of the world, and I thought so too. But it looks like we were both wrong.

'I remember telling you that, although a star generates enormous power, it's fundamentally a relatively elegant and simple system. Take our sun, for example. It's composed of just the two simplest elements: hydrogen and helium; its behavior is the balance of just the two mechanisms of nuclear fission and gravity. As a result, it's easier to model its activity mathematically than our Earth. Research on the sun has given us an extremely accurate mathematical model by this time, work to which I've contributed. Using this model, we can accurately predict the sun's behavior. This would allow us to take advantage of a tiny disturbance to rapidly disrupt the equilibrium conditions inside the sun. The method is simple: use the *Vechnyy Buran* to make a precision strike on the surface of the sun.

'Perhaps you think it no more than tossing a pebble into the sea. But that's not the case, Papa. This is dropping a grain of sand into an eye.

'From the mathematical model, we know that the sun is in an extremely fine-tuned and sensitive state of energy equilibrium. If correctly placed, a small disturbance will create a chain reaction from the surface to a considerable distance down, spreading to disrupt the local equilibrium. There are recorded precedents: the latest incident was in early August of 1972, when a powerful but highly localized eruption created a massive EMP that heavily affected Earth. Compasses in planes and boats jumped wildly, long-distance wireless communications failed, the sky shone with dazzling red lights in high northern latitudes, electric lights flickered in villages as if they were in the center of a thunderstorm. The reactions continued for more than a week. A well-accepted theory nowadays is that a celestial body even smaller than the *Vechnyy Buran* collided with the surface of the sun at that time.

'These disruptions on the sun's surface certainly occurred many times, but most would have happened before humanity invented wireless equipment, and therefore went undetected. In addition, since these collisions were placed by random chance, the disturbances in equilibrium wouldn't have been optimal in strength and area.

'But the *Vechnyy Buran*'s impact location has been meticulously calculated, and the disturbance it will create will be orders of magnitude larger than the natural examples mentioned. This time, the sun will blast powerful electromagnetic radiation into space in every frequency, from the highest to the lowest. In addition, the powerful X-ray radiation generated by the sun will collide violently with Earth's ionosphere, blocking off short-wave radio communications, which are reliant on the layer.

'During the disturbance, the majority of wireless communications outside of the millimeter radio range will fail. The effect will weaken somewhat at night, but during the day, it will even exceed your jamming of the previous two days. Based on calculations, the disturbances will last a week.

'Papa, the two of us always did live in worlds far away from each other's. We could never interact much with each other. But now our worlds have come together. We're fighting for the same goal, for which I'm proud. Papa, like all your soldiers, I await your order.'

'Everything Dr. Levchenko said is true,' said the general director. 'Last year, we sent a probe to enact a small-scale collision with the sun according to calculations based on the mathematical model. The experiment confirmed the model's predictions of the disturbance. Dr. Levchenko and his research group even hypothesized that this method could be used to alter Earth's climate in the future.'

Marshal Levchenko walked into a side room and picked up the red telephone that was a direct line to the president. A little later, he walked back out.

The historical records give different accounts of this moment: some claim that he spoke immediately, while others recount that for a minute he was silent. But they concur on the words he said.

'Tell Misha to carry out his plan.'

JANUARY 12TH, NEAR-SUN ORBIT,
ABOARD THE *VECHNYY BURAN*

The *Vechnyy Buran* fired all ten fission engines, jets of plasma hundreds of kilometers long erupting from every engine nozzle as it made final corrections to trajectory and orientation.

In front of the *Vechnyy Buran* was an enormous and lovely solar prominence, a current of superheated hydrogen wheeling upward from the sun's surface. Like long ribbons of gauze drifting high above the fiery sea of the sun, they shifted and changed like a dreamscape.

Their ends anchored to the surface of the sun, forming a gigantic gateway.

The *Vechnyy Buran* passed slow and stately through the four-hundred-thousand-kilometer-tall triumphal arch. More solar prominences appeared in front, one end attached to the sun, but the other extending into the depths of space. The *Vechnyy Buran* with its blinking blue engine lights threaded through them like a firefly amid burning trees. Then the blue lights slowly dimmed. The engines stopped. The *Vechnyy Buran*'s trajectory had been meticulously established; the rest depended on the law of gravity.

As the spaceship entered the corona, the outermost layer of the sun's atmosphere, the black backdrop of space above turned a magenta all-pervading in its radiance. Below was a clear view of the sun's chromosphere, twinkling with countless needle-shaped structures: discovered in the nineteenth century, they were jets of incandescent gas emanating from the surface of the sun. They made the atmosphere of the sun look like a burning grassland, where each stalk of grass was thousands of kilometers tall. Underneath the burning plain was the sun's photosphere, a sea of endless fire.

From the last images relayed from the *Vechnyy Buran,* people saw Misha rise to his feet in front of the giant monitoring screen. He pressed a button to retract the protective cover outside the transparent dome, revealing the magnificent sea of fire before him. He wanted to see the world of his childhood dreams with his own eyes. The view was distorting and rippling; that was the half-meter-thick insulation glass melting. Soon the glass barrier fell in a sheet of transparent liquid. Like someone who had never seen the sea facing the ocean wind in rapture, Misha spread his arms to greet the six-thousand-degree hurricane that roared toward him. In the last seconds of video before the camera and transmission equipment melted, one could see Misha's body catching alight, a slender torch melding into the sun's sea of fire . . .

What sight would have followed could only be conjecture. The *Vechnyy Buran*'s solar panels and protruding structures would have melted first, surface tension making silver beads of fluid of them on the spaceship's surface. As the *Vechnyy Buran* traversed the boundary between the corona and chromosphere, its main body would begin to melt, fully liquefying at a depth of two thousand kilometers into the chromosphere. The beads of liquid metal would cohere into a huge silvery droplet, diving unerringly toward the target its now-melted computers had calculated. The effect of the sun's atmosphere would become apparent: a pale blue flame would emanate from the droplet, trailing hundreds of meters behind it, its color gradating from the pale blue, to yellow, to a gorgeous orange at the tail.

At last, this lovely phoenix would disappear into the endless sea of flames.

JANUARY 13TH, EARTH

Humanity returned to the world as it had been before Marconi.

As night fell, undulating auroras flooded the sky, even into the equatorial zones.

Facing television screens filled with white noise, most people could only guess and imagine at the situation in that vast land where war raged.

JANUARY 13TH, MOSCOW FRONT LINE

General Baker pushed aside the division commander of the Eighty-second Airborne and the assorted NATO frontline commanders attempting to drag him onto a helicopter. He raised his binoculars to continue surveilling the horizon, where the Russian front was rumbling in advance.

'Calibrate to four thousand meters! Load number-nine ammunition, delayed fuse, fire!'

From the sounds of artillery behind him, Baker could tell that no more than thirty of their 105 mm grenade launchers, last of the defensive heavy artillery, could still fire.

An hour ago, the German tank battalion that had been the last remaining armored-vehicle force in the position had launched an admirably courageous counterattack. They'd achieved outstanding results: eight kilometers away, they'd destroyed half again their number of Russian tanks. But under the crushing disadvantage in numbers, they had disappeared under the Russian army's roaring torrent of steel like dew under the noon sun.

'Calibrate to thirty-five hundred meters, fire!'

The explosive missiles hissed as they flew, and flung up a barrier of earth and fire in front of the Russian tank lines. But they were like a landslide before a flood, the earth a short-lived impediment against the implacable waters.

Once the earth blasted up by the explosions fell back to the ground, the Russian armored cars reappeared in view through the dense smoke. Baker saw that they were arranged as densely as if they were receiving inspection. Attacking in this formation would have been suicide a few days ago, but now, with almost all of NATO's aerial and long-distance firepower jammed, it was a perfectly feasible way to concentrate armored-vehicle strength as much as possible, ensuring a break in the enemy line.

Baker had expected that the defensive line would be poorly arranged. Under the electromagnetic conditions on the battlefield, it had been effectively impossible to quickly and accurately determine the direction the main enemy assault would take. As to how the defense would proceed, he didn't know. With the C3I system completely down, quickly adjusting the defensive dispositions would be enormously difficult.

'Calibrate to three thousand meters, fire!'

'General, you were looking for me?' The French commander Lieutenant General Rousselle came over. Beside him were only a French lieutenant colonel and a helicopter pilot. He wasn't wearing camouflage, and the medals on his chest and general's stars on his shoulders shone brightly polished, making the steel helmet he wore and the rifle he held seem incongruous.

'I hear that the French Foreign Legion is withdrawing from the fortifications on our left wing.'

'Yes, General.'

'General Rousselle, seven hundred thousand NATO troops are in the process of retreat behind us. Their successful breakthrough of the enemy encirclement depends on our steadfast defense!'

'Depends on your steadfast defense.'

'Care to explain that comment?'

'You have plenty to explain yourself! You hid the real battle situation from us. You knew from the beginning that the Rightist allies would independently negotiate a cease-fire in the east!'

'As the commander in chief of the NATO forces, I had the right to do so. General, I think you're also clear on the duty placed on you and your troops to follow the orders given.'

A silence.

'Calibrate to twenty-five hundred meters, fire!'

'I only obey the orders of the president of the French Republic.'

'I do not believe you could have received orders to that effect right now.'

'I received them months ago, at the National Day reception at Élysée Palace. The president personally informed me of how the French army should conduct itself under the present conditions.'

Baker finally lost his temper. 'You bastards haven't changed a bit since de Gaulle's time!'*

'Don't make it sound so unpleasant. If you won't leave, I will stay here without my retinue as well. We will fight and die honorably together on the snowy plain. Napoleon lost here too. It's nothing to be ashamed of,' Rousselle said, gesturing with his French-made FAMAS rifle.

A silence.

'Calibrate to two thousand meters, fire!'

Baker turned slowly to face the frontline commanders in front of him. 'Relay these words to the American soldiers defending these lines: We didn't start out as an army dependent on computers to fight our battles. We come from an army of farming men. Decades ago, on Okinawa, we fought the Japanese foxhole by foxhole through the jungle. At Khe Sanh, we deflected the North Vietnamese soldiers' grenades with shovels. Even longer ago, on that cold winter night, our great Washington himself led his barefoot soldiers across the icy Delaware to make history—'

'Calibrate to fifteen hundred meters, fire!'

'I order you, destroy all documents and excess supplies—'

'Calibrate to twelve hundred meters, fire!'

General Baker put on his helmet, strapped on his Kevlar vest, and clipped his 9 mm pistol to his left side. The grenade launchers went

*In 1966, General de Gaulle withdrew all French armed forces from the NATO integrated military command, a serious blow to NATO's Cold War efforts at the time.

silent; the gunners were shoving the grenades into the barrels. Next sounded a mess of explosions.

'Troops,' Baker said, looking at the Russian tanks spread in front of them like the veil of death. 'Bayonets up!'

The sun faded in and out of the thick smoke of the battlefield, throwing shifting light and shadow onto the snowy plain as the battle raged.

THE MICRO-ERA

1

RETURN

The Forerunner now knew that he was the only person left in the universe. He'd realized when he crossed the orbit of Pluto. From here, the Sun was but a dim star, no different from when he had left the solar system thirty years ago.

The divergence analysis the computer had just performed, however, told him that Pluto's orbit had significantly shifted outward. Using this data, he could calculate that the Sun had lost 4.74 per cent of its mass since he had left. And that led to only one conclusion, one that sent shivers straight through his heart, chilling his soul.

It had already happened.

In fact, humanity had known about this long before he had embarked on his journey. They had learned this after thousands upon thousands of probes had been shot into the Sun. The probes' findings had allowed astrophysicists to determine that a short-lived energy flash would erupt from the star, reducing its mass by about five per cent.

If the Sun could think and could remember, it would have almost certainly been untroubled. In the billions of years of its life, it had already undergone much greater upheavals than this. When it was born from the turbulence of a spiraling stellar nebula, greater changes had been measured in milliseconds. In those brilliant and glorious moments, the Sun's gravitational collapse had ignited the fires of nuclear fusion, illuminating the grim, dark chaos of stellar dust.

It knew that its life was a process and, even though it was currently in the most stable phase of this progression, occasional minor, yet sudden, changes were inevitable. The Sun was like the calm surface of water: perfectly still for the most part, but every so often broken by the bursting of a rising bubble. The loss of energy and mass meant very little to it. The Sun would remain the Sun, a medium-sized star with an apparent visual magnitude of -26.8.

The flash would not even have a significant effect on the rest of the solar system. Mercury would probably dissolve, while the dense atmosphere of Venus would likely be stripped to nothing. The effect on the more distant planets would be even less severe. It could be expected that the surface of Mars would melt, likely scorching its color from red to black. As for Earth, its surface would only be heated to seven thousand degrees, probably for no longer than a hundred hours or so. The planet's oceans would certainly evaporate. On dry land, strata of continental rock would liquefy, but that would be all.

The Sun would then quickly revert to its previous state, albeit with reduced mass. This reduction would cause the orbits of all the planets to shift outward, but that would hardly be consequential. Earth, for example, would only experience a slight drop in temperature, falling to about -80 degrees on average. In fact, the cold would advance the re-solidification of the melted surface, and it would ensure that some of Earth's water and atmosphere would be preserved.

There was a joke that became popular in those days. It was a conversation with God, and it went like this:

'Oh, God, for you thousands of years are just a brief moment!'

God answered, 'Indeed, they are just a second to me.'

'Oh, God, for you vast riches are just small change!'

God answered, 'Just a nickel.'

'Oh, God, please spare me a nickel!'

To which God then answered, 'Certainly. Just give me a second.'

Now it was the Sun that was asking humanity for 'just a second'. It had been calculated that the energy flash would not happen for another eighteen thousand years.

For the Sun this was certainly no more than a second, but in humanity – faced with an entire 'second' of waiting – it engendered an attitude of apathy. 'Apathism' was even elevated to a kind of philosophy. All this did not occur without repercussions; with every passing day, humanity grew more cynical.

Then again, there were at least four or five hundred generations in which humankind could find a way out.

After two centuries, humanity took the first step: a spaceship was launched into interstellar space, tasked with finding a habitable planet within one hundred light-years to which humanity could migrate. This spaceship was called the *UNS Ark*, and its crew became known as the Forerunners.

The *Ark* swept past sixty stars, thus past sixty infernos. Only one was accompanied by a satellite. This satellite was a five- thousand-mile-wide droplet of incandescent molten metal, its liquid form in constant flux as it orbited.

This was the *Ark*'s only achievement, further proof of humanity's loneliness.

The *UNS Ark* sailed for twenty-three years. However, as she traveled close to light speed, this 'Ark Time' equated to twenty-five thousand years on Earth. Had it followed its mission plan, the *UNS Ark* should have returned to Earth long ago.

Flying close to the speed of light made communication with Earth impossible. Only by reducing its velocity to less than half the speed of light could the *Ark* be contacted by Earth. This maneuver, however, cost significant amounts of time and energy, and therefore the *Ark* would usually only do this once a month in order to receive a dispatch from Earth. When it slowed down, the *Ark* would pick up Earth's most recent message, sent more than a hundred years after the previous one. The relative time between the *Ark* and Earth made communication much like targeting a high-powered scope; if the scope was off by even the slightest degree, it would miss the target by a vast distance.

The *UNS Ark* had received its last message from Earth thirteen 'Ark Years' after its departure. On Earth, seventeen thousand years had passed since it had left. One month after that message, the *Ark* had again slowed, but it only received silence. The predictions made many millennia ago could certainly have been off. One month on the *Ark* was more than a hundred years on Earth. That was when it must have happened.

The *UNS Ark* had truly become an ark – one with a lone Noah. Of the other seven Forerunners, four had been killed by radiation when a star exploded in a nova four light-years from the *Ark*; two others had succumbed to illness and one man had, in the silence of that fateful slow-down, shot himself.

The last Forerunner had kept the *Ark* at communication speed for a long stretch. Finally, he had accelerated the *Ark* back to near-light-speed, but a tiny flame of hope burning within him had soon tempted him to reduce the ship's speed once more. Again he had listened anxiously, but all he heard was silence. And so it went on; his frequent cycles of acceleration and deceleration prolonged the return journey countless times.

And through it all, the silence remained.

The *Ark* returned to the solar system twenty-five thousand years after its departure from Earth, nine thousand years later than originally planned.

2

THE MONUMENT

Passing the orbit of Pluto, the *Ark* continued its flight deep into the solar system. For an interstellar vessel such as the *UNS Ark*, traveling in the solar system was like sailing in the calm of a harbor. Soon the Sun grew brighter. As the sunlight began to bathe the *Ark*, the Forerunner caught his first glimpse of Jupiter. Through his telescope he could see that the huge planet had changed almost beyond recognition. Its red spot was nowhere to be seen, and its tempestuous bands appeared more chaotic than ever. He paid no heed to the other planets and continued the tranquil last leg of his journey, straight on to Earth.

The Forerunner's hand trembled as he pushed the button. The massive metal shield covering the porthole slowly opened.

'Oh, my blue sphere, blue eye of the universe, my blue angel,' the Forerunner prayed, his eyelids firmly closed.

After a long while, he finally forced his eyes open.

The planet he saw was black and white.

The black was rock, melted and re-hardened, tombstone-black. The white was seawater, vaporized and refrozen, corpse- shroud white.

As the *Ark* entered low-Earth orbit, slowly passing over the black land and white oceans, the Forerunner spotted no vestiges of humanity; everything had been melted to nothing. Civilization was gone, lost in a wisp of smoke.

But surely there should have been a monument, some memorial capable of withstanding the seven thousand degrees that had destroyed all else.

Just as these thoughts crossed the Forerunner's mind, the monument appeared. It was a video signal, originating from the surface and transmitted to his spaceship. The computer streamed the signal's millennia-old contents onto his screen. Obviously shot by extremely heat-resistant cameras, it revealed the catastrophe that had befallen Earth. The moment when the energy flash hit was very different from what he had so often imagined. The Sun did not suddenly grow brighter; most of the cataclysmic radiation it blasted forth remained well outside the visible spectrum. He could see, however, the final moments of the blue sky. It suddenly turned inferno-red, only to change again to a nightmarish purple.

He saw the cities of that era, the so-familiar forms of skyscrapers, oozing with thick black smoke as the temperature surged by thousands of degrees. Soon they began to glow like the dim red of kindled charcoal but they could not last, finally melting like countless wax candles.

Scorching red magma streamed from the mountaintops, forming cascading waterfalls of molten rock. These incandescent rapids converged to form a massive crimson river of lava that buried the Earth under its pyroclastic floods. And from where there had been ocean waters now rose giant mushroom clouds of steam. The bellies of these ferociously billowing mountains shone with the red glow of the molten world beneath. Their crests were permeated with the sky's cruel purple. The endless ranges of steam clouds expanded with relentless speed and abandon. Soon they swallowed all of the Earth. . .

Years passed before this haze finally dispersed, revealing that there was still a planet beneath. The burned and melted world below had begun to cool, leaving all of it covered in rippling black rock. In some parts, magma still flowed, forming intricate webs of fire that spanned the Earth. All traces of humanity had disappeared. Civilization had vanished, forgotten like a dream from which the Earth had awoken.

A few years later, the Earth's water, having been dissociated to oxyhydrogen under the incredible heat, began to recombine. It fell in great torrents, once again covering the burning world in steam. It was as if the Earth had been trapped in a gigantic steamer: dark, moist and stiflingly hot. The deluge lasted for dozens of years as the Earth continued to cool. Slowly, the oceans began to fill again.

Centuries passed. The dark clouds of evaporated seawater had finally dispersed, and the sky turned blue once more. In the heavens, the Sun reappeared. Earth's new, more distant orbit forced a sharp decline in temperatures, freezing the oceans. Now the sky was without clouds, and the long-dead world below froze in complete silence.

The picture changed again, this time revealing a city. First, a forest of tall, slender buildings came into view. As the camera slowly descended from some unseen peak, a plaza came into view. Its spacious dimensions were filled with a sea of people. The camera descended further, allowing the Forerunner to discern that all of the faces in the forum were turned upward, appearing to look right at him. The camera finally stopped, hovering above a platform in the middle of the plaza.

A beautiful girl, probably in her teens, stood on this platform. Through the screen, she waved right at the Forerunner, and as she waved, she shouted, 'Hey, we can see you! You came to us like a shooting star!' Her voice was delicate and fair. 'Are you the *UNS Ark One*?'

In the final years of his voyage the Forerunner had spent most of his time playing a virtual reality game. To run this game, the computer directly interfaced with the player's brain signals, using his thoughts to generate three-dimensional images. The people and objects in these images were obviously restricted in many ways, bound by the limits of the player's imagination. In his loneliness, the Forerunner had created one virtual world after another, ranging from single households to entire realms.

Having spent so much time in unreal realities, he quickly recognized the city on his screen for what it was: just another virtual world – and one of inferior quality, at that – most likely the product of a distracted mind. Virtual projections such as this one, born from the imagination, were always prone to errors. The pictures he saw now, however, seemed to have more wrong with them than right.

First and worst, when the camera passed the skyscrapers the Forerunner had watched as numerous people exited the buildings through windows on the top floors. These people had jumped straight out, leaping hundreds of feet down to the ground below. After falling from such dizzying heights, they landed without a scratch, apparently completely unharmed. He also saw people leap off the ground only to rise, as if being pulled by invisible wires. These strange jumps carried them several stories up a skyscraper's side. They ascended even higher, pushing off from foot-holds that ran up the side of each of the buildings, as though they had been put there specifically for just that purpose. In this manner they could reach the top of any building or enter it through any of its countless windows. These skyscrapers seemed to have neither elevators nor doors. At least, the Forerunner never saw them use anything except a window to enter or leave a building.

When the virtual camera moved above that plaza, the Forerunner could see another error: amongst the sea of people hung crystal balls suspended by strings. These balls were about three feet in diameter each. Occasionally people would reach into these balls and pull out a segment of the crystal substance with great ease. As they removed the piece, the ball would immediately recover its spherical shape. The extracted segment would do the same; but even as the small piece became round, the person who had extracted it would put it into his mouth and swallow it . . .

In addition to these obvious mistakes, the confusion and irrationality of the image's creator was most evident in the bizarre objects that were floating through the city's sky. Some were large, ranging from five to ten feet long, while others were smaller, only a foot or so long. Some resembled pieces of broken sponge, while others brought to mind the crooked branches of some giant tree; all slowly floated through the air.

The Forerunner saw one large branch drifting toward the girl on the platform. She simply gave it a light push, sending it spiraling into the distance. The Forerunner suddenly understood: in a world on the brink of destruction, it must have been impossible to remain of sound mind and thought.

The image was most likely being sent out by an automated installation, which had probably been buried deep beneath the surface before the catastrophe struck. Shielded from the radiation and heat, it must have lain hidden and waited, automatically rising to the surface once it was safe. This installation, then, probably kept an unending vigil, monitoring space, projecting these images to any of the scattered remnants of humanity returning to Earth. Chances were that these comical and jumbled images had been created with good will, intended to comfort the survivors.

'Did you say that other *Ark* ships were launched?' the Forerunner asked, hoping to get something from this bizarre display.

'Of course. There were twelve others!' the girl answered enthusiastically. The absurdity of the other elements of the image notwithstanding, this girl was not half bad at all. Her beautiful face combined the best features typical of Eastern and Western cultures, and she beamed with pure innocence. To her, the entire cosmos was a great big playground. Her large, round eyes seemed to sing with every flutter of her eyelids, while her long hair floated and fanned in the air, appearing completely weightless. She reminded the Forerunner of a mermaid swimming in an unseen ocean.

'So, is anyone still alive?' the Forerunner asked, his final hope blazing like wildfire.

'Aren't you?' the girl innocently asked in return.

'Of course. I'm a real human. Not like you, a computer-generated virtual person,' the Forerunner replied, slightly exasperated.

'The last *Ark* arrived seven hundred and thirty years ago. You are the last *Ark* to return, but please tell us: do you have any women aboard?' the girl enquired with great interest.

'There is only me,' the Forerunner replied, his head heavy with the memories.

'So, you say that there are no women with you?' the girl asked again, her eyes widening in genuine shock.

'As I said, I am the only one. Are there no other spaceships out there that have yet to return?' the Forerunner enquired in return, desperate to keep the spark of hope alive.

The girl wrung her delicate, elfin hands. 'There are none! It's so sad, so very terribly sad! You are the last of them, if . . . oh . . .' She could barely contain her sobs. 'If not by cloning . . .' The girl was now crying uncontrollably. 'Oh,' she finished, her beautiful face now covered with tears. Around her, the people in the plaza were crying a sea of tears.

While he did not cry, the Forerunner, too, felt his breaking heart sink to new depths. Humanity's destruction had become a fact beyond denial.

'Why do you not ask me who I am?' the girl asked, raising her face again. She had reclaimed her innocent demeanor, her recent sorrow – merely seconds past – apparently forgotten.

'I couldn't care less,' the Forerunner answered flatly.

With tears in her eyes again, the girl shouted, 'But I am Earth's leader!'

'Yes! She is the High Counsellor of Earth's Unity Government!' the people in the plaza shouted in unison. Their rapid shift from sorrow to excitement reflected marked deficiencies in their programming.

The Forerunner felt himself growing tired of this senseless game, and he rose to turn away.

'How can you not care? All the capital has gathered here to welcome you, forefather! Do not ignore us!' the girl cried, emitting a tearful wail.

Remembering his original and still-unresolved question, the Forerunner turned and enquired, 'What has humanity left behind?'

'Follow our landing beacon, then you can learn for yourself!' came the happy reply.

3

THE CAPITAL

The Forerunner climbed into his landing module. Leaving the *UNS Ark* to orbit, he began his descent to Earth, following the landing beacon's directions. He wore a pair of video specs, their lenses displaying the images being broadcast from the planet below.

'Forefather, you must immediately come to Earth's capital. Even though it is not the planet's biggest city, it is certainly the most beautiful,' the girl calling herself Earth's leader prattled on. 'You will like it! Note, though, that the landing coordinates we have given you will lead you to a spot a good distance from the city, as we wish to avoid possible damage . . .'

The Forerunner changed the focus of his specs to show the area directly below his lander. Now, at only thirty thousand feet in the air, he could still see nothing but black wasteland below.

As he descended, the virtual image grew even more confusing. Perhaps its creator, thousands of years before, had been in the grip of an unimaginable depression; or perhaps the computer projecting it, left to its own devices for thousands upon thousands of years, was showing signs of its age. In any case, for some unfathomable reason the virtual girl had begun to sing:

Oh, you dear angel! From the macro-era you return!
Oh, glorious macro-era
Magnificent macro-era
Oh, beautiful macro-era
Oh, vanished vision! In the fires the dream did burn.

As this beautiful singer began her hymn, she leapt into the air. She lifted off the platform, jumping thirty feet into the air. After falling back to the platform, she sprang back up, this time clearing the plaza in a single bound. She landed on top of a building, and from there she jumped again, this time across the entire width of the plaza. Landing at its other side, she looked like a charming little flea.

She leapt once more, and in mid-air she caught one of the strange objects that was floating past her. Several feet long, the object looked like the trunk of a strange tree, and it carried her spiraling through the air, above the sea of people. Even as she rose, her svelte body continued to writhe rhythmically.

The sea of people below began to buzz with raw excitement, that soon boiled over into song: 'Oh, macro-era! Oh, macro-era!' As the song continued, they all began to jump. The crowd now looked like sand on a drum, rising in waves with every invisible beat.

The Forerunner simply refused to take any more of this, and he shut off both the image and the sound. He was certain now that the situation was even worse than he had first thought. Before the catastrophe had struck, the people of Earth must have felt venomous envy toward the survivors who had slipped through time and space, thus eluding their appointed destruction. Fuelled by such emotions, they had created this gross perversion to torment those who returned.

As his descent continued the annoyance the images had caused slowly began to ebb, and by the time he felt the shock of the landing that annoyance had almost completely left him. For a moment he succumbed to fantasy: maybe he had truly landed near a city that simply wasn't visible from up high.

All illusion dissolved as he stepped out of the lander. He was surrounded by boundless, black desolation. Despair chilled his entire body.

The Forerunner carefully slid open his visor. Immediately, he felt a surge of cold air against his face. The air was very thin, but it was thick enough for him to breathe. The temperature was somewhere around forty degrees below freezing. The sky was a dark blue, as it had been at dawn and dusk in the age before the catastrophe. It was neither time now, as the Sun hanging overhead clearly confirmed.

The Forerunner removed his gloves, but he could not feel the Sun's warmth. In the thin air, the sunlight was scattered and weak. He could see stars twinkling brightly in the sky above.

The ground beneath his feet had solidified about two thousand years before. All around, he could see the ripples of hardened magma. Even though the first signs of weathering were visible, the surface remained hard and jagged. No matter how closely he looked, he could only make out the barest traces of soil. Before him the undulating land stretched to the horizon, punctuated only by small hills. Behind him lay the frozen ocean, gleaming white against the skyline.

Scanning his surroundings, the Forerunner searched for the source of the transmission. He finally spotted a transparent shield dome embedded in the rocky ground. This shell was about three feet in diameter, and it covered what appeared to be an array of highly complex structures.

The Forerunner was soon able to make out several similar domes scattered in the distance. They were roughly fifty to one hundred feet apart. From where he stood, they looked a little like bubbles, frozen as they burst through the Earth's surface and now glinting under the Sun.

Reactivating the left lens of his video specs, the Forerunner opened a virtual window into the strange imaginary world created for him. It's shameless 'leader' was still floating through the air, riding her bizarre branch, singing and writhing deliriously. As she flew, she blew kisses toward the camera. The masses below, down to the last man, cheered:

Oh, great macro-era!
Oh, romantic macro-era!
Oh, melancholic macro-era!
Oh, frail macro-era . . .

Numbed, the Forerunner stopped cold. Standing beneath the deep blue sky in the light of the shining Sun under the sparkling stars, he felt the entire universe revolving around him. Him. The last human.

He was overcome by an avalanche of dark loneliness. Covering his face, he sank to his knees and began to sob.

As he descended into despair, the singing ceased. Everyone in the virtual image stared straight toward him, their myriad eyes filled with deep concern. The girl, still riding her branch through mid-air, beamed a sweet smile right up at him.

'Do you have so little faith in humanity?' she asked, her eyes twinkling.

She continued speaking, and, as she did, something that the Forerunner could not place sent a shiver through his body, heightening all his senses. Disturbed, he slowly began to rise back to his feet. As he stood, he suddenly saw it: a shadow was falling over the city in his left lens. It was as if a dark cloud had appeared out of the blue, blackening the entire sky in an instant. He took a step to the side. Light was immediately restored to the city.

He slowly approached the dome, intrigued. Standing before it, he bent forward, carefully studying it. Inside he could indistinctly make out a dense array of tiny, yet incredibly detailed, structures. He immediately noticed that something magnificently strange had completely dominated the sky in his video specs.

That something was his face.

'We can see you! Can you see us? Use a magnifier!' the girl shouted as loudly as she could. The sea of people below overflowed with exhilaration once more.

Now the Forerunner finally understood it all: he recalled the people jumping out of tall buildings, which made sense because gravity could cause them no harm in their microscopic environment. This also explained their leaps. In such an environment, people would easily be able to leap up a building a thousand feet high – or should that be a thousand microns? The large crystal balls must, in fact, be drops of water; in this tiny environment, their shape would be completely at the mercy of the water's surface tension. And when these microscopic people wanted a drink, they could simply pull out a tiny droplet. Finally, the strange, elongated things that floated through the urban landscape – and that the girl was riding – these, too, made sense. They were nothing other than tiny particles of dust.

This city was not virtual at all. It was a city just as real as any city twenty-five thousand years ago had been, only it was covered by a three-foot, transparent dome.

Humanity still existed. Civilization still existed.

In this microscopic city floated a girl on a branch of dust – the High Counsellor of Earth's Unity Government – confidently stretching her open hand toward the man who, at the moment, filled almost her entire cosmos: the Forerunner.

'Forefather, the micro-era welcomes you!'

4

MICRO-HUMANITY

'In the seventeen thousand years before the catastrophe,' the girl told the Forerunner, 'humanity left no stone unturned in its search for some way out. The easiest way out would have been migrating to another star. But no *Ark*, including yours, was able to locate even a single star with a habitable planet. And it did not really matter; a mere century before the catastrophe, our spaceship technology was still not developed enough to migrate even one-thousandth of humanity.

'Another plan,' she continued, 'was to have humanity migrate deep underground, well-hidden from the Sun's energy flash, ready to emerge once its effects subsided. That plan, however, would have done little other than prolong everyone's inevitable deaths. After the catastrophe, Earth's ecosystem was completely destroyed. Humanity could not have survived.

'There was a time when humanity fell into total despair. It was in that darkest night that an idea came to life in the mind of a certain genetic engineer: what if humanity's size could be reduced by nine orders of magnitude?' A pensive look crossed her face. 'Everything about human society could also be scaled to that size, creating a microscopic ecosystem, and such an ecosystem would only consume microscopic amounts of natural resources. It did not take long before all of humanity came to agree that this plan was the only way in which our species could be saved.'

The Forerunner listened intently, thoroughly considering the implications of this plan.

She continued. 'The plan relied on two types of technology. The first was genetic engineering: by modifying the human genome, humans would be reduced to the height of about ten microns, no larger than a single body cell. Human anatomy, however, would remain completely unchanged. This was a completely plausible goal. In essence, there is very little difference between the genome of a bacterium and that of a human. The other piece of the puzzle was nanotechnology. This technology had been developed as far back as the twentieth century, and even in those days people were able to assemble simple generators the size of bacteria. Based on these humble beginnings, humanity soon learned to build everything from nano-rockets to nano-microwave ovens; but the nano-engineers of ages past could have never imagined where their technologies would ultimately be put to use.

'Fostering the first batch of micro-humans was very similar to cloning: the complete genome was extracted from a human cell and then cultivated to form a micro-human that resembled the original in all ways except size. Later generations were born just like macro-humans. That, by the way,' she added, 'is what we call you. And you may have already guessed that we call your era the 'macro-era'.

'The first group of micro-humans took to the world stage in a rather dramatic fashion,' she told him. 'One day, about 12,500 years after the departure of your *Ark*, a classroom was shown on all of Earth's TV screens. Thirty students sat in this classroom. Everything seemed perfectly normal. The children were normal children, and the classroom was a normal classroom. There was nothing at all that would have seemed out of the ordinary. But then the camera panned out and humanity could see that this classroom in fact stood on the stage of a microscope.' The High Counsellor would have continued her account had she not been interrupted by the Forerunner's curiosity.

'I would like to ask,' he interjected, 'if micro-humans, with their microscopic brains, can achieve the intelligence levels of macro-humans?'

The girl shook her head, more bemused than angry. 'Do you take me for some kind of fool? Whales are no smarter than you are! Intelligence is not a matter of brain size. In regard to the number of atoms and quantum states in our brains, well, let us just say that our ability to process information easily matches that of a macro-human brain.' She paused, then continued with great curiosity in her voice. 'Could you please show us to your spacecraft?'

'Of course, very gladly.' It was the Forerunner's turn to pause. 'How exactly will you go?'

'Please wait just a moment!' the girl shouted exuberantly.

After saying this, the High Counsellor leapt into the air and onto a truly bizarre flying machine. The machine resembled a large, propeller-powered feather. Soon everyone on the plaza below was leaping into the air, competing for a spot on this 'feather'. It was apparent that this society had no concept or system of rank or status. The people indiscriminately jumping onto this strange vehicle were perfectly ordinary citizens, both young and old. Regardless of their age, they all wore the childish demeanor that seemed so inappropriate on the High Counsellor; the result was a noisy, excited, chaotic ruckus.

The feather was almost instantly jam-packed with people, but a continuous stream of new feathers was already coming into view. No sooner did one appear before it was covered with excited micro-humans. In the end, the city's sky was filled with several hundred feathers, each stuffed to capacity, or beyond, with people. They were all led by the High Counsellor's feather flier. The girl led this formidable flying armada through the city.

The Forerunner bent over the dome again, carefully observing the microscopic city within. This time he was able to make out the skyscrapers. To him, they looked like a dense forest of matchsticks. He strained his eyes and was finally able to spot the feather-like vehicles. They looked like tiny white grains of powder floating on water. If it had not been for the sheer number of them, they would have been impossible to see with the naked eye.

The picture in the left lens of the Forerunner's video specs remained as clear as ever. The micro-camera-person and their unimaginably small camera had evidently also boarded a feather, and from there they continued to stream a live feed. Through this feed, the Forerunner was able to catch a glimpse of traffic in the micro-city.

He was in for an immediate shock: it appeared that collisions were near-constant occurrences. The fast-flying feathers were continually knocking into each other and into the dust particles floating through the air. They even frequently hit the sides of the towering skyscrapers! But the flying machines and their passengers were no worse for wear, and no one seemed to pay any heed to these collisions.

This was actually a phenomenon that any junior high physics student could have explained: the smaller the scale of an object, the stronger its structural integrity. There is a vast difference between two bicycles colliding and two ten-thousand-ton ships ramming into each other. And if two dust particles collide, they will suffer no harm whatsoever. Because of this, the people of the micro-world seemed to have bodies of steel and could live lives free from the fear of injury.

As the feathers flew, people would occasionally jump out of the skyscraper windows, trying to board one of the machines in mid-air. They were not always successful, however, and some would fall from what seemed like hundreds of yards. The sheer height left the watching Forerunner with a feeling of vertigo. The falling micro-humans, on the other hand, plummeted with perfect grace and composure, even taking the time to greet acquaintances through skyscraper windows as they rushed toward the ground.

'Oh, your eyes are as black as the ocean, so very, very deep,' the High Counsellor said to the Forerunner. 'So deep with melancholy! Your melancholy shrouds our city. You should make them a museum! Oh, oh, oh . . .' She began to cry, clearly distressed.

The others, too, began to cry, and their feather fliers started bouncing between the skyscrapers, smashing into buildings left, right and center.

The Forerunner could see his own huge eyes in the image on his left video spec. Their melancholy, magnified a million times over, shocked even him. 'Why a museum?' he asked, perplexed.

'Because melancholy is only for museums. The micro-era is an age without worries!' Earth's leader loudly proclaimed. Even though tears still lingered on her tender face, there was no longer any trace of sorrow to be found behind them.

'We live in an age without worries!' the others joined in excitedly, shouting in unison.

It seemed to the Forerunner that moods in the micro-era shifted hundreds of times faster than they had ever done in the macro-era. These shifts seemed particularly pronounced when it came to negative emotions such as sadness and melancholy. Micro-humans could bounce back from such feelings in the blink of an eye.

However, there was another aspect of this discovery that was even harder for the Forerunner to truly fathom. All negative emotions were incredibly rare in this era; so rare, in fact, that they were like fascinating artefacts to the people of the micro-era. When they encountered them, they grasped the opportunity to experience them.

'Don't be depressed like a child! You will quickly see that there is nothing to worry about in the micro-era!' the High Counsellor shouted, now full of joy.

Hearing her words, the Forerunner could not help but do a double-take. He had previously observed that the general mental state of the micro-humans seemed much like that of macro-era children, but he had just assumed that their children would be even more, well, childish. 'Are you saying,' he asked in astonishment, 'that in this era, as people age, they grow . . .?' He almost couldn't believe what he was asking. 'Grow more childish?'

'We grow happier with age!' The High Counsellor giggled.

'Yes! In the micro-era we grow happier with age!' the crowd echoed loudly.

'But melancholy can be very beautiful,' the girl continued. 'Like the moon's reflection on a lake; it reflects the romanticism of the macro-era. Oh, oh, oh . . .' The Earth's leader emitted plaintive cries at the thought.

'Yes! What a beautiful age it was!' the others chimed in, their eyes brimming with tears.

The Forerunner could not help but laugh. 'You little people really don't understand melancholy. Real melancholy sheds no tears.'

'You can show us!' the High Counsellor shouted, returning to her exuberant state.

'I hope not,' the Forerunner said, sighing gently.

'Look, this is our monument to the macro-era!' the High Counsellor announced as the feathers flew over another square in the city.

The Forerunner saw the monument. It was a massive black pillar, vaguely reminding him of a giant broadcast tower. Its rough exterior was covered with countless tiles, each about the size of a wheel. It called to mind the pattern of fish scales.

Staring at the towering structure, it took the Forerunner a long while to understand: it was a strand of macro-human hair.

5

THE BANQUET

Flying upwards, the feather fliers emerged from the transparent dome, passing through some unseen hole. As they left their city's cover behind, the High Counsellor turned to the Forerunner through the video screen in his specs.

'We are now a hundred miles or so from your spacecraft. If we can land on your fingers, you can carry us. It would greatly speed up our journey.'

The Forerunner turned his head to his lander, which was right behind him. Her reference could only mean that units of measurement had also shrunk in the micro-era. He stretched out his hand, and the feather-fliers landed. They looked like a fine white powder drifting onto his fingers.

In the video lens he could now see his fingerprints. They looked like massive, semi-translucent ranges of mountains that seemed to swallow these feathers as they floated into their great canyons. The High Counsellor was the first to leap from a feather. Immediately she fell, sprawling prone on the Forerunner's finger.

'Your oily skin is far too slippery!' she complained loudly, taking off her shoes. In frustration, she tossed them into the distance. Now barefoot, she turned, looking around curiously as the others also leapt onto his skin. A sea of people soon gathered between the semi-opaque cliffs of his fingers. By the Forerunner's best guess, there were now more than ten thousand micro-humans gathered on his hand.

The Forerunner raised himself and very, very carefully walked toward his lander, keeping his hand stretched out and steady before him.

He had not even fully entered the lander when the crowd of micro-humans began to shout. 'Wow! Just look, a metal sky! An artificial Sun!'

'Don't be so dramatic; you're being silly! This is just a small shuttle. The ship above is much larger!' the High Counsellor chastened her people. But she, too, was staring in wonder, looking in all directions. As she did this, the crowd again began singing its strange song:

Oh, glorious macro-era
Magnificent macro-era
Melancholic macro-era
Oh, vanished vision! In the fires the dream did burn.

As the lander took off, setting out on its flight to the *UNS Ark*, the High Counsellor finally continued her account of the history of the micro-era.

'For a time, micro- and macro societies co-existed. During this period, the early micro-humans came to fully absorb the knowledge of the macro-world, and so we inherited macro-human culture,' she told the Forerunner. 'At the same time, micro-humanity began developing its own extremely technologically advanced society. It was a society based on nanotechnology. This transitional era between the macro-era and micro-era lasted for about . . . hmm . . .' The High Counsellor's tiny mouth twitched ever so slightly as she recalled. 'About twenty generations or so.

'Then, as the catastrophe approached, the macro-humans ceased bearing children, and their numbers dwindled day by day. At the same time, the micro-human population skyrocketed, and the scope of our society expanded along with it. Soon it exceeded that of macro-human society. At this point the micro-humans requested that they be handed the reins of global governance. This demand shook macro-society to its core and led to a powerful backlash. Some diehards refused to surrender political power; they claimed it would have been like a batch of bacteria ruling mankind. It ended with a global war between macro- and micro-humanity!'

'How horrible for your people!' The Forerunner gasped in sympathy.

'Horrible for the macro-humans, since they were quickly defeated,' the High Counsellor replied.

'How did that happen? A single macro-human with a sledgehammer could obliterate a micro-city of millions,' the perplexed Forerunner objected.

'But micro-humanity did not fight them in its cities, and macro-humanity's arsenal was utterly unsuitable for fighting an unseen enemy,' she told him. 'The only real weapon at their disposal was disinfectant. Throughout the history of their civilization they had used it to battle micro-organisms, yet it had never achieved a decisive victory. Now that they were seeking to vanquish micro-humans, an enemy equal to them in intelligence, their chances of victory were even slimmer. They could not track the movements of the micro-armies, and so we could corrupt their computer chips right under their noses. And what could they do without their computers? Power does not come from size,' the High Counsellor explained.

The Forerunner nodded in agreement. 'Now that I think about it . . .'

The High Counsellor continued, a fierce fire now burning brightly in her eyes. 'Those war criminals met their just fate. Several thousand micro-human special forces armed with laser drills parachuted onto their retinas . . .' She let the Forerunner's imagination do the rest before continuing more calmly. 'After the war, the micro-humans had claimed control of Earth. As the macro-era ended, the micro-era began.'

'Very interesting!' the Forerunner exclaimed.

The lander docked with the *Ark* in low-Earth orbit. The micro-humans immediately boarded their feather-fliers again and began exploring their new surroundings. The enormous size of the spacecraft left them dumbstruck. The Forerunner initially thought their utterances reflected admiration, but the High Counsellor soon explained her feelings about the ship.

'Now we understand. Even without the Sun's energy flash, the macro-era could not have endured,' she said. 'You consume billions of times more resources than we do!'

'But consider that this spaceship is capable of traveling at near-light speed. It can reach stars hundreds of light-years away. This is something, small people, which could only be produced in the great macro-era,' the Forerunner countered.

'At the moment, we certainly cannot create its equal. Our spaceships at present can only reach one-tenth of the speed of light,' the High Counsellor conceded.

'You are capable of space travel?' the Forerunner stammered. The sheer surprise was enough to drain the color from his face.

'Certainly not as capable as you were. The spaceships of the micro-era can reach no further than Venus. In fact, we have just heard back from them, and they tell us that as things stand, it seems far more habitable than Earth,' the High Counsellor answered, paying no heed to his shock.

'How big are your ships?' the Forerunner asked, as he regained his composure.

'The big ones are the size of your age's . . . hmm . . .' She paused, searching for the right analogy. 'Soccer ball,' she finally said. 'They can carry hundreds of thousands of passengers. The small ones, on the other hand, are only the size of a golf ball – a macro-era golf-ball, of course.'

These words shattered the Forerunner's sense of superiority.

'Forefather, would you please offer us something to eat? We are starving!' the High Counsellor asked, speaking for her people as the feather fliers gathered on the *Ark*'s control console.

The Forerunner could see ten thousand micro-humans on his command console, looking at him eagerly.

'I never thought I would be asked to invite so many to lunch,' he answered with a smile.

'We would certainly not want to ask too much of you!' the girl said, bristling with anger.

The Forerunner retrieved a tin of canned meat from storage. He opened it then used a small knife to carefully scoop out a tiny piece. He then cautiously placed it to one side of the crowd standing on the command console. The Forerunner could make out the crowd's location with his naked eye. It was a tiny, circular area on the console, about the size of a coin. This area was less smooth than the surrounding area, like someone's breath on a cold surface.

'Why did you take so much? That is very wasteful!' the Earth's leader scolded.

Now using a large monitor, the Forerunner could see her; and behind her stood a towering mountain of meat toward which her people were swarming. As they reached the pink pillar, they extracted small pieces and ate them.

Looking back to the console before him, the Forerunner could not make out even the slightest change in the size of that small piece of meat. On the screen, he could see that the crowd had quickly dispersed, some discarding half-eaten pieces of meat on the way. The High Counsellor picked a piece for herself and took a bite.

As she chewed, she began shaking her head. 'This is not very nice at all,' she commented as she finally finished.

'Of course not; it was synthesized in the eco-cycler. It was impossible to make it taste any better – the machine has limited capacity for taste production,' the Forerunner acknowledged apologetically.

'Give us some alcohol to wash it down!' The Earth's leader issued another request almost immediately. This demand caused a cheer to erupt among the gathered micro-humans. The Forerunner raised an eyebrow; after all, he knew that alcohol could kill micro-organisms!

'You drink beer?' he asked cautiously.

'No, we drink Scotch or vodka!' the Earth's leader replied with gusto.

'Mao-tai would also do!' someone shouted.

In fact, the Forerunner still had a bottle of Mao-tai, a bottle he had kept on the *Ark* ever since its departure from Earth. He had intended it for the day they found a colonizable world. He fetched it.

Wistfully holding the white porcelain bottle, he removed its cap. He then carefully poured some of the spirits into the cap, setting it down next to the crowd.

On the screen, he could see that the micro-humans had begun to scale the unassailable cliff face that was the cap. On the micro-scale, the seemingly smooth surface of the cap offered many hand-holds. Using the climbing skills they had honed on their city's skyscrapers, the micro-humans were quickly able to ascend to the cap's rim.

'Wow, what a beautiful lake!' the chorus of micro-humans shouted in admiration.

On the screen, the Forerunner could see the surface of that vast lake of alcohol bulge upward in a giant arc formed by the forces of its surface tension. The micro-human camera operator followed the High Counsellor as she first tried to scoop out some of the liquid with her hand. This attempt failed, however, as her tiny arms could not reach. Instead, she then sat herself down on the edge of the cap. From there, she let a slender foot brush the surface of the alcohol. Her delicate foot was immediately encased in a clear bead of liquid. Lifting her leg, she used her hands to extract a small drop of alcohol from the bead. She let the drop fall into her mouth.

'Wow!' she exclaimed, nodding in satisfaction. 'Macro-era alcohol really is a lot better than our micro-era spirits.'

'I am very glad to hear that we still have something that is better. But using your feet to drink like that – that's very unhygienic,' the Forerunner noted.

'I don't understand,' she replied, looking up at him in confusion.

'You walked around on your bare feet for quite a while; they must be covered in germs,' the Forerunner explained.

'Oh, now I see!' the Earth's leader called out. She was handed a box that one of her attendants had been carrying. She opened the box, and immediately a strange animal emerged. It was a round football-sized organism with tiny, chaotically twitching legs. The High Counsellor lifted the creature by one of its small legs and explained. 'Look, this is one of our city's gifts to you! A lacto-chicken!'

The Forerunner strained his mind trying to recall his microbiology education. 'Are you saying that that is a . . .' He paused in disbelief. 'A lactobacillus?'

'That is what it was called in the macro-era. It is a creature that gives yogurt its taste. A very useful animal indeed!' the High Counsellor replied.

'A very useful bacterium,' the Forerunner corrected. 'But I now understand that bacteria cannot harm you at all. Our concept of hygiene has become meaningless in the micro-era.'

Earth's leader shook her head. 'Not necessarily. Some animals— Ah,' she caught herself, 'some bacteria can seriously hurt us. For example, there are the coli-wolves. Overpowering one of them is a great feat. But most animals, like the yeast pigs, are quite lovable.' As she spoke, she took another drop from her foot and placed it into her mouth. When she shook off the remains of the alcohol bead from her foot and stood up, the High Counsellor was already quite tipsy, and her speech had begun to slur.

'I never would have expected for alcohol to still be around!' the Forerunner frowned, genuinely astonished.

'We,' the Earth's leader said, her speech faltering, 'we have inherited all that was beautiful about civilization, even though those Macros thought that we had no right to.' She stumbled. 'The right to become the carriers of human civilization,' she slurred. Looking slightly dizzy, she plopped herself back down.

'We inherited all of humanity's philosophy – Western, Eastern, Greek and Chinese!' the crowd shouted with one voice.

Now seated, the Earth's leader stretched her hands toward heaven and intoned, 'No man ever steps in the same river twice. The Tao gave birth to One. The One gave birth to Two. The Two gave birth to Three. The Three gave birth . . .' Her words trailed off, but she quickly slurred on: 'Gave birth to all of creation! We appreciate the paintings of van Gogh. We listen to Beethoven's music. We perform Shakespeare's plays. To be or not to be; that is . . .' Again she paused. 'That is the question.' She rose again, stumbling tipsily as she gave her best Hamlet performance.

'In our era, we never would have imagined a girl like you becoming the world's leader,' the Forerunner noted.

'The macro-era was a melancholic age with melancholic politics. The micro-era is a carefree age. We need happy leaders,' the High Counsellor replied, already looking a good deal more sober.

'We have not finished our discussion.' She paused, gathering herself. 'Our discussion of history. We had just talked about . . .' She paused again, thinking. 'Ah, yes, war. After the war between macro- and micro-humanity, a world war broke out amongst micro-humanity.'

The Forerunner interrupted in shock. 'What? Certainly not for territory?'

'Of course not,' the High Counsellor answered. 'If there is one thing that is truly inexhaustible in the micro-era, it is territory. It was because of some,' here she again paused, this time for reasons only known to her before continuing, 'some reasons that a macro-human could not understand. But know that in one of our largest campaigns, the battlefields were so large they covered . . .' She paused once more. 'Oh, in your units, more than three hundred feet. Imagine an area that vast!'

'You inherited much more from the macro-era than I could have ever imagined,' the Forerunner stated soberly.

'Later, the micro-era focused all of its energies on preparing for the impending catastrophe. Over five centuries, we built thousands of super-cities, deep within the Earth's crust. These cities would have looked to you like six-foot-wide, stainless-steel balls, and each one could house tens of millions. These cities were built fifty thousand miles underground . . .'

'Wait just a second; the Earth's radius is just under four thousand miles,' the Forerunner interjected.

'Oh, I again used our units,' the Earth's leader apologized. 'In your units, it would be about . . .' She did the calculation in her head. 'Yes, half a mile! When the first signs of the Sun's energy flash were observed, the entire micro-world migrated beneath the Earth's surface. Then, then the catastrophe struck.

'Four hundred years after the catastrophe, the first group of micro-humans made its way up through a massive tunnel roughly the size of a macro-era water pipe. Boring their way through the solidified magma with a laser drill, they made it to the surface,' she explained. 'It would, however, be another five centuries before micro-humanity could establish a new world for itself on the surface. When we finally did, we built a world with tens of thousands of cities, a world of eighteen billion inhabitants.

'We were full of optimism about humanity's future then. It was an all-pervading, boundless optimism that would have been unimaginable in the macro-era. We were optimistic precisely because of our micro-society's tiny scale. It meant that humanity's ability to survive in this universe had been increased many millions of times over. For example,' she said, 'the contents of that can you just opened could feed our entire city for two years. And the can itself could supply our city with all the metal it needed for those two years.'

'As a macro-human, I now have a much better understanding of the enormous advantages of the micro-era. It's all so mythical, so very epic!' the Forerunner exclaimed in admiration.

The High Counsellor smiled and continued. 'Evolution trends toward the small. Size does not equal greatness. Microscopic life has a much easier time coexisting with nature in harmony. When the giant dinosaurs died out, their contemporaries, the ants, persisted. Now, should another great disaster approach, a spaceship the size of your lander could evacuate all of humanity. Micro-humanity could rebuild its civilization on a smallish asteroid and live comfortably.'

A long silence followed.

Finally, the Forerunner, firmly focusing on that coin-sized sea of humanity before him, solemnly stated, 'When I saw the Earth again, when I thought myself the last human in the universe, I was heartbroken, and I felt all hope die. No one had ever faced such heartrending agony. But, now! Now I am the happiest person alive; at least, I am the happiest macro-human there ever was. I see that humanity's civilization has persisted. In fact, civilization has achieved much more than just survival; yours is the true apex of civilization! We are all human, originating from the same source. So now, I entreat micro-humanity to accept me as a citizen of your society.'

'We accepted you when we first detected the *Ark*. You can come live on Earth. It will be no problem for the micro-era to support one macro-human,' the Earth's leader replied in equally solemn tones.

'I will live on Earth, but all I need can come from the *Ark*. The ship's life eco-cycler will be able to sustain me for the rest of my natural life. There is no reason for a macro-human to ever again consume Earth's resources,' the Forerunner said, his face glowing with deep, silent joy.

'But our situation is improving. Not only has Venus's climate become far more hospitable to human life, Earth's temperature is also warming again. Maybe next year, we will even have rainfall in many parts of the world. Then plants will be able to grow again,' the Earth's leader stated.

'Speaking of plants, have you ever seen any?' the Forerunner asked.

The High Counsellor answered. 'We grow lichen on the inside of our protective dome. They are huge plants, every filament as tall as a ten-story building! Then there's also the chlorella in the water . . .'

The Forerunner interjected. 'But have you ever heard of grass? Or trees?'

'Are you talking about the macro-era plants that grew as tall as mountains? My, they are legends of ancient times,' she replied.

The Forerunner smiled slightly and said, 'I just want to do one thing. When I return, I will show you the gifts I bring the micro-era. I think you will greatly enjoy them!'

6

REBIRTH

Alone again, the Forerunner made his way to the *Ark*'s cold storage, which was filled with tall, neatly arranged racks. Thousands upon thousands of sealed tubes filled these racks. It was a seed bank, storing the seeds of millions of Earth's plant species. The *Ark* had been meant to carry these seeds to the distant world that humanity would eventually adopt.

There were also a few rows that constituted the embryo storage. Here the embryonic cells of millions of Earth's animal species were banked.

When the temperatures warmed the following year, the Forerunner would plant grass on the Earth below. Amongst these millions of kinds of seeds, there were strains of grass hardy enough to grow in ice and snow. They would certainly be able to grow on the present-day Earth.

If only a tenth of the planet's ecosphere could be restored to what it had been in the macro-era, the micro-era would become a heaven on Earth. In fact, much more could probably be restored. The Forerunner indulged in the warm bliss of imagination: he could picture the micro-humans' wild joy when they would first see a colossal green blade of grass rising to the heavens. And what about a small meadow? What would a meadow mean to micro-humanity?

An entire grassland! What would a grassland mean? A green cosmos for micro-humanity! And a small brook in the grassland? What a majestic wonder the sight of the brook's clear waters snaking through the grassland would be in the eyes of micro-humans. Earth's leader had said there could be rain soon. If rain fell, there could be a grassland and that brook could spring to life! Then there could certainly be trees! My God, trees!

The Forerunner envisioned a group of micro-human explorers setting out from the roots of a tree, beginning their epic and wondrous journey upward. Every leaf would be a green plain, stretching to the horizon.

There could be butterflies then. Their wings would be like bright clouds, covering the heavens. And birds, their every call angelic trumpets blaring from the heavens.

Indeed, one-trillionth of the Earth's ecological resources could easily support a micro-human population of a trillion! Now the Forerunner finally understood the point that the micro-humans had so repeatedly emphasized.

The micro-era was an age without worries.

There was nothing that could threaten this new world, nothing but . . .

A terrible thought darkened the Forerunner's mind and soul as he realized what he must do; and it had to be done immediately. There was no time to delay. He went over to one of the racks and retrieved one hundred sealed tubes.

They contained the embryonic cells of his contemporaries – the embryonic cells of macro-humans.

The Forerunner took these tubes and dropped them into the laser waste incinerator. He then went back to cold storage, walking up and down the rows several times, carefully checking every nook and cranny. Only when he was absolutely certain that no macro-human tubes had been left behind did he return to the laser incinerator. He felt a sense of deep tranquility as he pushed the button.

The laser beam burned at tens of thousands of degrees. In its blazing light, the tubes and the embryos they contained were vaporized in the blink of an eye.

FIBERS

'Hello? You've gone along the wrong fiber.'

This was the first sentence I heard after reaching this world. At the time, I was piloting an F-18 back to the USS Roosevelt, completing a routine patrol in the skies over the Atlantic, when I was suddenly propelled into this place. Even though I put thrusters at maximum, my fighter remained suspended motionless in that transparent dome, as if held in place by some unseen force field. And there was also that huge yellow planet up in the sky, a shadow cast down on it by a paper-thin ring. I wasn't like those amateurs. I didn't believe I was dreaming, I knew this was real. Reason and composure were my strong suits, and that's precisely what got me to the top of the pack, flying F-18s.

'Please direct yourself to the registration office for accidental entry. You must first exit your plane.' The voice spoke again through my headset.

I looked down. The plane was suspended over a glass station at a height of some fifty meters.

'You may jump down. Gravity here is not as strong.'

This turned out to be the case. I opened up the canopy and stood up steadily, but the thrust of my legs sent me into a jump, my whole body flying out of the cockpit as if thrown by the ejector seat, before floating down to the ground. I saw several people pacing idly on the gleaming glass.

The most unusual thing about them was that there wasn't anything unusual all. From their appearance and clothing, they certainly wouldn't have attracted any special attention in New York

— but in this strange place, their normality stood out as anything but. And then I saw the registration office, with three people already there, along with the person working behind the desk. Perhaps they were all accidental entrants, like myself. I went over.

'Name, please?' asked the official. The guy was very tanned and thin. He didn't seem different to any other low-level civil servant on Earth. 'If you do not understand the language here, just use the translation device.' He waved his hand at a pile of odd-looking devices on the desk next to him. 'Though I doubt we'll need to, as our fibers neighbor each other.'

'David — Scott,' I answered. And then I asked, 'What is this place?'

'This is a cross-fiber transfer station. Don't worry, going down the wrong fiber is a common mistake. What is your profession?'

I pointed to the yellow planet with the ring outside. 'And that, what is that?'

The registration officer lifted his head to look me in the eye, and I noticed he had the bored expression of someone who did this sort of thing every single day. And hated it.

'Earth, of course,' he said.

'How could that be Earth?' I cried out, incredulously. But I was at the same time stuck by another possibility. 'What date is this?'

'You mean today? It's January twentieth, 2001. And your profession, sir?'

'Are you sure?'

'What? Of the date? Of course I'm sure. Today is the inauguration of the new president of the United States.'

Hearing this, I relaxed for a moment, a feeling of familiarity coming over me. These people were certainly from Earth.

'That idiot, Gore, how could he be elected president?' said one of the three people next to me. He had a brown overcoat draped over his shoulders.

'But you're wrong, it was Bush who was elected president,' I said to him.

'No, Gore,' he insisted. We began to argue.

'What are you two are going on about?' asked the man behind us, who was wearing a traditional, straight-collared Chinese suit.

'Their fibers are very close,' explained the registration clerk. Then he asked me again, 'Sir. Your profession, please?'

'Oh, who cares about professions? I want to know where I am! That planet out there can't be Earth — how could Earth be yellow?!'

'Yeah, that's right! Earth can't be that color. You think we're idiots or something!' the man with the brown coat draped over him barked at the staffer.

The registration clerk just shook his head, flabbergasted. 'That's what I hear the most from people who have come out of wormholes.'

I immediately felt a sense of kinship with the man in the brown coat. I asked him, 'So you took the wrong fiber, too?' Even though I myself didn't understand what that meant.

He nodded. 'So have those two.'

'You flew in on an airplane?'

He shook his head. 'No, I got here on my morning jog somehow. And those other two had their own ways here. But it was basically the same. There they were, going along, when suddenly everything changed, and now they're here.'

I nodded, beginning to understand. 'So you know what I mean when I say the planet out there can't be Earth.'

The three of them nodded in unison. I shot a smug look back at the official.

'How could Earth be that color — do you take us for idiots?' repeated the man in the brown coat.

I nodded again.

'Even an idiot knows Earth looks dark purple from space!'

A sudden look of bemusement come over me. The man in the Chinese suit asked, 'What, are you color blind?'

I nodded to affirm this new comment. 'Yeah, or maybe he's the idiot.'

The man in the Chinese suit went on, 'Everybody knows the color of the Earth is determined by the scattering qualities of its atmosphere and oceans. Meaning that the color is. . .'

I kept on nodding. Mr. Chinese suit nodded back at me.

'. . .grey.'

'What, are you all stupid?' It was the first time the woman among us had spoken. She had a curvaceous, sensual figure, and a way of holding herself that said she knew it. If I hadn't been so disoriented by everything that was happening, I might have found her attractive. 'Everybody knows the Earth is pink! Its sky is pink, and so is its ocean. Haven't you ever heard the song, 'I'm so adorable, so pretty, with blue clouds for my eyes, and my face in these pink skies. . ."

'Your profession, sir?' asked the registration clerk once more.

I rushed up to him now, snapping, 'Bud, let's not worry about my damned profession for the moment. Right now, I want you to tell me where I am. That is not Earth. Even if we pretended that the Earth was yellow, what's that ring around it?'

And then the four of us who'd taken the wrong fiber were on the same page again. The other three agreed that Earth has no rings, and only Saturn and Neptune have rings.

'Although,' the young woman said, 'Earth does have three moons.'

'No! Earth has only one moon!' I shouted.

'Then how boring your love affairs must be, since you can't walk along the beach, hand in hand, with the romance of all six shadows as three moons shine down overhead.'

'I find such an image horrific and not romantic in the least,' said the Chinese suit.

'Everybody knows that Earth has no moons at all.'

'Then love affairs for you,' replied the young woman, 'must be even more boring and bland.'

'How could you say that? Two lovers watching Jupiter rising from the beach, that's boring to you?'

I stared at him in confusion. 'What's this about Jupiter? You can see Jupiter when you're on a date?'

'What are you, blind?'

'I'm a pilot and my eyes are better than all of yours.'

'Then how could you not see a star? Why are you looking at me like that? I guess you don't know that the energy level of Jupiter was so great, its gravity brought on nuclear reactions some eighty or ninety million years ago, and it became a star. I guess you also don't know that's the reason the dinosaurs went extinct? How educated are you, anyway? Even if you've never been to school, you must have seen the silvery dawn light of Jupiter rising, right? You must have seen those gorgeous dusks when Jupiter and the Sun descend together? God, you're hopeless!'

It felt like I had come to a mental institution. I turned to face the registration clerk again. 'You asked me my profession, just now. All right, I'm a pilot with the U.S. Air Force.'

'Wow,' cried the young woman. 'You're an American?'

I nodded.

'Then you must be a gladiator! I saw from the first that you weren't the usual kind of guy. My name's Wawani. I'm Indian. Let's be friends!'

'Gladiator? What does that have to do with the United States of America?' I asked, bewildered.

'I know the U.S. Congress has plans to ban gladiators and coliseums, but the bill hasn't passed yet, has it? And Bush, Jr. is as bloodthirsty his father was, so with him about to step in, the bill has even less chance of getting through. You think I don't know? I was at the gladiator games at the Olympics in Atlanta, but man, I couldn't afford the tickets, so I just sat way in the back and saw one bout. For all the good it did me. The guys got in a pile-on and both of them lost their knives. I didn't see any blood at all.'

'Are you sure you're not talking about ancient Rome?'

'Ancient Rome? Heh! That was an age of weakness, an age when there were no men. Back then the worst punishment was making criminals watch a chicken be killed. And they'd all faint straight away.' She leaned against me, warmly. 'You must be a gladiator.'

I didn't know what to say, or even what kind of expression to take. I turned back to the staffer. 'What else?'

The clerk turned back to me and nodded. 'That's fine, we ten should stick together. We can get this done faster that way.'

I, Wawani, Brown Coat guy, and Mr. Chinese Suit all looked around. 'Aren't there only five of us?'

'What's "five"?' The official looked confused. 'The four of you, and then add me in, and that's ten.'

'You really are idiots,' said Mr. Chinese suit. 'If you must know, I'll teach you: ten is what comes after *dada*!'

Now it was my turn not to know a number. 'What's "*dada*"?'

'How many are your fingers and toes? Twenty! Now cut one off, and what you have left is *dada* digits.'

I nodded, 'Oh, dada is nineteen — so you go by a base-twenty number system. And they,' I pointed at the registration clerk, 'have a base-five system.'

'You must be a gladiator. . . .' Wawani said, tracing along my face with her finger. It felt good.

Chinese suit guy looked at the clerk with condescension in his eyes. 'What a stupid number system — you have two hands and two feet, yet you make use of only one fourth of that.'

'It's you who's stupid!' the official shot right back. 'You could calculate just fine with the fingers of one hand. There's no need to stick out both your crummy claws and hooves!'

'Does everyone here have a number system for machine calculation?' I asked. 'I mean, you guys have computers, yes?'

We reached a consensus again when they said these were binary systems.

'Naturally they are binary,' said Brown Coat. 'Otherwise computing could hardly have been invented! Because there are only two states: the bean falls into the hole of the bamboo slat, or else it doesn't.'

I was confused again. 'Bamboo slat? Bean?'

'It seems you have no education! Though it ought to be common knowledge that King Wen of the Zhou invented the computer.'

'King Wen of the Zhou? That Oriental necromancer?'

'Careful there! You can't talk like that about the creator of cybernetics.'

'So computers. . . You must mean the Chinese abacus?'

'What do you mean, 'I must mean the Chinese abacus'. Why, that's what a computer is! They're as big as football fields, made of pine wood and bamboo slats, with small yellow soybeans as the operation media. It takes a hundred head of cattle to set them moving! But their CPUs are exquisite, being only as big as a small building. The bamboo integrated circuits inside exhibit absolutely first-rate craftsmanship.'

'How do you code on it?'

'You mean how do you perforate the bamboo slats? King Wen's bronze drill was excavated and is now at the National Palace Museum in Beijing! King Wen of Zhou's *Yijing*, distribution 3.2, has over one million lines of code, filling over one thousand kilometers of perforated bamboo strips. . .'

'You really are a gladiator. . .' Wawani said, nestling closer into me.

'Can we just get registered?' asked the clerk, impatiently. 'After that I can try explaining it all again.'

I looked outside and thought about the yellow Earth with the ring. 'I think I understand,' I said. 'I am educated, and I know a little about quantum mechanics.'

'I also understand some,' the man in the Chinese suit said. 'It seems the multiverse theory from quantum mechanics is correct.'

Brown Coat guy seemed to be the most educated of us. He nodded his head. 'When a quantum system makes a choice, the universe splits into two or more, to include all the possibilities for that choice. From this are produced a great bundle of parallel universes. This is the result of the quantum multi-states on a universal scale.'

The registration official said, 'We call this parallel universe 'a fiber'. The multiverse is a bundle of fibers, and you all come from neighboring strands, so your worlds are all comparatively similar.'

'We can understand each other's language, at least.' Though as soon as I said that, Wawani proved me wrong. At least partly.

'How odd all this is! What are you all talking about?' She was the least educated, but the sweetest. I think that word must have had made sense somehow in her world. She sidled up to me again, warm as ever. 'You really are a gladiator.'

'Your world has connected the fibers?' I asked the clerk.

He nodded his head. 'It came with faster-than-light travel. The wormholes are very small, and disappear quickly, but new ones also appear simultaneously. And especially when faster-than-light travel is achieved in your fibers, the number of wormholes will increase, and so more people step through the wrong door.'

'And what do we do now?'

'None of you may remain in our fiber. After you register, you have to return to your original fiber.'

'I want the gladiator to return to my fiber with me,' said Wawani.

'If he wishes, that is of course fine with us. As long as he doesn't stay in this fiber.' He pointed at the yellow Earth.

I said, 'I wish to return to my own fiber.'

'What color is your Earth?' asked Wawani.

'Blue, and dotted with white clouds.'

'How awful! Come back with me to the pink Earth,' cooed Wawani, as she beckoned me.

'Well I think it's swell, and I want to return to my own fiber,' I said, coldly.

We quickly finished registering. Wawani asked the registration clerk, 'Can I have a souvenir?'

'Take a fiber lens with you. One per person.' The clerk pointed at several globes placed on the glass table nearby. 'If you connect links on the globes before you part, after you return to your fiber, you can see an image of the corresponding fiber.'

Wawani exclaimed in happy surprise, 'If my world is connected to the gladiator's, then after I return home, I can see his fiber?!'

'Not only that, but any corresponding fiber — not just the one.'

I didn't quite follow what the clerk meant, but I took a globe anyway and connected the lead on it to Wawani's globe. After a beep indicated successful connection, I returned to my F-18. Inside the cockpit, I found it hard to put down the globe. After a few minutes, the mid-fiber interchange station and the yellow Earth both disappeared in an instant, and I was back in the skies over the Atlantic. I saw the blue skies and seas I was used to. When I landed the plane on the USS Roosevelt, the control tower reported that I was not at all delayed, nor had radio communication at any point been lost.

But that globe proved that I had been to another fiber. I found a way to sneak it off the plane. That evening the carrier docked at Boston, and I brought the globe back to the officers' quarters. When I took it out of my bag, there really was a clear image on the globe. I saw pink skies and blue clouds. Wawani was walking idly at the foot of some sparkling, crystalline mountains. I turned the sphere in my hands and saw that in the other hemisphere, a different image was on display. The pink sky and blue clouds were present still, but there was someone else there besides Wawani, a person in an American Air Force jacket. Me.

It was all quite simple, actually: when I decided not to follow Wawani, the universe split into two, so what I was seeing now was the fiber of the other possibility.

The fiber lens remained with me my whole life. I watched the love between myself and Wawani on the pink Earth, how they lived as recluses on the crystal mountain, how they got old there, how they raised a whole brood of pink children.

And in the fiber in which Wawani returned alone, she hadn't forgotten me. Thirty years to the day after we had gone down the wrong fiber, I saw her in the globe, guiding an old man by the hand as they sauntered intimately along a beach. The three moons cast six shadows on the surface of the sandy beach. Just then, Wawani looked up at me from within her globe. Her eyes no longer resembled the blue clouds, and her face was no longer like the pink skies. But her smile was as alluring as ever. And I could clearly hear her say, 'You really are a gladiator!'

THE MESSENGER

The old man had only yesterday noticed the listener downstairs. His spirits were quite low these days, and except for when he played his violin, he didn't look out the window much. He meant to isolate himself from the outside world with the window curtain, and with his music, but it was impossible.

Many years ago, over on the other side of the Atlantic, when he rocked a baby pram in a narrow garret and flipped through uninteresting patent applications in a bustling patent office, his ideas were still immersed in a beautiful world. In that world, he ran at the speed of light. Now he was in the quiet, secluded little town of Princeton. The detachment of his youth was gone. The outside world was constantly perplexing and disturbing.

Two matters in particular troubled him. One was quantum theory, originated by Max Planck and now the obsession of so many young physicists. It made him uneasy, particularly the theory's indeterminacy. 'God doesn't play dice,' he often said to himself these days. He had, in the latter half of his life, devoted himself to concocting a unified field theory, but had made no progress. What he'd built was pure math and no physics. The other matter that troubled him was the atom bomb. It had been a long time since Hiroshima and Nagasaki, a long time since the war, but his pain, which had been a dull wound, had now flared with agony. Such a small, simple formula. All it did was relate mass to energy. Truth be told, before Fermi's reactor pile was built, the old man thought humans turning mass into energy at the atomic level was a wild fantasy. Helen Dukas had been consoling him a lot lately. But she didn't realize he was unconcerned with his own merits, errors, honor, or disgrace – his worries were more far-reaching.

In recent dreams, he kept hearing a fearful sort of din, like a deluge or a volcano. Finally, one night, the clamor woke him and he discovered it was only a small puppy snoring on the patio. The noise never invaded his dreams again. He dreamt of a wasteland, the setting sun reflected on melting snow. He tried to escape this wasteland, but it was too big, seemingly limitless. Later he saw an ocean, the setting sun again, the sea bloodred, and he understood. The whole world was a wasteland covered in melting snow. He woke with a start once more. This time, a question emerged in his mind like a dark reef at ebb tide:

Does humanity still have a future?

The question tormented him like a raging fire, nearly intolerable.

The person downstairs was young. He wore a stylish nylon jacket. The old man realized this visitor was listening to his violin. For the next three days, whenever the old man began his evening playing, the visitor would arrive and stand quietly in the fading glow of the Princeton sunset. Around nine o'clock the old man would put down his violin, and the listener would slowly depart. Maybe he was a Princeton University student, or just someone who'd heard the old man lecture. The old man had long ago grown weary of his countless worshippers, the sycophants of every kind, from kings to housewives. But this stranger downstairs, this friend so interested in his musical talent, this one gave him a kind of consolation. On the fourth night, the old man had just begun to play when it started raining. He looked out the window and saw the young man standing under the only available shelter: a Chinese parasol tree. The rain worsened, and the tree's sparse autumnal foliage provided little cover. The old man stopped playing, wishing to release his audience early. But the young man seemed to know this wasn't the concert's proper ending time. He remained standing there, unmoving, his saturated jacket shining under the streetlamp. The old man put down his violin. He went unsteadily down the stairs and out into the misty rain, and finally he was standing before the young visitor.

'If you . . . eh, would like to listen, why not come upstairs?'

Not waiting for an answer, the old man turned and went back inside. The visitor stood there staring, as if into limitless distance, as if what just happened had been a dream. The music resumed upstairs. The visitor entered the front door in a kind of trance. He went upstairs, as if drawn by the spirit of the music. The old man's door was half open. The visitor went inside. The old man faced the window and watched the rain as he played. He didn't turn his head, but he sensed the young man had arrived. He felt a bit apologetic toward his audience, this person so infatuated with his violin's voice. He didn't play particularly well. Today's selection in particular, his favorite Mozart rondo, he often played out of tune. Sometimes he forgot a phrase and used his imagination to fill the gap. He still had this cheap violin, his old friend, its voice far from precise. But the young listener seemed calm and content. The two of them were soon immersed in the instrument's flawed but imaginative sound.

This was an unremarkable night in the mid-twentieth century. The Iron Curtain separated East from West. Humanity's future, recently fallen under the nuclear shadow, was like the dim, misty, rainy autumn evening. On this night, in the rain, Mozart's rondo floated out of this little house in Princeton, New Jersey.

Time seemed to pass faster than usual. Nine o'clock rolled around soon enough. The old man stopped playing and looked up to see his guest bow, then turn to go.

'Eh, will you come and listen tomorrow?' the old man asked.

The young man stood at the door and didn't turn around. 'I'm afraid not, Professor. Tomorrow you will have a visitor.' He opened the door, then seemed to recall something. 'Oh, that's right. Your guest will leave at 8:10. Will you still play afterward?'

The old man nodded distractedly, not grasping the implication of these words.

'Very well then, I will come. Thank you.'

The rain continued unabated the next day, and evening did indeed bring a guest, the Israeli ambassador. The old man had always given that remote, newborn country his blessing – they were his people over there, his tribe – and he'd donated the proceeds from selling his original manuscripts to the cause. But this time, the ambassador wanted something else. The old man didn't know whether to laugh or cry. They wanted him to be president of Israel! He firmly declined. He accompanied the ambassador back into the rain, and fished out his pocket watch just before the man got in his car. Under the streetlamp, the timepiece showed 8:10. A memory stirred.

'Your . . . eh, your visit . . . did anyone else know about it?'

'Rest assured, Professor. This is all a rigorously kept secret. Nobody knows.'

Perhaps that young visitor knew, but somehow he also knew . . . The old man asked a very odd question: 'So, had you planned on leaving at 8:10?'

'Pardon me? Well, no. I hoped to chat with you at length, but since you've refused, I've no wish to disturb you. We understand, Professor.'

The old man returned upstairs, perplexed, but when he took out his little violin, he forgot his bewilderment. The music had just begun when the young man appeared.

Their concert ended at ten o'clock, and the old man repeated yesterday's invitation: 'Will you come and listen tomorrow?' He thought a bit and added, 'I think this is nice.'

'Well, tomorrow I can listen from below again.'

'But I think it will still be raining tomorrow. These are cloudy days.'

'You're right, it will rain tomorrow, but not when it comes time for you to play. The next day, when you play again, I'll come up to listen. The rain won't stop until 11 A.M. the following morning.'

The old man laughed, thinking the young visitor very funny indeed, but watching him leave, he had a sudden premonition that none of this was a joke.

His premonition was correct. The weather over the next few days bore out the young man's predictions. On the rainless evening, he remained downstairs listening. It was raining at concert time the following day, and he came upstairs. It stopped raining in Princeton at precisely 11 A.M. the next morning.

The first clear night after the weather, the young visitor forwent listening downstairs and came up to the old man's room, bringing with him a small violin. Saying nothing, he presented it with both hands to the old man.

'No no, please. I have no use for another violin.' The old man waved it away. Many people had offered him violins, among them famous and valuable Italian instruments, ones that had belonged to celebrated players – and he'd politely refused them one by one, feeling his skill did not merit such great violins.

'I'm lending this to you. After a while you'll return it to me. Sorry, Professor, you can't keep it.'

The old man took it, and on close inspection it seemed a common sort of violin. It didn't seem to have strings, surprisingly, though a more careful look revealed that it did, but the strings were extremely fine, like spider threads. The old man didn't dare press down on them. The gossamer seemed a breath away from breaking. He looked up at the visitor, who smiled and nodded, so he lightly pressed the strings. They didn't snap, indeed they felt impossibly strong beneath his fingertips. He brought the bow to bear, inadvertently sliding it along one string and making it sound – and it was like hearing the cry of Nature itself.

It was the voice of the Sun, the Sun of all voices.

The old man launched upon the rondo, and right away he was one with the boundless cosmos. He saw light waves propagating through space, slowly, like mist blown by a morning breeze; undulating gravitational swells of the vast space-time membrane, and the countless stars floating on that membrane like sparkling dewdrops; a mighty gale of energy blowing across the membrane, conjuring dreamlike secondary rainbows.

When the old man woke from his musical reverie, the young visitor had gone.

The old man was fascinated with the violin. He played every day, and into the late hours of the night. Dukas and his doctor both urged him to consider his health, but they also knew that every time that violin music started, a vigor he'd never known would surge through his veins.

The young visitor had yet to return.

After ten days, he started playing the strange violin less, even sometimes going back to his original violin, that old friend. He'd started worrying that excessive use might wear down or even break the fine gossamer strings. But he couldn't resist the sounds that came out of that instrument. It was like he was enchanted. He began to think of the young visitor's return, whenever that might be, and having to give up the violin, and he resumed playing it all night long like he had at first. Every night, in the wee hours, when he reluctantly stopped playing, he would carefully examine the strings. His vision had gone dim with age, but he had Dukas find a magnifying glass, under which the strings showed no sign of wear or abrasion. Their surface was like precious stone, glossy, sparkling, translucent, in the dark, even fluorescing blue.

Another ten days passed.

It was late, and it had become his habit to gaze at the violin just before falling asleep. Something about the strings struck him as peculiar. He picked up the magnifying glass and examined the strings closely, confirming his suspicion. Actually, the inkling had begun several days before, but only now had the change become pronounced enough to easily perceive.

The strings were thickening with use.

The next night, when the old man had just put bow to string, the young visitor suddenly appeared.

'You've come for this, haven't you?' the old man asked uneasily.

The visitor nodded.

'Eh . . . perhaps you could let me have it?'

'Absolutely not. My apologies, Professor, but it's impossible. I can't leave anything behind now.'

The old man thought about this and began to understand. He offered up the violin with both hands. 'It's not from this time, is it?'

The young man shook his head, standing by the window. Outside, the Milky Way traversed the vast sky, the stars resplendent. He was a black silhouette before this magnificent backdrop.

The old man understood more. He recalled the visitor's mysterious predictive talents. It was quite simple really. He hadn't been predicting. He'd been remembering.

'I'm a messenger. In our time, we unexpectedly saw how worried you are, so I was dispatched.'

'And you brought me what?' the old man said, unamazed. 'This violin?' Throughout his life, the cosmos had been one big wonder to him. It was precisely because of this that he'd surpassed others and been the first to glimpse the universe's deepest mystery.

'No, the violin is just proof that I'm from the future.'

'Proof?'

'In this era of yours, people convert mass into energy. You have the atom bomb and very soon you'll have the fusion bomb. In our era, we can turn energy into mass. You see . . .' He pointed at the violin strings. '. . . they're getting thicker. The increased mass is converted sonic energy, from when you play.'

The old man shook his head in bafflement.

'I know these revelations go against your theory. Firstly, I can't possibly travel back in time. Secondly, according to your formula, it would take a huge amount of energy to increase the strings' mass as much as you have.'

The old man was silent awhile. He smiled indulgently. 'Eh . . . theory is ambiguous, gray.' He sighed. 'And the tree of my life has also turned gray. Okay, child, what have you brought for me?'

'Two pieces of news.'

'And the first is?'

'Humanity has a future.'

The old man sank into an armchair, relieved. He was like every old man who finally settles his life's ultimate and long-cherished wish. A sense of well-being suffused him from head to toe. He could really rest. 'I suppose I should have known that, child, since you are here.'

'The atom bombs used on Japan will be the last nuclear weapons used in combat. By the end of the 1990s, most countries will have signed an international agreement banning nuclear weapons testing and preventing proliferation. Fifty years after that, the last warhead will be destroyed. And I'll be born two hundred years after that.'

The young man picked up the violin he meant to reclaim. 'I should go. I've already delayed many journeys in order to hear your music. I still have three eras to visit, and five people to meet, among them the creator of the unified field theory. I'm afraid that's a matter for a century hence.'

What he didn't mention was that he always chose a time near death to pay these formal visits to great people, to minimize affecting the future.

'And what is the second piece of news you have for me?'

The young man had opened the door. He turned, smiling apologetically.

'Professor, I'm afraid God does indeed play dice.'

The old man watched through his window as the visitor left the house. It was quite late and the street was empty. The young man began to undress. It seemed he didn't want to bring this era's clothes with him. The skintight suit he wore underneath fluoresced in the dim light – his era's garb, obviously. He didn't exit by transforming into white light, as the old man had imagined. He rose into the air, rapidly, at an angle, and a few seconds later he vanished among the brilliant stars of the night sky. His speed had been constant – no acceleration. Clearly, he had not risen as such. Earth had revolved while he had remained static, at absolute rest in this space-time. The old man reckoned the messenger could use his absolute space-time coordinates as a starting point, like standing on the bank of the long river of space-time, and watch time surging by, and if he wanted, go anywhere he liked upriver or down.

Albert Einstein stood there for a while in silence, then slowly turned, and once more picked up his old violin.

DESTINY

We discovered the asteroid 1,800,000 kilometers from Earth.

It was an irregular ovoid with a diameter of about ten kilometers. It revolved slowly, the many little planes and facets of its surface reflecting sunlight like blinking eyes. Our shipboard computer showed its orbit would intersect with Earth in eighteen days. This massive chunk of space rock would strike near the Gulf of Mexico.

Earth's lookout network should have noticed this a year before, but we hadn't heard anything about it in the news. We contacted Earth, but after the expected five-second lag, our earpieces were still quiet. We tried several more times and received no answer. It was like humanity was in collective shock. We'd exchanged words with Earth only ten minutes before. The radio silence amazed us more than our asteroid discovery.

Twenty days before, Emma and I had chartered this small ship for a space-cruising honeymoon. It was an old ship under traditional propulsion. In this era of space-time jump flights, our snail-slow old-school cutter seemed romantic and sentimental. We had toured synchronously orbiting Space City, then Luna, and then flown more than a million kilometers up-system. The journey had gone smoothly, idyllic as an old pastoral song, but on the eve of our planned return, things took a turn for the abnormal.

There it was, fifty kilometers off our bow, clear against the dark backdrop of space, real as a museum exhibit on black satin, and I was sure this wasn't a nightmare.

'We have to do something,' I said.

As always, once I'd issued a call to action, Emma set about planning the details: 'We could fire an engine at it, blow it off course.'

A computer sim confirmed this was feasible, but it would have to be done within twenty-four minutes. If the planetoid moved beyond that window undisturbed, it would be too late.

We didn't hesitate any longer. We moved to a safe distance of one hundred kilometers from the asteroid, then issued the order to the computer. The engine separated from the tail section of our hull. We watched through a porthole as the cylinder spouted blue flame and headed for the rock. The blaze soon became a radiant little star. We held our breaths watching it collide with that massive boulder floating in space. After the initial flash, an immense fireball erupted from the asteroid, expanding fast, as if a new sun had suddenly instantiated before us, and was coming for us. Just when it seemed the inferno would engulf our ship, the expansion slowed, and suddenly it was shrinking, and then it was gone. There was the asteroid again, its surface marked by the engine detonation, the diameter of the crater at least three thousand meters. Countless points of light were flying out from the asteroid, impact ejecta, among them a fragment that swept past our ship. The computer was determining the asteroid's new trajectory, and we nervously waited.

'Course change successful. The body will not collide with Earth. It will be captured at an orbit of 58,037 kilometers and become an Earth satellite.'

Emma and I hugged, overjoyed.

'Think the leasing company will make us pay for that engine?' she asked, half joking.

'Would they dare ask that of humankind's saviors? Besides, we're entitled to proprietary rights on this planetoid. Mineral extraction alone will make us billions!'

With the joy and pride of saviors, we fired the remaining engine and headed for Earth. But once again we got no answers to our hails, leaving us again in suspense. We just couldn't imagine what was going on at home.

Our going was slow on one engine, and the asteroid passed us, soon vanishing in Earth's direction. Emma, who'd been watching its progress on-screen, cried out: 'God! Earth! Look at Earth!'

I looked, but at this distance it was baseball-sized, a glittering blue sphere, and I saw nothing strange. Emma pointed at the magnified image on-screen. After a quick scan I began to grow afraid: It was the continents. They'd changed. They looked like nothing I'd ever seen.

We turned to the computer for help, and it responded: 'You're seeing the continent shapes and distribution of the Late Cretaceous, including the supercontinent Gondwana.'

'The Cretaceous? How . . . long ago was that?'

'Approximately sixty-five million years. But your question may be framed incorrectly. Many signs indicate that the Cretaceous is now.'

The computer was right. Now we understood why Earth had gone radio-quiet: Humanity didn't exist yet.

In our home era, space-time jump flights made interstellar travel possible. Every time an interstellar ship jumped, it left behind one or more wormholes, which then drifted in near-Earth space. If an interplanetary ship accidentally entered one, it might be flung instantaneously tens of thousands of light-years, far forward or back in time. Later, improved interstellar ships led to a purge of the spatial dimensions in these left-behind wormholes; that is, they would no longer change your location in space, but might still produce a time jump. Such wormholes were vastly less dangerous. If you accidentally went through one, all you had to do was retrace your route and go back through the other way, returning to the exact moment you left. We'd gone through such a time-oriented wormhole without sensing it at all.

Accidental time-hole jumps occurred from time to time, but the backward-jumping ships always returned, among them a planet-mining ship that found itself in the Cambrian period. The astronauts saw an Earth glowing dark red, without oceans, the dry land flowing with magma.

Meanwhile, the forward-jumping ships never returned, a cause for great optimism about the future.

But Earth governments were still most focused on the backward jumps. There were strict ordinances. If you happened into a wormhole, by law you had to return. If you couldn't return because of wormhole drift (the probability of this was very low), you had to get a sufficient distance from Earth and then self-destruct, to avoid changing Earth history.

'God,' Emma cried, 'what have we done?'

My spirits were also low. In a flash, we'd gone from saviors to devils.

'Don't worry, dear,' I consoled, 'not every little disturbance triggers a butterfly effect.'

'Little disturbance? That's what you call what we did?' She remembered something and asked the computer, 'This is the Cretaceous?'

The computer replied in the affirmative. We both understood. What we'd nudged off course was none other than that fateful asteroid, the dinosaur killer.

After a long silence, Emma said, 'Let's go back.'

We promptly turned the ship around and carefully sped back along our original course.

'But what are we returning to?' I sighed. 'A trial?'

'Ideally. If humanity still exists, never mind judges, we can die easy.'

Smiling, I shook my head. 'You worry too much, Emma. Think about it. Why did humans come out ahead of other species? Why not ants? Or dolphins, or other such animals? They have societies, intelligence . . . but their degree of civilization doesn't measure up to our scraps. Opportunities for species evolution are fair and impartial.'

'Okay then, why?'

'Because humanity is the spirit, the soul, of all living things. The cosmos chose us. Look how far our civilization has come. This confidence is warranted! The world we go back to might be changed somewhat, but humanity will exist, and so will human civilization!'

Emma smiled a bit. 'I forgot what a believer in human selection theory you are.' She made a sign of the cross over her chest. 'I can only hope you're right.'

When we passed back through the wormhole, it felt like the cosmos vanished and reappeared. The process was very short. It was like space blinked, and that was that. No wonder we hadn't noticed the first time through. During the instant of passage, Earth's silence was replaced by a clamor of EM signals, but our excitement turned immediately to disappointment. The signals seemed to be nothing but muffled bursts of chirps and hoots. Neither we nor the computer could interpret them. We shouted at Earth and still got no answer. Once again, we saw Earth on the screen, the continents now restored to their familiar arrangement, and this at least let me breathe and relax for a moment. If there really had been a butterfly effect, at least it hadn't inverted heaven and earth.

Our little ship flew on its remaining engine toward Earth. We entered low Earth orbit two days later and had just enough fuel left for descent. We splashed down in the Pacific, near Australia, and the ship quickly began to sink. We had to repair to a small life raft, and then we were adrift. It was the wee hours of the morning. The sun hadn't risen. I looked around and the ocean seemed like the same old ocean, the sky the familiar sky. The world seemed unchanged.

After drifting half an hour, we saw a large vessel in the distance. We shot a signal flare and the ship came speedily toward us.

'Humanity!' Emma yelled, her eyes shining with excited tears. 'It really still exists!'

'I said so, didn't I? Humans are the soul of all living things. We're destined to have the peak civilization.'

'But this world isn't the one we set out from.' She was afraid again. 'Look at that ship. I don't think humans have entered the technological era yet.'

The ship appeared quite ancient, nothing like the vessels of our modern world. But that didn't mean this world was technologically backward. I noticed the ship had no sails and wondered about its motive power.

It sped toward us and then came to a halt. A rope ladder came down the side. Emma and I climbed up. The crew were tanned and weathered-looking and dressed in rough gray-green clothes. I addressed them but no one responded; then one of them motioned for us to follow him.

We went up a long flight of steps, ascending the ship's central tower-like structure, which commanded a view of the whole vessel. Our guide presented us to a powerfully built, silver-bearded old man, and said something to us. We didn't understand, but the computer I wore on my chest did. It said: 'Their tongue is similar to ancient Latin, with some differences. The sentence may be understood as . . . *This is our captain.*'

The captain also spoke to us, and the computer translated: 'You two were drifting alone on the sea. Such bravery! Aren't you afraid of getting devoured?'

'Devoured?' I said, the computer translating and amplifying my words. 'By what?'

The captain gestured at the ocean. By now the sun had risen, and a thin morning fog on the sea's surface scattered golden sunlight. The water, tranquil until moments before, now surged with waves, which soon broke, and an immense monster breached the surface. Then came another, and amid the roaring water, a whole pod of the beasts soon emerged. Emma and I finally understood the consequences of what we'd done 65 million years before.

Dinosaurs had never gone extinct.

One came toward the ship, halting alongside, its immense body like a frightful mountain peak, and we were in its vast shadow. I saw black, crisscrossing blood vessels under the gray, satiny skin, like vines and tendrils entangling the great gray summit. The dinosaur's massive neck extended forward, suspending the huge head above us, and seawater came down like torrential rain, flooding the deck. A pair of colossal eyes watched us fixedly. Our blood almost congealed under that grim, cold gaze. Emma pressed against me, shuddering from head to toe.

'Don't be afraid,' the captain said. 'It can't hurt anyone. This is a zoo.'

Sure enough, the dinosaur watched us for a while, then turned and swam away, its wake surging against the side of the ship and rocking it. We spotted another big ship like ours, far off upon the sea, with two dinosaurs swimming before it.

'You've domesticated dinosaurs?' Emma said. 'Amazing!'

I too was astonished. 'We thought dinosaurs would pose a threat to human evolution. Now we see they've only made human civilization stronger!'

Emma nodded. 'Exactly! As beasts of burden they're clearly stronger than oxen or horses. I guess they could move a small mountain without much effort! Darling, you really were right. Humans are the soul of all living things. From now on, I'm a confirmed believer in human selection theory!'

The computer translated our words, and the captain watched us, seemingly baffled. 'This is a zoo,' he said. 'They don't harm people.'

Just then I made another surprising discovery: a vision of towering, pillar-like structures on the horizon, their altitude truly shocking. A cloud bank floated about halfway up the immense columns. We were like ants looking at a titanic forest. I asked the captain what it was.

'A building complex,' the captain said, indifferent. 'A coastal skyscraper complex.'

'God!' Emma cried. 'How tall are they?'

'Some ten thousand of you.'

'A building over ten thousand meters high?' I said. 'That would mean, what, several thousand floors?'

The captain shook his head. 'A hundred or so.'

'Each level a hundred meters high?' Emma exclaimed. 'What a grand palace!'

'A grand civilization,' I said. 'A grand *human* civilization!'

'Those structures were built by the tourists,' the captain said.

'Tourists?' I said. 'Ah yes, you said this is a zoo, but . . . tourists? You lot are obviously not tourists.'

'It's early,' Emma said. 'Maybe the zoo is still closed?'

The captain stared at us in amazement, then turned to look at the distant swimming dinosaurs. This confused us, gave us pause, as did the slow, unsophisticated manner of these humans before us.

A howling chorus erupted from the pod of dinosaurs. The clamor was familiar: we'd heard it in space, coming from Earth via radio. We again marveled at the ten-thousand-meter buildings on the horizon, before a revelation burst in my mind like a thunderclap. At my side, Emma cried out in dismay and fell to the deck, as if suddenly paralyzed.

She surely understood now, like I did.

The cosmos had not chosen humanity after all. In the old timeline, humans had created the apex civilization on Earth, but that had been a one-time and accidental chance. In our human conceit, we'd taken the accidental for the inevitable. Now nature had tossed the evolutionary coin again, and it had come up tails instead of heads.

We were indeed in a zoo, but the dinosaurs were the tourists.

My legs went weak. I fell down and sat with Emma on the deck. The world before our eyes was a dark abyss. We heard the computer translation of the captain's words:

'You two are rather exquisite looking. I think it will be okay if you stay with us. Both of you will be approved as ornamental humans.'

'Ornamental humans?' I asked, stupefied. The world gradually came back into focus. There was the grand city on the horizon.

'No,' Emma muttered, 'I want to go ashore . . .'

'Are you mad?' the captain said. 'Ashore, you would become a food human!'

'A . . . food human?'

'Food for *them*. Several thousand food humans are supplied to that city every day! Only in the zoo can you be an ornamental, saved from being food. All humans aspire to this.'

The world seemed suddenly changed into a grim, sinister meat locker. We were thoroughly desperate, and despairing. I was ready to give up on survival, had already begun to plan how to end my life, when Emma pointed skyward and cried, 'Look!'

And there it was, a shining celestial body. It had, until a moment before, been hiding in the morning sun's brilliance. Now we could see it clearly. It was orbiting fast, fast enough for us to perceive it moving. Watching carefully, I could see it wasn't just a point of light, but a mass with definite shape.

'The Demon Star,' the captain said. 'A tourist scientist says they are researching it. They say it was on a collision course with Earth, long ago, and their Savior used a violent explosion to push it away. The tourists claim their ancestors thus avoided extinction. They say there is a crater from this fateful explosion still on the Demon Star's surface. Look there . . .' The captain pointed toward the distant city, at its tallest tower. 'That is the cathedral. The tourists worship their Savior inside.'

'Do you know where we come from?' I said. I couldn't help it.

The captain shook his head. He wasn't interested. Curiosity belonged to the apex species, it seemed. These humans didn't have it. They might as well have been ants or bees.

'Evolutionary fate is callous,' I said to Emma, to myself, maybe even to those other humans who could never understand me. 'Callous and unfeeling. Indifferent. Humanity once enjoyed good fortune. We were lucky and we didn't even know it. But now . . . well, we're not ants or bees, not yet. We still have opportunities, and we should seize them, and not yield to fate.'

'You're right,' Emma said. 'We've changed history once, if unintentionally. Why not change it again?'

I looked at the distant, towering cathedral, then pointed at the pod of dinosaurs and asked the captain, 'Those . . . tourists. They must really worship their Savior, right?'

The captain nodded. 'As far as they are concerned, the Savior is supreme.'

Emma and I connected to the computer through our retinal screens. We retrieved the ship's flight files, finding every detail of the course alteration 65 million years ago, including data and images. Everything had been recorded.

'Can you speak their language?' Emma asked the captain, who nodded.

'Excellent,' I said. 'Tell them we are the Saviors who pushed away the Demon Star. Tell them we have irrefutable proof.'

The captain and his crew stared at us, dumbfounded.

'Quickly, if you don't mind! Later I'll tell you the other story of humanity, but for now, please relay our message to the tourists, and be quick about it!'

The captain cupped his hands around his mouth and yelled in the dinosaurs' direction. His voice was tenuous and weak compared with their howls. It was hard to believe he was speaking their language.

But the pod of dinosaurs immediately stopped playing. They turned their heads toward us as one, and as one they swam toward our big ship.

BUTTERFLY

The modern study of chaos began with the creeping realization in the 1960s that quite simple mathematical equations could model systems every bit as violent as a waterfall. Tiny differences in input could quickly become overwhelming differences in output – a phenomenon given the name 'sensitivity dependence on initial conditions.' In weather, for example, this translates into what is only half-jokingly known as the Butterfly Effect – the notion that a butterfly stirring the air today in Peking can transform storm systems next month in New York.

. . . Sensitive dependence on initial conditions was not an altogether new notion. It had a place in folklore:

For want of a nail, the shoe was lost;
For want of a shoe, the horse was lost;
For want of a horse, the rider was lost;
For want of a rider, the battle was lost;
For want of a battle, the kingdom was lost!

—James Gleick, *Chaos: Making a New Science*

March 23, Belgrade

Four-year-old Katya heard the first few explosions from her sickroom on the fifth floor of the Children's Hospital. She looked out the window, but the night sky appeared unchanged. Louder and more frightening than the dull blasts was the tumultuous sound of footsteps in the corridors, which seemed to shake the whole building.

Katya's mother Elena picked up her daughter and ran out of the room. They joined the crowd rushing through the ward in the direction of the basement. Her father Aleksandar and his Russian friend Reznik exited the room close behind them, but split off and ran upstairs, against the stream of people. Elena did not notice them. Over the past year, she had devoted her body and soul to Katya's care. She had donated one of her own kidneys in order to save her daughter from the ravages of uremia. Today was the day Katya was to be discharged from the hospital, and Elena's joy at her daughter's new lease on life overrode any concerns about the outbreak of war.

But this was not the case for Aleksandar. When the explosions quieted, war would occupy his entire life. He stood next to Reznik on the roof of the building and surveyed the fires flickering to life in the distance. Overhead, the tracers of the antiaircraft guns punctuated the night with brilliant ellipses.

'There is a joke,' said Aleksandar, 'about a family who had a lovely, stubborn daughter. One day, the military erected barracks next to their home. The privates stationed there were a rakish bunch, and they often teased the girl, which caused her father to worry to no end. Before long, someone told him his daughter was pregnant! Upon hearing the news, he let out a long sigh of relief and said, 'Thank god, it finally happened.''

'That is not a Russian joke,' frowned Reznik.

'I didn't understand it at first either, but now I get it. When the thing you have feared for a long time happens, sometimes it comes as a relief.'

'You are not God, Aleksandar.'

'Or so I have been reminded by the bastards in the Department of Defense,' Aleksandar replied dryly.

'You are saying you went to the government? They did not believe you could find the atmospheric sensitivity points?'

'Can you believe it?'

'Not at first, but I came around once I saw how your mathematical model operated.'

'Nobody there will look closely at my model, but they mostly don't believe me anyway.'

'But you are not opposed to the party.'

'I'm not anything! I'm not interested in politics. Maybe it's because I mouthed off during the civil war years.'

By now, the sound of explosions had ceased, but the fires in the distance had grown brighter, suffusing the two tallest buildings in the city with a dull red glow. The towers stood on opposite banks of the Sava River. In New Belgrade, the white façade of the headquarters of the Socialist Party of Serbia stood out against the flames. Across the river loomed the specter of the Belgrade Palace, its black exterior indistinct, like a strange reflection of the first building.

'Theoretically speaking, your model might work, but there is something you may have overlooked,' Reznik mused. 'To calculate one sensitivity point for the weather of the whole country and its activation mechanism, even with all of Yugoslavia's fastest computers, would take a month or more to complete.'

'That is exactly the reason I came to find you. I want to use that computer of yours in Dubna.'

'What makes you so certain I will agree?'

'I'm not certain. But your grandfather was a military adviser to Tito, and he was wounded at the Battle of Sutjeska.'

'Fine. But how will I obtain the initial atmospheric data for the entire globe?'

'It's public. You can download it from the World Meteorological Network. The feed aggregates real-time data from every weather satellite around the world, as well as every participating observation point on land and sea. It's a huge volume of data, though, so a phone line won't cut it. You'll need a dedicated cable with a transmission rate of at least a million bits per second.'

'This I have.'

Aleksandar handed Reznik a small briefcase with a combination lock. 'Everything God himself might possibly need is inside, but the CD is the most important thing. I burned a copy of my atmospheric modeling software, about six hundred megabytes, or almost the entire capacity of the disc. It's the uncompiled C language source code, so your monster machine ought to be able to run it,' he explained. 'There's also a satellite phone connected to a modified GPS receiver. With this, you can see my precise location anywhere on Earth.'

Reznik took the case and said, ‘I leave tonight for Romania to catch a flight to Moscow. If everything goes smoothly, I will call you on the satellite phone by this time tomorrow to share the details of your miracle sensitivity point. But I doubt its effect can be amplified as planned. Commanding the elements is really best left to God.’

After Reznik departed, Aleksandar left the hospital and returned home with his wife and daughter. When they reached the confluence of the Sava and Danube Rivers, he stopped the car, and the three of them got out to quietly observe the dark surface of the water.

After a long silence, Aleksandar spoke: ‘I said once that when war broke out, I would have to leave home.’

‘Are you scared of the bombs, Papa? Take me with you, I’m scared, too. They are really loud!’ said Katya.

‘No, sweetie, I am going to find a way to stop the bombs from falling on our land. Papa may have to go somewhere far away, so he can’t bring Katya. Actually, Papa doesn’t even know where he will go.’

‘How will you stop the bombs from falling? Can you find a strong army to protect us?’

‘There’s no need for an army, Katya. Papa just needs to do one little thing at the right time and right place on Earth, like pouring a bucket of hot water or smoking a cigar, and all of Yugoslavia will be covered by clouds and fog. Then the bombs and the people who drop them won’t be able to find their targets!’

‘Why are you telling her this?’ Elena cut in.

‘It doesn’t matter. No one will believe her, including you.’

‘A year ago, you went to the Australian coast and turned on an industrial fan, under the delusion that this would bring rain to dusty Ethiopia . . .’

‘I didn’t succeed that time, but it wasn’t because of errors in my theory or my mathematical model. I didn’t have a computer that was fast enough, so in the time it took to calculate the sensitivity point, atmospheric variation had already desensitized it!’

‘Aleksandar, you are always living in a dream! But I will not stand in your way. I would not have married you if those dreams had not moved me once . . .’ Elena recalled the past in mute sorrow. She had been born into a Muslim household in Bosnia. Five years ago, when she fled the besieged city of Sarajevo and wed her Serbian college classmate, her obstinate father and brother had nearly turned their Kalashnikovs on her.

After he drove Elena and Katya home, Aleksandar turned his car toward Romania. It was not an easy drive. The road was snarled with checkpoints and wartime traffic, and he did not cross the border until noon the next day. It was smooth sailing thereafter, and he arrived at Bucharest Otopeni International Airport before nightfall.

March 25, Dubna

One hundred miles to the north of Moscow, there was a small town untainted by the decadence and decline of the capital. The spruce little town reposed amid meadows and dappled shade. Here, the passage of time had stopped, as evidenced by scattered busts of Lenin. At the entrance to the town, the mouth of the tunnel that ran beneath the Volga River was still adorned with a Soviet-era slogan in big letters: LABOR IS GLORIOUS. Sixty thousand people lived here, and almost all of them were scientists. The town was called Dubna, and it was home to the former Soviet Union's research center for high technology and nuclear weapons.

In the center of town stood a newly constructed building, whose elegant, even avant-garde appearance offered a striking contrast to the Soviet-style architecture around it. There was a fully enclosed computer lab on the second floor of the building, which was unexpectedly equipped with an American-made Cray supercomputer. Although it was an older model, at the time it belonged to the list of equipment strictly prohibited from export to the Eastern Bloc under the now-defunct COMECON. Four years prior, with Russia's cooperation, the United States, the United Kingdom, Germany, and France jointly established a high-technology research center. It was the Western countries' hope that generous compensation and a good research environment might tempt Russian scientists away from non-Western countries, particularly those nuclear physicists who could otherwise earn only a measly hundred US dollars per month. At the same time, Russia and the West would share the fruits of the center's research. The building in Dubna was merely a branch facility of the larger center. Due to Russia's lagging supercomputing infrastructure, researchers faced considerable operational difficulties. To remedy the situation, the Americans installed the Cray supercomputer. The huge machine was controlled by US engineers, who were also responsible for vetting any software that ran on it.

If the computer could feel, it would certainly have felt lonely. Since it had taken up residence here three years ago, the vast majority of its time was spent idling, or periodically running self-diagnostic tests. There were a handful of graduate students from the Moscow State University College of Electronics who occasionally fed it computation programs via the terminal on the first floor, but if it ever slept, it might have handled those programs in its sleep just as easily.

Late in the evening of March 25, the Cray supercomputer received a program written in C language from the network terminal, followed by a compilation command. It was an enormous piece of software – the largest it had ever seen, in fact – but the computer remained unenthused. It had seen programs containing more than ten million lines of code before, only to discover at runtime that most of the code represented mechanized loops and pixel conversions, designed to generate uninspired 3-D animation models. It launched the compiler and began absently translating line after line of C code into the ones and zeros of its native tongue, funneling the unimaginably long string of numbers into external storage. Just as it finished compiling the code, it received a command to execute. The computer immediately sucked the mountain of ones and zeros it had spat out only moments before back into its internal memory. Plucking a fine thread from the tangled skein of code, it began to run the program.

There was a sharp, involuntary intake of breath and a shudder from the Cray supercomputer. In an instant, the program had spawned over a million high-order matrices, three million ordinary differential equations, and eight million partial differential equations. The little mathematical monsters stretched their greedy maws wide and waited for the initial data. Soon, a torrent of data began to surge through a separate 10 Mbps transmission channel. The computer could just barely distinguish the elements that composed the flood – set after set of pressure, temperature, and humidity parameters. The initial data, like incandescent lava, flowed into the sea of matrices and equations and set everything to a seething boil. Each of the supercomputer's thousand-plus CPUs reached maximum capacity. A typhoon of logic howled across the vast electronic world of its memory, whipping up turbid, monstrous waves of data.

The storm lasted for forty minutes, which, to the computer, seemed like centuries. At last, it let out a breath. Stretching its power to the limit, it narrowly conquered the raging world within. The typhoon slackened, and the breakers gradually subsided. Soon, the typhoon dispersed completely, and the sea began to solidify and shrink rapidly. It finally condensed into a tiny kernel of data, which twinkled continuously in the boundless void of the computer's internal memory. Then, the seed split open, displaying a few lines of data on the screen of the first-floor terminal.

From where he sat in front of the screen, Reznik picked up the satellite phone.

'The first sensitivity point has appeared. It is drifting in the area bounded by latitudes twenty-two degrees and twenty-five degrees north and longitudes thirteen degrees and fifteen degrees west. Activation mechanism: Sharply cool the sensitivity point. Where is it? Let me see. . . . Oh! You must go to Africa, Aleksandar!'

March 27, Mauritania

As the helicopter skimmed low over the sunbaked desert, Aleksandar thought he might suffocate in the sweltering heat. The pilot, however, seemed completely unfazed. He kept up a steady stream of chatter the entire way. This peculiar white man had piqued his curiosity. After stepping off his flight at Nouakchott International Airport, the man had immediately engaged the service of his light helicopter. Then, he had purchased a freezer from a restaurant next to the terminal, in which he placed a large block of ice. Finally, he had loaded both the freezer and a large sledgehammer into the helicopter. The man could not identify his destination, and had simply directed him to fly the helicopter into the desert in the direction in which he pointed. He kept a large, strange-looking phone pressed to his ear the entire flight. The phone was connected to what looked like a game console. The pilot had seen a similar device when he had worked for a copper-prospecting team, and he knew it was a GPS receiver.

'Hey, friend, you came from Cairo?!' the pilot shouted over the pulsing roar of the engine in stilted French.

'I came from the Balkans, and changed planes in Cairo,' answered Aleksandar, only half listening.

'*Pardon?* The Balkans! There's a war on, yes?'

'Seems like it.'

Six thousand kilometers away, Reznik's voice in Aleksandar's earpiece informed him that his position was clear. The sensitivity point had stabilized, and was currently drifting very slowly at a distance of five kilometers.

'The Americans have dropped many bombs there, even Tomahawks, no?' The pilot imitated the sound of a missile whizzing overhead, followed by a cartoonish explosion. 'Hey, friend, do you know how much one Tomahawk costs?'

'One and a half million US dollars, I think.'

Aleksandar, pay attention. Just thirty-five hundred meters to go.

'Wow! White people are always so extravagant. That much money here could build a plantation, or a reservoir. It could feed a lot of people, no?'

Three thousand meters, Aleksandar!

The pilot continued. 'Why is America fighting? You don't know?! Oh, I heard Milošević killed four thousand people in someplace called Kosovo . . .'

Two thousand meters, Aleksandar. It's drifting again, to the left!

'Turn left!' barked Aleksandar.

'. . . what? Left? Okay, is this all right?'

Aleksandar repeated the question to Reznik. *Ah, too far to the left.* 'Too far, bring it back a little bit!'

'You should give me a clear direction,' the pilot grumbled. 'Are we okay now?'

'Okay, Reznik?' Aleksandar muttered into the satellite phone. *Dead ahead, Aleksandar. Fifteen hundred meters to go.* 'Perfect, hold it steady. Thank you, friend.'

'Do not mention it. You are paying me a very fair price! Oh, as I was saying, he killed four thousand people. But, do you remember, two years ago there was killing in Africa, too . . .'

One thousand meters!

'. . . in Rwanda . . .'

Five hundred meters!

'. . . killed five hundred thousand people . . .'

One hundred meters!

'. . . did anyone care? . . .'

Aleksandar, you are on top of the sensitivity point!

'Land the helicopter!' Aleksandar interrupted.

'. . . you have probably already forgotten it . . . what, land it? Here? Got it! I hope the sand will not trap the landing skids . . . Okay, you have arrived. Wait a moment before you get out, or you will be blinded!'

With the pilot's assistance, Aleksandar lifted the freezer down from the cabin, and then pulled out the ice block that had already started to melt and placed it on the sand. All around them, the desert shimmered in the blistering heat.

'Take care not to burn yourself,' chuckled the pilot, as Aleksandar raised the sledgehammer over the ice.

For my suffering homeland, I flap the wings of a butterfly . . .

He silently mouthed the phrase in Serbian, his eyes half closed. Then, he brought the hammer crashing down onto the ice, shattering the block into glittering shards, which melted on contact with the sand, like a fleeting reverie. A cool, invigorating draft rose and dispersed, quickly engulfed by the hot desert air.

'What on earth are you doing, friend?' The pilot eyed him with a bemused look on his face.

'A ritual of sorts. A totemic rite, like your fire dances,' laughed Aleksandar, wiping sweat from his brow.

'The ritual, and that mysterious spell – you are praying to your god for something?'

'Rain and fog, rain and fog to cover my distant homeland.'

March 29, Belgrade

It was Katya's best night of sleep yet. Her body had rejected her new kidney, and she had grown feverish. After her mother asked a neighbor who worked as a nurse to administer an immunosuppressant injection brought back from the hospital, she felt a little better. More importantly, that evening, the thunder of explosions diminished to a few scattered rumbles, and the residents of their apartment building did not bolt to the basement at midnight to wait for dawn. The next day, Katya discovered the reason why.

That morning, Katya got up late. It was already past eight, but it was still very dark outside. She went out onto the balcony and saw that the sky was overcast with dark, heavy clouds. Streamers of mist twined through the trees.

'My God . . .' Elena uttered a low cry at the sight.

'Mama, did Papa do this?'

'Probably not. But if it stays cloudy for a few weeks, then maybe he really did it.'

'Where is Papa now?'

'I don't know. He is a butterfly, winging his way around the world.'

'There are no butterflies that ugly!' Katya pronounced. 'Anyway, I don't like cloudy days.'

March 29, Allied Air Forces Combat Directive No. 1362

Sent from: AIRCOM Operations Center.

Full text distributed to: AFSOUTH, SETAF, and Commanding General, US 6th Fleet.

Intelligence Report M441 from sources EAM and NM proved erroneous (see Field Conditions Database 'ASD119,' meteorological section), and was corrected in Intelligence Report M483.*

Combat Directives No. 1351, No. 1353, and No. 1357 are hereby amended as follows.

The following section was distributed to all Forward Operating Bases in: Italy (Comiso, Aviano, Caserma Ederle, La Maddalena, Sigonella, Brisindi) and Greece (Souda Bay, Iraklion, Athens, Nea Makri).

It was also forwarded to: Mediterranean Carrier Strike Group.

*Cancel all B3** strikes issued under Combat Directives No. 1351 and No. 1357 against target groups GH56, IIT773, NT4412,*

---

* EAM and NM refer respectively to the US Air Force Europe Weather Agency and the US National Weather Service.

** Refers to laser-guided missiles and television-guided missiles.

BBH091145, LO88, 1123RRT, and 691HJ (indexed under 'TAG471' in Target Database).

Continue B3 strikes issued under Combat Directive No. 1353 against target groups PA851 and SSF67 (see index above).

A2 strikes issued under Combat Directives No. 1351, No. 1353, and No. 1357 remain in effect.*

The following section was distributed to: Aviano Air Base.

Increase low-altitude observation flights to evaluate the AF3 effects of the remaining B3 strikes.

TOP SECRET

Number of Copies: 0

March 29, Dubna

'Aleksandar, Aleksandar! Listen, the second sensitivity point has formed, between latitudes twenty-nine degrees and thirty degrees north and longitudes one hundred and thirty-three degrees and one hundred and thirty-four degrees west. It is moving fast, but it is stabilizing. Activation mechanism: Violently disturb the water. Oh, it is out at sea, you know.'

March 31, Off the West Coast of the Ryukyu Islands

The surface of the sea was calm and smooth like blue satin. The little fishing vessel was traveling at full speed, cutting a long, foaming wake behind it.

On the aft deck, an Okinawan fisherman, skin dark from exposure, was busy wrapping a bundle of TNT in waterproof paper. His equally leathery partner had set about connecting the electric blasting cap that was strapped to the explosive to an igniter with a long fuse wire. Aleksandar stood to the side and looked on. The two men chatted while they worked. Out of respect for Aleksandar, they spoke in accented but fluent English. Like the rest of the world, their discussion revolved around war.

---

* Refers to Tomahawk cruise missiles.

'I think it's good news for us,' said one of the men. 'Sets a precedent. If a problem with North Korea or Taiwan arises in the future, our Saberhawks and the Americans' aircraft carrier can cruise up, guns blazing. Magnificent!'

'Fucking Americans, I can't stand them! They can get the hell out of Okinawa, and they can take their noisy planes, too!'

'Use your head, you idiot. If there was no military base, who would buy our fish? More importantly, you're Japanese. You should consider what's best for Japan.'

'How do I put this? Iwata-kun, you and I are different. Your family came over from Kyushu ten years ago, but as for me, my family has lived in Okinawa for generations. It was once an independent kingdom, which makes you and the Americans outsiders.'

'Hirose-kun, just listen to yourself. Governor Ota is full of shit, and you're not the first person he has led astray. . . . Oh, mister, it's ready.'

Aleksandar carried the neatly wrapped explosive to the stern. Pressing the satellite phone to his ear, he waited.

'Mister, if you want to catch fish with that thing, listen to me and pick a different direction!'

'I don't want to blast any fish, just the water,' replied Aleksandar.

'It's your money, so we'll do it your way, of course. There are more and more weirdos like you visiting Okinawa these days.'

Aleksandar, Aleksandar! You are on top of the sensitivity point! Create a disturbance!

Aleksandar cast the explosive into the sea.

'Careful! Don't let the wire foul the propeller!' yelled one of the fishermen, as the fuse wire uncoiled and snaked rapidly over the stern. Aleksandar placed a finger on the trigger button.

For my suffering homeland, I flap the wings of a butterfly . . .

There was a dull, shuddering roar from beneath the surface, and a huge column of water erupted thirty meters from the stern, white spray glittering in the sunlight. The great mass of water fell back into the sea, and the surface boiled and frothed for a time, but soon everything was quiet again.

'I told you you wouldn't catch anything,' muttered one of the Okinawans, gazing at the smooth patch of sea.

April 1, Belgrade

'Mama, it's been cloudy for three days now! It must be Papa!' exclaimed Katya from where she stood by the window.

The pale sky of the last two days had grown dark and steely, and the clouds pressed low against the city. The white tower and the black palace, shrouded in fog, stood sentry over the Sava River in the drizzling rain.

Elena shook her head. 'I am convinced it is an act of God.'

April 1, Airspace over Yugoslavia, F-117 Attack Squadron

Forward Air Controller: 'Black Beauty, Black Beauty, you are flying over your target.'

F-117: 'Cyclops, Cyclops, target visibility is zero. I am flying above the clouds at forty-five hundred meters.'

Forward Air Controller: 'I am flying below the clouds at eighteen hundred meters. I have just tested the laser target designator. The target cannot be identified with sufficient accuracy to initiate an airstrike. The fog is too thick.'

F-117: 'Cyclops, test television guidance.'

Forward Air Controller: 'Testing television guidance . . . Black Beauty, the target can be identified with sufficient accuracy. You will have to descend through the cloud layer to attack. Cloud base over the target is at two thousand meters.'

F-117: 'I am ready to strike. Cyclops, please record blast damage.'

Forward Air Controller: 'Black Beauty, Black Beauty, do not descend! Artillery fire is heavy below the clouds, and I am detecting Tamala radiation* on the ground!'

F-117: 'Cyclops, I am going in low. We cannot return empty-handed again!'

---

* Tamala radar was a system produced by the Czechs that utilized unique 'passive detection' methods. It was said to be capable of detecting F-117 and B-2 stealth fighter jets, and also, that it was deeply feared by the Allied Air Forces.

Forward Air Controller: 'Black Beauty, pull up! Remember the rules of engagement! Major Grant, do you want to be court-martialed?!'

Grant pulled the control stick back toward his chest, and then tilted it to the right. The angular black body of the F-117 rose lazily upward and then made a sudden, sharp turn, streaking across the vast expanse of clouds in the direction of Italy. Inside his helmet, Grant sighed.

Damn, before I took off from Aviano, I signed my name on those two MK-12 laser-guided bombs below me.

April 1, Allied Air Forces Combat Directive No. 1694

From: AIRCOM Operations Center.

Full text distributed to: AFSOUTH, SETAF, and CG, US 6th Fleet.

Intelligence Reports M769 and M770 from sources EAM and NM proved erroneous for a second time (see Field Conditions Database 'ASD119,' meteorological section). The intelligence reliability rating of the aforementioned sources has been reduced from T1 to T3.

Combat Directives No. 1681 through No. 1690 are hereby amended according to Post-Strike Aerial Damage Assessment ND224 and ground intelligence from S24.

The following section was distributed to all Forward Operating Bases in Italy (Comiso, Aviano, Caserma Ederle, La Maddalena, Sigonella, Brisindi) and Greece (Souda Bay, Iraklion, Athens, Nea Makri).

It was also forwarded to: Mediterranean Carrier Strike Group.

Cancel all B3 strikes issued under Combat Directive No. 1681 and all subsequent Directives against target groups TA67 through TA71, 110LK, TU81, GH1632, SPT4418, MH703, and BR45 through BR67 (indexed under 'TAG471' in Target Database).

TOP SECRET

Number of Copies: 0

April 2, Dubna

'Aleksandar, the third sensitivity point! Region: Bounded by latitudes seventy-six degrees and seventy-seven degrees south and longitudes ninety-two degrees and ninety-three degrees east. Activation mechanism: Sharply raise the temperature of the sensitivity point.

'You must go to Antarctica, friend. First go to Puerto Natales, Patagonia, but do not charter a vessel. There is not enough time! I have a friend there who was on the team that conducted the last survey of the Antarctic ozone hole. He is very resourceful. He has a private plane, and can fly you directly to the sensitivity point in Marie Byrd Land. He might still have a foothold there. It may take some time for you to catch up to this sensitivity point, and when you do, the effect of the second point will likely have faded. We must let the skies over your country clear up for two or three days. But do not worry – this sensitivity point is very stable. It will not drift too far, and it can last for a long time, which may be related to Antarctica's constant freezing temperatures. More importantly, it can be activated multiple times! This way, you can stay there – naturally, it will not be very comfortable – and in half a month clouds and fog will cover the Balkans!

'Well done, Aleksandar, unbelievably well done!'

April 4, Belgrade

'It's sunny, Mama!' squealed Katya, looking at the blue sky from the balcony.

Elena released a small sigh. 'Aleksandar, you're not really the Messiah.'

There was a huge roar followed by the sound of rattling glass. Another roar, and dust showered down from the ceiling.

'Katya, we need to get to the basement!'

'No,' whined the little girl, 'I like sunny days!'

April 6, Marie Byrd Land, Antarctica

'What a pure and quiet world! I could stay here forever,' exclaimed Aleksandar.

From two thousand meters above, the endless ice sheet was tinged with a faint, bewitching blue by the hazy sun on the horizon.

The pilot, a strapping Argentinian man named Alfonso, glanced at Aleksandar and said, 'This purity will be gone soon. Tourism in Antarctica is developing rapidly. At first, it was limited to the Shetland Islands, but now it is expanding inland. Sea cruises and scenic flights are arriving in droves. My tour company is thriving, and I will never have to fish or ranch like my father's generation.'

'But it's not just tourism – isn't your government planning to allow immigration to the mainland?'

'Why not? After all, Argentina is the closest country to Antarctica! The world is going to leave this land battered and bleeding sooner or later, just like what's happening in the Balkans.'

Just then, Reznik's voice came over the satellite phone connection: *Aleksandar, we have a small problem. The Americans have closed off access to the Cray computer lab!*

'Do you think we've been detected?'

Not at all. I told them we were running a piece of global atmospheric modeling software, which is true. Relations with the West are strained right now, and the research center was bound to feel the effects. You stay put – I will straighten things out soon.

As the plane coasted to a halt on the snowy plain, Aleksandar saw a small cabin up ahead. The cabin was constructed from thermal insulation boards, and was raised on four upright posts to prevent the accumulation of snowdrifts.

'This was left here by a British survey team, and I fixed the place up a little,' said Alfonso, pointing to the outpost. 'There's enough food and fuel inside to last us a month.'

April 7, Belgrade

Katya's body had rejected the transplant again. The fever had returned, and the little girl mumbled fitfully in her sleep. The injections Elena had brought home on the day of Katya's discharge had been used up, and she would have to return to the hospital to replenish their supply. The hospital was all the way on the other side of the city.

It was another sunny day.

'Mama, tell me a story before you go.' Katya propped herself up in bed and took her mother's arm.

'Sweetie, Mama has already told you all the fairy tales she knows. Mama will tell you one last story, but Katya is a big girl now, and after this there will be no more.

'In the not-so-distant past, only three years before Katya was born, we lived in a much bigger country than we do now. Our country stretched almost all the way down the eastern shore of the Adriatic Sea. In this country, Serbians, Croatians, Slovenians, Macedonians, Montenegrins, and Bosnians were one big family. They lived together in peace and harmony, and treated each other like brothers and sisters . . .'

'Even the Albanians in Kosovo?'

'Yes, even the Albanians. A powerful man called Tito led our country. We were strong and proud, and our culture was rich and colorful. The whole world respected us . . .'

Elena stared absently at the patch of blue sky outside the window, tears glistening in the corners of her eyes.

'Then what happened?' asked Katya.

Elena stood. 'Child, stay at home and rest while I am gone. If the bombs come, listen to Uncle Letnić next door. Don't forget to put on more clothes before you go to the basement, or the cold and damp will aggravate your illness.' She picked up her bag and walked out the door.

'What happened to the country?' Katya called after her mother's retreating figure.

There was no gas in the family car, so Elena had to take a taxi. She had to wait much longer than usual, but she still managed to hail a passing cab. It was a relatively smooth ride. There were few other cars and people on the streets, and plumes of smoke were visible in the distance. When she arrived at the Children's Hospital, she discovered that the shelling had left the hospital without power. Nurses stood clustered in the premature infant station, delivering oxygen to the sealed incubators by hand. Medicine was in short supply, but she was able to retrieve the immunosuppressants Katya needed.

As soon as she had the drugs in hand, Elena rushed back. This time, she waited even longer for a taxi, and in the end, she had to catch a ride on a mostly empty bus. When she spotted the Danube River from the window, Elena let out a sigh of relief. She was already halfway home. The sky was vast and cloudless, and the city sat beneath it like a target painted on the surface of Earth.

'You are not the Messiah, Aleksandar,' Elena muttered inwardly.

The bus drove onto a bridge that spanned the Danube. In the absence of other traffic, it soon reached the center. A cool river breeze was blowing through the bus window, and Elena could not smell the gun smoke. Except for the distant trickles of smoke, the city seemed tranquil in the bright sunshine, perhaps even more so than before.

It was then that Elena saw it.

She saw it low above the ground in the distance. At first, it appeared as a black speck that flashed against the background of the blue sky; as it grew closer, she could make out its elongated form. It cruised through the air at a steady pace. Elena had not imagined that it would fly so slowly, as if it were searching for something. It dipped low over the river, tracing a graceful arc through the air. Elena had to peer downward to see it skimming along the river's surface. It was close enough that Elena could clearly see its smooth, innocuous exterior. It did not resemble the ferocious shark described by the newspapers; it was closer to a guileless, innocent dolphin that had leapt clear of the Danube's waters.

The Tomahawk missile struck the bridge and brought it crashing down into the Danube. Days later, when the overturned bus was removed from the river, rescue workers recovered the charred corpses of several passengers. Among them was the body of a woman, her arms still clutched tightly around a handbag that contained two boxes of injections. Even in death, she had protected the handbag well: half of the syringes had not shattered, and the prescription name was still visible on the labels of the boxes. The firefighter in charge of the salvage efforts remarked that it was an uncommon drug.

April 7, Marie Byrd Land, Antarctica

'I'll teach you how to dance the tango,' said Alfonso, and so he and Aleksandar sprang to their feet and whirled across the snow. Here, it was as if Aleksandar had stumbled onto another planet. In the perpetual twilight of the snowfield, he forgot the passage of time, even forgot the war.

'You dance quite well, but that is not a real Argentinian tango.'

'I can never get the head snaps right.'

'That's because you don't understand the meaning of the movements. When Argentinian cowboys first began to dance the tango, they did not move their heads. Later, the cowboys who crowded around to watch the dance grew jealous of the cowboys with pretty girls on their arms, so they began to pelt them with stones. So from then on, you had no choice but to stay vigilant and swivel your head in all directions.'

Aleksandar's laughter trailed off into a deep sigh. 'Yes, that's the way of the outside world.'

April 10, Dubna

'Aleksandar, things have gone south. The Western countries have halted all cooperation projects at the research center, and the Americans plan to dismantle and remove the Cray supercomputer. . . . I am trying to find a way to access another computer. There is a nuclear detonation simulation center in Dubna. It is a military facility, and they have a supercomputer there. A Russian-made machine might run more slowly, but it should be adequate to complete these calculations. But I need to run this idea by my superiors, and it might need to go even higher. Hold on for two more days! Though we cannot track it, I believe the sensitivity point is still in Antarctica!'

April 13, Belgrade

In the dim basement, which trembled with the force of the dull explosions above, Katya was fighting for every last breath.

The neighbors had exhausted every possibility. Two days prior, Uncle Letnić had sent his own son out to get the drugs, but the shelves of every hospital in the city were bare. The injections could only be imported from Western Europe – a virtual impossibility now.

There had been no news of Katya's mother.

In her stupor, Katya cried out for her mother over and over again, but it was her father who appeared in the remnants of her consciousness. He transformed into an immense butterfly, with wings as broad as football fields. As he ceaselessly flapped his enormous wings high overhead, the clouds and fog dissipated, and the sun shone brightly over Belgrade and the Danube . . .

'I like sunny days . . .' Katya mumbled.

April 17, Dubna

'Aleksandar, we have failed. I could not obtain access to the supercomputer. Yes, I appealed the matter to the highest level through my channels at the Academy of Sciences, but. . . . No, no, no. They did not say they disbelieved it, nor did they say they believed it. It is not important either way. I have been dismissed from my post. They drove off an academician like a stray dog, and you ask why? Because I played a part in all this. . . . Yes, they permitted a volunteer force to enter Yugoslavia, but what I did was different. . . . I do not know, either. They are politicians, and we will never be able to understand the inner workings of their minds, just like they will never understand us. . . . Don't be naïve. Believe me, it is absolutely impossible. There are only a few computers in the entire world that can complete such complicated calculations in a short time . . .

'Go home? No, do not go back. Katya . . . how can I tell you this, my friend? Katya passed three days ago. The rejection reaction took her in the end. Elena went to fetch medicine from the hospital eight days ago and never came back. No one has heard from her since . . . I do not know. It was not easy to get through to your home telephone. I heard this from your neighbors. Aleksandar, my friend, come to Moscow! Come to my home. We still have your software, at least, and it can change the world!

'Hello? Hello? Aleksandar!

'. . . . . .'

April 14, Marie Byrd Land, Antarctica

'Alfonso, you go back to Argentina. I want to be here alone.' Standing in front of the cabin on the snowfield, Aleksandar wore a sorrowful smile. 'Thank you for everything you have done. Truly, thank you.'

'You aren't from Greece, as Reznik claimed.' Alfonso stared at Aleksandar. 'You are from Yugoslavia. I don't know what you came here to do, but I am certain it is connected to the war.'

'I suppose it was, but it doesn't matter anymore.'

'I read it on your face when you were listening to the news on the radio. I saw that expression many times a decade ago on the Islas Malvinas. Back then I was a soldier, and I fought heroically. Yes, I was very brave. All of Argentina was very brave. We did not lack for courage and zeal, just a few Exocets. . . . I still remember the day we surrendered. It was cloudy on the island that day – cloudy and wet and cold. But it was not so bad, the British let us keep our guns.' Alfonso paused. 'Very well, friend, I will return in a few days. Do not stray too far from the cabin. There have been many storms lately.'

Aleksandar watched Alfonso's plane vanish into the white Antarctic sky, and then turned and went into the cabin. A moment later, he emerged with a bucket.

He never entered the cabin again.

Bucket in hand, Aleksandar walked aimlessly across the vast plain of snow. He did not know how much time had passed before he came to a halt.

. . . *Activation mechanism: Sharply raise the temperature of the sensitivity point.*

He opened the bucket, and fumbled for a lighter with frozen fingers.

For my suffering homeland, I flap the wings of a butterfly . . .

He lit the gasoline in the bucket, and then sat down in the snow and gazed at the rising flames. It was an ordinary fire. It lacked the intensity to activate the sensitivity point, and it would not bring clouds and fog to his homeland.

For want of a nail, the shoe was lost;
For want of a shoe, the horse was lost;
For want of a horse, the rider was lost;
For want of a rider, the battle was lost;
For want of a battle, the kingdom was lost!

July 10, AFSOUTH Headquarters, Italy

When it was all over, the weekend dance was reinstated, and the men could finally strip off the fatigues they had worn for three long months and don crisp dress uniforms. Between the grand marble columns of the Renaissance hall, the gold stars of the general officers and the silver stars of the field officers glimmered under the soft light of an enormous crystal chandelier. The ladies of Italian high society, who were not only glamorous but well-read and quick to engage in witty repartee, dotted the hall like blossoms. Together with the scintillating flow of wine, their presence made for an intoxicating night. Everyone congratulated themselves for having participated in such a glorious and romantic expedition.

When General Wesley Clark appeared in the company of his staff, the hall erupted into applause. The applause conferred upon him was not just in recognition of his meritorious service during the war. General Clark cut a tall, lean figure, and had the refined bearing of a scholar. He stood in marked contrast with the last war's General Schwarzkopf.

After two waltzes, the partygoers began to square dance. It was a popular dance within the Pentagon, but most of the ladies were unfamiliar with the steps, so the younger officers very enthusiastically began to teach them. General Clark decided to step out for a stroll. He left through a side entrance and came to a small lake in a vineyard. Another figure slipped out of the hall behind the general and followed him at a discreet distance. The general wound his way along the path through the secluded garden to the water's edge, seemingly entranced by the beautiful evening landscape.

But without warning, he spoke: 'Hello, Colonel White.'

The general's keen sixth sense caught White off guard, and he hastily stepped forward and saluted. 'You still recognize me, General, sir?'

General Clark did not turn to face him. 'I was very impressed by your work these past three months, Colonel. You and everyone else in the situation room have my thanks.'

'General, please forgive me for interrupting, but there is a matter I wish to discuss with you. It's . . . rather personal. If I don't raise it now, I'm afraid I may not get another chance.'

'By all means, tell me.'

'Over the first few days of the campaign, some of the meteorological intelligence from the target zone was . . . a bit unreliable.'

'Not unreliable, Colonel, just plain wrong,' corrected the general. 'We were left twiddling our thumbs through four days of rain and fog. If the forecast had been accurate, we would have delayed the first strike.'

The sun had set some time ago, and mountains in the distance cut black silhouettes against the lingering twilight. The lake was mirror-calm, and a gondolier's song drifted across the water. . . . It was a poor occasion for this sort of discussion, but the colonel knew this was his only opportunity, so he kept on talking.

'But some people will not let the matter drop. The Senate Armed Services Committee wants to know how the Air Force Weather Agency spent its two-billion-dollar budget over the last three years. They have formed an investigative subcommittee, and they want to hold hearings. It looks like they want to make a big show of it.'

'I don't want it to blow out of proportion, but someone needs to be held responsible, Colonel.'

White was sweating profusely. 'That's not fair, sir. Everyone knows forecasting is a tremendously random business. The atmosphere is a complex chaotic system, and it's almost impossible to predict its behavior . . .'

'Colonel, if I remember correctly, you are responsible for target discrimination, which bears no relation to meteorology.'

'That's right, sir, but . . . Colonel Katherine Davey of the USAF-E Weather Agency was responsible for meteorological intelligence in the Balkan target zone . . .' White hesitated. 'Uh, you've seen her, she often comes to the Operations Center.'

'Ah, yes, I remember, the doctor from Massachusetts.' Clark suddenly whirled around. 'Very tall, olive skin, slender legs – a beauty.'

'Yes, sir, I . . .' White began, but the general interrupted his stammering.

'Colonel, I recall you said this was a personal matter.'

White did not answer.

General Clark wore a stern expression. 'Colonel, not only do I remember your name, but I also remember that you are married. I also know that your wife is not Colonel Davey.'

'Yes, General, but . . . this is not America.'

General Clark nearly burst out laughing, but he held back. He could not bear to destroy the quiet beauty of the place.

Afterword: The events described in this story are beyond the realm of possibility, not because of the limitations of human ability, but because of fundamental impossibilities in the fields of physics and mathematics. One of the charms of science fiction, however, is that it can change the laws of nature and then show how the universe would operate according to those revisions.

DEVOURER

1
THE CRYSTAL FROM ERIDANUS

It was right in front of him, but the Captain could still barely make out its translucent crystalline structure. Floating through the black void of space, it was hidden by the darkness, like a piece of glass sunken in the murky depths. Only the slight distortion of starlight provoked by its passage allowed the Captain to make out its position. Soon it was lost again, disappearing in the space between the stars.

Suddenly the Sun distorted, its distant, eternal light twisting and twinkling before his eyes. It gave the Captain a start, but he maintained his proverbial 'Asian cool'. Unlike the dozen soldiers floating beside him, he managed not to gasp in shock. The Captain immediately understood; the crystal, a mere thirty feet away, had moved in front of the Sun, shining sixty million miles in the distance. In the three centuries to come, this strange vista would frequently play across his mind and he would wonder if this had been an omen of humanity's fate.

As the highest ranking officer of the United Nations' Earth Protection Force in space, the Captain commanded the force's interplanetary assets. It was a tiny unit, but it was equipped with the most powerful nuclear weapons humanity had ever devised. Its enemies were lifeless rocks hurtling through space: asteroids and meteorites that the early warning system had determined to be a threat to Earth. The mission of the Earth Protection Force was to redirect or to destroy these objects.

They had been on space patrol for more than two decades, yet they had never had a chance to deploy their bombs. All rocks large enough to warrant their use seemed to avoid Earth, wilfully denying them their chance for glory.

Now, however, a sweep had discovered this crystal at a distance of two astronomical units. The crystal's trajectory was as precipitous as it was utterly unnatural, propelling it straight toward Earth.

The Captain and his unit cautiously approached, their spacesuits' boosters spinning a web of trails around the strange object. Just as they closed to thirty feet, a misty light flashed to life inside the crystal, clearly revealing a prismatic outline about ten feet long. As the space patrol drew nearer, they could make out the intricate, crystalline pipes of its propulsion system. The Captain was now floating directly in front of it. Stretching his gloved right hand toward the crystal, he initiated humanity's first contact with extra-terrestrial intelligence.

As he reached out, the crystal became transparent once more. A brilliantly colored image now sprang to life inside it. It was a manga girl, with huge, rolling eyes and long hair that cascaded down to her feet. She was wearing a beautiful, flowing skirt and she seemed to drift dreamily in invisible waters.

'Warning! Alert! Warning! The Devourer approaches!' she shouted immediately, stricken with obvious panic. Her large eyes stared at the Captain, a lithe arm pointing away from the Sun in unmistakable alarm. There could be little doubt the unseen pursuer was hot on her dainty heels.

'Where do you come from?' the Captain enquired, by all appearances unperturbed.

'Epsilon Eridani, as you apparently call it, and by your reckoning of time I have traveled for sixty thousand years,' she replied, before again raising her cry. 'The Devourer approaches! The Devourer approaches!'

The Captain continued his enquiry. 'Are you alive?'

'Of course not. I am merely a message,' came the response. But it was only a short reprieve. 'The Devourer approaches! The Devourer approaches!'

'How is it that you can speak English?' the Captain continued.

The girl again replied without hesitation. 'I learned in transit,' she said, only to carry on: 'The Devourer approaches! The Devourer approaches!'

'And that you look as you do . . .?' The Captain let his question trail off.

'I saw it in transit,' she said, before continuing to shout with ever greater urgency. 'The Devourer approaches! The Devourer approaches! Oh, surely the Devourer must terrify you.'

'What is the Devourer?' the Captain finally asked.

'In appearance, it resembles a gigantic tire. Hm, yes, that would be an analogy that works for you,' the girl from Eridanus began her explanation.

'You are very well acquainted with how things work on our world,' the Captain interrupted, raising an eyebrow behind his visor.

'I became acquainted in transit,' the girl replied, before again crying out: 'The Devourer approaches!' With that last cry, she flashed to one end of the crystal. Where she had been a second ago an image of the 'tire' appeared, and it indeed closely resembled a tire, even though its surface glowed with phosphorescent light.

'How large is it?' one of the other officers queried.

'Thirty-one thousand miles in total diameter. The "tire"'s body is six thousand miles wide, and the hole in the middle has a diameter of nineteen thousand miles.'

There was a long pause before someone asked the question now on everyone's mind. 'Are the miles you are talking about *our* miles?'

The girl answered immediately and calmly. 'Of course. It is so large that it can encircle an entire planet, just as one of your tires might fit around a soccer ball. Once it has encased a world, it begins plundering the planet's natural resources, only to spit out the remains like a cherry pit when it is done!'

There was another pause before the officer spoke again, his voice quivering with trepidation. 'But we still do not understand what the Devourer really is.'

The girl in the crystal offered more information without hesitation. 'It is a generation ship, although we do not know where it came from or where it is going. In fact, even the giant lizards that pilot the Devourer surely do not know. Having wandered the Milky Way for tens of millions of years, they have certainly forgotten both their origin and their original purpose. But this much is certain: in the distant past, when the Devourer was built, it was much smaller. It eats planets in order to grow, and it devoured our world!'

As she fell silent, the image of the Devourer in the crystal grew, eventually dominating the screen's entire surface. It soon became apparent that it was slowly descending upon the unseen camera operator's world. Seen through the eyes of the planet's inhabitants, their world had become nothing more than the bottom of a slowly spinning, cosmic well. Complex structures were clearly visible, covering the walls of this titanic well. At first, they reminded the Captain of infinitely magnified microprocessor circuitry. Then he realized that they were an endless string of cities stretching the entire inner ring of the Devourer. Looking up, the image in the crystal revealed a circle of blue radiance emanating from the well's mouth. In the sky above, it formed a gigantic halo of fire, encircling the stars.

The girl from Eridanus told them that they were seeing the jets of the Devourer's aft ring engine. As she spoke, her entire body erupted into flowing tendrils, with even her cascading hair waving like countless twisting arms. Every last part of her expressed boundless terror.

'What you are seeing is the devouring of the third planet of Epsilon Eridani,' she told them. 'The first thing you would have noticed, had you been on our world then, was your body becoming lighter. You see, the Devourer's gravitational pull was powerful enough to counteract our planet's gravity. The destruction this wrought was devastating. First, our oceans surged to meet the Devourer as it passed over our planet's pole. Then, as the Devourer moved to fully encircle our world, the waters followed it to the equator. As the oceans swept the globe, the waves towered high enough to engulf the clouds.

'The incredible gravitational forces tore at our continents, ripping them apart as if they were nothing but tissue paper. Our sea floor and dry land were pockmarked by countless volcanic eruptions.' The girl paused in her narrative, only to pick it up with a flutter of her eyelids. 'Once it had encircled our equator, the Devourer stopped, perfectly matching our planet in its orbit around our Sun. Our world was right in its maw.

'When the plunder of a world commences, countless cables thousands of miles long are lowered from the Devourer's inner wall to the planet's surface below. An entire world is trapped, like a fly in the web of a cosmic spider. Giant transport modules are then sent back and forth between the planet and the Devourer, taking with them the planet's oceans and atmosphere. As they shuttle to and fro, other huge machines begin to drill deep into the planet's crust, frenziedly extracting minerals to satisfy the Devourer's hunger.' The girl paused again, her eyes staring intensely into the distance. She resumed as abruptly as she had stopped. 'Devourer and planet cancel out each other's gravity, creating a low-gravity zone between this tire-like entity and the planet. This zone makes it that much easier to bring the planet's resources to the Devourer. The epic plunder is extremely efficient.

'Expressed in Earth time, the Devourer only needs to chew on a world for a century or so. After it is done, all of the planet's water and its atmosphere will have been reduced to nothing. As the Devourer ravages, its gravity will also eventually deform the planet, slowly stretching it along its equator. In the end, the planet will become . . .' the girl paused a third time, this time struggling for words rather than for effect, 'how would you call it? Yes, disc-shaped. The Devourer, having sucked the planet completely dry, will move on, spitting the planet out. When it leaves, the planet will return to its spherical shape. As it re-forms, the entire world will suffer a final global catastrophe, its surface resembling the molten sea of magma that heralded its birth many billions of years ago. Much like then, no trace of life will survive this inferno.'

'How far is the Devourer from our solar system?' the Captain asked as soon as she finished.

'It is just behind me!' she warned urgently. 'In your reckoning, it will arrive in a mere century! Alert! The Devourer approaches! The Devourer approaches!'

2

EMISSARY FANGS

Just as the debate over the crystal's credibility began to rage in earnest, the first small Devourer ship entered the solar system. It was heading straight toward Earth.

The first contact was again initiated by the space patrol led by the Captain. The mood of this contact could not have been more different than the last, and the mood was, by far, not the only contrast. The exquisitely wrought structure of the Eridanus Crystal bore all the hallmarks of the ethereal technology of a refined civilization. The Devourer's ship was the polar opposite. Its exterior appeared exceedingly crude and ungainly, somewhat like a frying pan that had spent the better part of a century forgotten in the wilderness. It immediately reminded onlookers of a giant steampunk machine.

The envoy of the Devourer Empire matched his vehicle in appearance: a massive, awkward lizard covered in huge slabs of scales. Erect, he stood nearly thirty feet tall. He introduced himself as 'Faingsh', but his appearance and later behavior quickly led to him being called 'Fangs' instead.

When Fangs landed at the feet of the United Nations Building, his craft's engines blasted a large crater, the splattering concrete leaving the surrounding buildings scarred and battered. Since the alien emissary's massive size prevented him from entering the Assembly Hall, the delegates gathered on the United Nations Plaza in front of the building to meet him. Some among them now covered their faces with bloody handkerchiefs, staunching foreheads gashed open by flying glass and concrete.

The ground shook with every step Fangs took toward them, and when the alien spoke, he roared. It was a sound like the screaming horns of a dozen train engines, and it made the hair of all who heard it stand on end. Although he had learned English in transit, Fangs spoke through an unwieldy translator hanging around his neck, the device repeating his words back in English. The rough male voice the translator produced, despite being much quieter than Fangs' real voice, nonetheless made his listeners' flesh crawl.

'Ha! Ha! You white and tender worms, you fascinating little worms,' Fangs began jovially.

All around, people covered their ears until the thunderous roar had ended, only removing their hands slightly to hear the translation.

'You and I will live together for a century, and I believe we shall come to like each other,' Fangs continued.

'Your honor, you must know that we are very concerned as to the purpose of your great mothership's arrival in our solar system!' the Secretary-General stated, raising his head to address Fangs. Even though he was shouting at the top of his lungs, he still managed to sound no louder than a mosquito's buzz.

Fangs adopted a human-like posture, raising himself on his hind legs. As he shifted his weight, the ground trembled. 'The great Devourer Empire will consume the Earth so that it may continue its epic journey!' he proclaimed. 'This is inevitable!'

'What, then, of humanity?' the Secretary-General asked, his voice quivering ever so slightly.

'That is something I will determine today,' Fangs replied.

In the pause that followed, the heads of state exchanged meaningful glances. The Secretary-General finally nodded and said, 'It is necessary that we discuss this fully amongst ourselves.'

Fangs shook his massive head, interrupting before they could speak further. 'It is a very simple matter: I must merely have a taste . . .'

And with that, his giant claw reached into the gathered crowd and snatched up a European head of state. He gracefully tossed the man, a throw of twenty-odd feet, straight into his mouth. Then he carefully began to chew. From the first crunch to the last, his victim remained completely mute; it was impossible to tell whether it was dignity or terror that stayed his screams.

In the terrible moments that followed, the only sound was that of the man's skeleton snapping and cracking between Fangs' giant, dagger-like teeth. After about half a minute, Fangs spat out the man's suit and shoes, much as a human might spit out watermelon seeds.

Even though the clothes were covered in oozing blood, they remained horrifyingly intact.

All the world seemed to have fallen completely silent, until a human voice broke the deathly quiet.

'How, sir, could you just pick him up and eat him?' the Captain asked as he stood amongst the crowd.

Fangs walked toward him with colossal, thundering steps. The crowd scattered in his wake. He stood before the Captain and lowered his gaze of pitch black, basketball-sized eyes until he was staring right at him. He asked, 'I shouldn't have?'

'Sir, how could you have known that you can eat him?' the Captain asked flatly. 'From a biochemical perspective, it is almost impossible that a being from such a distant world should be edible.'

Fangs nodded, his large maw almost seeming to grin. 'I have had my eye on you. You watched me with cool detachment, lost in thought. What is it that you were contemplating?'

The Captain returned his smile and replied, 'Sir, you breathe our air and speak using sound waves. You have two eyes, a nose and a mouth. You have four limbs arranged along a bilateral symmetry . . .' He let his thought drift off into silence.

'And you don't understand it?' Fangs asked, snaking his giant head right in front of the Captain's face. With a hiss, he exhaled a nauseating breath reeking of blood and gore.

'That is correct. I do understand the principles of the matter well enough to find it incomprehensible that we should be so similar,' the Captain answered, showing no signs of revulsion or fear.

'There is something I do not understand. Why are you so calm? Are you a soldier?' Fangs asked in response.

'I am warrior who defends of Earth,' the Captain answered.

'Hm, but does pushing around small stones really make you a warrior?' Fangs countered with more than a hint of mockery.

'I am ready for greater tests,' the Captain stated solemnly, lifting his chin.

'You fascinating little worm.' Fangs laughed, nodding. Raising his body to its full height, he turned back to the heads of state. 'But let us return to the real topic at hand: humanity's fate. You are tasty. There is a smooth and mild quality about you that reminds me of certain blue berries we found on a planet in Eridanus. I therefore congratulate you. Your species will continue. We will raise you as livestock in the Devourer Empire. We will allow you to live a good sixty years before we bring you to market.'

'Sir, do you not think that our meat will be too gamey at that age?' the Captain asked with a cold chuckle.

Fangs roared with laughter, his voice like an erupting volcano. 'Ha, ha, ha, ha! The Devourers like chewy snacks!'

3

ANTS

The United Nations engaged Fangs in several further meetings. Even though no one else was eaten, the verdict on humanity's fate remained unchanged.

A meeting was scheduled to take place at a meticulously prepared archaeological excavation site in Africa.

Fangs' ship landed right on schedule, about fifty feet away from the dig site. The deafening explosion and storm of debris that accompanied the craft's arrival had, by this point, become all too familiar.

The girl from Eridanus had advised them that the vessel's engine was powered by a miniature fusion reactor. The concept, like most of the information she had provided on the Devourers, was easy enough for the human scientists to understand; the things she told them about the technology of Eridanians, on the other hand, never failed to baffle the people of Earth. Her crystal, for example, began to melt in Earth's atmosphere. In the end, the entire section containing its propulsion system dissolved, leaving nothing but a thin slice of crystal floating gracefully through the air.

As Fangs arrived at the excavation site, two UN staffers presented him with a large album, a full square yard in size. It had been meticulously designed to accommodate the Devourer's huge stature. The album's hundreds of beautifully constructed pages revealed all aspects of human culture in brilliantly colored detail. In some ways, it resembled an opulent primer for children.

Inside the large pit of the excavation site itself, an archaeologist vividly described the glorious history of Earth's civilizations. He threw all his passion into his desperate attempt to make this alien understand, to comprehend that there was so much on this blue planet worth cherishing. As he spoke, his fervor moved him to tears. It was a pitiable spectacle.

Finally, he pointed to the excavation and intoned: 'Honorable emissary, what you see here are the newly discovered remains of a town. This fifty-thousand-year-old site is the oldest human settlement discovered to date. Could the hearts of your people truly be hard enough to destroy this magnificent civilization of ours? A civilization that has developed, step by slow step, over fifty thousand years?'

While all this was going on, Fangs was leafing through the album with obvious, playful amusement. As the archaeologist finished, Fangs raised his head and glanced at the excavation pit. 'Hey, archaeologist worm, I care neither for your hole nor your old city in the hole. I would, however, very much want to see the earth you removed from the pit,' he said, pointing at a large pile of dirt.

The archaeologist went from baffled to completely stunned as the artificial voice of the translator finished relaying Fangs' request. 'The earth?' he asked, fumbling for words. 'But there's nothing in that pile of dirt.'

'That is your opinion,' Fangs said, approaching the mound of dirt. Bending his gigantic body toward the ground, he reached into the pile with two of his huge claws and began digging. A circle of onlookers quickly formed, many gasping at the deceptive deftness of Fangs' seemingly unwieldy claws. Prodding the soft earth, he repeatedly retrieved tiny specks from the soil, only to place them on the album. Fangs seemed completely engrossed in this strange labor for a good ten minutes. Having finished whatever he had been up to, he carefully lifted the album with both claws and straightened his body. Walking toward the gathered humans, he gave them a chance to see what it was that he had placed on the album.

Only by looking very carefully could those gathered make out that it was hundreds of ants. They were gathered in a tight bunch: some alive, others curled up in death.

'I want to tell you a story,' Fangs said as the humans studied the ants. 'It is the story of a kingdom. This kingdom was descended from a great empire, and it could trace its ancestry all the way back to the ends of Earth's Cretaceous period, during which its founders built a magnificent city in the shadow of the towering bones of a dinosaur.' Fangs paused, deep in thought, before continuing. 'But that is long-lost, ancient history, and when winter suddenly fell only the last in a long line of queens remembered those glory days. It was a very long winter indeed, and the land was covered by glaciers. Tens of millions of years of vigorous life were lost as existence became ever more precarious.

'After waking from her last hibernation, the queen could not rouse even one out of every hundred of her subjects. The others had been entombed by the cold, some being frozen to nothing but transparent, empty shells. Feeling the walls of her city, the queen realized that they were as cold as ice and hard as steel. She understood that the Earth remained frozen. In this age of terrible cold, even summer brought no thaw. The queen decided it was time to leave the homeland of her ancestors and to seek out unfrozen earth to establish a new kingdom.

'And so the queen led her surviving subjects to the surface to begin their long and arduous journey in the shadow of looming glaciers,' Fang said. 'Most of her remaining subjects perished during their protracted wanderings, consumed by the deadly cold. But the queen and a few straggling survivors finally found a patch of earth that remained untouched by frost. Overflowing geothermal energy warmed this sliver of land. The queen, of course, knew nothing of this. She did not understand why there should be moist and soft soil anywhere in this frozen world, but she was in no way surprised that she had found it: a race that persevered through sixty million long years could never suffer extinction!

'In the face of a glacier-covered Earth and a dim Sun, the queen proclaimed that it was here that they would found a new mighty kingdom – a kingdom that would endure for all eternity. Standing under the summit of a tall, white mountain, she declared that this new kingdom would be known as the "Realm of the White Mountain",' he said grandly.

'In fact, the eponymous summit was the skull of a mammoth,' he continued. 'It was the zenith of the Late Pleistocene of the Quaternary Glaciation. In those days, you human worms were still dumb animals, shivering in your scattered caves. It would still be ninety thousand years before the first flicker of your civilization would appear a continent away on the plains of Mesopotamia.

'Living off the frozen remains of mammoths in the vicinity of the Realm of the White Mountain, the new settlement survived ten thousand hard years. Then, as the ice age ended, spring returned to Earth and the land was again draped in green. In this great explosion of life, the Realm of the White Mountain quickly entered a golden age of prosperity. Its subjects were beyond number, and they ruled a vast domain. Over the next ten thousand years the kingdom was ruled by countless dynasties, and countless epics told its stories.'

As he continued, Fangs pointed at the large pile of earth in front of them. 'That is the final resting place of the Realm of the White Mountain. As you archaeologist worms were preoccupied by your excavations of a lost and dead fifty-thousand-year-old city, you completely failed to realize that the soil above those ruins was teeming with a city that was very much alive. In scale it was easily comparable to New York, and the latter is a city on merely two dimensions. The city here was a grand three-dimensional metropolis with numerous layers. Every layer was densely packed with labyrinthine streets, spacious forums and magnificent palaces. The design of the city's drainage and fire prevention systems handily outshone those of New York.

'The city was home to a complex social structure and a strict division of labor,' he told his captive audience. 'Its entire society ran with machine-like precision and harmonious efficiency. The vices of drug use and crime did not exist here, and hence there was neither depravity nor confusion. But its inhabitants were by no means devoid of emotion, showing their abiding sorrow whenever a subject of the Realm passed away. They even had a cemetery on the surface at the edge of the city, and there they would bury their dead an inch under the ground.

'However, the greatest acclaim must be reserved for the grand library nestled in the lowest layer of this city. In this library, one could find a multitude of ovoid containers. Each container was a book filled with pheromones. The exceedingly complex chemistry of these pheromones stored the city's knowledge. Here the epics detailing the enduring history of the Realm of the White Mountain were recorded. Here you could have learned that in a great forest fire all the subjects of the kingdom embraced each other to form countless balls, and that, with heroic effort, they were able to escape a sea of fire by floating down a stream. You could have learned the history of the hundred-year war against the White Termite Empire or of the first time that an expedition from the kingdom saw the great ocean . . .' Fangs let his translator's voice trail off.

Then his booming voice rang out again. 'But it was all destroyed in three short hours. Destroyed when, with an earth-shattering roar, the excavators came, blackening the sky. Then their giant steel claws came cutting down, grabbing the soil of the city, utterly destroying it and crushing all within. They even destroyed the layer where all the city's children and the tens of thousands of snow-white eggs, yet to become children, rested.'

All of the world again seemed to have fallen deathly quiet. This silence outlasted the quiet that had followed Fangs' horrible feast. Standing before the alien emissary, humanity was, for the first time, at a loss of words.

Finally Fangs said, 'We still have a very long time to get along and very many things to talk about, but let us not speak of morals. In the universe, such considerations are meaningless.'

4
ACCELERATION

Fangs left the people at the dig site in a state of deep shock and despair. The Captain was again the first to break the silence. He turned to the surrounding dignitaries of all nations and said, 'I know that I am a mere nobody and that the only reason I am fortunate enough to attend these occasions is because I was the first to come into contact with the two alien intelligences. Nonetheless, I want to say a couple of things: first, Fangs is right; second, humanity's only way out is to fight.'

'Fight? Oh, Captain, fight . . .' The Secretary-General shook his head with a bitter simile.

'Right! Fight! Fight! Fight!' the girl from Eridanus shouted from her crystal pane as she flitted several feet above the heads of those assembled. In her sun-drenched crystal, the long-haired girl's entire body began writhing and flowing.

'You people from Eridanus fought them. How did that end?' someone called out. 'Humanity must think of its survival as a species, not of satisfying your twisted desire for vengeance.'

'No, sir,' the Captain said, turning to face the assembled crowd. 'The Eridanians engaged an enemy they knew nothing about in a war of self-defense. Furthermore, they were a society that had historically not known war. Given the circumstances, it is hardly surprising that they were defeated. Nonetheless, in a century of bitter warfare they meticulously acquired a deep understanding of the Devourer. We now have been handed that vast reservoir of knowledge by this spaceship. It will be our advantage.

'Careful preliminary studies of the material have shown that the Devourer is by no means as terrible as we had first feared,' he told them. 'Foremost, beyond the fact that it is inconceivably large, there is little about the Devourer that exceeds our understanding. Its life forms, the ten-billion-plus Devourers themselves, are carbon-based, just like us. They even resemble us on a molecular level, and because we share a biological basis with the enemy nothing about them will remain beyond our grasp. We should count our blessings; consider that we could just as well have been faced with invaders made of energy fields and the stuff of neutron stars.

'But there is even more cause for hope,' he said. 'The Devourer possesses very little, shall we say, 'super-technology'. The Devourer's technology is certainly very advanced when compared to humanity's, but that is primarily a question of scale, not of theoretical complexity. The main energy source of the Devourer's propulsion system is nuclear fusion. In fact, the primary use for water plundered from planets – beyond providing basic life support – is fuel for this system. The Devourer's propulsion technology is based on the principle of recoil and the conservation of momentum; it is not some sort of strange, space-time bending nonsense.' The Captain paused, studying the faces before him. 'All of this may dismay our scientists; after all, the Devourer, with its tens of millions of years of continuous development, clearly shows us the limits of science and technology, but it also clearly shows us that our enemy is no invincible god.'

The Secretary-General mulled over the Captain's words and then asked, 'But is that enough to ensure humanity's victory?'

'Of course, we have more specific information. Information that should allow us to formulate a strategy that will give a good shot at victory. For example—'

'Acceleration! Acceleration!' the girl from Eridanus shouted over their heads, interrupting the Captain.

The Captain explained her outburst to the baffled faces around him. 'We have learned from the Eridanian data that the Devourer ship's ability to accelerate is limited. The Eridanians observed it for two long centuries, and they never once saw it exceed this specific limit. To confirm this, we used the data we received from the Eridanian spaceship to establish a mathematical model that accounts for the Devourer's architecture and the material strength of its structural components. Calculations using this model verify the Eridanians' observations. There is a firm limit to the speed at which the Devourer can accelerate, and this limit is determined by its structural integrity. Should it ever exceed this mark, the colossus will be torn to pieces.'

'So what?' the head of a great nation asked, underwhelmed.

'We should remain level-headed and carefully consider it,' the Captain answered with a laugh.

5

THE LUNAR REFUGE

Humanity's negotiations with the alien emissary finally showed some small signs of progress: Fangs yielded to the demand for a lunar refuge.

'Humans are nostalgic creatures,' the Secretary-General had explained in one of their meetings, tears in his eyes.

'So are the Devourers, even though we no longer have a home,' Fangs had sympathetically answered, nodding his head.

'So, will you allow a few of us to stay behind? If you permit, they will wait for the great Devourer Empire to spit out the Earth after it has finished consuming the planet. After waiting for the planet's transformed geology to settle, they will return to rebuild our civilization.'

Fangs shook his gargantuan head. 'When the Devourer Empire consumes, it consumes completely. When we are done, the Earth will be as desolate as Mars. Your worm-technology will not be enough to rebuild a civilization.'

The Secretary-General would not be dissuaded. 'But we must try. It will soothe our souls, and it will be especially important for those of us in the Devourer Empire being raised as livestock. It will surely fatten them if they can think back on their distant home in this solar system, even if that home no longer necessarily exists.'

Fangs now nodded. 'But where will those people go while the Earth is being devoured? Besides Earth, we will also consume Venus. Jupiter and Neptune are too large for us to consume, but we will devour their satellites. The Devourer Empire is in need of their hydrocarbons and water. We will also take a bite out of the barren worlds of Mars and Mercury, as we are interested in their carbon dioxide and metals. The surfaces of all these worlds will become seas of fire.'

The Secretary-General had an answer ready. 'We can take refuge on the Moon. We understand that the Devourer Empire plans to push the Moon out of orbit before consuming the Earth.'

Fangs nodded. 'That is correct. The combined gravitational forces of the Devourer and the Earth will be very powerful. They could crash the Moon into our ship. Such a collision would be enough to destroy our Empire.'

The Secretary-General smiled ever so slightly as he replied. 'All right then, let a few of us live up there. It will be no great loss to you.'

'How many do you plan to leave behind?' Fangs queried.

'The minimum to preserve our civilization: one hundred thousand,' the Secretary-General answered flatly.

'Well then, you should get to work,' Fangs concluded.

'Get to work? What work?' the Secretary-General asked, perplexed.

'Pushing the Moon out of its orbit. For us, that is always a great inconvenience,' Fangs answered dismissively.

'But,' said the Secretary-General, grasping his hair in despair. 'Sir, that would be no different than denying humanity our meagre and pitiable request. Sir, you know that we do not possess such technological prowess!'

'Ha, worm, why should I care? And besides, don't you still have an entire century?' Fangs concluded with a chuckle.

6

PLANTING THE BOMBS

On the gleaming white plains of the Moon, a spacesuit-clad contingent stood next to a tall drilling tower. The emissary of the Devourer Empire stood somewhat apart, his giant frame another towering silhouette against the horizon. All eyes were firmly focused on a metal cylinder being slowly lowered from the top of the drilling tower down into the drill well below. Soon the cable was speeding into the well. On Earth, 240,000 miles away, an entire world was glued to the unfolding events. Then came the signal: the payload had reached the bottom of the well. All observers, including Fangs, broke into applause as they celebrated the arrival of this historic moment.

The last nuclear bomb that would propel the Moon out of orbit had been put in place. A century had passed since the Eridanus Crystal and the emissary of the Devourer Empire had arrived on Earth. For humanity, it had been a century of despair, a hundred years of bitter struggle.

In the first half of the century, the entire Earth had zealously thrown itself at the task of constructing an engine that could propel the Moon. The technology needed to build such an engine, however, utterly failed to materialize. All that was accomplished was that the Moon's surface had gained a few scrap metal mountains, the remains of failed prototypes. Then there were also the lakes of metal, formed where experimental engines had melted under the heat of nuclear fusion.

Humanity had asked Fangs for technological assistance; after all, the lunar engines would not even have to be a tenth of the scale of the countless super-engines the Devourer possessed.

Fangs, however, refused and instead quipped, 'Don't assume that you can build a planetary engine just because you understand nuclear fusion. It's a long way from a firecracker to a rocket. Truth be told, there is no reason at all for you to work so hard at it. In the Milky Way, it is perfectly commonplace for a weaker civilization to become the livestock of a stronger civilization. You will discover that being raised for food is a splendid life indeed. You will have no wants and will live happily to the end. Some civilizations have sought to become livestock, only to be turned down. That you should feel uncomfortable with the idea is entirely the fault of a most banal anthropocentrism.'

Humanity then placed all its hopes in the Eridanus Crystal, but again they were disappointed. The technology of the Eridanian civilization had developed along completely different lines from Earth's or those of the Devourer. Their technology was wholly based on their planet's organisms. The crystal, for example, was a symbiont to a kind of plankton that floated in their world's oceans. The Eridanians merely synthesized and utilized the unusual abilities of their planet's life forms without ever truly understanding their secrets. And so, without Eridanian life forms, their technology remained completely unworkable.

After over fifty valuable years were wasted, in desparation humanity suddenly produced an exceedingly eccentric scheme to propel the Moon. It was the Captain who first came up with this plan. At the time, he had a leading role in the Moon propulsion program and had advanced to the rank of marshal. Even though his plan was unapologetically illogical, its technological demands were modest and humanity's available technology was fully capable of making it work; so much so, in fact, that many were surprised that no one had come up with it earlier.

The new plan to propel the Moon was very simple: a large array of nuclear bombs would be installed on one side of the Moon. These bombs would, for the most part, be buried roughly two miles under the lunar surface. Their spacing would ensure that no bomb was destroyed by the blast of another. According to this plan, five million nuclear bombs were to be installed on the Moon's 'propulsion side'. Compared to these bombs, humanity's most powerful Cold War-era nuclear bombs were mere toy weapons.

When the time came to detonate these super-powerful nuclear bombs under the lunar surface, the force of their explosions would be wholly incomparable to the nuclear tests of earlier ages, suffocated deep underground. These denotations would blow off a complete stratum of lunar matter. In the Moon's low gravity, the exploded strata's rocks and dust would reach escape velocity. As they launched into space, they would exert an enormous propulsive force on the Moon itself.

If a certain number of bombs were detonated in rapid succession, this momentum could become a continual propelling force, just as if the Moon had been fitted with a powerful engine. By detonating nuclear bombs in different places it would be possible to control the Moon's flight path.

The plan would even go one step further, calling for not one but two layers of nuclear bombs within the lunar surface. The second layer would be installed at a depth of about four miles. After the top layer had been completely used up, two miles of lunar matter would be stripped from the propulsion side of the Moon. The unceasing denotations would then smoothly transition to the second layer. This would double the duration for which the 'engine' could propel the Moon.

When the girl from Eridanus heard of this plan, she came to the conclusion that humanity was truly insane. 'Now I understand. If you had technology to match the Devourers, you might be even more brutal than they are!' she exclaimed.

Fangs, on the other hand, was full of praise. 'Ha, ha! What a wonderful idea you worms managed to dream up. I love it. I love your vulgarity. Vulgarity is the highest form of beauty!' he exclaimed.

'Absurd! How can vulgarity be beautiful?' the girl from Eridanus retorted.

'The vulgar is naturally beautiful, and nothing is more vulgar than the universe! Stars burn manically in the pitch-black cold abyss of space. Isn't that vulgar? Do you understand that the universe is masculine? Feminine civilizations, like yours, are fragile, fine and delicate, a sickly abnormality in a tiny corner of the universe. And that is that!' Fangs replied.

A hundred years had passed, and Fangs' huge frame still brimmed with vitality. The girl from Eridanus was still vivid and bright, but the Captain felt the weight of years. He was 130 years old, an old man.

At the time, the Devourer had just passed the orbit of Pluto. It was awakening after its long, sixty-thousand-mile journey from Epsilon Eridani. In the dark of space, its huge ring was lit up brilliantly, and its immense society set to work, preparing to plunder the solar system.

After the Devourer had plundered the peripheral planets it flung itself onto a precipitous trajectory toward Earth.

7

HUMANITY'S FIRST AND LAST SPACE WAR

The acceleration of the Moon away from Earth had begun.

The Moon was hanging in the sky of Earth's day side when the first bombs were detonated. The flare from each explosion briefly lit up the Moon in the blue sky, giving it the appearance of a giant silver eye frantically blinking in the heavens. When night fell on Earth, the one-sided flashes of the Moon still shone the light of human handiwork to the surface twenty-five thousand miles below. A pale silver trail following the Moon's dark side was now visible. It was composed of the rocks blasted into space from the Moon's surface. Cameras installed on the propulsion side of the Moon showed strata of rock being blasted into space like billowing floodwaters. The waves of rock quickly faded into the distance, becoming thin strands trailing the Moon. Turning toward the Earth's other side, the Moon circumscribed an accelerating orbit.

Humanity's attention, however, was now squarely focused on the great and terrible ring that had appeared in the sky: the Devourer loomed over the Earth. The enormous tides that its gravity caused had already destroyed Earth's coastal cities.

The Devourer's aft engines flashed in a circle of blue light as it engaged in final orbital adjustments on its approach. It eventually perfectly matched the Earth's orbit around the Sun, while at the same time it aligned its axis of rotation with Earth's. Having completed these adjustments, it ever so slowly began to move toward the Earth, ready to surround the planet with its huge ring body.

The Moon's acceleration continued for two months. During this time, a bomb had exploded within its surface every two or three seconds, resulting in an almost incomprehensible total of 2.5 million nuclear explosions. As it entered into its second orbit around the Earth, the Moon's acceleration had forced its once circular orbit into a distinctly elliptical shape. As the Moon moved to the far end of this ellipse, Fangs and the Captain arrived on its forward-facing side, away from the exploding bombs. The Captain had expressly invited the alien emissary for this occasion.

As they stood on the lunar plain surrounded by craters, they felt the tremors from the other side shake deep beneath their feet. It almost seemed as if they could sense the powerful heartbeat of Earth's satellite. In the pitch-black sky beyond, the Devourer's giant ring dazzled with its brilliant light, its huge shape consuming half the sky.

'Excellent, Captain-worm, most excellent indeed!' Fangs applauded, his voice full of sincere praise. 'But,' he continued, 'you should hurry. You only have one more orbit to accelerate. The Devourer Empire is not accustomed to waiting for others. And I have another question: the cities you built below the surface a decade ago are still empty. When will their inhabitants arrive? How can your spaceships transport one hundred thousand humans here from Earth in only one month?'

'We will bring no one here,' the Captain calmly replied. 'We will be the last humans to stand on the Moon.'

Hearing this, Fangs twisted his body in surprise. The Captain had said 'we', meaning the five thousand officers and soldiers of Earth's space force. They formed a perfect phalanx on the crater-covered lunar plain. At the front of the phalanx a soldier brandished a blue flag.

'Look! This is our planet's banner. We declare war upon the Devourer Empire!' the Captain announced defiantly.

Fangs stood dumbfounded, more confused than surprised. Immediately, his body began to reel as he was thrown onto his back by the Moon's sudden gravitational surge. Fangs was knocked prone to lunar ground, stunned beyond any thought of movement. All around him lunar dust kicked up by his massive fall slowly began to drift to the ground.

But the dust was quickly thrown up again, stirred by massive shock waves reverberating from the other side of the Moon. These shocks soon left the entire plain covered in a layer of white dust.

Fangs realized the frequency of nuclear explosions on the other side of the Moon had abruptly increased several times over. Judging by the sharp increase of gravity, he could infer that the Moon's acceleration must have increased several times as well. Rolling over, he retrieved a large handheld computer from a pocket in the front of his spacesuit. He brought up the Moon's current orbital trajectory on it. Immediately, he realized that this tremendous increase of acceleration would take the Moon out of orbit. The Moon would break free of Earth's gravity and shoot off into space. A flashing red line of dots showed its predicted course.

It was on a collision course with the Devourer.

Discarding his computer without a second thought, Fangs slowly rose to his feet. Straining his neck against the explosive increase in gravity, he peered through the billowing clouds of lunar dust. Standing in front of him was Earth's army, still upright, stalwart like standing stones.

'A century of conspiracy and deceit,' Fangs mumbled under his breath.

The Captain just nodded in agreement. 'You now realize that it is too late,' he pointed out gravely.

Fangs spoke after a long sigh. 'I should have realized that the humans of Earth were a completely different breed from the Eridanians. Life on their world had evolved symbiotically, free of natural selection and the struggle for survival. They did not even know what war was.' He halted, digesting what had happened. 'We let that guide our assessment of Earth's people. You have ceaselessly butchered one another from the day that you climbed down from the trees. How could you be easily conquered? I . . .' Again he paused. 'It was an unforgivable dereliction of duty!'

When the Captain spoke, his steady, level tone explained further what Fangs was realizing. 'The Eridanians brought us vast quantities of vital information. The information included the limits of the Devourer's ability to accelerate. It is this information that formed the basis of our battle plan. As we detonate the bombs that change the Moon's trajectory, its maneuvering acceleration will come to exceed the Devourer's acceleration limit three-fold. In other words,' he said, 'it will be thrice as agile as the Devourer. There is no way you can avoid the coming collision.'

'Actually, we were not completely off guard,' Fangs said. 'When the Earth began producing large quantities of nuclear bombs, we began to monitor their whereabouts. We made sure that they were installed deep within the Moon, but we did not think . . .' Fangs trailed off.

Behind his visor, the Captain smiled faintly. 'We aren't so stupid as to directly attack the Devourer with nuclear bombs,' he said. 'We know that the Devourer Empire has been steeled by hundreds of battles. Earth's simple and crude missiles would certainly have been intercepted and destroyed, one and all. But you cannot intercept something as large as the Moon. Perhaps the Devourer, with its immense power, could have eventually broken or diverted the Moon, but it is far too close for that now. You are out of time.'

Fangs snarled. 'Crafty worms. Treacherous worms, vicious worms!' He shook his head, bristling. 'The Devourer Empire is an honest civilization. We put all things out in the open, yet we have been cheated by the deceitful treachery of the Earth worms.' He gnashed his huge teeth as he finished speaking, his fury almost goading him to lock his giant claws around the Captain. The soldiers, with their rifles aimed right at him, however, stayed his talons. Fangs had not forgotten that his body, too, was but flesh and blood. One burst of bullets would end him.

With his eyes firmly fixed on Fangs, the Captain stated, 'We will leave, and you, too, should make your way off the Moon, otherwise you will surely be killed by the Devourer Empire's nuclear weapons.'

The Captain was quite correct. Just as Fangs and the human space forces left the Moon's surface, the interceptor missiles of the Devourer struck. Both sides of the Moon now flashed with brilliant light. The forward-facing side of the Moon exploded as huge waves of rocks were blasted into space. All around the Moon, lunar matter was violently scattered in every imaginable direction. Seen from the Earth, the Moon, on its collision course with the Devourer, looked like a warrior, wild hair ablaze with rage. There was no force that could have stopped it now! Wherever on Earth this spectacle was visible, seas of people erupted into feverish cheers.

The Devourer's interception action was short-lived and soon ceased. It realized that it's attack had been completely futile. In the moments it would take for the Moon to close the short distance between them, there was no way to divert its course or to destroy it.

The nuclear explosions that the Moon's pulled propulsion had also ceased. It had reached a suitable velocity, and Earth's defenders wanted to preserve enough nuclear bombs to carry out any last-minute maneuvers. All was silent.

In the cold tranquility of space, the Devourer and the Earth's satellite floated toward each other in complete silence. The distance between the two rapidly decreased. As it dwindled to thirty thousand miles, the control ship of Earth's Supreme Command could already see the Moon overlapping the giant ring of the Devourer. From there, it looked like a ball bearing in a track.

Up to this point, the Devourer had not made any changes to its trajectory. It was easy to understand why: the Moon could have easily matched any premature orbital maneuver. Any meaningful evasive action would have to be taken in the final moments before the Moon's impact. The two cosmic giants were almost like ancient knights in a joust. They were charging toward one another, galloping across the distance separating them, but the victor would only be decided in the blink of an eye before they made contact.

Two great civilizations of the Milky Way held their breath in rapt anticipation, awaiting that decisive moment.

At twenty thousand miles, both sides began their maneuvers. The Devourer's engines were the first to flare, shooting blue flames more than five thousand miles out into space. It began its evasion. On the Moon, nuclear bombs were once again ignited, ferociously detonating with unprecedented intensity and frequency. It carried out its adjustments, matching its course to ensure a collision. Its arcing tail of debris clearly described its change of direction. The blue light of the Devourer's five-thousand-mile flames merged with the silver flashes of the Moon's nuclear blasts; it was the most magnificent vista ever to grace the solar system.

Both sides maneuvered like this for three hours. The distance between them had already shrunk to three thousand miles when the computer displays showed what no one in the control ship ever would have believed to be possible: the Devourer was changing course with an acceleration speed four times greater than the limit the Eridanians had claimed possible!

All this time they had unreservedly believed in this limit. They had made it the foundation of Earth's victory. Now, the nuclear bombs remaining on the Moon no longer had the capacity to make the necessary adjustments to give chase. Calculations showed that in three short hours, even if they did all they could, the Moon would brush pass the Devourer, falling short by 250 miles.

One last burst of dizzying flashes washed over the control ship, exhausting all of the Earth's nuclear bombs. At almost exactly the same moment, the Devourer's engines fell silent. In a deathly quiet, the laws of inertia told the final verses of this magnificent epic: the Moon scraped past the Devourer's side, barely missing. Its velocity was so high that the Devourer's gravity could not catch it, only twisting its trajectory a little as it zoomed past. After the Moon had passed the Devourer, it silently sped away from the Sun.

On the control ship, the Supreme Command fell into a complete silence. Minutes passed.

'The Eridanians betrayed us,' a commander finally whispered in shock.

'The crystal was probably just a trap set by the Devourer Empire!' a staff officer shouted.

In an instant, the Supreme Command descended into utter chaos. Most people began to scream and shout: some to vent their utter despair, others to conceal it. All were on the verge of hysteria. A few of the non-military personnel wept; others tore the hair from their heads. Spirits stood teetering on the verge of the abyss, ready to fall forever.

Only the Captain remained serene, standing quietly in front of a large screen. He slowly turned and with one simple question calmed the chaos. 'I would ask all of you to pay attention to one detail: why did the Devourer cut its engine?'

Pandemonium was immediately replaced by deep thought. Indeed, after the Moon had used its last nuclear bomb, the enemy had no reason to shut down its engine. They had no way of knowing whether or not there were any bombs left on the Moon. Furthermore, there was the danger of the Devourer's gravity catching the Moon. Had the Devourer continued to accelerate, it could have easily extended the distance to the Moon's trajectory. It could have – should have – made it farther than those tiny, barely adequate 250 miles.

'Give me a close up of the Devourer's outer hull,' the Captain commanded.

A holographic image was displayed on the screen. It was a picture being transmitted by a miniature, high-speed reconnaissance probe flying three hundred miles above the Devourer's surface. The splendidly illuminated surface of the Devourer came into clear view. In awe, they beheld the massive steel peaks and valleys of its giant ring body slowly turn past their view. A long black seam caught the Captain's attention. In the past century, he had become very familiar with every detail of the Devourer's surface, but he was absolutely certain that *that* gap had not existed before. Others quickly noticed it as well.

'What is that? Is it . . . a crack?' someone asked.

'It is. A crack. A three-thousand-mile-long crack,' the Captain said, nodding. 'The Eridanians did not betray us. The data in the crystal was accurate. The acceleration limit is real, but as the Moon approached the despairing Devourer decided to risk the consequences and to exceed the limit by four-fold, desperate to avoid the collision. This, however, had a cost: the Devourer has cracked.'

Then they found more cracks.

'Look, what's going on now?' someone shouted as its rotation brought another part of Devourer's surface into view. A dazzling bright light began glowing on the edge of its metal surface, as if dawn were creeping over its vast horizon.

'It's the rotational engine!' an officer called out.

'Indeed. It is the rarely used equatorial rotational engine,' the Captain explained. 'It is firing at full power, trying to stop the Devourer's rotation!'

'Captain, you were spot on, and this proves it!'

'We must act now and use all available means to gather detailed data so that we can run a simulation!' the Captain commanded. Even as he spoke, the entire Supreme Command was already executing the task.

Over the past century, a mathematical model had been developed that precisely described the Devourer's physical structure. The required data was gathered and processed very efficiently, and so the results were quickly produced: it would take nearly forty hours for the rotational engine to reduce the Devourer's rotation to a speed at which it could avoid destruction. Yet in only eighteen hours the centrifugal forces would completely break the Devourer into pieces.

A cheer rose among the Supreme Command. The big screen shone with the holographic image of the Devourer's impending demise: the fragmentation process would be very slow, almost dreamlike. Against the pitch blackness of space, this giant world would disperse like milk sinking into coffee, its edges gradually breaking off, only to be swallowed by the darkness beyond. The Devourer would look like it was melting into space. Only the occasional flash of an explosion now revealed its disintegrating form.

The Captain did not join the others as they watched this soul-soothing display of destruction. He stood apart from the group, focused on another screen, carefully observing the real Devourer. His face betrayed no trace of triumph. As calm returned to the bridge, the others began to take notice of him. One after another they joined him at the screen, where they discovered that the blue light at the Devourer's aft had reappeared.

The Devourer had restarted its engine.

Given the critical state that the ring structure was already in, this seemed like an utterly baffling decision. Any acceleration, no matter how minute, could cause a catastrophic collapse. But it was the Devourer's trajectory that truly baffled the onlookers: it was ever so slowly retracing its steps, returning to the position it had held before its evasive maneuvers. It was carefully re-establishing its synchronous orbit and re-aligning its axis of rotation with Earth's.

'What? Does it still want to devour the Earth?' an officer exclaimed, both shocked and confused.

His question provoked a few scattered laughs. All laughter, however, soon fell silent as the others became aware of the look on the Captain's face. He was no longer looking at the screen. His eyes were closed. His face was blank and drained of all color. In the past hundred years, the officers and personnel who had made fending off the Devourer their life's work had become very familiar with the Captain's countenance. They had never seen him like this. A calm fell over the gathered Supreme Command as they turned back to the screen. Finally, they understood the gravity of the situation.

The Devourer still had a way out.

The Devourer's flight toward the Earth had begun. It had already matched the Earth in both orbital speed and rotation as it approached the planet's South Pole.

If it took too long, the Devourer's own centrifugal forces would tear it apart; if it went too fast, the power of its propulsion would rip it to pieces. The Devourer's survival was hanging a thin thread. It had to hold a perfect balance between timing and speed.

Before the Earth's South Pole was enveloped by the Devourer's giant ring, the Supreme Command could see the shape of the frozen continent change rapidly. Antarctica was shrinking, like butter in a hot frying pan. The world's oceans were being pulled toward the South Pole by the immense gravity of the Devourer, and now the Earth's white tip was being swallowed by their billowing waters.

As this happened, the Devourer, too, was changing. Countless new cracks began to cover its body, and all of them were growing longer and wider. The first few tears were now no longer black seams but gaping chasms glowing with crimson light. They could easily have been mistaken for the portals to hell, thousands of miles in length.

In the midst of all this destruction, a few fine white strands rose from the ring's massive body. Then, more and more of these filaments emerged, flowing from every part of the ship. It almost looked like the huge ship had sprouted a sparse head of white hair. In fact, they were the engine trails of ships being launched from the great ring. The Devourers were fleeing their doomed world.

Half of the Earth had already been encircled by the Devourer when things took a turn for the worse: the Earth's gravity was acting like the invisible spokes of a cosmic wheel, holding the disintegrating Devourer. No new cracks were appearing on its surface and the already open rips had ceased growing. Forty hours later, the Earth was completely engulfed by the Devourer. The effect of the planet's gravity was stronger at this point, and the cracks on the Devourer's surface were beginning to close. Another five hours later, they had completely closed.

In the control ship, all the screens of the Supreme Command had gone black, and even the lights were now dark. The only remaining source of illumination was the deathly pale rays of the Sun piercing through the portholes. In order to generate artificial gravity, the mid-section of the ship was still slowly rotating. As it did, the Sun rose and fell, porthole to porthole. Light and shadow wandered, as if it were replaying humanity's bygone days and nights.

'Thank you for a century of dutiful service,' the Captain said. 'Thank you all.' He saluted the Supreme Command. Under the gaze of the officers and personnel, he calmly folded up his uniform. The others followed his example.

Humanity had been defeated. The defenders of Earth had done their utmost to discharge their duties and, as soldiers, they had done their duty gloriously. In spirit, they all accepted their unseen medals with clear consciences. They were entitled to enjoy this moment.

8

EPILOGUE: THE RETURN

'There really is water!' a young lieutenant shouted with joyous surprise. It was true; a vast surface of water stretched out before them. Sparkling waves shimmered under the dusky heavens.

The Captain removed the gloves of his spacesuit. With both hands, he scooped up some water. Opening his visor, he ventured a taste. As he quickly closed his visor again, he called, 'It's not too salty.' When he saw that the lieutenant was about to open his own visor, he stopped him. 'You'll suffer decompression sickness. The composition of the atmosphere is actually not the problem; the poisonous sulphuric components in the air have already thinned out. However, the atmospheric pressure is too low. Without a visor, it is like what being at thirty thousand feet was before the war.'

A general dug in the sand at his feet. 'Maybe there's some grass seeds,' he said, smiling as he raised his head to look at the Captain.

The Captain shook his head. 'Before the war, this was the bottom of the ocean.'

'We can go have a look at New Land Eleven. It's not far from here. Maybe we can find some there,' the lieutenant suggested.

'Any will have been burnt long ago,' someone commented with a sigh.

Each of them scanned the horizon in all directions. They were surrounded by an unbroken chain of mountains only recently born by the orogenic movements of the Earth. They were dark blue massifs made of bare rock. Rivers of magma spilling from their peaks glowed crimson, like blood oozing from the body of a slain stone titan.

The magma rivers of the Earth below had burned out.

This was Earth, 230 years after the war.

After the war had ended, the more than one hundred people

aboard the control ship had entered the hibernation chambers. There they waited for the Devourer to spit out the Earth; then they would return home. During their wait, their ship had become a satellite, circling the new joint planet of Devourer and Earth in a wide orbit. In all that time, the Devourer Empire had done nothing to harass them.

One hundred and twenty-five years after the war, the command ship's sensors picked up that the Devourer was in the process of leaving the Earth. In response, it roused some of those in hibernation. By the time they woke, the Devourer had already left the Earth and flown on to Venus. The Earth had been transformed into a wholly alien world, a strange planet, perhaps best described as a lump of charcoal freshly out of the oven. The oceans had all disappeared, and the land was covered in a web of magma rivers.

The personnel of the control ship could only continue their hibernation. They reset their sensors and waited for the Earth to cool. This wait lasted another century.

When they again woke from hibernation, they found a cooled planet, its violent geology having subsided; but now the Earth was a desolate, yellow wasteland. Even though all life had disappeared, there was still a sparse atmosphere. They even discovered remnants of the oceans of old.

So they landed at the shore of such a remnant, barely the size of a pre-war continental lake.

A blast of thunder, deafening in this thin atmosphere, roared above them as the familiar, crude form of a Devourer Empire ship landed not far from their own vessel. Its gigantic doors opened, and Fangs took his first tottering steps out, leaning heavily on a walking stick the size of a power pole.

'Ah, you are still alive, sir!' the Captain greeted him. 'You must be around five hundred now?'

'How could I live that long? I, too, went into hibernation, thirty years after the war. I hibernated just so I could see you again,' Fangs retorted.

'Where is the Devourer now?' the Captain asked.

Fangs pointed into the sky above as he answered. 'You can still see it at night; it is but a dim star now, just having passed Jupiter's orbit.'

'It is leaving the solar system?' the Captain queried.

Fangs nodded. 'I will set out today to follow it.'

The Captain paused before speaking. 'We are both old now.'

Fangs sadly nodded his giant head. 'Old . . .' he said, his walking stick trembling in his hand. 'The world, now . . .' He continued pointing from heaven to Earth.

'A small amount of water and atmosphere remains. Should we consider this an act of mercy from the Devourer Empire?' the Captain asked quietly.

Fangs shook his head. 'It has nothing to do with mercy; it is your doing.'

The Earth's soldiers looked at Fangs in puzzlement.

'Oh, in this war the Devourer Empire suffered an unprecedented wound. We lost hundreds of millions in those tears,' Fangs admitted. 'Our ecosystem, too, suffered critical damage. After the war, it took us fifty Earth years just to complete preliminary repairs, and only once that was done could we begin to chew the Earth. But we knew that our time in the solar system was limited. If we did not leave in time, a cloud of interstellar dust would float right into our flight path. And if we took the long way round, we would lose seventeen thousand years on our way to the next star. In that time, the star's state would have already changed, burning the planets that we wished to consume. Because of this we had to chew the planets of the Sun in great haste and could not pick them clean,' Fangs explained.

'That fills us with great comfort and honor,' the Captain said, looking at the soldiers surrounding him.

'You are most worthy of it. It truly was a great interstellar war. In the lengthy annals of the Devourer's wars, ours was one of the most remarkable battles! To this day, all throughout our world, minstrels sing of the epic achievements of the Earth's soldiers,' Fangs stated.

'We would sooner hope that humanity would remember the war. So, how is humanity?' the Captain asked.

'After the war, approximately two billion humans were migrated to the Devourer Empire, about half of all of humanity,' Fangs answered, activating the large screen of his portable computer where pictures of life on the Devourer appeared. The screen revealed a beautiful grassland under blue skies. On the grass, a group of happy humans was singing and dancing. At first it was difficult to distinguish the gender of these humans. Their skin was a soft, subtle white, and they were all dressed in fine, gauzy clothes with beautiful wreaths of flowers on their heads. In the distance, one could make out a magnificent castle, clearly modelled on something from an Earth fairytale. Its vibrant colors made it look as if it were made of cream and chocolate.

The camera's lens drew closer, giving the Captain a chance to study these people's countenances in detail. He was soon completely convinced that they were truly happy. It was an utterly carefree happiness, pure as crystal. It reminded him of the few short years of innocent childhood joy that pre-war humans had experienced.

'We must ensure their absolute happiness,' Fangs said. 'It is the minimum requirement for raising them. If we do not, we cannot guarantee the quality of their meat. And it must be said that Earth people are seen as food of the highest quality; only the upper class of the Devourer Empire society can afford to enjoy them. We do not take such delicacies for granted.' Fangs paused for a moment. 'Oh, Captain. We found your great-grandson, sir. We recorded something from him to you. Do you care to see it?'

The Captain gazed at Fangs in surprise then nodded his head.

A fair-skinned, beautiful boy appeared on the screen. Judging by his face he was only ten years old, but his stature was already that of a grown man. He held a flower wreath in his effeminate hands, having obviously just been called from a dance.

Blinking his large, shimmering eyes, he said, 'I hear that my great-grandfather still lives. I ask only one thing of you, sir. Never, ever come see me. I am nauseated! When we think of humanity's life before the war, we are all nauseated. What a barbaric life that was, the life of cockroaches! You and your soldiers of Earth wanted to preserve that life. You almost stopped humanity from entering this beautiful heaven. How perverse! Do you know how much shame, how much embarrassment you have caused me? Bah! Do not come looking for me! Bah! Go and die!' After he had finished, he skipped off to join the dancing on the grassland.

Fangs was first to break the awkward silence that followed. 'He will live past the age of sixty. He will have a long life and will not be slaughtered.'

'If it is because of me, then I am truly grateful,' the Captain said, smiling miserably.

'It is not. After learning about his ancestry, he became very depressed and filled with feelings of hatred toward you. Such emotions prevented his meat from meeting our standards,' Fangs explained.

As Fangs looked at these last few humans before him, genuine emotions played across his massive eyes. Their spacesuits were extremely old and shabby, and the many years that have since past were etched into their faces. In the pale yellow of the Sun, they looked like a group of rust-stained statues. Fangs closed his computer and, full of regret, said, 'At first, I did not want you to see this, but you are all true warriors, more than capable of dealing with the truth, ready to recognize,' he paused for a long moment before continuing 'that human civilization has come to an end.'

'You certainly destroyed Earth's civilization,' the Captain said, staring into the distance. 'You have committed a monstrous crime!'

'We finally have started to talk about morals again,' Fangs said with a laugh and a grin.

'After invading our home and brutally devouring everything in it, I would think that you had forfeited all right to talk about morals,' the Captain said coldly.

The others had already stopped paying attention; the extreme, cold brutality of the Devourer civilization was just beyond human understanding. Nothing could have been less interesting to the others than a discussion with them about morals.

'No, we have the right. I now truly wish to talk about morals with humanity,' Fangs said before again pausing. '"How, sir, could you just pick him up and eat him?"' he continued, quoting the Captain. Those last words left nobody unshaken. They did not emanate from the translator, but came directly from Fangs' mouth. Even though his voice was deafening, Fangs somehow managed to imitate those three-hundred-year-old words with perfection.

Fangs continued, resuming his use of the translator. 'Captain, three hundred years ago your intuition did not mislead you: When two civilizations – separated by interstellar space – meet, any similarities should be far more shocking than their differences. It certainly shouldn't be as it is with our species.'

As all present focused their gaze on Fangs' frame, they were overcome with a sense of premonition that a world-shaking mystery was about to be revealed.

Fangs straightened himself on his walking-stick and, looking into the distance, said, 'Friends, we are both children of the Sun; and while the Earth is both our species' fraternal home, my people have the greater claim to her! Our claim is 140 million years older than yours. All those millennia ago, we were the first to live on this beautiful planet, and this is where we established our magnificent civilization.'

The Earth's soldiers stared blankly at Fangs. The waters of the remnant ocean rippled in the pale yellow sunlight. Red magma flowed from the distant new mountains. Sixty million years down the rivers of time, two species, each the ruler of this Earth in their own time, met in desolation on their plundered home world.

'Dino . . . saur!' someone exclaimed in a shocked whisper.

Fangs nodded. 'The Dinosaur Civilization arose one hundred million years ago on Earth, during what you call the Cretaceous period of the Mesozoic. At the end of the Cretaceous, our civilization reached its zenith, but we are a large species, and our biological needs were equally great. In the wake of our population increase, the ecosystem was stretched to its limit, and the Earth was pushed to its brink as it struggled to support our society. To survive, we completely consumed Mars' elementary ecosystem.

'The Dinosaur Civilization lasted twenty thousand years on Earth,' he continued, 'but its true expansion was a matter of a few thousand years. From a geological perspective its effects are indistinguishable from those of an explosive catastrophe; what you call the Cretaceous–Tertiary extinction event.

'Finally, one day all the dinosaurs boarded ten giant generation ships and, with these ships, sailed into the vast sea of stars. In the end, all ten of these ships were joined together. Then, whenever this newly united ship reached another star's planet, it expanded. Sixty million years later, it has become the Devourer Empire you now know.'

'Why would you eat your own home world? Are dinosaurs bereft of all sentiment?' someone asked.

Fangs answered, lost in thought. 'It is a long story. Interstellar space is indeed vast and boundless, but it is also different than you would imagine. The places that truly suit us, as advanced carbon-based life forms, are few and far between. A dust cloud blocks the way to the center of the Milky Way just two thousand light-years from here. There is no way for us to pass through it and no way for us to survive in it. And after that it becomes an area of powerful radiation and a large group of wandering black holes.' Fangs paused, before continuing, still speaking more to himself than to the humans before him. 'If we should travel in the opposite direction, we would just come to the end of the Milky Way's spiral arm and then, not far beyond, there is nothing but a limitless, desolate void. The Devourer Empire has already completely consumed almost all the planets that could be found in the habitable areas that exist between these two barriers. Now the only way out is to fly to another arm of the Milky Way. We have no idea what awaits us there, but if we stay here we will certainly be doomed. It will be a journey of fifteen million years, taking us right through the void. To survive it, we must build large stocks of all possible expendables.

'Right now, the Devourer Empire is just like a fish in a drying stream. It must make a desperate leap before its water completely evaporates. It realizes that the most likely end is reaching dry land and succumbing to death under the scorching Sun but there is the slight chance that it may fall into a neighboring water hole and thereby survive.' Fangs lowered his gaze toward the humans, bending down to almost eye level. 'As far as sentiment is concerned, we have lived through tens of millions of arduous years and fought stellar wars beyond number. The hearts of the dinosaur race have long since hardened. Now the Devourer Empire must consume as much as it possibly can in preparation for our million-year journey.' Fangs again paused, deep in thought. 'What is civilization? Civilization is devouring, ceaselessly eating, endlessly expanding; everything else comes second.'

The Captain, too, was deep in thought. Looking at Fangs, he asked, 'Can the struggle for existence be the universe's only law of biological and cultural evolution? Can we not establish a self-sufficient, introspective civilization where all life exists in symbiosis? A civilization like that of the Eridanians?'

Fangs answered without hesitation or pause. 'I am no philosopher; perhaps it can be done. The crux is, who will take the first step? If one's survival is based on the subjugation and consumption of others and if that should be the universe's iron law of life and civilization, then whoever first rejects it in favor of introspection will certainly perish.'

With that Fangs returned to his spaceship, but he soon re-emerged carrying a thin, flat box in both talons. The box was about ten feet square, and it would have easily taken four men to carry it. Fangs placed the box on the ground and opened its top. To the humans' surprise, the box was filled with dirt, and grass was growing on it. On this lifeless world, its green left no heart untouched.

As Fangs opened the box, he turned to the humans. 'This is pre-war soil. After the war, I put all of our planet's plants and all of its insects into suspended animation. Now, after more than two centuries, they have awoken. Originally, I wanted to take this soil with me as a memento. Alas, I have thought more about it, and I have changed my mind. I have decided to return it to where it truly belongs. We have taken more than enough from our home world.'

As they gazed upon this tiny piece of Earth, so full of life, the humans' eyes began to moisten. They now knew the dinosaurs' hearts had not turned to stone. Behind those scales, colder and crueler than steel and rock, beat hearts that longed for home.

Fangs rattled his claws, almost as if he wanted to cast off the emotions that had gripped him. Slightly shaken, he said, 'All right then, my friends, we will go together, back to the Devourer Empire.' Seeing the expression on the humans' faces, he raised a claw before continuing. 'You will, of course, not be food there. You are great warriors and you will be made citizens of the Empire. And there is still work that needs your attention. A museum to the human civilization needs to be built.'

The eyes of every single Earth soldier turned to the Captain. He stood deep in thought, then slowly nodded.

One after the other, the Earth's soldiers boarded Fangs' spaceship. Because its ladder was intended for dinosaurs, they had to pull the full length of their bodies up each rung to climb inside. The Captain was the last human to board the ship. Grasping the lowest rung of the ship's ladder, he pulled his body off the ground. Just at that moment, something in the ground beneath his feet caught his eye. He stopped in mid-pull, looking down. For a long time he hung there, motionless.

He had seen . . . an ant.

The ant had climbed out of that box of soil. Never losing sight of the tiny insect, the Captain let go of the ladder and squatted down. Lowering his hand, he let the ant clamber onto his glove. Raising it to his face, he carefully studied the small creature, its obsidian body glinting in the sunlight. Holding it, the Captain walked over to the box, where he cautiously returned the ant to the tiny blades of grass. As he lowered his hand, he noticed more ants climbing about the soil beneath the grass.

Raising himself, he turned to Fangs who was standing right by his side. 'When we leave, this grass and these ants will be the dominant species on Earth.'

Fangs was at a loss for words.

'Earth's civilized life seems to be getting smaller and smaller. Dinosaurs, humans and now probably ants,' the Marshal said, squatting back down. He looked on, his eyes deep with love and admiration as he watched these small beings live their lives in the grass. 'It is their turn.'

As he spoke, the Earth's soldiers re-emerged from the spaceship. Climbing down to Earth, they returned to the box of living soil. Standing around it they, too, were filled with deep love.

Fangs shook his head. 'The grass cannot survive. It might eventually rain here at the seaside, but it won't be enough for the ants.'

'Is the atmosphere too thin? They seem to be doing just fine at the moment,' someone noted.

'No, the air is not the problem. They are not like humans and can live well in this atmosphere. The real crux of the matter is that they will have nothing to eat,' Fangs replied.

'Can't they eat the grass?' another voice joined in.

'And then? How will they live on? In this thin air, the grass will grow very slowly. Once the ants have eaten all the blades, they will starve. In many ways, their situation mirrors the destiny of the Devourer civilization,' Fangs mused.

'Can you leave behind some food from your spaceship for them?' another soldier asked, almost pleadingly.

Fangs shook his massive head again. 'There is nothing on my spaceship besides water and the hibernation system. On that note, we will hibernate until we catch up with the Devourer. But what about your spaceship – do you have any food on board?'

Now it was the Captain's turn to shake his head. 'Nothing but a few injections of nourishment solution. Useless.'

Pointing to the spaceship, Fangs interrupted the discussion. 'We must hurry. The Empire is accelerating quickly. If we tarry, we will not catch up.'

Silence.

'Captain, we will stay behind.' It was the young lieutenant who broke the silence.

The Captain nodded forcefully.

'Stay behind? What are you up to?' Fangs asked in astonishment, turning from one to the other. 'The hibernation equipment on your spaceship is almost completely depleted and you have no food. Do you plan to stay and wait for death?'

'Staying will be the first step,' the Captain answered calmly.

'What?' Fangs asked, ever more perplexed.

'You just mentioned the first step toward a new civilization,' the Captain explained.

'You,' Fangs could hardly believe his own words, 'want to be the ants' food?'

Earth's soldiers all nodded. Without a word, Fangs gazed at them for what seemed like forever, before turning and slowly hobbling back to his spaceship, leaning heavily on his walking stick.

'Farewell, friend,' the Captain called after Fangs.

Fangs replied with a long, drawn-out sigh. 'An interminable darkness lies before me and my descendants: the darkness of endless war and a vast universe. Oh, where in it could there be a home for us?'

As he spoke, the humans saw that the ground beneath his feet had grown damp, but they could not tell if he had, or even could, shed tears.

With a thunderous roar, the dinosaur's spaceship lifted off and quickly disappeared into the sky. Where it had vanished, the Sun was now setting.

The last warriors of Earth seated themselves around the living soil in silence. Then, beginning with the Captain, they all, one by one, opened their visors and stretched out on the sandy earth.

As time passed, the Sun set. Its afterglow bathed the plundered Earth in a beautiful red. As it faded, a few stars began to twinkle in the sky. To his surprise, the Captain saw that the dusky sky was a beautiful blue. Just as the thin atmosphere began to render him unconsciousness, the Captain felt the tiny movements of an ant on his temple, filling him with a deep sense of contentment. As the ant climbed up to his forehead, he was transported back to his distant childhood. He was at the beach, lying in a small hammock that hung between two palm trees. Looking up to the splendid sea of stars above, he felt his mother's hand gently stroke his forehead . . .

Darkness fell. The remnant ocean lay flat as a mirror, pristinely reflecting the Milky Way above. It was the most tranquil night in the planet's history.

In this tranquility, the Earth was reborn.

SEA OF DREAMS

FIRST HALF

The Low-Temperature Artist

It was the Ice and Snow Arts Festival that lured the low-temperature artist here. The idea was absurd, but once the oceans had dried, this was how Yan Dong always thought of it. No matter how many years passed by, the scene when the low-temperature artist arrived remained clear in her mind.

At the time, Yan Dong was standing in front of her own ice sculpture, which she'd just completed. Exquisitely carved ice sculptures surrounded her. In the distance, lofty ice structures towered over a snowfield. These sparkling and translucent skyscrapers and castles were steeped in the winter sun. They were short-lived works of art. Soon, this glittering world would become a pool of clear water in the spring breeze. People were sad to see them melt but the process embodied many of life's ineffable mysteries. This, perhaps, was the real reason why Yan Dong clung dearly to the ice and snow arts.

Yan Dong tore her gaze away from her own work, determined not to look at it again before the judges named the winners. She sighed, then glanced at the sky. It was at this moment that she saw the low-temperature artist for the first time.

Initially, she thought it was a plane dragging a white vapor trail behind it, but the flying object was much faster than a plane. It swept a great arc through the air. The vapor trail, like a giant piece of chalk, drew a hook in the blue sky. The flying object suddenly stopped high in the air right above Yan Dong. The vapor trail gradually disappeared from its tail to its head, as though the flying object were inhaling it back in.

Yan Dong studied the bit of the vapor trail that was the last to disappear. It was flickering oddly, and she decided it had to be from something reflecting the sunlight. She then saw what that *it* was – a small, ash-gray spheroid. Then quickly realized that the spheroid wasn't small – it looked small in the distance, but was now expanding rapidly. The spheroid was falling right toward her, it seemed, and from an incredibly high altitude. When the people around her realized, they fled in all directions. Yan Dong also ducked her head and ran, darting in and around the ice sculptures.

An enormous shadow hung over the area, and for a moment, Yan Dong's blood seemed to freeze. The expected impact never came, though. The artists and judges and festival spectators stopped running. They gazed upward, dumbstruck. She looked up, too. The massive gray spheroid floated a hundred meters over their heads. It wasn't wholly spheroid, as if the vapor expelled during its high-speed flight had warped its shape. The half in the direction of its flight was smooth, glossy, and round. The other half sprouted a large sheaf of hair, making it look like a comet whose tail had been trimmed. It was massive, well over one hundred meters in diameter, a mountain suspended in midair. Its presence felt oppressive to everyone beneath it.

After the spheroid halted, the air that had driven it charged the ground, sending up a rapidly expanding ring of dirt and snow. It's said that when people touched something they didn't expect to be as cold as an ice cube, it'd feel so hot that they'd shout as their hand recoiled. In the instant that the mass of air fell on her, that's how Yan Dong felt. Even someone from the bitterly cold Northeast would have felt the same way. Fortunately, the air diffused quickly, or else everyone on the ground would have frozen stiff. Even so, practically everyone with exposed skin suffered some frostbite.

Yan Dong's face was numb from the sudden cold. She looked up, transfixed by the spheroid's surface. It was made of a translucent ash-gray substance she recognized intimately: ice. This object suspended in the air was a giant ball of ice.

Once the air settled, large snowflakes were fluttering around the floating mountain of ice. An oddly pure white against the blue sky, they glittered in the sunlight. However, these snowflakes were only visible within a certain distance around the spheroid. When they floated farther away, they dissolved. They formed a snow ring with the spheroid as its center, as though the spheroid were a streetlamp lighting the snowflakes around it on a cold night.

'I am a low-temperature artist!' a clear, sharp voice emitted from the ball of ice. 'I am a low-temperature artist!'

'This ball of ice is you?' Yan Dong shouted back.

'You can't see my true form. The ball of ice you see is formed by my freeze field from the moisture in the air,' the low-temperature artist replied.

'What about those snowflakes?'

'They are crystals of the oxygen and nitrogen in the air. In addition, there's dry ice formed from the carbon dioxide.'

'Wow. Your freeze field is so powerful!'

'Of course. It's like countless tiny hands holding countless tiny hearts tight. It forces all the molecules and atoms within its range to stop moving.'

'It can also lift this gigantic ball of ice into the air?'

'That's a different kind of field, the antigravity field. The ice-sculpting tools you all use are so fascinating. You have small shovels and small chisels of every shape. Not to mention watering cans and blowtorches. Fascinating! To make low-temperature works of art, I also have a set of tiny tools. They are various types of force fields. Not as many tools as you have, but they work extremely well.'

'You create ice sculptures, too?'

'Of course. I'm a low-temperature artist. Your world is extremely suitable for the ice- and snow-molding arts. I was shocked to discover they've long existed in this world. I'm thrilled to say that we're colleagues.'

'Where do you come from?' the ice sculptor next to Yan Dong asked.

'I come from a faraway place, a world you have no way to understand. That world is not nearly as interesting as yours. Originally, I focused solely on the art. I didn't interact with other worlds. However, seeing exhibitions like this one, seeing so many colleagues, I found the desire to interact. But, frankly, very few of the low-temperature works below me deserve to be called works of art.'

'Why?' someone asked.

'Excessively realistic, too reliant on form and detail. Besides space, there's nothing in the universe. The actual world is just a big pile of curved spaces. Once you understand this, you'll see how risible these works are. However, hm, this piece moves me a little.'

Just as the voice faded away, a delicate thread extended from the snowflakes around the ball of ice, as if it flowed down following an invisible funnel. The snowflake thread stretched from midair to the top of Yan Dong's ice sculpture before dissolving. Yan Dong stood on her tiptoes, and tentatively stretched a gloved hand toward the snowflake thread. As she neared it, her fingers felt that burning sensation again. She jerked her hand back, but it was already painfully cold inside the glove.

'Are you pointing to my work?' Yan Dong rubbed her frozen hand with the other. 'I, I didn't use traditional methods. That is, carve it from ready-made blocks of ice. Instead, I built a structure composed of several large membranes. For a long time, steam produced from boiling water rose from the bottom of the structure. The steam froze to the membrane, forming a complex crystal. Once the crystal grew thick enough, I got rid of the membrane and the result is what you see here.'

'Very good. So interesting. It so expresses the beauty of the cold. The inspiration for this work comes from . . .'

'Windowpanes! I don't know whether you will be able to understand my description: When you wake during a hard winter's night just before sunrise, your bleary gaze falls on the windowpane filled with crystals. They reflect the dark blue first light of early dawn, as though they were something you dreamed up overnight . . .'

'Yes, yes, I understand!' The snowflakes around the low-temperature artist danced in a lively pattern. 'I have been inspired. I want to create! I must create!'

'The Songhua River is that way. You can select a block of ice, or . . .'

'What? Your form of art is as pitiable as bacteria. Do you think my form of low-temperature art is anything like that? This place doesn't have the sort of ice I need.'

The ice sculptors on the ground looked bewildered at the interstellar low-temperature artist. Yan Dong said, blankly, 'Then, you want to go . . .'

'I want to go to the ocean!'

Collecting Ice

An immense fleet of airplanes flew at an altitude of five kilometers along the coastline. This was the most motley collection of airplanes in history. It was composed of all types, ranging from Boeing jumbo jets to mosquito-like light aircraft. Every major press service in the world had dispatched news planes. In addition, research organizations and governments had dispatched observation planes. This chaotic air armada trailed closely behind a short wake of thick white vapor, like a flock of sheep chasing after its shepherd. The wake was left by the low-temperature artist. It constantly urged the planes behind it to fly faster. To wait for them, it had to endure a rate of flight slower than crawling. (For someone who jumped through space-time at will, light speed was already crawling.) The whole way, it grumbled that this pace would kill its inspiration.

In the airplanes behind it, reporters rattled away, asking endless questions over the radio. The low-temperature artist had no desire to answer any of them. It was only interested in talking to Yan Dong, sitting in the Harbin Y-12 that China Central Television had rented. As a result, the reporters grew quiet. They listened carefully to the conversation between the two artists.

'Is your home within the Milky Way?' Yan Dong asked. The Harbin Y-12 was the plane closest to the low-temperature artist. She could see the flying ball of ice intermittently through the white vapor. This wake trailing it was formed from oxygen, nitrogen, and carbon dioxide in the atmosphere condensing in the ultralow temperatures around the ice ball. Sometimes, the plane would accidentally brush the wake's billows of white mist. A thick coat of frost would immediately coat the plane's windows.

'My home isn't part of any galaxy. It sits in the vast and empty void between galaxies.'

'Your planet must be extremely cold.'

'We don't have a planet. The low-temperature civilization developed in a cloud of dark matter. That realm is indeed extremely cold. With difficulty, life snatched a little heat from the near-absolute-zero environment. It sucked in every thread of radiation that came from distant stars. Once the low-temperature civilization learned how to leave, we couldn't wait to go to the closest warm planet in the Milky Way. On this world, we had to maintain a low-temperature environment to live, so we became that warm planet's low-temperature artists.'

'The low-temperature art you're talking about is sculpting ice and snow?'

'Oh, no. No. Using a temperature far lower than a world's mean temperature to affect the world so as to produce artistic effects, this is all part of the low-temperature art. Sculpting ice and snow is just the low-temperature art that suits this world. The temperature of ice and snow is what this world considers a low temperature. For a dark-matter world, that would be a high temperature. For a stellar world, lava would be considered low-temperature material.'

'We seem to overlap in what art we consider beautiful.'

'That's not unusual. So-called warmth is just a brief effect of an equally brief spasm produced after the universe was born. It's gone in an instant like light after sunset. Energy dissipates. Only the cold is eternal. The beauty of the cold is the only enduring beauty.'

'So you're saying the final fate of the universe is heat death?!' Yan Dong heard someone ask over her earpiece. Later, she learned the speaker was a theoretical physicist sitting in one of the planes following behind.

'No digressions. We will discuss only art,' the low-temperature artist scolded.

'The ocean is below us!' Yan Dong happened to glance out the porthole. The crooked coastline passed below.

'Further ahead, we'll reach the deepest part of the ocean. That will be the most convenient place to collect ice.'

'Where will there be ice?' Yan Dong asked, uncomprehending, as she looked at the vast, blue ocean.

'Wherever a low-temperature artist goes, there will be ice.'

*

The low-temperature artist flew for another hour. Yan Dong stared out the window as they traveled. The view had long become a boundless surface of water. At that moment, the plane suddenly pulled up. She nearly blacked out from acceleration.

'We almost hit it!' the pilot shouted.

The low-temperature artist had stopped suddenly. Taken by surprise, the planes behind it scrambled to change direction.

'Damn it! The law of inertia doesn't apply to the fucker. Its speed seemed to drop to zero in an instant. By all rights, this sort of deceleration should have cracked the ball of ice into pieces,' the pilot said to Yan Dong.

As he spoke, he steered the plane around. The other pilots did the same. The ball of ice, rotating majestically, lingered in midair. It produced oxygen and nitrogen snowflakes, but due to strong wind at the altitude, the snowflakes were all blown away. They seemed like white hair whirling in the wind around the ball of ice.

'I am about to create!' the low-temperature artist said. Without waiting for Yan Dong to respond, it suddenly dropped straight down as if the giant invisible hand that had held it suddenly let it go. It free-fell faster and faster until it disappeared into the blue backdrop that was the ocean, leaving only a faint thread of atoms stretching down from midair. A ring of white spray shot up from the sea surface. When it fell, a wave spread out in a circle on the water.

'This alien threw itself into the ocean and committed suicide,' the pilot said to Yan Dong.

'Don't be ridiculous!' Yan Dong stretched out her Northeastern accent and glared at the pilot. 'Fly a little lower. The ball of ice will float back up any moment now.'

But the ball of ice didn't float back up. In its place, a white dot appeared on the ocean. It quickly expanded into a disk. The plane descended and Yan Dong could observe in detail.

The white disk was actually a white fog that covered the ocean. Soon, between its quick expansion and the airplane's continued descent, the only ocean she could see oozed a white fog from its surface. A noise from the sea covered the roaring of the plane's engine. It sounded both like rolling thunder and the cracking of the plains and mountains.

The airplane hovered close to sea level. Yan Dong peered at the surface of the ocean below the fog. The light the ocean reflected was mild, not like moments ago when glints of gold had slashed Yan Dong's eyes. The ocean grew deeper in color. Its rough waves grew level and smooth. What shocked her, though, was the next discovery: The waves became solid and motionless.

'Good heavens. The ocean froze!'

'Are you crazy?' The pilot turned his head to look at Yan Dong.

'See for yourself. . . . Hey! Why are you still descending? Do you want to land on the ice?!'

The pilot yanked the control stick. Once again, the world in front of Yan Dong grew black. She heard the pilot say, 'Ah, no, fuck, how strange . . .' The pilot looked as though he were sleepwalking. 'I wasn't descending. The ocean, no, the ice is rising by itself!'

At that moment, Yan Dong heard the low-temperature artist's voice: 'Get your flying machine out of the way. Don't block the path of the rising ice. If there weren't a colleague in the flying machine, I would simply crash into you. I can't stand disruptions to my inspiration while I'm creating. Fly west, fly west, fly west. That direction is closer to the edge.'

'Edge? The edge of what?' Yan Dong asked.

'The cube of ice I'm taking!'

Planes took off like a flock of startled birds, climbing into the sky and heading in the direction the low-temperature artist indicated. Below, because the white fog created by the temperature drop had dissipated, the dark blue ice field stretched to the horizon. Even though the plane was climbing, the ice field climbed even faster. As a result, the distance between the planes and the ice field continued to shrink.

'The Earth is chasing us!' the pilot screamed.

The plane now flew pressed against the ice field. Frozen dark blue waves roiled past the plane's wings.

The pilot yelled, 'We have no choice but to land on the ice field. My god, climbing and landing at the same time. That's just too strange.'

Just at that moment, the Harbin Y-12 reached the end of the ice. A straight edge swept past the fuselage. Below them, liquid sea reemerged, rippling and shimmering. It was like what a fighter jet saw the instant it leapt off the deck of an aircraft carrier, except the 'aircraft carrier' was several kilometers tall.

Yan Dong snapped her head around. Behind them, an immense, dark blue cliff could be seen. The bottom of the massive block of ice had cleared the ocean.

As the chunk of ice continued to rise, Yan Dong finally understood what the low-temperature artist had meant: This was literally a giant block of ice. The dark blue cube occupied two-thirds of the sky. Afterward, radar observation indicated that the block of ice was sixty kilometers long, twenty kilometers wide, and five kilometers tall, a thin and flat cuboid. Its flat surface reflected the sunlight, like streaks of eye-piercing lightning high in the sky.

The giant block of ice kept rising, casting an unimaginably large shadow onto the sea. And when it shifted, it revealed the most terrifying sight since the dawn of history.

The planes were flying over a long, narrow basin, the empty space in the ocean that was left once the giant block of ice was removed. On each side was a mountain of seawater five kilometers high. Hundred-meter-high waves surged at the bottom of these liquid cliffs. At the top, the cliffs were collapsing, advancing as they did. Their surface rippled, but they remained perpendicular to the seafloor. As the seawater cliffs advanced, the basin shrank.

This was the reverse of Moses parting the Red Sea.

What startled Yan Dong the most was how slow the entire process seemed. This was, she assumed, due to the scale. She'd seen the Huangguoshu waterfalls. The water had seemed to fall slowly there, too. And these cliffs of seawater before her were magnitudes larger than those waterfalls. Watching them felt like an endless moment of unparalleled wonder.

The shadow cast by the block of ice had completely disappeared. Yan Dong looked up. The block of ice was now just the size of two full moons.

As the two seawater cliffs advanced, the basin shrank into a canyon. Then the two seawater cliffs, tens of kilometers long, five thousand meters high, crashed into each other. An incredible roar echoed between the sea and sky. The space in the ocean the ice block left was gone.

'We aren't dreaming, are we?' Yan Dong said to herself.

'If this were a dream, everything would be fine. Look!'

The pilot pointed below. Where the two cliffs had crashed into each other, the sea hadn't yet settled. Two waves as long as those cliffs rose, as if they were the reincarnation of those two seawater cliffs on the sea's surface. They parted, heading in opposite directions. From high above, the waves weren't that impressive, but careful measurements showed they were over two hundred meters tall. Viewed from up close, they'd seem like two moving mountain ranges.

'Tidal waves?' Yan Dong asked.

'Yes. Could be the largest ever. The coast is in for a disaster.'

Yan Dong looked up. She could no longer see the frozen block in the blue sky. According to radar, it had become an ice satellite of Earth.

For the rest of the day, the low-temperature artist removed, in the same way, hundreds of blocks of ice of the same size from the Pacific Ocean. It sent them into orbit around the Earth.

By nightfall, a cluster of twinkling points could be seen flying across the sky every couple of hours. You could distinguish them from the usual stars because, on careful inspection, someone could make out the shape of each point. They were each a small cuboid. They all, in their own orientations, spun on their own axes. As a result, they reflected the sunlight and twinkled at different rates.

People thought for a long time, but were never quite able to adequately describe these small objects in space. Finally, a reporter came up with an analogy that got some traction.

'They're like a handful of crystalline dominoes scattered by a space giant.'

A Dialogue Between Two Artists

'We ought to have a chat,' Yan Dong said.

'I asked you to come just to do that, but only about art,' the low-temperature artist said.

Yan Dong stood on a giant block of ice suspended five thousand meters in the air. The low-temperature artist had invited her here. The helicopter that had brought her had landed and now waited to the side. Its rotors were still spinning, ready to take off at any moment.

Ice fields stretched to the horizon on all sides. The ice surface reflected the dazzling sunlight. The layer of blue ice below her seemed bottomless. At this altitude, the sky was clear and boundless. The wind blew stiffly.

This was one of the five thousand giant blocks of ice the low-temperature artist had taken from the oceans. Over the past five days, it had taken, on average, one thousand blocks a day from the oceans and sent them into orbit. All across the Pacific and Atlantic oceans, giant blocks of ice were being frozen and then carried into the air to become one of an increasing number of glittering 'space dominoes.' Tidal waves assaulted every major city along the world's coasts. Over time, though, these disasters became less frequent. The reason was simple: The sea level had dropped.

Earth's oceans had become blocks of ice revolving around it.

Yan Dong stamped her feet on the hard ice surface. 'Such a large block of ice, how did you freeze it in an instant? How did you do it in one piece without it cracking? What force are you using to send it into orbit? All of this is beyond our understanding and imagination.'

The low-temperature artist said, 'This is nothing. In the course of creation, we've often destroyed stars! Didn't we agree to discuss only art? I, creating art in this way, you, using small knives and shovels to carve ice sculptures, from the view from the perspective of art, aren't all that different.'

'When those ice blocks orbiting in space are exposed to intense sunlight, why don't they melt?'

'I covered every ice block with a layer of extremely thin, transparent, light-filtering membrane. It only allows cold light, whose frequencies don't generate heat, to get into the block of ice. The frequencies that do generate heat are all reflected. As a result, the block of ice doesn't melt. This is the last time I'll answer this sort of question. I didn't stop work to discuss these trivial things. From now on, we'll discuss only art, or else you might as well leave. We'll no longer be colleagues and friends.'

'In that case, how much ice do you ultimately plan to take from the oceans? This is surely relevant to the creation of art!'

'Of course, I'll only take as much as there is. I've talked to you before about my design. I'd like to realize it perfectly. Initially, I planned to take ice from Jupiter's satellites if it had turned out that Earth's oceans aren't enough, but it seems there's enough to make do.'

The wind mussed Yan Dong's hair. She smoothed it back into place. The cold at this altitude made her shiver. 'Is art important to you?'

'It's everything.'

'But . . . there are other things in life. For example, we still need to work to survive. I'm an engineer at the Changchun Institute of Optics. I can only make art in my spare time.'

The low-temperature artist's voice rumbled from the depths of the ice. The vibrating ice surface tickled Yan Dong's feet. 'Survival. Ha! It's just the diaper of a civilization's infancy that needs to be changed. Later, that's as easy as breathing. You'll forget there ever was a time when it took effort to survive.'

'What about societal and political matters?'

'The existence of individuals is also a troublesome part of infant civilizations. Later, individuals melt into the whole. There's no society or politics as such.'

'What about science? There must be science, right? Doesn't a civilization need to understand the universe?'

'That is also a course of study infant civilizations take. Once exploration has carried out to the proper extent, everything down to the slightest will be revealed. You will discover that the universe is so simple, even science is unnecessary.'

'So that just leaves art?'

'Yes. Art is the only reason for a civilization to exist.'

'But we have other reasons. We want to survive. The several billion people on this planet below us and even more of other species want to survive. You want to dry our oceans, to make this living planet a doomed desert, to make us all die of thirst.'

A wave of laughter propagated from the depths of the ice. Again, it tickled Yan Dong's feet.

'Colleague, look, once the violent surge of creative inspiration had passed, I talked to you about art. But, every time, you gossip with me about trivialities. It disappoints me greatly. You ought to be ashamed. Go. I'm going to work.'

Yan Dong finally lost her patience. 'Fuck your ancestors!' she shouted, then continued to swear in a Northeastern dialect of Chinese.

'Are those obscenities?' the low-temperature artist asked placidly. 'Our species is one where the same body matures as it evolves. No ancestors. As for treating your colleague like this . . .' It laughed. 'I understand. You're jealous of me. You don't have my ability. You can only make art at the level of bacteria.'

'But, you just said that our art requires different tools but there's no essential difference.'

'I've just now changed my perspective. At first, I thought I'd run into a real artist, but, as it turns out, you're a mediocre, pitiful creature who chatters on about the oceans drying, ecological collapse, and other inconsequential things that have nothing to do with art. Too trivial, too trivial, I tell you. Artists cannot be like this.'

'Fuck your ancestors anyway.'

'Yes, well. I'm working. Go.'

For a moment, Yan Dong felt heavy. She fell ass-first onto the slick ice as a gust of wind swept down from above. The ice block was rising again. She scrambled into the helicopter, which, with difficulty, took off from the nearest edge of the block of ice, nearly crashing in the tornado produced as the block of ice rose.

Communication between humanity and the low-temperature artist had failed.

Sea of Dreams

Yan Dong stood in a white world. The ground below her feet and the surrounding mountains were covered in a silvery white cloak. The mountains were steep and treacherous. She felt as though she were in the snow-covered Himalayas. But in fact, it was the opposite; she was at the lowest place on Earth. The Marianas Trench. Once the deepest part of the Pacific Ocean. The white material that covered everything was not snow but the minerals that had once made the water salty. After the seawater froze, these minerals separated out and were deposited on the seafloor. At the thickest, these deposits were as much as one hundred meters deep.

In the past two hundred days, the oceans of the Earth were exhausted by the low-temperature artist. Even the glaciers of Greenland and Antarctica were completely pillaged.

Now, the low-temperature artist invited Yan Dong to participate in its work's final rite of completion.

*

In the ravine ahead lay a surface of blue water. The blue was pure and deep. It seemed all the more touching among so many snow-white mountain peaks. This was the last ocean on Earth. It was about the area of Dianchi Lake in Yunnan. Its great waves had long ceased. Only gentle ripples swayed on the water, as though it were a secluded lake deep in the mountains. Three rivers converged into this final ocean. These were great rivers that had survived by luck, trudging through the vast, dehydrated seafloor. They were the longest rivers on Earth. By the time they'd arrived here, they'd become slender rivulets.

Yan Dong walked to the oceanfront. Standing on the white beach, she dipped her hand into the lightly rippling sea. Because the water was so saturated with salt, its waves seemed sluggish. A gentle breeze blew Yan Dong's hand dry, leaving a layer of white salt.

The sharp sound that Yan Dong knew so well pierced the air. It tore through the air whenever the low-temperature artist slid toward the ground. Yan Dong spotted it in the sky as it approached.

The low-temperature artist didn't greet Yan Dong. The ball of ice fell into the middle of this last ocean, causing a tall column of water to spout. Afterward, once again, a familiar scene emerged: A disk of white fog oozed out from the point where the low-temperature artist hit the water. Rapidly, the white fog covered the entire ocean. The water quickly froze with a loud cracking sound. Once again, the fog dissipating revealed a frozen ocean surface. Unlike before, this time, the entire body of water was frozen. There wasn't a drop of liquid water left. The ocean surface also didn't have frozen waves. It was as smooth as a mirror. Throughout the freezing process, Yan Dong felt a cold draft on her face.

The now-frozen final ocean was lifted off the ground. At first, it was lifted only several careful centimeters off the ground. A long black fissure emerged from the edge of the ice field between the ice and white salt beach. Air, forming a strong wind low to the ground, rushed into the long fissure, filling the newly created space. It blew the salt around, so that it now buried Yan Dong's feet. The rate the lake was rising at increased. In the blink of an eye, the final ocean was in midair. So much volume rising so quickly produced violent, chaotic winds. A gust swirled up the salt into a white column in the ravine. Yan Dong spit out the salt that flew into her mouth. It wasn't salty like she'd imagined. It tasted bitter in a way that was hard to express, like the reality that humanity was up against.

The final ocean wasn't a cuboid. Its bottom was an exact impression of the contours of the seafloor. Yan Dong watched it rise until it became a small point of light that dissolved into the mighty ring of ice.

The ring of ice was about as wide as the Milky Way in the sky. Unlike the rings of Uranus and Neptune, the surface of the ring of ice was neither perpendicular nor parallel to the surface of the Earth. It was like a broad belt of light in space. A broad belt composed of two hundred thousand blocks of ice completely surrounding the Earth. From the ground, one could clearly make out every block of ice. Some of them rotated while others seemed static. Throughout the day, the ring of ice varied with dramatic changes in brightness and color. The two hundred thousand points of light, some twinkling, some not, formed a majestic, heavenly river that flowed solemnly across the Earth's sky.

Its colors were the most dramatic at dawn and dusk. The ring of ice changed gradually from the orange-red of the horizon to a dark red and then to dark green and dark blue, like a rainbow in space.

During the daytime, the ring of ice assumed a dazzling silver color against the blue sky, like a great river of diamonds flowing across a blue plain. The daytime ring of ice looked most spectacular during an eclipse, when it blocked the sun. Massive blocks of ice refracted the sunlight. Like a strange and magnificent fireworks show in the sky.

How long the sun was blocked by the ice ring depended on whether it was an intersecting eclipse or a parallel eclipse. What was known as a parallel eclipse was when the sun followed the ring of ice for some distance. Every year, there was one total parallel eclipse. For a day, the sun, from sunrise to sunset, followed the path of the ice ring for its entire journey. On this day, the ring of ice seemed like a belt of silver gunpowder set loose on the sky. Ignited at sunrise, the dazzling fireball burned wildly across the sky. When it set in the west, the sight was magnificent, too difficult to put into words. Some people proclaimed, 'Today, God strolled across the sky.'

Even so, the ring of ice's most enchanting moment was at night. It was twice as bright as a full moon. Its silver light filled the Earth. It was as though every star in the universe had lined up to march solemnly across the night sky. Unlike the Milky Way, in this mighty river of stars, one could clearly make out every cuboid star. Of these thickly clustered stars, half of them glittered. Those hundred thousand twinkling stars formed a ripple that surged, as though driven by a gale. It transformed the river of stars into an intelligent whole . . .

With a sharp squeal, the low-temperature artist returned from space for the last time. The ball of ice was suspended over Yan Dong. A ring of snowflakes appeared and wrapped itself tightly around it.

'I've completed it. What you do think?' it asked.

Yan Dong stayed silent for a long time, then said only one short phrase: 'I give up.'

She had truly given up. Once, she'd stared up at the ring of ice for three consecutive days and three nights, without food or drink, until she collapsed. Once she could get out of bed again, she went back outside to stare at the ice ring again. She felt she as if she could gaze at it forever and it wouldn't be enough. Beneath the ring of ice, she was sometimes dazed, sometimes steeped in an indescribable happiness. This was the happiness of when an artist found ultimate beauty. She was completely conquered by this immense beauty. Her entire soul was dissolved in it.

'As an artist, now that you're able to see such work, are you still striving for it?' the low-temperature artist asked.

'Truly, I'm not,' Yan Dong answered sincerely.

'However, you're merely looking. Certainly, you can't create such beauty. You're too trivial.'

'Yes. I'm too trivial. We're too trivial. How can we? We have to support ourselves and our children.'

Yan Dong sat on the saline soil. Steeped in sorrow, she buried her head in her hands. This was the deep sorrow that arose when an artist saw beauty she could never produce, when she realized she would never be able to transcend her limitations.

'So, how about we name this work together? Call it – *Ring of Dreams,* perhaps?'

Yan Dong considered this. Slowly, she shook her head. 'No, it came from the sea or, rather, was sublimated from the sea. Not even in our dreams could we conceive that the sea possessed this form of beauty. It should be called – *Sea of Dreams.*'

'*Sea of Dreams* . . . very good, very good. We'll call it that, *Sea of Dreams.*'

Then, Yan Dong remembered her mission. 'I'd like to ask, before you leave, can you return *Sea of Dreams* to become our actual seas?'

'Have me personally destroy my own work? Ridiculous!'

'Then, after you leave, can we restore the seas ourselves?'

'Of course you can. Just return these blocks of ice and everything should be fine, right?'

'How do we do that?' Yan Dong asked, her head raised. All of humanity strained to hear the answer.

'How should I know?' the low-temperature artist said indifferently.

'One final question: As colleagues, we all know that works of art made from ice and snow are short-lived. So *Sea of Dreams* . . .'

'*Sea of Dreams* is also short-lived. A block of ice's light-filtering membrane will age. It'll no longer be able to block heat. But they will dissolve differently than your ice sculptures. The process will be more violent and magnificent. Blocks of ice will vaporize. The pressure will cause the membrane to burst. Every block of ice will turn into a small comet. The entire ring of ice will blur into a silver fog. Then *Sea of Dreams* will disappear into that silver fog. Then the silver fog will scatter and disappear into space. The universe can only look forward to my next work on some other distant world.'

'How long until this happens?' Yan Dong's voice quavered.

'The light-filtering membrane will become ineffective, as you reckon time, hm, in about twenty years. Oh, why are we talking about things other than art again? Trivial, trivial! Okay, colleague. Goodbye. Enjoy the beauty I have left you!'

The ball of ice shot into the air, disappearing into the sky. According to the measurements of every major astronomical organization in the world, the ball of ice flew rapidly along a perpendicular to the ecliptic plane. Once it had accelerated to half the speed of light, it abruptly disappeared thirteen astronomical units away from the sun, as if it'd squeezed into an invisible hole. It never returned.

SECOND HALF

Monument and Waveguide

The drought had already lasted for five years.

Withered ground swept past the car window. It was midsummer and there was not a bit of green anywhere on the ground. The trees were all withered. Cracks like black spiderwebs covered the ground. Frequent dry, hot winds kicked up sand that concealed everything. Quite a few times, Yan Dong thought she saw the corpses of people who had died of thirst along the railroad tracks, but they might have just been fallen, dry tree branches, nothing to be afraid of. This harsh, arid world contrasted sharply with the silver *Sea of Dreams* in the sky.

Yan Dong licked her parched lips. She couldn't bring herself to drink from her water flask. That was four days' rations for her entire family. Her husband had forced it on her at the train station. Yesterday, her workmates had protested, demanding to be paid in water. In the market, nonrationed water grew scarcer and scarcer. Even the rich weren't able to buy any. . . . Someone touched her shoulder. It was the person in the seat beside her.

'You're that alien's colleague, aren't you?'

Since she'd become the low-temperature artist's messenger, Yan Dong had also become a celebrity. At first, she was considered a role model and a hero. However, after the low-temperature artist left, the situation changed. One way of looking at things is, it was her work that had inspired the low-temperature artist at the Ice and Snow Arts Festival. Without that, none of this would have happened. Most people understood that this was utter nonsense, but having a scapegoat was a good thing. So, in people's eyes she was eventually seen as the low-temperature artist's conspirator. But fortunately, after the artist had left, there were bigger issues to worry about. People gradually forgot about Yan Dong. However, this time, even though she was wearing sunglasses, she had been recognized.

'Ask me to drink some water!' the man beside her said, his voice rasping. Two flakes of dry skin fell from his lips.

'What are you doing? Are you robbing me?'

'Be smart, or else I'll scream!'

Yan Dong felt obliged to hand over her water flask. The man drained the flask in one swallow. The people around them watched this with shock on their faces. Even the train attendant who had been passing by stopped in the aisle and stared at him, stupefied. That anyone could be so wasteful was nearly beyond belief. It was like back in the Oceaned Days (what people called the age before the arrival of the low-temperature artist), watching a rich person eat a sumptuous dinner that cost one hundred thousand yuan.

The man returned the empty flask to Yan Dong. Patting Yan Dong's shoulder again, the man said in a low voice, 'It doesn't matter. Soon, it'll all be over.'

Yan Dong understood what the man meant.

The capital seldom had cars on its streets anymore. The rare few had all been retrofitted to be air-cooled. Using a conventional liquid-cooled car was strictly prohibited. Fortunately, the Chinese branch of the World Crisis Organization had sent a car to pick her up. Otherwise, she'd absolutely have had no way to reach their offices. On the way, she saw that sandstorms had covered all the roads with yellow sand. She didn't see many pedestrians. For anyone dehydrated, walking around in the hot, dry wind was too dangerous.

The world was like a fish out of water, already begging for a breath.

When she arrived at the World Crisis Organization, Yan Dong reported to the bureau chief. The bureau chief brought her to a large office and introduced her to the group she would be working with. Yan Dong looked at the office door. Unlike the other ones, this one had no nameplate. The bureau chief said:

'This is a secret group. Everything done here is strictly confidential. In order to avoid social unrest, we call this group the Monument Division.'

Entering the office, Yan Dong realized the people here were all somewhat eccentric: Some had hair that was too long. Some had no hair at all. Some were immaculately dressed, as if the world weren't falling apart around them. Some wore only shorts. Some seemed dejected, others abnormally excited. Many oddly shaped models sat on a long table in the middle of the office. Yan Dong couldn't guess what they might be for.

'Welcome, Ice Sculptor.' The head of the Monument Division enthusiastically shook Yan Dong's hand after the bureau chief's introduction. 'You'll finally have the opportunity to elaborate on the inspiration you received from the alien. Of course, this time, you can't use ice. What we want to build is a work that must last forever.'

'What for?'

The division head looked at the bureau chief, then back at Yan Dong. 'You still don't know? We want to establish a monument to humanity!'

Yan Dong felt even more at a loss with this explanation.

'It's humanity's tombstone,' an artist to her side said. This person had long hair and tattered clothes, and gave the impression of decadence. One hand held a bottle of sorghum liquor that he'd drunk until he was somewhat tipsy. The liquor was left over from the Oceaned Days and now much cheaper than water.

Yan Dong looked all around, then said, 'But . . . we're not dead yet.'

'If we wait until we're dead, it'll be too late,' the bureau chief said. 'We ought to plan for the worst case. The time to think about this is now.'

The division head nodded. 'This is humanity's final work of art, and also its greatest work of art. For an artist, what can be more profound than to join in its creation?'

'Fucking, actually. . . . Much more,' the long-haired artist said, waving the bottle. 'Tombstones are for your descendants to pay homage to. We'll have no descendants, but we'll still erect a fucking tomb?'

'Pay attention to the name. It's a monument,' the division head corrected solemnly. Laughing, he said to Yan Dong, 'However, the idea he put forth is very good: He proposed that everyone in the world donate a tooth. Those teeth can be used to create a gigantic tablet. Carving a word on each tooth is sufficient to engrave the most detailed history of human civilization on the tablet.' He pointed at a model that looked like a white pyramid.

'This is blasphemy against humanity,' a bald-headed artist shouted. 'The worth of humanity lies in its brains, but he wants to commemorate us with our teeth!'

The long-haired artist took another swig from his bottle. 'Teeth. . . . Teeth are easy to preserve.'

'The vast majority of people are still alive!' Yan Dong repeated solemnly.

'But for how long?' the long-haired artist said. As he asked this question, his enunciation suddenly became precise. 'Water no longer falls from the sky. The rivers have dried. Our crops have utterly failed for three years now. Ninety percent of the factories have stopped production. The remaining food and water, how long can that sustain us?'

'You heap of waste.' The bald-headed artist pointed at the bureau chief. 'Bustling around for five years and you still can't bring even one block of ice back from space.'

The bureau chief laughed off the bald-headed artist's criticism. 'It's not that simple. Given current technology, forcing down one block of ice from orbit isn't hard. Forcing down one hundred, up to one thousand blocks of ice is doable. But forcing back all two hundred thousand blocks of ice orbiting the Earth, that's another matter completely. If we use conventional techniques, a rocket engine could slow a block of ice enough that it would fall back into the atmosphere. That would mean building a large number of reusable high-power engines, then sending them into space. That's a massive-scale engineering project. Given our current technology level and what resources we've stockpiled, there are many insurmountable obstacles. For example, in order to save the Earth's ecosystem, if we start now, we'd need to force down half the blocks of ice within four years, an average of twenty-five thousand per year. The weight of rocket fuel required would be greater than the amount of gasoline humanity used in one year during the Oceaned Days! Except it isn't gasoline. It's liquid hydrogen, liquid oxygen, dinitrogen tetroxide, unsymmetrical dimethylhydrazine, and so on. They need over a hundred times more energy and natural resources to produce than gasoline. Just this one thing makes the entire plan impossible.'

The long-haired artist nodded. 'In other words, doomsday is not far away.'

The bureau chief said, 'No, not necessarily. We can still adopt some nonconventional techniques. There is still hope. While we're working on this, though, we must still plan for the worst.'

'This is exactly why I came,' Yan Dong said.

'To plan for the worst?' the long-haired artist asked.

'No, because there's still hope.' She turned to the bureau chief. 'It doesn't matter why you brought me here. I came for my own purpose.' She pointed to her bulky travel bag. 'Please take me to the Ocean Recovery Division.'

'What can you do in the Ocean Recovery Division? They're all scientists and engineers there,' the bald-headed artist wondered.

'I'm a research fellow in applied optics.' Yan Dong's gaze swept past the artists. 'Besides daydreaming along with you, I can also do some practical things.'

*

After Yan Dong insisted, the bureau chief brought her to the Ocean Recovery Division. The mood here was completely different from the Monument Division. Everyone was tense, working on their computers. A drinking fountain stood in the middle of the office. They could take a drink whenever they wanted. This was treatment worthy of kings. But considering that the hope of the world rested on the people in this room, it wasn't so surprising.

When Yan Dong saw the Ocean Recovery Division's lead engineer, she told her, 'I've brought a plan for reclaiming the ice blocks.'

As she spoke, she opened her travel bag. She took out a white tube about as thick as an arm, followed by a cylinder about a meter long. Yan Dong walked to a window that faced the sun. She stuck the cylinder out the window, then shook it back and forth. The cylinder opened like an umbrella. Its concave side was plated with a mirror coating. That turned it into something like a parabolic reflector for a solar stove. Next, Yan Dong pushed the tube through a small hole at the bottom of the paraboloid, then adjusted the reflector so that it focused sunlight at the end of the tube. Immediately, the other end of the tube cast an eye-stabbing point of light on the floor. Because the tube lay flat on the floor, the point was an exaggerated oval.

Yan Dong said, 'This uses the latest optical fiber to create a waveguide. There's very little attenuation. Naturally, an actual system would be much larger than this. In space, a parabolic reflector only about twenty meters in diameter can create a point of light at the other end of the waveguide with a temperature of over three thousand degrees.'

Yan Dong looked around. Her demonstration hadn't produced the reaction she'd expected. The engineers took a look, then returned to their computer screens, paying her no mind. It wasn't until a stream of dark smoke rose from the point of light on the antistatic floor that the nearest person came over and said, 'What did you do? I doubt it's hot.'

At the same time, the person nudged back the waveguide, moving the light coming through the window away from the focal length of the parabolic reflector. Although the point was still on the floor, it immediately darkened and lost heat. Yan Dong was surprised at how adept the person was at adjusting the thing.

The lead engineer pointed at the waveguide. 'Pack up your gear and drink some water. I heard you took the train. The one to here from Changchun is still running? You must be extremely thirsty.'

Yan Dong desperately wanted to explain her invention, but she truly was thirsty. Her throat burned and it was painful to speak.

'Very good. This is a really practical plan.' The lead engineer handed Yan Dong a glass of water.

Yan Dong drained the glass of water in one gulp. She looked blankly at the lead engineer. 'Are you saying that someone has already thought of this?'

The lead engineer laughed. 'Spending time with aliens has made you underestimate human intellect. In fact, from the moment the low-temperature artist sent the first block of ice into space, many people have come up with this plan. Afterward, there were lots of variants. For example, some used solar panels instead of reflectors. Some used wires and electric heating elements instead of waveguides. The advantage is that the equipment is easy to manufacture and transport. The disadvantage is the efficiency is not as high as waveguides. We've been researching this for five years now. The technology is already mature. The equipment we need has mostly been manufactured.'

'Then why haven't you carried the plan out?'

An engineer next to them said, 'With this plan, the Earth will lose twenty-one percent of its water. Either during propulsion as vaporized steam or during reentry from high-temperature dissociation.'

The lead engineer turned to that engineer. 'We don't know that yet. The latest American simulations show, below the ionosphere, the hydrogen produced by high-temperature dissociation during reentry will immediately recombine with the surrounding oxygen into water. We overestimated the high-temperature-dissociation loss. The total loss estimate is around eighteen percent.' She turned back to Yan Dong. 'But this percentage is high enough.'

'Then do you have a plan to bring back all of the water from space?'

The lead engineer shook her head. 'The only possibility is to use a nuclear fusion engine. But, right now, on Earth, controlled nuclear fusion isn't within our capabilities.'

'Then why aren't you acting more quickly? You know, if you dither around, the Earth will lose one hundred percent of its water.'

The lead engineer nodded. 'So, after a long time of hesitation, we've decided to act. Soon, the Earth will be in for the fight of its life.'

Reclaiming the Oceans

Yan Dong joined the Ocean Recovery Division, in charge of receiving and checking the waveguides that had been produced. Although this wasn't a core posting, she found it fulfilling.

One month after Yan Dong arrived at the capital, humanity's project to reclaim the oceans started.

Within one short week, eight hundred large-scale carrier rockets shot into the sky from every launch site in the world, sending fifty thousand tons of freight into Earth orbit. Then, from the North American launch site, twenty space shuttles ferried three hundred astronauts into space. Because launches generally followed the same route, the skies above the launch sites all had a single rocket contrail that never dispersed. Viewed from orbit, it seemed like threads of spider silk stretching up from every continent into space.

These launches increased human space activity by an order of magnitude, but the technology used was still twentieth-century technology. People realized, under existing conditions, if the entire world worked together and risked everything on one attempt, it could do anything.

On live television, Yan Dong and everyone else witnessed the first time a deceleration propulsion system was installed on a block of ice.

To make things less difficult, the first blocks of ice they forced back weren't the ones that rotated about their own axes. Three astronauts landed on a block of ice. They brought with them the following equipment: an artillery-shell-shaped vehicle that could drill a hole into the block of ice, three waveguides, one expeller tube, and three folded-up parabolic reflectors. It was only now that anyone could get the sense of the immense size of a block of ice. The three people seemed to land on a tiny crystalline world. Under intense sunlight in space, the giant field of ice under their feet seemed unfathomable.

Near and far, innumerable similar crystalline worlds hung in the black sky. Some of them still rotated about their own axes. The surrounding rotating and nonrotating blocks of ice reflected and refracted the sunlight. On the ice the three astronauts stood on, they cast a dazzling pattern of ever-changing light and shadow. In the distance, the blocks of ice in the ring looked smaller and smaller, but gathered closer and closer together, gradually shrinking into a delicate, silver belt twisting toward the other side of the Earth. The closest block of ice was only three thousand meters away from this one. Because it rotated about its minor axis, in their eyes, such a rotation had a breathtaking momentum, as though they were three tiny ants watching a crystalline skyscraper collapsing over and over again. Due to gravity, these two ice blocks would eventually crash into each other. The light-filtering membranes would rupture and the blocks of ice would disintegrate. The smashed blocks of ice would quickly evaporate in the sunlight and disappear. Such collisions had already happened twice in the ring of ice. This was also why this block was the first block of ice to be forced back.

First, an astronaut started the driller vehicle. As the drill head spun, crumbs of ice flew out in a cone-shaped spray, twinkling in the sunlight. The driller vehicle broke through the invisible light-filtering membrane. Like a twisting screw, it dug into the ice, leaving a round hole in its wake. Along with the hole that stretched into the depths of the ice, a faint white line could be seen in the ice itself. Once the hole reached the prescribed depth, the vehicle headed out toward another part of the ice. It then bored another hole. At last, it drilled four holes in total. They all intersected at one point deep in the ice.

The astronauts inserted the three waveguides into three of the holes, then inserted the expeller into the wider fourth hole. The expeller tube's mouth was pointed in the direction of the motion of the block of ice. After that, the astronauts used a thin tube to caulk the gap the three waveguides and the expeller tube left against their holes' walls with a fast-sealing liquid to create a good seal. Finally, they opened the parabolic reflectors. If the initial phase of ocean reclamation employed the latest technology, it was these parabolic reflectors. They were a miracle created by nanotechnology. Folded up, each was only a cubic meter. Unfolded, each formed a giant reflector five hundred meters in diameter. These three reflectors were like three silver lotus leaves that grew on the block of ice. The astronauts adjusted each waveguide so that its receiver coincided with the focal point of its reflector.

A bright point of light appeared where the three holes intersected deep in the ice. It seemed like a tiny sun, illuminating within the block of ice spectacular sights of mythic proportions: a school of silver fish, dancing seaweed drifting with the waves . . . Everything retained its lifelike appearance at the instant it was frozen. Even the strings of bubbles spat from fishes' mouths were clear and distinct. Over one hundred kilometers away, inside another ice block being reclaimed, the sunlight that the waveguides led into the ice revealed a giant black shadow. It was a blue whale over twenty meters long! This had to be the Earth's seas of old.

Deep in the ice, steam soon blurred the point of light. As the steam dispersed, the point changed into a bright white ball. It swelled in size as the ice melted. Once the pressure had built up to a predetermined level, the expeller mouth cover was broken open. A violent gush of turbulent steam exploded out. Because there were no obstructions, it formed a sharp cone that scattered in the distance. Finally, it disappeared in the sunlight. Some portion of the steam entered another ice block's shadow and condensed into ice crystals that seemed like a swarm of flickering fireflies.

The deceleration propulsion system in the first batch of one hundred blocks of ice activated. Because the blocks of ice were so massive, the thrust the system produced was, relatively speaking, very small. As a result, they needed to orbit fifteen days to a month before they could slow the blocks of ice down enough for them to fall into the atmosphere. Later, reclaiming ice blocks that rotated was much more complicated. The propulsion system had to stop the rotation first, then slow down the block of ice.

Before the blocks of ice entered the atmosphere, astronauts would land on them again to recover the waveguides and reflectors. If they wanted to force all two hundred thousand blocks down, this equipment had to be reused as much as possible.

Ice Meteors

Yan Dong and members of the Crisis Committee arrived together at the flatlands in the middle of the Pacific Ocean to watch the first batch of ice meteors fall.

The ocean bed of former days looked like a snowy white plain, reflecting the intense sunlight – no one could open their eyes unless they were wearing sunglasses. But the white plain before them didn't make Yan Dong think of the snowfields of her native Northeast because, here, it was as hot as hell. The temperature was near fifty degrees Celsius. Hot winds kicked up salty dirt, which hurt when it hit her face. A hundred-thousand-ton oil tanker was in the distance. The gigantic hull lay tilted on the ground. Its propeller, several stories tall, and rudder completely covered the salt bed. An unbroken chain of white mountains stood even farther in the distance. That was a mountain range on the seafloor humanity had never seen until now. A two-sentence poem came to Yan Dong's mind: *The open sea is a boat's land. Night is love's day.*

She laughed bitterly then. She'd experienced this tragedy, yet she still couldn't shake off thinking like an artist.

Cheers erupted. Yan Dong raised her head and looked to where everyone was pointing. In the distance, a bright red point had appeared in the silver ring of ice that traversed the sky. The point of light drifted out of the ring. It swelled into a fireball. A white contrail dragged behind the fireball. This contrail of steam grew ever longer and thicker. Its color became even denser, even whiter. Soon, the fireball split into ten pieces. Each piece continued to split. A long white contrail dragged behind every small piece. This field of white contrails filled half the sky, as though it were a white Christmas tree and a small, bright lamp hung on the tip of every branch . . .

Even more ice meteors appeared. Their sonic booms shook the earth like rumbles of spring thunder. As old contrails gradually dissipated, new contrails appeared to replace them. They covered the sky in a complex white net. Several trillion tons of water now belonged to the Earth again.

Most of the ice meteors broke apart and vaporized in the air, but one large fragment of ice fell to the ground about forty kilometers from Yan Dong. The loud crash shook the flatlands. A colossal mushroom cloud rose from somewhere in the distant mountain range. The water vapor shone a dazzling white in the sunlight. Gradually, it dispersed in the wind and became the sky's first cloud layer. The clouds multiplied and, for the first time, blocked the sun that had been scorching the earth for five years. They covered the entire sky.

For a while, Yan Dong felt a pleasant coolness that oozed into her heart and lungs.

The cloud layer grew thick and dark. Red light flickered within it. Maybe it was lightning or the light from the continuous waves of ice meteors falling toward the earth.

It rained! This was a downpour so heavy it would have been rare even in the Oceaned Days. Yan Dong and everyone else there ran around screaming wildly in the storm. They felt their souls dissolve in the rain. Then they retreated into their cars and helicopters because, right now, people would suffocate in the rain.

The rain fell nonstop until dusk. Waterlogged depressions appeared on the seafloor flatlands. A crack in the clouds revealed the golden, flickering rays of the setting sun, as though the Earth had just opened its eyes.

Yan Dong followed the crowd, stepping through the thick salty mud. They ran to the nearest depression. She cupped some water in her hands, then splashed that thick brine on her face. As it fell, mixed with her tears, she said, choking with sobs:

'The ocean, our ocean . . .'

Epilogue

TEN YEARS LATER

Yan Dong walked onto the frozen-over Songhua River. She was wrapped in a tattered overcoat. Her travel bag held the tools that she'd kept for fifteen years: several knives and shovels of various shapes, a hammer, and a watering can. She stamped her feet to make sure that the river had truly frozen. The Songhua River had water as early as five years ago, but this was the first time it had frozen, and during the summer, no less.

Due to the arid conditions and, at the same time, the potential energy of the many ice meteors converting into thermal energy in the atmosphere, the global climate had stayed hotter than ever. But in the final stage of ocean reclamation, the largest blocks of ice were forced down. These blocks of ice broke into larger fragments. Most of them crashed onto the ground. This not only destroyed a few cities but also kicked up dust that blocked the sun's heat. Temperatures fell rapidly all over the world. Earth entered a new ice age.

Yan Dong looked at the night sky. This was the starscape of her childhood. The ring of ice had disappeared. She could only make out the vestiges of the remaining small blocks of ice from their rapid motion against the background of stars. *Sea of Dreams* had turned back into actual seas again. This magnificent work of art, its cruel beauty as well as nightmare, would forever be inscribed in the collective memory of humanity.

Although the ocean-reclamation effort had been a success, Earth's climate would be a harsh one from now on. The ecosystem would take a long time to recover. For the foreseeable future, humanity's existence would be extremely difficult. Nevertheless, at least existence was possible. Most people felt content with that. Indeed, the Ring of Ice Era made humanity learn contentment, and also something even more important.

The World Crisis Organization would change its name to the Space Water Retrieval Organization. They were considering another great engineering project: Humanity intended to fly to distant Jupiter, then take water from Jupiter's moons and the rings of Saturn back to Earth in order to make up for the 18 percent lost in the course of the Ocean Reclamation Project.

At first, people intended to use the technology for propelling blocks of ice that they'd already mastered to drive blocks of ice from the rings of Saturn to Earth. Of course, that far away, the sunlight was too weak. Only using nuclear fusion to vaporize the cores of the blocks of ice could provide the necessary thrust. As for the water from Jupiter's moons, that required even larger and more complex technology to acquire. Some people had already proposed pulling the whole of Europa out of Jupiter's deep gravity well, pushing it to Earth, and making it Earth's second moon. This way, Earth would receive much more water than 18 percent. It could turn Earth's ecosystem into a glorious paradise. Naturally, this was a matter for the far future. No one alive hoped to see it during their lifetime. However, this hope made people in their hard lives feel a happiness they'd never felt before. This was the most valuable thing humanity received from the Ring of Ice Era: Reclaiming *Sea of Dreams* made humanity see its own strength, taught it to dream what it had never before dared to dream.

Yan Dong saw in the distance a group of people gathered on the ice. She walked to them, gliding with each step. When they spotted her, they began to run toward her. Some slipped and fell, then picked themselves up and raced to catch up with the others.

'Our old friend! Hello!' The first one to reach Yan Dong wrapped her in a warm hug. Yan Dong recognized him. He was one of the ice sculpture judges from so many ice and snow festivals before the Ring of Ice Era.

As they neared, she recognized the others, most of them ice sculptors from before the Ring of Ice Era. Like everyone else of this era, they wore tattered clothes. Suffering and time had dyed the hair on their temples white. Yan Dong felt as though she'd come home after years of wandering.

'I heard that the Ice and Snow Arts Festival has started back up again?' she asked.

'Of course. Otherwise, what are we all doing here?'

'I've been thinking. Times are so hard . . .'

Yan Dong wrapped her large overcoat tighter around herself. She shivered in the cold wind, constantly stamping her numb feet against the ice. Everyone else did the same, shivering, stamping their feet, like a group of begging refugees.

'So what if times are hard? Even in hard times, you can't not make art, right?' an old ice sculptor said through chattering teeth.

'Art is the only reason for a civilization to exist!' someone else said.

'Fuck that, I have plenty of reasons to go on,' Yan Dong said loudly.

Everyone laughed, then fell silent as they thought back on ten years of hard times. One by one, they counted their reasons to go on. Finally, they changed themselves from survivors of a disaster back to artists again.

Yan Dong took a bottle of sorghum liquor from her bag. They warmed up as each one took a swig then passed it on to the next. They built a fire on the vast riverbank and heated up a chainsaw until it would start in the bitter cold. They all stepped onto the river, and the chainsaw growled as it cut into the ice. White crumbs of ice fell around them. Soon, they pulled their first block of glittering, translucent ice from the Songhua River.

HEARD IT IN THE MORNING

> The Master said, 'If I should hear the Way in the morning, I would feel all right to die in the evening.'
>
> —Confucius, *The Analects*, 4.8, translated by Annping Chin

Einstein Equator

'There's something I've been meaning to tell you,' Ding Yi said to his wife and daughter. 'Most of my mind is occupied with physics. I've only ever cleared away a small corner of it for you two. It's painful to admit, but there's nothing I can do about it.'

'You've said that before,' replied Fang Lin, Ding Yi's wife. 'About two hundred times.'

'Yeah!' added his ten-year-old daughter, Wenwen. 'And I've said so, too, a hundred times.'

'But you've never really understood, either of you,' said Ding Yi, shaking his head. 'You don't really get physics.'

'That's fine,' laughed Fang Lin. 'I know it's not another woman. And that's all I care about.'

The three of them were riding in a small vehicle traveling at five hundred kilometers per hour, along a steel tube five meters in diameter. The length of the tube was thirty thousand kilometers, encircling the entire planet at latitude 45° north.

The vehicle was entirely self-propelled, with a transparent carriage that had absolutely no apparatus for locomotion. When looking out from the vehicle, the steel tube projected forward, straight as a line. The vehicle within shot through like a bullet in a rifle barrel, albeit a rifle with no trigger or stock. The opening ahead seemed fixed at some infinitely distant point, unmoving, sharp as a needle. If not for the surrounding tube walls slipping by like gurgling water currents, there would hardly be any sense of movement at all. When the vehicle came to a stop, one could see that the tube walls were mounted with countless large instruments, as well as a great many hoops, all placed an equal distance apart. At full speed, the hoops became a blur, invisible to the naked eye. Ding Yi told his wife and daughter these hoops were used to produce a superconducting coil with a strong magnetic field, and the thin tube within the tube they could see suspended outside the window was a particle channel.

They were riding in the largest particle accelerator ever constructed by humanity, a device with a path around the planet, dubbed the 'Einstein equator.' With it, physicists could fulfill the fondest dream of the previous century's great scientists: a grand unified theory of the universe.

The vehicle was intended for use by engineers to service and repair the accelerator, but just now Ding Yi was using it to take his family on a trip around the world. He had long promised such a trip to his wife and daughter, though they never thought this was the route they'd take. The trip took sixty hours in total, and all they ever saw was the perfectly straight iron tube. But that was okay for Fang Lin and Wenwen, who were just happy to be together as a family for a couple of days.

And it's not like the trip was boring. Ding Yi would point at the tube walls from time to time and say to Wenwen, 'Well, we are now passing Mongolia – can you see the grassy plains? Look, there are herds of sheep, too. . . . Now we are going past Japan, though actually we're only just brushing against the northernmost tip of the country. Look, the sun is shining on snowy Kunashiri Island. You know, these are the first rays of light to fall on Asia each morning. . . . And now we are way down at the bottom of the Pacific Ocean. It's so dark, we can't see anything. Or, wait, no, there are some rays of light here, dark reds. Ah, yes, we can clearly see, there is an ocean floor volcano. The magma exuding from it cools so fast, it's just dark red flashes that ignite and then extinguish again, like a big bonfire at the bottom of the ocean. Wenwen, here is where new continents are born!' And so on.

Later, they went past the entire United States in the vehicle, slipping past the Atlantic Ocean to the European mainland via France, driving past Italy and the Balkan peninsula, then entering Russia once again, and onward across the Caspian Sea back to Asia, passing into China via Kazakhstan. And now, they were on the last stage of the journey, returning to the Einstein equator's starting point in the Taklamakan Desert, at the World Nuclear Center, which was also the main control center for the particle accelerator.

It was dark outside when Ding Yi and his family emerged from the control center building. The wide desert lay spread out beneath the stars, and all was quiet. The world was simple, yet so profound.

'All right, then,' Ding Yi said to Fang Lin and Wenwen, excited now. 'We three fundamental particles have now completed one accelerator experiment in the Einstein equator.'

'Father, how long does it take for real particles to go around in the big tube like that?' Wenwen pointed at the accelerator tube behind them, stretching out from the control center east and west, away into the distance.

'Tomorrow, the accelerator will operate for the first time, with the largest particles it can handle, and each particle in it will receive a push like a nuclear weapon,' Ding Yi answered his daughter. 'They will accelerate to nearly the speed of light. At that speed each particle in the tube requires only a tenth of a second to travel the rotation course that just took us more than two days.'

'Don't imagine that trip means you've kept your promise to us,' Fang Lin teased. 'That didn't count as a trip around the world!'

'That's right!' nodded Wenwen, playing along. 'When you are free again, Papa, you have to take us along the outside of the tube, so we can see where we were when we were inside. Now that would be a real trip around the world!'

'Oh, there's no need for that,' Ding Yi said to his daughter. He continued, with great feeling, 'If you just use your imagination, this trip was enough. Why, you've seen everything already! From inside the tube, I mean. In your imagination. Remember: True beauty is not visible to the eye, but only to the imagination. It's not like the oceans or the flowers and forests; it has no color and form. You can grasp the universe as a whole, make the whole thing a toy for your own mind. But only with your imagination. And mathematics. Only then will you see this kind of beauty.'

Ding Yi saw his wife and daughter off, but did not return home himself, instead heading back into the control center. Only a few staff remained on the overnight shift, marking it as one of the quietest times the site had seen after two years of construction and testing.

Ding Yi went up to the top floor and stood on the rooftop, open to the sky. As he looked at the accelerator tube bisecting the earth below, it seemed to him that all the stars were eyes and all the eyes were trained on the line below.

Ding Yi returned to his office below, lay down on the sofa, and went to sleep. It was then that a dream came to him, the kind only a physicist could have.

He was riding in a small vehicle, right at the starting point of the Einstein equator. It began to move, and he felt the massive power of the accelerator. He whipped along the forty-fifth parallel, one revolution after the other, like a ball on a roulette wheel. As he approached the speed of light, the dramatic increase in mass caused his body to feel like a solid hunk of metal. He grew conscious of the fact that his body contained the power to create worlds, and at once knew the pleasure of a god. On the last revolution, he was drawn down a side road and charged off to a strange place, where all was only void. He saw the color of the void: neither black nor white, but the color of colorlessness, though not transparent, either. Here, space and time themselves awaited creation. His creation.

In front of him, he saw a small black dot. It expanded dramatically, and he could make out that it was another vehicle, and inside there was another Ding Yi. Himself. They careened and collided at the speed of light, and disappeared, leaving only a dimensionless singularity in the midst of the void. This seed of all things exploded into a rapidly expanding high-energy ball of fire. Red light gradually faded, infusing into the universe, energy falling cold in the sky like snow. At first, a thin cloud of nebulae, and then fixed stars, star clusters, galaxies.

In this new universe, Ding Yi possessed a quantized self. He could leap from one end of the universe to the other in an instant. And not leap, even, but rather exist at all points in the universe simultaneously. He was like a boundless fog that permeated the cosmos. The silver desert of the fixed stars was igniting inside his body. He was everywhere even as he was nowhere. He knew his whole existence was an illusion of probability. His multi-centered spirit, churning in and out of existence, scanning the universe, seeking a vision of itself collapsing into a dense body. Even as he searched, this vision appeared. It came from two eyes which were floating in the cosmos, behind a silver curtain of star clusters. The eyes had the beauty and the long lashes of Fang Lin, but the lively spirit of Wenwen. These eyes scanned the boundless distance. But in the end, they could not perceive Ding Yi's quantized self. The wave function trembled, like a breeze over a placid lake, but it couldn't collapse into being. Just as Ding Yi was about to give up hope, the endless sea of stars did begin to coalesce. Nebulae began to swirl and surge. Then everything went quiet. The stars of the universe formed into a single large eye, an eye one billion light-years wide, its image like diamond dust scattered on velvet. It stared at Ding Yi. Then, in an instant, the wave function collapsed, like a film of fireworks played backward. Ding Yi's quantized existence cohered at last, at some tiny, insignificant point within the universe. He opened his eyes and returned to reality.

It was the control center's chief engineer who'd woken him. Ding Yi opened his eyes and saw the physicists and technicians of the nuclear center standing around him as he lay on the sofa. They looked at him like they had just seen a monster.

'What is it? Have I overslept?' Ding Yi looked out the window, and saw that the sky had brightened, though the sun had not yet risen.

'No,' said the chief engineer. 'But . . . something's happened.' It was only then that Ding Yi realized that they weren't concerned with him, but something else entirely. The chief engineer dragged Ding Yi to the window. Ding Yi had only gone two paces when suddenly someone stopped him, held him fast. He turned. It was Matsuda Seiichi, the Japanese physicist and one of the previous year's Nobel Prize laureates.

'Dr. Ding,' said Matsuda. 'You may find your mind unprepared for what you are about to see. I . . . I wouldn't be too concerned about it. We might all be dreaming, at this very moment.' Matsuda's face was pale; Ding Yi saw that the hand grasping him was trembling.

He could hardly suppress a shudder. 'But I've just woken from a dream!' said Ding Yi. 'What happened?' They all simply stared, agape. The chief engineer resumed dragging Ding Yi to the window. He looked out. What he saw made him immediately doubt the very words he'd spoken. The reality in front of his eyes was stranger than the dream he'd just had.

In the pale blue of the early morning light, the familiar accelerator tube bisecting the desert had been replaced with a band of green grass. Now a belt of green ran east and west, out to the horizon.

'Back to the control room!' called the chief engineer. Ding Yi followed them there and received yet another unbelievable shock: The control room was completely empty. Every piece of equipment had disappeared without a trace. Instead, all was grass, even growing directly out of the antistatic floor panels.

Ding Yi rushed madly out of the control room, around the building, and onto the band of grass, looking at how it disappeared off in the east, near the spot where the sun was about to rise. His breath came out in a fog in the cold desert air of the early morning.

'Where is the rest of the accelerator?' he asked the chief engineer, gasping.

'It has disappeared entirely – the parts aboveground, and underground, and in the ocean.'

'And turned to grass?!'

'Uhm, no. The grass is only on the desert surface near us. In other parts, it has simply disappeared. The surface and the seabed parts are left with only empty abutments and the underground parts left with only an empty tunnel.'

Ding Yi bent down and picked up a blade of the grass. Anywhere else, it would have been unremarkable, but here it was very unusual indeed: it looked nothing like the succulents or tamarisks of the desert, plants adapted to low-water conditions, but rather plum and crisp. Bursting with moisture, in fact. The kind of plant that could only grow in the south, with its higher rainfall. Ding Yi ground the blade of grass between his fingers, staining them green. A faint clean, grassy smell wafted toward his nose. Ding Yi stared for a long time into his hands. Then finally he said, 'This does look like a dream.'

But a voice from the east replied, 'No, this is real!'

Vacuum Decay

At the end of the green grass road, the sun was already half risen in the sky, its light shining straight in their eyes. Out of the rays of the sun came a person, moving toward them along the grassy road. At first it was only a silhouette backed by the sun, the edges swallowed up in the bright emerging wheel of light, making the figure seem like a mirage. But as it came closer, people saw he was an adult man. He wore a white shirt and black pants, but no tie. Closer still, his face also became clear: mixed Asian and European features, which was not unusual in this region, though no one would confuse this man for a local. There was something too regular about his features – they weren't quite realistic, more like an illustration of a human being on a public sign. When he came closer still, it became clear he was not of this world at all. Because he was not walking. No, his legs stood straight as pens, the bottoms of his shoes floating just above the grass. Then, just two or three meters from them, he stopped.

'Hello to you all. I have taken this external form so that we can communicate better. I do hope you can accept this, my best attempt at a human figure.' The person spoke in English, and his voice was just like his face, extremely standard and without any distinguishing features.

'Who are you?' someone asked.

'I am the dehazardification officer of this universe.'

This universe. Those two words left a deeper impression on the physicists than the rest.

'Did you have something to do with the disappearance of the accelerator?' asked the chief engineer.

'Yes. It was evaporated last night, as your planned experiment had to be stopped. By way of compensation I sent you this grass, which grows quickly in the desert.'

'But . . . why?'

'Your accelerator, if actually operated to its maximum potential, can accelerate particles to power levels exceeding ten to the twentieth power gigaelectron volts, which approaches those of the big bang itself. And this could bring disaster to the universe.'

'What disaster?'

'Vacuum decay.'

Hearing this response, the chief engineer turned to look at the physicists by his side. They remained silent, their brows furrowed, as they thought it over.

'Do you need a more in-depth explanation?' asked the dehaz officer.

'No, there is no need,' said Ding Yi, with a slight shake of his head. The physicists had thought the dehaz officer might bring up some concepts too difficult for humans to understand, but to their surprise, he referred to an idea proposed as early as the 1980s. At the time, most people thought it just a novel conjecture, with no relation to reality. Ideas like that had been all but forgotten by most.

The vacuum decay concept had made its earliest appearance in a 1980 article in the journal *Theoretical Physics*, by Sidney Coleman and Frank De Luccia, titled 'Gravitational Effects of and on Vacuum Decay.' Even earlier, Paul Dirac had theorized that what seemed to be vacuum in our universe could be a false vacuum, where in seemingly empty space, phantomlike virtual particles emerged and disappeared on unimaginably short time scales. In these instants, the living drama of creation and destruction went on endlessly at every point, making what we called a vacuum actually a teeming sea of particles. So it followed that a vacuum actually had an energy level. Coleman and De Luccia's contribution was to discover that certain high-energy processes might produce another vacuum state, one without the energy level of the present universal vacuum. The result might then be a 'true vacuum' of energy level zero. Such a vacuum might only be the size of a single atom at first, but once produced, the higher-energy vacuum neighboring the lower-level vacuum would fall to the lower level, and so on, in a process whereby the low-energy vacuum volume would expand spherically and rapidly. The expansion rate of the sphere would quickly accelerate to the speed of light, and all protons and neutrons within the sphere's volume would instantly decay. All the matter in the world would evaporate, leading to total destruction.

'Within 0.03 seconds, the zero-energy vacuum sphere expanding at the speed of light would destroy the Earth. Five hours later it would destroy the solar system. Four years after that, it would destroy the closest star systems, and a hundred thousand years after that, the entire Milky Way galaxy. . . . Nothing would be able to stop the expansion of the sphere, so in time nothing in the universe would escape.' So said the dehaz officer, his words connecting precisely with what the physicists were thinking. Could he actually read their thoughts?! The dehaz officer spread his arms in a gesture of embrace.

'If we look at our universe as a wide sea, we are the fish in the sea. The boundless sea around us is so utterly transparent we forget it even exists. But I have to tell you: This is no seawater. It is liquid dynamite. A single spark could set off an inferno that destroys everything. As the universe's dehazardification officer, my job is to extinguish all potential sparks.'

'I'm sure that's not easy,' said Ding Yi. 'Our universe already has a radius of twenty billion light-years, which must be a wide expanse even for a superior civilization like yours.'

The dehaz officer smiled then – it was the first time he had smiled, and yet this smile, too, was entirely without distinguishing characteristics. 'It's not as complex as you think. You already understand that our present universe is merely the embers of a big bang. Stars and galaxies are no more than scattered ashes that still retain some heat. You see, this is a low-base-energy universe, and the high-energy star systems you all see now only existed in the distant past. In the current natural universe, even the highest-energy processes, for example large masses cast into black holes, are all many orders of magnitude smaller than the big bang. In the present universe, the only chance for a big bang–level energy process comes from intelligent civilizations exploring with all their might the ultimate secrets of the universe. By concentrating great quantities of energy, they might create that level of power at microcosmic points. Hence, we only have to maintain surveillance over all the civilized worlds in the universe.'

'But, how long have you been paying attention to humans?' asked Matsuda. 'Perhaps since the age of Max Planck?'

The dehaz officer shook his head.

'So, was it the age of Newton? Also no? Surely not as far back as Aristotle?'

'All incorrect,' replied the dehaz officer. 'The universe's dehazardification systems operation agencies work like this: Many sensors have already been placed around the universe wherever life has appeared. When a civilization with the ability to produce big bang–level energy processes is discovered, the sensors issue a warning. A dehaz officer like myself receives the warning and then goes in person to observe the civilization on this world. But unless these civilizations are actually going to carry out experiments with energy levels on the order of the big bang, we absolutely do not interfere in any way.'

Just then, a black square appeared above the dehaz officer's head, about two meters on each side. The surface of the square was of such a deep, bottomless blackness it looked like a hole dug out of reality. A few seconds later, the shadowy outline of a blue globe emerged from the black space. Pointing at this image, the dehaz officer said, 'This is the image taken by the sensor placed at your planet.'

'When was this sensor placed there?' someone asked.

'According to your geological division of time, during the Carboniferous period of the Paleozoic era.'

'Paleo . . . what?!'

'But that was . . . three hundred million years ago!'

'Surely not as early as that?' said the chief engineer, his tone now one of awe and veneration.

'Early, you say? No, in fact, that was too late! When we first arrived at Earth during the Carboniferous period, we saw the Gondwana supercontinent, with its moist amphibious animals crawling in the primeval forests and swamps. Why, it all sent us into cold sweats of alarm! Clearly, Earth already long had the potential for a technological civilization, so the sensor should really have been in place from the Cambrian or Ordovician periods.'

The image of the planet came forward, filling the square, the lens focused on the movements of the continents. Suddenly it felt like the scientists were carrying out the inspection themselves.

The dehaz officer said, 'The image you are seeing was shot during the Pleistocene epoch, three hundred seventy thousand years ago, which to us is practically yesterday.'

The surface on the image of the planet stopped moving, with the lens fixed on the continent of Africa, which was just then on the nightside of the planet, appearing as a large ink-dark patch surrounded by lighter ocean. Something had caught the sensor's attention: the image zoomed in, and Africa expanded into a more detailed view, quickly taking up all of the scene, as if the observer were on a nosedive toward the planet's surface. Darkness gave way to greater color contrasts: white at the accumulated snows of the fourth ice age and the darker parts remaining vague and unclear – whether they were forests or scattered rocks upon the plains, the audience could only guess. The lens continued to close in, until a snowy plain filled the scene, turning the display square entirely a single color, that of snow on the ground at night: grayish white, with a hint of dark blue. Then black spots on the snowy plain, quickly resolving into human figures. Next, one could see they were all hunched over, with long skins draped over their shoulders blowing in the wind. The image shifted once again, and the face of a person looked up to fill the screen. In the weak rays of evening light, there was no way to make out facial details, but they could see that humans had very high brows and cheekbones, and long, thin lips. The lens continued to zoom in, until it seemed it could go no further. A pair of deeply sunken eyes filled the screen, the pupils of the dark eyes filled with silvery dots of light at the center. These were the stars, reflected in the eyes.

The image froze on this frame and a sharp sound of alarm arose. This was the system warning, the dehaz officer informed them.

'Why?' asked the chief engineer, not understanding.

'When this early person looked up at the starry sky, the threshold for a warning was reached. For they have now expressed curiosity about the universe. And by then there have been ten of these supercondition events at different points, matching the conditions for a system warning.'

'But if I'm not mistaken, you said just now that the sensor will only deliver its warning when a civilization capable of generating power levels equal to those at the creation of the universe emerges.'

'Is not what you are looking at just such a civilization?'

The people looked at each other, all at a loss.

The dehaz officer smiled his traitorous smile. 'Is it so hard to understand? Once life becomes conscious of the existence of the mysteries of the universe, it is only one step away from unlocking these mysteries.' Seeing that the people still did not understand, he continued. 'For example, life on this planet took four hundred million years to realize for the first time that the mysteries of the universe exist, but since then, only four hundred thousand years have passed, and you have constructed this Einstein equator. And the most accelerated phase of that development all happened in fewer than five hundred years. If you will, with their eyes on the universe in those moments, that human saw treasure. All of what you call human civilization since then has been little more than bending over to pick it up.'

Ding Yi nodded his head as if he had begun to understand. 'When you put it that way, the moment that person gazed up at the stars was monumentally important!'

The dehaz officer went on, 'It is for that reason that I have come to your world, and set up surveillance over the progress of your civilization. It's as if I were looking over a child playing with fire, and the surrounding universe, illuminated by the fire, fascinates the child. But this child might lose control over the flames. And now, the universe stands in danger of being incinerated.'

Ding Yi thought deeply on this. When he finally looked up, he asked what would become the most important question in the history of human science. 'So what you are saying is, we can never obtain the grand unified theory? We will never plumb the ultimate mysteries of the universe?'

At this, all the scientists gazed questioningly at the dehaz officer, like souls awaiting their final judgment.

'There are many tragedies to a life of wisdom and this is one of them,' the dehaz officer said blandly.

Matsuda, his voice quavering, asked, 'As a higher civilization, how do you all accept such a terrible thing?'

'We are truly fortunate children in this universe, for we have obtained the unified theory.'

Immediately, the fires of hope were reignited in the hearts of the scientists.

But Ding Yi thought of another terrifying possibility. 'You mean . . . vacuum decay has actually happened, somewhere?'

The dehaz officer shook his head. 'We used another method to obtain the unified model, which we cannot speak of now, though at a later time I may explain it to you in detail.'

'And can we not repeat that method?'

The dehaz officer continued to shake his head. 'Its time has passed, and no civilization in this universe may repeat it.'

'Well, but, please, then tell us humans of the unified theory of the universe!'

The dehaz officer shook his head again.

'We beg of you! This is very important to us – no, it's everything to us!' Ding Yi rushed forward to grasp the dehaz officer by the arm, but his hands passed through the form of the man, feeling nothing at all.

'The Knowledge Protection Directive prohibits doing so.'

'Knowledge Protection Directive?!'

'It is the highest directive regarding civilized worlds in the universe: A higher-level civilization is not permitted to transmit knowledge to a lower-level civilization. We call this behavior 'knowledge pipeline delivery.' Lower-level civilizations can only obtain knowledge by their own investigation.'

'But that isn't rational!' cried Ding Yi in a petulant voice. 'Better you all explained the unified theory to all of the civilizations seeking the deepest secrets of the universe, so they would not try to arrive at them via high-energy experiments. Wouldn't the universe be safer then?'

'Your thinking is too simplistic. The unified theory only covers this universe. As soon as you had it you would know that countless other universes exist, and then you would thirst for the trans-unified theory, to comprehend all of these universes. Plus, the grand unified theory would supply you with the knowledge to build technology that could generate even higher-energy processes, which you would use to try to tunnel through the barriers between different universes. But there are differences in the vacuum energies of different universes, so this would lead to vacuum decay, simultaneously destroying both universes, and maybe more. Knowledge pipeline delivery would also involve even more direct negative results and disasters in the lower civilization, for reasons that you all presently cannot understand. Therefore, the Knowledge Protection Directive must never be violated. What this directive refers to as 'knowledge' not only includes the deep secrets of the universe, but also refers to all of the knowledge you presently do not possess, including knowledge at each level. Imagine, for example, if human beings still did not know Newton's three laws or calculus – I would similarly not be able to give these to you.'

The scientists fell silent. In their eyes, the sun which had just risen so high had sunk at once into darkness. To them, the whole universe in an instant became a grand tragedy, the depth of which they could not grasp immediately, but which would trickle over and through them for the rest of their lives. It would be torture. In fact, the rest of their lives would hold little meaning.

Matsuda sat down on the grass, dazed. What he said next would be famous later. 'In a universe that cannot be known, my heart hardly cares to keep on beating.'

These words expressed precisely what all the physicists were feeling, with their glazed and sluggish eyes. It looked as if they wanted to cry, but the tears wouldn't come. They were like that for some indeterminate time, until Ding Yi suddenly broke the silence.

'I've got it! I've thought of a way to get the grand unified theory without breaking the Knowledge Protection Directive.'

The dehaz officer nodded at him. 'Let's hear it.'

'You tell me the ultimate secret of the universe. Then, you destroy me.'

'I'll give you three days' time to consider this,' the dehaz officer said, answering Ding Yi with neither surprise nor hesitation.

Ding Yi was wild with joy. 'You mean this will work?!'

The dehaz officer nodded his head.

The Altar of Truth

What should people call the huge half-spherical body, its flat surface facing up and its round surface lodged in the desert, looking from far away like an overturned hill? The dehaz officer had constructed the half sphere out of sand, somehow causing a huge tornado to spring up out of the desert. In the midst of the wind, a tall pillar of sand had finally condensed into this form. No one knew what he had used to form so much sand into such a precise hemisphere shape, and of such strength and durability it could sit, lodged round side down, without collapsing. But the hemisphere was unstable in this position, swaying visibly as gusts of wind passed over the desert.

The dehaz officer had told them that on his world this sort of hemisphere served as an altar. During the ancient age of that civilization, scholars had collected on such altars to discuss the secrets of the universe. Because of the instability of a hemisphere placed in this way, the scholars on the altar had to distribute themselves carefully over its surface, or else the hemisphere would tilt to one side, causing the people on it to slide off. The dehaz officer said little more about any deeper meaning the shape might have, but people guessed that it might symbolize the unbalanced and unstable state of the universe.

To one side of the hemisphere, there was a long sloping path, also made out of sand, that led from the ground up to the altar. In the dehaz officer's world, this path was not necessary, for even before they had become omnipotent, his race had been a transparent life-form equipped with two pairs of wings, and so they could fly directly onto the altar. The slope, then, was constructed especially for humans. Some three hundred of them would travel up the path to the altar of truth, where they would give their lives in exchange for the deepest secrets of the universe.

Three days before, after the dehaz officer had agreed to Ding Yi's request, new developments were driving the world to despair: in the space of a single short day, hundreds of people had made the same request. Besides the world's core scientists, other scholars from all over the world wanted it. At first it was only physicists, but later physicists and cosmologists, and then scientists from mathematics, biology, and all the basic sciences, and then even economists, historians, and others from outside the natural sciences. These people who asked to trade their lives for truth were all at the cutting edge of their fields, the elite even among the elite, with half of them winners of Nobel Prizes. The altar of truth had attracted the cream of the crop, as far as the human sciences were concerned.

The altar of truth was no longer in a desert, as the grass the dehaz officer had planted three days before had quickly spread, the band doubling in width, its unruly margins now just beneath the altar. More than ten thousand people had assembled on the grass: besides the scientists aiming to give up their lives and reporters from media organizations around the world, there were also the family and friends of the scientists. Two days and two nights of ceaseless pleading had left them all exhausted and sick at heart. But even with spirits at the edge of collapse, they still decided to give it their all, until the last minute. Helping them at this task were representatives from all the world's governments, including more than ten heads of state, all trying their hardest to hold on to the scientific elite of their countries.

*

'How could you bring our child here?!' Ding Yi demanded of Fang Lin, aghast. Behind them, Wenwen sat and played on the grassy ground, totally unaware of what was going on. She had the only happy face in a crowd of dark expressions.

'I want her to see you die,' Fang Lin said coldly, her face pale and wan, her two eyes focused on the distance.

'Do you think her presence will stop me?'

'I don't hold out any hope for that, but I hope I can at least stop your daughter from being like you.'

'You can punish me, but the child . . .'

'No one can punish you, and don't you pretend that what is about to happen is a punishment to you. You're finally making your dreams come true!' Lin yelled as she turned to face him.

Ding Yi looked straight into the eyes of his wife and said, 'I guess you finally know me, on a deeper level.'

'I don't know anyone. There's nothing in my heart now. Nothing except hatred.'

'You of course have the right to hate me.'

'I hate physics!'

'But if it weren't for physics, humans now would still be just animals living in forests or caves.'

'Well, I'm hardly happier than them!'

'But I'm happy. I wish you could share in my happiness.'

'Let your child share it with you, when she sees with her own eyes her father leaving her forever. At least then, after she's grown, she will stay away from physics. What poison it is!' Lin scoffed in disgust.

The heads of state were holding forth with the dehaz officer on the altar of truth, beseeching him to refuse the scientists' requests.

The president of the United States said, 'Sir – if I may call you that? Our world's best scientists are all here. Surely you don't really want to destroy science on this planet?'

'It's not as severe as all that,' said the dehaz officer. 'Another batch of scientific elite will quickly surge forth and take their place, for exploring the secrets of the universe is the basic instinct of all intelligent life.'

'Given we are all intelligent life-forms, how could you kill fellow scholars? Isn't that too cruel?'

'This is their own choice. Their lives are their own. And of course, can be exchanged for what they think is highest and most valuable.'

'You needn't remind us of that!' exclaimed the Russian president. 'We humans are long used to exchanging our lives for something higher. During the wars of the last century, more than twenty million in our countries did just that. But the fact now is that those scientists' lives get us nothing in return! Only they themselves will gain the knowledge they seek, and then you allow them only ten minutes more of life! They have become slaves to their desire for the final truth. Surely you too understand this to be the case?'

'What I understand to be the case is this: They are the only correct and reasonable living individuals in this star system.'

The heads of state exchanged looks, then looked back in confusion and puzzlement at the dehaz officer.

The dehaz officer spread his arms as if to embrace the heavens: 'Life is a small price to pay for the chance to glimpse the beauty of universal harmony.'

'But after they see this beauty they only have ten minutes to live!'

'Even without the ten minutes, it would still be worth it to experience this ultimate beauty.'

The heads of state looked at each other, all shaking their heads with wry and bitter smiles.

'With the progress of civilization, people like these will gradually increase in number,' said the dehaz officer, pointing at the scientists gathered beneath the altar. 'In the end, when the problems of existence are completely solved, when love disappears because individuation gives way to connection, and when art finally dies out upon reaching the final peaks of exquisiteness and obscurity, the pursuit of extreme beauty of the universe will become the only thing civilization can put its faith in. Then what these people want now will align with the basic values of the world.'

The heads of state were silent a moment, trying to understand what the dehaz officer had said, when the president of the United States suddenly began to laugh. 'Haha! Sir, you are having us on – you are playing a game with all of humanity!'

The dehaz officer looked confused. 'I do not understand . . .'

'Humanity is not as stupid as you imagine,' said the prime minister of Japan in reply. 'Even a child could grasp fallacies in your logic!'

At this, the dehaz officer seemed even more confused. 'I don't see any logical fallacies in what I've said.'

The American president went on, after another wry laugh. 'A trillion years from now, our universe will be filled with highly progressed civilizations. Well, if it is as you say, and the desire for the state of final truth will become the basic value of the entire universe, at that time all the civilizations of the universe will agree, use high-energy experiments to investigate the trans-unified theory that comprehends all of the universes – will they not worry that they will destroy everything, including themselves, in the course of these experiments? Do you wish to tell us that this will happen?!'

The dehaz officer stared at the heads of state for a long time without speaking, a strange gaze that made them shiver with its creepiness. One of them seemed to have a realization.

'Wait. You're saying . . .'

The dehaz officer raised a hand to stop him from going on, then walked toward the edge of the altar of truth. There, in a loud, bright voice, he said to all:

'You all certainly wish to know how we obtained the grand unified theory. Now this can be told to you.

'Long, long ago, our universe was much smaller than it is today, and very hot, too. The fixed stars had not appeared, but there were materials that had condensed from the energy, forming nebulae that permeated the red glow of space. Life appeared at this time – a kind of life formed from thin clouds of matter bound in force fields, with bodies that looked like tornadoes. This kind of nebulae life progressed rapidly as a flash, quickly producing an advanced civilization that spread all over the universe. When the nebulae civilization's own desire for the ultimate truths of the universe reached its peak, all the worlds of the whole universe agreed to risk the vacuum decay danger to advance experiments with big bang–level energies, in order to explore the grand unified theory of the universe.

'The nebulae life-forms' methods for controlling matter were entirely different from those of life in the universe today. Owing to the severe lack of matter in general, they made their own bodies into the things they wanted. After they made their final decision, some of the bodies on some of the worlds rapidly transformed themselves into accelerator parts. Finally, more than a million of these nebulae linked themselves up, forming a particle accelerator that could reach the energy levels at the creation of the universe. When the accelerator went into operation, a dazzling blue ring of light flashed among the dark red nebulae.

'They knew well the dangers of this experiment. As they recorded the results of the experiment, they transmitted the data through a gravity wave propelled outward, this being the only form that could carry information through a vacuum decay event.

'After the accelerator operated for a time, the vacuum decay event did occur. The lower-energy vacuum sphere expanded from atomic size at the speed of light, expanding in the blink of an eye to astronomical size, evaporating and utterly destroying everything inside. Eventually, the speed of vacuum sphere expansion exceeded the expansion of the universe itself, and after enough time had passed, the entire universe was destroyed.

'A long time passed, and the universe had nothing in it at all. Then, the material which had been evaporated slowly began to re-condense. Nebulae appeared again, but the universe was entirely dead and alone. Until, that is, the fixed stars and planets appeared, when life finally once again sprouted in the universe. In those early days, the gravity wave sent forth by the extinct nebulae civilization continued to reverberate, though the appearance of solid matter caused it to swiftly diminish. But just before it was entirely lost, the earliest civilization to appear in the universe intercepted it, and the information it carried was decoded, so that from this ancient experimental data the new civilization obtained the grand unified theory. They discovered that the most crucial data for building the model was produced in the last one ten-thousandth of a second before the vacuum decay.

'Let us consider the situation of the nebulae universe. Even as the vacuum sphere expanded and destroyed the universe, the worlds outside the sphere, beyond the sphere's event horizon as they were, could not have seen the catastrophe coming. So up until the moment the vacuum arrived, these worlds were entirely focused on receiving data from their accelerator. One ten-thousandth of a second after they had enough data to build the grand unified model, the vacuum sphere destroyed everything. However, the speed of thought among the nebulae was so high, one ten-thousandth of a second was a relatively long time for them. Therefore, they could have deduced the grand unified model in their last moment of life. Of course, this could be mere self-consolation. More likely, they did not deduce anything. Which means the nebulae civilization ripped open the fabric of the universe, but they themselves were destroyed before glimpsing the ultimate beauty of the universe. Perhaps they deserve our respect all the more, when we realize they knew the risks even before they began their experiments, and sacrificed themselves even as they supplied the data on the ultimate secrets of the universe to distant future civilizations.

'Now you all should understand that the pursuit of the most ultimate truth of the universe is the final aim of civilization.'

The dehaz officer's story made everyone enter a long period of silent thought. Whether the humans of Earth agreed with his last sentence or not, one thing was sure: He had just left a permanent impression on human thought and culture.

The American president broke the silence. 'You have painted a dark vision for civilization! Is it really true that in the long course of time, all humanity's hope and hard work just comes down to the moth flying into the flame?'

'The moth certainly does not find it dark. To the moth, there is at least a brief period of light.'

'Humanity absolutely cannot accept such a view of life!'

'This is entirely understandable. In our universe reborn after vacuum decay, civilization is still in its early stages, and every world has its own ways, pursuing different aims. To the majority of worlds, the pursuit of ultimate truth does not possess the highest meaning. To risk the danger of destroying the universe for it would not be fair to the majority of lives in the universe. Even on my own world, certainly not all members agree to sacrifice all. Therefore, we ourselves have not continued trans-unified model high-energy experiments, and have set up the dehazardification system throughout the entire universe. But we believe that with the advance of civilization, there will finally come a day when all of the worlds of the universe will agree on the ultimate aim of civilization. Even right now in your infant civilization, there are already people who agree with this view.

'All right, the time has come. If any of you do not wish to exchange your life for truth, then please go back down and allow those who do so to come up.'

The heads of state went down from the altar of truth and, when face-to-face with those scientists, made their last effort.

The president of France said, 'How about this: Let us put the matter off a bit! Come with me! There is more to life for us to experience. Let's relax. Listen to the songs of the birds at dusk. We'll stare at the silver moon, as old familiar music plays. We'll drink our wine, and think of those we love. . . . Yes, yes, you will discover that the ultimate truth is not so important as you first thought. There is more beauty in life than in the harmony of the universe!'

'All life follows reason,' replied a physicist, coldly. 'You will never understand.'

The French president wanted to say more, but the president of the United States lost patience. 'Fine! It's no good playing fiddle for the cows! Can you not see what a group of irresponsible people this is? What a bunch of con artists and deceivers they are?! They all whooped it up about doing research for the benefit of all mankind, when actually they just take society's wealth to satisfy their own perverted desires for some kind of mysterious beauty. Is there really any difference between that and using public money to visit a prostitute?'

Ding Yi rushed up and patted the president on the shoulder, saying with a laugh, 'Well, Mr. President, science has come all this way and now, at least, someone can better define its fundamental character and substance.'

Matsuda, off to one side, said, 'We have long admitted his point and told you so; it's just that you never believed us.'

The Exchange

The exchange of life for truth began.

The first group of eight mathematicians came up the long sloping path to the altar of truth. There was no wind over the desert sands, as if nature itself held its breath. All was silent. The just-risen sun threw long shadows from the humans onto the desert, and these shadows were all that moved in a world now frozen.

The figures of the mathematicians disappeared onto the altar of truth, invisible now to the people below. All kept still, listening with bated breath. Then came the voice of the dehaz officer, crystal clear in the tomb-like silence:

'Please ask your question.'

Then the voice of a mathematician said, 'We wish to know the final proofs of the conjectures of Fermat and Goldbach.'

'All right. But the proof is very long, and there is only time for you to see the key portions. The rest can be explained in writing.'

Just how the dehaz officer conveyed the knowledge to the scientists would forever remain a mystery to humanity. In images from a distant surveillance plane, the scientists all turn their heads up at the sky, though there didn't seem to be anything in the direction they looked. It was commonly held that the aliens had used some kind of thought waves to directly input the information into their brains. But in fact, the actual situation was considerably simpler: The dehaz officer projected the information into space. To the people on the altar of truth, the entire sky had become a display screen, but the information was not visible from any other angle.

An hour passed before someone broke the silence on the altar of truth. 'We are finished,' they said.

'You all have ten minutes,' came the placid, if solemn, answer of the dehaz officer.

The altar of truth filled with the surreptitious sounds of many people deep in conversation. The people below could only make out fragments of what was being said, though their excitement and joy was all too evident. They sounded like a group of people who had been traversing dark tunnels for a year or more, suddenly coming to the light at the mouth of a cave.

'. . . This is totally new . . .'

'. . . How could it be . . .'

'. . . before we intuited that . . .'

'Good god, it's really . . .'

When the ten minutes were about to conclude, another clear voice sounded on the altar of truth: 'Please accept the sincerest thanks from the eight of us.'

A strong light flashed on the altar of truth. When it was over, the people below saw eight orbs of ionic flame rise up from the altar, floating lightly upward, fluttering as they rose, gradually fading, bright yellow turning soft orange, and then red. Finally, they disappeared one by one into the blue sky. The whole process went on in complete silence. From the surveillance plane, one could see that only the dehaz officer remained on the altar of truth, standing in the center.

'The next group may ascend!' he called out in a loud voice.

As nearly ten thousand people fixed their eyes on the scene, another eleven people walked up to the altar of truth.

'Please ask your question.'

'We are paleontologists. We want to know the real reason the dinosaurs were destroyed.'

The paleontologists also looked up at the sky. They took much less time than the mathematicians who had been there before, and soon after someone said to the dehaz officer, 'Now we know! Thank you.'

'You all have ten minutes.'

'Well, the puzzle pieces all fit . . .'

'I wouldn't have thought of that in my wildest dreams . . .'

'. . . did you ever see anything so . . .'

And then the strong light appeared and disappeared. Eleven flaming orbs rose from the altar of truth, and were quickly lost in the skies over the desert.

Group after group of scientists walked onto the altar of truth, completed the exchange of life for truth, and then with a flash of a bright light were transformed into beautiful flaming orbs that floated away.

All was conducted in quiet austerity. Under the altar of truth, people avoided creating scenes of wailing for loved ones never again to be seen. Rather, the people of the world quietly watched the majestic scene, their own souls deeply cowed as some of their fellow humans experienced the greatest spiritual baptism in history.

A full day passed without anyone seeming to notice. The sun had fallen halfway toward the horizon in the west, the dusk scattering on the altar of truth with a layer of golden, shimmering light. The physicists began their ascent to the altar. These formed the biggest group, with eighty-six people. Just when they began, the voice of a child broke the silence that had held until that moment.

'Papa!' Wenwen, in tears, rushed out from among the crowd on the grass, ran straight to the sloping path, and charged into the group of physicists, clutching Ding Yi by his leg. 'Papa, I won't let you turn into one of those balls of fire that floats away!'

Ding Yi lightly embraced his daughter. 'Wenwen,' he asked. 'Tell Papa, can you remember the worst thing that ever happened to you?'

Wenwen, sniffing back her tears, thought for several seconds, then said, 'I've been growing up out here in the desert, and I . . . I wanted so bad to go to the zoo. Last time, Papa went south for a meeting. You brought me to a big zoo, but as soon as we went in, your phone rang, and you said something urgent happened at work. The zoo only allowed children with adults, so I had to leave with you. You never took me there again. Papa, this was the worst thing that happened to me. I cried on the plane the whole way back.'

Ding Yi said, 'But, my child! You will certainly have a chance to visit that zoo again. Mama can take you. With Papa now, it's different. He's also at the entrance to the big zoo, and inside are the mysterious things Papa always dreamed of seeing. But if Papa does not go now, later there will never be another chance.'

Wenwen stared at her father with her tear-filled eyes a moment, nodded her head and said, 'Then . . . then go, Papa.'

Fang Lin came up, took her daughter from Ding Yi's arms, eyes glaring at the altar of truth that loomed before her, and said, 'Wenwen, your father may be the most selfish papa in the world . . . but he really does want to go to that zoo.'

Ding Yi's eyes were fixed on the ground as he spoke again, his voice soft as a prayer. 'Yes, Wenwen, Papa really wants to go.'

Fang Lin fixed her baleful stare at Ding Yi one last time. 'You are a fundamental particle all right – utterly cold. Go on, then. Off to your final experiment.'

The group was about to turn and go when another female voice made them stop again.

'Matsuda-san, if you are going up there, I'll die right here in front of you!'

The woman speaking was a petite young Japanese woman, standing on the grass by the edge of the platform slope, a small silver handgun held against her temple.

Matsuda walked out from the group of physicists and up to the young woman. 'Motoko,' he said, looking her straight in the eye, 'do you remember that cold morning in Sapporo? You said you wanted to test whether I truly loved you or not. You asked me, if your face were disfigured in a fire, what would I do? I said I would stay loyally by your side for the rest of your life. But you were disappointed when you heard this. You said that if I truly loved you, I would say I would blind myself, so that a beautiful Motoko would always exist in my heart.'

The gun Motoko held did not move, but her dark eyes filled up with tears.

Matsuda Seiichi went on, 'So, my darling, you know deeply the importance of beauty to a human life. And now, the ultimate beauty of the universe is before me. I must see her.'

'If you take another step I'll shoot!'

Matsuda Seiichi smiled at her, then said softly, 'Goodbye, Motoko.' Then he turned and joined the other physicists as they started up again. Neither the sharp report of the gun, nor the splatter of brain material onto the grass, nor the soft thud of the body hitting the ground could make Matsuda turn around again.

The physicists reached the round surface of the altar of truth. In the center, the dehaz officer smiled warmly in greeting. The last light of the dusk went out as the sun set below the western horizon. Desert and grass alike went dim. The altar of truth seemed to suspend over the infinite black depths of space, reminding all of the physicists of the dark night before the creation of the universe, before a single star existed. The dehaz officer waved his hand. The physicists saw a golden star appear, in the distant black depths. At first it was too small to make out, but gradually it grew from a bright point to something with surface area and shape. They saw that it was a spiral galaxy floating toward them. The galaxy grew rapidly, displaying its roiling gases and nebulae. As the distance closed in still more, they discovered the stars in this galaxy were all numbers and symbols, the waves and structures forming one full, organized equation.

The grand unified theory of the universe had begun its slow and majestic passage before the physicists.

When the eighty-six orbs rose from the altar of truth, Fang Lin's eyes fell to the grassy ground. But she heard her daughter ask in a faint voice, 'Mama, which one is Papa?'

The final person to ascend was Stephen Hawking, his electric wheelchair moving slowly up the long slope like a bug crawling up the branch of a tree.

At last, the wheelchair reached the altar and the dehaz officer at its center. By then, the sun had already gone down, and the indigo sky was scattered with stars, the desert and grass below too dim to make out.

'Your question, Dr. Hawking?' asked the dehaz officer, expressing no more respect for him than for any other, but facing him with his featureless smile as he listened to the impersonal inflections of the voice on the scientist's wheelchair loudspeaker.

'What is the purpose of the universe?'

No answer appeared from the sky. The smile disappeared from the dehaz officer's face, and some slight expression – despair? – seemed to flash across his eyes.

'Sir?' asked Hawking.

Silence. The sky still was a dark expanse. Behind some thin wisps of cloud, the star systems of the universe continued to churn.

'Excuse me? Sir?' asked Hawking, again.

'Professor Hawking, the exit is to your rear,' said the dehaz officer.

'This is your answer?'

The dehaz officer shook his head. 'I'm saying that you can go back where you came from.'

'You do not know?'

The dehaz officer nodded. 'I do not.' Just then, he appeared not only human, but an individual with a full personality, as a dark flush of sorrow came into his face. Seeing him then, one could not doubt that he was indeed a person. And all too human, perhaps.

'How could I know,' murmured the dehaz officer.

Epilogue

One night, fifteen years later, on the grassy plain that had once been the Taklamakan Desert, a mother and daughter were having a conversation. The mother was in her forties, but white hair had long appeared at her temples, her weather-beaten eyes filled with worry, exhaustion, and little else. The daughter was a slim and delicate young woman, her large and limpid pupils glittering with the reflection of starlight.

The mother sat upon the soft lush grass, her eyes looking dispiritedly at the distant horizon. 'Wenwen, first you were admitted to the physics department at your father's alma mater, and now you are about to undertake doctoral studies in quantum gravity. And I've never tried to stop you. You can become a theoretician, and you can put all your spirit into this one field, if you like, but Wenwen, listen to your mother. Please, dear, no more than that. Don't cross the line!'

Wenwen looked up at the glittering Milky Way, saying, 'Mama, can you imagine, all this came from a small point, twenty billion years ago? The universe crossed its line long ago.'

Fang Lin stood, grabbed her daughter by the shoulders, said, 'Child, please don't be like that!'

Wenwen's eyes were still fixed on the stars, unmoving.

'Wenwen, are you listening to Mama? What's the matter with you?!' Fang Lin shook her daughter, but Wenwen's eyes were still absorbed by the sea of stars.

Instead of answering, she asked her mother, 'Mama, what is the purpose of the universe?'

'Ah. . . . Noooo.' Fang Lin gave up. She fell back to the grassy ground, her hands over her teary face. 'Child, no, no, not this.'

Wenwen finally turned her gaze back, squatted down, and held her mother by the shoulders, saying softly to her, 'Then, Mama, what is the purpose of humanity?'

Like a block of ice, the question chilled Fang Lin's burning heart. She turned to look her daughter in the eye. Then she looked out into the distance, in thought. Just as fifteen years earlier she had looked in that direction. Where the altar of truth had loomed, and beyond, where the Einstein equator had once crossed the desert.

A light breeze sprang up, rippling the soft grassy sea, as if it were the sea of humans roiling beneath the infinitude of the stars, singing quietly to the universe.

'I don't know. How could I know,' murmured Fang Lin.

SUN OF CHINA

PROLOGUE

Shui Wah took the small parcel from his mother's trembling hands. It contained one pair of thick-soled shoes she had sewn herself, three steamed buns, two heavily patched coats and twenty yuan. His father squatted by the roadside, sullenly smoking a long-stemmed pipe.

'Our son is leaving home. Would it kill you to put on a good face?' Ma scolded Pa. When she met with stony silence, she added, 'Fine, don't let him go. Can you afford to build him a house and find him a wife?'

'Go, then! East, west, they all leave in the end! I'd have been better off raising a litter of puppies!' Pa bawled, without looking up.

Shui lifted his eyes to the village in which he had been born and raised. Condemned to perpetual drought, the villagers scraped by on what little rainwater they could collect in cisterns. Shui's family had no money to build a cistern out of cement and had to make do with an earthen one instead. On hot days, the water stank. In years past, the foul water had been safe to drink after boiling, just a little bitter, a bit astringent. This summer, however, even the boiled water gave them diarrhea. They had heard from a local military doctor that some toxic mineral had leached into the water from the ground.

With one last glance at his father, Shui turned and walked away. He did not look back. He did not expect Pa to watch him go. When Pa felt miserable, he would crouch over his pipe for hours, unmoving, as if he had become a clod of dirt on the yellow earth. But he still clearly saw Pa's face, or perhaps it was better to say he walked upon it. Northwestern China stretched around him, a vast expanse of parched ocher, lined with cracks and gullies carved by erosion. Was the face of an old farmer any different? The trees, the soil, the houses, the people – everything was blackened, yellowed, wrinkled. He could not see the eyes of this face that stretched toward the horizon, but he could feel their presence, staring toward the sky. In youth, that gaze had been filled with longing for rain; in old age, it had grown glassy.

In fact, this giant visage had always been dull and impassive. He did not believe this land had ever been young.

There was a sudden gust of wind, and the path out of the village was swallowed in yellow dust. Shui followed this road, taking his first step toward his new life. It was a road that would lead him to places beyond his wildest dreams.

LIFE GOAL #1:

DRINK SOME WATER THAT IS NOT BITTER, MAKE SOME MONEY.

'Oh, there are so many lights!'

Night had fallen by the time Shui reached the cluster of many small, unauthorized coal pits and kilns that constituted the mining district.

'Those? Hardly. Now in the city, that's a lot of lights,' said Guo Qiang, who had come to meet him. Guo was from the same village as Shui, but he had left many years before.

Shui followed Guo to the workers' bunkhouse for the night. At dinnertime, he was delighted to discover that the water tasted pleasantly sweet. Guo told him a deep well had been drilled in the district, so naturally the water was good. 'But go to the city,' he added, '*that's* sweet water!'

Before bed, Guo handed Shui a hard, wrapped bundle to use as a pillow. He opened it and saw round sticks covered in black plastic. Peeling back the plastic, he saw that the sticks were yellowish, like soap.

'Dynamite,' Guo mumbled before he rolled over and started snoring. Shui noticed that his head rested on the same sort of 'pillow'. There was a stack of dynamite beneath the bed, and a cluster of blast caps dangled above his head. Later, Shui learned that there were enough explosives in the bunkhouse to blow his whole village sky-high. Guo was the mine's blast technician.

Work at the mine was hard and tiring. Shui ran back and forth, digging coal, pushing carts, erecting props and doing other odd jobs. He was dead tired at the end of each day. But Shui had grown up with hardship, and he did not fear it. What did frighten him were the conditions in the pit. The descent felt like burrowing into a dark anthill. At first, it felt like a waking nightmare, but later he grew accustomed this, too. He was paid a piece rate, and he could make 150 yuan every month. He could even earn 200 when the work was good. He was quite content with this.

But what satisfied Shui most of all was the water. After his first day of work, his entire body was blackened with soot, so he followed his fellow miners to the showers. When he entered, he watched as they used washbasins to ladle water from a large pool. They then rinsed themselves, letting the water stream down from head to toe, black rivulets running across the earth. He was utterly astounded. *Ma, how can they waste such sweet water like this?* In Shui's eyes, it was that sweet, fresh water that made this dusty, blackened world beautiful beyond comparison.

Guo, however, urged Shui to move to the city. He had previously worked as a laborer there, but because he had stolen from a construction site he had been labeled a vagrant and sent back to his registered home. He assured Shui that he could earn more money in the city. Moreover, he could do so without having to work himself to death, as in the mine.

Shui hesitated, but as he struggled to make up his mind, Guo met with an accident in the pit. He was removing a dud stick of dynamite when it exploded. He had to be carried from the pit, his body riddled with shards of rock. Before he died, he turned to Shui and rasped, 'Go to the city . . . there are more lights there . . .'

LIFE GOAL #2:

GO TO A CITY WITH MORE LIGHTS AND SWEETER WATER, MAKE MORE MONEY.

'Night here is as bright as day!' exclaimed Shui. Guo had not been mistaken. There really were many more lights in the city. At that moment, he was following Junior, carrying a shoeshiner's trunk on his back. They were walking along the main thoroughfare of the provincial capital toward the train station. Junior was from a village that neighbored Shui's home, and he had once worked together with Guo in the provincial capital. Despite Guo's directions, it had taken Shui a while to track him down. Junior, it turned out, no longer worked in construction; he had switched to shining shoes. But luck was on Shui's side: not only did he find the shoeshiner but one of Junior's flatmates, who plied the same trade, had just returned home to attend to a personal matter. Junior quickly walked Shui through the polishing process and then told him to pick up the other guy's trunk and follow behind.

As he walked, Shui decided he had very little confidence in his new trade. He could see the use in repairing shoes. But shining shoes? Anyone who spent one yuan on a shine – three yuan for the good polish – surely had a screw loose. In front of the station, however, their first customer arrived before they had even finished setting up their stall. To his surprise, by eleven o'clock that night, Shui had earned fourteen yuan!

Junior, on the other hand, wore a surly expression on his face as they returned home. He griped that business had been bad that day, and Shui did not miss the implication that he had stolen Junior's business.

'What are those big metal boxes under the windows?' Shui asked, pointing at a building up ahead.

'Air-conditioning units. It feels like early spring in there.'

'The city is incredible!' Shui exclaimed, wiping the sweat from his face.

'Life here is tough. It's easy to earn enough money for a bowl of rice, but if you want to marry and settle down, forget about it,' Junior said, gesturing with his chin toward the building. 'An apartment in there costs two, three thousand per square meter!'

'What's a square meter?' Shui asked innocently.

Shaking his head in disdain, Junior did not reply.

Shui split the rent on a small makeshift apartment with a dozen other men. Most of them were migrant laborers or farmers peddling their produce in the city. But the man who occupied the mattress right next to Shui was a proper city-dweller, although he did not come from this city. He was really no different from the other men. He ate no better than anyone else, and at night he, too, would strip to the waist to enjoy the cool evening air. Every morning, however, he would don a sharp suit and leather shoes. As he walked out the door, he seemed to become a different person. It was like watching a golden phoenix soar out of a chicken coop.

The man's name was Zhuang Yu. The others did not resent him, mainly because of something he had brought with him. It looked liked a large umbrella to Shui, only it was made from mirrors. The inside was very bright and reflective. Zhuang first placed the upturned umbrella on the ground beneath the sun. Then, he set a pot of water on a bracket where the handle should be. The reflected glare heated the bottom of the pot and the water quickly came to a boil. Later, Shui learned it was called a solar cooker. The men used it to boil water and cook food, which saved them quite a bit of money. On overcast days, however, it was useless.

The so-called 'solar cooker' umbrella had no ribs; it was just a very thin sheet. Shui looked on with fascination when Zhuang collapsed the umbrella. A long thin electrical wire ran from the top of the cooker into the apartment. To close it, Zhuang simply pulled the plug from the socket. The umbrella drooped to the ground with a small puff of air, suddenly transformed into a length of silver cloth. Shui picked up the cloth and inspected it carefully. It was soft and smooth and so light that it hardly seemed to weigh anything all. His own distorted likeness was reflected on its surface, glinting with the iridescent sheen of a soap bubble. As soon as he relaxed his grip, the silver cloth slipped through his fingers and fell to the ground without a sound, like an airy handful of quicksilver. When Zhuang reinserted the plug into the power socket, the cloth lazily unfurled like a lotus in full blossom. After a short time, it reverted to its round, upside-down umbrella shape. When he touched the surface again, it was thin and firm. Giving it a light tap, he was rewarded with a pleasant, metallic ping. In this state, it was extremely strong, able to support a full pot or kettle once fixed to the ground.

'It's a type of nanomaterial,' Zhuang told Shui. 'The surface finish possesses excellent reflective properties, and it is also very strong. Most importantly, it is soft and flexible under normal conditions but becomes rigid when a weak electric current is applied.'

Shui later learned that this 'nano mirror film' was one of Zhuang's own research achievements. After applying for a patent, he had invested everything he had into bringing products made from the new material to market. But no one had showed any interest in his products, even his portable solar cooker, and he lost all of his capital. Now he was so poor that he had to borrow money from Shui to make rent. But even though he had fallen so low, he remained relentlessly upbeat. Day in and day out, he scoured the city in pursuit of outlets for his new material. He told Shui that this was the thirteenth city he had visited in search of opportunities.

Besides the solar cooker, Zhuang also owned a smaller sheet of the mirror film. Normally, it rested on his bedside table, looking like a small silver handkerchief.

Every morning before he went out, Zhuang would hit a tiny power switch, and the silver handkerchief would immediately stiffen into a thin panel. Using it as a small mirror, he would groom and dress himself in front of it. One morning, as he brushed his hair in the mirror, he cast a sidelong glance at Shui, who had just rolled out of bed.

'You really ought to pay attention to your appearance,' he remarked. 'Wash your face regularly, tame your hair a bit. Not to mention your clothes. Can't you spare a little money for new ones?'

Shui reached for the mirror and held it to his face. Finally he laughed and shook his head. It was too much hassle for a shoeshiner.

'Modern society is full of opportunities,' Zhuang said, leaning toward Shui. 'The skies are thick with golden birds. Perhaps one day you will reach out and seize one, but only if you learn to take yourself seriously.'

Shui looked around, but he did not see a single golden bird. He shook his head and said, 'I never got an education.'

'That is certainly regrettable, but who knows? Maybe it will turn out to your advantage in the end. The greatness of this era lies in its unpredictability. Miracles can happen to anyone.'

'You,' Shui asked haltingly, 'went to university, right?'

'I have a doctorate in solid-state physics. Before I resigned, I was a professor.'

For a long time after Zhuang left, Shui sat with his mouth agape. Finally, he shook his head. If someone like Zhuang Yu could not catch a bird in thirteen different cities, he stood no chance. He felt like Zhuang was making fun of him, but in any case the guy was pitiable and ridiculous himself.

That night, while some of the men slept and others played a game of poker, Shui and Zhuang went to watch television in the small restaurant just a few doors down.

It was already midnight, and a news broadcast was on. The screen showed only the anchor, and there were no other graphics.

'In a press conference held this afternoon, a State Council spokesperson revealed that the remarkable China Sun Project has formally launched. The largest ecological engineering project since the Three-North Shelterbelt, its construction is expected to fundamentally transform our nation's soil . . .'

Shui had heard of the project before, and he knew it involved constructing another sun in the sky. The second sun would bring more rain to the arid Northwest.

It all sounded very farfetched to Shui. He wanted to ask Zhuang about it, as he usually did when he encountered such matters. When he turned his head, however, his friend was staring with wide eyes at the television, slack-jawed, as if the screen had snatched the soul from his body.

Shui waved his hand in front of the other man's face, but received no response. Zhuang did not recover his senses until long after the broadcast had ended. 'Really,' he mumbled to himself, 'how did I not think of the China Sun?'

Shui looked at him blankly. If even he knew about it, there was no way Zhuang was not aware of the China Sun. Who in China had not heard of it? Of course he knew about it – he just hadn't thought about it until now. But what new possibility had captured his attention? What could this project possibly have to do with Zhuang Yu, a down-and-out tramp living in a stuffy, ramshackle apartment?

'Do you remember what I said this morning?' Zhuang asked. 'Right now, a golden bird has swooped in front of me, and it is *huge*. It has been right overhead all this time, but I never fucking noticed!'

Shui continued to stare at him in total confusion.

'I am going to Beijing,' Zhuang announced, rising. 'I'll catch the 2:30 train. Come with me, brother!'

'To Beijing? To do what?'

'Beijing is so big, what can't be done?' he replied. 'Even if you just shine shoes, you'll still make much more money there than you do here!'

And so, that very night, Shui and Zhuang boarded a train so crowded that there was not a single seat available. All through the night, the train rolled across the vast open spaces of the West, racing toward the rising sun.

LIFE GOAL #3:

GO TO A BIGGER CITY, SEE MORE OF THE WORLD, MAKE EVEN MORE MONEY.

When Shui saw the capital for the first time, one thing became clear: some things had to be seen to be understood. The power of his imagination alone was inadequate. For instance, he had imagined nighttime in Beijing countless times. At first, he had simply doubled or trebled the lights in his village or at the mining district; after he moved to the provincial capital, he repeated the trick with the lights there. But when the bus he and Zhuang had boarded at Beijing West Railway Station turned onto Chang'an Avenue, he knew he could multiply the lights of the provincial capital a thousand times and never match the spectacle of Beijing at night. Of course, the lights of Beijing were not really a thousand times brighter than those of the provincial capital, but there was something about central Beijing that the cities out west could never hope to capture.

Shui and Zhuang stayed the night in a cheap basement motel and then went their separate ways in the morning. Before he took his leave, Zhuang wished Shui good luck and said that, if he ran into any trouble, he could always come find him. But when Shui asked him for a telephone number or address, he admitted he had neither.

'Then how will I find you?' asked Shui.

'Just wait a while. Soon, you'll know where I am by glancing at the television or the newspaper.'

As he watched Zhuang's receding figure, Shui shook his head in bewilderment. What a puzzling response! The man did not have a cent to his name. Today, he had not been able to afford the room at the motel, and Shui had bought their breakfast. Before they left for Beijing, he had even given his solar cooker to the landlord in place of rent. Now, he was no better than a beggar with a dream.

After he parted from Zhuang, Shui immediately went out in search of work, but the city shocked him so deeply he soon forgot his original objective. He spent the entire day strolling aimlessly through the city streets. It was as though he had walked into a fairyland, and he did not feel tired in the slightest. As dusk fell, he stood before one of the new symbols of the capital. Completed just last year, the Unity Tower stood five hundred meters tall. Shui craned his neck to look up at the glass precipice that rose above the clouds. On its surface, the fading glow of the sunset and the swiftly brightening sea of lights below staged a breathtaking performance of light and shadow. Shui watched until his neck grew sore. Just as he turned to leave, the lights of the tower itself came on. The potent spectacle took possession of Shui, and he stood transfixed, his gaze turned skyward.

'You've been staring for a long time. Are you interested in this sort of work?'

Shui turned to see who had addressed him. It was a young man. He was dressed like any other resident of the city, but he held a yellow hardhat in his hand.

'What work?' Shui asked, confused.

'What were you looking at just then?' the man asked in return, pointing upward with the hand that still held the helmet.

Shui lifted his head and looked in the direction the man was pointing. To his surprise, he spotted several people high up on the glass precipice. From the ground, they looked like little black dots.

'What are they doing so high up there?' Shui asked as he strained for a closer look. 'Cleaning the glass?'

The man nodded. 'I'm the human resources manager of the Blue Skies Window Cleaning Company. Our company primarily provides high-rise cleaning services. Are you willing to do that kind of job?'

Shui raised his head again. Looking at the antlike black dots high above him, he felt dizzy. 'It seems . . . scary.'

'If you are concerned about safety, you can rest assured. The job looks dangerous, and that does make recruitment quite difficult. We're short of hands right now. But I guarantee you that our safety precautions are very thorough. As long as you follow the operating procedures to the letter, there is absolutely no danger. And we pay higher wages than companies in similar industries. You could make fifteen hundred per month plus free lunch on work days, and the company would buy you personal insurance.'

Shui was taken aback by the sum. Astonished, he just stared at the manager. The other man misunderstood his silence. 'Fine, I'll cancel your probation period and throw in another three hundred. That's eighteen hundred per month. I can't go any higher than that. The base pay for this kind of work used to be four or five hundred yuan, plus additional piece work. Now we pay a fixed monthly salary, which is not bad in comparison.'

So Shui became a high-rise window cleaner, otherwise known as a 'spiderman'.

LIFE GOAL #4:
BECOME A BEIJINGER.

Together with four other window cleaners, Shui cautiously descended from the top floor of the Aerospace Tower. It took them forty minutes to reach the eighty-third floor, where they had left off the previous day. One of the spidermen's biggest headaches was cleaning canted facades, those that formed angles smaller than ninety degrees with the ground. The architect of the Aerospace Tower, in a display of his own pathological creativity, had designed the entire building on a slant. The top of the tower was supported by a slender column driven into the ground. According to the celebrity architect, the slanted design was supposed to impart the sensation of rising upward. His statement seemed reasonable, and the skyscraper became famous throughout the world as a landmark of Beijing. But the architect and eight generations of his ancestors were routinely and inventively cursed by Beijing's spidermen. For them, cleaning the Aerospace Tower was a nightmare. The entirety of one side was at an incline, which stood four hundred meters tall and met the ground at a sixty-five-degree angle.

Once he reached his workstation, Shui looked up. Above him, the huge glass face looked like it was toppling down on him. With one hand, he removed the cap from his detergent container. With his other hand, he clutched the handle of his suction cup. This kind of suction was specially made for cleaning surfaces beyond the vertical, but even so, it was difficult to use and often came unsealed. When this happened, the spiderman would swing away from the wall, dangling from his safety line. Such accidents were frequent while cleaning the Aerospace Tower, and each time, it would near frighten the soul out of the cleaner's body. Just yesterday, Shui's workmate lost suction and swung far out from the building. As he swung back in, he was caught by a gust of wind and sent crashing into the building, shattering a large sheet of glass. His forehead and arms were cut to ribbons, and the cost of replacing the expensive coated architectural glass set him back an entire year's wages.

Shui had joined the ranks of the spidermen more than two years ago, but the work had not grown easier with time. Category 2 winds on the Beaufort scale on the ground strengthened to Category 5 winds at one hundred meters. On buildings that exceeded four or five hundred meters, the winds were stronger still. That the job was hazardous went without saying. Plummeting to one's death in the streets below wasn't an unusual fate for spidermen. In winter, strong winds felt as sharp as knives, and the hydrofluoric acid solution commonly used to clean glass windows was so corrosive that it would cause their fingernails to turn black and fall off. To protect themselves from the detergent, the spidermen had to wear watertight jackets, pants, and boots, even in summer. When cleaning coated glass, the blazing sun would beat down on their backs, and the reflected glare in front of them was so blinding it was difficult to keep their eyes open. It made Shui feel like he had been placed into Zhuang's solar cooker.

But Shui loved his job. The past two years had been the happiest time of his life. It undoubtedly helped that the spidermen were highly paid relative to the other uncultured migrant laborers who flocked to Beijing. More importantly, however, he derived a wonderful sense of fulfillment from his work. He relished the jobs his fellow spidermen were unwilling to do: cleaning newly constructed super-skyscrapers. Each of these buildings stood at least two hundred meters tall, and the tallest topped five hundred meters. Hanging off the sides of these skyscrapers, Shui commanded a magnificent view of Beijing, stretched out below him. The so-called 'high-rises' built during the previous century looked squat from up there. A little farther away, they became small bunches of twigs stuck in the ground. In the heart of the city, the Forbidden City looked like it had been built with golden toy blocks. From this height, he could not hear the clamor of Beijing, and he could survey the city with a single glance. It breathed quietly below him, a super-organism surrounded by a spider's web of arterial roads. Sometimes, a skyscraper he was cleaning would push through the clouds. The world below his waist could be enveloped in a dark and dreary rainstorm even as the sun shined brightly overhead. Looking at the endless sea of clouds billowing beneath his feet, Shui always felt as though the howling winds above blew right through him.

The experience taught Shui a philosophical truth: some things only became clear when seen from above. Swallowed up in the capital, everything around him seemed hopelessly complicated. On the ground, the city was like an unending labyrinth. Up here, it was nothing more than an anthill with ten million inhabitants, and the world around it was so vast!

The first time he received his paycheck, Shui had gone for a stroll through a large shopping mall. Riding the elevator to the third floor, he was met by a peculiar scene. Unlike the bustling floors below, this hall was empty except for a few staggeringly large, low tables. The broad tabletops were covered with clusters of tiny buildings, each one no taller than a book. The space between the buildings was filled with bright green grass, dotted with white pavilions and winding corridors. The little structures were lovely, like they were carved from ivory or cheese. Together with the green lawn, they formed an exquisite miniature world. In Shui's eyes, it looked like a model of paradise. At first he guessed that these were some sort of toys, but he did not see any children in the hall. All of the adults at the tables wore attentive, serious expressions. Bewitched, he stood next to one of the tiny paradises and studied it for a long time. It was not until an attractive young woman came over to greet him that he realized this was a real estate office. He pointed to a building at random and asked how much the apartment on the top floor cost. The saleslady told him it was a three-bedroom, one-den apartment and that it cost thirty-five hundred yuan per square meter, which worked out to three hundred and eighty thousand yuan in total. Shui drew a sharp gasp when he heard the number, but the woman's next statement softened the brutal figure considerably: 'You can pay by monthly installments of fifteen hundred to two thousand yuan.'

'I-I'm not from Beijing. Could I still buy it?' he asked carefully.

The saleslady flashed him a winning smile. 'You are too funny. The household registration system was dismantled years ago. Is there such a thing as a 'real' Beijinger anymore? If you settle down here, doesn't that make you a Beijinger?'

After Shui left the mall, he had wandered aimlessly through the streets for a long time. All around him, Beijing's brilliant mosaic of lights glittered in the night. In his hand he held the colorful fliers the saleslady had given him, and every so often he stopped to look at them. Just two years ago, in that rundown room in that distant western city, even owning an apartment in the provincial capital had seemed like a fairytale. Now, he was still a long way away from buying an apartment in Beijing, but it was a fairytale no longer. It was a dream, and like those delicate little models, it was right before his eyes. He could reach out and touch it.

Just then, someone rapped on the window Shui was cleaning, interrupting his daydream. This was a common nuisance. For white-collar workers, the appearance of high-rise window cleaners at their office windows was a source of indescribable irritation. It was like the cleaners really were large, aberrant spiders, as their nickname suggested, and far more than a single pane of glass separated the workers without from those within.

While the spidermen worked, the people inside would complain that they were too noisy, or that they were blocking the sunlight, or about any of the million other ways in which the cleaners had ruined their day. The glass of the Aerospace Tower was semi-reflective, and Shui had to strain to see through it. When he finally made out the man inside, he was astonished to see Zhuang Yu.

After they parted ways, Shui had often worried about Zhuang. In his mind, the man had remained a dapper tramp, making his way through the big city step by arduous step. Then, one night in late autumn, as Shui sat in his dormitory silently fretting about Zhuang's winter wardrobe, he saw him on television. The China Sun Project had begun the selection process for the critical technology at the heart of the project: the material that would be used to build its reflector. In the end, Zhuang's nano mirror film was chosen from among a dozen other materials. Overnight, the scientifically inclined vagrant was transformed into one of the chief scientists of the China Sun Project, recognized the world over. Afterward, even though Zhuang made frequent media appearances, Shui gradually forgot about him. He believed they no longer had anything to do with each other.

When Shui arrived in that spacious office, he saw that Zhuang had not changed one bit over the past two years. He even wore the same suit. Shui now saw that the attire he had once considered so luxurious was, in truth, very shabby. He told Zhuang all about his life in Beijing. 'It looks like we've both done well here,' he concluded, grinning.

'Yes, yes, very well!' Zhuang agreed, nodding excitedly. 'To tell the truth, that morning when I told you about the opportunities of these times, I had lost faith in just about everything. I was mostly saying those things for my own benefit, but these days the world truly is brimming with opportunities!'

Shui nodded too. 'There are golden birds everywhere.'

Shui took stock of the large, modern-looking office around him. A few unusual decorations stood out from the rest of the room. A holographic image of the night sky was projected across the entire ceiling of the office; anyone who stood in the center of the room would feel as though they had been transported to a courtyard beneath the brilliant stars. A curved silver plate hung suspended against the background of stars. It was a mirror that looked very similar to Zhuang's solar cooker, but Shui knew that the real thing was likely twenty or thirty times larger than Beijing.

In one corner of the ceiling, there was a spherical lamp. Like the mirror, it floated in the air without any means of support, shining with a bright yellow light. The mirror reflected its rays onto a globe next to Zhuang's desk, creating a circle of light on its surface. As the lamp slowly floated across the ceiling, the mirror rotated to track it, throwing its light upon the globe without interruption. The starlit sky, the mirror, the lamp, its light, the globe and the illuminated spot composed an abstract and mysterious mural.

'This is the China Sun? Shui asked in awe, pointing to the mirror.

Zhuang nodded. 'It is a thirty-thousand-square-kilometer reflector. From geosynchronous orbit – at an altitude of thirty-six thousand kilometers – it will reflect sunlight onto Earth. Viewed from the surface, it will look like there is another sun in the sky.'

'There's something I don't understand. How does an extra sun in the sky bring more rain?'

'This artificial sun can employ many different methods to influence the weather. For instance, by disturbing the thermodynamic equilibrium of the atmosphere, it can influence atmospheric circulation, increase ocean evaporation or shift weather fronts,'

Zhang answered. 'But that doesn't really explain it. In fact, the orbital reflector is just one part of the China Sun Project. The other part is a complex model of atmospheric motion, which will run on multiple supercomputers. It will be able to accurately simulate motion in any given region of the atmosphere and then identify a critical point. If heat from the artificial sun is brought to bear upon this point, the effect would be dramatic enough to completely transform the climate of a targeted area for a period of time.' He paused. 'The process is extremely complicated, and it is outside my area of expertise. I don't quite understand it myself.'

Shui decided to ask another question which Zhuang could certainly answer. He knew his question was foolish, but he steeled his nerve and asked anyway. 'How can something so big hang in the sky without falling down?'

Zhuang gazed silently at Shui for several long seconds. Finally, he glanced down at his watch and then clapped Shui on the shoulder. 'Let's go. I'm treating you to dinner. I'll explain why the China Sun will not fall while we eat.'

The explanation did not turn out to be as easy as Zhuang expected. He was forced to set aside his original topic and start with the basics. While Shui knew he lived on a round planet, the traditional Chinese model of a heavenly dome over a square Earth was still rooted deep in his mind. It required a great deal of effort from Zhuang to make Shui really understand that the world in which he lived was a small spherical rock floating through an endless void. Although Shui came no closer to understanding why the China Sun would not fall, the universe was greatly changed in his mind's eye that evening. He entered his own Ptolemaic Era. The second evening, Zhuang ate dinner with Shui at a roadside food stall and successfully dragged him into the Copernican Era. Over the next two evenings, Shui slogged through the Newtonian Era, acquiring an elementary understanding of universal gravitation. The evening after that, with the help of the globe in his office, Zhuang ushered Shui into the Space Age. On the next public holiday, in front of that globe, Shui finally grasped the meaning of a geosynchronous orbit. At last, he understood why the China Sun would not fall down.

That day, Zhuang took Shui on a tour of the China Sun Command Center. At the center, a massive monitor displayed a panoramic view of the ongoing construction of the China Sun in geosynchronous orbit. Several thin silver sheets floated in the blackness of space, so large that the space shuttles hovering next to them seemed like tiny mosquitoes.

But what shook Shui the most was an image on another monitor. It showed Earth from an altitude of thirty-six thousand kilometers. The continents floated on the oceans like large scraps of brown packing paper. Mountain ranges became creases in the paper, and clouds looked like residual smudges of powdered sugar on its surface.

Zhuang showed Shui the location of his home village and Beijing. He gawked at the monitor for a long minute before he blurted, 'People must think differently up there.'

The main construction of the China Sun was finished three months later. As night fell on National Day, the reflector was turned towards the night-shrouded Earth, training its immense spotlight on Beijing and Tianjin. That night, standing amid a crowd of several hundred thousand people gathered in Tiananmen Square, Shui witnessed a magnificent sunrise. In the western sky, a star began to brighten dramatically, creating a little ring of blue around itself. As the China Sun approached peak luminosity, the halo expanded, filling half the sky. Around its edges, the clear blue bled into yellow and then orange-red and dark purple, forming a circular rainbow that became known as the 'Wreath of Dawn'.

By the time Shui returned to his dormitory, it was already four o'clock in the morning. As he lay on his narrow upper bunk, the light of the China Sun streamed through his window, illuminating the real estate fliers pasted to the wall above his pillow. He ripped the glossy pages down.

Under the divine radiance of the China Sun, the ideal that had once thrilled him now seemed dull and insignificant.

Two months later, the manager of the cleaning company came to find Shui. He told him that Director Zhuang of the China Sun Command Center wished to see him. Shui had not seen Zhuang since he had finished his work on the Aerospace Tower.

'Your sun is really something!' Shui exclaimed in heartfelt admiration when he met Zhuang in his office at the Aerospace Tower.

'It is our sun, and yours especially!' answered Zhuang. 'Right now you cannot see it from Beijing because it is bringing snow to your village!'

'My parents mentioned in their letter that they were getting more snow than usual this winter!'

'However, the China Sun has a big problem,' said Zhuang, pointing to a large monitor behind him. Two images of a single circular spot of light were displayed on the screen. 'These images of the China Sun were taken from the same location, two months apart. Can you see the difference?'

'The one on the left is brighter.'

'You see, the decrease in reflectivity can be seen with the naked eye after just two months.'

'How can that be? Has the mirror grown dusty?'

'There is no dust in space, but there is the solar wind, or the stream of particles ejected by the sun. With time, the wind will transform the China Sun's mirrored surface. As the reflector accumulates a fine film of particles, its reflectivity will decrease. One year from now, it will look like it is covered with water vapor. Then, the China Sun will have become the China Moon, and it will be useless,' explained Zhuang.

'You didn't think of this earlier?'

'Of course we thought of it!' Zhuang paused. 'Let's talk about you. How do you feel about switching jobs?'

'Switching jobs? What else could I do?'

'You would still be working as a high-altitude cleaner, but you would be working for us.'

Shui glanced around in confusion. 'Wasn't your tower just cleaned? Why would you need to specially employ a high-rise window cleaner?'

'No, we don't want you to clean buildings. We want you to clean the China Sun.'

LIFE GOAL #5: FLY TO SPACE, CLEAN THE CHINA SUN.

There was a meeting of the senior directors of the China Sun Project Operations Division to discuss the establishment of a reflector cleaning unit. Zhuang introduced Shui to the assembled parties and explained his profession to them. When someone inquired about his educational background, Shui honestly replied that he had only finished three years of primary school.

'But I can recognize characters and can read without problems,' he told the attendees.

The conference room dissolved into laughter.

'Director Zhuang, is this a joke?' someone shouted indignantly.

'I'm not joking,' Zhuang replied evenly. 'If we assembled a crew of thirty cleaners, it would take them six months to clean the entire China Sun if they worked around the clock. In reality, we would need at least sixty to ninety people working in shifts. If the new aerospace labor protection law goes into effect as scheduled, we may need even more, perhaps one hundred and twenty to one hundred and fifty cleaners. Can we really send one hundred and fifty astronauts with doctorates and three thousand flight hours in high-performance fighter jets up into space to do the job?'

'Surely we can find more qualified candidates? Higher education is practically universal in the cities these days. How can we send an illiterate hick into space?'

'I am not illiterate!' Shui objected.

The man ignored him and continued speaking to Zhuang. 'You would debase this great project!'

The other participants nodded in agreement.

Zhuang nodded, too. 'I thought you might react like this. Ladies and gentlemen, except for this cleaner, you all hold doctorates.

Well then, let us see the quality of your cleaning work! Please come with me.'

A dozen bewildered participants followed Zhuang out of the conference room and into the elevator. Three types of lifts had been installed in the tower: standard, fast, and express. They boarded the fastest elevator and shot up at breakneck speed to the top floor of the building.

'This is my first time in this elevator,' someone remarked. 'I feel like I am blasting off in a rocket!'

'After we enter geosynchronous orbit, everyone will experience what it is like to clean the China Sun,' said Zhuang, drawing strange glances from the people around him.

After they stepped out of the elevator, Zhuang led the group up a narrow flight of stairs. Finally, they emerged from a low metal door onto the open roof of the tower. They were immediately thrust into bright sunlight and powerful winds. The blue sky overhead seemed even clearer than usual, and the directors looked all around, admiring the panoramic view of Beijing. Another small group of people stood waiting for them. Shui was startled to see his company's manager and his fellow spidermen!

'Now, everyone will try their hand at Shui's profession!' Zhuang announced in a loud voice.

The spidermen stepped forward and strapped each director into a safety harness. They then led them to the edge of the roof and carefully helped them onto narrow suspended platforms that normally served as a workstation for a dozen or more spidermen. The boards were slowly lowered until they were suspended five or six meters beneath the edge of the rooftop, where they halted. Screams of unadulterated terror rose from where the directors dangled against the glass face of the tower.

'Ladies and gentlemen, let us continue the meeting where we left off!' Zhuang called down to his colleagues below, leaning over the edge of the roof.

'You bastard! Quick, pull us up!'

'Every one of you has to clean a pane of glass before I let you up!'

It was an impossible demand. The people below could only cling to their safety harnesses or the ropes supporting the platforms for dear life, not daring to move. They were utterly incapable of loosening one hand to pick up a squeegee or remove the lid from the detergent bucket. Every day, these aerospace officials dealt with altitudes as high as tens of thousands of kilometers in the form of blueprints and documents; but now, as they gained a first-hand feel for four hundred meters, they were scared witless.

Zhuang rose and walked to the spot above an air force colonel. Of the dozen people hanging off the side of the building, he was the only one who remained calm and collected. The colonel began to clean the glass, keeping his motions steady and controlled. What astonished Shui most, however, was that the man was working with both hands, and he had relinquished his grip on anything he might use to steady himself. Even so, his board remained motionless against the wall in the strong wind, a feat that only veteran spidermen could accomplish. When Shui recognized the man, the scene in front of him no longer seemed as strange; he was an astronaut who had flown on the Shenzhou 8 spacecraft more than a decade earlier.

'Colonel Zhang, in your candid opinion, is the task before you really easier than a spacewalk in orbit?' asked Zhuang.

'With respect to the physical ability and skill required, the difference is not great,' the former astronaut replied.

'Well said. According to studies conducted at the Aerospace Training Center, from an ergonomic standpoint, there are many similarities between cleaning skyscrapers and cleaning the reflector in space. Both tasks require workers to constantly maintain their balance in the face of danger, while performing repetitive, monotonous, physically demanding labor. Both tasks require constant vigilance, as the slightest carelessness can lead to an accident. For an astronaut, that might mean deviation from orbit, lost tools or materials, or a malfunction in his life support system. For a spiderman, that might mean shattered glass, dropped tools or detergent, or breakage or slippage of his safety harness. In terms of physical strength, technical skill, and psychological fortitude, the spidermen are fully qualified to work as reflector cleaners.'

The former astronaut lifted his head and nodded at Zhuang. 'I am reminded of that old parable about the oil peddler who could pour oil into a bottle through the square hole in a copper coin. He was every bit as skilled as a general who never missed a bull's-eye. The only difference between them was their social status.'

'Columbus discovered America and Cook discovered Australia, but these New Worlds were settled by ordinary people, pioneers who came from the lowest rungs of European society,' added Zhuang. 'The development of space is no different. In the next Five-Year Plan, we have designated near-Earth space as a second western frontier. The era of exploration has ended, and the aerospace industry will never again be the exclusive domain of an elite minority. Sending ordinary people into orbit is the first step toward the industrialization of space!'

'Okay! Fine! You have made your point! Now quickly, let us up!' his colleagues shouted hoarsely below.

In the elevator on the way down, the manager of the cleaning company leaned toward Zhuang and whispered in his ear, 'Director Zhuang, that was a moving and impassioned speech back there, but wasn't it a little much? But of course, it is difficult to discuss the key issue at hand in front of Shui and my boys.'

'Eh?' Zhuang shot him an inquiring look.

'Everyone knows that the China Sun Project is a quasi-commercial operation. Halfway to completion, a funding shortfall nearly led to the project's cancellation, and now you have next to no operations budget. In the commercial aerospace sector, the annual salary of a qualified astronaut is over one million yuan. My guys will save you tens of millions every year.'

Zhuang smiled enigmatically. 'You think such a paltry sum would be worth the risk? Today, I deliberately slashed the educational standards required of reflector cleaners to set a precedent. After this, I will be able to hire ordinary university graduates to fill the jobs in orbit needed to operate the China Sun. This way, we will save a lot more money than just a few tens of millions. As you said, it is the only course of action available. We really don't have any money left.'

'Growing up, going to space was such a romantic endeavor. I can clearly remember that, when Deng Xiaoping visited the Johnson Space Center, he called an American astronaut a god. Now,' said the manager with a bitter smile, shaking his head and slapping Zhuang on the back, 'I am no better or worse than you.'

Zhuang turned to look at the young spidermen and then told the manager in a raised voice, 'But, sir, the salary I am offering is eight to ten times better than what you pay them!'

The next day, Shui and sixty of his fellow spidermen arrived at the National Aerospace Training Center in Shijingshan. Each and every one of them was a farm boy who had come from some remote corner of China's vast countryside to Beijing, looking for work.

MIRROR FARMERS

At the Xichang Space Center, the nose cone of the space shuttle *Horizon* emerged from the billowing white clouds of exhaust produced by its engines. With a thunderous roar, it rose straight into the clear blue sky. Shui and fourteen other reflector cleaners sat strapped into their seats in the cabin. After three months of training on the ground, they had been chosen from the sixty candidates to be part of the first crew assigned to actual operations in space.

To Shui, the lift-off g-forces were not nearly as terrible as the tales said they would be. He even found a familiar comfort in them. It was the feeling of being held tightly in his mother's arms as a child. Outside the porthole to his upper right, the blue sky began to deepen. There was a faint pop of bolts blasting apart outside the cabin, and the booster rockets separated. As they left the rockets behind, the earsplitting roar of the engines became a mosquito-like drone. The sky faded to dark purple and then full black. The stars appeared, unblinking and intensely luminous.

The drone ceased abruptly, and silence fell over the cabin. The vibration of Shui's seat disappeared along with the pressure pinning his torso to the seatback. They had entered microgravity. Shui and the other spidermen had trained in a colossal swimming pool to prepare for weightlessness. It really did feel like he was floating in water.

But it was not yet safe to unfasten his seatbelt. The hum of the engine returned, and the shuttle's acceleration pressed the men back into their seats. The long maneuver into orbit had begun. The starry sky and the ocean appeared by turns in the tiny porthole. One moment the cabin flooded with the blue glow reflected by Earth, the next with the white light of the Sun. Each time Earth appeared in the porthole, the curvature of the horizon grew more conspicuous, and more of the planet's surface came into view. From start to finish, it took six hours to maneuver into geosynchronous orbit. The continuous alternation of sky and earth outside the porthole had a hypnotic effect on Shui, lulling him into an unexpected sleep. He was jarred awake by the commander's voice over the intercom. He informed them that the orbit insertion maneuver was complete.

One after another, his companions floated from their seats, pressing their faces to the viewing ports to peer outside. Shui unfastened his own seatbelt and, using swimming motions, floated clumsily through the air to the nearest porthole. For the first time, he saw Earth in its entirety with his own eyes. Most of the other men, however, had gathered in front of the viewing ports on the other side of the cabin. He pushed off against the bulkhead with his foot and shot across to join them. Unable to control his speed, he bumped his head on the opposite wall. As he gazed through a porthole, he realized the *Horizon* was already directly beneath the China Sun. The reflector took up most of the starry sky. Their space shuttle seemed like a small mosquito trapped under a silver dome. As the *Horizon* continued its approach, Shui gradually came to appreciate the sheer immensity of the reflector. Its mirrored surface occupied the entire view from the porthole, and its curvature was imperceptible, as if they were flying above a boundless silver plain. A reflection of the *Horizon* appeared on its surface as the distance continued to shrink. Shui could see long seams on the silver ground, which formed a grid like the latitude and longitude lines on a map. The grid was his sole reference point for judging the shuttle's relative velocity. After a time, the longitude lines no longer ran parallel. They began to converge in one direction, gradually at first and then more sharply, as if the *Horizon* was bound for a pole on this great map. Soon, the pole came into view. All of the longitudinal seams met at a small black dot. As the shuttle began its descent toward the dot, Shui realized with a start that it was actually a gigantic tower rising above the silver plain. He knew that this hermetically sealed cylinder was the China Sun Control Station. For the next three months, it would be their only home in the desolation of space.

And so the spidermen began their new lives in space. Every day – the China Sun orbited Earth once every twenty-four hours – they piloted small tractor-like machines onto the mirrored surface to polish it.

They drove their tractors to and fro across the wide expanse of the reflector, as if they were tilling the silver earth. As a result, the Western media coined a more poetic name for the spidermen. They were now 'mirror farmers'.

The world in which these farmers lived was quite peculiar. A silver plain lay beneath their feet. Though the reflector's curved form caused the plain to rise slowly in the distance in every direction, it was so vast that it looked as flat and calm as still water. Overhead, both Earth and the Sun were visible. The latter appeared much smaller than Earth, as if it was the planet's radiant satellite. On the surface of the Earth, which occupied most of the sky, they could see a slowly moving circle of light. It was a particularly striking sight when it drifted onto the nighttime hemisphere. This was the region illuminated by the China Sun. The reflector could change the size of the light spot by adjusting its own shape. When the silver plain rose steeply in the distance, the spot grew smaller and brighter. When the slope was gentler, the spot grew larger and dimmer.

The work of the reflector cleaners was extremely difficult. They soon realized that buffing the reflector was far more monotonous and draining than scrubbing skyscrapers on Earth. When they returned to the control station at the end of each day, they were often too exhausted to even take off their spacesuits. As more personnel arrived from Earth, the control station began to feel cramped, and they lived like crewmen aboard a submarine. Nonetheless, they considered themselves fortunate if they could return to the station at all. The most remote point on the reflector was nearly one hundred kilometers from the station. Cleaners working on the reflector's outer rim often could not make it back after a day on the job and had to spend the 'night' in the 'wilderness'. After suctioning a liquid dinner from their suit, they would fall asleep suspended in space.

The work was incredibly dangerous, to boot. Never before in the history of human spaceflight had so many people performed space walks. In the 'wilderness', the slightest malfunction in one's space suit could mean death. There were also micrometeorites, bits of space debris, and solar storms to worry about. The control station engineers carped bitterly about these living and working conditions, but the mirror farmers, who had been born into hardship, adapted to their new circumstances without complaint.

On his fifth day in space, Shui received a call from his family. He was working more than fifty kilometers away from the control station, and the China Sun had its beam trained on his home village.

He heard Pa's voice. 'Wah, are you on that sun? It's shining above our heads right now. The night is as bright as day!'

Shui replied, 'Yeah, Pa, I'm right above you.'

Then Ma spoke. 'Wah, is it hot up there?'

'You could say it's both hot and cold. Right now, everything outside of my shadow is hotter than ten summers in our village, but inside my shadow is colder than ten winters.'

'I can see our Wah,' Ma told Pa. 'That little black dot on the Sun right there!'

Shui knew this was impossible, but as tears rolled down his cheeks, he said, 'Pa, Ma, I can see you, too. There are two little black dots on the Asian continent where you are! Dress warmly tomorrow. I can see a cold front moving in from the north!'

Three months later, the second cleaning crew arrived to relieve the first of its duties, and Shui and his coworkers returned to Earth for three months' leave. After they landed, the first thing that every one of them did was buy a high-powered monocular telescope. When they returned to the China Sun three months later, they used their new purchases to observe the planet below during the breaks between work. They most often turned their lenses toward home, but at an altitude of nearly forty thousand kilometers it was impossible to see their villages. One of the men scrawled a simple, inelegant poem on the reflector with a felt-tip pen:

From this silver earth, I watch my distant home
On the edge of the village, my mother looks up at the China Sun
Its disc is the image of her son's eye
The yellow earth is clad in green under his gaze

The mirror farmers did an outstanding job. Over time, they began to take on responsibilities beyond the scope of their cleaning work. At first, they simply repaired damage done to the reflector by meteor strikes, but later they were tasked with more demanding work: monitoring and reinforcing sections at risk for overstress failure.

As the China Sun moved in orbit, it was constantly reorienting itself. These adjustments were made by three thousand engines distributed across the back face of the reflector. The actual mirrored surface of the reflector was very thin, and it was joined to the whole structure with a great number of slender beams. When the engines fired, parts of the reflector surface could become overstressed. If the engine outputs were not corrected in time, or the location was not reinforced, the unchecked overstress could tear the mirrored surface. Discovering and reinforcing stress points required both great technical skill and ample experience.

Apart from reorientation or reshaping periods, overstress was most likely to occur during an 'orbital haircut', or a 'Radiation Pressure and Solar Wind-Induced Drag Correction', as the operation was formally known. Together, solar wind and radiation exerted a significant force on the enormous surface of the reflector. Approximately two kilograms of pressure pushed against every square kilometer of the reflector, causing an outward drift in its orbit. The earthbound control center constantly monitored these changes, comparing the altered track to the intended orbit on a large screen. On screen, it looked as if long, wavy hairs were sprouting from the intended orbit, hence the curious nickname for the operation.

The reflector's acceleration was much greater during an orbital haircut than during reshaping or reorientation, and the work of the mirror farmers was critical during this period. Flying above the silver plain, they would scrutinize every anomaly on its surface and perform emergency reinforcements when necessary. They acquitted themselves splendidly and their salaries were raised accordingly. But the greatest beneficiary was Zhuang Yu, who rose to the highest office of the China Sun Project –without having to hire a single university graduate.

Nevertheless, it was clear to the mirror farmers that they would be the first and last group of workers in space to receive only a primary school education. Those who followed them would be university graduates at the very least. Still, they served the purpose envisioned by Zhuang. They had proven that skill, experience, and the ability to adapt to adverse circumstances were more important than knowledge and creativity in the blue-collar jobs created by space development. Ordinary people were fully up to the task.

However, space did alter the way the mirror farmers thought. No one else had the privilege of gazing down upon Earth from thirty-six thousand kilometers every day. With a glance, they could take in the whole planet. To them, the global village was no longer just a metaphor but a reality before their very eyes.

As the first laborers in space, the mirror farmers had been a global sensation, but the industrial development of near-Earth orbit was now in full swing. Mega-projects were commissioned, including vast solar power stations that beamed microwave energy down to the planet below, microgravity processing plants, and many others. Construction even began on an orbital city that could accommodate one hundred thousand residents. Industrial workers arrived in space in droves. They, too, were ordinary people, and so the world gradually forgot about the mirror farmers.

Several years passed. Shui bought a house in Beijing, married, and had a child. He spent half of every year at home, and the other half in space. He loved his job. His long patrols on that silver land more than thirty thousand kilometers above Earth filled his heart with detached peacefulness. He felt as though he had found his ideal life, and the future stretched before him as level and smooth as the silver plain underfoot. But then something happened that shattered his tranquility and thoroughly changed the course of his mental journey. Shui encountered Stephen Hawking.

No one had expected that Hawking would live to be one hundred. It was a medical miracle, but it was also a testament to his force of will. After the first low-gravity assisted living facility was constructed in near-Earth orbit, he became its first resident. However, the hypergravity of launch nearly claimed his life. Because he would have to endure the same forces during reentry, returning to Earth was out of the question, at least until the invention of a space elevator, antigravity cabin module or similar delivery vehicle. In fact, his doctors advised him to permanently settle in space, as the weightless environment perfectly suited his body.

At first, Hawking expressed little interest in the China Sun. Only a survey of anisotropy in the cosmic background radiation was sufficient to persuade him to subject himself to the g-forces generated by the trip from near-Earth orbit to geosynchronous orbit (though, of course, these forces were smaller than those he had experienced during launch). The observation station had been installed on the back face of the China Sun, as the reflector would block all interference from the Sun and Earth. But when the survey was complete, the observation station dismantled and the survey team withdrawn, Hawking did not want to leave. He said he liked it there and wished to stay a while longer. Something had drawn his attention to the China Sun. The press had a field day with speculations of all kinds, but only Shui knew the whole truth.

What Hawking enjoyed most about his life on the China Sun were his daily excursions across the surface of the reflector. To the consternation of many, he would simply drift along the underside of the reflector for several hours every day. Shui, who by now was the China Sun's most experienced spacewalker, was assigned to accompany the professor on his outings. At that time, Hawking's fame rivaled Einstein's – even Shui had heard of him. Nevertheless, Shui was shocked when they met for the first time in the control center. He had never imagined that someone with such a severe disability could achieve so much – not that he understood the great scientist's achievements in the slightest. On their excursions, however, Hawking betrayed no hint of his paralysis. Perhaps it was his experience controlling an electric wheelchair that allowed him to operate the micro-engines in his spacesuit as nimbly as any able-bodied person.

Hawking found it difficult to communicate with Shui. He did have an implant that allowed him to control a speech synthesizer with his brain waves, which made speaking less of a chore than it had been in the previous century. However, his words still had to be run through a device that provided real-time translation into Chinese so that Shui could understand him. Shui's superiors instructed him that he was never to initiate conversation with the professor in case he disturbed his thoughts. Hawking, however, was more than willing to talk to him.

He first asked Shui for an account of his life and then began to reminisce about his own early years. Hawking told Shui about his cold, sprawling childhood home in St Albans; in winter, the frigid, lofty parlor would ring with the music of Wagner. He told him about the Gypsy caravan his parents placed in a field at Osmington Mills, and how he and his younger sister Mary would ride it to the seashore. He talked about the times he and his father visited the Ivinghoe Beacon in the Chiltern Hills. Shui marveled at the centenarian's memory, but he was even more amazed that they shared a common vocabulary. The professor greatly enjoyed Shui's accounts of life in his home village. Floating on the outer rim of the reflector, he asked Shui to point out its location.

After a while, their conversations inevitably turned to science. Shui feared this would bring their discussions to an end, but it was not the case. For the professor, it was relaxing to discuss deep topics in physics and cosmology using language that even ordinary people could follow. He told Shui about the Big Bang, black holes, and quantum gravity. When Shui returned to the station, he began to wrestle with the thin little book Hawking had written in the previous century, consulting the station's engineers and scientists when he encountered something he did not understand. He grasped far more of its contents than anyone thought he would.

One day, the two men traveled to the outskirts of the reflector. 'Do you know why I like this place?' the professor asked Shui, facing a sliver of Earth visible beyond the rim of the reflector. 'This huge mirror separates us from Earth below. It lets me forget about the world and devote my entire focus to the cosmos.'

'The world below is complicated,' agreed Shui, 'but seen from so far away, the universe seems so simple, just stars scattered in space.'

'Yes, my boy, it does indeed,' said the professor.

Just like the reflector's front face, its back face was also mirrored. The only real difference was that it was dotted with the engines that adjusted the reflector's orientation and shape, which resembled small black towers. On their daily strolls, Shui and Hawking would leisurely float along, staying just above the ground. They often drifted all the way from the control station to the outer rim. When the Moon was not visible, the back face of the reflector was extremely dark, and its surface reflected the starlit sky. Compared to the front face, the horizon was closer here, and visibly curved. By the light of the stars, the black latitude and longitude lines formed by the support beams passed beneath their feet, as if they were skimming above the surface of a tiny, tranquil planet. Whenever the reflector was reoriented or reshaped, the engines on the back face would ignite. Illuminated by countless jets of flame, the surface of this tiny planet seemed even more beautiful and mysterious. And shining above, always, the Milky Way, bright and unwavering.

It was here that Shui first encountered the deepest secrets of the cosmos. He learned that the starry sky that filled his vision was but a speck of dust in the unimaginable vastness of the universe, and that this entire creation was nothing but the embers of a ten-billion-year-old explosion.

Many years ago, when he had taken his first step as a spiderman onto the roof of a skyscraper, Shui had seen all of Beijing. When he arrived on the China Sun, he had seen all of Earth. Now, Shui faced the third such glorious moment of his life. Standing on the roof of the cosmos, he could see things beyond his wildest dreams. Although he possessed only a superficial understanding of those distant worlds, they still held an irresistible attraction for him.

Once Shui expressed his confusion to an engineer in the station. 'Humanity landed on the Moon in the sixties. And what next? Even now, we have not set foot on Mars. We don't even visit the Moon anymore.'

'Humans are practical creatures,' replied the engineer. 'What was driven by idealism and faith in the middle of the last century was not viable in the long term.'

'What's wrong with idealism and faith?'

'There's nothing wrong with them per se, but economic interests are better. If in the sixties humanity had spared no expense in the pursuit of spaceflight and racked up enormous losses, Earth might still be mired in poverty. Ordinary people like you and me would never have made it to space at all, even if we are no further than near-Earth orbit. Pal, don't let Hawking poison you. Normal folk shouldn't toy with the things he does.'

The conversation changed Shui. On the surface he appeared calm, working as hard as ever, but deep down he was contemplating new horizons.

Twenty years flew by. From an altitude of thirty-six thousand kilometers, Shui and his compatriots commanded a clear view of two decades of changes creeping across the globe. They watched as the Three-North Shelter Belt formed a verdant ribbon that traversed northwestern China, slowly turning the yellow desert green. Their home villages would never lack rain or snow again. The dry riverbeds on the outskirts of the villages flowed once more with clear, clean water.

The China Sun deserved the credit for all of this. It had played a major role in the great campaign to transform the climate of northwestern China. Not only that, it also performed a number of innovative extracurricular activities: once it melted the snows of Mount Kilimanjaro to ease a drought in Africa; on another occasion it turned an Olympic host city into a city that truly never slept.

But with the advent of newer technologies, the China Sun's methods of manipulating the weather began to seem clumsy and encumbered with too many side effects. The China Sun had accomplished its mission.

The Ministry of Space Industry held a grand ceremony to decorate the first group of industrial workers in orbit. They were honored not only for their twenty years of exceptional hard work, but more importantly, these sixty men were recognized for the singular accomplishment of entering space as youths with nothing but an elementary or middle-school education. In doing so, they had thrown the doors of space development wide open to everyone. Economists unanimously agreed that this had been the true beginning of the industrialization of space.

The ceremony attracted widespread attention from the press. In addition to the aforementioned reasons, the mirror farmers' story had acquired a legendary quality in the hearts of the public. It was also an excellent opportunity to indulge in nostalgia in an age where things were rapidly acquired and then forgotten.

Those simple and honest lads were already well into middle age, but they did not appear greatly changed. Audiences could still recognize them on their holographic television sets. Over the years most of the men had attained some form of higher education, and a few had even earned the title of space engineer. In their own eyes and the eyes of the public, however, they remained that same group of migrant laborers from the countryside.

Shui gave a speech on behalf of his companions. 'With the completion of the electromagnetic conveyor system, the cost of entering near-Earth orbit is only half the cost of a flight across the Pacific Ocean,' he said. 'Space travel has become an ordinary, unglamorous affair. New generations are hard-pressed to imagine what traveling to space meant to an ordinary person twenty years ago, how the opportunity would excite him, how it would make his blood boil. We were the lucky ones.

'We are ordinary men, and there is little to be said about us. Our extraordinary experience was entirely thanks to the China Sun. Over the past twenty years, it has become our second home. In our hearts, it is like a miniature Earth. At first, we used the seams on the reflector's mirrored surface to represent the latitude and longitude lines of the northern hemisphere. When we marked our positions, we would specify our coordinates in degrees north and degrees east or west. Later, as we grew familiar with the reflector, we gradually blocked out the continents and oceans on it. We would say were in Beijing or Moscow. Each of our home villages had a corresponding position on the reflector's surface, and we cleaned those areas the hardest.'

Shui became momentarily lost in thought. 'We worked hard on that small, silver Earth, and we did our duty. All in all, five reflector cleaners gave their lives for the China Sun. Some had no time to take cover from solar magnetic storms, and others were hit by meteors or space debris. Soon, our silver world, where we lived and worked for two decades, will vanish. It is difficult to express our feelings in words.'

Shui fell silent. Zhuang, who had risen to the office of Minister for Space Industry, picked up the thread. 'I completely understand how you must feel, but I am pleased to be able to tell everyone that the China Sun will not disappear! As I expect you all know, such a massive object cannot be allowed to burn up in the atmosphere, as was common practice in the last century. But there is another, rather elegant, way to find the China Sun a final resting place. If we simply discontinue the orbital haircuts and make the appropriate adjustments to its orientation, solar wind and radiation pressure will accelerate it until it reaches the second cosmic velocity. In the end, it will escape Earth's orbit and become a satellite of the Sun. Perhaps, many years in the future, interplanetary spaceships will rediscover it. We could turn it into a museum and return to that silver plain and reminisce about these unforgettable years.'

Shui lit up with sudden excitement. 'Minister, do you really think that day will come?' he asked Zhuang in a loud voice. 'Do you really think there will be interplanetary spaceships?'

Zhuang stared at him, at a loss for words.

'In the middle of the last century,' Shui continued, 'when Armstrong left the very first footprint on the Moon, almost everyone believed that humanity would land on Mars within the next ten to twenty years. Now, many decades have passed. No one has returned to the Moon, let alone Mars. The reason is simple: it is a losing proposition.

'Since the end of the Cold War, economics has come to rule our day-by-day lives, and under its rule humanity has made great strides. Today, we have eliminated war and poverty and restored the environment. Truly, Earth is becoming a paradise. This has reinforced our belief in the efficiency of the economic principle. It has grown paramount, permeating our very DNA. There is no doubt human society has become an economic society. Never again will we undertake any endeavor that yields less than the investment it requires. The development of the Moon makes no economic sense, the large-scale manned exploration of the planets would qualify as an economic crime, and as for interstellar flight, that is downright lunacy! Now humanity knows only input, output and consumption.'

Zhuang nodded. 'In this century, human development of space has been confined to near-Earth space. That is a fact,' he said. 'There are many underlying reasons for it, but they are beyond the scope of today's topic.'

'No, they are well within it! We have been given an opportunity. If we just spend a little money, we can leave near-Earth space behind and embark on a great voyage into the cosmos. Just as solar radiation pressure can push the China Sun out of orbit around Earth, it can also push it to more distant places.'

Zhuang chuckled and shook his head. 'Oh, you mean to use the China Sun as a solar sail? That might work in the abstract. The body of the reflector is thin and light, and its surface area is large. After a long period of acceleration by radiation pressure, it would become the fastest spacecraft ever launched by humanity. However, I am only speaking in a theoretical sense. In reality, a ship with only a sail cannot travel far. It needs a crew. An unmanned sailboat will only drift in circles on the ocean without ever sailing out of the harbor – I recall Stevenson's *Treasure Island* contained a particularly vivid description of such a ship. Returning from a long voyage by means of radiation pressure requires precise, complex control over the reflector's orientation. But the China Sun was designed to operate in orbit around Earth. Without human control, it will follow an aimless path as it drifts blindly through space, and it will not make it far.'

'Yes, but it will have a crew aboard. I will pilot it,' Shui replied calmly.

At that moment, the audience measurement system indicated that the channel's ratings had risen sharply. The eyes of the entire world were focused upon them.

'But you cannot control the China Sun by yourself. Its orientation controls require at least—'

'At least twelve people,' Shui interrupted. 'Taking other factors of interstellar travel into account, at least fifteen to twenty people. I believe we will have that many volunteers.'

Zhuang gave a helpless laugh. 'I truly did not expect that today's conversation would take this turn.'

'Minister Zhuang, over twenty years ago, you changed the course of my life on more than one occasion.'

'But I never, ever imagined you would travel so far, much further than I have.' Zhuang sighed deeply. 'Well, this is very interesting. Let us continue our discussion! Ah,' he said, frowning, 'I'm afraid your idea is not feasible. The most sensible target for the China Sun is Mars, but you have not considered that the China Sun cannot land. If you want to land, it will require a huge expenditure, and the plan will lose its economic viability. If you do not want to land, the whole endeavor is tantamount to launching an unmanned probe. What would be the point?'

'The China Sun is not bound for Mars.'

Zhuang looked at Shui, baffled. 'Then where? Jupiter?'

'Not Jupiter, either. Even farther afield.'

'Farther? To Neptune? Pluto?' Zhuang abruptly stopped. For a long while, he gazed at Shui in disbelief. 'My god, you don't mean to say—'

Shui nodded firmly. 'Yes, the China Sun will fly beyond the solar system and become the first interstellar spaceship!'

All around the world, people stared at their televisions with the same open-mouthed incredulity as Zhuang.

Zhuang stared straight ahead and nodded mechanically. 'Well, if you are not joking, let me make a quick estimate . . .' he said, his eyes half-closed as he began to do mental calculations. 'I have it figured out. Using solar radiation pressure, the China Sun would accelerate to one-tenth of the speed of light. Taking into account the time needed to accelerate, it would reach Proxima Centauri in forty-five years. The China Sun would then use the radiation pressure of Proxima Centauri to decelerate. After you complete a survey of the Alpha Centauri system, you would accelerate in the opposite direction, returning to the solar system after another few decades. It sounds like a marvelous plan, but in fact, it is a dream that cannot be realized.'

'Wrong again,' Shui replied. 'When we reach Proxima Centauri, the China Sun will not decelerate. We will skim by it at a speed of thirty-thousand kilometers per second, using its radiation pressure to accelerate even faster as we fly toward Sirius. If possible, we will continue to leapfrog through space, to a third star, a fourth . . .'

'What the hell is your game plan here?' Zhuang shouted, losing patience.

'All we ask of Earth is a highly reliable but small-scale ecological life support system—'

'And you would use this system to sustain the lives of twenty people for over a century?'

'Let me finish,' Shui replied. 'And a cryogenic hibernation system. We will spend most of the voyage in a dormant state, only powering up the life support system when we approach Proxima Centauri. At the current level of technology, this should be enough to let us travel through the cosmos for over a thousand years. Of course, these two systems do not come cheap, but it will require just one-thousandth of the capital required to build a manned interstellar probe from scratch.'

'Even if you did not want a cent, the world cannot permit twenty people to commit suicide.'

'This is not suicide, it is exploration,' Shui countered. 'Maybe we will not even make it past the asteroid belt right in front of us, but maybe we will reach Sirius or beyond. If we do not try, how will we know?'

'But there is something that sets this expedition apart from exploration,' said Zhuang. 'There is no possibility of return.'

Shui nodded. 'Yes, we will not return. Some people are satisfied with a wife, children and a warm bed, never so much as glancing at the parts of the world that do not concern them. But some people will spend their whole lives trying to glimpse something humanity has never seen before. I have been both of these people, and I have the right to choose the life I want to lead,' he concluded. 'That includes living out my days on a mirror, drifting through space ten light-years away.'

'One final question,' Zhuang said. 'In one thousand years' time, as you race past stars at speeds of tens or hundreds of thousands of kilometers per second, it will take decades or even centuries for humanity to receive the weak radio signals you send out. Is it worth the sacrifice?'

With a smile, Shui announced to the whole world, 'As the China Sun flies beyond the solar system, humans will look away from all our creature comforts and up toward the starry sky again. We will recall our dream of space travel and rekindle our desire for interstellar exploration.'

LIFE GOAL #6:
FLY TO THE STARS, DRAW HUMANITY'S GAZE BACK TO THE DEPTHS OF THE COSMOS.

Zhuang stood on the roof of the Aerospace Tower and gazed at the China Sun as it moved swiftly through the sky. Its light caught the capital's high-rises and threw countless fast-moving shadows, as if Beijing was an upturned face following the China Sun.

This was the China Sun's last revolution around Earth. It had already reached escape velocity and would soon fly beyond the planet's gravitational field, entering into orbit around the Sun. There were twenty people aboard humanity's first manned interstellar spaceship. Besides Shui, the others had been selected from among more than one million volunteers. They included three other mirror farmers who had worked with Shui for many years. The China Sun had accomplished its goal before it ever began its journey. Humanity's enthusiasm for exploring beyond the solar system was reborn.

Zhuang's thoughts returned to that sultry summer night in that northwestern city twenty-three years ago, when he and a farm boy from the arid countryside had boarded the night train to Beijing.

In parting, the China Sun trained its spot of light on each major city in turn, giving humanity one last look at its radiance. Finally, the spot of light came to rest on northwestern China. At its center lay the little village in which Shui had been born.

By the side of the road on the outskirts of town, Shui's parents stood together with their neighbors, watching the China Sun fly east.

Pa shouted into the phone, 'Wah, you are going somewhere far away?'

'Yeah, Pa,' Shui replied from space. 'I am afraid I will not come home.'

'Is it very far away?' Ma asked.

'Very far, Ma,' Shui answered.

'Farther than the Moon?' Pa asked.

Shui fell silent for a few seconds. Then, in a voice much lower than before, he said, 'Yeah, Pa, a little farther than the Moon.'

Shui's parents were not especially distraught. Their son was going to do great things at that place beyond the Moon! Besides, these were extraordinary times. Even from the remotest corners of the Earth, they could talk to him at any time, they could even see him on their little television. It was no different from speaking to him face-to-face. It did not occur to them that there would be an ever longer delay; that Shui's answers to their concerned questions would come slower and slower. At first, it would only be a few seconds, but the pauses would grow. In a year's time, every question would require hours for a response.

Finally, their son would vanish. They would be told that Shui had gone to sleep and that he would not wake for forty years.

After that, Shui's parents would continue to tend that plot of once-barren but now fertile land and live out the remainder of their once-backbreaking but now satisfying lives. Their last wish would be that, someday in the distant future, their son would return to see an even more beautiful homeland.

As the China Sun left Earth's orbit, it steadily dimmed in the eastern sky, its blue halo shrinking to a star-like point as it dissolved into the night. Then dawn arrived, and its light was completely swallowed by the glow of the morning Sun.

The morning Sun also shone down on the path that led out of the village. White poplars now lined the path, and a short distance away a small river ran parallel to it. On that day twenty-four years ago, in the small hours of the morning, under the same light of dawn, the son of northwestern peasants gradually disappeared into the distance on this very road, nursing vague hopes.

It was now broad daylight in Beijing, but Zhuang remained standing on the roof of the Aerospace Tower, gazing at the point where the China Sun had vanished. It had embarked on its endless voyage of no return. The China Sun would first pass Venus' orbit, getting as close as possible to the sun to boost radiation pressure and maximize the distance it had in which to accelerate. This would be realized through a complex series of orbital transfer maneuvers, much like the way ocean-going vessels of the Age of Navigation would tack and jibe upwind. After seventy days, it would pass Mars' orbit. After one hundred and sixty days, it would sweep by Jupiter. After two years, it would fly beyond Pluto's orbit and become an interstellar spaceship, and its crew would enter hibernation. After forty years, it would fly past Alpha Centauri, and its crew would briefly reawaken. One century after the China Sun began its journey, Earth would receive information obtained during their exploration of Alpha Centauri. By then, the China Sun would already be soaring toward Sirius. Thanks to the speed boost from Alpha Centauri's three suns, it would have reached fifteen percent of the speed of light. Another sixty years later, one hundred and sixty years after setting out from Earth, it would reach Sirius. After passing the binary star system formed by Sirius A and Sirius B, its speed would increase to twenty percent of the speed of light, and it would hurtle even deeper into the night sky. Given the limits of the onboard cryogenic hibernation system's lifespan, the China Sun might reach ε Eridani or – though the probability was quite small – even 79 Ceti. Both star systems were thought to harbor planets.

No one knew how far the China Sun would fly, or what strange worlds Shui and the others would behold. Perhaps one day they would send a message to Earth, but it would be over a thousand years before they received a reply.

No matter what happened, Shui would always remember a country called China on his mother planet. He would always remember a little village in that country's arid northwest. He would always remember the path that led out of that village, the path on which his journey began.

THE THINKER

The Sun

He still remembered how he felt the first time he saw the Mount Siyun Astronomical Observatory thirty-four years ago. After his ambulance crossed the mountain ridge, Mount Siyun's highest peak emerged in the distance. Its observatories' spherical roofs reflected the golden light of the setting sun like pearls inlaid into the mountain peak.

At the time, he'd just graduated from medical school. A brain-surgery intern assisting the chief of surgery, he'd been rushed here to save a visiting research scholar from England who'd fallen on a hike. The scholar had injured his head too seriously to be moved. Once the ambulance arrived, they drilled a hole in the patient's skull, then drained some blood out to reduce brain swelling. Once the patient had been stabilized enough to move, the ambulance took him to the hospital for surgery.

It was late at night by the time they could leave. Out of curiosity, while others carried the patient into the ambulance, he examined the several spherical observatories that surrounded him. How they were laid out seemed to imply some sort of hidden message, like a Stonehenge in the moonlight. Spurred on by some mystical force that he still didn't understand even after a lifetime of contemplation, he walked to the nearest observatory, opened its door, then walked inside.

The lights inside were off except for numerous small signal lamps. He felt as though he'd walked from a moonlit starry sky to a moonless starry sky. The only moonlight was a sliver that penetrated the crack in the spherical roof. It fell on the giant astronomical telescope, partially sketching out its contours in silver lines. The telescope looked like a piece of abstract art in a town square at night.

He stepped silently to the bottom of the telescope. In the weak light, he saw a large pile of machinery. It was more complex than he'd imagined. He searched for an eyepiece. A soft voice came from the door:

'This is a solar telescope. It doesn't have an eyepiece.'

A figure wearing white work clothes walked through the door, as though a feather had drifted in from the moonlight. The woman walked over to him, bringing a light breeze along with her.

'A traditional solar telescope casts an image onto a screen. Nowadays, we usually use a monitor. . . . Doctor, you seem to be very interested in this.'

He nodded. 'An observatory is such a sublime and rarefied place. I like how it makes me feel.'

'Then why did you go into medicine? Oh, that was very rude of me.'

'Medicine isn't just some trivial skill. Sometimes, it, too, is sublime, like my specialty of brain medicine, for example.'

'Oh? When you use a scalpel to open up the brain, you can see thoughts?' she said.

Her smiling face in the weak light made him think of something he'd never seen before, the sun cast onto a screen. Once the violent flares disappeared, the magnificence that remained couldn't help but make his heart skip a beat. He smiled, too, hoping she could see his smile.

'Oh, we can look at the brain all we want,' he said, 'but consider this: Say a mushroom-shaped thing you can hold in one hand turns out to be a rich and varied universe. From a certain philosophical viewpoint, this universe is even grander than the one you observe. Even though your universe is tens of billions of light-years wide, it's been established that it's finite. My universe is infinite because thought is infinite.'

'Ah, not everybody's thoughts are infinite but, Doctor, yours seem to be. As for astronomy, it's not as rarefied as you think. Several thousand years ago on the banks of the Nile and several hundred years ago on a long sea voyage, it was a practical skill. An astronomer of the time often spent years marking the positions of thousands of stars on star charts. A census of the stars consumed their lives. Nowadays, the actual work of astronomical research is dull and meaningless. For example, I study the twinkling of stars. I make endless observations, take notes, then make more observations and take more notes. It's definitely not sublime as well as not rarefied.'

His eyebrows rose in surprise. 'The twinkling of stars? Like the kind we can see?' When he saw her laugh, he laughed, too, shaking his head. 'Oh, I know, of course, that's atmospheric refraction.'

'However, as a visual metaphor, it's pretty accurate. Get rid of the constant terms, just show the fluctuations in their energy output, and stars really do look like they're twinkling.'

'Is it because of sunspots?'

She stopped smiling. 'No, this is the fluctuation of a star's total energy. It's like how when a lamp flickers, it's not because of the moths surrounding it, but because of fluctuations in voltage. Of course, the fluctuations of a twinkling star are minuscule, detectable only by the most precise measurements. Otherwise, we'd have been burned by the twinkling of the sun long ago. Researching this sort of twinkling is one way of understanding the deep structure of stars.'

'What have you discovered so far?'

'It'll be a while before we discover anything. For now, we've only observed the twinkling of the star that's the easiest to observe – the sun. We can do this for years while we gradually expand out to the rest of the stars. . . . You know, we could spend ten, twenty years taking measurements of the universe before we make any discoveries and come to some conclusion. This is my dissertation topic, but I think I'll be working on this for a long while, perhaps my whole life.'

'So you don't think astronomy is dull, after all.'

'I think what I'm working on is beautiful. Entering the world of stars is like entering an infinitely vast garden. No two flowers are alike. . . . You have to think that's a weird analogy, but it's exactly how I feel.'

As she spoke, seemingly without realizing it, she gestured at the wall. A painting hung there, very abstract, just a thick line undulating from one end to the other. When she noticed what he was looking at, she took it down, then handed it to him. The thick, undulating line was a mosaic of colorful pebbles from the area.

'It's lovely, but what does it represent? The local mountain range?'

'Our most recent measurements of the sun twinkling, it was so intense and we'd rarely ever seen it fluctuate like that this year. This is a picture of the curve of the energy radiated as it twinkled. Oh, when I hike, I like to collect pebbles, so . . .'

The scientist was only partially visible in the surrounding shadow. She looked like an elegant ink line a brilliant artist drew on a piece of fine, white calligraphy paper. The curve's intelligence of spirit filled that perfect white paper immediately with vitality and intention. . . . In the city he lived in outside the mountains, at any given moment, more than a million young women, like a large group of particles in Brownian motion, chased the showy and vain, without even a moment of reflection. But who could imagine that on this mountain in the middle of nowhere, there was a gentle and quiet woman who stared for long stretches at the stars . . .

'You can reveal this kind of beauty from the universe. That's truly rare and also very fortunate.' He realized he was staring and looked away. He returned the painting to her but, lightly, she pushed it back to him.

'Keep it as a souvenir, Doctor. Professor Wilson is my advisor. Thank you for saving his life.'

After ten minutes, the ambulance left under the moonlight. Slowly, he realized what he'd left on the mountain.

First Time

Once he married, he abandoned his effort to fight against time. One day, he moved his things out of his apartment to the one he now shared with his wife. Those things that two people shouldn't share, he brought to his office at the hospital. As he riffled through them, he found a mosaic made of colorful pebbles. Seeing the multicolored curve, he suddenly realized that the trip to Mount Siyun was ten years ago.

Alpha Centauri A

The hospital's young employees' group had a spring outing. He cherished this outing particularly, because it was getting less and less likely they'd invite him again. This time, the trip organizer was deliberately mysterious, pulling down the blinds on all the coach windows and having everyone guess where they were once they arrived. The first one to guess correctly won a prize. He knew where they were the instant he stepped off the coach, but he kept quiet.

The highest peak of Mount Siyun stood before him. The pearl-like spherical roofs on its summit glittered in the sunlight.

After someone guessed where they were, he told the trip organizer that he wanted to go to the observatory to visit an acquaintance. He left on foot, following the meandering road up the mountain.

He hadn't lied, but the woman whose name he didn't even know wasn't part of the observatory staff. After ten years, she probably wasn't here anymore. He didn't actually want to go inside, just to look around at the place where, ten years ago, his soul, hot, dry, and as bright as the sun, spilled into a thread of moonlight.

One hour later, he reached the mountaintop and the observatory's white railings. Its paint had cracked and faded. Silently, he took in the individual observatories. The place hadn't changed much. He quickly located the domed building that he'd once entered. He sat on a stone block on the grass, lit a cigarette, then studied the building's iron door, spellbound. The scene he'd long cherished replayed from the depths of his memory: with the iron door half open, in the midst of a ray of moonlight like water, a feather drifted in . . .

He was so completely steeped in that long-gone dream that when the miracle happened, he wasn't surprised: the observatory's iron door opened for real. The feather that once had emerged from the moonlight drifted into the sunlight. She left in a hurry to go into another observatory. This couldn't have taken more twenty seconds, but he knew he wasn't mistaken.

Five minutes later, they reunited.

This was the first time he'd seen her with adequate light. She was exactly as he'd imagined. He wasn't surprised. It'd been ten years, though. She shouldn't have looked exactly like the woman barely lit by a few signal lamps and the moon. He was puzzled.

She was pleasantly surprised to see him, but no more than that. 'Doctor, I make a round of every observatory for my project. In a given year, I'm only here for half a month. To run into you again, it must be fate!'

That last sentence, tossed off lightly, confirmed his initial impression: She didn't feel anything more about seeing him again besides surprise. However, she still recognized him after ten years. He took a shred of comfort in that.

They exchanged a few words about what had happened to the visiting English scholar who'd suffered the brain injury. Finally, he asked, 'Are you still researching the twinkling of stars?'

'Yes. After observing the sun's twinkling for two years, I moved on to other stars. As I'm sure you understand, the techniques necessary to observe other stars are completely different from those to observe the sun. The project didn't have new funding. It halted for many years. We just started it back up three years ago. Right now, we are only observing twenty-five stars. The number and scope are still growing.'

'Then you must have produced more mosaics.'

The moonlit smile that had surfaced so many times from the depths of memory over the past ten years now emerged in the sunlight. 'Ah, you still remember! Yes, every time I come to Mount Siyun, I collect pretty pebbles. Come, I'll show you!'

She took him into the observatory where they'd first met. A giant telescope confronted him. He didn't know whether it was the same telescope from ten years ago, but the computers that surrounded it were practically new. Familiar things hung on a tall curved wall: mosaics of all different sizes. Each one was of an undulating curve. They were all of different lengths. Some were as gentle as the sea. Others were violent, like a row of tall towers strung together at random.

One by one, she told him which waves came from which stars. 'These twinklings, we call type A twinklings. They don't occur as much as other types. The difference between type A twinklings and those of other types, besides that their energy fluctuations are orders of magnitude larger, is that the mathematics of their curves is even more elegant.'

He shook his head, puzzled. 'You scientists doing basic research are always talking about the elegance of mathematics. I guess that's your prerogative. For example, you all think that Maxwell's equations are incredibly elegant. I understood them once, but I couldn't see where the elegance was . . .'

Just like ten years ago, she suddenly grew serious. 'They're elegant like crystals, very hard, very pure, and very transparent.'

Unexpectedly, he recognized one of the mosaics. 'Oh, you re-created one?' Seeing her uncomprehending expression, he continued. 'That's the waveform of the sun twinkling in the mosaic you gave me ten years ago.'

'But . . . that's the waveform from a type A twinkling from Alpha Centauri A. We observed it, um, last October.'

He trusted that she was genuinely puzzled, but he trusted his own judgment as well. He knew that waveform too well. Moreover, he could even recall the color and shape of every stone that made up the curve. He didn't want her to know that, until he got married last year, that mosaic had always hung on his wall. There were a few nights every month when moonlight would seep in after he'd turned out the lights, and he could make out the mosaic from his bed. That was when he'd silently count the pebbles that made up the curve. His gaze crawled along the curve like a beetle. Usually, by the time he'd crawled along the entire curve and gone halfway back, he'd fallen asleep. In his dreams, he continued to stroll along this curve that came from the sun, like stepping from colorful stone to colorful stone to cross a river whose banks he'd never see . . .

'Can you look up the curve of the sun twinkling from ten years ago? The date was April twenty-third.'

'Of course.'

She gave him an odd look, obviously startled that he remembered that date so easily. At the computer, she pulled up that waveform of the sun twinkling followed by the waveform of Alpha Centauri A twinkling that was on the wall. She stared at the screen, dumbfounded.

The two waveforms overlapped perfectly.

When her long silence grew unbearable, he suggested, 'Maybe these two stars have the same structure, so they also twinkle the same way. You said before that type A twinkling reflects the star's deep structure.'

'They are both on the main sequence and they both have spectral type G2, but their structures are not identical. The crux, though, is that even for two stars with the same structure, we still wouldn't see this. It's like banyan trees. Have you ever seen two that were absolutely identical? For such complex waveforms to actually overlap perfectly, that's like having two large banyan trees where even their outermost branches were exactly the same.'

'Perhaps there really are two large banyan trees that are exactly the same,' he consoled, knowing his words were meaningless.

She shook her head lightly. Suddenly, she thought of something and leapt to stand. Fear joined the surprise already in her gaze.

'My god,' she said.

'What?'

'You. . . . Have you ever thought about time?'

He quickly caught on to what she was thinking. 'As far as I know, Alpha Centauri A is our closest star. It's only about . . . four light-years away.'

'1.3 parsecs is 4.25 light-years.' She was still in the grip of astonishment. It was as if she couldn't believe the things she herself was saying.

Now it was all clear: The two identical twinklings occurred eight years and six months apart, just long enough for light to make a round trip between the two stars. After 4.25 years, when the light of the sun's twinkling reached Alpha Centauri A, the latter twinkled in the same way, and after the same amount of time, the light of Alpha Centauri's twinkling was observed here.

She hunched over her computer, making calculations and talking to herself. 'Even if we take into account the several years where the two stars regressed from each other, the result still fits.'

'I hope what I said doesn't cause you too much worry. There's ultimately nothing we can do to confirm this, right? It's just a theory.'

'Nothing we can do to confirm this? Don't be so sure. That light from the sun twinkling was broadcast into space. Perhaps that'll lead to another star twinkling in the same way.'

'After Alpha Centauri, the next closest star is . . .'

'Barnard's Star, 1.81 parsecs away, but it's too dim. There's no way to measure it. The next star out, Wolf 359, 2.35 parsecs away, is just as dim. Can't measure it. Yet farther out, Lalande 21185, 2.52 parsecs away, is also too dim. . . . That leaves Sirius.'

'That seems like a star bright enough to see. How far is it?'

'2.65 parsecs away, just 8.6 light-years.'

'The light from the sun twinkling has already traveled for ten years. It's already reached there. Perhaps Sirius has already twinkled back.'

'But the light from it twinkling won't arrive for another seven years.' She seemed to wake all of a sudden from a dream, then laughed. 'Oh, dear, what am I thinking? It's too ridiculous!'

'So you're saying, as an astronomer, the idea is ridiculous?'

She studied him earnestly. 'What else can it be? As a brain surgeon, how do you feel when someone discusses with you where thought comes from, the brain or the heart?'

He had nothing to say. She glanced at her watch, so he started to leave. She didn't urge him to stay, but she accompanied him quite a distance along the road that led down the mountain. He stopped himself from asking for her number because he knew, in her eyes, he was just some stranger who bumped into her again by chance ten years later.

After they said goodbye, she walked up toward the observatory. Her white lab coat swayed in the mountain breeze. Unexpectedly, it stirred up in him how it had felt when they'd said goodbye ten years ago. The sunlight seemed to change into moonlight. That feather disappeared in the distance . . . like a straw of rice, sinking into the water, that someone desperately tries to grab. He decided he wanted to maintain that cobweb-like connection between them. Almost instinctively, he shouted at her back:

'If, seven years from now, you see Sirius actually twinkles like that . . .'

She stopped walking and turned toward him. With a smile, she answered, 'Then we'll meet here!'

Second Time

With marriage, he entered a completely different life, but what changed his life thoroughly was a child. After the child was born, the train of life suddenly changed from the local to the express. It rushed past stop after stop in its never-ending journey onward. He grew numb from the journey. His eyes shut, he no longer paid attention to the unchanging scenery. Weary, he went to sleep. However, as with so many others sleeping on the train, a tiny clock deep in his heart still ticked. He woke the minute he reached his destination.

One night, his wife and child slept soundly but he couldn't sleep. On some mysterious impulse, he threw on his clothes, then went to the balcony. Overhead, the fog of city lights dimmed the many stars in the sky. He was searching for something, but what? It was a good while before his heart answered him: He was looking for Sirius. He couldn't help but shiver at that.

Seven years had passed. The time left before the appointment he'd made with her: two days.

Sirius

The first snow of the year had fallen the day before, and the roads were slippery. The taxi couldn't make it up the last stretch to the mountain's peak. He had to go, once again, on foot, clambering to the peak of Mount Siyun.

On the road, more than once, he wondered whether he was thinking straight. The probability she'd keep the appointment was zero. The reason was simple: Sirius couldn't twinkle like the sun had seventeen years earlier. In the past seven years, he had skimmed a lot of astronomy and astrophysics. That he'd said something so ridiculous seven years ago filled him with shame. He was grateful that she hadn't laughed at him there and then. Thinking about it now, he realized she had merely been polite when she seemed to take it seriously. In the intervening seven years, he'd pondered the promise she'd made as they left each other many, many times. The more he did, the more it seemed to take on a mocking tone . . .

Astronomical observations had shifted to telescopes in Earth orbit. Mount Siyun Observatory had shut down four years ago. The buildings there became vacation villas. No one was around in the off-season. What was he going to do there? He stopped. The seven years that'd passed had taken their toll. He couldn't climb up the mountain as easily anymore. He hesitated for a moment, but ultimately abandoned the idea of turning back. He continued upward.

He'd waited so long, why not finally chase a dream just this once?

When he saw the white figure, he thought it was a hallucination. The figure wearing the white windbreaker in front of the former observatory blended into the backdrop of the snow-packed mountain. It was difficult to make out at first, but when she saw him, she ran to him. She looked like a feather flying over the snowfield. He could only stand dumbstruck, and wait for her to reach him. She gasped for air, unable to speak. Except that her long hair was now short, she hadn't changed much. Seven years wasn't long. Compared to the lifetimes of stars, it didn't even count as an instant, and she studied stars.

She looked him in the eyes. 'Doctor, at first, I didn't have much hope of seeing you. I came only to carry out a promise or perhaps to fulfill a wish.'

'Me too.'

'I almost let the observation date slip by, but I never truly forgot it, just stowed it in the deepest recesses of my memory. A few nights ago, I suddenly thought of it . . .'

'Me too.'

Neither of them spoke. They just listened to the gusts of wind that blew through the trees reverberate among the mountains.

'Did Sirius actually twinkle like that?' he asked finally, his voice trembling a little.

'The waveform of its twinkling overlaps precisely the sun's from seventeen years ago and Alpha Centauri A's from seven years ago. It also arrived exactly on time. The space telescope Confucius 3 observed it. There's no way it can be wrong.'

They fell again into another long stretch of silence. The rumble of wind through the trees rose and fell. The sound spiraled among the mountains, filling the space between earth and sky. It seemed as though some sort of force throughout the universe thrummed like a deep and mystical chorus. . . . He couldn't help but shiver. She, evidently feeling the same way, broke the silence, as though to cast off her fears.

'But this situation, this strange phenomenon, goes beyond our current theories. It requires many more observations and much more evidence in order for the scientific community to deal with it.'

'I know. The next possible observable star is . . .'

'It would have been Procyon, in Canis Minor, but five years ago, it rapidly grew too dark to be worth measuring. Maybe it drifted into a nearby cloud of interstellar dust. So, the next measurable star is Altair, in the constellation Aquila.'

'How far is it?'

'5.1 parsecs, 16.6 light-years. The sun's twinkling from seventeen years ago has just reached it.'

'So we have to wait another seventeen years?'

'People's lives are bitter and short.'

Her last sentence touched something deep in his heart. His eyes, blown dry by the winter wind, suddenly teared. 'Indeed. People's lives are bitter and short.'

'But at least we'll still be around to keep this sort of appointment again.'

He stared at her dumbly. Did she really want to part ways again for seventeen years?!

'Excuse me. This is all a bit overwhelming,' he said. 'I need some time to think.'

The wind had blown her hair onto her forehead. She brushed it away. She saw into his heart, then laughed sympathetically. 'Of course. I'll give you my number and email address. If you're willing, we'll keep in touch.'

He let out a long breath, as if a riverboat on the misty ocean finally saw the lighthouse on the shore. His heart filled with a happiness he was too embarrassed to admit to.

'But. . . . Why don't I escort you down the mountain.'

Laughing, she shook her head and pointed to the domed vacation villa behind her. 'I'm going to stay here awhile. Don't worry. There's electricity and good company. They live here, forest rangers . . . I really need some peace and quiet, a long time of peace and quiet.'

They made their quick goodbyes. He followed the snow-packed road down the mountain. She stood at Mount Siyun's peak for a long while watching him leave. They both prepared for a seventeen-year wait.

Third Time

After the third time he returned from Mount Siyun, he was suddenly aware of the end of his life. Neither of them had more than seventeen years left. The vast and desolate universe made light as slow as a snail. Life was as worth mentioning as dirt.

They kept in touch for the first five of the seventeen years. They exchanged emails, occasionally called each other, but they never met. She lived in another city, far away. Later, they each walked toward the summit of their own lives. He became a celebrated brain-medicine expert and the head of a major hospital. She became a member of an international academy of science. They had more and more to worry about. At the same time, he understood that, with the most prominent astronomer in academic circles, it was inappropriate to discuss too much this myth-like thing that linked them together. So, they gradually grew further and further apart. Halfway through their seventeen years, they stopped contacting each other entirely.

However, he wasn't worried. He knew that, between them, they had an unbreakable bond, the light from Altair rushing through vast and desolate space to Earth. They both waited silently for it to arrive.

Altair

They met at the peak of Mount Siyun in the dark of night. Both of them wanted to show up early to avoid making the other wait. So around three in the morning, they both clambered up the mountain. Their flying cars could have easily reached the peak, but they both parked at the foot of the mountain and then walked up, as if they wanted to re-create the past.

Mount Siyun was designated as a nature preserve ten years ago, and it had become one of the few wild places left on Earth. The observatory and vacation villas of old became vine-covered ruins. It was among these ruins that they met under the starlight. He'd recently seen her on TV, so he knew the marks that time had left on her. Even though there was no moon tonight, no matter what he imagined, he felt that the woman before him was still the one who stood under the moonlight thirty-four years ago. Her eyes reflected starlight, making his heart melt in his feelings of the past.

She said, 'Let's not start by talking about Altair, okay? These past few years, I've been in charge of a research project, precisely to measure the transmission of type A twinkling between stars.'

'Oh, wow. I hadn't let myself hope that anything might actually come from all this.'

'How could it not? We have to face up to the truth that it exists. In the universe that classical relativity and quantum physics describes, its oddity is already inconceivable. . . . We discovered in these few years of observation that transmitting type A twinkling between stars is a universal phenomenon. At any given moment, innumerable stars are originating type A twinklings. Surrounding stars propagate them. Any star can initiate a twinkling or propagate the twinkling of other stars. The whole of space seems to be a pool flooded with ripples in the midst of rain. . . . What? Aren't you excited?'

'I guess I don't understand: Observing the transmission of twinkling through four stars took over thirty years. How can you . . .'

'You're a smart person. You ought to be able to think of a way.'

'I think . . . Is it like this: Search for some stars near each other to observe. For example, star A and star B, they're ten thousand light-years from Earth, but they're only five light-years from each other. This way, you only need five years to observe the twinkle they transmitted ten thousand years ago.'

'You really are a smart man! The Milky Way has hundreds of billions of stars. We can find plenty of stars like those.'

He laughed. Just like thirty-four years ago, he wished she could see him laugh in the night.

'I brought you a present.'

As he spoke, he opened a traveling bag, then took out an odd thing about the size of a soccer ball. At first glance, it seemed like a haphazardly balled-up fishing net. Bits of starlight pierced through its small holes. He turned on his flashlight. The thing was made of an uncountably large number of tiny globes, each about the size of a grain of rice. Attached to each globe was a different number of sticks so slender they were almost invisible. They connected one globe to another. Together, they formed an extremely complex netlike system.

He turned off the flashlight. In the dark, he pressed a switch at the base of the structure. A dazzling burst of quickly moving bright dots filled the structure, as though tens of thousands of fireflies had been loaded into the tiny, hollow, glass globes. One globe lit, then its light propagated to surrounding globes. At any given moment, some portion of the tiny globes produced an initial point of light or propagated the light another globe produced. Vividly, she saw her own analogy: a pond in the midst of rain.

'Is this a model of the propagation of twinkling among the stars? Oh, so beautiful. Can it be . . . you'd already predicted everything?!'

'I'd guessed that propagating the twinkling among the stars was a universal phenomenon. Of course, it was just intuition. However, this isn't a model of the propagation of stellar twinkling. Our campus has a brain-science research project that uses three-dimensional holographic-microscopy molecular-positioning technology to study the propagation of signals between neurons in the brain. This is just the model of signal propagation in the right brain cortex, albeit a really small part of it.'

She stared, captivated by the sphere with the dancing lights. 'Is this consciousness?'

'Yes. Just as a computer's ability to operate is a product of a tremendous amount of zeros and ones, consciousness is also just a product of a tremendous amount of simple connections between neurons. In other words, consciousness is what happens when there is a tremendous amount of signal propagation between nodes.'

Silently, they stared at this star-filled model of the brain. In the universal abyss that surrounded them, hundreds of billions of stars floating in the Milky Way and hundreds of billions of stars outside the Milky Way were propagating innumerable type A twinklings between each other.

She said lightly, 'It's almost light. Let's wait for sunrise.'

They sat together on a broken wall, looking at the model of the brain in front of them. The flicker light had a hypnotic effect. Gradually, she fell asleep.

Thinker

She flew against a great, boundless gray river. This was the river of time. She was flying toward time's source. Galaxies like frigid moraines floated in space. She flew fast. One flutter of her wings and she crossed over a hundred million years. The universe shrank. Galaxies clustered together. Background radiation shot up. After one billion years had passed, moraines of galaxies began to melt in a sea of energy, quickly scattering into unconstrained particles. Afterward, the particles transformed into pure energy. Space began to give off light, dark red at first. She seemed to slink in a bloodred energy sea. The light rapidly grew in intensity, changing from the dark red to orange, then again to an eye-piercing pure blue. She seemed to fly within a giant tube of neon light. Particles of matter had already melted in the energy sea. Shining through this dazzling space, she saw the borders of the universe bend into a spherical surface, like the closing of a giant palm. The universe shrank down to the size of a large parlor. She was suspended in its center waiting for a strange particle to arrive. Finally, everything fell into pitch darkness. She knew she was already within a strange particle.

After a blast of cold, she found herself standing on a broad white plain. Above her was a limitless black void. The ground was pure white, covered by a layer of smooth, transparent, sticky liquid. She walked ahead to the side of a bright red river. A transparent membrane covered the river surface. The red river water surged under the membrane. She left the ground, soaring into the sky. Not far away, the blood river branched into many tributaries, forming a complex network of waterways. She soared even higher. The blood rivers grew slender, mere traces against the white ground, which still stretched to the horizon. She flew forward. A black sea appeared. Once she flew over the sea, she realized it wasn't black. It seemed so because it was deep and completely transparent. The mountain ranges on the vast seafloor came into view. These crystalline mountain ranges stretched radially from the center of the sea to the shore. . . . She pushed herself up even higher and didn't look down again until who knows how long. Now, she saw the entire universe at once.

The universe was a giant eye calmly looking at her.

She woke suddenly. Her forehead was wet. She wasn't sure if it was sweat or dew. He hadn't slept, always at her side silently looking at her. Sitting on the grass in front of them, the model of the brain had exhausted its battery. The starlight that pierced it had extinguished.

Above them, those stars hovered as before.

'What are 'they' thinking?' she asked, breaking the silence.

'Now?'

'In these thirty-four years.'

'The twinkling the sun originated could just be a primitive neural impulse. Those happen all the time. Most of them are like mosquitoes causing tiny ripples on a pond, insubstantial. Only those impulses that spread through the whole universe can become an actual experience.'

'We used up a lifetime, and saw of 'him' just one twinkling impulse that 'he' couldn't even feel?' she said hazily, as though still in the middle of a dream.

'Use an entire human civilization's life span, and we still might not see one of 'his' actual experiences.'

'People's lives are bitter and short.'

'Yes. People's lives are bitter and short . . .'

'A truly insightful, solitary person.'

'What?' He looked at her, uncomprehending.

'Oh, I said 'he,' apart from completeness, is nothingness. 'He' is everything. Still thinking, or maybe dreaming. But dreaming about what . . .'

'Let's not try to be philosophers!' He waved his hand as though he were shooing something away.

Out of the blue, something occurred to her. She got off of the broken wall. 'According to the big bang theory of modern cosmology, while the universe is expanding, the light emitted from a given point can never spread widely across the universe.'

'In other words, 'he' can never have even one actual experience.'

Her eyes focused infinitely far away. She stayed silent for a long time, before speaking. 'Do we?'

Her question sank him into his recollection of the past. Meanwhile, the woods of Mount Siyun heard its first birdcall. A ray of light appeared on the eastern horizon.

'I have,' he answered confidently.

Yes, he had. It was thirty-four years ago during a peaceful moonlit night on this mountain peak. A feather-like figure in the moonlight, a pair of eyes looking up at the stars. . . . A twinkling in his brain quickly propagated through the entire universe of his mind. From then on, that twinkling never disappeared. That universe contained in his brain was more magnificent than the star-filled exterior universe that had already expanded for about fourteen billion years. Although the external universe was vast, the evidence ultimately showed it was finite. Thought, however, was infinite.

The eastern sky grew brighter and brighter, starting to hide its sea of stars. Mount Siyun revealed its rough contours. On its highest peak, at the vine-covered ruins of the observatory, these two nearly sixty-year-old people gazed eastward expectantly, waiting for that dazzling brain cell to rise over the horizon.

GLORY AND DREAMS

AN OLYMPICS DELAYED

The dawn light now lit up half the sky. But in the Republic of West Asia the land was still mired in the dark, as if the receding night had congealed into a black sludge that covered all.

Mr. Grant drove a small truck filled with garbage out the main gate of a United Nations humanitarian aid station. The native West Asians employed at the base had all left, leaving him to take out the trash himself these last few days. But this was the last final time. The next day, the last group of UN workers, including himself, would also be leaving. In all likelihood it was just a matter of days before war would descend on this country again.

Grant pulled the truck up to the nearby dump, got down from the vehicle and picked up a bag of garbage. But as he reached for the second bag, his hand paused in midair. There was something alive out there, in this dead place, a small black dot on the horizon, leaping and in motion, as if refusing to be a part of the dark backdrop of this land. It was like a sunspot against the bright solar background.

A sudden sound brought Grant's attention back to his immediate surroundings. Several black shadows were moving toward the garbage bag he had just put down, like stones on the ground come to life and on the move. These were the scavengers who showed up every day, male and female, young and old. After seventeen years of blockade, famine had choked this country to its last gasps of life.

Grant looked back to the horizon. He could now make out that the distant dot was a human being, running.

Against the brightening sky, the black point seemed just then like a bug dancing before a flame.

At that moment, something stirred up the scavengers. Someone had found half a sausage, and had stuffed it into his mouth, chewing and swallowing blissfully as the others stopped to watch, listlessly, for several seconds. And then they were back at the torn trash bag. To their hunger-addled minds, food among the garbage was brighter than the rising sun.

Grant raised his head again. The runner was closer now, and he could make out the body of a woman. A very thin young woman. She seemed like a tree sapling, swaying in the morning light. When she was close enough for him to hear her labored breathing, he found he still could not hear her footsteps. She had run all the way up to the garbage dump when her legs gave out and she sat down hard on the ground. She was a teenage girl, with jet-black skin, dressed in an old racing vest and worn-out running shorts.

Something about her eyes drew Grant in. They stood out prominently from her small thin face, making her look like some kind of nocturnal animal. There was a light in them that set them apart from the listless looks of the scavengers. Something in these eyes ignited under the dawn light. It was desire, suffering and fear mixed all together. Her existence was concentrated in these eyes, which made the rest of her face and body seem little more than a withered branch and leaf attached to the fruit. She breathed hard, struggling to catch her breath, a sound like a faraway wind. Her lips were pale and parched.

One of the scavengers murmured something to her in the West Asian language, which Grant understood a little. The meaning was more or less: 'Cinnie, you are late again. Don't think others will save you anything to eat!'

The level gaze of the girl called Cinnie shifted down to the trash bag, laboriously, as if something was drawing her far away from there. But her hunger was soon evident, as she started to search the garbage for food with the others. Now almost all of the remaining food had been taken, but she found an open can of fish. She snatched at some of the fish bones inside and began to chew, forcing them down in a single swallow. She was just about to get up, seemingly to look for some more, only to collapse immediately. Grant went over to her and tried to help her sit up. Her body, covered in sweat, was unbelievably light. It was like he held only a bolt of folded cloth in his arms.

'It's the hunger. She's been like this several times before.' Someone spoke in perfect English to Grant, who gently placed Cinnie back on the ground. Grant stood up, took out a bottle of milk from the cab of his truck, then squatted down to feed her. Cinnie could taste the milk, even as faint as she was. She began to drink it down in gulps.

'Where is your home?' asked Grant in hard, foreign-sounding West Asian when he saw she was slightly more awake.

'She is mute.'

'Does she live far from here?' Grant lifted his head and spoke to the scavenger speaking English. The man wore glasses and had a scraggly beard.

'No, she lives in the refugee camp nearby, but every morning she runs to the river and back again.'

'The river! But that's. . . more than ten kilometers. Is she crazy?'

'No, she is training.' Seeing Grant even more confused, the scavenger said, 'She is the top marathon runner in the Republic of West Asia.'

'Oh. . . But this country has not held a national championship in years, I thought?'

'In any case, that is what everyone says.'

Cinnie had recovered now, taking up the milk bottle herself and drinking all that remained. Grant, squatting beside her, shook his head with a sigh. 'It's true. Wherever you go, there are those who live in their dreams.'

'I was once such a person,' said the scavenger.

'Your English is good.'

'I was an English literature professor at the University of West Asia. These seventeen years of sanctions and blockade have made us lose our dreams. In the end, we all become like this.' He pointed at the other scavengers still picking through the trash as he spoke. Cinnie's collapse hadn't attracted the slightest attention from them. 'My only dream now is to drink any booze you've got leftover.'

Grant looked down at Cinnie with sorrow. 'She'll kill herself like this.'

'What difference does it make?' shrugged the English literature professor. 'In two or three days, war will break out, all of you will have left, international aid will be cut off, and the roads will be closed. And we will all die, either from bombs or from starvation.'

'But the war will end quickly, I think. The people of West Asia are tired of war. The country is already a complete mess."

'Exactly. All we wish for now is food. And to stay alive. Look at him.' The professor pointed at a young person picking in the trash pile, hair dirty and wild. 'He is a fugitive soldier.'

Just then Cinnie, held up one thin arm and pointed at the UN base not far away, a cluster of several white prefab buildings. She used two hands to gesture toward it.

'It seems she wants to enter,' said the professor.

'Can she hear?' asked Grant. Seeing the professor nod, he turned to Cinnie. Motioning with one hand and speaking in his shaky West Asian, he explained. 'You cannot. You cannot enter. I will give you more, some things to eat. Tomorrow. Do not come. Tomorrow we go.'

Cinnie used her fingers to write several words in the sand, in West Asian. The professor read them and told Grant, 'She wants to watch the opening ceremony of the Olympics on your television.' He shook his head sadly. 'Ah, this child. There's no point helping her. She's incorrigible.'

'The Olympics have been delayed one day,' said Grant.

'Because of the war?

'What, you didn't know?' Grant looked at the people around him in surprise.

'Well, what do the Olympics have to do with us?' The professor shrugged again.

Just then, they were interrupted by the harsh sound of an approaching engine. An old-fashioned bus, the kind now seen only in West Asia, was heading their way up the road. It stopped in front of them, and a man jumped down from the bus. He looked to be about fifty, with salt and pepper hair. He came running up, yelling, 'Is Cinnie here? I'm looking for Cinnie Wydia!'

Cinnie tried to stand, but her legs gave way and she lay back down again. The man spotted her and rushed over. 'Child, what has happened? Do you recognize me?'

Cinnie nodded her head.

'Where did you come from?' the professor asked.

'I am Clark, Director of the National Athletics Agency,' answered the man before lifting Cinnie off the ground.

CLOUD OF POEMS

A yacht bore Yi Yi and his two companions across the South Pacific on a voyage dedicated to poetry. Their destination was the South Pole. Upon a successful arrival in a few days, they would climb through the Earth's crust to view the Cloud of Poems.

Today, the sky and seas were clear. For the purposes of poem making, the workings of the world seemed to be laid out in glass. Looking up, one could see the North American continent in rare clarity in the sky. On the vast world-encompassing dome as seen from the eastern hemisphere, the continent looked like a patch of missing plaster on a wall.

Oh, yes, humanity lived inside the Earth nowadays. To be more accurate, humanity lived inside the Air, for the Earth had become a gas balloon. The Earth had been hollowed out, leaving only a thin shell about a hundred kilometers thick. The continents and oceans remained in their old places, only they had all migrated to the inside of the shell. The atmosphere also remained, moved inside as well. So now the Earth was a balloon, with the oceans and continents clinging to its inner surface. The hollow Earth still rotated, but the significance of the rotation was much different than before: It now produced gravity. The attractional force generated by the bit of mass forming Earth's crust was so weak as to be insignificant, so now the Earth's 'gravity' had to come from the centrifugal force of rotation. But this kind of 'gravity' was unevenly distributed across the regions of the world.

It was strongest at the equator, being about 1.5 times Earth's original gravity. With increase of latitude came a gradual decrease in gravity—the two poles experienced weightlessness. The yacht was currently at the exact latitude that experienced 1.0 gees as per the old scale, but Yi Yi nonetheless found it difficult to recall the sensation of standing on the old, solid Earth.

At the heart of the hollow Earth hovered a tiny sun, which currently illuminated the world with the light of noon. The sun's luminosity changed continuously in a twenty-four-hour cycle, from its maximum to total darkness, providing the hollow Earth with alternating day and night. On suitable nights, it even gave off cold moonlight. But the light came from a single point; there was no round, full moon to be seen.

Of the three people on the yacht, two of them were not, in fact, people. One was a dinosaur named Bigtooth. The yacht swayed and tilted with every shift of his ten-meter-tall body, to the annoyance of the one reciting poetry at the boat's prow. This was a thin, wiry old man, garbed in the loose, archaic robes of the Tang Dynasty, whose snow-white hair and snow-white whiskers flowed in the wind as one. He resembled a bold calligraphy character splashed in the space between sea and sky.

This was the creator of the new world, the great poet Li Bai.

The Gift

The matter began ten years ago, when the Devouring Empire completed its two-century-long pillage of the solar system. The dinosaurs from Earth's ancient past departed for Cygnus in their ring-shaped world fifty thousand kilometers in diameter, leaving the sun behind them. The Devouring Empire took 1.2 billion humans with them as well, to be raised as livestock. But as the ring world approached the orbit of Saturn, it suddenly began to decelerate, before, incredibly, returning along its earlier route to the inner reaches of the solar system.

One ring-world week after the Devouring Empire began its return, the emissary Bigtooth piloted away from the ring in his spaceship shaped like an old boiler, a human named Yi Yi in his pocket.

'You're going to be a present!' Bigtooth told Yi Yi, eyes on the black void outside the window port. His booming voice rattled Yi Yi's bones.

'For whom?' Yi Yi threw his head back and shouted from the pocket. From the opening, he could see the dinosaur's lower jaw, like a boulder jutting out from the top of a giant cliff.

'You'll be given to a god! A god came to the solar system. That's why the Empire is returning.'

'A real god?'

'Their kind controls unimaginable technology. They've transformed into beings of pure energy, and can instantaneously jump from one side of the Milky Way to the other. They're gods, all right. If we can get just a hundredth of their ultra-advanced technology, the Devouring Empire will have a bright future ahead. We're entering the final step of this important mission. You need to get the god to like you!'

'Why did you pick me? My meat is very low-grade,' said Yi Yi. He was in his thirties. Next to the tender, pale-fleshed humans cultivated with so much care by the Devouring Empire, he appeared rather old and world-worn.

'The god doesn't eat bug-bugs, just collects them. I heard from the breeder that you're really special. Apparently you have many students?'

'I'm a poet. I currently teach Classic literature to the livestock humans on the feedlot.' Yi Yi struggled to pronounce 'poet' and 'literature,' rarely used words in the Devourer language.

'Boring, useless knowledge. Your breeder turns a blind eye to your classes because their spiritual effects improve the bug-bugs' meat quality. . . . From what I've observed, you think highly of yourself and give little notice to others. They must be very interesting traits for a head of livestock to have.'

'All poets are like this!' Yi Yi stood tall in the pocket. Even though he knew that Bigtooth couldn't see, he raised his head proudly.

'Did your ancestors participate in the Earth Defense War?'

Yi Yi shook his head. 'My ancestors from that era were also poets.'

'The most useless kind of bug-bug. Your kind was already rare on Earth back then.'

'They lived in the world of their innermost selves, untouched by changes to the outside world.'

'Shameless . . . ha, we're almost there.'

Hearing this, Yi Yi stuck his head out of the pocket. Through the huge window port, he could see the two white, glowing objects ahead of the ship: a square and a sphere, floating in space. When the spaceship reached the level of the square, the latter briefly disappeared against the backdrop of the stars, revealing that it had virtually zero thickness. The perfect sphere hovered directly above the plane. Both shone with soft, white light, so evenly distributed that no features could be distinguished on their surfaces. They looked like objects taken from a computer database, two concise yet abstract concepts in a disorderly universe.

'Where's the god?' Yi Yi asked.

'He's the two geometric objects, of course. Gods like to keep it nice and simple.'

As they approached, Yi Yi saw that the plane was the size of a soccer field. The spaceship descended upon the plane thruster side down, but the flames left no marks on the surface, as if the plane were nothing but an illusion. Yet Yi Yi felt gravity, and the jarring sensation when the spaceship touched down proved that the plane was real.

Bigtooth must have come here before; he opened the hatch without hesitation and walked out. Yi Yi's heart seized up when he saw that Bigtooth had simultaneously opened the hatches on both side of the airlock, but the air inside the chamber didn't howl outward. As Bigtooth walked out of the ship, Yi Yi smelled fresh air from inside his pocket. When he poked his head out, a soft, cool breeze caressed his face. This was ultra-advanced technology beyond the comprehension of either humans or dinosaurs. Its comfortable, casual application astounded Yi Yi, in a way that pierced the soul more deeply than what humanity must have felt in its first encounter with Devourers. He looked up. The sphere floated overhead against the backdrop of the radiant Milky Way.

'What little gift have you brought me this time, Emissary?' asked the god in the language of the Devourers. His voice was not loud, seeming to come from a boundless distance away, from the deep void of outer space. It was the first time Yi Yi had found the crude language of the dinosaurs pleasing to the ear.

Bigtooth extended a claw into his pocket, caught Yi Yi, and set him down on the plane. Yi Yi could feel the elasticity of the plane through the soles of his feet.

'Esteemed god,' Bigtooth said. 'I heard you like to collect small organisms from different star systems, so I brought you this very entertaining little thing: a human from Earth.'

'I only like *perfect* organisms. Why did you bring me such a filthy insect?' said the god. The sphere and the plane flickered twice, perhaps to express disgust.

'You know about this species?' Bigtooth raised his head in astonishment.

'Not intimately, but I've heard about them from certain visitors to this arm of the galaxy. They made frequent visits to Earth in the brief course of these organisms' evolution, and were revolted at the vulgarness of their thoughts, the lowliness of their actions, the disorder and filth of their history. Not a single visitor would deign to establish contact with them up to the destruction of Earth. Hurry and throw it away.'

Bigtooth seized Yi Yi, rotating his massive head to look for a place to throw him. 'The trash incinerator is behind you,' said the god. Bigtooth turned and saw that a small, round opening had appeared in the plane behind him. Inside shimmered a faint blue light . . .

'Don't dismiss us like that! Humanity created a magnificent civilization!' Yi Yi shouted with all his might in the language of the Devourers.

The sphere and plane again flickered twice. The god gave two cold laughs. 'Civilization? Emissary, tell this insect what civilization is.'

Bigtooth lifted Yi Yi to his eye level; Yi Yi could even hear the *gululu* of the dinosaur's giant eyeballs turning in their sockets. 'Bug-bug, in this universe, the standard measure of any race's level of civilization is the number of dimensions it can access. The basic requirement for joining civilization at large is six or more. Our esteemed god's race can already access the eleventh dimension. The Devouring Empire can access the fourth dimension in small-scale laboratory environments, and only qualifies as a primitive, uncivilized tribe in the Milky Way. You, in the eyes of a god, are in the same category as weeds and lichen.'

'Throw it away already, it's disgusting,' the god urged impatiently.

Having finished speaking, Bigtooth headed for the incinerator's aperture. Yi Yi struggled frantically. Numerous pieces of white paper fluttered loose from his clothing. The sphere shot out a needle-thin beam of light, hitting one of the sheets, which froze unmoving in midair. The beam scanned rapidly over its surface.

'Oh my, wait, what's this?'

Bigtooth allowed Yi Yi to dangle over the incinerator's aperture as he turned to look at the sphere.

'That's . . . my students' homework!' Yi Yi managed laboriously, struggling in the dinosaur's giant claw.

'These squarish symbols are very interesting, and the little arrays they form are quite amusing too,' said the god. The sphere's beam of light rapidly scanned over the other sheets of paper, which had since landed on the plane.

'They're Ch-Chinese characters. These are poems in Classical Chinese!'

'Poems?' the god exclaimed, retracting its beam of light. 'I trust you understand the language of these insects, Emissary?'

'Of course, esteemed god. Before the Devouring Empire ate Earth, we spent a long time living on their world.' Bigtooth set Yi Yi down on the plane next to the incinerator, bent over, and picked up a sheet of paper. He held it just in front of his eyes, trying with effort to distinguish the small characters on it. 'More or less, it says—'

'Forget it, you'll distort the meaning!' Yi Yi waved a hand to interrupt Bigtooth.

'How so?' asked the god interestedly.

'Because this is a form of art that can only be expressed in Classical Chinese. Even translating these poems into other human languages alters them until they lose much of their meaning and beauty.'

'Emissary, do you have this language in your computer database? Send me the relevant data, as well as all the information you have on Earth history. Just use the communications channel we established during our last meeting.'

Bigtooth hurried back to the spaceship and banged around on the computer inside for a while, muttering, 'We don't have the Classical Chinese portion here, so we'll have to upload it from the Empire's network. There might be some delay.' Through the open hatchway, Yi Yi saw the morphing colors of the computer screen reflected off the dinosaur's huge eyeballs.

By the time Bigtooth got off the ship, the god could already read the poem on one sheet of paper with perfect modern Chinese pronunciation.

'Bai ri yi shan jin,
Huang he ru hai liu,
Yu qiong qian li mu,
Geng shang yi ceng lou.'

'You're a fast learner!' Yi Yi exclaimed.

The god ignored him, silent.

Bigtooth explained, 'It means, the star has set behind the orbiting planet's mountains. A liquid river called the Yellow River is flowing in the direction of the ocean. Oh, the river and the ocean are both made of the chemical compound consisting of one oxygen atom and two hydrogen atoms. If you want to see further, you must climb further up the edifice.'

The god remained silent.

'Esteemed god, you visited the Devouring Empire not long ago. The scenery there is almost identical to that of the world known to this poem's author bug-bug, with mountains, rivers, and seas, so . . .'

'So I understand the meaning of the poem,' said the god. The sphere suddenly moved so it was right above Bigtooth's head. Yi Yi thought it looked like a giant pupilless eye staring at Bigtooth. 'But, didn't you feel something?'

Bigtooth shook his head, confused.

'That is to say, something hidden behind the outward meaning of that simple, elegant array of square symbols?'

Bigtooth looked even more confused, so the god recited another Classical poem:

'Qian bu jian gu ren,
Hou bu jian lai zhe,
Nian tian di zhi you,
Du cang ran er ti xia.'

Bigtooth hurried eagerly to explain. 'This poem means, looking in front of you, you can't see all the bug-bugs who lived on the planet in the distant past. Looking behind you, you can't see all the bug-bugs who will live on the planet in the future. So you feel how time and space are just too big and end up crying.'

The god brooded.

'Ha, crying is one way for Earth bug-bugs to express their grief. So at that point their visual organs—'

'Do you still feel nothing?' the god interrupted Bigtooth. The sphere descended further, nearly touching Bigtooth's snout.

Bigtooth shook his head firmly this time. 'Esteemed god, I don't think there's anything inside. It's just a simple little poem.'

Next, the god recited several more poems, one after the other. They were all short and simple, yet imbued with a spirit that transcended their topics. They included Li Bai's 'Downriver to Jiangling,' 'Still Night Thoughts,' and 'Bidding Meng Haoran Farewell at Yellow Crane Tower'; Liu Zongyuan's 'River Snow'; Cui Hao's 'Yellow Crane Tower'; Meng Haoran's 'Spring Dawn'; and so forth.

Bigtooth said, 'The Devouring Empire has many historical epic poems with millions of lines. We would happily present them all to you, esteemed god! In comparison, the poems of human bug-bugs are so puny and simple, like their technology—'

The sphere suddenly departed its position above Bigtooth's head, drifting in unthinking arcs in midair. 'Emissary, I know your people's greatest hope is that I'll answer the question 'The Devouring Empire has existed for eight million years, so why is its technology still stalled in the Atomic Age?' Now I know the answer.'

Bigtooth gazed at the sphere passionately. 'Esteemed god, the answer is crucial to us! Please—'

'Esteemed god,' Yi Yi called out, raising a hand. 'I have a question too. May I speak?'

Bigtooth glared resentfully at Yi Yi, as if he wanted to swallow him in one bite. But the god said, 'Though I continue to despise Earth insects, those little arrays have won you the right.'

'Is art common throughout the universe?'

The sphere vibrated faintly in midair, as if nodding. 'Yes – I'm an intergalactic art collector and researcher myself, in fact. In my travels, I've encountered the various arts of numerous civilizations. Most are ponderous, unintelligible setups. But using so few symbols, in so small and clever an array, to encompass such rich sensory layers and subtle meaning, all the while operating under such sadistically exacting formal rules and rhyme schemes? I have to say, I've never seen anything like it. . . . Emissary, you may now throw away this insect.'

Once again, Bigtooth seized Yi Yi with his claw. 'That's right, we ought to throw it away. Esteemed god, we have fairly abundant resources on human civilization stored in the Devouring Empire's central networks. All those resources are now in your memory, while this bug-bug probably doesn't know any more than a couple of the little poems.' He carried Yi Yi toward the incinerator as he spoke.

'Throw away those pieces of paper too,' the god said. Bigtooth hurriedly returned and used his other claw to collect the papers. At this point, Yi Yi hollered from between the massive claws.

'O god, save these papers with the ancient poems of humanity, as a memento! You've discovered an unsurpassable art. You can spread it throughout the universe!'

'Wait.' The god once again stopped Bigtooth. Yi Yi was already hanging above the incinerator aperture, feeling the heat of the blue flames below him. The sphere floated over, coming to a stop a few centimeters from Yi Yi's forehead. Yi Yi, like Bigtooth earlier, felt the force of the enormous pupilless eye's gaze.

'Unsurpassable?'

Bigtooth laughed, holding up Yi Yi. 'Can you believe the pitiable bug-bug, saying these things in front of a magnificent god? Hilarious! What remains to humanity? You've lost everything on Earth. Even the scientific knowledge you've managed to bring with you has been largely forgotten. One time at dinner, I asked the human I was about to eat, what were the atomic bombs used by the humans in the Earth Defense War made of? He told me they were made of atoms!'

'Hahahaha . . .' The god joined Bigtooth in laughter, the sphere vibrating so hard it became an ellipsoid. 'It's certainly the most accurate answer of them all, hahaha . . .'

'Esteemed god, all these dirty bug-bugs have left are a couple of those little poems! Hahaha—'

'But they cannot be surpassed!' Yi Yi said solemnly in the middle of the claw, puffing out his chest.

The sphere stopped vibrating. It said, in an almost intimate whisper, 'Technology can surpass anything.'

'It has nothing to do with technology. They are the quintessence of the human spiritual realm. They cannot be surpassed!'

'Only because you haven't witnessed the power of technology in its ultimate stage, little insect. Little, little insect. You haven't seen.'

The god's tone of voice became as gentle as a father's, but Yi Yi shivered at the icy killing edge hidden deep within. The god said, 'Look at the sun.'

Yi Yi obeyed. They were in the vacuum between the orbits of Earth and Mars. The sun's radiance made him squint.

'What's your favorite color?' asked the god.

'Green.'

The word had barely left his lips before the sun turned green. It was a bewitching shade; the sun resembled a cat's eye floating in the void of space. Under its gaze, the whole universe looked strange and sinister.

Bigtooth's claw trembled, dropping Yi Yi onto the plane. When their reason returned, they realized a fact even more unnerving than the sun turning green: the light should have taken more than ten minutes to travel here from the sun, but the change had occurred instantaneously!

Half a minute later, the sun returned to its previous condition, emitting brilliant white light once more.

'See? This is technology. This is the force that allowed my race to ascend from slugs in ocean mud to gods. Technology itself is the true God, in fact. We all worship it devotedly.'

Yi Yi blinked his dazzled eyes. 'But that god can't surpass this art. We have gods too, in our minds. We worship them, but we don't believe they can write poems like Li Bai and Du Fu.'

The god laughed coldly. 'What an extraordinarily stubborn insect,' it said to Yi Yi. 'It makes you even more loathsome. But, for the sake of killing time, let me surpass your array-art.'

Yi Yi laughed back. 'It's impossible. First of all, you aren't human, so you can't feel with a human's soul. Human art to you is only a flower on a stone slab. Technology can't help you surmount this obstacle.'

'Technology can surmount this obstacle as easily as snapping your fingers. Give me your DNA!'

Yi Yi was confused. 'Give the god one of your hairs!' Bigtooth prompted him. Yi Yi reached up and plucked out a hair; an invisible suction force drew the hair into the sphere. A while later, the hair fell from the sphere, drifting to the plane. The god had only extracted a bit of skin from its root.

The sphere roiled with white light, then gradually became clear. It was now filled with transparent liquid in which strings of bubbles rose. Next, Yi Yi spotted a ball the size of an egg yolk inside the liquid, made pale red by the sunlight shining through, as if it were luminous in and of itself. The ball soon grew. Yi Yi realized that it was a curled-up embryo, its bulging eyes squeezed shut, its oversized head crisscrossed with red blood vessels. The embryo continued to mature. The tiny body finally uncurled and swam frog-like in the sphere of liquid. The liquid gradually became cloudy, so that the sunlight coming through the sphere revealed only a blurry silhouette that continued to rapidly mature until it became that of a swimming grown man. At this point, the sphere reverted to its original opaque, glowing state, and a naked human fell out of it and onto the plane.

Yi Yi's clone stood up unsteadily, the sunlight glistening off his wet form. He was long-haired and long-bearded, but one could tell that he was only in his thirties or forties. Aside from the wiry thinness, he didn't look at all like the original Yi Yi.

The clone stood stiffly, gazing dully into the infinite distance, as if completely oblivious to the universe he'd just joined. Above him, the sphere's white light dimmed, before extinguishing altogether. The sphere itself disappeared as if evaporating. But just then, Yi Yi thought he saw something else light up, and realized that it was the clone's eyes. The dullness had been replaced with the divine gleam of wisdom. In this moment, Yi Yi would learn, the god had transferred all his memories to the clone body.

'Cold . . . so this is cold?' A breeze had blown past. The clone had wrapped his arms around his slick shoulders, shivering, but his voice was full of delighted surprise. 'This is cold! This is pain, immaculate, impeccable pain, the sensation I scoured the stars for, as piercing as the ten-dimensional string through time and space, as crystalline as a diamond of pure energy at the heart of a star, ah . . .' He spread his emaciated arms and beheld the Milky Way. '*Qian bu jian gu ren, hou bu jian lai zhe, nian yu zhou zhi—*' A spate of shivers left the clone's teeth chattering. He hurriedly stopped commemorating his birth and ran over to warm himself over the incinerator.

The clone extended his hands over the blue flames inside the aperture, shivering as he said to Yi Yi, 'Really, this is something I do all the time. When researching and collecting a civilization's art,

I always lodge my consciousness inside a member organism of that civilization, to ensure my complete understanding of the art.'

The flames inside the incinerator's aperture suddenly flared. The plane surrounding it roiled with multicolored light as well, so that Yi Yi felt as if the entire plane were a sheet of frosted glass floating on a sea of fire.

'The incinerator has turned into a fabricator,' Bigtooth whispered to Yi Yi. 'The god is performing energy-matter exchange.' Seeing Yi Yi's continued puzzlement, he explained again, 'Idiot, he's making objects out of pure energy, the handicraft of a god!'

Suddenly, a white mass burst from the fabricator, unfurling in midair as it fell – clothing, which the clone caught and put on. Yi Yi saw that it was a loose, flowing Tang Dynasty robe, made of snow-white silk and trimmed with a wide band of black. The clone, who had appeared so pitiable earlier, looked like an ethereal sage with it on. Yi Yi couldn't imagine how it had been made from the blue flames.

The fabricator completed another object. Something black flew from the aperture and thudded onto the plane like a rock. Yi Yi ran over and picked it up. He might not trust his eyes, but his hand clearly registered a heavy inkstone, icy cold at that. Something else smacked onto the plane; Yi Yi picked up a black rod. No doubt about it – it was an inkstick! Next came several brush pens, a brush holder, a sheet of snow-white mulberry paper (paper, out of the flames!), and several little decorative antiques. The last object out was also the largest: an old-fashioned writing desk! Yi Yi and Bigtooth hurriedly righted the desk and arranged the other objects on top of it.

'The amount of energy he converted into these objects could have pulverized a planet,' Bigtooth whispered to Yi Yi, his voice shaking slightly.

The clone walked over to the desk, nodding in satisfaction when he saw the arrangement on it. One hand stroked his newly dry beard. He said, 'I, Li Bai.'

Yi Yi examined the clone. 'Do you mean you want to become Li Bai, or do you really think you're Li Bai?'

'I'm Li Bai, pure and simple. A Li Bai to surpass Li Bai!'

Yi Yi laughed and shook his head.

'What, do you question me even now?'

Yi Yi nodded. 'I concede that your technology far exceeds my understanding. It's indistinguishable from human ideas of magic and acts of God. Even in the fields of art and poetry, you've astonished me. Despite such an enormous cultural, spatial, and temporal gap, you've managed to sense the hidden nuances of Classical Chinese poetry. . . . But understanding Li Bai is one matter, and exceeding him is another. I continue to believe that you face an unsurpassable body of art.'

A mysterious amusement appeared on the clone's – Li Bai's – face, only to quickly vanish. He pointed at the desk. 'Grind ink!' he bellowed to Yi Yi, before striding away. He was nearly at the edge of the plane before he stopped, stroking his whiskers, gazing toward the distant Milky Way, descending into thought.

Yi Yi took the Yixing clay pot on the desk and poured a trickle of clear water into the depression in the inkstone. Then he began to grind the inkstick against the stone. It was the first time he'd done this; he clumsily angled the stick to scrape at its corners. As he watched the liquid thicken and darken, Yi Yi thought of himself, 1.5 astronomical units away from the sun, perched on this infinitely thin plane in the vastness of outer space. (Even while it was making things out of pure energy, a distant viewer would have perceived zero thickness.) It was a stage floating in the void of the universe, on which a dinosaur, a human raised as dinosaur livestock, and a technological god in period dress planning to surpass Li Bai were performing bizarre live theater. With that thought, Yi Yi shook his head and laughed wanly.

Once he thought the ink was ready, Yi Yi stood and waited next to Bigtooth. The breeze on the plane had ceased by this time; the sun and Milky Way shone calmly, as if the whole universe were waiting in anticipation.

Li Bai stood steadily at the edge of the plane. The layer of air above the plane created almost no scattering effect, so that the sunlight cast him in crispest light and shadow. Aside from the movements of his hand when he smoothed his beard now and then, he was practically a statue hewn from stone.

Yi Yi and Bigtooth waited and waited. Time flowed past silently. The brush on the desk, plump with ink, began to dry. The position of the sun changed unnoticed in the sky; they, the desk, and the spaceship cast long shadows, while the white paper that was spread out on the desk appeared as if it had become part of the plane.

Finally, Li Bai turned and slowly stepped over to the desk. Yi Yi hurriedly re-dipped the brush in ink and offered it with both hands, but Li Bai held up a hand in refusal. He only stared at the blank paper on the desk in continued deep thought, something new in his gaze.

Yi Yi, with glee, saw that it was perplexity and unease.

'I need to make some more things. They're all . . . fragile goods. Be sure to catch them.' Li Bai pointed at the fabricator; the flames within, which had dimmed, grew bright once more. Just as Yi Yi and Bigtooth ran over, a tongue of blue flame pushed out a round object. Bigtooth caught it agilely. Upon closer inspection, it was a large earthen jar. Next, three large bowls sprang out of the blue flames. Yi Yi caught two of them, but the third fell and shattered. Bigtooth carried the jar to the desk and carefully unsealed it. The powerful fragrance of wine emerged. Bigtooth and Yi Yi exchanged astonished looks.

'There wasn't much documentation on human winemaking in the Earth-related data I received from the Devouring Empire, so I'm not sure I fabricated this correctly,' said Li Bai, pointing to the jar of wine to indicate that Yi Yi should taste it.

Yi Yi took a bowl, scooped a little from the jar, and took a sip. Fiery heat ran past his throat down into his belly. He nodded. 'It's wine, albeit much too strong compared to the kind we drink to improve our meat quality.'

Li Bai pointed to the other bowl on the desk. 'Fill it up.' He waited for Bigtooth to pour a bowlful of the strong wine, then picked it up and glugged the whole thing down. Then he turned and once again walked off into the distance, weaving a stagger here and there along the way. Once he reached the edge of the plane, he stood there and resumed his pondering in the direction of the stars, only this time his body swayed rhythmically left and right, as if to some unheard melody. Li Bai didn't ponder for long before returning to the desk once more, and on the walk back he staggered every step. He grabbed the brush being proffered by Yi Yi and threw it into the distance.

'Fill it up,' Li Bai said, eyes fixed on the empty bowl . . .

An hour later, Bigtooth's two immense claws carefully lowered a passed-out Li Bai onto the cleared desk, only for him to roll over and fall right off, muttering something in a language incomprehensible to dinosaur and human alike. He'd already vomited a particolored pile (although no one knew when he'd had the occasion to eat in the first place), some of it staining his flowing robes. With the white light of the plane passing through, the vomit formed some sort of abstract image. Li Bai's mouth was black with ink: after finishing his fourth bowl, he'd tried to write something on the paper, but had ended up merely stabbing his ink-plump brush heavily upon the table. After that, he'd tried to smooth the brush with his mouth, like a child at his first calligraphy lesson . . .

'Esteemed god?' Bigtooth bent down and asked carefully.

'Wayakaaaaa . . . kaaaayiaiwa,' said Li Bai, tongue lolling.

Bigtooth straightened, shook his head, and sighed. He said to Yi Yi, 'Let's go.'

The Second Path

Yi Yi's feedlot was located on the Devourers' equator. While the planet had lain within the inner reaches of the solar system, this had been a beautiful prairie between two rivers. When the Devourers left the orbit of Jupiter, a harsh winter had descended, the prairie disappearing and the rivers freezing. The humans raised there had all been relocated to an underground city. After the Devourers received the summons from the god and returned, spring had come back to the land with the approach of the sun. The two rivers quickly defrosted, and the prairie began to turn green as well.

In times of good weather, Yi Yi lived alone in the crude grass hut he'd built himself by the riverside, tilling the land and amusing himself. A normal human wouldn't have been allowed, but as Yi Yi's feedlot lectures on ancient literature had edifying properties, imparting a unique flavor to the flesh of his students, the dinosaur breeder didn't stop him.

It was dusk, two months after Yi Yi had first met Li Bai, the sun just tipping over the perfectly straight horizon line of the Devouring Empire. The two rivers reflected the sunset, meeting at the edge of the sky. In the riverside hut, a breeze carried faint, distant sounds of song and celebration over the prairie. Yi Yi was alone, playing weiqi with himself.

He looked up and saw Li Bai and Bigtooth walking along the riverbank toward him. Li Bai was much changed from before: his hair was unkempt, his beard even longer, his face sun-browned. He had a rough cloth pack slung over his left shoulder and a large bottle-gourd in his right hand. His robes had been reduced to rags; his woven-straw shoes were mangled with wear. But Yi Yi thought that he now seemed more like a human being.

Li Bai walked over to the weiqi table. Like the last few times, he slammed the gourd down without looking at Yi Yi and said, 'Bowl!' When Yi Yi had brought over the two wooden bowls, Li Bai uncorked the gourd and filled them with wine, then took a paper package from his pack. Yi Yi opened it to discover cooked meat, already sliced, its aroma greeting his nose enthusiastically. He couldn't help but grab a piece and start chewing.

Bigtooth only stood, a few meters away, watching them silently. He knew from before that the two of them were going to discuss poetry again, a topic in which he had no interest and no ability.

'Delicious,' Yi Yi said, nodding approvingly. 'Is the beef made directly from energy too?'

'No, I've gone natural for a long while now. You might not know, but there's a pasture a long distance away from here where they raise Earth cows. I cooked the beef myself in the Shanxi Pingyao style. There's a trick to it. When you stew the meat, you have to add . . .' Li Bai whispered mysteriously into Yi Yi's ear, 'Urea.'

Yi Yi looked at him uncomprehendingly.

'Oh, that's what you get when you take human urine, let it evaporate, and extract the white stuff. It makes the cooked meat red and juicy with a tender texture, while keeping the fatty parts from being cloying and the lean parts from being leathery.'

'The urea . . . it's made from pure energy, right?' Yi Yi asked, horrified.

'I told you, I've gone natural! It took me a lot of work to collect the urea from several human feedlots. This is a very traditional folk cuisine technique, faded from use long before the destruction of Earth.'

Yi Yi had already swallowed his bite of beef. He picked up the wine bowl to prevent himself from vomiting.

Li Bai pointed at the gourd. 'Under my direction, the Devouring

Empire has built a number of distilleries, already capable of producing many of the wines famous on Earth. This is bona-fide zhuyeqing, made by steeping bamboo leaves in sorghum liquor.'

Yi Yi only now discovered that the wine in his bowl was different from what Li Bai had brought previously. It was emerald green, with a sweet aftertaste of herbs.

'Looks like you've really mastered human culture,' Yi Yi said feelingly to Li Bai.

'That's not all. I've also spent a lot of time on personal enrichment. As you know, the scenery of many parts of the Devouring Empire is near identical to what Li Bai saw on Earth. In these two months, I've wandered the mountains and waters, feasting my eyes on picturesque landscapes, drinking wine under moonlight, declaiming poetry on mountain summits, even having a few romantic encounters in the human feedlots everywhere . . .'

'Then, you should be ready to show me your works of poetry.'

Li Bai exhaled and set down his wine bowl. He stood and paced uneasily. 'I've composed some poems, yes, and I'm certain you'd be astonished at them. You'd find that I'm already a remarkable poet, even more remarkable than you and your great-grandfather. But I don't want you to see the poems, because I'm equally certain you'd think they fail to surpass Li Bai's. And I . . .' He looked up and far away, at the residual radiance of the setting sun, his gaze dazed and pained. 'I think so too.'

On the distant prairie, the dances had ended. People were happily turning to their abundant dinner. A group of girls ran to the riverbank to splash in the shallows near shore. Circlets of flowers adorned their heads, and light gauze like mist draped over their bodies, forming an intoxicating scene in the lighting of dusk. Yi Yi pointed at one girl near the hut. 'Is she beautiful?'

'Of course,' Li Bai said, looking uncomprehendingly at Yi Yi.

'Imagine cutting her open with a sharp knife, removing her every organ, plucking out her eyes, scooping out her brain, picking out all her bones, slicing apart her muscles and fat according to position and function, gathering her blood vessels and nerves into two bundles. Finally, imagine laying out a big white cloth and arranging all those pieces, classified according to anatomical principles. Would you still think her beautiful?'

'How do you think of such a thing while drinking? Disgusting,' Li Bai said, wrinkling his brow.

'How is it disgusting? Is this not the technology you worship?'

'What are you trying to say?'

'Li Bai saw nature like you see the girls down by the riverside. But in technology's eyes, nature is its components, perfectly arrayed and dripping blood on a white cloth. Therefore, technology is antithetical to poetry.'

'Then you have a suggestion for me?' Li Bai said thoughtfully, stroking his beard.

'I still don't think you stand a chance at surpassing Li Bai, but I can point your energies in the correct direction. Technology has clouded your eyes, blinding you to the beauty of nature. Therefore, you must first forget all your ultra-advanced technological knowledge. If you can transplant all your memories into your current brain, you can certainly delete some of them.'

Li Bai exchanged looks with Bigtooth. Both burst into laughter. 'Esteemed god, I told you from the start, these are tricky bug-bugs,' said Bigtooth. 'A moment of carelessness and you'll fall into one of their traps.'

'Hahahaha, tricky indeed, but entertaining as well,' Li Bai said to Bigtooth, before turning toward Yi Yi with cold amusement. 'Did you really think I came here to admit defeat?'

'You could not surpass the pinnacle of human poetry. That's a fact.'

Abruptly, Li Bai raised a finger and pointed to the river. 'How many ways are there to walk to the riverbank?'

Yi Yi looked uncomprehendingly at Li Bai for a few seconds. 'It seems . . . there's only one.'

'No, there's two. I can also walk in this direction,' Li Bai indicated the direction opposite from the river, 'and keep going, all the way around the Devouring Empire, crossing the river from the other side to reach this bank. I can even make a full circuit around the Milky Way and return here. With our technology, it's just as easy. Technology can surpass anything! I am now forced to take the second path!'

Yi Yi pondered this for a long time before shaking his head in bewilderment. 'Even if you have the technology of a god, I can't think of a second path to surpassing Li Bai.'

Li Bai stood. 'It's simple. There are two ways to surpass Li Bai. The first is to write poems that surpass his. The other is to write every poem!'

Yi Yi looked even more confused, but Bigtooth beside him seemed to have had an epiphany.

'I will write every five-character-line and seven-character-line poem possible. They were Li Bai's specialty. In addition, I'm going to write down every possible lyrical poem for the common line formats! How do you not understand? I'm going to try every possible permutation of Chinese characters that fits the format rules!'

'Ah, magnificent! What a magnificent undertaking!' Bigtooth crowed, forgetting all dignity.

'Is this hard?' Yi Yi asked ignorantly.

'Of course, incredibly so! The largest computer in the Devouring Empire might not be able to finish the calculations before the death of the universe!'

'Surely not,' Yi Yi said, skeptical.

'Of course yes!' Li Bai nodded with satisfaction. 'But by using quantum computing, which you're still a long way from mastering, we can complete the calculations in an acceptable length of time. Then I'll have written every single poem, including everything that's been written in the past, and, much more importantly, everything that may be written someday in the future! This will naturally include poems that surpass Li Bai's best works. In fact, I've ended the art of poetry. Every poet from now on to the destruction of the universe, no matter how great, will be no more than a plagiarist. Their works will turn up in a search of my enormous storage device.'

Bigtooth suddenly gave a guttural cry, his gaze on Li Bai changing from excitement to shock. 'An enormous . . . storage device? Esteemed god, do you mean to say, you're going to . . . *save* all the poems the quantum computer writes?'

'What's the fun in deleting everything right after I write it? Of course I'm going to save them! It will be a monument to the artistic contributions my race has made to this universe!'

Bigtooth's expression changed from shock to horror. He extended his bulky claws and bent his legs, as if trying to kneel to Li Bai. 'You mustn't, esteemed god,' he cried. 'You mustn't!'

'What's got you so scared?' Yi Yi regarded Bigtooth with astonishment.

'You idiot! Don't you know that atomic bombs are made of atoms? The storage device will be made of atoms too, and its storage precision can't possibly exceed the atomic level! Do you know what atomic-level storage is? It means that all of humanity's books can be stored in an area the size of the point of a needle! Not the couple of books you have left, but all the books that existed before we ate Earth!'

'Ah, that sounds plausible. I've heard that a glass of water contains more atoms than the Earth's oceans contained cups of water. Then, he can just write down those poems and take the needle with him,' Yi Yi said, pointing at Li Bai.

Bigtooth nearly burst with outrage. He had to rapidly pace a few steps to summon a little more patience. 'Okay, okay, tell me, if the god writes all those five-character- and seven-character-line poems, and the common lyrical poetry formats, one time each, how many characters would that be?'

'Not many, no more than two or three thousand, right? Classical poetry is the most concise art form there is.'

'Fine, you idiot bug-bug, let me show you how concise it really is!' Bigtooth strode to the table and pointed at the game board with one claw. 'What is it you call this stupid game . . . ah yes, weiqi. How many grid intersections are on the board?'

'There are nineteen lines in both the vertical and horizontal directions, for a total of three hundred and sixty-one points.'

'Very good, each intersection can be occupied by a black piece, a white piece, or no piece, a total of three states in all. So you can think of each game state as using three characters to write a poem of nineteen lines and three hundred and sixty-one characters.'

'That's a clever comparison.'

'Now, if we exhaust all the possible permutations of these three characters in this poem format, how many poems can we write? Let me tell you: 3^{361}, or, let me think, 10^{172}!'

'Is . . . is that a lot?'

'Idiot!' Bigtooth spat the word at him for the third time. 'In all the universe, there are only . . . gargh!' He was too infuriated to speak.

'How many?' Yi Yi still wore a befuddled expression.

'10^{80} atoms! You idiot bug-bug—'

Only now did Yi Yi show any sign of astonishment. 'You mean to say, if we could save one poem in every atom, we might use up every atom in the universe and still not be able to fit all of his quantum computer's poems?'

'Far from it! Off by a factor of 10^{92}! Besides, how can one atom store a whole poem? The memory devices of human bug-bugs would have needed more atoms to store one poem than your population. As for us, *ai,* technology to store one bit per atom is still in the laboratory stage . . .'

'Here you display your shortsightedness and lack of imagination, Emissary, one of the reasons behind the laggardly advancement of Devouring Empire technology,' Li Bai said, laughing. 'Using quantum storage devices based on the quantum superposition principle, the poems can be stored in very little matter. Of course, quantum storage is none too stable. To preserve the poems forever, it needs to be used in tandem with more traditional storage techniques. Nonetheless, the amount of matter required is minuscule.'

'How much?' Bigtooth asked, looking as if his heart were in his throat.

'Approximately 10^{57} atoms, a pittance really.'

'That's . . . that's exactly the amount of matter in the solar system!'

'Correct, including all the planets orbiting the sun, and of course including the Devouring Empire.'

Li Bai said this last sentence easily and naturally, but it struck Yi Yi like a bolt out of the blue. Bigtooth, on the other hand, seemed to have calmed down. After the long torment of sensing disaster on the horizon, the actual onslaught only left a sense of relief.

'Can't you convert pure energy into matter?' asked Bigtooth.

'You should know how much energy it would take to create such an enormous amount of matter. The prospect is unimaginable even to us. We'll go with ready-made.'

'His Majesty's concerns weren't unjustified,' Bigtooth murmured to himself.

'Yes, yes,' Li Bai said happily. 'I informed the Emperor of the Devourers the day before yesterday. This great ring-world empire shall be used for an even greater goal. The dinosaurs should feel honored.'

'Esteemed god, you'll see how the Devouring Empire feels,' Bigtooth said darkly. 'I also have one more concern. Compared to the sun, the amount of matter in the Devouring Empire is insignificantly minuscule. Is it really necessary to destroy a civilization millions of years of evolution in the making, just to obtain a few scraps?'

'I fully understand your reservations. But you must know, extinguishing, cooling, and disassembling the sun will take a long time. The quantum calculations should begin before then, and we need to save the resulting poems elsewhere so that the computer can clear its internal storage and continue work. Therefore the planets and the Devouring Empire, which can immediately provide matter for manufacturing storage devices, are crucial.'

'I understand, esteemed god. I have one last question: Is it necessary to store all the results? Why can't you add an analytical program at the end, to delete all the poems that don't warrant saving? From what I know, Classical Chinese poetry has to follow a strict structure. If we delete all the poems that violate the formal rules, we'll greatly decrease the volume of the results.'

'Formal rules? Ha.' Li Bai shook his head contemptuously. 'Shackles upon inspiration, and nothing more. Classical Chinese poetry wasn't bound by these rules before the Northern and Southern Dynasties. Even after the Tang Dynasty, which popularized the strict jintishi form, many master poets ignored the rules to write some extraordinary biantishi works. That's why, for this ultimate poetry composition, I won't take formal rules into consideration.'

'But, you should still consider the poem's content, right? Ninety-nine percent of the results are obviously going to be rubbish. What's the point of storing a bunch of randomly generated character arrays?'

'Rubbish?' Li Bai shrugged. 'Emissary, you are not the one who decides whether a poem is meaningful. Neither am I, nor any other person. Time decides. Many poems once considered worthless at the time of their writing were later lauded as masterpieces. Many of the masterpieces of today and tomorrow would have been considered worthless in the distant past. I'm going to write all the poems there are. Trillions of years from now, who knows which of them mighty Time will choose as the finest?'

'That's absurd!' Bigtooth bellowed, startling several birds hidden in the distant grass into flight. 'If we go by the human bug-bugs' preexisting Chinese character database, the first poem your quantum computer writes should be:

'a a a a a
a a a a a
a a a a a
a a a a ai

'Might I ask, would mighty Time choose *this* as a masterpiece?!'

Yi Yi broke his silence to cheer. 'Wow! Who needs mighty Time to choose? It's a masterpiece right now! The first three lines and the first four characters of the fourth are the exclamations – *ah!* – of living beings witnessing the majestic grandeur of the universe. The last character is the clincher, where the poet, having witnessed the vastness of the universe, expresses the insignificance of life in the infinity of time and space with a single sigh of inevitability.'

'Hahahaha . . .' Li Bai stroked his whiskers, unable to stop smiling. 'A fine poem, my bug-bug Yi Yi, a fine poem indeed, hahaha . . .' He took up the gourd and poured Yi Yi wine.

Bigtooth raised his massive claws and flung Yi Yi into the distance with one swat. 'Nasty bug-bug, I know you're happy now. But don't forget, once the Devouring Empire is destroyed, your kind won't survive either!'

Yi Yi rolled all the way to the riverbank. It took a long time before he could crawl back up. A grin cracked across his dirt-covered face; he was laughing despite his pain, truly happy. 'This is great! This universe is motherfucking incredible!' he yelled with no thought to dignity.

'Any other questions, Emissary?' asked Li Bai. Bigtooth shook his head. 'Then I'll leave tomorrow. The day after the next, the quantum computer will execute its poetry-writing software, commencing the ultimate poetry composition. At the same time, the work to extinguish the sun and dismantle the planets and the Devouring Empire shall commence.'

Bigtooth straightened. 'Esteemed god, the Devouring Empire will complete preparations for battle tonight!' he said solemnly.

'Good, very good, the coming days will be interesting. But before all else, let us finish this gourd.' Li Bai nodded happily as he took up the gourd and poured the remaining wine. He looked at the river, now shrouded in night, and continued to savor those words: 'A fine poem indeed, the first, haha, the first and already so fine.'

The Ultimate Poetry Composition

The poetry-composition software was in fact very simple. Represented in humanity's C language, it would be no more than two thousand lines of code, with an additional database of modest size appended storing the Chinese characters. Once the software was uploaded onto the quantum computer in the orbit of Neptune, an enormous transparent cone floating in the vacuum, the ultimate poetry composition began.

Only now did the Devouring Empire learn that the god version of Li Bai was merely one individual member of his ultra-advanced civilization. The dinosaurs had previously assumed that any society that had advanced to this level of technology would have melded their consciousness into one being long ago; all five of the ultra-advanced civilizations they'd met in the past ten million years had done so. That Li Bai's race had preserved their individual existences also somewhat explained their extraordinary ability to grasp art. When the poetry composition began, more individuals from Li Bai's race jumped into the solar system from various places in distant space and began construction on the storage device.

The humans living in the Devouring Empire couldn't see the quantum computer in space, or the new arrivals from the race of gods. To them, the process of the ultimate poetry composition was simply the increase and decrease of the number of suns in space.

One week after the poetry software began execution, the gods successfully extinguished the sun, reducing the sun count to zero. But the cessation of nuclear fission inside the sun caused the star's outer layer to lose support, and it quickly collapsed into a new star that illuminated the darkness once more. However, this sun's luminosity was a hundred times greater than before; smoke rose from the grass and trees on the surface of the Devouring Empire. The new star was once again extinguished, but a while later it burst alight again. So it went on, lighting only to be extinguished, extinguishing only to light once more, as if the sun were a cat with nine lives, struggling stubbornly. But the gods were highly practiced at killing stars. They patiently extinguished the new star again and again, until its matter had, as much as possible, fused into the heavier elements needed in the construction of the storage device. Only after the eleventh star dimmed was the sun snuffed out for good.

At this point, the ultimate poetry composition had run for three Earth months. Long before then, during the appearance of the third new star, other suns had appeared in space. These suns rose and fell in succession throughout space, brightening and dimming. At one point, there were nine new suns in the sky. They were releases of energy as the gods dismantled the planets. With the star-sized sun diminishing in brightness later on, people could no longer tell the suns apart.

The dismantlement of the Devouring Empire commenced the fifth week after the start of the poetry composition. Before it, Li Bai had made a suggestion to the Empire: The gods could jump all the dinosaurs to a world on the other side of the Milky Way. The civilization there was much less advanced than the gods', its members being unable to convert themselves into pure energy, but still much more advanced than the Devourers' civilization. There, the dinosaurs would be raised as a form of livestock and live happy lives with all their needs taken care of. But the dinosaurs would rather break than bend, and angrily refused this suggestion.

Next, Li Bai made another request: that humanity be allowed to return to their mother planet. To be sure, Earth had been dismantled, and most of it went toward the storage device. But the gods saved a small amount of matter to construct a hollow Earth, about the same size as the original, but with only a hundredth of its mass. To say that the hollow Earth was Earth hollowed-out would be incorrect, because the layer of brittle rock that originally covered the Earth could hardly be used to make the spherical shell. The shell material was perhaps taken from the Earth's core. In addition, razor-thin but extremely strong reinforcing hoops crisscrossed the shell, like lines of latitude and longitude, made from the neutronium produced in the collapse of the sun.

Movingly, the Devouring Empire not only immediately agreed to Li Bai's request, allowing all humans to leave the great ring world, but also returned the seawater and air they'd taken from Earth in their entirety. The gods used them to restore all of Earth's original continents, oceans, and atmosphere inside the hollow Earth.

Next, the terrible battle to defend the great ring began. The Devouring Empire launched barrages of nuclear missiles and gamma rays at the gods in space, but these were useless against their foe. The gods launched a powerful, invisible force that pushed at the Devourers' ring, spinning it faster and faster, until it finally fell apart under the centrifugal forces of such rapid rotation. At this time, Yi Yi was en route to the hollow Earth. From twelve million kilometers away, he witnessed the complete course of the Devouring Empire's destruction:

> The ring came apart very slowly, dreamlike. Against the pitch-black backdrop of space, this immense world dispersed like a piece of milk foam on coffee, the fragments at its edges slowly sinking into darkness, as if being dissolved by space. Only by the flashes of sporadic explosions would they reappear.
>
> Excerpt from Devourer

The great, fierce civilization from ancient Earth was thus destroyed, to Yi Yi's deepest lament. Only a few dinosaurs survived, returning to Earth with humanity, including the emissary Bigtooth.

On the return journey to Earth, the humans were largely in low spirits, but for different reasons than Yi Yi: Once they were back on Earth, they'd have to farm and plow if they wanted to eat. To humans accustomed to having every need provided for in their long captivity, grown indolent and ignorant of labor, it really did seem like a nightmare.

But Yi Yi believed in Earth's future. No matter how many challenges lay ahead, humans were going to become people once more.

The Cloud of Poems

The poetry voyage arrived on the shores of Antarctica.

The gravity here was already weak; the waves cycled slowly in a dreamlike dance. Under the low gravity, the impact of waves upon shore sent spray dozens of meters into the air, where the seawater contracted under surface tension into countless spheres, some as large as soccer balls, some as small as raindrops, which fell so slowly that one could draw rings around them with one's hand. They refracted the rays of the little sun, so that when Yi Yi, Li Bai, and Bigtooth disembarked, they were surrounded by crystalline brilliance.

Due to the forces of rotation, the Earth was slightly stretched at the North and South Poles, causing the hollow Earth's pole regions to maintain their old chilly state. Low-gravity snow was a wonder, loose and foamy, waist-high in the shallow parts and deep enough at others that even Bigtooth disappeared beneath it. But having disappeared, they could still breathe normally inside the snow! The entire Antarctic continent was buried underneath this snow-foam, creating an undulating landscape of white.

Yi Yi and company rode a snowmobile toward the South Pole. The snowmobile skimmed across the snow-foam like a speedboat, throwing waves of white to either side.

The next day, they arrived at the South Pole, marked by a towering pyramid of crystal, a memorial dedicated to the Earth Defense War of two centuries ago. Neither writing nor images marked its surface. There was just the crystal form in the snow-foam at the apex of the Earth, silently refracting the sunlight.

From here, one could gaze upon the entire world. Continents and oceans surrounded the radiant little sun, so that it looked as if it had floated up from the waters of the Arctic Sea.

'Will that little sun really be able to shine forever?' Yi Yi asked Li Bai.

'At the very least, it will last until the new Earth civilization is advanced enough to create a new sun. It is a miniature white hole.'

'White hole? Is that the inverse of a black hole?' asked Bigtooth.

'Yes, it's connected through a wormhole to a black hole orbiting a star, two million light-years away. The black hole sucks in the star's light, which is released here. Think of the sun as one end of a fiber-optic cable running through hyperspace.'

The apex of the monument was the southern starting point of the Lagrangian axis, the thirteen-thousand-kilometer line of zero gravity between the North and South Poles of the hollow Earth, named after the zero-gravity Lagrangian point that had existed between the Earth and moon before the war. In the future, people were certain to launch various satellites onto the Lagrangian axis. Compared to the process on Earth before the war, this would be easy: one would only have to ship the satellite to the North or South Pole, by donkey if one wanted to, and give it a good kick up with one's foot.

As the party viewed the memorial, another, larger snowmobile ferried over a crowd of young human tourists. After disembarking, the tourists bent their legs and jumped straight into the air, flying high along the Lagrangian axis, turning themselves into satellites. From here, one could see many small, black specks in the air, marking out the position of the axis: tourists and vehicles drifting in zero gravity. They would have been able to fly directly to the North Pole if it weren't for the sun, placed at the midpoint of the Lagrangian axis. In the past, some tourists flying along the axis had discovered their handheld miniature air-jet thrusters broken, been unable to decelerate, and flown straight into the sun. Well, in truth, they vaporized a considerable distance from it.

In the hollow Earth, entering space was also easy. One only needed to jump into one of the five deep wells on the equator (called Earthgates) and fall (fly?) a hundred kilometers through the shell, then be flung by the centrifugal forces of the hollow Earth's rotation into space.

Yi Yi and company also needed to pass through the shell to see the Cloud of Poems, but they were heading through the Antarctic Earthgate. Here, there were no centrifugal forces, so instead of being flung into space, they would only reach the outer surface of the hollow Earth. Once they'd put on lightweight space suits at the Antarctic control station, they entered the one-hundred-kilometer well – although, without gravity, it was better termed a tunnel. Being weightless here, they used the thrusters on their space suits to move forward. This was much slower than the free fall on the equator; it took them half an hour to arrive on the outside.

The outer surface of the hollow Earth was completely barren. There were only the crisscrossing reinforcing hoops of neutronium, which divided the outside by latitude and longitude into a grid. The South Pole was indeed where all the longitudinal hoops met. When Yi Yi and company walked out of the Earthgate, they saw that they were located on a modestly sized plateau. The hoops that reinforced Earth resembled many long mountain ranges, radiating in every direction from the plateau.

Looking up, they saw the Cloud of Poems.

In place of the solar system was the Cloud of Poems, a spiral galaxy a hundred astronomical units across, shaped much like the Milky Way. The hollow Earth was situated at the edge of the Cloud, much as the sun had been in the actual Milky Way. The difference was that Earth's position was not coplanar with the Cloud of Poems, which allowed one to see one face of the Cloud head-on, instead of only edge-on as with the Milky Way. But Earth wasn't nearly far enough from the plane to allow people here to observe the full form of the Cloud of Poems. Instead, the Cloud blanketed the entire sky of the southern hemisphere.

The Cloud of Poems emitted a silvery radiance bright enough to cast shadows on the ground. It wasn't that the Cloud itself was made to glow, apparently, but rather that cosmic rays would excite it into silver luminescence. Due to the uneven spatial distribution of the cosmic rays, glowing masses frequently rippled through the Cloud of Poems, their varicolored light rolling across the sky like luminescent whales diving through the Cloud. Rarely, with spikes in the cosmic radiation, the Cloud of Poems emitted dapples of light that made the Cloud look utterly unlike a cloud. Instead, the entire sky seemed to be the surface of a moonlit sea seen from below.

Earth and the Cloud did not move in sync, so sometimes Earth lay in the gaps between the spiral arms. Through the gap, one could see the night sky and the stars, and most thrillingly, a cross-sectional view of the Cloud of Poems. Immense structures resembling Earthly cumulonimbuses rose from the spiraling plane, shimmering with silvery light, morphing through magnificent forms that inspired the human imagination, as if they belonged to the dreamscape of some super-advanced consciousness.

Yi Yi tore his gaze from the Cloud of Poems and picked up a crystal chip off the ground. These chips were scattered around them, sparkling like shards of ice in winter. Yi Yi raised the chip against a sky thick with the Cloud of Poems. The chip was very thin, and half the size of his palm. It appeared transparent from the front, but if he tilted it slightly, he could see the bright light of the Cloud of Poems reflect off its surface in rainbow halos. This was a quantum memory chip. All the written information created in human history would take up less than a millionth of a percent of one chip. The Cloud of Poems was composed of 10^{40} of these storage devices, and contained all the results of the ultimate poem composition. It was manufactured using all the matter in the sun and its nine major planets, of course including the Devouring Empire.

'What a magnificent work of art!' Bigtooth sighed sincerely.

'Yes, it's beautiful in its significance: a nebula fifteen billion kilometers across, encompassing every poem possible. It's too spectacular!' Yi Yi said, gazing at the nebula. 'Even I'm starting to worship technology.'

Li Bai gave a long sigh. He had been in a low mood all this time. '*Ai,* it seems like we've both come around to the other person's viewpoint. I witnessed the limits of technology in art. I—' He began to sob. 'I've failed . . .'

'How can you say that?' Yi Yi pointed at the Cloud of Poems overhead. 'This holds all the possible poems, so of course it holds the poems that surpass Li Bai's!'

'But I can't get to them!' Li Bai stomped his foot, which shot him meters into the air. He curled into a ball in midair, miserably burying his face between his knees in a fetal position; he slowly descended under the weak gravitational pull of the Earth's shell. 'At the start of the poetry composition, I immediately set out to program software that could analyze poetry. At that point, technology once again met that unsurpassable obstacle in the pursuit of art. Even now, I'm still unable to write software that can judge and appreciate poetry.' He pointed up at the Cloud of Poems. 'Yes, with the help of mighty technology, I've written the ultimate works of poetry. But I can't find them amid the Cloud of Poems, *ai* . . .'

'Is the soul and essence of intelligent life truly untouchable by technology?' Bigtooth loudly asked the Cloud of Poems above. He'd become increasingly philosophical after all he'd endured.

'Since the Cloud of Poems encompasses all possible poems, then naturally some portion of those poems describes all of our pasts and all of our futures, possible and impossible. The bug-bug Yi Yi would certainly find a poem that describes how he felt one night thirty years ago while clipping his fingernails, or a menu from a lunch twelve years in his future. Emissary Bigtooth, too, might find a poem that describes the color of a particular scale on his leg five years from now . . .'

Li Bai had touched down once more on the ground; as he spoke, he took out two chips, shimmering under the light of the Cloud of Poems. 'These are my parting gifts for you two. The quantum computer used your names as keywords to search through the Cloud of Poems, and found several quadrillion poems that describe your various possible future lives. Of course, these are only a tiny portion of the poems with you as subject in the Cloud of Poems. I've only read a couple dozen of these. My favorite is a seven-character-line poem about Yi Yi describing a romantic riverbank scene between him and a beautiful woman from a faraway village . . .

'After I leave, I hope humanity and the remaining dinosaurs can get along with each other, and that humanity can get along with itself even better. If someone nukes a hole into the shell of the hollow Earth, it's going to be a real problem. . . . The good poems in the Cloud of Poems don't belong to anyone yet. Hopefully humans will be able to write some of them.'

'What happened to me and the woman, afterward?' Yi Yi asked.

Under the silver light of the Cloud of Poems, Li Bai chuckled. 'Together, you lived happily ever after.'

CANNONBALL

PROLOGUE

Since mankind had depleted the Earth's natural resources, the world turned its gaze towards the last pristine continent: Antarctica. This shifted the Earth's political center of gravity and led to the Antarctic Treaty being discarded. Due to their proximity to Antarctica, two South American countries suddenly emerged as global powers, attaining a geopolitical status that rivaled their status on the soccer field. Mankind had also entered into the final phase of the complete eradication of nuclear weapons. This victory of enlighted reason over barbarism made humanity's struggle for Antarctica devoid of the fearful shadow of a thermonuclear apocalypse.

1

NEW SOLID STATE

In the immense cavern, Shen Huabei felt as if he were walking on a dark plain under a starless sky. Beneath his feet, rock that had melted in the heat of a nuclear blast had already cooled and solidified, though a powerful warmth still penetrated the thermal insulation of his boots, causing the soles of his feet to sweat. Farther inside, a section of cavern wall had not yet cooled. It glowed faintly red in the darkness, like a murky dawn sky.

Shen Huabei's wife, Zhao Wenjia, walked to his left, and their eight-year-old son, Shen Yuan, was in front of them. Shen Yuan skipped ahead, seemingly unconstrained by his heavy radiation suit. They were joined by members of the UN Nuclear Inspection Team whose headlamps sent long beams of light into the darkness.

Two methods were employed to destroy nuclear weapons: disassembly and underground detonation. This was one of China's subterranean detonation sites.

Professor Kavinsky, leader of the inspection team, caught up to Shen Huabei. His headlamp shined on the three people ahead of him and threw their long, swaying shadows across the cavern floor.

'Doctor Shen, why did you bring your family? This is no place for a picnic.'

Shen Huabei halted to allow the Russian physicist to catch up. 'My wife is a geological engineer working for the central command of the Eradication Operation. As for my son, I think he likes it here.'

'Our son has always been fascinated by the strange and the extreme,' Wenjia agreed, more to her husband than the head of the team. Even though her face was partially concealed by the radiation suit's visor, Huabei could still clearly see the unease in his wife's eyes.

The boy was practically dancing in front of them. 'When they started, this hole was only as big as our basement. After just two blasts, it got gigantic! Think of the fireballs those blasts made – it was probably like there were huge *babies* under the ground having tantrums, kicking and screaming. It must have been amazing!'

Shen Huabei and Zhao Wenjia exchanged glances. He was grinning slightly, but the worry in her expression had only deepened.

'My boy, there were eight babies!' Professor Kavinsky said to Shen Yuan with a laugh. He turned to face Shen Huabei. 'Doctor Shen, this is what I meant to discuss with you. In the last blast, you detonated the warheads of eight Giant Wave submarine-launched ballistic missiles, each with a yield of one hundred kilotons. The warheads were on a rack, stacked in a cube—'

'What is the issue?'

'Before the detonation, I clearly saw on the monitor that there was a white sphere in the center of the cube.'

Shen Huabei stopped walking again. Looking squarely at Kavinsky, he said, 'Professor, the provisions of the Destruction Treaty prohibit us from detonating less than our mandated quota, but I do not believe they restrict us from detonating more. There were five independent observations that verified the size of the blast. Anything else is immaterial.'

Kavinsky nodded. 'That is why I waited until after the detonation to raise this issue with you. I am simply curious.'

'I imagine you have heard of "sugar coating".'

Shen Huabei's words fell like a curse over the site. The cavern went silent as everyone stopped walking, and the beams of light from their headlamps became still, shining in every direction. They conducted their conversation over a wireless intercom system in their radiation suits, so even the people far ahead had heard Shen Huabei's words. The silence ended as the members of the inspection team walked over and gathered around Shen Huabei. Everyone in this select group, no matter what part of the world they hailed from, was a luminary in the field of nuclear weapons research, and they had all clearly understood.

'It really exists?' an American asked, gawping at Shen Huabei.

The latter just nodded his head.

There is a story claiming that after receiving news of China's initial nuclear test in the middle of the last century Mao Zedong's first question was: 'Was there a nuclear explosion?' Whether he knew it or not, this was an excellent question. The key to designing fission weapons is the ability to apply compression. When a nuclear bomb goes off, a package of conventional explosives detonates around a mass of fissile material, compressing it into a dense sphere. When that sphere reaches critical density, a violent chain reaction begins, which results in a nuclear explosion. All of this takes place within a millionth of a second, so the pressure on the fissile core must be calibrated with extreme precision, as even a minuscule imbalance can easily result in the core failing to reach critical density. If that happens, the weapon will only produce a normal chemical blast. Since the inception of nuclear weapons, researchers have used complex mathematical models to design a variety of compression charge arrays. New technologies developed in recent years had enabled researchers to design compression mechanisms with groundbreaking accuracy, and 'sugar coating' was one of the techniques that allowed them to achieve this.

A 'sugar coat' was a kind of nanomaterial that was used to encase the core of a nuclear weapon. Once applied, it was, in turn, covered in a layer of conventional explosive charges. 'Sugar coating' had the function of automatically balancing compressive stress, so even if the outer layer of explosives did not produce uniform pressure the 'sugar coat' would balance its distribution, resulting in the precise compression necessary to bring fissile material to critical density.

'The white sphere you saw between the warheads was an alloyed material wrapped in a "sugar coat",' Shen Huabei said. 'It ought to have undergone extreme compressive stress in the explosion. This is part of a research project we plan to continue throughout the process of weapon destruction. Once all the nuclear weapons on Earth have been destroyed, it will be difficult to produce momentary compressive stress of this magnitude – for a while, at least. It will be interesting to see what happens to the test material under such pressure – to see what it will turn into. We hope this research can help us find some promising uses for 'sugar coating' in civilian hands.'

One UN official, considering the possibilities, said, 'You should encase graphite in 'sugar coating', so we could produce a large diamond with every explosion. Maybe this costly project of nuclear weapon destruction could turn a profit.'

Laughter erupted in their headphones. Officials without technical backgrounds were often the butt of jokes in situations like this. 'Let's see, eight hundred kilotons. . . . How many orders of magnitude greater is that than the pressure needed to turn graphite into a diamond?' someone asked.

'Of course it didn't make a diamond!' Shen Yuan's bright voice crackled in their earphones. 'I bet it made a black hole! A tiny black hole! It's going to suck us in, suck the whole world in, and we'll wind up in a prettier universe on the other side!'

'Haha, the explosion wasn't quite that large, my boy. Doctor Shen, your son has a fascinating mind!' said Kavinsky. 'So, what were the test results? What did the alloy turn into? I assume you could not find most of it.'

'I don't know yet. Let's go see,' said Shen Huabei, pointing ahead. The explosion had blasted an enormous, spherical cavity into the Earth, and its curved bottom formed a small basin. In the basin's center, the lights of several headlamps flitted around. 'Those are people from the 'sugar coating' research team.'

They walked down the gentle slope towards the center of the basin. Suddenly, Kavinsky stopped. He then laid his hands flat against the ground. 'There's a tremor!'

The others felt it too. 'It couldn't have been induced by the explosion, could it?'

Zhao Wenjia shook her head. 'We have carried out repeated surveys of the geological structure of the area around the destruction site. There is no way for an explosion to cause an earthquake here. The tremor began after the explosion and has continued uninterrupted since. Doctor Deng Yiwen said it has something to do with the 'sugar coating' experiment, though I don't know the details.'

As they approached the center of the basin, the tremor became stronger, emanating from deep below the ground. Soon it was strong enough to send a tingling sensation up their legs, as if a giant train was rumbling wildly in the Earth beneath them. Upon reaching the center, a suited researcher at the bottom of the basin rose to greet them. It was Doctor Deng Yiwen, the scientist responsible for the experiments involving the compression of materials with nuclear explosions.

'What's that you're holding?' Shen Huabei asked, pointing at a large, white ball in Doctor Yiwen's hand.

'Fishing line,' said Doctor Yiwen. Around him, a ring of people crouched on the ground, peering into a small hole in the surface of the rock that had melted and re-condensed in the explosion. The hole's rim was a near-perfect circle, around ten centimeters in diameter, and its edge was quite smooth, as if it had been bored with a drill. One end of the fishing line in Doctor Yiwen's hand was in the hole, and he unraveled more line in a continuous stream.

'We've already fed more than ten thousand meters of line into the hole and we're nowhere near the bottom. Our radars say it's more than thirty thousand meters deep and getting deeper.'

'How did it form?' someone asked.

'The compressed test alloy sank into the Earth like a stone in the sea. That's what made this hole. The alloy is passing through dense layers of rock as we speak, which is what's causing the tremor.'

'My God, that is astonishing!' Kavinsky exclaimed. 'I assumed the alloy would be vaporized in the heat of the blast.'

'If it had not been 'sugar coated', that would have been the result.' Doctor Yiwen agreed. 'As it was, it didn't have time to evaporate – the 'sugar coat' redistributed the force of the blast, compressing the alloy into a new state of matter that ought to be called a super-solid-state. That name was taken, so we are calling it "new-solid-state".'

'Are you saying that this thing's density, compared to the density of the earth below, is analogous to the density of a stone dropped into water?' Professor Kavinsky asked, still somewhat incredulous.

'It's much denser than that. The main reason stones sink in water is unrelated to either material's density; it's the fact that water is a liquid – when water freezes its density doesn't change considerably, but if you place a stone on ice it won't sink through it. New-solid-state matter, however, actually *sinks through* rocks, so we can only imagine how dense it must be.'

'You mean it turned into something like neutron-star material?'

Doctor Deng Yiwen shook his head. 'We haven't determined its precise density yet, but just by looking at the speed of its descent we can be certain that it's not as dense as the degenerate matter of a neutron star. If it were, it would be falling as fast as a meteorite through the atmosphere, and it would cause volcanic eruptions and large earthquakes. It's a state of matter somewhere between ordinary solid-state and degenerate matter.'

'Will it sink to the center of the Earth?' asked Shen Yuan.

'It is possible. Below a certain depth, the rock strata of the Earth's crust and mantle give way to the liquid core, where it will be even easier for the thing to sink.'

'Awesome!'

While everyone's attention was on the hole, Shen Huabei and his family quietly parted from the group and walked off into the darkness. Except for the hum of the tremor, it was silent away from the hole. The beams of their headlamps dissolved into the immense darkness around them, and their presence was subsumed into the vast, featureless void. They turned their intercoms to a private channel. Here, Shen Yuan was to make a choice that would determine the course of his life: would he follow his father or his mother?

Shen Yuan's parents faced a problem worse than divorce: his father had terminal leukemia. Shen Huabei did not know whether his work in nuclear research had caused the disease, but he knew he had no more than six months to live. Fortunately, the technology existed to induce artificial hibernation. Shen Huabei would enter a state of suspended animation until there was a cure for leukemia. Shen Yuan could either enter hibernation with his father or continue his life with his mother. The second choice seemed more prudent, but it was hard for a child to resist the idea of following his father into the future. Shen Huabei and Zhao Wenjia each tried once again to win him over.

'Mom, I'm going to stay with you. I won't go to sleep with daddy!' said Shen Yuan.

'You changed your mind?' asked Zhao Wenjia, overjoyed.

'Yes! I don't need to go to the future to have fun. There is plenty of fun stuff around now, like that thing – the one that's sinking into the ground. I want be around to see that!'

'That's your decision?' asked Shen Huabei. Zhao Wenjia glared at him, worried her son might change his mind again.

'Yeah,' said Shen Yuan. 'I'm gonna go try to see what's down that hole.' He took off running towards the basin, where the others' headlamps flickered.

Zhao Wenjia watched her son run off. 'I worry I won't be able to give him what he needs. He's just like you – lost in his dreams. Maybe the future would suit him better.'

Shen Huabei put his hands on his wife's shoulders. 'No one knows what the future will be like. And what's wrong with him being like me? The present needs dreamers, too.'

'There's nothing wrong with being a dreamer. That's why I fell in love with you. But you must know he has another side to him – he was chosen as class head of two of his classes!'

'Yes, I heard. I don't know how he managed that.'

'He has a thirst for power, and he knows what it takes to achieve it. In that way, he's nothing like you at all.'

'Yes. How can he reconcile that with his fantasies?'

'I'm more worried about what will happen when he does.'

Shen Yuan had arrived at the basin, his headlamp indistinguishable from the others. His parents stopped watching him, turned off their headlamps and sank into darkness.

'No matter what, life will continue. They may develop a cure next year, or it might be a century, or . . . they may never develop one. Without question, you'll live at least another forty years. I need you to promise me something: in forty years, if there is still no cure, I need you to wake me up. I want to see you and our son again. This can't be our final goodbye.'

'You want to see an old woman and a grown man ten years your senior in the future? But it is as you said, life goes on.' In the dark, Zhao Wenjia managed a miserable smile.

In that giant cavern hollowed out by nuclear blasts, they spent a final, silent moment together. The next day, Shen Huabei was to enter into a dreamless sleep. Zhao Wenjia would be left to live with Shen Yuan, whose life was consumed by his dreams. Together, they would continue down the treacherous road of life, toward an unknown future.

2

AWAKENING

It took a day for him to wake up fully. When he first opened his eyes, he saw only a white mist from which blurred, white figures gradually emerged over the next ten hours. After a further ten hours, he was able to recognize them as doctors and nurses. People in suspended animation are unaware of the passage of time, and Shen Huabei initially thought that his weak consciousness was part of the process of entering hibernation, that perhaps the hibernation systems had suffered a malfunction as he was going under. As his vision continued to improve, he examined the hospital ward around him, which was softly lit by sconces on its white walls. This place was familiar, which confirmed to him the idea that he had not yet entered hibernation.

In the next moment, it became clear that he was mistaken. The white ceiling of the ward began to glow blue, and against this backdrop, sharp, white letters emerged.

> Greetings! Living Earth Cryogenics, your suspended animation provider, filed for bankruptcy in 2089. Responsibility for your care was transferred to Jade Cloud Corporation. Your hibernation serial number is WS368200402-118. You retain all rights and privileges granted to you in your contract with Living Earth Cryogenics. You underwent medical treatment before being awoken, and you are successfully cured of all disease. Please accept Jade Cloud Corporation's congratulations on your new life.
>
> You have been in hibernation for 74 years, 5 months, 7 days, and 13 hours. Your account is paid in full.
>
> The current date is 16 April 2125. Welcome to the future.

His hearing gradually began to return, and three hours later he was able to speak. After 74 years of deep sleep, his first words were, 'Where are my wife and son?'

A tall, thin doctor stood next to his bed. She handed him a folded piece of paper. 'Doctor Shen, this is a letter from your wife.'

Shen Huabei cast a strange glance at the doctor. *Even before I went under, people hardly ever wrote paper letters*, he thought to himself. He managed to unfold the letter, though his hands were still half-numb. Here was more proof that he had traveled through time: the paper, blank at first, began to emit an azure light that formed letters as it traveled down the page. Soon, the page was full of writing.

Before entering cryo-sleep, he had on countless occasions imagined the first words his wife might say to him as he woke up, but he could never have imagined what was written on the paper:

> Huabei, my love, you are in great danger!
>
> By the time you read this letter, I will no longer be alive. The person who gave you this letter is Doctor Guo. You can trust her; in fact, she may be the only person left on Earth you can trust. Follow whatever directions she gives you.
>
> Forgive me for breaking my promise. I did not wake you in forty years. You cannot imagine the person Yuan has become, the things he has done. As his mother, I felt unable to look you in the eye. My heart is broken. My life has been wasted. Please take care of yourself.

'My son – where is Shen Yuan?' shouted Huabei, rising with great effort onto his elbows.

'He died five years ago.' The doctor's answer was icy, utterly indifferent to the heartache this message inflicted. As if realizing this, she softened and added, 'Your son was 78 years old.'

Doctor Guo took a card from her coat pocket and handed it to Huabei. 'This is your new identity card. The information it contains is explained in your wife's letter.'

Huabei examined the paper, checking it back and front. There was nothing on it except for Wenjia's brief note. As he turned it over, the creases in the paper seemed to ripple, like the LCD screens of his day did when touched. Doctor Guo reached over and pressed on the letter's lower right corner, and the paper's display switched over to a spreadsheet.

'Sorry about that. Paper as you know it no longer exists.'

Huabei looked at her quizzically.

'There are no forests anymore,' she explained, shrugging. She then returned to the spreadsheet. 'Your new name is Wang Ruo. You were born in 2097. Your parents are deceased, and you have no close family. You were born in Hohhot, Inner Mongolia, but you now reside here,' she said, indicating a cell on the spreadsheet. 'It is a remote village in the mountains of Ningxia. It was the best place we could find, considering. You won't attract attention there. Before you depart, you will need to undergo plastic surgery. Under no circumstances should you talk about your son. Do not even express an interest in him if someone else mentions him.'

'But I am Shen Yuan's father! I was born in Beijing!'

Doctor Guo stiffened and became cold again. 'If you say that publicly, your hibernation and treatment will have been for nothing. You'll be dead in an hour.'

'Whatever happened?' Huabei needed to know – *now*.

The doctor smiled coldly as she began. 'There is much in this world that you probably don't know.' She shook her head ever so slightly. 'Well, we should hurry. You should first get out of bed and learn to walk again. We then need to get you out of here as quickly as possible.'

Just as Huabei opened his mouth to ask another question, a loud banging erupted from behind the door. It crashed open, and six or seven people rushed in and surrounded Huabei's bed. They were all of different ages and they had different clothes, except for a strange sort of hat that some of them wore and some carried. The hats had brims wide enough to cover their wearers' shoulders, like the straw hats farmers used to wear. Each of them also had a transparent oxygen mask, which some of them had removed when they entered the room. They all stared at Huabei menacingly.

'This is Shen Yuan's father?' one of them asked. He appeared to be the oldest member of the group, at least 80 years old, and he had a long, white beard. Without waiting for the doctor to answer, he turned to the rest of his group and nodded his head.

'He looks just like his son. Doctor, you've done your duty. He's ours now.'

'How did you know he was here?' asked Doctor Guo coolly.

Before the doctor could answer, a nurse spoke up from the corner of the room. 'I told them.'

Doctor Guo turned and glared angrily at the nurse. 'You betrayed a patient's confidence?'

'Happily,' said the nurse, her pretty face twisted into a grimace.

A young man grabbed Huabei's gown and dragged him off the bed. He lay paralyzed on the ground, still too weak to move. A girl kicked him in the gut so hard that the sharp toe of her boot almost pierced his stomach; the pain was excruciating, and he writhed on the floor like a fish. The old man took hold of Huabei's collar and hauled him to his feet with an unexpected strength. He held Huabei upright in a futile effort to make him stand. He released his grip and Huabei fell backwards, smacking his head on the floor. His eyes blurred with pain. Someone said, 'Great, that'll cover a small bit of this bastard's debt to society.'

'Who are you people?' asked Huabei weakly. From his position on the floor between their feet, he felt as if his captors were a menacing group of giants.

'You should know who I am, at least,' said the old man, sneering vindictively. Seen from below, his face appeared twisted and grotesque. Huabei shuddered. 'I am Deng Yang, Deng Yiwen's son.'

The name made Huabei's stomach lurch. He turned and grabbed the hem of the old man's trousers. 'Your father was my co-worker and close friend! You were my son's classmate! Don't you remember? My goodness, you're Yiwen's son? I can't believe it! Back then, you were—'

'Get your filthy hands off me!' shouted Deng Yang.

The young man who had pulled Huabei off the bed crouched down and leaned close to his face, his eyes full of malice. 'Listen. You aren't any older than you were when you went to sleep. This man is your elder, and you need to show him some respect.'

'If Shen Yuan were still alive, he'd be old enough to be your father,' said Deng Yang loudly, eliciting a round of laughter. He pointed at one of his companions. 'When this young man was four years old, both his parents died in the Central Breach Disaster,' he said to Huabei. 'And this young lady lost her parents in the Lost Bolt Disaster. She wasn't even two years old.' Deng Yang gestured towards two more members of his group. 'These people invested their life savings in the Project. When this man learned it had failed, he attempted suicide. And this man simply lost his mind.' He paused, then added, 'And as for me, I was tricked by your bastard son. I threw my youth and my talent into that goddamn hole, and the whole world hates me for it.'

Huabei still lay on the floor, shaking his head in confusion.

'Shen Huabei, this is a court, and we, the victims of the Antarctic Entry Project, are your judge and jury! Everyone in this country is a victim, but we have the special privilege of administering your justice. We could have sent you to a real court, but our justice system is even more convoluted now than it was in your day. Lawyers would have spent a year spewing bullshit about your case, and then you'd probably have been acquitted, like your son was. We won't take more than an hour to deliver our righteous judgment, and believe me: once we have, you'll wish the leukemia had taken you 70 years ago.'

They began jeering at Huabei. Two people lifted him by his arms and hauled him towards the door. He was too weak to struggle, and his legs dragged on the floor.

'Mr Shen, I did what I could,' said Doctor Guo as Huabei neared the door. He wanted to look back at her, the only person he could trust in these vicious times, according to his wife's letter, but the position he was held in made it impossible. She spoke again from behind him.

'Don't despair too much. Living in these times isn't easy, either.'

As he was dragged out the door, Huabei heard Doctor Guo call out, 'Close the door and turn up the air purifiers! Do you want to choke to death?' Her tone was urgent, and it was clear that she was already indifferent to his fate.

Once they got out of the hospital ward, Huabei understood Doctor Guo's last words: the air was acrid and hard to breathe. He was dragged out through the hospital's main corridor. As they exited the building, the two people dragging him put his arms over their shoulders and began to carry him. He took a deep breath, relieved to be outside of the hospital, but what he inhaled was not the fresh, outdoor air he expected; instead it was a gas even more noxious than the air in the hospital. His lungs erupted in pain, and he was racked by a sudden, violent cough that did not stop. As he began to suffocate, he heard someone say, ‘Give him a respirator. We don’t want him to die before we can administer justice.’ Someone fitted a device over his nose and mouth. The air it provided had a strange taste, but at least he could breathe. Someone else said, ‘You don’t need to give him a screen hat. He won’t be alive long enough for the UV to give him leukemia again.’ This drew a burst of cruel laughter from the group. Huabei’s breathing became somewhat more regular, and the tears caused by his cough began to dry, restoring his vision. He raised his head and took his first look at the future.

The first thing he noticed was the people on the street; all of them were wearing transparent respirator masks and every head was covered by one of those large straw hats his kidnappers had just called a ‘screen hat’. He also noticed that despite the warm weather, everyone was swaddled in clothes, without an inch of skin showing. The street was lined with enormous skyscrapers on both sides, so tall that he felt like he was in a deep valley. ‘Skyscraper’ was an apt term for these buildings – they literally stretched into the gray clouds overhead. In the narrow strip of sky between the buildings, the sun shone indistinctly behind the clouds. Streaks of smoke passed in front of the sunlight, and he soon realized that the clouds themselves were in fact plumes of pollution.

‘A great time to be alive, isn’t it?’ asked Deng Yang. His friends laughed heartily, as if they hadn’t laughed for ages.

They carried him towards a nearby car – similar in size to a sedan and able to accommodate four or five people. As they approached it, two people passed by them, walking with purpose in another direction. They wore helmets, and though their uniforms were unfamiliar to Huabei, he could guess at their profession. He called out to them.

‘Help! I’m being kidnapped! Help me!’

The two police officers abruptly turned around and ran over to Huabei. They looked him up and down, taking special notice of his hospital gown and bare feet. One of them asked, ‘You’re just out of cryo, aren’t you?’

Huabei nodded weakly. ‘They’re kidnapping me . . .’

The other police officer nodded at this. 'Sir, this sort of thing is common. Many people have been waking from cryo-sleep recently, and getting them established in society takes a lot of resources. People are resentful and angry, and they often lash out.'

'That's not what's happening here—' began Huabei, but the officer cut him off with a wave of his hand.

'Sir, you're safe now.' The police officer turned toward Deng Yang and his co-conspirators. 'This man obviously still requires medical attention. Two of you have to take him back to the hospital. We will investigate this matter thoroughly, but for now, all seven of you are under arrest on suspicion of kidnapping.' He lifted the radio on his wrist to his mouth and called for reinforcements.

Deng Yang rushed over and interrupted him. 'Officer, wait a moment. We aren't anti-cryo thugs. Look closely at this man. Doesn't he look familiar?'

The police officers peered at Huabei's face for a long time. One of them pulled down his respirator for a moment to see him better.

'It's Mi Xixi!'

'He's not Mi Xixi, he's Shen Yuan's father!'

Mouths agape, the two policemen looked back and forth between Shen Huabei and Deng Yang. The young man whose parents had died in the Central Breach disaster pulled the policemen over to him and whispered to them. As he spoke, the policemen glanced occasionally over at Huabei, and with each glance their eyes grew colder. The last time they looked at him, his heart sank. Deng Yang had two more accomplices.

The policemen walked over, avoiding Huabei's eye. One of them stood sentry and the other approached Deng Yang. In an urgent whisper, he said, 'We saw nothing. Whatever you do, don't let anyone figure out who he is – there'd be a riot.'

It wasn't just the policeman's words that terrified Huabei, but the way he said them. He spoke without regard to whether Huabei heard, as if Huabei were part of the landscape. The members of Deng Yang's gang quickly pushed Huabei into the car and entered behind him. As soon as the car's engine revved up, its windows grew darker, preventing the sun from shining in and Huabei from looking out. The car was self-driving and completely devoid of any visible means of manual control. No one spoke as they took to the road.

At last, Huabei ventured a question, if only to break the ominous silence.

'Who is Mi Xixi?'

'A movie star,' the Lost Bolt orphan sitting next to him said. 'He is famous for playing your son. Shen Yuan and alien monsters are the media's villains of the day.'

Huabei squirmed in his seat, trying to move away from the girl. As he did, he inadvertently brushed his arm against a button beneath the window. The window's glass immediately turned clear again. Through it, Huabei saw they were driving on an enormous, complex highway overpass. The structure was packed with vehicles separated by no more than two meters. Alarmingly, the cars were not stopped in traffic, as their proximity suggested they should be – they were all moving at full speed, at least one hundred kilometers per hour. The whole overpass looked like an unsafe amusement park ride.

Their car sped ahead towards a junction in the road. As they approached the junction, their car turned to change lanes, and just as it seemed they would crash into another car, a gap opened in the lane beside them, allowing them to merge. In fact, a gap opened for every merging vehicle, with an action so quick and so smooth that the two lanes seemed to meld into one. Huabei had already realized that the car was self-driving; now, he realized that the AI operating the car enabled an extremely efficient use of the highway.

A person in the back seat reached over and hit the button to darken the window again.

'I don't know anything that's going on, and you still want to kill me?' asked Huabei.

From his seat in front, Deng Yang turned to face Huabei. After a pause, he unenthusiastically said, 'Well, then I guess I'll just have to tell you.'

3

THE ANTARCTIC DOORSTEP

'People rich in imagination are usually weak, and most strong people – the people who make history – lack imagination. Your son was a remarkable exception: a man with imagination and the strength of will to bring his visions into being. To him, reality was just a small, remote island in a vast ocean of fantasies; but when he wanted to, he could reverse the two, making his fantasies into an island and reality into the ocean. He navigated both oceans with incredible skill—'

Huabei interrupted him. 'I know my own son. Stop wasting my time.'

'No matter how well you knew him, you could never have imagined the status that Shen Yuan attained, the power he held. He was in a position to bring his darkest visions to life. Unfortunately, the world did not recognize how dangerous this was until it was too late. Perhaps there have been others like him in history, but they were like asteroids that flew by the Earth. They never made impact – they just flew off into the vastness of space. History gave Shen Yuan the means to realize his twisted vision. His asteroid made impact, to our great misfortune.'

'In your fifth year of cryogenic hibernation, the world took a preliminary step towards resolving the problem of who should control Antarctica. The continent was declared a shared region of global economic development. Strong nations circumvented this declaration and carved out large areas of the continent for their own exclusive benefit. Each of those nations wanted to exploit the resources of its own region as quickly as possible. Doing so was their only hope to escape the economic depression that resource depletion and pollution had brought about. There was a saying back then – the future lies at the bottom of the world. It was then that your son proposed his insane idea. He claimed that implementing it would turn Antarctica into China's backyard, that he could make it simpler to get from Beijing to Antarctica than to Tianjin. This was not a metaphor – it actually was faster to get to Antarctica than to Tianjin, and the trip used fewer resources and created less pollution. When he began announcing his plan in a televised press conference, the whole country laughed, as if they were watching a ludicrous comedy. But before the conference was over, we had all stopped laughing. We realized it really was possible! Thus began the disastrous Antarctic Doorstep Project.

Deng Yang abruptly stopped talking.

'Well, what is the Antarctic Doorstep Project?' asked Huabei, urging Deng Yang to continue.

'You'll know soon enough,' said Deng Yang icily.

'Can you at least tell me what I have to do with any of this?'

'You are Shen Yuan's father. What else is there to say?'

'So we've regressed to genetic determinism now?'

'Of course not, but by your son's own admission, bloodline is relevant in this case. After he became internationally famous, he said in countless interviews that his way of thinking and his personality were already largely formed by the time he was eight years old and that it was his father who had formed them. He said that all his work over the years was meant only to supplement the knowledge his father gave him. He even declared outright that his father was the original innovator of the Antarctic Doorstep Project.'

'What? Me? Antarctica? That is simply—'

'Let me finish. You also provided the technological foundation for the project.'

'What are you talking about?'

'New-solid-state matter. Without it, the Antarctic Doorstep Project would have been a pipe dream. It made it possible to turn this twisted fantasy into a reality.'

Shen Huabei shook his head in confusion. He was completely unable to imagine how super-dense new-solid-state matter could enable such fast travel to Antarctica.

Just then, the car came to a stop.

4

THE GATE OF HELL

They got out of the car, and Huabei saw a strange, small hill in front of them. It was the color of rust and completely barren, without even a single blade of grass on its surface.

Deng Yang nodded towards the slope, 'That's an iron hill.' Seeing the surprise on Huabei's face, he added, 'It's a single, huge piece of metal.' Huabei looked around and saw there were several more 'iron hills' nearby, jutting out from the ground at odd intervals, their color strange against the large plain on which they stood. It looked like an alien landscape.

By now, Huabei was able to walk again, though shakily. He staggered along behind his captors, towards a large structure in the distance. The structure was a perfect cylinder, more than three hundred feet tall, and its surface was completely smooth, with no visible entrance. As they approached, a heavy iron panel slid open in the side of the structure, allowing them to enter. It closed tightly behind them.

Shen Huabei saw that he was in a dimly-lit room that resembled an airlock chamber. On the smooth, white wall hung a long row of what looked like spacesuits. Each person took one off the wall and put it on, and two people helped Huabei into one. He looked around the room and saw another sliding door on the far wall. Above the door glowed a red light, and next to the light was a digital display that showed the current atmospheric pressure in the room. When his heavy helmet was tightened into place, a transparent liquid crystal display appeared in the upper right corner of his visor, showing a string of numbers and figures in quick succession. He recognized that it was the suit's internal diagnostic system. Then, he heard the deep drone of machinery start up. The number on the atmospheric pressure display above the door was falling fast. In less than three minutes, it hit zero. The red light turned green and the door slid open, revealing the dark interior of the airtight structure.

Huabei's guess had been correct: the room they were in was an airlock chamber that enabled passage between an area with atmosphere and one without any. The interior of the huge cylinder was a vacuum.

The group walked through the door, which shut behind them, leaving them in pitch darkness. The lights on a few people's helmets turned on, sending feeble shafts of light into the void. A feeling of déjà-vu came over Huabei, and he shivered with dread.

'Walk forward,' crackled Deng Yang's voice in Huabei's headphones. His helmet light illuminated a small bridge ahead of them, no more than three feet wide. Its far end was obscured by darkness, so he couldn't see how long it was. Beneath the bridge was blackness. With trembling steps, Huabei walked on. The heavy boots of his airtight suit produced a hollow clang against the metal surface of the bridge. He walked a few yards out onto the bridge and turned his head to see if anyone had followed him. As he did, everyone's helmet lamps suddenly turned off, and all was engulfed in darkness. A few seconds later, a blue light suddenly began to glow beneath the narrow bridge. Huabei looked behind him and saw that he was the only one on the bridge – everyone else had gathered at its foot, and they were all looking at him. Lit from below by the blue light, they looked like ghosts. Tightly grasping the bridge's railing, Huabei looked down, and what he saw made his blood run cold.

He was standing above a deep well.

The well was around thirty feet in diameter. Rings of light were evenly spaced along its interior wall; it was only by their glow that was he able to discern the well's presence. The bridge spanned the mouth of the well, and he stood in its exact center. He couldn't see the well's bottom. He saw only countless rings of light on the wall of the well, shrinking with perspective into the distance and finally coming to a point. It was like looking down at a glowing blue target.

'Your judgment is at hand – you will pay your son's debt!' shouted Deng Yang. He grabbed hold of a wheel at the foot of the bridge and began to turn it, muttering, 'This is for my stolen youth, my wasted talent . . .' The bridge tilted to one side, and Huabei tightly gripped the higher railing, trying with all his might to keep his footing.

Deng Yang gave control of the wheel to the Central Breach orphan, who turned it forcefully. 'This is for my mother and father, for their melted bodies . . .' The incline of the bridge increased.

The girl whose parents died in the Lost Bolt Disaster stepped up. She turned the wheel, her wrathful gaze on Huabei. 'This is for vaporizing my parents . . .'

The man who had attempted suicide after losing his fortune took the girl's place at the wheel. 'This is for my money – my Rolls Royce, my Lincoln, my villa on the beach, my swimming pool. This is for my ruining my life, for making my wife and son stand in that long, cold welfare line . . .'

The bridge was now tilted on its side, leaving Huabei hanging on to the top railing as he desperately caught a foothold on the railing now below him.

The man who had lost his mind joined the man who had attempted suicide at the wheel, and they turned it together. He was clearly still ill, and he said nothing – he just looked down into the well and laughed. The bridge flipped over completely. Huabei clutched the railing with both hands and dangled over the pit.

His fear had actually subsided somewhat. As he gazed through the gate of hell into the bottomless pit beneath him, Huabei's life flashed before his eyes. His childhood and youth had been a drab and joyless time for him. He had found success as a student and a researcher, yet even after inventing 'sugar coating' technology, he still felt ill at ease in the world. Personal relationships had always felt to him like a spider's web whose strands bound him more tightly the more he struggled. He had never known true love; he had married out of obligation. As soon as he decided never to have children, a child came to him and his wife. He was a man who lived in a world of dreams and fantasies, the sort of man most people despise. He had never found his place among other people. His life was one of isolation, of going against the current. He used to put all his hope in the future. Now, the future had arrived: he was a widower whose son was the enemy of humanity, in a polluted city, surrounded by hateful, twisted people. . . . He was nearly overcome with disappointment in the era in which he found himself and in his own life. He had once resolved to learn the true nature of things before he died; now, that no longer mattered to him. He was simply a weary traveler whose only desire was to rest.

Cheers rose as Huabei's grip finally failed and he plummeted towards his fate, towards the glowing blue rings beneath him.

He shut his eyes and gave himself over to weightlessness. It felt like his body was dissolving away, and with it, the crushing burden of existence. In these, the last few seconds of his life, a song suddenly popped into his mind. His father had taught it to him – an old Soviet tune, already forgotten by the time he had entered cryogenic hibernation. He had once gone to Moscow as a visiting scholar, and while there, he tried to find someone who knew the song. No one had heard of it, so it became his own, private song. He would only have time to hum a note or two in his head before he hit the bottom of the well, but he was sure that after his soul left his body, it would enter the next world humming.

Before he knew it, Huabei had already hummed half of the song's slow melody to himself. He suddenly became aware of how much time must have passed. Opening his eyes, he saw himself flying past ring after ring of blue light.

He was still falling.

'Ha ha ha ha!' Deng Yang's maniacal laugh came through his headphones. 'You're about to die – what a feeling that must be!'

Huabei looked down at the row of concentric rings glowing blue beneath him. They whizzed by him, one after the other, and each time he passed through the largest circle a new one emerged at its center, tiny at first but growing rapidly. He looked up at the concentric rings of light above him, whose expansion off into the distance mirrored the sight below.

'How deep is this well?' he asked.

'Don't worry, you'll hit the bottom soon enough. There's a hard steel plate down there, and you're going to splat against it like a bug on a windshield! Ha ha ha ha!'

As Deng Yang spoke, Huabei noticed that the small display in the upper right corner of his visor had flickered back to life. In glowing red letters, it read:

You have reached a depth of fifty miles.

Your speed is 0.86 miles per second.

You have passed the Mohorovičić discontinuity.

Having passed the crust, you are now entering the Earth's mantle.

Huabei shut his eyes again. This time, there was no music. His mind was like a computer, dispassionate and quick, and after thirty seconds of thought he opened his eyes. Now he understood everything. This was the Antarctic Doorstep Project. There was no steel plate at the end. This well was bottomless.

This was a tunnel straight through the Earth.

5

THE TUNNEL

'Is its path tangential or does it go straight through the Earth's core?' wondered Huabei aloud.

'Clever! You figured it out!' exclaimed Deng Yang.

'As clever as his son,' someone added – the Central Breach orphan, by the sound of his voice.

'It goes through the Earth's core, from Mohe to the easternmost part of the Antarctic Peninsula,' said Deng Yang, responding to Huabei's question.

'The city we were just in was Mohe?'

'Yes, it experienced a boom once the tunnel was constructed.'

'As far as I know, a tunnel from there straight through the Earth would reach the southern part of Argentina.'

'That's correct, but this tunnel curves slightly.'

'If that's the case, won't I hit the wall?'

'No – in fact, you would hit the wall if the tunnel went to Argentina. A perfectly straight tunnel would only be workable between the Earth's poles, along its axis. To make a tunnel at an angle to the axis, you must consider the rotation of the Earth. This tunnel's curvature is necessary for smooth passage.'

'This tunnel is a remarkable achievement!' exclaimed Huabei sincerely.

You have reached a depth of 185 miles.

Your speed is 1.5 miles per second.

You have entered the Earth's asthenosphere.

Huabei saw that he was passing through the rings of light at an increasing rate. The concentric circles of light above and below him now appeared considerably denser.

Deng Yang spoke. 'Digging a tunnel through the Earth isn't exactly a new idea. As early as the 18th century, at least two people had already considered it. One was the mathematician Pierre Louis Maupertuis. The second was none other than Voltaire. After them, the French astronomer Flammarion raised the idea again, and he was the first to take into account the rotation of the Earth.'

Huabei interrupted him. 'So how can you say the idea came from me?'

'Because those people were just doing thought experiments, while your idea influenced someone – someone talented, with vision, who went on to make this outlandish idea a reality.'

'I don't remember mentioning anything like that to Shen Yuan.'

'Then you have a poor memory. You had a vision that changed the course of human history, and you forgot it!'

'I honestly can't recall.'

'Surely you remember a man called Delgado, from Argentina, and the birthday present he gave your son.'

You have reached a depth of 930 miles.

Your speed is 3.2 miles per second.

You have entered the Earth's mesosphere.

Huabei finally remembered. It was Shen Yuan's sixth birthday, and Huabei had invited the Argentine physicist Doctor Delgado, who happened to be in Beijing, to his home. Argentina was one of the two South American nations that emerged from the struggle for Antartica as a superpower. It had vast territorial claims on the continent, and large numbers of Argentine citizens had gone to live there. Argentina had also begun rapidly augmenting its nuclear arsenal, to the great alarm of the international community.

In the subsequent process of global nuclear disarmament, it was natural that Argentina, as a nuclear-armed state, should join the UN's Nuclear Eradication Committee. Shen Huabei and Delgado were both serving as technical experts within that committee.

Delgado had given Shen Yuan a globe. It was made of a novel kind of glass, one of the products of Argentina's rapid technological development. The refractive index of this glass was equal to that of air, so it was entirely invisible. On the globe, the continents appeared as if they were floating in space between the Earth's poles. Shen Yuan loved his gift.

As they chatted after dinner, Delgado took out a prominent Chinese newspaper and showed Huabei a political cartoon. It was a drawing of a famous Argentine soccer player kicking the Earth like a soccer ball.

'I don't like this cartoon,' said Delgado. 'China knows nothing about Argentina except that we play soccer well, and this limited understanding affects international politics. The Chinese see Argentina as an aggressive nation.'

'Well, Doctor, Argentina is the furthest nation from China on Earth. We are at opposite ends of the globe,' said Zhao Wenjia, smiling. She took the transparent globe from Shen Yuan and held it up. China and Argentina overlapped through the perfectly clear glass.

'I know a way to improve communication between our countries,' said Huabei, taking the globe. 'We'd just need to dig a tunnel through the center of the Earth.'

'That tunnel would be more than 7,500 miles long. That's not much shorter than a direct flight path,' said Delgado.

'But the travel time would be much shorter than flying. Think about it – you'd pack your bags, hop into one end of the tunnel, and . . .'

Huabei had only raised this idea to turn the conversation away from politics. It worked. Delgado's interest was piqued, and he said, 'Shen, your way of thinking is truly original. Let's see – after I jumped into the hole, the speed of my fall would continuously accelerate. The deeper I fell, the slower my acceleration would be, but I would continue to accelerate all the way to the center of the Earth. At the center, I will have achieved my maximum velocity, and my acceleration would be zero. Then, as I began to ascend the far side of the hole, I would decelerate, and my rate of deceleration would increase the further I ascended. When I arrived at the surface of the Earth in Argentina, my speed would be exactly zero. If I wanted to return to China, I could simply jump back into the hole. I could continue this sort of travel forever, if I wished, moving in simple harmonic vibration between the Northen and Southern hemispheres. Yes, it's a wonderful idea, but the travel time . . .'

'Let's calculate it,' said Huabei. He turned on his computer.

Completing the calculation took only a moment. Based on the planet's average density, if you jumped into the tunnel in China, traveled 7,917 miles through the Earth and emerged from the tunnel in Argentina, your travel time would be forty two minutes and twelve seconds.

'Now that's what I call fast travel!' said Delgado, clearly pleased.

You have reached a depth of 1,740 miles.

Your speed is four miles per second.

You are passing the Gutenberg discontinuity and entering the Earth's core.

As Huabei continued to fall, Deng Yang spoke. 'You certainly didn't notice it at the time, but clever little Shen Yuan hung onto your every word that evening. You also wouldn't know that he didn't sleep a wink that night. He just stared at the transparent globe next to his bed. Your influence on his thinking was enormous. Over the years, you planted countless seeds in his imagination. This one happened to bear fruit.'

The wall of the tunnel was around fifteen feet from Huabei, and he watched it fly upwards. The rings of light now sped by so rapidly that they appeared as a blur on the wall.

'Is this wall made of new-solid-state material?' he asked.

'What else could it be? Is there another material strong enough to construct a tunnel like this?'

'How did you produce such an enormous quantity? How can you transport and operate a material so dense that it sinks through the Earth?

'The short answer is this: new-solid-state material is produced in a continuous series of small nuclear explosions, using your 'sugar coating' technology, of course. Producing it is a long and complex process. We can produce new-solid-state material in a range of densities. Lower-density material does not sink into the ground, so it is used to build large foundations that can bear the weight of high-density material without sinking, by dispersing its pressure. The same principle can be applied in transporting the material.

The technology used to machine the material is more complex; you don't have the background knowledge to understand it. Suffice it to say that new-solid-state material is an enormous industry, larger in scale than steel production. The Antarctic Doorstep Project is not the material's only application.'

'How was this tunnel built?'

'I'll tell you first that the basic component of the tunnel's structure is a wellbore casing. Each section of casing is around 320 feet long, and the tunnel is made of around 240,000 sections linked together. As to the specific construction process, you're a smart man – you figure it out.'

'A caisson?'

'Yes, we used a caisson. First we sank the wellbore casing from sites in China and Antarctica. Linked together, the sections of casing formed an unbroken line through the Earth. The second step was to excavate the material from inside the casing, forming the tunnel. The metal hills you saw outside the entrance to the tunnel are made of excavated material, iron and nickel alloys from the core of the Earth. The actual work of linking the casing was carried out by 'subterranean ships', machines made of new-solid-state material that are capable of travel among and between the strata of the Earth. Some models are able to operate at core depth. We used these machines to maneuver the sinking sections of casing into place.

'By my calculation, the process you describe would only require 120,000 sections of casing.'

'Super dense solids are able to withstand the high pressures and temperatures found in the interior of the Earth, but the movement of liquid matter within the Earth is more problematic. There is magma at relatively shallow depths, but the real danger is in the core, where the flow of liquid iron and nickel produces enormous shearing force against the tunnel. New-solid-state matter is strong enough to withstand these forces, but the joints in the casing aren't. Therefore, the tunnel is constructed out of two layers of casing, one wrapped tightly around the other. By staggering the joints of the two layers, we were able to achieve sufficient resistance to the shearing forces.'

You have reached a depth of 3,350 miles.

Your speed is 4.8 miles per second.

You are approaching the Earth's solid core.

'I suppose you'll tell me next about the disasters that this project caused.'

6

DISASTER

'Twenty-five years ago, the Antarctic Doorstep suffered its first disaster, just as the project entered the final phase of survey and design,' Deng Yang continued. 'This stage required substantial underground navigation. On one exploratory voyage, a ship called *Sunset 6* experienced a malfunction while in the Earth's mantle and sank down to the core. Two members of the three-person crew were killed. Only the young, female pilot survived. She is still down there, sealed off in the core of the Earth, doomed to live out her remaining days encased in that subterranean ship. The neutrino communication device on the ship is no longer able to transmit messages, though it might still receive ours. Oh, that's right – her name is Shen Jing. She is your granddaughter.'

Huabei's heart skipped a beat.

At this speed, the rings of light on the wall of the tunnel were completely indistinct, making the wall itself appear to glow with a harsh, blue light. Huabei felt as if he were falling into a tunnel through time, into the recent past, the past he had not known.

You have reached a depth of 3,600 miles.

Your speed is 4.8 miles per second.

You have entered the solid core and are approaching the center of the Earth.

'In the sixth year of construction, the tragic Central Breach Disaster struck. As I mentioned before, the tunnel's wall is composed of two staggered layers of casing. Before installing a section of the inner layer, it was necessary to join the adjacent outer sections and extract all material from inside them, as any debris could have compromised the seal between the layers. This was time-sensitive work, especially in the liquid core. After two sections of the outer ring were coupled and before the inner section was inserted, the outer layer had to hold on its own against the force of the nickel-iron flow. The riveting used to join the rings was exceptionally strong. Its design was projected to be able to withstand the force of the flow almost indefinitely. Three hundred miles into the core, two sections of outer ring that had just been coupled were struck by an aberrant surge in the nickel-iron flow, five times more forceful than anything observed in prior surveys. The force of the surge dislocated the sections, and in an instant, high-temperature, high-pressure core material rushed through the breach, into the caisson, and up the tunnel. As soon as the breach was detected, Shen Yuan, as general director of the project, immediately ordered the closure of the Gutenberg Gate, a safety valve located at the Gutenberg Discontinuity. More than 2,500 engineers were working in the five hundred miles of tunnel beneath the valve at the time. These workers boarded high-speed freight elevators to evacuate the tunnel as soon as they became aware of the breach. The final elevator departed around twenty miles ahead of the crest of the nickel-iron flow. In the end, only sixty-one elevators made it through the Gutenberg Gate before it closed; everyone else was trapped on the wrong side, swallowed by torrents of the core flow, burning at over seven thousand degrees. One thousand five hundred and twenty-seven people lost their lives.

'News of the disaster shook the world. There was a consensus that Shen Yuan was to blame, but people disagreed about how he should have responded. One group asserted he had had time to wait for all the elevators to pass through the Gutenberg Gate before closing it. The last elevator was twenty miles ahead of the flow – it would have been a close call, but possible. Even if the flow had overtaken the Gutenberg Gate before it could be closed, there was still the Moho Gate, another safety valve at the Mohorovičić discontinuity. Outraged members of the victims' families accused Shen Yuan of murder. His public response was a single sentence: I had to act fast. He wasn't wrong – hesitating might have caused a cataclysm. There was a whole subgenre of disaster films about the Antarctic Doorstep. The most famous, Metal Fountain, was a nightmarish depiction of what would have happened if the core material had breached the surface. In it, a column of liquid nickel and iron shot out of the tunnel into the stratosphere, where it blossomed outwards like a flower of death. It glowed with a blinding white light that illuminated the whole Northern hemisphere, and a rain of molten metal began to fall over the Earth, turning all of Asia into a furnace. Humanity met the same fate as the dinosaurs.

'This wasn't artistic license; it was a probable outcome. Because of this, Shen Yuan faced another line of accusation that contradicted the first: he should have closed the Gutenberg Gate immediately, without waiting for sixty-one elevators to ascend. This was the more popular view, and its adherents labelled Shen Yuan's crime 'criminal negligence against humanity'. There was no proper legal basis for either accusation, but Shen Yuan resigned from his leadership position on the Project. He refused to be reappointed elsewhere, and he continued his work on the tunnel as an ordinary engineer.'

The light on the wall of the tunnel suddenly turned from blue to red.

You have reached a depth of 3,900 miles.

Your speed is five miles per second.

You are passing through the center of the Earth.

Deng Yang's voice came through Huabei's earphones once again. 'Your current speed would be fast enough to carry you into orbit, but your location at the center of the planet means that the world is revolving around you. The continents and oceans of Earth, its cities and people, are all orbiting you.'

Bathed in the solemn red light, another piece of music came to Huabei, this time a magnificent symphony. He was traveling at first cosmic velocity in a tunnel through the center of the Earth – a tunnel whose glowing, red walls gave Huabei the impression that the Earth itself was alive and that he was floating through one of its veins. His heart raced.

Deng Yang continued: 'New-solid-state material is an excellent insulator, but the air around you is still above 2,700 degrees. Your suit's cooling system is running at full power.'

After about ten seconds, the red light on the wall suddenly turned back to a tranquil blue.

You have passed through the center of the Earth and begun your ascent and deceleration.

You have ascended three miles.

Your speed is 4.8 miles per second.

You are in the Earth's solid core.

The blue light soothed Huabei. He had already gotten used to weightlessness, and he slowly turned his body so that he was moving head-first. In this position, he felt he was rising rather than falling. 'Wasn't there a third disaster?' he asked.

'The Lost Bolt Disaster happened five years ago, after the Antarctic Doorstep Project had been completed and officially opened for use. Core trains traveled through the tunnel nonstop. The cars of the trains were cylindrical, twenty-seven feet in diameter and 165 feet long; a single train was made up of as many as two hundred cars that could carry twetnty-two thousand tons of freight or nearly ten-thousand passengers. A one-way trip through the center of the Earth took only forty-two minutes and required no resources besides gravity.

'At the Mohe Station, a repair technician carelessly dropped a bolt into the tunnel. It was no thicker than five inches in diameter, but it was made of a new material that is able to absorb electromagnetic waves, so the radar safety system was unable to detect it. The bolt fell down the tunnel, through the Earth, and arrived at the Antarctic Station, where it began to fall again. Near the center of the Earth, it struck a core train ascending to Antarctica. The speed of the bolt relative to the train was close to ten miles per second; its kinetic energy made it like a missile. It penetrated the first two cars of the train, vaporizing everything in its path, and the explosion sent the rest of the train off course. It crashed into the wall of the tunnel at five miles per second, tearing it to shreds in an instant.

'Debris from the crash oscillated back and forth in the tunnel. Some pieces rose as high as the surface, but most of the debris had lost momentum in the crash and simply swung around near the core.

It took a month to clean the shards out the tunnel. We were unable to recover the bodies of the three thousand passengers on board – they had been incinerated in the heat of the core.'

You have ascended 1,360 miles from the center of the Earth.

Your speed is 4.6 miles per second.

You have re-entered the Earth's liquid core.

'The biggest disaster of all was the Project itself. The Antarctic Doorstep Project may have been an unprecedented feat of engineering, but from an economic standpoint, it was incredibly stupid. People still can't figure out how such a patently foolish project could ever have made it off the drawing board. Shen Yuan's reckless ambition certainly played a role, but the true reason it succeeded was people's frenzied desire for new lands to claim and their blind worship of technology. The economic benefits of the Project dried up on the day it was completed. It was true that the tunnel enabled extremely fast travel through the Earth and consumed almost no resources – people used to say 'just toss it in the tunnel' or 'just hop in the tunnel'. But it had been a huge investment, and the transport fees on core trains were astronomical. Despite its speed, the high cost of using the tunnel eliminated its competitive advantage over traditional modes of transport.'

'Humanity's Antarctic dream was soon shattered. The last pristine land on Earth was overexploited and destroyed in a swarm of industry, and Antarctica became like everywhere else: used up, covered in refuse – a landfill. The ozone layer over Antarctica was completely destroyed, which affected the whole world. Even in the Northern hemisphere, strong UV rays made it necessary for people to cover their skin outdoors. The melting of the Antarctic ice sheet accelerated sharply, causing a dramatic rise in sea levels across the globe. In the midst of these crises, human reason once again prevailed. Member States of the United Nations unanimously signed a new Antarctic Treaty that mandated an immediate, complete withdrawal from the continent. It is once again a wilderness, and we expect its environment to recover gradually. The treaty caused a sudden, sharp drop in demand for shipping to Antarctica, and after the Lost Bolt Disaster, all core train operations ceased. The tunnel has now been closed for eight years, but its effects on the economy still linger. Thousands of people who had bought stock in the Antarctic Doorstep Company lost everything, which caused serious social unrest. The tunnel was a black hole for investors, and it brought the country's economy to the brink of collapse. Even today, we are still mired in the troubles and pain it caused.

'That is the story of the Antarctic Doorstep Project.'

As Huabei's speed decreased, the blur of blue light on the wall of the tunnel began to flicker, and soon he was again able to distinguish each ring as it passed. In each direction, the lights appeared once again as the dense, concentric rings of a target.

You have reached a height of 2,980 miles above the Earth's core.

Your speed is 3.1 miles per second.

You are passing through the Earth's mesosphere.

7

THE DEATH OF SHEN YUAN

'What became of my son?' asked Huabei.

'After the tunnel was closed, Shen Yuan stayed on as part of a skeleton crew at the Mohe Station. I called him on the phone one day; he said he was 'with his daughter' and hung up. I didn't learn the truth behind those cryptic words until several years later. It nearly defies description. He spent all his time in an airtight suit, falling back and forth through the tunnel. He slept in the tunnel. He only returned to the station to eat and recharge his suit. He passed through the Earth roughly thirty-two times each day. Day after day, year after year, he traveled from Mohe to the Antarctic Peninsula and back again, in a simple harmonic wave with a cycle of eighty-four minutes and an amplitude of 7,830 miles.'

> You have ascended 3,730 miles from the center of the Earth.
>
> Your speed is 1.5 miles per second.
>
> You are passing through the Earth's asthenosphere.

'No one knows exactly what Shen Yuan did during his endless fall. According to his colleagues, each time he passed through the center of the Earth, he used a neutrino communicator to hail his daughter. He often had long conversations with her as he fell – one-sided, of course. But Shen Jing, trapped in the *Sunset 6* as it drifted in the nickel-iron flow of the Earth's core, was probably able to hear him.

'He subjected his body to long periods of weightlessness, interrupted by two or three exposures each day to the normal force of Earth's gravity when he returned to the station to eat and recharge his suit. He was an old man, and the constant change in gravity weakened his heart. His heart gave out as he fell. No one noticed. His body continued to travel through the tunnel for two days until his sealed suit exhausted its charge. The tunnel was his crematorium. His final pass through the center of the Earth burned his body to ashes. I believe your son would have been satisfied with this fate.'

'That will be my fate as well, won't it?' asked Huabei, calmly.

'It should satisfy you, too. You saw everything you wanted to see before your death. We had originally planned to throw you into the tunnel without a suit, but in the end, we decided that you should get a thorough look at the thing your son made.'

'Yes, I am satisfied. This life has been enough. I am sincerely grateful to each of you.'

There was no answer. The hum of Huabei's headphones abruptly disappeared as his executioners, standing on the other side of the world, cut off communications.

Huabei looked up. The concentric rings of light above him were quite sparse now. It took two or three seconds to pass each one, and the interval was getting longer. A beeping sound came through his headphones, and words appeared on his visor:

> You have reached a height of 3,850 miles above the Earth's core.
>
> Your speed is 0.9 miles per second.
>
> You have passed through the Mohorovičić Discontinuity, and are entering the Earth's crust.
>
> Attention!
>
> You are approaching the Antarctic Terminal.

At the center of the rings above him there was only emptiness, which grew as he approached the final ring of blue light. He passed it and rose slowly towards a bridge spanning the mouth of the tunnel, identical to the bridge on the other end. On the bridge stood several people in airtight suits. As he ascended through the mouth of the tunnel, they reached out to grab him and pulled him up onto the bridge.

The interior of the Antarctic station was also dark, lit only from below by the glow of the blue rings. Huabei looked up and saw a huge cylindrical object suspended above him. Its diameter was slightly smaller than that of the tunnel. He walked along the bridge to the rim of the tunnel and looked up again. There was a whole row of cylinders hanging above the mouth of the tunnel. He counted four of them and guessed that there were more in the darkness above those. This, he knew, had to be the decommissioned core train.

8

ANTARCTICA

Half an hour later, Huabei walked out of the tunnel's Antarctic Terminal station, accompanied by the police officers who had saved his life. He stood on a snowless expanse of Antarctic plain. There was an abandoned city in the distance. The sun hung low over the horizon, casting its weak rays over the vast and otherwise uninhabited continent. The air here was cleaner than on the other side of the Earth, and no respirator was necessary.

A policemen told Huabei that they were members of a small police force left to guard the empty city. They had rushed to the station after receiving an alert from Doctor Guo. The tunnel's mouth was sealed when they arrived, so they immediately contacted the tunnel's management department and lodged an urgent request to remove the cover. Huabei was approaching the mouth of the tunnel just as it opened, and they saw him rise towards them in the blue light, like something floating up from the depths of the ocean. If it had opened a few seconds later, Huabei would have certainly perished. The tunnel's seal would have blocked his ascent, and he would have begun falling again towards the Northern hemisphere. His suit would have run out of power before he reached the core, and he would have been burned to ashes, just as his son was.

'Deng Yang and his co-conspirators have been arrested and will be charged with attempted murder. However . . .' The police officer paused and glared at Huabei. 'I understand what drove them.'

Huabei was still dizzy from the weightlessness of his fall. He looked off towards the sun at the edge of the sky and sighed. 'This life has been enough,' he said.

'If that's how you feel, you'll find it easier to accept your fate,' said another officer.

'My fate?' Huabei's senses came back to him and he turned his head to face the second officer.

'You can't live in these times or this sort of thing will happen again. Fortunately for you, the government has a 'temporal emigration program' aimed at reducing population pressures on the environment. Under this program, a portion of the population is obliged to enter cryogenic hibernation, to be awoken at some future date. We have already received our orders – you will be a temporal emigrant. I don't know how long it will be until you are awoken.'

It took Huabei a long time to fully comprehend what he had been told. Once he did, he gave the police officer a deep bow. 'Thank you. How am I always so lucky?'

'Lucky?' asked the officer, clearly confused. 'Temporal emigrants from this era will have a hard enough time adapting to the society of the future. There is no hope for someone from the past like you!'

A faint smile crossed Huabei's face. 'That doesn't matter. What matters is that I will have the chance to see the Earth Tunnel restored to glory!'

The policemen scoffed. 'I wouldn't bet on it. The Project was a catastrophe! It will stand forever as nothing more than a monument to you and your son's failure.'

'Ha ha ha ha!' Huabei burst into laughter. He was still weak from weightlessness and could barely stand straight, but his spirit soared. 'The Great Wall and the Pyramids were utter failures, too. The Mongols invaded China from the north, and the pharoah's mummy never came back to life. But is that how we think of these colossal projects now? No, we think of them as glorious monuments to the human spirit!' He pointed behind him, at the towering cylinder of the tunnel station. 'This tunnel is a Great Wall through the center of the Earth itself, and here you are at its edge, weeping like Lady Meng Jiang! How pitiful! Ha ha ha ha!'

Huabei opened his arms to embrace the cold Antarctic wind. 'Yuan, our lives were enough,' he said happily.

EPILOGUE

The next time Huabei awoke half a century had passed. His experience was almost identical to the last time: he was taken by a group of people to a car, which drove to the tunnel's Mohe Terminal station. He was put into an airtight suit – for some reason, much heavier than the one he had worn 50 years before – and was thrown, once again, into the tunnel. After fifty years, the tunnel looked much the same as it did before – a bottomless hole, lit by an endless series of blue, ring-shaped lights on its walls.

This time, however, someone had jumped in with him. She was young and beautiful, and she introduced herself as his tour guide.

'A tour guide? So my prediction was right – the tunnel has become a wonder of the world, like the Great Wall or the Pyramids!' Huabei said excitedly as he fell.

'No, not like those places. The tunnel has become . . .' She was holding Huabei's hand, to ensure that they fell at the same speed, and her speech trailed off as she carefully adjusted her grip.

'What has it become?'

'The World Cannon!'

'What?' Huabei looked again at the walls of the tunnel as they flew by, trying to understand.

The tour guide explained, 'After you entered hibernation, the environment became even worse. Pollution and the destruction of the ozone layer killed what little vegetation remained on Earth. Breathable air became a commodity. At the time, we were left with one option if we wanted to save the Earth: shut down all heavy energy industries.'

'That may help the environment, but it would also mean the end of civilization,' Huabei interrupted.

'Many people were willing to accept that as a side effect, given the size of the problem. However, some continued looking for another way out. The most feasible alternative was to move all the planet's industrial operations to the moon and to outer space.'

'You built a space elevator?'

'No, though we tried. It turned out to be even harder than digging the Earth Tunnel.'

'Did you invent anti-gravity spacecraft?'

'No. In fact, that has been proven to be theoretically impossible.'

'Nuclear-powered rockets?'

'Those we have, but they're not much cheaper to operate than traditional rockets. Using them to move all industry to space would have been an economic disaster of the same scale that this tunnel was.'

'So you weren't able to move anything to space in the end.' Huabei smiled grimly. 'Has the world entered . . . a post-human age?'

The guide did not respond. Together they fell in silence into the abyss as the rings of light flying past them grew denser and blended together into a single, luminescent surface on the wall of the tunnel. Ten minutes later, the light turned red, and they wordlessly passed through the center of the Earth at five miles per second. The walls soon turned blue again, and Huabei's guide deftly turned her body 180 degrees, so that she ascended head-first. Huabei followed her motion clumsily.

'Oh!' Huabei shouted in surprise. The display in the upper right corner of his visor said their current speed was 5.3 miles per second.

They had passed the center of the Earth, but they were still accelerating.

Something else alarmed Huabei: he felt the force of gravity. The process of falling through the Earth was supposed to take place entirely in weightlessness, but he distinctly felt his own weight. His scientist's intuition told him that what he felt was not in fact gravity – it was thrust. Some force was thrusting them forward and causing them to continue to accelerate, even as gravity should have been slowing them down.

'I take it you've read *From the Earth to the Moon*, by Jules Verne?' asked the guide suddenly.

'When I was young. It was the dumbest book I'd ever read,' Huabei answered, absent-mindedly. His attention was on his surroundings as he tried to figure out what strange force was acting on them.

'It's not dumb at all. To implement large-scale, fast transportation into space, a cannon is ideal.'

'Unless the speed of the launch squashes you flat.'

'The reason you'd get squashed would be if you accelerated too quickly, and you'd only accelerate too quickly if the barrel of the cannon was too short. With a long enough barrel, the payload could accelerate gently, just as we are right now.'

'So we're in Verne's cannon?'

'As I said, it's called the World Cannon.'

Huabei looked up at the blue tunnel and tried to imagine it as the barrel of a cannon. At this speed, the wall appeared as a single, uninterrupted object, so he had no sense of movement. He felt as if they were motionless, hovering in a glowing, blue tube.

'In your fourth year of hibernation, we developed a novel type of new-solid-state material. It possesses all the properties of the previous material, but it is also an excellent conductor. A thick wire made of this material is wrapped around the exterior of the Antarctic half of the tunnel, making it function as a four-thousand-mile-long electromagnetic coil.

'What powers the coil?'

'There is a strong electric current in the core of the Earth. It's what produces the Earth's magnetic field. We used core ships to assemble more than one hundred thousand-mile-long loops of conductive solid-state wire in the core. These loops collect the current in the core and transfer it to the coil around the tunnel, filling the tunnel with a powerful electromagnetic field. In the shoulders and midsections of our suits are two superconducting coils that produce the opposite magnetic field. That's how we achieve thrust.'

Continuing to accelerate, they quickly approached the end of the tunnel. As they did, the walls again began to glow red.

'Our speed is 9.3 miles per second, well above escape velocity. We're about to be fired from the World Cannon!'

The towering Core Train Station above had long been dismantled, replaced with nothing but a sealed gate, covering a simple opening right up into the sky.

A recorded message played over their headphones:

> Attention passengers: the World Cannon is about to commence today's forty-third launch. Please put on your protective eyewear and insert your earplugs. Failure to do so will cause permanent damage to your eyesight and hearing.

Ten seconds later, the sealed mouth of the tunnel slid open loudly, revealing its thirty-foot-wide mouth. Air roared into the vacuum of the tunnel's interior. With a noise like thunder, a long tongue of flame leapt out of the mouth of the tunnel, so bright that it outshone the weak, low-hanging Antarctic sun. Instantly, the sealed gate slid closed again, the tunnel's air pumps roaring to life. Soon they had removed all the air that had rushed into the tunnel during the three seconds that the gate had been open; then the cannon was ready for the next launch.

People looked up to see two shooting stars, trailing tails of fire as they streaked upwards and disappeared into the deep blue Antarctic sky.

Huabei looked back to see the ground receding beneath his feet. He recognized the city next to the tunnel's terminal, which soon appeared only as big as a basketball court. He saw the color of the sky quickly transitioning from blue to black, as if a screen were being dimmed. Turning his gaze below, he saw the long arc of the Antarctic Peninsula surrounded by ocean. A long tail of flame trailed behind him, emanating from the red-hot surface of his suit. He was enveloped in a thin cloak of fire.

He looked over at his guide, some thirty feet away. She was also wrapped in flames, like some fantastic creature of living fire. The air resistance felt like a giant hand pressing relentlessly down on his head and shoulders. As the sky grew darker, this giant hand was conquered by another, more powerful, force and the pressure subsided. Looking down, he saw all of Antarctica, noticing with joy that it was white once again. In the distance, the curvature of the Earth became clear. The sun appeared to move upwards from the arc of the horizon, scattering its resplendent light throughout the planet's thin atmosphere. Once more, Huabei looked up and saw the constellations spread out above him. He had never seen the stars shine so brightly.

The fire surrounding his body was extinguished as they shot out of the atmosphere. They were now floating through the vast silence of space.

Huabei felt as light as a feather. His sealed suit, or spacesuit, was much thinner than before, as its top layer of heat-dispersing material had burned off in the friction of the atmosphere. Their communications had been interrupted by atmospheric disturbance, but now they were back online. Huabei's guide spoke: 'Atmospheric resistance slowed us down a bit, but we are still traveling at escape velocity. We're leaving the Earth. Look over there.'

She pointed beneath them at the Antarctic Peninsula, which was now tiny. Huabei saw a flash of light from the spot where the tunnel emerged, and a shooting star shot upwards into the sky, trailing fire behind it. As it exited the atmosphere, the fire dimmed and went out.

'That was a spaceship leaving the World Cannon. It's going to pick us up. At every moment, five or six 'payloads' are traveling through the barrel of the cannon, firing off at eight-to-ten minute intervals, so getting into space is as fast and easy as taking the subway. It fired even more rapidly when the great industrial migration began twenty years ago. There were often more than twenty ships accelerating through the barrel at a time, with two- or three-minute intervals between shots. Back then, the spaceships shot into the sky like a never-ending shower of meteors. The job was enormous, but humanity's fate hung in the balance. It was truly magnificent!'

Huabei spotted numerous streaking stars, easy to see against the stillness of the stars in the background, and Huabei realized that they were in fact objects in orbit around the Earth. Squinting, he was able to make out some of their shapes: some were ring-shaped, others were circular and some appeared to be irregular assemblies of many different shapes. They looked like jewels against the deep blackness of space.

'That one is Baoshan Iron & Steel Company,' said Huabei's guide, pointing towards a glowing, ring-shaped object. She pointed out several other bright objects. 'Those are Sinopec which, of course, no longer handles oil. Those cylindrical ones are the European Metallurgy Association. Over there are solar power stations – they collect solar energy and send it to the surface using microwaves. The shining parts are just their control centers; their panels and transmission arrays are invisible from here.'

Huabei was enraptured by the sight. He looked down at the lush, blue orb of Earth, and tears flowed from his eyes. His heart went out to everyone, living or dead, who had participated in the Antarctic Doorstep Project. He wished that all of them could see this. And one of them especially – a certain young woman, who would remain forever young in his heart.

'Did they find my granddaughter?' he asked.

'No. We don't have the technology to conduct long-range scans in the core. The search area is vast, and no one knows where the iron-nickel flow has carried her.'

'Can we send this image to the core as a neutrino transmission?'

'We already are. I believe she can see it all.'

MIRROR

As research delves deeper, humanity is discovering that quantum effects are nothing more than surface ripples in the ocean of existence, shadows of the disturbances arising from the deeper laws governing the workings of matter. With these laws beginning to reveal themselves, quantum mechanics' ever-shifting picture of reality is once again stabilizing, deterministic variables once again replacing probabilities. In this new model of the universe, the chains of causality that were thought eliminated have surfaced once more, and clearer than before.

Pursuit

In the office were the flags of China and the CCP. There were also two men, one on either side of the broad desk.

'I know you're very busy, sir, but I must report this. I've honestly never seen anything like it,' said the man in front of the desk. He wore the uniform of a police superintendent second class. He was near fifty, but he stood ramrod-straight, and the lines of his face were hard and vigorous.

'I know the weight of that last sentence coming from you, Xufeng, veteran investigator of thirty years.' The Senior Official looked at the red and blue pencil slowly twirling between his fingers as he spoke, as if all his attention were focused on assessing the merit of its sharpening. He tucked away his gaze like this much of the time. In the years Chen Xufeng had known him, the Senior Official had looked him in the eyes no more than three times. Each time had come at a turning point in Chen's life.

'Every time we take action, the target escapes one step ahead of us. They know what we're going to do.'

'Surely you've seen similar things before,' the Senior Official said.

'If it were simply that, it wouldn't be a big deal, of course. We considered the possibility of an inside job right off.'

'Knowing your subordinates, I find that rather improbable.'

'We found that out for ourselves,' Chen said. 'Like you instructed, we've reduced the participants in this case as much as possible. There are only four people in the task force, and only two know the full story. But just in case, I planned to call a meeting of all the members and question them one by one. I told Chenbing to handle it – you know him, the one from the Eleventh Department, very reliable, took care of the business with Song Cheng – and that's when it happened.

'Don't take this for a joke, sir. What I'm going to say next is the honest truth.' Chen Xufeng laughed a little, as if embarrassed by his own defensiveness. 'Right then, they called. Our target called me on the phone! I heard them say on my cell phone, *You don't need this meeting, there's no traitor among you.* Less than thirty seconds after I told Chenbing I wanted to call a meeting!'

The Senior Official's pencil stilled between his fingers.

'You might be thinking that we were bugged, but that's impossible. I chose the location for the conversation at random to be the middle of a government agency auditorium while it was being used for chorus rehearsals for National Day. We had to talk right into each other's ears to hear.

'And similar funny business kept happening after that. They called us eight times in total, each time about things we had just said or done. The scariest part is, not only do they hear everything, they see everything. One time, Chenbing decided to search the target's parents' home. He and the other task force member were just standing up, not even out of the department office, when they got the target's call. *You guys have the wrong search warrant,* they told them. *My parents are careful people. They might think you guys are frauds.* Chenbing took out the warrant to check, and sir, he really had taken the wrong one.'

The Senior Official set the pencil lightly on his desk, waiting in silence for Chen Xufeng to continue, but the latter seemed to have run out of steam. The Senior Official took out a cigarette. Chen Xufeng hurriedly patted at his coat pockets for a lighter, but couldn't find one.

One of the two phones on the desk began to ring.

Chen Xufeng swept his gaze over the caller ID. 'It's them,' he said quietly.

Unperturbed, the Senior Official motioned at him. Chen pressed the speaker button. A voice immediately sounded, worn and very young. 'Your lighter is in the briefcase.'

Chen Xufeng glanced at the Senior Official, then began to rummage through the briefcase on the desk. He couldn't find anything at first.

'It's wedged in a document, the one on urban household registration reform.'

Chen Xufeng took out the document. The lighter fell onto the desk with a clatter.

'That's one fine lighter there. French-made S. T. Dupont brand, solid palladium-gold alloy, thirty diamonds set in each side, worth . . . let me look it up . . . 39,960 yuan.'

The Senior Official didn't move, but Chen Xufeng raised his head to study the office. This wasn't the Senior Official's personal office; rather, it had been selected at random from the rooms in this office building.

The target continued the demonstration of their powers. 'Senior Official, there are five cigarettes left in your box of Chunghwas. There's only one Mevacor cholesterol tablet left in your coat pocket – better have your secretary get some more.'

Chen Xufeng picked up the box of cigarettes on the desk; the Senior Official took out the blister pack of pills from his pocket. The target was correct on both counts.

'Stop coming after me. I'm in a tricky situation just like you. I'm not sure what to do now,' the target continued.

'Can we discuss this in person?' asked the Senior Official.

'Believe me, it would be a disaster for both sides.' With that, the phone went dead.

Chen Xufeng exhaled. Now he had the proof to back up his story – the thought of disbelief from the Senior Official unsettled him more than his opponent's antics. 'It's like seeing a ghost,' he said, shaking his head.

'I don't believe in ghosts, but I do see danger,' said the Senior Official. For the fourth time in his life, Chen Xufeng saw that pair of eyes bore into his.

The Inmate and the Pursued

In the No. 2 Detention Center at the city outskirts, Song Cheng walked under escort into the cell. There were already six other prisoners inside, mostly other inmates serving extended terms.

Cold looks greeted Song Cheng from all directions. Once the guard left, shutting the door behind him, a small, thin man came up.

'Hey, you, Pig Grease!' he yelled. Seeing Song Cheng's confusion, he continued, 'The law of the land here ranks us Big Grease, Second Grease, Third Grease . . . Pig Grease at the bottom, that's you. Hey, don't think we're taking advantage of the latecomer.' He pointed his thumb at a heavily bearded man leaning in the corner. 'Brother Bao's only been here three days, and he's already Big Grease. Trash like you may have held a pretty government rank before, but here you're lowest of the low!' He turned toward the other man and asked respectfully, 'How will you receive him, Brother Bao?'

'Stereo sound,' came the careless reply.

Two other inmates sprang up from the bunks and grabbed Song Cheng by the ankles, dangling him upside down. They held him over the toilet and slowly lowered him until his head was largely inside.

'Sing a song,' Skinny Guy commanded. 'That's what stereo sound means. Give us a comrade song like 'Left Hand, Right Hand'!'

Song Cheng didn't sing. The inmates let go, and his head pitched all the way into the toilet.

Struggling, Song Cheng pulled his head out. He immediately began to vomit. Now he realized that the story designed by those who had framed him would make him the target of all his fellow inmates' contempt.

The delighted prisoners around him suddenly scattered and dashed back to their bunks. The door opened; the police guard from earlier came in. He looked with disgust at Song Cheng, still crouched in front of the toilet. 'Wash off your head at the tap. You have a visitor.'

Once Song Cheng rinsed off, he followed the guard into a spacious office where his visitor awaited. He was very young, thin-faced with messy hair and thick glasses. He carried an enormous briefcase.

Song Cheng sat down coldly without looking at the visitor. He had been permitted a visit at this time, and here, not in a visitation room with a glass partition; from that, Song Cheng had a good guess as to who sent him. But the first words out of his visitor's mouth made Song lift his head in surprise.

'My name's Bai Bing. I'm an engineer at the Center for Meteorological Modeling. They're coming after me for the same reason they came after you.'

Song Cheng looked at the visitor. His tone of voice seemed odd: this was a subject that should have been discussed in whispers, but Bai Bing spoke at a normal volume, as if he wasn't talking about anything that needed hiding.

Bai Bing seemed to have noticed his confusion. 'I called the Senior Official two hours ago. He wanted to talk face-to-face with me, but I turned him down. After that, they got on my trail, followed me all the way to the detention center doors. They haven't seized me because they're curious about our meeting. They want to know what I'll tell you. They're listening in to our conversation right now.'

Song Cheng shifted his gaze from Bai Bing to the ceiling. He found it hard to trust this person, and regardless, he wasn't interested in the matter. The law might have spared him the death penalty, but it had sentenced and executed his spirit all the same. His heart was dead. He could no longer muster interest in anything.

'I know the truth, all of it,' Bai Bing said.

A smirk flickered at the corner of Song Cheng's mouth. *No one knows the truth but them,* but he didn't bother to say that out loud.

'You began working for the provincial-level Commission for Discipline Inspection seven years ago. You were promoted to this rank just last year.'

Song Cheng remained silent. He was angry now. Bai Bing's words had dragged him back into the memories he'd worked so hard to escape.

The Big Case

At the beginning of the century, the Zhengzhou Municipal Government began a policy of setting aside a number of deputy-level positions for holders of Ph.D.s. Many other cities followed its example, and later, provincial governments began to adopt the same practice, even removing graduation-year requirements and offering higher starting positions. It was an excellent way to demonstrate the recruiters' magnanimity and vision to the world, but in reality, the attractive concept amounted to little more than political record engineering. The recruiters were farsighted indeed – they knew perfectly well that these book-smart, well-educated young people lacked any sort of political experience. When they entered the unfamiliar and vicious political sphere, they found themselves swallowed whole in labyrinthine bureaucracy, unable to gain any foothold. The whole business was no big loss in job vacancies, while substantially padding the recruiters' political résumés.

An opportunity like this led Song Cheng, already a law professor at the time, to leave his peaceful campus study for the world of politics. His peers who chose the same road didn't last a year before they left in utter despair, beaten men and women, their only achievement being the destruction of their dreams. But Song Cheng was an exception. He not only stayed in politics, but did exceptionally well.

The credit belonged to two people. One was his college classmate Lu Wenming. In their last year as undergraduates, he'd placed in the civil service even as Song Cheng tested into grad school. With his advantageous family background and his own dedicated effort, ten years later he'd become the youngest provincial secretary of discipline inspection in the nation, head of the organization in charge of maintaining discipline within the provincial-level Party. He was the one who'd advised Song Cheng to give up his books for governance.

When the simple scholar first began, Lu didn't lead him by the hand so much as he toddled him along by the feet, hand-placing Song's every step as he taught him how to walk. He'd steered Song Cheng around traps and treachery that the latter could never have spotted himself, allowing him to progress up the road that had led to today. The other person he should thank was the Senior Official . . . on that thought, Song Cheng's heart gave a spasm.

'You have to admit, you chose this for yourself. You can't say they didn't give you a way out.'

Song Cheng nodded. Yes, they'd given him a way out, a boulevard with his name in lights at that.

Bai Bing continued, 'The Senior Official met with you a few months ago. I'm sure you remember it well. It was in a villa out in the exurbs, by the Yang River. The Senior Official doesn't normally see outsiders there.

'Once you were out of the car, you found him waiting for you at the gate, a very high honor. He clasped your hand warmly and led you into the drawing room.

'The décor would've given off a first impression of unassuming simplicity, but you'd be wrong there. That aged-looking mahogany furniture is worth millions. The one plain scroll painting hanging on the wall looks even older, and there's insect damage if you look closely, but that's *Dangheqizi* by the Ming Dynasty painter Wu Bin, bought at a Christie's auction in Hong Kong for eight million HKD. And the cup of tea the Senior Official personally steeped for you? The leaves were ranked five stars at the International Tea Competition. It goes for nine hundred thousand yuan per half kilo.'

Song Cheng really could recall the tea Bai Bing spoke of. The liquid had sparkled the green of a jewel, a few delicate leaves drifting in its clarity like the languid notes from a mountain saint's zither. . . . He even recalled how he'd felt: *If only the outside world could be this lovely and pure.* The tarp of apathy was torn from Song Cheng's stifled thoughts, his blurred mind snapping back into focus. He stared at Bai Bing, eyes wide with shock.

How could he know all this? The whole affair had been dispatched to the deepest oubliettes, a secret among secrets. No more than four people in all the world knew, and that was counting himself.

'Who are you?!' He opened his mouth for the first time.

Bai Bing smiled. 'I introduced myself earlier. I'm an ordinary person. But I'll tell you straight off, not only do I know a lot, I know everything, or at least have the means to know everything. That's why they want to get rid of me like they got rid of you.'

Bai Bing continued his account. 'The Senior Official sat close, one hand on your shoulder. That benevolent gaze he turned on you would have moved anyone from the junior ranks. From what I know (and remember, I know everything), he'd never shown anyone else the same intimacy. He told you, *Don't worry, young man, we're all comrades here. Whatever the matter, just speak honestly and trust that you'll get honesty in return. We can always come to a solution . . . you have ideas, you're capable, you have a sense of duty and a sense of mission. Those last two in particular are as precious as an oasis in a desert among young cadres nowadays. This is why I think so highly of you. In you, I see the reflection of what I was once like.*

'I should mention that the Senior Official may have been telling the truth. Your official work didn't give you many chances to interact with him, but quite a few times, you'd run into him in the hallways of the government building or coming out of a meeting, and he'd always be the one to come up to you to chat. He very rarely did that with lower-ranking officials, especially the younger ones. People took notice. He might not have said anything to help you at organizational meetings, but those gestures did a lot for your career.'

Song Cheng nodded again. He'd known all this, and had been immensely grateful. All that time, Song had wanted the opportunity to repay him.

'Then the Senior Official raised his hand and gestured behind him. Immediately, someone entered and quietly set a big stack of documents and materials on the table. You must have noticed that he wasn't the Senior Official's normal secretary.

'The Senior Official passed a hand over the documents and said, *The project you just completed fully demonstrates those priceless assets of yours. It required such an immense and difficult investigation to collect evidence, but these documents are ample, detailed, and reliable, the conclusions drawn profound. It's hard to believe you did it all in half a year. It would be the Party's great fortune to have more outstanding Discipline Inspection officials like you.* . . . I don't need to tell you how you felt at that moment, I think.'

Of course he didn't. Song Cheng had never been so horrified in his life. That stack of documents first sent him shaking as if electrocuted, then froze him into stone.

Bai Bing continued: 'It all started with the investigation into the illegal apportionment of state-owned land you undertook on behalf of the Central Commission, yes . . .

'I recall that when you were a child, you and two of your friends went exploring in a cave, called Old Man Cavern by the locals. The entrance was only half a meter high, and you had to crouch down to enter. But inside was an enormous, dark vault, its ceiling too high for your flashlights to reach. All you could see were endless bats swishing past the beams of light. Every little sound provoked a rumbling echo from the distance. The dank cold seeped into your bones. . . . It's a lively metaphor for the investigation: walking along, following that seemingly run-of-the-mill trail of clues, only to find yourself led toward places that made you afraid to believe your own eyes. As you deepened your investigation, a grand network of corruption spanning the entire province unfolded before you, and every strand of the web led in one direction, to one person. And now, the top-secret Discipline Inspection report you'd prepared for the Central Commission was in his hands! In this investigation, you'd considered all sorts of worst-case scenarios, but you never dreamed of the one that you faced now. You were thrown into total panic. You stammered, *H-how did this end up in your hands, sir?* The Senior Official smiled indulgently and lifted his hand to gesture lightly again. You immediately got your answer: The secretary of discipline inspection, Lu Wenming, walked into the room.

'You stood and glared at Lu Wenming. *How – how could you do this? How could you go against our organization's rules and principles like this?* Lu Wenming cut you off with a wave of his hand and asked in the same furious tone of voice as you, *How could you go ahead with something like this without telling me?*

'*I've taken over your duties as secretary for the year you're undergoing training at the Central Party School,* you shot back. *Of course I couldn't tell you, it was against the rules of the organization!*

'Lu Wenming shook his head sorrowfully, looking as if he wanted to weep in despair. *If I hadn't caught this report in time . . . can you even imagine the consequences? Song Cheng, your fatal flaw is that insistence on dividing the world into black and white, when reality is nothing more than gray!*'

Song Cheng exhaled long and slow. He remembered how he'd stared dumbly at his classmate, unable to believe that he could say something like that. He'd never revealed thoughts in that vein before. Was the hatred of internal corruption he'd shown in their many late-night conversations, the steadfast courage he displayed as they tackled sensitive cases that drew pressure from all directions, the deeply personal concern for the Party and the nation he'd expressed at so many dawns, after grueling all-nighters at work – was all that nothing but pretense?

'It's not that Lu Wenming was lying before. It's more that he never delved *that* deeply into his soul in front of you. He's like that famous dessert, Baked Alaska, flash-cooked ice cream. The hot parts and the cold parts are both real. But the Senior Official didn't look at Lu Wenming. Instead, he slammed a hand onto the table. *What gray? Wenming, I really can't stand this side of you! What Song Cheng did was outstanding, faultless. In that respect he's better than you!* He turned to you and said, *Young man, you did exactly as you should have done. A person, especially a young person, is gone forever if they lose that faith and sense of mission. I look down on people like that.*'

The part that had struck Song Cheng the deepest was that, although he and Lu Wenming were the same age, the Senior Official only called him 'young,' and emphasized it repeatedly at that. The unspoken implication was clear: *With me as an opponent, you're still nothing but a child.* In the present, Song Cheng could only concede that he was right.

'The Senior Official continued on. *Nonetheless, young man, we still need to mature a little. Let's take an example from your report. There really are problems with the Hengyu Aluminum Electrolysis Base, and they're even worse than you discovered in your investigations. Not only are domestic officials implicated, foreign investors have collaborated with them in serious legal trespasses. Once the matter is dealt with, the foreigners will withdraw their investments. The largest aluminum-electrolysis enterprise in the country will be put out of business. Tongshan Bauxite Mines, which provides the aluminum ore for Hengyu, will be in deep trouble too. Next comes the Chenglin nuclear power plant. It was built too big due to the energy crisis the last few years, and with the severe domestic overproduction of electricity now, most of this brand-new power plant's output goes to the aluminum-electrolysis base. Once Hengyu collapses, Chenglin Nuclear Facility will face bankruptcy as well. And then Zhaoxikou Chemical Plant, which provides the enriched uranium for Chenglin, will be in trouble. . . . With that, nearly seventy billion yuan in government investment will be gone without a trace, and thirty to forty thousand people will lose their jobs. These corporations are all located within the provincial capital's outskirts – this vital city will be instantly thrown into turmoil. . . . And the Hengyu issue I went into is only a small part of this investigation. The case implicates one provincial-level official, three sub-provincial-level officials, two hundred and fifteen prefectural-level officials, six hundred and fourteen county-level officials, and countless more in lower ranks. Nearly half of the most successful large-scale enterprises and the most promising investment projects in the province will be impacted in some way. Once the secrets are out, the province's entire economy and political structure will be dead in the water! And we don't know, and have no way of predicting, what even worse consequences might arise from so large-scale and severe a disturbance. The political stability and economic growth our province has worked so hard to attain will be gone without a trace. Is that really to the benefit of the Party and the country? Young man, you can't think like a legal scholar anymore, demanding justice by the law come hell or high water. It's irresponsible. We've progressed along the road of history to today because of balance, arising from the happy medium between various elements. To abandon balance and seek an extreme is a sign of immaturity in politics.*

'When the Senior Official finished, Lu Wenming began. *I'll take care of things with the Central Commission. You just make sure you take over properly from the cadres in that project group. I'll break off training at the Central Party School next week and come back to help you—*

'*Scoundrel!* The Senior Official once again slammed the table. Lu Wenming jumped in fright. *Is that how you took my words? You thought I was trying to get this young man to abandon his principles and duty?! Wenming, you've known me for years. From the depths of your heart, do you really think I have so little sense of Party and principle? When did you become so oily? It saddens me.* Then he turned to you. *Young man, you've done a truly exceptional job so far on your work. You must stand fast in the face of interference and pressure, and hand the corrupt elements their comeuppance! This case hurts the eyes and heart to look upon. You must not spare them, in the name of the people, in the name of justice! Don't let what I just said burden you. I was just reminding you as an old Party member to be careful, to avoid serious consequences beyond your prediction. But there's one thing I know – you must get to the bottom of this terrible corruption case.* The Senior Official took out a piece of paper as he spoke, handing it to you solemnly. *Is this wide enough in scope for you?*'

Song Cheng had known right then that they'd set up a sacrificial altar and were ready to lay out the offerings. He looked at the list of names. It was wide enough in scope, truly enough, enough in both rank and quantity. It would be a corruption case to astound the entire nation, and with the case's triumphant conclusion, Song Cheng would become known throughout the country as an anti-corruption hero, revered by the people as a paragon of justice and virtue.

But he was clear in his heart that this was nothing more than a lizard severing its own tail in a crisis. The lizard would escape; the tail would grow back in no time. He saw the Senior Official watching him, and in that moment he really did think of a lizard, and he shivered. But Song Cheng knew, too, that the Senior Official was afraid, that he'd made him afraid, and it made Song Cheng proud. The pride made him vastly overestimate his own capabilities at that moment, but more vitally, there was that ineffable thing running in the blood of every scholar-idealist. He made the fatal choice.

'You stood and took up the pile of documents with both hands. You said to the Senior Official, *By the Internal Supervision Regulations of the CCP, the secretary of discipline inspection has the authority to conduct inspections upon Party officials of the same rank. According to the rules, sir, these documents can't stay with you. I'll take them.*

'Lu Wenming went to stop you, but the Senior Official gently tugged him back. At the door, you heard your classmate say in a low voice behind you, *You've gone too far, Song Cheng.*

'The Senior Official walked you to your car. As you were about to leave, he took your hand and said slowly, *Come again soon, young man.*'

Only later did Song Cheng fully realize the deeper meaning to his words: *Come again soon. You don't have much time left.*

The Big Bang

'Who the hell are you?' Song Cheng stared at Bai Bing fearfully. How could he know this much? No one could know this much!

'Okay, we'll end the reminiscing here.' Bai Bing cut off his narrative with a wave of his hand. 'Let me go into the whys and wherefores, to clear up the questions you have. Hmm . . . do you know what the big bang is?'

Song Cheng stared blankly at Bai Bing, his brain unable to immediately process Bai's words. At last he managed the response of a normal human and laughed.

'Okay, okay,' Bai Bing said. 'I know that was sudden. But please trust that I'm all there in the head. To go through everything clearly, we really do need to start with the big bang. This. . . . Damn, how do I even explain it to you? Let's return to the big bang. You probably know at least a little.

'Our universe was created in a massive explosion twenty billion years ago. Most people picture the big bang like some ball of fire bursting forth in the darkness of space, but that's incorrect. Before the big bang, there was nothing, not even time and space. There was only a singularity, a single point of undefined size that rapidly expanded to form our universe today. Anything and everything, including us, originated from the singularity's expansion. It is the seed from which all living things grew! The theory behind it all is really deep, and I don't fully understand it myself, but the relevant part is this: With the advancement of physics and the appearance of 'theories of everything' like string theory, physicists are starting to figure out the structure of that singularity and create a mathematical model for it. This is different from the quantum-theory models they had before. If we can determine the fundamental parameters of the singularity before the big bang, we can determine everything in the universe it forms too. An uninterrupted chain of cause and effect running through the entire history of the universe . . .' He sighed. 'Seriously, how am I supposed to explain it all?'

Bai Bing saw Song Cheng shake his head, as if he didn't understand, or as if he didn't even want to keep listening.

Bai Bing said, 'Take my advice and stop thinking about the suffering you've gone through. Honestly, I haven't been much luckier. Like I said, I'm just an ordinary person, but now they're hunting me, and I may end up even worse than you, all because I know everything. You can hold on to the fact that you were martyred for your sense of duty and faith, but I'm . . . I just have really shitty luck. Enough shit luck for eight reincarnations. I've been screwed over even worse than you.'

Song Cheng only continued to look at him, silently, as if to say: *No one can be screwed over worse than me.*

Framed

A week after he met with the Senior Official, Song Cheng was arrested for murder.

To be fair, Song Cheng had already known they'd take extraordinary measures against him. The usual administrative and political methods were too risky to use on someone who knew so much and was already in the process of taking action. But he hadn't imagined his opponent would move so quickly, or strike so viciously.

The victim was a nightclub dancer called LuoLuo, and he'd died in Song Cheng's car. The doors were locked from the outside. Two canisters of propane, the type used to refill cigarette lighters, had been tossed into the car, both slit open. The liquid inside had completely evaporated, and the high concentration of propane vapor in the car had fatally poisoned the victim. When the body was discovered, it was clutching a battered, broken cell phone in one hand, clearly used in an attempt to smash the car windows.

The police produced ample evidence. They had two hours of recordings to prove that Song Cheng had been in most irregular association with LuoLuo for the last three months. The most incriminating piece of evidence was the 110 call LuoLuo had made to the police shortly before his death.

```
LuoLuo
... Hurry. Hurry! I can't open the car doors! I
can't breathe, my head hurts ...
110
Where are you? Can you clarify your situation?!
LuoLuo
... Song ... Song Cheng wants to kill me ...
[End of transmission]
```

Afterward, the police found a short phone-call recording on the victim's cell, preserving an exchange between Song Cheng and the victim.

Song Cheng

Now that we've gone this far, how about you break things off with Xu Xueping?

LuoLuo

Why the need, Brother Song? Me and Sister Xu just have the usual man-woman relations. It won't affect our thing. Hell, it might help.

Song Cheng

It makes me uncomfortable. Don't make me take action.

LuoLuo

Brother Song, let me live my life.

[End of transmission]

This was a highly professional frame-up. Its brilliance lay in that the evidence the police held was just about 100 percent real.

Song Cheng really had been associating with LuoLuo for a while, in secret, and it could indeed be called irregular. The two recordings weren't faked, although the second had been distorted.

Song Cheng met LuoLuo because of Xu Xueping, director general of Changtong Group, who held intimate financial ties to many nodes of the network of corruption and no doubt considerable knowledge of its background and inner workings. Of course, Song Cheng couldn't get any information directly from her, but with LuoLuo he had an in.

LuoLuo didn't provide Song Cheng information out of any inner sense of righteousness. In his eyes, the world was already good for nothing but wiping his ass on. He was in it for revenge.

This hinterland city shrouded in industrial smog and dust might have been ranked at the bottom of the list of similar-sized Chinese cities for average income, but it had some of the most opulent nightclubs in the nation. The young scions of Beijing's political families had to watch their image in the capital city, unable to indulge their desires like the rich without Party affiliations. Instead, they got in their cars every weekend and zipped four or five hours along the highway to this city, spent two days and one night in hedonistic extravagance, and zipped back to Beijing on Sunday night.

LuoLuo's Blue Wave was the highest-end of all the nightclubs. Requesting a song cost at least three thousand yuan, and bottles of Martell and Hennessy priced at thousands each sold multiple cases every night. But Blue Wave's real claim to fame was that it catered exclusively to female guests.

Unlike his fellow dancers, LuoLuo didn't care about how much his clients paid, but how much that money meant to them. A white-collar foreign worker making just two or three hundred thousand yuan a year (rare paupers in Blue Wave) could give him a few hundred and he'd accept. But Sister Xu wasn't one. Her fortune of billions had made waves south of the Yangtze the last few years, and likewise she was smashing the opposition in her expansion northward. But after several months spent together, she'd sent LuoLuo off with a mere four hundred thousand.

It had taken a lot to catch Sister Xu's eye; after she had broken it off, any other dancer would have, in LuoLuo's words, swigged enough champagne to make his liver hurt. But not LuoLuo, who was now filled with hatred for Xu Xueping. The arrival of a high-ranking Discipline Inspection official gave him hope of revenge, and he used his talents to entangle himself with Sister Xu once more. Normally, Xu Xueping was closemouthed even with LuoLuo, but once they had too many drinks or snorted too many lines, it was a different story. LuoLuo knew how to take the initiative, too; in the darkest hours before dawn, while Sister Xu slept soundly beside him, he'd silently climb out of bed and search her briefcase and drawers, snapping pictures of documents that he and Song Cheng needed.

Most of the video recordings the police used to prove Song Cheng's association with LuoLuo had been taken in the main dance hall in Blue Wave. The camera liked to start with the pretty young boys dancing enthusiastically on the stage, before shifting to the expensively dressed female guests gathered in the dim areas, pointing at the stage, now and then smiling confidentially. The final shot always captured Song Cheng and LuoLuo, often sitting in some corner in the back, seeming very intimate as they conversed quietly with heads bent close. As the only male guest in the club, Song Cheng was instantly recognizable . . .

Song Cheng didn't have anything to say to that. Most of the time, he could only find LuoLuo at Blue Wave. The lighting in the dance hall was always dim, but these recordings were high resolution and clear. They could only have been taken with a high-end low-light camera, not the sort of equipment normal people would have. That meant they'd noticed him from the very beginning, showing Song Cheng how very amateur he had been compared to his opponent.

That day, LuoLuo wanted to report his latest findings. When Song Cheng met him at the nightclub, LuoLuo uncharacteristically asked to talk in the car. Once they were done, he'd told Song that he felt unwell. If he went back to the club now, his boss would make him get on stage for sure. He wanted to rest for a while in Song Cheng's car.

Song Cheng had thought that LuoLuo's addiction might have been acting up again, but he didn't have a choice. He could only drive back to his office to take care of the work he hadn't finished during the day, parking in front of the department building with LuoLuo waiting in the car. Forty minutes later, when he came back out, someone had already found LuoLuo dead in a car full of propane fumes. Song Cheng had to open the car door from the outside.

Later, a close friend in the police force who'd participated in the investigation told Song that the lock on his car door didn't show any signs of sabotage, and the evidence elsewhere really was enough to rule out the possibility of another killer. Logically enough, everyone assumed that Song Cheng had killed LuoLuo. But Song Cheng knew the only possible explanation: LuoLuo had brought the two propane canisters into the car himself.

This was too much for Song Cheng to fight against. He gave up his attempts to clear his name: if someone had used his own life and death as a weapon to frame him, he didn't have a chance of escape.

Really, LuoLuo committing suicide didn't surprise Song Cheng; his HIV test had returned positive. But someone else must have prompted him to use his death to frame Song Cheng. What would have been in it for him? What would money be worth to him now? Was the money for someone else? Or maybe his recompense wasn't money. But what was it, then? Was there some temptation or fear even stronger than his hatred of Xu Xueping? Song Cheng would never know now, but here he could see even more clearly his opponent's capabilities, and his own naïveté.

This was his life as the world knew it: a high-ranked Discipline Inspection cadre living a secret life of corruption and affairs, arrested for murdering his paramour in a lover's spat. The temperance he'd previously displayed in his heterosexual relationship only became further proof in the public mind. Like a trampled stinkbug, everything he had possessed disappeared without a trace.

Now Song Cheng realized that he'd been so prepared to sacrifice everything for faith and duty only because he hadn't even understood what sacrificing everything entailed. He'd of course imagined that death would be the bottom line. Only later did he realize that sacrifice could be far, far crueler. The police took him home one time when they searched his house. His wife and daughter were both there. He reached toward his daughter, but the child shrieked in disgust and buried her face in her mother's arms, shrinking into a corner. He'd seen the look they gave him only once before, one morning when he'd found a mouse in the trap under the wardrobe, and showed it to them . . .

'Okay, let's set aside the big bang and the singularity and all the abstract stuff for now.' Bai Bing broke off Song Cheng's painful reminiscences and hauled the large briefcase onto the table. 'Take a look at this.'

Superstring Computer, Ultimate Capacity, Digital Mirror

'This is a superstring computer,' Bai Bing said, patting the briefcase. 'I brought it over, or, if you prefer, stole it from the Center for Meteorological Modeling. I'll depend on it to escape pursuit.'

Song Cheng shifted his gaze to the briefcase, clearly confused.

'These are expensive. There are only two in the province as of now. According to superstring theory, the fundamental particles of matter aren't point-like objects, but an infinitely thin one-dimensional string vibrating in eleven dimensions. Nowadays, we can manipulate this string to store and process information along the dimension of its length. That's the theory behind a superstring computer.

'A CPU or piece of internal storage in a traditional electronic computer is just an atom in a superstring computer! The circuits are formed by the particles' eleven-dimensional microscale structure. This higher-dimensional subatomic array has given humanity practically infinite storage and operational capacity. Comparing the supercomputers of the past to superstring computers is like comparing our ten fingers to those supercomputers. A superstring computer has ultimate capacity, that is to say, it has the capacity to store the current status of every fundamental particle existing in the known universe and perform operations with them. In other words, if we only look at three dimensions of space and one of time, a superstring computer can model the entire universe on the atomic level . . .'

Song Cheng alternately looked at the briefcase and Bai Bing. Unlike before, he seemed to be listening to Bai Bing's words with full attention. In truth, he was desperately seeking any kind of relief, letting this mysterious visitor's rambling extricate him from his painful memories.

'Sorry for going on and on like this – big bang this and superstring that. It must seem completely unrelated to the reality we're facing, but to give a proper explanation I can't sidestep it. Let's talk about my career next. I'm a software engineer specializing in simulation software. That is, you create a mathematical model and run it in a computer to simulate some object or process in the real world. I studied mathematics, so I do both the model-creating and the programming. In the past I've simulated sandstorms, soil erosion on the Loess Plateau, energy generation and economic development trends in the Northeast, so on. Now I'm working on large-scale weather models. I love my work. Watching a piece of the real world running and evolving inside a computer is honestly fascinating.'

Bai Bing looked at Song Cheng, who was staring at him unblinkingly. He seemed to be listening attentively, so Bai Bing continued.

'You know, the field of physics has had huge breakthroughs one after another in recent years, a lot like at the beginning of the last century. Now, if you give us the boundary conditions, we can lift the fog of quantum effects to accurately predict the behavior of fundamental particles, either singly or in a group.

'Notice I mentioned groups. A group of enough particles means a macroscopic body. In other words, we can now create a mathematical model of a macroscopic object on the atomic level. This sort of simulation is called a digital mirror. I'll give an example.

If we used digital mirroring to create a mathematical model of an egg – as in, we input the status of every atom in the egg into the model's database – and run it in the computer, given suitable boundary conditions, the virtual egg in memory will hatch into a chick. And the virtual chick in memory would be perfectly identical to the chick hatched from the egg in real life, down to the tips of every feather! And think further, what if the object being modeled were bigger than an egg? As big as a tree, a person, many people. As big as a city, a country, or even all of Earth?' Bai Bing was getting worked up, gesturing wildly as he spoke.

'I like to think this way, pushing every idea to its limit. This led me to wonder, what if the object being digitally mirrored were the entire universe?' Bai Bing could no longer control his passion. 'Imagine, the entire universe! My god, an entire universe running in RAM! From creation to destruction—'

Bai Bing broke off his enthusiastic account and stood up, suddenly on guard. The door swung open soundlessly. Two grim-faced men entered. The slightly older one turned to Bai Bing and raised his hands to show that he should do the same. Bai Bing and Song Cheng saw the leather handgun holster under his open jacket; Bai Bing obediently put his hands up. The younger man patted Bai Bing down carefully, then shook his head at the older man. He picked up the large briefcase as well, setting it down farther from Bai Bing.

The older man walked to the door and made a welcoming gesture outward. Three more people entered. The first was the city's chief of police, Chen Xufeng. The second was the province's secretary of discipline inspection, his old classmate, Lu Wenming. Last came the Senior Official.

The younger cop took out a pair of handcuffs, but Lu Wenming shook his head at him. Chen Xufeng turned his head minutely toward the door, and the two plainclothes police left. One of them removed a small object from the table leg as he left, clearly a listening device.

Initial State

Bai Bing's face didn't show any sign of surprise. He smiled placidly. 'You've finally caught me.'

'More accurately, you flew into our net on purpose. I have to admit, if you really wanted to escape, we would've had a hard time catching you,' said Chen Xufeng.

Lu Wenming glanced at Song Cheng, his expression complicated. He seemed to want to say something, but stopped himself.

The Senior Official slowly shook his head. He intoned solemnly, 'Oh, Song Cheng, how did you fall so low . . .' He stood silent for a long time, hands resting on the table's edge, his eyes a little damp. No onlooker could have doubted that his grief was real.

'Senior Official, I don't think you need to playact here,' Bai Bing said, coldly watching the proceedings.

The Senior Official didn't move.

'You were the one who arranged to frame him.'

'Proof?' the Senior Official asked indulgently, still unmoving.

'After that meeting, you only said one thing about Song Cheng, to him.' Bai Bing pointed at Chen Xufeng. '*Xufeng, you know what that whole business with Song Cheng means, of course. Let's put a little effort into it.*'

'What does that prove?'

'It won't count for anything in court, of course. With your cleverness and experience, you didn't let anything slip, even in a secret conversation. But he,' Bai Bing pointed again at Chen Xufeng, 'got the message loud and clear. He's always understood you perfectly. He ordered one of the two people earlier to carry out the framing. His name is Chenbing, and he's his most competent subordinate. The whole process was one formidable engineering project. I don't think I need to go into detail here.'

The Senior Official slowly turned around and sat down in a chair by the office table. He looked at the ground as he said, 'Young man, I have to admit, your sudden appearance has been astonishing in many ways. To use Chief Chen's words, it's like seeing a ghost.' He was silent for a while, and then his voice rang out with sincerity. 'How about you tell us your real identity? If you really were sent by the central officials, please trust that we'll assist you however we can.'

'I wasn't. I've said again and again that I'm an ordinary guy. My identity is nothing more than what you've already looked up.'

The Senior Official nodded. It was impossible to tell whether Bai Bing's words had reassured him, or added to his concern.

'Sit, let's all sit.' The Senior Official waved a hand at Lu and Chen, both still standing, and drew closer to Bai Bing. 'Young man,' he said solemnly. 'Let's get to the bottom of all this today, okay?'

Bai Bing nodded. 'That's my plan too. I'll start from the beginning.'

'No, that won't be necessary. We heard everything you said to Song Cheng earlier. Just continue where you left off.'

Bai Bing was momentarily at a loss for words, unable to remember where he'd stopped.

'Atomic-level model of the entire universe,' the Senior Official reminded him, but seeing that Bai Bing still couldn't figure out how to start talking again, he added his own input. 'Young man, I don't think your idea is feasible. Superstring computers have ultimate capacity, yes, providing the hardware basis for running this sort of simulation. But have you considered the problem of the initial state? To make a digital mirror of the universe, you must start the simulation from some initial state – in other words, to construct a model that represents the universe on an atomic level, for the instant the model starts at, you'll have to input the status at that instant of every atom in the universe into the computer, one by one. Is this possible? It wouldn't be possible with the egg you mentioned, let alone the universe. The number of atoms in that egg outnumber the number of eggs ever laid since the beginning of time by orders of magnitude. It wouldn't even be possible with a bacterium, which still contains an astonishing number of atoms. Taking a step back, even if we put forth the near unimaginable manpower and computing power needed to find the initial state of a small object like the bacterium or the egg on an atomic level, what about the boundary conditions for when the model runs? For example, the outside temperature, humidity, and so on needed for a chicken egg to hatch. Taken on the atomic level, these boundary conditions will require unimaginable quantities of data too, perhaps even more than the modeled object itself.'

'You've laid out the technical problems beautifully. I admire that,' Bai Bing said sincerely.

'The Senior Official was once a star student in the field of high-energy physics. After Deng Xiaoping's reforms restored university degrees, his was one of the first classes to receive master's degrees in physics in China,' said Lu Wenming.

Bai Bing nodded in Lu Wenming's direction, then turned toward the Senior Official. 'But you forget, there's a moment in time in which the universe was extremely simple, even simpler than eggs and bacteria, simpler than anything in existence today. The number of atoms in it at the time was zero, see. It had no size and no composition.'

'The big bang singularity?' the Senior Official said immediately, almost no delay between Bai Bing's words and his. It was a glimpse at the quick, agile mind beneath his slow and steady exterior.

'Yes, the big bang singularity. Superstring theory has already established a perfect model of the singularity. We just need to represent the model digitally and run it on the computer.'

'That's right, young man. That really is the case.' The Senior Official stood and walked to Bai Bing's side to pat his shoulder, revealing rare excitement. Chen Xufeng and Lu Wenming, who hadn't understood the exchange that had just taken place, looked at them with puzzled expressions.

'Is this the superstring computer you brought out of the research center?' the Senior Official asked, pointing at the briefcase.

'Stole,' said Bai Bing.

'Ha, no matter. The software for the digital mirror of the big bang is on it, I expect?'

'Yes.'

'Run it for us.'

Creation Game

Bai Bing nodded, hauled the briefcase onto the desk, and opened it. Beside the display equipment, the briefcase also contained a cylindrical vessel. The superstring computer's processor was in fact only the size of a pack of cigarettes, but the atomic circuitry required ultralow temperatures to operate, so the processor had to be kept submerged in the insulated vessel of liquid nitrogen. Bai Bing set the LCD screen upright and moved the mouse, and the superstring computer awoke from sleep mode. The screen brightened, like a dozing eye blinking open, displaying a simple interface composed of just a drop-down text box and a header reading:

Please Select Parameters to Initiate Creation of the Universe

Bai Bing clicked the arrow beside the drop-down text box. Row upon row of data sets, each composed of a sizable number of elements, appeared below. Each row seemed to differ considerably from the others. 'The properties of the singularity are determined by eighteen parameters. Technically, there's an infinite number of possible parameter combinations, but we can determine from superstring theory that the number of parameter combinations that could have resulted in the big bang is finite, although their exact number is still a mystery. Here we have a small selection of them. Let's select one at random.'

Bai Bing selected a group of parameters, and the screen immediately went white. Two big buttons appeared in striking contrast at the center of the screen.

Initiate Cancel

Bai Bing clicked Initiate. Now only the white background was left. 'The white represents nothingness. Space doesn't exist at this time, and time itself hasn't begun. There really is nothing.'

A red number 'o' appeared in the lower left corner of the screen.

'This number indicates how long the universe has been evolving. The zero appearing means that the singularity has been generated. Its size is undefined, so we can't see it.'

The red number began to increment rapidly.

'Notice, the big bang has begun.'

A small blue dot appeared in the middle of the screen, quickly growing into a sphere emitting brilliant blue light. The sphere rapidly expanded, filling the entire screen. The software zoomed out, and the sphere once again shrank into a distant dot, but the ballooning universe quickly filled the screen once more. The cycle repeated again and again in rapid frequency, as if marking the beats to some swelling symphony.

'The universe is currently in the inflationary epoch. It's expanding at a rate far exceeding the speed of light.'

As the sphere slowed in its growth, the field of view began to zoom out less frequently, too. With the decrease in energy density, the sphere turned from blue to yellow, then red, before the color of the universe stabilized at red and began to darken. The field of view no longer zoomed out, and the now-black sphere expanded very slowly now on the screen.

'Okay, it's ten billion years after the big bang. At this point, this universe is in a stable stage of evolution. Let's take a closer look.' Bai Bing moved the mouse, and the sphere rushed forward, filling the whole screen with black. 'Right, we're in this universe's outer space.'

'There's nothing here?' said Lu Wenming.

'Let's see . . .' As Bai Bing spoke, he right-clicked and pulled up a complicated window. A script began to calculate the total matter present in the universe. 'Ha, there are only eleven fundamental particles in this universe.' He pulled up another massive data report and read it carefully. 'Ten of the particles are arranged in five mutually orbiting pairs. However, in each pair, the two particles are tens of millions of light-years apart. They take millions of years to move one millimeter with respect to each other. The last particle is free.'

'Eleven fundamental particles? But after all that talk, there's still nothing here,' said Lu Wenming.

'There's space, nearly a hundred billion light-years in diameter! And time, ten billion years of it! Time and space are the true measures of existence! This particular universe is actually one of the more successful ones. In a lot of the universes I created before, even the dimensions of space quickly disappeared, leaving only time.'

'Dull,' harrumphed Chen Xufeng, turning away from the screen.

'No, this is very interesting,' said the Senior Official delightedly. 'Do it again.'

Bai Bing returned to the starting interface, selected a new set of parameters, and initiated another big bang. The formation process of the new universe looked to be about the same as the earlier one, an expanding and dimming sphere. Fifteen billion years after creation, the sphere became fully black: the evolution of the universe had stabilized. Bai Bing moved the viewpoint into the universe. Even Chen Xufeng, least interested out of all of them, exclaimed. Beneath the vast darkness of space, a silvery surface extended endlessly in all directions. Small, colorful spheres decorated the membrane like multicolored dewdrops tumbling on the broad surface of a mirror.

Bai Bing brought up the analysis window again. He looked at it for a while and said, 'We were lucky. This is a universe rich in variety, about forty billion light-years in radius. Half of its volume is liquid, while the other half is empty space. In other words, this universe is a massive ocean, forty billion light-years in depth and radius, with the solid celestial bodies floating on its surface!' Bai Bing pushed the field of view closer to the ocean's surface, allowing them to see that the silvery ocean surface was gently rippling. A celestial body appeared in their close-up view. 'This floating object is . . . let me see, about the size of Jupiter. Whoa, it's rotating by itself! The mountain ranges look amazing when they're coming in and out of – let's just call this liquid water! See the water being flung up by the mountain ranges, along its orbit. It forms a rainbow arc above the surface!'

'It's beautiful, indeed, but this universe goes against the basic laws of physics,' the Senior Official said, looking at the screen. 'Never mind an ocean forty billion light-years deep, a body of liquid four light-years deep would have collapsed into a black hole due to gravity long ago.'

Bai Bing shook his head. 'You've forgotten a fundamental point: This isn't our universe. This universe has its own set of laws of physics, completely different from ours. In this universe, the gravitational constant, Planck's constant, the speed of light, and other basic physical constants are all different. In this universe, one plus one might not even equal two.'

Encouraged by the Senior Official, Bai Bing continued the demonstration, creating a third universe. When they entered for a closer look, a chaotic jumble of colors and shapes appeared on the screen. Bai Bing immediately exited. 'This is a six-dimensional universe, so we have no way of observing it. In fact, this is the most common case, and we were lucky to get two three-dimensional universes on our first two tries. Once the universe cools down from its high-energy state, the odds of having three available dimensions on the macroscopic scale is only three out of eleven.'

A fourth universe manifested. To the bafflement of everyone: the universe appeared as an endless black plane, with countless bright, silvery lines intersecting it perpendicularly. After reading the analysis profile, Bai Bing said, 'This universe is the opposite of the previous one – it has fewer dimensions than our own. This is a two-and-a-half-dimensional universe.'

'Two and a half dimensions?' The Senior Official was astonished.

'See, the black two-dimensional plane with no thickness is this universe's outer space. Its diameter is around five hundred billion light-years. The bright lines perpendicular to the plane are the stars in space. They're hundreds of millions of light-years long, but infinitely thin, because they're one-dimensional. Universes with fractional dimensions are rare. I'm going to make note of the parameters that produced this one.'

'A question,' said the Senior Official. 'If you use these parameters to initialize a second big bang, would it produce a universe exactly the same as this one?'

'Yes, and the evolution process would be identical too. Everything was predetermined at the time of the big bang. See, after physics got past the obfuscation of quantum effects, the universe once again displayed an inherently causal and deterministic nature.' Bai Bing looked at the others one by one. He said seriously, 'Please keep this point in mind. This will be key to understanding the terrifying things we'll be seeing later.'

'This really is fascinating.' The Senior Official sighed. 'Playing God, aloof and ethereal. It's been a long time since I've felt this way.'

'I felt the same,' Bai Bing said as he stood up from the computer to pace back and forth, 'so I played the creation game again and again. By now, I've initiated more than a thousand big bangs. The awe-inspiring wonder of those thousand-plus universes is impossible to describe with words. I felt like an addict . . . I could have kept going like that, never coming into contact with you, never getting involved. Our lives would have continued along our orbits. But . . . ah, hell. . . . It was a snowy night at the beginning of the year, nearly two in the morning, really quiet. I ran the last big bang of the day. The superstring computer gave birth to the one thousand two hundred and seventh universe – this one . . .'

Bai Bing returned to the computer, scrolled to the bottom of the drop-down list, and selected the last set of parameters. He initiated the big bang. The new universe rapidly expanded in a glow of blue light before extinguishing to black. Bai Bing moved the mouse and entered his Universe No. 1207 at nineteen billion years after creation.

This time, the screen displayed a radiant sea of stars.

'1207 has a radius of twenty billion light-years and three dimensions. In this universe, the gravitational constant is 6.67 times 10^{-11}, and the speed of light in a vacuum is three hundred thousand kilometers per second. In this universe, an electron has a charge of 1.602 times 10^{-19} coulombs. In this universe, Planck's constant is

6.62 . . .' Bai Bing leaned in toward the Senior Official, watching him with a chilling gaze. 'In this universe, one plus one equals two.'

'This is our own universe.' The Senior Official nodded, still steady, but his forehead was now damp.

Searching History

'Once I found Universe No. 1207, I spent more than a month building a search engine based on shape and pattern recognition. Then I looked through astronomy resources to find diagrams of the geometrical placement of the Milky Way with respect to the nearby Andromeda Galaxy, Large and Small Magellanic Clouds, and so on. Searching for the arrangement within the entire universe gave me more than eighty thousand matches. Next I searched those results for matches for the internal arrangement of the galaxies themselves. It didn't take long to locate the Milky Way in the universe.' Onscreen, a silver spiral appeared against a backdrop of pitch-black space.

'Locating the sun was even easier. We already know its approximate location in the Milky Way—' Bai Bing used his mouse to click and drag a small rectangle over the tip of one arm of the spiral.

'Using the same pattern-recognition method, it didn't take long to locate the sun in this area.' A brilliant sphere of light appeared onscreen, surrounded by a large disk of haze.

'Oh, the planets in the solar system haven't formed yet right now. This disk of interstellar debris is the raw material they're made up of.' Bai Bing pulled up a slider bar at the bottom of the window. 'See, this lets you move through time.' He slowly dragged the slider forward. Two hundred million years passed before them; the disk of dust around the sun disappeared. 'Now the nine planets have formed. The video window shows real distances and proportions, unlike your planetarium displays, so finding Earth is going to take more work. I'll use the coordinates I saved earlier instead.' With that, the nascent planet Earth appeared on the screen as a hazy gray sphere.

Bai Bing scrolled the mouse wheel. 'Let's go down . . . good. We're about ten kilometers above the surface now.' The land below was still shrouded in haze, but crisscrossing glowing red lines had appeared in it, a network like the blood vessels in an embryo.

'These are rivers of lava,' Bai Bing said, pointing. He kept scrolling down, past the thick acidic fog. The brown surface of the ocean appeared, and the point of view plunged lower, into the ocean. In the murky water were a few specks. Most were round, but a few were more complicated in shape, most obviously different from the other suspended particles in that they were moving on their own, not just floating with the current.

'Life, brand new,' Bai Bing said, pointing out the tiny things with the mouse.

He rapidly scrolled the mouse wheel in the other direction, raising their point of view back into space to once again show the young Earth in full. Then he moved the time slider. Countless years flew past; the thick haze covering Earth's surface disappeared, the ocean began to turn blue, and the land began to turn green. Then the enormous supercontinent Pangaea split and broke apart like ice in spring. 'If you want, we can watch the entire evolution of life, all the major extinctions and the explosions of life that followed them. But let's skip them and save some time. We're about to see what this all has to do with our lives.'

The fragmented ancient continents continued to drift until, at last, a familiar map of the world appeared. Bai Bing changed the slider-bar settings, advancing in smaller increments through time before coming to a stop. 'Right, humans appear here.' He carefully shifted the slider a little further forward. 'Now civilization appears.

'You can only see most of distant history on a macro scale. Finding specific events isn't easy, and finding specific people is even harder. Searching history mainly relies on two parameters: location and time. It's rare that historical records give them accurately this far back. But let's try it out. We're going down now!' Bai Bing double-clicked a location near the Mediterranean Sea as he spoke. The point of view hurtled downward with dizzying speed. At last, a deserted beach appeared. At the far side of the yellow sand was an unbroken grove of olive trees.

'The coast of Troy in the time of the ancient Greeks,' said Bai Bing.

'Then . . . can you move the time to the Trojan Horse and the Sack of Troy?' Lu Wenming asked excitedly.

'The Trojan Horse never existed,' Bai Bing said coolly.

Chen Xufeng nodded. 'That sort of thing belongs in children's stories. It would be impossible in a real war.'

'The Trojan War never happened,' said Bai Bing.

'If that's the case, did Troy fall due to other reasons?' The Senior Official sounded surprised.

'The city of Troy never existed.'

The other three exchanged looks of astonishment.

Bai Bing pointed at the screen. 'The video window is now displaying the real coast of Troy at the time the war supposedly happened. We can look five hundred years forward and back . . .' Bai Bing carefully shifted the mouse. The beach onscreen flashed rapidly as night and day alternated, and the shape of the trees changed quickly, too. A few shacks appeared at the far end of the beach, human silhouettes occasionally flickering past them. The shacks grew and fell in number, but even at their greatest they formed no more than a village. 'See, the magnificent city of Troy only ever existed in the imaginations of the poet-storytellers.'

'How is that possible?' Lu Wenming cried. 'We have archaeological evidence from the beginning of the last century! They even dug up Agamemnon's gold mask.'

'Agamemnon's gold mask? Fuck that!' Bai Bing laughed harshly. 'Well, as the historical records improve in quality and quantity, later searches get increasingly easy. Let's do it again.'

Bai Bing returned their point of view to Earth's orbit. This time, he didn't use the mouse, but entered the time and geographical coordinates by hand. The view descended toward western Asia. Soon, the screen displayed a stretch of desert, and a few people lying under the shade of a cluster of red willows. They wore ragged robes of rough cloth, their skin baked dark, their hair long and matted into strands by sweat and dust. From a distance, they looked like heaps of discarded rubbish.

'They aren't far from a Muslim village, but the bubonic plague has been going around and they're afraid to go there,' Bai Bing said.

A tall, thin man sat up and looked around. After checking that the others were soundly asleep, he picked up a neighbor's sheepskin canteen and took a swig. Then he reached into another neighbor's battered pack and took out a piece of traveler's bread, broke off a third, and put it in his own bag. Satisfied, he lay back down.

'I've run this at normal speed for two days and seen him steal other people's water five times and other people's food three times,' Bai Bing said, gesturing with his mouse at the man who'd just lain down.

'Who is he?'

'Marco Polo. It wasn't easy to search him up. The Genoan prison where he was imprisoned gave me fairly precise times and coordinates. I located him there, then backtraced to that naval battle he was in to extract some identifying traits. Then I jumped much earlier and followed him here. This is in what used to be Persia, near the city of Bam in modern Iran, but I could have saved myself the effort.'

'That means he's on his way to China. You should be able to follow him into Kublai Khan's palace,' said Lu Wenming.

'He never entered any palace.'

'You mean, he spent his time in China as just a regular commoner?'

'Marco Polo never went to China. The long and even more dangerous road ahead scared him off. He wandered around West Asia for a few years, and later told the rumors he heard along the way to his friend in prison, who wrote the famous travelogue.'

His three listeners once again exchanged looks of astonishment.

'It's even easier to look up specific people and events later on. Let's do it one more time with modern history.'

The room was large and very dim. A map – a naval map? – had been spread out on the broad wooden table, surrounded by several men in Qing Dynasty military uniforms. The room was too dark to see their faces.

'We're in the headquarters of the Beiyang Fleet, quite a ways to go before the First Sino-Japanese War. We're in the middle of a meeting.'

Someone was talking, but the heavy southlands accent and the poor sound quality made the words unintelligible. Bai Bing explained, 'They're saying that for coastal defense purposes, given their limited funds, purchasing heavy-tonnage ironclads from the West is less worthwhile than buying a large number of fast, steam-powered torpedo boats. Each vessel could hold four to six gas torpedoes, forming a large, fast attack force, maneuverable enough to evade Japanese cannon fire and strike at close range. I asked a number of naval experts and military historians about this. They unanimously believe that if this idea had been implemented, the Beiyang Fleet would have won their battles in the First Sino-Japanese War. He's brilliantly ahead of his time, the first in naval history to discover the weaknesses of the traditional big-cannons-and-big-ships policy with the new innovations in armaments.'

'Who is it?' Chen Xufeng asked. 'Deng Shichang?'

Bai Bing shook his head. 'Fang Boqian.'

'What, that coward who ran away halfway through the Battle of the Yellow Sea?'

'The very one.'

'Instinct tells me that all this is what history was really like,' the Senior Official mused.

Bai Bing nodded. 'That's right. I didn't feel so aloof and ethereal after this stage. I started to despair. I had discovered that practically all the history we know is a lie. Of all the noble, vaunted heroes we hear about, at least half were contemptible liars and schemers who used their influence to claim achievements and write the histories, and managed to succeed. Of those who really did give everything for truth and justice, two-thirds choked to death horribly and quietly in the dust of history, forgotten by everyone, and the remaining one-third had their reputations smeared into eternal infamy, just like Song Cheng. Only a tiny percentage were remembered as they were by history, less than the exposed corner of the iceberg.'

Only then did everyone notice Song Cheng, who'd remained silent throughout. They saw him quietly stir, his eyes alight. He looked like a felled warrior rising to stand once more, taking up his weapon astride a fresh warhorse.

Searching the Present

'Then you came to Universe No. 1207's present day, am I correct?' asked the Senior Official.

'That's right, I set the digital mirror to our time.' As he spoke, Bai Bing moved the time slider to the far end. The point of view once again returned to space. The blue Earth below didn't look particularly different from how it had appeared in ancient times.

'This is our present day shown through the mirror of Universe No. 1207: after decades of continuous exporting of natural resources and energy, our hinterland province still doesn't have a presentable industry to its name aside from mining and power generation. All we have is pollution, most of the rural areas still below the poverty line, severe unemployment in the cities, deteriorating law and order . . . naturally, I wanted to see how our leaders and planners did their jobs. What I saw, well, I don't need to tell you that.'

'What were you after?' asked the Senior Official.

Bai Bing smiled bitterly, shaking his head. 'Don't think I had some lofty goal like him,' he said, pointing at Song Cheng. 'I was just an ordinary person, happy to mind my own business and live out my days in peace. What do your antics have to do with me? I wasn't planning to mess with you, but . . . I put so much work into this supersimulation software, and naturally I wanted to get some material benefits out of it. So I called a couple of your people, hoping they'd give me a bit of cash for keeping quiet . . .' He abruptly swelled with indignation.

'Why did you have to overreact? Why did I have to be eliminated? If you'd just given me the money, we'd all be done here! . . . Anyway, I've finished explaining everything.'

The five people sank into a long silence, all of them watching the image of Earth on the screen. This was the digital mirror of the current Earth. They were in there, too.

'Can you really use this computer to observe everything in the world that's ever happened?' Chen Xufeng said, breaking the silence.

'Yes, every detail of history and the present day is data in the computer, and that data can be freely analyzed. Anything, no matter how secret, can be observed by extracting the corresponding information from the database and processing it. The database holds an atomic-level digital replica of the entire world, and any part of it can be extracted at will.'

'Can you prove it?'

'That's easy. You leave the room, go anywhere you want, do anything you want, and come back.'

Chen Xufeng looked at the Senior Official and Lu Wenming in turn, then left the room. He returned two minutes later and looked at Bai Bing wordlessly.

Bai Bing moved the mouse so that the point of view rapidly descended from space to hover above the city, which seamlessly filled the screen. He panned around, searching carefully, and quickly found the No. 2 Detention Center at the city outskirts, then the three-story building they were in. The point of view entered the building, gliding along the empty hallway on the second floor. The two plainclothes detectives sitting on the bench outside appeared onscreen, Chenbing lighting a cigarette. At last, the screen displayed the door of the office they were in.

'Right now, the simulation only lags behind reality as it happens by 0.1 seconds. Let's go back a few minutes.' Bai Bing nudged the time slider left.

Onscreen, the door swung open and Chen Xufeng walked out. The two police on the bench immediately stood; Chen waved them an all's-well and walked in the opposite direction. The point of view followed closely, as if someone were filming from right behind him with a camera. In the digital mirror, Chen Xufeng entered the restroom, took a handgun from his trouser pocket, pulled the trigger, and returned it to his pocket. Bai Bing paused the simulation here and rotated the view around to different angles as if it were a 3-D cartoon. Chen Xufeng walked out of the restroom, and the point of view followed him back to the office, revealing the four people waiting for him.

The Senior Official watched the screen expressionlessly. Lu Wenming raised his head warily and eyed Chen Xufeng. 'That thing really is impressive,' Lu Wenming said with a dark expression.

'Next I'll demonstrate an even more impressive feature,' said Bai Bing, pausing the simulation. 'Since the universe is stored in the digital mirror on the atomic level, we can search up any and every detail in the universe. Next, let's see what's in Chief Chen's coat pocket.'

On the paused screen, Bai Bing clicked and dragged a rectangle over the area of Chen Xufeng's coat pocket, then opened an interface to process it. With a series of actions, he removed the cloth on the outside of the pocket, revealing a small piece of folded-up paper inside. Bai Bing pressed Ctrl+C to copy the piece of paper, then started up a 3-D model-processing program and pasted in the copied data. A few more actions unfolded the piece of paper. It was a foreign exchange check for 250,000 USD.

'Next, we'll track this check to its origin.' Bai Bing closed the model-processing software and returned to the paused video window. Bai

Bing right-clicked the already-selected check in Chen Xufeng's coat pocket, then chose Trace from the list of options. The check flashed, and the still screen jumped to life. Time was flowing backward, showing the Senior Official and his retinue backing out of the office, then out of the building, then into a car. Chen Xufeng and Lu Wenming put on earphones, clearly listening in on Bai Bing and Song Cheng's conversation. The trace search continued, the surroundings continuing to change, but the flashing check remained at the center of the screen as the subject of the search, seeming to tug Chen Xufeng with it through scene after scene. Finally, the check jumped out of Chen's coat pocket and slipped into a small basket, which then jumped from Chen's hand into another person's. At that moment, Bai Bing paused the simulation.

'I'll resume playing here,' said Bai Bing, selecting normal playback speed. They seemed to be looking at Chen Xufeng's living room. Onscreen, a middle-aged woman in a black suit stood with the fruit basket in her hand, as if she'd just entered. Chen Xufeng was sitting on the sofa.

'Chief Chen, Director Wen sent me to visit you, and to express his gratitude for last time. He wanted to come in person, but thought it was best not to show up here too often to prevent idle gossip.'

Chen Xufeng said, 'When you go back, tell Wen Xiong that he'd better stay on the straight and narrow, now that he's in good shape. Going too far all the time doesn't do anyone good. He'd better not blame me for losing patience!'

'Yes, of course, how could Brother Wen forget your advice? Nowadays, he's been actively contributing to society – he's built four elementary schools in impoverished districts. He's also dedicated to making progress in politics. The city has already elected him as its delegate to the National People's Congress!' As she spoke, the visitor set the fruit basket onto the coffee table.

'Take that with you,' Chen Xufeng said, waving a hand.

'We would never bring anything too fancy, Chief Chen. We know how you'd hate it. This is just some fruit as a token of our gratitude. I suppose you haven't seen the way Chief Wen tears up whenever he mentions you. He calls you our loving parents reborn, you know.'

Once the visitor left, Chen Xufeng shut the door and returned to the coffee table. He tipped all the fruit out of the basket, picked up the check at the bottom, and slid it in his pocket.

The Senior Official and Lu Wenming eyed Chen Xufeng coldly. Clearly they hadn't known any of this. Wen Xiong was the director general of Licheng Group, an enormous corporation spanning dining, long-distance travel, and many other services. Its start-up money had come from drug profits from Wen Xiong's crime syndicate, which had made this city into a crucial hub in the Yunnan-Russia drug-trafficking route. With Wen Xiong's successful expansion into aboveboard commerce, his underground business, drawing nourishment from the former, grew even more rapidly. The result in the hinterland city was the proliferation of drugs and the decline of public safety. And Chen Xufeng, the backstage supporter, was a powerful safeguard for its continued survival.

'You took payment in dollars? It must have gone to your son,' Bai Bing said cheerfully. 'The money that's paying for his American college education all came from Wen Xiong, after all. . . . Speaking of which, don't you want to see what he's doing right now, on the other side of the planet? That's easy enough. It's midnight in Boston right now, but the last two times I saw him, he wasn't sleeping yet.' Bai Bing sent the point of view up into space, twirled the Earth 180 degrees, then zoomed in on North America. He found the city splendid with lights on the Atlantic coast, then located the apartment building so quickly it was clear he must have searched it before. The point of view entered an apartment bedroom, exposing an awkward scene: the boy in his room with two prostitutes, one white and one black.

'See how your son's spending your money, Chief Chen?'

Furious, Chen Xufeng tipped the monitor screen-side down onto the briefcase.

The deeply stunned group once again sank into a long silence. At last Lu Wenming asked, 'Why did you spend all this time just running away? Didn't you consider using more . . . conventional means to free yourself from this predicament?'

'You mean, report to Discipline Inspection? Excellent idea, yes. I had the same idea at first, so I used the digital mirror to run a search on the Discipline Inspection leadership.' Bai Bing raised his head to look at Lu Wenming. 'You can guess what I saw. I didn't want to end up like your old college buddy here. In that case, could I go to the public prosecutors or the Anti-Corruption Bureau? I'm sure Director Guo and Chief Chang process the vast majority of serious accusations strictly by the law, and very carefully tiptoe around a small portion. For what I'd report, they'd join you in hunting me down the moment I told them. Where else could I go? Could I get the press to run an exposé? I think you're all familiar with those certain key figures in the provincial news media groups. After all, weren't they the ones who came up with the Senior Official's shining résumé? The only difference between those reporters and prostitutes is that they sell a different body part. It's all tied together in one big web, not a strand safe to touch. I didn't have anywhere to go.'

'You could go to the Central Commission,' the Senior Official said neutrally, closely observing Bai Bing for a reaction.

Bai Bing nodded. 'It's the only choice left. But I'm a nobody. I don't know anyone. I came to see Song Cheng first to find reliable connections, pursuit or no.' Bai Bing paused, then continued, 'But this decision wasn't an easy one. You're all smart people. You know the ultimate consequences of doing this.'

'It means that this technology will be revealed to the world.'

'That's right. Every bit of the fog that covers history and reality will be swept away. Anything and everything, in light and darkness, past and present, will be stripped naked and paraded before the light of day. At that time, light and dark will be forced into a deciding battle for supremacy unlike anything in history. The world's going to descend into chaos—'

'But the end result will be the victory of the light,' said Song Cheng, who'd been silent until then. He walked in front of Bai Bing and looked straight at him. 'Do you know how shadows derive their power? It comes from their very nature of secrecy. Once they're exposed to the light, their power is gone. You see that with most cases of corruption. And your digital mirror is the burning brand that will tear the darkness open.'

The Senior Official exchanged looks with Chen and Lu.

Silence fell. On the superstring computer screen, the atomic-level digital mirror of Earth hovered placidly in space.

The Senior Official put a hand on Bai Bing's shoulder. 'Why don't you move the time slider in the simulation farther forward?'

Bai Bing, Chen Xufeng, and Lu Wenming looked uncomprehendingly at the Senior Official.

'If we can accurately predict the future, we can change the present and control the course the future will take. We'd control everything – young man, don't you think this is possible? Perhaps, together, we can shoulder the great duty of shaping the history to come.'

Bai Bing realized what he was saying and gave a pained smile, shaking his head. He stood and walked over to the computer. He clicked and dragged the time slider bar, extending its length beyond Now into the future. Then he said to the Senior Official, 'Try it for yourself.'

Infinite Recursion

The Senior Official leapt toward the computer, quicker than anyone had ever seen him move, bringing to mind the dark image of a hungry eagle spotting a baby chick on the ground. He moved the mouse with practiced motions, sliding the time past the Now. In the instant that the slider entered the future, an error window popped up.

Stack Overflow

Bai Bing took the mouse from the Senior Official's hand. 'Let's run a debugging program and trace that step by step.'

The simulation software returned to the state it had been in before the error and began to run line by line. When the real Bai Bing moved the slider past the present, the simulation Bai Bing in the digital mirror did the same. The debugging program immediately zoomed in on the digital mirror's superstring computer display, allowing them to see that, on the simulated screen, the simulated simulated Bai Bing two layers down was also moving the slider past the present. Then the debugging program zoomed in on the superstring computer display in the third layer. . . . In this way the debugger progressed layer after layer deeper, each layer's Bai Bing in the process of moving the slider past the present time, an infinite Droste image.

'This is recursion, a programming approach where a piece of code calls itself. Under normal circumstances, it finds its answer a finite number of layers down, after which the answer follows the chain of calls back to the surface. But here we see a function calling itself without end, forever unable to find an answer, in infinite recursion. Because it needs to store resources used by the previous layer on the stack at every call, it created the stack overflow we saw earlier. With infinite recursion, even a superstring computer's ultimate capacity can be used up.'

'Ah.' The Senior Official nodded.

'As a result, even though the course of the universe was decided at the big bang, we still can't know the future. For people who hate the determinist idea that everything comes from a chain of cause and effect, this probably provides some consolation.'

'Ah . . .' The Senior Official nodded again. He dragged out the sound for a long, long time.

The Age of the Mirror

Bai Bing discovered that a strange change had overcome the Senior Official, as if something had been sucked out of him. His whole body seemed to be withering, swaying as if it had lost the strength to keep itself upright. His face was pale, his breathing rapid. He put both hands on the chair's arms and lowered himself into the seat, the movement difficult and painstaking, as if he were afraid his bones would snap.

'Young man, you have destroyed my life's work,' the Senior Official said eventually. 'You win.'

Bai Bing looked at Chen Xufeng and Lu Wenming, finding that they were at a loss like himself. But Song Cheng stood straight-backed and unafraid among them, his face alight with victory.

Chen Xufeng slowly stood, drawing his gun from his trouser pocket.

'Stop,' said the Senior Official, not loudly, but with unsurpassed authority in his voice. The gun in Chen Xufeng's hand stilled in midair. 'Put the gun down,' the Senior Official commanded, but Chen didn't move.

'Sir, at this stage, we have to act decisively. We can explain away their deaths, shot and killed while resisting arrest and attempting escape—'

'Put the gun down, you mad dog!' the Senior Official roared.

The hand holding the gun fell to Chen Xufeng's side. He slowly turned toward the Senior Official. 'I'm no mad dog. I'm a loyal dog, a dog who understands gratitude! A dog who will never betray you, sir! You can trust someone like me, who's crawled step by step up from the bottom, to know right and wrong like a good dog toward the superior who made him into who he is today. I don't think the slick thoughts of intelligentsia.'

'What are you trying to say?' Lu Wenming, who had long been silent, got to his feet.

'Everyone knows what I mean. I'm not like some people, taking a step only after making sure there's two or three steps of retreat open. Where's my road out? At a time like this, if I don't protect myself, who will do it for me?!'

Bai Bing said calmly, 'It's useless to kill me. That's the fastest way to expose the digital mirror technology to the public.'

'Even an idiot would have realized he'd take precautionary measures. You've really lost all reason,' Lu Wenming said quietly to Chen Xufeng.

Chen Xufeng said, 'Of course I know the bastard wouldn't be that stupid, but we have our own technological resources. If we put in everything we have, we might be able to completely wipe out the digital mirror technology.'

Bai Bing shook his head. 'That's impossible. Chief Chen, this is the era of the internet. Concealing and distributing information is easy, and I have the defender's advantage. You can't beat me at my game, not even if you put in your best tech experts. I could tell you where I've hidden the digital mirror software backups and how I plan to release them after my death, and you wouldn't be able to do a thing. The initialization parameters are even easier to hide and distribute. Forget about that idea.'

Chen Xufeng slowly put the gun back into his pocket and sat down.

'You think you're already standing on the summit of history, yes?' the Senior Official said tiredly to Song Cheng.

'Justice stands on the summit of history,' Song Cheng said solemnly.

'Indeed, the digital mirror has destroyed us all. But its power to destroy far exceeds this.'

'Yes, it will destroy all evil.'

The Senior Official nodded slowly.

'Then it will destroy all the corruption and immorality that comes short of evil.'

The Senior Official nodded again. 'In the end, it will destroy all of human civilization.'

His words made the others take pause. Song Cheng said, 'Human civilization has never beheld such a bright future. This battle between good and evil will wash away all its grime.'

'And then?' the Senior Official asked softly.

'And then, the great age of the mirror will arrive. All of humanity will face a mirror in which every action can be perfectly seen and no crime can be hidden. Every sinner will inevitably meet their judgment. It will be an era without darkness, where the sun shines into every crevice. Human society will become as pure as crystal.'

'In other words, society will be dead,' the Senior Official said. He raised his head to look Song Cheng in the eyes.

'Care to explain?' Song Cheng said, with the mocking note of a victor looking at a loser.

'Imagine if DNA never made mistakes, always replicating and inheriting with perfect fidelity. What would life on Earth become?'

While Song Cheng considered this, Bai Bing answered for him. 'In that case, life would no longer exist on Earth. The basis of the evolution of life is mutation, caused by mistakes in DNA.'

The Senior Official nodded at Bai Bing. 'Society is the same way. Its evolution and vitality is rooted in the myriad urges and desires departing from the morality laid out by the majority. A fish can't live in perfectly clear water. A society where no one ever makes mistakes in ethics is, in reality, dead.'

'Your attempt to defend your crimes is laughable,' Song Cheng said contemptuously.

'Not completely,' Bai Bing said immediately, surprising the others. He hesitated for a few seconds, as if to steel his resolve. 'To be honest, there was another reason I didn't want to make the mirror simulation software public. I . . . I don't much like the idea of a world armed with the digital mirror either.'

'Are you afraid of the light like them?' Song Cheng demanded.

'I'm an ordinary guy. I'm not involved in any shady business, but there are different kinds of the light you're talking about. If someone beams a searchlight through your bedroom window in the middle of the night, that's called light pollution. . . . I'll give an example. I've only been married two years, but I've already experienced that . . .

wearying of the aesthetics, so to speak. So I got . . . uh, *involved* with a coworker. My wife doesn't know, of course. Everyone's lives are good – better this way even I suspect. I wouldn't be able to live this kind of life in the age of the mirror.'

'It's an immoral and irresponsible life to begin with!' Song Cheng said, anger entering his voice.

'But doesn't everyone live like that? Who doesn't have some sort of secret? If you want to be happy these days, sometimes, you have to bend a little. How many people can be shining spotless saints like you? If the digital mirror makes everyone into perfect people who can't take a step out of line, then – then what's even fucking left?'

The Senior Official laughed, and even Lu and Chen, who'd been grim-faced all this time, cracked a smile. The Senior Official patted Bai Bing on the shoulder. 'Young man, your argument might not be particularly high-minded, but you've thought far deeper than our scholar over here.' He turned toward Song Cheng as he spoke. 'There's no way we can extricate ourselves now, so you can put aside your hatred and thirst for vengeance toward us. As one so well-learned on the subject of social philosophy, surely you're not so shallow-minded as to think that history is made from virtue and justice?'

The Senior Official's words were a potent tranquilizer for Song Cheng. He recovered from the fever of victory. 'My duty is to punish the evil, protect the virtuous, and uphold justice,' he said after a moment of hesitation, his tone much calmer.

The Senior Official nodded, satisfied. 'You didn't give a straight answer. Very good, it shows that you're not quite that narrow-minded yet.'

Here, the Senior Official suddenly shuddered all over, as if someone had dumped cold water over him. He broke out of his daze. The weakness was gone; whatever vitality had deserted him earlier seemed to have returned. He stood, gravely buttoned his collar, and meticulously smoothed the wrinkles from his clothes. Then he said with utmost solemnity to Lu Wenming and Chen Xufeng, 'Comrades, from now on, everything can be seen in the digital mirror. Please take care with your behavior and image.'

Lu Wenming stood, his expression heavy. He attended to his appearance as the Senior Official had, then gave a long sigh. 'Yes, from now on, Heaven watches from above.'

Chen Xufeng stood unmoving with his head hanging.

The Senior Official looked at everyone in turn. 'Very well, I'll be leaving now. I have a busy day at work tomorrow.' He turned toward Bai Bing. 'Young man, come to my office tomorrow at six in the evening. Bring the superstring computer.' Then he turned toward Chen and Lu. 'As for you two, do your best. Xufeng, keep your chin up. We may have committed sins beyond pardon, but we don't need to feel so ashamed. Compared to them,' he pointed to Song Cheng and Bai Bing, 'what we've done really doesn't amount to much.'

He opened the door and left with his head held high.

Birthday

The next day really was a busy day for the Senior Official.

As soon as he entered the office, he summoned key officials in charge of industry, agriculture, finance, environmental protection, and more, one by one, to debrief them on their next orders of business. Though each meeting was short, the Senior Official drew on his ample experience to zero in on important aspects of the work and problems requiring attention. With his well-honed conversational skills, too, each official left thinking that this was only another typical work debriefing. They noticed nothing unusual.

At ten thirty in the morning, after sending away the last official, the Senior Official settled down to document his views on the province's economic development, and problems he foresaw with large- and medium-scale province-owned enterprises. The compilation wasn't long, less than two thousand characters, but it distilled decades of reflection and work experience. Anyone familiar with the Senior Official's philosophies would be astonished reading this document – it differed considerably from his previous views. In his long years at the apex of power, this was the first time he expressed views unadulterated by personal considerations, solely coming from concern for the Party and the country's best interests.

It was past noon by the time the Senior Official finished writing. He didn't eat, only drank a cup of tea, and continued work.

The first indication of the age of the mirror occurred then. The Senior Official was informed that Chen Xufeng had shot himself in his office; meanwhile, Lu Wenming seemed to be in a trance, compulsively reaching for his collar button and straightening his clothes, as if someone could be snapping a picture of him at any instant. The Senior Official met the two pieces of news with only a smile.

The age of the mirror had not yet arrived, but the darkness was already breaking.

The Senior Official ordered the Anti-Corruption Bureau to immediately assemble a task force; with the cooperation of the police and the related Departments of Finance and Commerce, they were to immediately seize all records and accounts belonging to his son's Daxi Trade and Commerce Group and his daughter-in-law's Beiyuan Corporation, and contain the legal entities according to the law. He took care of his other relatives' and cronies' various financial bodies in the same manner.

At four thirty, the Senior Official began to draft a list of names. He knew that, upon the arrival of the age of the mirror, thousands of officials at or above the county rank throughout the province would be sacked. The immediate concern was to seek suitable successors for key roles within each organization, and the list, meant for the provincial and central leadership, presented his suggestions. In reality, this list had existed in his mind long before the appearance of the digital mirror. These were the people he'd planned to eliminate, supplant, and retaliate against.

It was already five thirty, time to leave work. He felt a gratification he had never experienced before: he had spent at least today as a human being.

Song Cheng entered the office, and the Senior Official handed him a thick stack of documents. 'This is the evidence you obtained on me. You should report to the Central Commission as soon as possible. I wrote a confession last night complete with supporting evidence and added them here. Aside from looking through and checking the results of your investigations, I also supplemented some material to fill in the gaps.'

Song Cheng accepted the documents, nodding solemnly. He didn't say anything.

'In a moment, Bai Bing will arrive with the superstring computer. You should tell him that you're about to inform your superiors of the digital mirror software. The central officials, after considering the matter from all directions, will use it conservatively to begin with. He should therefore make sure the software doesn't leak to the public beforehand. That would pose serious dangers and adverse effects. Therefore, you will have him delete all the backup copies, whether online or elsewhere, that he made to protect himself. As for the initialization parameters, if he told them to anyone else, have him make a list of names. He trusts you. He'll do as you say. You must make sure all the backups are gone.'

'We already plan to,' said Song Cheng.

'Then,' the Senior Official looked Song Cheng in the eye, 'kill him, and destroy his superstring computer. At this point, you can hardly think I'm plotting for my own sake.'

Once Song Cheng recovered from his surprise, he shook his head, smiling.

The Senior Official smiled, too. 'Very well, I've said everything I have to say. Whatever happens next has nothing to do with me. The mirror has recorded these words of mine; perhaps one day, in the distant future, someone will listen.'

The Senior Official waved away Song Cheng, then leaned against the back of the chair. He exhaled, slowly, subsumed in a sense of relief and release.

After Song Cheng left, the clock struck six. Bai Bing entered the office on the dot, carrying the briefcase that contained the digital mirror of history and reality.

The Senior Official invited him to sit. Looking at the superstring computer resting on the table, he said, 'Young man, I have something to ask of you: May I see my own life in the digital mirror?'

'Of course you can, no problem!' Bai Bing said, opening the briefcase and booting up the computer. He opened the digital mirror software, then set the time to the present and the location to the office. The two occupants appeared in real time on the screen. Bai Bing selected the Senior Official, right-clicked, and activated the tracking capability.

The image onscreen began to change rapidly, so rapidly that the whole image window filled with a blur. But the Senior Official, as the subject of the search, remained in the middle of the screen the entire time, steady like the center of the world. He was flickering rapidly, too, but the figure was discernibly becoming younger. 'This is a reverse chronology tracking search. The image recognition software can't use your current form to identify younger versions of you, so it has to track you step by step through your age-related changes to find the beginning.'

Several minutes later, the screen stopped flashing through time, now displaying a newborn baby's slick, wet face. The maternity ward nurse had just removed him from the scale. The little creature didn't laugh or scream; his eyes were open and charming, taking stock of the new world around him.

The Senior Official chuckled. 'That's me, all right. My mother always told me that I opened my eyes as soon as I was born,' the Senior Official said, smiling. He was clearly feigning lightheartedness to conceal the breach in his calm; this time, unlike many other times, he wasn't particularly successful.

'Look here, sir,' Bai Bing said, pointing to a menu bar below the image. 'These buttons let you zoom and change angles. This is the time slider bar. The digital mirror program will continue to move forward in time following you as the search object. If you want to find a particular time or event, it's not that different from how you'd use the scrollbar to look up things in a large document in a word processor. First find the approximate location with large steps through time, then make smaller adjustments, moving the slider left or right based on scenes you recognize. You should be able to find it. It's also similar to the fast-forward and rewind functions on a DVD player, although, of course, this disk playing at normal speed would take—'

'I believe nearly five hundred thousand hours,' said the Senior Official, doing the mental math for Bai Bing. He accepted the mouse and zoomed out, revealing the young mother on the maternity bed, and the rest of the hospital room. There were a bedside table and lamp in the plain style of that era, and a window with a wooden frame. What caught his attention was a spot of red-orange light on the wall. 'I was born in the evening, about the same time as now. Perhaps this is the last ray of the setting sun.'

The Senior Official shifted the time slider, and the image again began to jump rapidly. Time flew past. When he stopped, the screen showed a small circular table lit by a bare bulb hanging from the ceiling. At the table, his plainly dressed, bespectacled mother was tutoring four children. An even younger child of three or four, clearly the Senior Official himself, was clumsily feeding himself from a small wooden bowl. 'My mother was an elementary school teacher. She liked to bring the students having trouble with schoolwork back home for tutoring. That way, she could pick me up from nursery school on time.' The Senior Official watched for a while. His child self accidentally spilled the bowl of porridge all over himself. His mother hurriedly got up, reaching for a towel. Only then did the Senior Official move the time slider.

Time skipped forward a few years. The screen suddenly lit up in a blaze of red, apparently the mouth of a blast furnace. Several workers in dirty asbestos work suits were moving, their silhouettes flickering in and out of the furnace flames. The Senior Official pointed to one of the figures. 'That's my father, a furnace worker.'

'You can change the angle to the front,' said Bai Bing. He tried to take the mouse from the Senior Official, who refused him politely.

'Oh, no. This year, the factory worked everyone overtime to increase production. The workers had to be brought meals by family members, and I went. This was the first time I saw my father at work, from this exact angle. His silhouette against the furnace fire impressed itself into my mind very deeply.'

Once more, years passed in the wake of the time slider, stopping on a clear, sunny day. The bright red flag of the Young Pioneers of China waved against the azure sky. A boy in a white shirt and blue trousers gazed up at it as other hands fastened a red scarf around his neck. The boy's right hand flew above his head in a salute, passionately announcing to the world that he would always be prepared to struggle for the cause of Communism. His eyes were as clear as the cloudless blue sky.

'I joined the Young Pioneers in second grade of elementary school.'

Time jumped forward, and a different flag appeared: that of the Communist Youth League, against the backdrop of a memorial to the fallen. A small group of older children were swearing their oaths to the flag. He stood in the back row, his eyes as bright as before, but tinged with new fervor and longing.

'I joined the Youth League first year of secondary school.'

The slider moved. The third red flag of his life appeared, the flag of the Communist Party this time, in what appeared to be an enormous lecture hall. The Senior Official zoomed in on one of the six teenagers taking their oaths, letting his face fill the screen.

'I joined the Party sophomore year of college.' The Senior Official pointed at the screen. 'Look at my eyes. What do you see in them?'

In that pair of young eyes could still be seen the spark of childhood, the fervor and longing of youth, but there was a new and yet immature wisdom, too.

'I feel you were . . . sincere,' Bai Bing said, looking at those eyes.

'You'd be right. Until then, I still meant every word of the oath.' The Senior Official wiped at his eye, the motion minute enough that Bai Bing didn't notice it.

The slider moved forward another few years. This time it sped too far, but after a few small adjustments, a tree-shaded path appeared on the screen. He stood there, looking at a young woman turning to leave. She turned her head to look at him one last time, her eyes bright with tears. She gave a powerful impression, solemn but resolute. Then she left, disappearing into the distance between the two rows of tall poplars. Tactfully, Bai Bing got up and prepared to leave some space, but the Senior Official stopped him.

'Don't worry, this is the last time I saw her.' He put down the mouse, his gaze leaving the screen. 'Very well, thank you. You may turn off the computer.'

'Don't you want to keep watching?'

'That's all I have worth reminiscing.'

'We can find where she is right now, no problem!'

'That won't be necessary. It's getting late; you should leave. Thank you, truly.'

Once Bai Bing left, the Senior Official telephoned the security station, requesting that the building guard come up to his office for a moment. Soon after, the armed police guard entered and saluted.

'You're . . . Yang, yes?'

'You have an excellent memory, sir.'

'I didn't call you up here for anything important. I just wanted to tell you that today is my birthday.'

Taken by surprise, the guard was momentarily lost for words.

The Senior Official smiled indulgently. 'Send my regards to the ranks. You may go.' The guard saluted, but just as he turned to leave, the Senior Official seemed to think of something. 'Oh, leave the gun behind.'

The guard hesitated, but pulled out his handgun. He walked over and carefully set it on one end of the broad office desk, before saluting again and leaving.

The Senior Official picked up the gun, detached the magazine, and took out the bullets, one by one, until there was only the last. Then he pushed the magazine back in. The next person to handle this gun could be his secretary, or the janitor who came in at night. An empty gun was always safer.

He put down the gun, then stood the removed bullets on the table in a circle, like the candles on a birthday cake. After that he strode to the window, looking across the city to the sun on the verge of setting. Behind the outer city's industrial air pollution, it appeared as a deep red disk. He thought it looked like a mirror.

The last thing he did was to take the small 'Serve the People' pin from his lapel and set it on the flag stand on the desk, beneath the miniature flags of China and the CCP.

Then he sat at his desk, calmly awaiting the last ray of the setting sun.

The Future

That night, Song Cheng entered the main computer room of the Center for Meteorological Modeling. He found Bai Bing alone, looking quietly at the screen of the booting superstring computer.

Song Cheng came over and patted his shoulder. 'Hey, Bai, I've already notified your manager. A special car will arrive shortly to take you to Beijing. You'll give the superstring computer to a central official. Some other experts in the field might listen to your report too. With such an extraordinary technology, it won't be easy to get people to understand and believe it all. You'll have to be patient when you explain and give the demonstrations . . . Bai Bing, what's wrong?'

Bai Bing remained quiet, not turning from his seat. In the mirrored universe on the screen, the Earth floated suspended in space. The ice caps had altered in shape, and the ocean was a grayer shade of blue, but the changes weren't obvious. Song Cheng didn't notice them.

'He was right,' Bai Bing said.

'What?'

'The Senior Official was right.' Bai Bing turned slowly toward Song Cheng. His eyes were bloodshot.

'Did you spend an entire day and night coming up with that conclusion?'

'No, I got the future-time recursion to work.'

'You mean . . . the digital mirror can simulate the future now?'

Bai Bing nodded listlessly. 'Just the very distant future. I thought of a completely new algorithm last night. It avoids the relatively near future, which allows it to sidestep the disruption in the causal chain resulting from knowledge of the future changing the present. I jumped the mirror directly into the far future.'

'How far?'

'Thirty-five thousand years later.'

'What's society like, then?' Song Cheng asked cautiously. 'Is the mirror having its effect?'

Bai Bing shook his head. 'The digital mirror won't exist by that time. Society won't either. Human civilization already disappeared.'

Song Cheng was speechless.

On the screen, the viewing angle descended rapidly, coming to a stop above a city surrounded by desert.

'This is our city. It's empty, already dead for two thousand years.'

The first impression the dead city gave was of a world of squares. All the buildings were perfect cubes, arrayed in neat columns and rows to form a perfectly square city. Only the clouds of sandy dust that rose at times in the square grid streets prevented one from mistaking the city for an abstract geometrical figure in a textbook.

Bai Bing maneuvered the viewing angle to enter a room in one of the cube-shaped edifices. Everything in it had been buried by countless years of sand and dust. On the side with the window, the accumulated sand rose in a slope, already high enough to touch the windowsill. The surface of the sand bulged in places, perhaps indicating buried appliances and furniture. A few structures like dead branches extended from one corner; that was a metal coatrack, now mostly rust. Bai Bing copied part of the view and pasted it into another program, where he processed away the thick layer of sand on top, revealing a television and refrigerator rusted down to the bare frames, as well as a writing desk. A picture frame, long fallen over, lay on the desk. Bai Bing adjusted the viewing angle and zoomed in so that the small photo in the frame filled the screen.

It was a family portrait of three, but the three people in the photo were practically identical in appearance and dress. One could guess their gender only by the length of hair, and age only by height. They wore matching outfits similar to Mao suits, orderly and stiff, buttoned to the collar. When Song Cheng looked closer, he found that their features still displayed some variation. The effect of indistinguishability had come from their identical expressions, a sort of wooden serenity, a sort of dead graveness.

'Everyone in the photos and video fragments I could find had the same expression on their face. I haven't seen any other emotion, certainly not tears or laughter.'

'How did it end up like this?' Song Cheng asked, horrified. 'Can you look through the historical records they left?'

'I did. The course of history after us goes something like this: The age of the mirror will start in five years. During the first twenty years, digital mirrors will only be used by law enforcement, but they'll already be substantially affecting human society and causing structural changes. After that, digital mirrors will seep into every corner of life and society. History calls it the beginning of the Mirror Era. For the first five centuries of the new era, human society still gradually develops. The signs of total stagnation first appear in the mid-sixth century ME. Culture stagnates first, because human nature is now as pure as water, and there is nothing left to depict and express. Literature disappears, then all of the humanities. Science and technology will grind to a standstill after them. The stagnation of progress lasts thirty thousand years. History calls that protracted period the Middle Age of Light.'

'What happens after?'

'The rest is straightforward. Earth runs out of resources, and all the arable land is lost to desertification. Meanwhile, humanity still doesn't have the technology to colonize space, or the power to excavate new resources. In those five thousand years, everything slowly winds down. . . . In the era I showed you, there are still people living on all the continents, but there's really not much to see.'

'Ah . . .' The sound Song Cheng made resembled the Senior Official's slow sigh. A long time passed before his shaking voice could ask, 'Then . . . what do we do? Do we destroy the digital mirror right now?'

Bai Bing took out two cigarettes, handing one to Song Cheng. He lit his own and drew deeply, blowing the smoke at the three dead faces on the screen. 'I'm definitely destroying the digital mirror. I only kept it around until now so you can see. But nothing we do now matters. That's one bit of consolation: everything that happens afterward has nothing to do with us.'

'Someone else created a digital mirror too?'

'The theory and technology for it are both out there, and according to superstring theory, the number of viable initialization parameter sets is enormous, but still finite. If you keep going down the list, you'll eventually run into that one set. . . . More than thirty thousand years from now, till the last days of civilization, humanity will still be thanking and worshiping a guy named Nick Kristoff.'

'Who is he?'

'According to the historical records: a devout Christian, physicist, and inventor of the digital mirror software.'

Mirror Era

FIVE MONTHS LATER, AT THE PRINCETON UNIVERSITY CENTER OF EXPERIMENTAL COSMOLOGY

When the radiant sea of stars appeared on one of the fifty display screens, all of the scientists and engineers present erupted into cheers. Five superstring computers stood here, each simulating ten virtual machines, for a total of fifty sets of big bang simulations running day and night. This newly created virtual universe was the 32,961st.

Only one middle-aged man remained unmoved. He was heavy-browed and alert-eyed, imposing in appearance, the silver cross at his breast all the more striking against his black sweater. He made the sign of the cross, and asked:

'Gravitational constant?'
'6.67 times 10^{-11}!'
'Speed of light in a vacuum?'
'2.998 times 10^{5} kilometers per second!'
'Planck's constant?'
'6.626 times 10^{-34}!'
'Charge of electron?'
'1.602 times 10^{-19} coulombs!'
'One plus one?' He gravely kissed the cross at his chest.
'Equals two! This is our universe, Professor Kristoff!'

OF ANTS AND DINOSAURS

PROLOGUE

BRIGHT SPARKS

If the entire history of the Earth were condensed into a single day, one hour would equate to 200 million years, one minute to 3.3 million years and one second to 55,000 years. Life would appear as early as eight or nine o'clock in the morning, but human civilisation would not emerge until the last tenth of the last second of the day. From the morning that philosophers held the first ever debate on the steps of a temple in Ancient Greece . . . from the day slaves laid the first foundation stone of the Great Pyramid . . . from the minute that Confucius welcomed his first disciple into the candlelit gloom of his thatched hut . . . right up until the moment you turned the first page of this book, only one-tenth of a tick of the clock would have elapsed.

But in the hours before this tenth of a second, what was life on Earth doing? Was every single living being doing nothing but swimming, roaming around, breeding and sleeping for . . . well . . . billions of years? Was every other organism universally and unremittingly stupid – for aeon after aeon? Of the countless branches on the tree of life, was our small twig really the only one to have been graced with the light of intelligence? It seems unlikely.

Nevertheless, for a germ of intelligence to grow into a great civilisation is no easy feat. It requires that many conditions be met simultaneously, a one-in-a-million coincidence. Nascent intelligence is as precarious as a tiny flame in an open field. It's liable to be snuffed out in the slightest breeze, and even if it does catch and manages to set the surrounding weeds alight, the little fire will likely find its path blocked by a stream or an empty clearing, causing it to die out without so much as a whimper. Should it somehow muster sufficient energy and spread like wildfire, a heavy rainstorm will probably extinguish it. All in all, the chances of a tiny flame becoming a raging conflagration are exceedingly slim. And so we can assume that, through the endless night of antiquity, budding intelligences flickered on and then off again like the brief, brilliant twinkles of fireflies.

At approximately twenty minutes to midnight – that is, approximately twenty minutes before our arrival – two flames of intelligence appeared on Earth. We might call them bright sparks. This twenty-minute period was no mere flash in the pan, for it equates to more than 60 million years. It's an era unimaginably distant from ours. Humanity's ancestors would not emerge for another few tens of millions of years. There were no humans back then, and even the continents were shaped very differently than they are today. On the geologic timescale, it was the Late Cretaceous period.

At that time, gigantic animals called dinosaurs inhabited Earth. There were many different types of dinosaurs, and most of them were ludicrously large. The heaviest weighed 80 tonnes, or as much as 800 people, and the tallest grew to thirty metres, the height of a four-storey building. They had already lived on Earth for 70 million years, which is to say that they appeared on Earth more than a billion years ago from now.

Compared with humanity's several hundred thousand years on Earth, 70 million years is a very long time indeed. Time enough for the patter of raindrops drip-dripping steadily onto the same spot to carve great chasms out of the Earth; time enough for the gentlest of air currents blowing continuously against a mountain to level it. A species undergoing continual evolution over the same timespan, no matter how stupid to begin with, will become intelligent. And that's what happened to the dinosaurs.

Over those millions of years, the dinosaurs discovered how to uproot the biggest trees, strip away the branches and leaves, and tie massive boulders to their ends with rattan. If the boulder was round or square, the tree became a hammer so humongous that it could have flattened one of our cars with a single blow. If the stone was flat, the dinosaurs used it as a megalithic axe. If the stone was pointed, they left intact some of the tree's upper branches and crafted the trunk into a spear tens of metres long. The branches stabilised the spear during flight, and it flew like a dud missile.

The dinosaurs formed primitive tribes and dwelt in enormous caves they excavated themselves. They learnt to use fire, preserving the embers left by lightning strikes to illuminate their cavernous abodes and to cook food. For candles they co-opted entire pine trees several arm-spans around. They even wrote on the walls of their caves with the charred tree-trunks, recording in simple strokes how many eggs were laid yesterday and how many baby dinosaurs hatched today. More importantly, the dinosaurs already possessed a rudimentary language. To our ears, their conversations would have sounded like the whistling of trains.

At the same time, another species on Earth was showing signs of budding intelligence. Ants. They too had undergone a long process of evolution; in fact, by this point, the scale of ant society far outstripped that of dinosaur society. Ants had raised cities on every continent – some of these took the form of towering ant-hills, others were subterranean labyrinths – and many of their kingdoms had populations exceeding 100 million. These vast societies developed ingenious, tightly organised structures and hummed along to an efficient, systematic rhythm. The ants communicated with each other using pheromones – extremely sophisticated odour molecules that could convey the most detailed information – and this endowed them with a more advanced language than that of the dinosaurs.

However, although the first glimmers of intelligence had appeared in two species on Earth – one great and one small – both species were beset with fatal flaws, and their respective paths to civilisation were strewn with insurmountable obstacles.

The dinosaurs' biggest disadvantage was that they lacked dexterous hands. Their huge, clumsy claws were matchless in a fight (one type of dinosaur, *Deinonychus*, had claws as sharp as sabres, which it used to disembowel its rivals) and could fashion crude tools, but they were incapable of performing fiddly tasks, manufacturing sophisticated implements or writing anything complicated. This was problematic because manual dexterity is a prerequisite for the development of civilisation. Only when a species has versatile hands can a virtuous circle form between brain evolution and survival activities.

The ants, conversely, could execute extraordinarily fiddly tasks, and they constructed the most intricate architecture both above ground and beneath it. But they lacked flair and a certain richness of thought. When a gathering of ants reached critical mass they exhibited a collective intelligence that was literal and unerring, much like a computer program. Guided by these programs, which developed over extended periods of time, ant colonies built city after labyrinthine city. Their society operated like a vast, precisely engineered piece of machinery, but separate an ant cog from that machine and you'd find that the individual's thought processes were disappointingly shallow and pedestrian. This was the ants' downfall, for the sort of creative thinking required to progress civilisation is the province of individuals – individuals like our Newton and Einstein, for example. The very nature of collective intelligence, its intrinsic principle of redundancy, is antithetical to the production of advanced thought; 100 million of us humans, though we might rack our brains as hard as we can, would still not come up with the three laws of motion or the theory of relativity.

In the ordinary run of things, therefore, neither ant society nor dinosaur society could have continued to evolve. As with countless such examples before and since, the flames of intelligence that had flared into life within these two species should have fizzled out in the waters of time, a couple of ephemeral bright sparks in the long night of Earth's history.

But then a curious thing happened.

1

THE FIRST ENCOUNTER

It was an ordinary day in the Late Cretaceous. It is impossible to determine the exact date, but it was truly an ordinary day, and Earth was at peace.

Let us examine the shape of the world that day. At that time, the profiles and positions of the continents differed radically from their current forms. Antarctica and Australia made up a single landmass greater in size than either continent today, India was a large island in the Tethys Sea, and Europe and Asia were two separate landmasses. Dinosaurs were found predominantly on two supercontinents. The first, Gondwana, had been Earth's only continuous landmass several billion years earlier. It had since broken up, and its area was greatly reduced, but it was still as big as present-day Africa and South America combined. The second, Laurasia, had split from Gondwana and would later come to form what we now know as North America.

That day, every creature on every continent was occupied with the business of survival. In that uncivilised world, they knew not where they'd come from and cared not where they were headed. When the Cretaceous sun was directly overhead and the shadows cast by the leaves of the cycads were at their smallest, their sole concern was where they were going to get lunch.

In a sunlit clearing amid a stand of tall sago palms in central Gondwana, one as yet quite unexceptional *Tyrannosaurus rex* had just lynched a plump, good-sized lizard for its midday meal. With its fearsome claws it ripped the still wriggling lizard in two and tossed the tail end into its gaping jaws. As it munched away with relish, the dinosaur felt entirely happy with the world and its own place within it.

Things below ground were far from calm, however. The *Tyrannosaurus*'s pursuit of the lizard had caused a powerful earthquake in the subterranean ant town located a mere metre from the dinosaur's left foot. Fortunately, the town had just avoided being trampled, but now hordes of its thousand or so residents scuttled to the surface to see what had happened.

The *Tyrannosaurus* had blocked out more than half their sky; it was like a towering peak piercing the clouds. For the ants massed in the mountain's shadow, it was as if the day had suddenly become overcast. They squinted up, up, high into the sky, watching as the lizard's tail arced through the air and into the fathomless mouth of the *Tyrannosaurus*. They listened to the sound of the dinosaur chewing, to the cracking and rumbling that was like thunder from the heavens. On previous occasions, this thunder had often been accompanied by a heavy downpour of splintered bones and chunks of flesh. Even a light drizzle of the dinosaur's leftovers would provide lunch for the entire town. But this *Tyrannosaurus* kept its mouth tightly closed, and nothing rained down from the sky. After a few moments, it tossed the other half of the lizard into its mouth. Thunder boomed overhead again, but still the shower of bones and flesh held off.

When the *Tyrannosaurus* had finished, it took a couple of steps back and lay down contentedly for a nap in the shade. The ground shuddered, the peak collapsed into a distant mountain range, and brilliant sunshine flooded the clearing once more. The ants shook their heads and sighed. The dry season was long this year, and life was getting harder by the day. They had already gone hungry for two days.

Just as the crestfallen critters were turning back towards the entrance to their town, another earthquake rocked the clearing. The mountain range was rolling agitatedly back and forth across the ground! The ants watched intently as the *Tyrannosaurus* stuck one of its monstrous claws into its mouth and began to dig furiously between its teeth. Immediately, they understood why the dinosaur could not sleep: lizard flesh had got stuck in its teeth and was getting on its nerves.

The mayor of the ant town had a sudden idea. It climbed onto a blade of grass and released a pheromone towards the colony below. As the pheromone spread, the ants understood the mayor's meaning and passed the message on. Antennae waved as a tide of excitement swept through the crowd.

Led by the mayor, the ants marched towards the *Tyrannosaurus*, streaming across the ground in orderly black rivulets. At first the mountain range seemed impossibly far away, visible on the horizon but unreachable. But then the restless *Tyrannosaurus* rolled towards them again, closing the gap between itself and the procession of ants in an instant. As it shifted, one of its huge claws fell from the sky and landed with an earth-shaking thump right in front of the mayor. The impact bounced the entire procession clear off the ground, and the dust it raised mushroomed before the ants like an atomic cloud.

Without waiting for the dust to settle, the ants followed their mayor onto the dinosaur's claw. The dinosaur's palm had come to rest perpendicular to the ground, forming a craggy, precipitous cliff. But to the ants, who excelled at climbing, this was no obstacle. They quickly darted up the cliff-face and onto the dinosaur's forearm. Still in formation, they navigated the rough skin of the forearm, winding their way across its plateau-like surface, down and up the steep sides of its countless gullies and on towards the upper arm and the *Tyrannosaurus*'s maw.

Just then, the *Tyrannosaurus* raised its massive claw to pick at its teeth again. The ants advancing across its forearm felt the ground beneath them tilting, followed by an alarming increase in G-force. They clung on for dear life. Half their view of the sky was now taken up by the dinosaur's colossal head. Its slow breathing was like wind gusting through the heavens and its oceanic eyes peering down at them made them tremble with fear.

Spotting the ants on its forearm, the *Tyrannosaurus* raised its other arm to brush them off. Its palm blotted out the midday sun like a vast stormcloud, casting a threatening shadow over the ant army. They stared up at it in horror, twitching their antennae frantically. The mayor quickly raised one of its front legs and the rest of the troop immediately did the same, the entire colony now one long, quivering black arrow pointing at the dinosaur's mouth.

The *Tyrannosaurus* was stunned for a few seconds but eventually grasped the ants' intention and lowered its arm. The stormcloud dispersed and sunlight returned. Then the dinosaur opened its mouth wide and placed a single clawed finger against its titanic teeth, forming a bridge between arm and jaw. There was a fraction of hesitation, but the mayor took the lead once again and the rest of the colony marched on without demur.

The first group of ants swiftly reached the end of the finger. Standing on the smooth, conical claw-tip, they gazed into the dinosaur's mouth in awe. Before them was a night-time world where a storm was brewing. A fierce, damp wind reeking of gore blasted their faces, and rumblings rose up from the dark, chasmic depths. When the ants' eyes adjusted to the gloom, they could just make out a patch of even denser darkness in the distance, the borders of which kept changing shape. It took them a long time to realise that this was the dinosaur's throat. It was also the source of the rumbling, which was coming from the *Tyrannosaurus*'s stomach. The ants instinctively recoiled in fright. Then, one by one, they climbed onto the dinosaur's huge teeth and crawled down the smooth white enamel cliffs.

With their powerful mandibles, the ants tore at the pink lizard flesh that was lodged in the ravines between the teeth. As they chewed, they stared up at the enormous white columns rising skywards to either side of them. High above them, on the dinosaur's palate, another row of gnashers gleamed menacingly in the sunlight, looking for all the world as if they might come chomping down at any moment. But the *Tyrannosaurus* had already moved its finger to its upper jaw, and an unbroken stream of ants was now scaling those teeth and devouring the meat stuck between them, creating a mirror-image of the scene on its lower jaw.

More than a thousand ants bustled about the dozen or so crevices and soon the scraps of meat had been picked clean. The dinosaur's dental discomfort had been dealt with! The *Tyrannosaurus* was not yet evolved enough to say thank you, so it merely let out a long sigh of satisfaction. This sudden hurricane blasted every last ant out of the dinosaur's mouth and into the air in a cloud of black dust, but because their bodies were incredibly light, they landed unscathed about a metre from the *Tyrannosaurus*'s head. With their stomachs now full, the ants pattered back to the entrance of their town, thoroughly sated. The *Tyrannosaurus*, meanwhile, rolled over into the cool shade and fell into an easy sleep.

And that was that.

As the Earth quietly turned, the sun slid silently towards the west, the cycad shadows lengthened, and butterflies and bugs flitted through the trees. In the distance, the waves of the primeval ocean lapped against the shores of Gondwana.

Unbeknown to all, in this most tranquil of moments the history of the Earth had taken a sharp turn in a new direction.

2

THE AGE OF EXPLORATION OF THE DINOSAUR BODY

Two days after the encounter between the ants and the dinosaur, on an equally sweltering afternoon, the inhabitants of the ant town were shaken by another quake. They scampered up to the surface and were met by the towering figure of a *Tyrannosaurus*, which they straightaway recognised as the same one from before. It had hunkered down and was scouring the ground for something. When it saw the colony, it lifted a claw and jabbed at its teeth. The ants understood immediately, and in a single uniform gesture all 1,000 of them waved their antennae excitedly. The *Tyrannosaurus* placed one of its forearms flat on the ground and allowed the ants to climb on. And just like that, the scene from two days earlier was replayed: the colony made a meal of the scraps of meat stuck between the dinosaur's teeth, and the dinosaur was relieved of a minor dental discomfort.

For some time after that, the *Tyrannosaurus* routinely sought out the town of ants so they could pick its teeth. The ants could feel its footfalls from a kilometre away and were able to accurately distinguish them from those of other dinosaurs. They could even tell from the vibrations in what direction the *Tyrannosaurus* was moving. If it was heading towards the town, the ants rushed eagerly to the surface, knowing that their food supply for the day was assured. Even though one party in this cooperative endeavour was very large and the members of the other party were undeniably very little, it didn't take long for the interactions between the two to become well honed.

One day the vibrations coming through the ants' earthen ceiling sounded different, unfamiliar. When they streamed up into the clearing to investigate, they saw that their partner had brought along three other *Tyrannosaurus rex* and a *Tarbosaurus bataar*! All five dinosaurs gestured at their teeth, requesting the ants' help. The mayor, recognising that its colony couldn't possibly undertake such a massive task on its own, sent several drones post-haste to contact other ant towns in the area. Soon, three mighty rivers of ants came pouring in from between the trees, and an army of more than 6,000 ants converged on the clearing. Each dinosaur required the services of 1,000 ants, or, rather, the meat between the teeth of one dinosaur could satisfy 1,000 ants.

The next day, eight dinosaurs came to have their teeth cleaned, and a few days later that number increased to ten. Most of them were exceedingly big carnivores and they had a correspondingly big impact on their surroundings. They trampled the nearby cycads, enlarging the clearing significantly, and at the same time they solved the food problems of a dozen ant towns in the vicinity.

However, the basis for this cooperation between the two species was by no means secure. For a start, compared to the myriad hardships faced by the dinosaurs – hunger when prey was scarce, thirst when water sources had dried up, injuries sustained in fights with their own or other kinds of dinosaur, not to mention a host of fatal diseases – getting meat trapped between their teeth was a mere piddling inconvenience. Quite a few of the dinosaurs who sought out the ants for a teeth-clean did so out of curiosity or for a lark. Equally, once the dry season was over, food would become plentiful again for the ants, and they would no longer need to rely on this unorthodox method of sourcing their daily meat. Attending those terrible banquets in the dinosaurs' mouths – so very like the gates of hell – was not something most of the ants relished.

It was the arrival of a *Tarbosaurus* with tooth decay that marked a major step forward in dinosaur–ant cooperation. That afternoon, nine dinosaurs had come to have their teeth cleaned, but this particular *Tarbosaurus* still seemed restless even after its procedure had been completed; one might even describe its mood as antsy. It held its forearm high to prevent the cleanser ants from leaving and with its other claw gestured insistently at its teeth.

The mayor in charge of that colony led a few dozen ants back into the *Tarbosaurus*'s mouth and examined the row of teeth carefully. They quickly discovered several cavities in the smooth enamel walls, each large enough to admit two or three ants side by side. In went the mayor, braving one of the cavities, and several other ants crawled in after it. They scrutinised the walls of the wide passageway. The dinosaur's teeth were very hard, and anything that could tunnel through material as tough as that was indisputably a digger to rival the ants themselves.

As the ants felt their way forward, a black worm twice their size suddenly erupted from a branch passage, brandishing a fearsome pair of razor-sharp mandibles. With a click, it bit off the mayor's head. A bundle of other worms then burst out of nowhere, divided the column of ants in the tunnel and launched a ferocious attack against them. The ants were too exhausted to defend themselves and in an instant more than half were slaughtered. Those that did manage to break through the encirclement raced past the black worms but quickly became disoriented in the labyrinthine passages.

Of the original crew, only five ants escaped the cavity, one of whom was carrying the mayor's head. An ant's head retains life and consciousness for a relatively long time after being separated from its body, and so, bizarre though it sounds – and how much more bizarre must it have looked – the disembodied mayor's head was able to address the thousand ants still standing on the dinosaur's forearm. In a meeting that was clearly far larger than a simple tête-à-tête, the bodiless head explained the situation regarding the *Tarbosaurus*'s teeth, issued a final command and only then expired.

A crack team of 200 soldier ants now marched into the dinosaur's mouth and made straight for that first tooth. Though the soldier ants were skilled at fighting, the black worms were many times their size. Owing to their familiarity with the structure of the tunnels, the worms successfully checked the soldier ants' attack, killing a dozen of them and forcing the rest to retreat.

Just as morale began to flag, reinforcements from another town arrived. These troops were a different type of soldier ant. Though smaller, they possessed a deadly power: they were able to deliver devastating attacks with formic acid. The fresh battalion surged into the tunnel, got into position, pivoted 180 degrees, aimed their posteriors at the enemy and ejected a fine spray of formic acid droplets. The black worms were reduced to scorched masses within seconds. Dark smoke poured from their remains.

Another detachment of soldier ants flooded in. They were also relatively small, but their mandibles were venomous – so venomous that a tiny bite could cause a black worm to twitch twice and drop dead. With the battle now in full swing, the ant army moved from tooth to tooth, rooting out the black worms. Acidic smoke leaked from every cavity. A team of worker ants ferried the corpses out of the dinosaur's mouth and deposited them on a leaf in its palm. Soon the leaf was piled high with dead black worms, many of them still smoking. Several other dinosaurs gathered around the *Tarbosaurus*, looking on in amazement.

Half an hour later, the last of the black worms had been purged and the battle was over. The *Tarbosaurus*'s mouth was filled with the strange taste of formic acid, but the dental complaint that had troubled it for most of its life was gone. It began to roar excitedly, sharing the miracle with all the dinosaurs present.

The news spread quickly through the forest and there was a dramatic spike in the number of dinosaurs visiting the ants. Some of them still wanted their teeth picked, but most came seeking treatment for dental ailments, because tooth decay was prevalent among carnivores and herbivores alike. On the busiest days, several hundred dinosaurs would congregate in the clearing, striding along carefully between great streams of ants. It was a bustling, prosperous scene. Accordingly, there was also a sharp increase in the number of ants who came to service the dinosaurs, and, unlike their patients, the ants, once arrived, rarely left. And so, what had started off as a normal-sized town exploded into a megalopolis of more than a million ants. It was called the Ivory Citadel and became famous as the first gathering place of ants and dinosaurs on Earth.

With the boom in business and the end of the dry season, the ants were no longer satisfied with scraps scavenged from between the dinosaurs' teeth. Their clients began to pay for their medical services with fresh bones and meat. Since the ants of the Ivory Citadel no longer needed to forage for food, they became professional dentists. This specialisation led to rapid advances in the ants' medical technology.

In the course of their anti-toothworm campaigns, the ants often travelled along the cavities to the roots of the dinosaurs' teeth. At the junction of the teeth and the gums they found thick translucent pipes. When these pipes were touched, for example during combat, violent earthquakes would shake the dinosaurs' mouths. Over time, the ants came to understand that stimulating these pipes caused the dinosaurs pain; later, they would call these structures nerves.

The ants had for a long time known of a certain two-leafed herb that could make their own limbs go numb – numb enough that they felt no pain when a leg was torn off – and that could also put them to sleep, sometimes for several days. They now applied the juice of this herb to the nerves in the roots of the dinosaurs' teeth, and the consequence was that contact with the nerves no longer triggered earthquakes. The gums of dinosaurs with dental diseases were frequently septic, but the ants knew of another herb whose juice could promote wound healing. So they spread the juice of this herb across the ulcers on the dinosaurs' gums, which closed up quickly.

The introduction of these two pain- and inflammation-reducing techniques not only enabled the ants to cure dinosaurs of toothworm infestations but also allowed them to treat other ailments not caused by the worms, such as toothaches and periodontitis. However, the real revolution in the ants' medical technology was brought about by the exploration of the dinosaur body.

The ants were natural explorers, not out of curiosity – they were incurious creatures – but out of an instinctive urge to expand their living space. Every so often, while exterminating worms or pouring medicine onto a dinosaur's teeth, they would peek into the abysmal reaches of its mouth. That dark, moist, interior world awakened in them a desire to travel into the great beyond, but fear of the attendant perils had always stopped them in their tracks.

The Age of Exploration of the Dinosaur Body was eventually ushered in by an ant named Daba – the first named ant in the recorded history of Cretaceous civilisation. After much preparation, Daba capitalised on the opportunity presented by a toothworm treatment and led a small expedition of ten soldier ants and ten worker ants into the dank depths of a *Tyrannosaurus*'s mouth.

Battling extreme humidity, the expedition began its traverse of the long narrow isthmus of the tongue. Tastebuds speckled the surface like a vast megalithic structure of slimy white boulders extending far into the gloom. The ant explorers picked their way between them.

As the dinosaur opened and closed its mouth, light from the outside world streaked through the gaps between its teeth, flickering like lightning on the horizon and casting long, wavering shadows behind the tastebud megaliths. When its tongue squirmed, the entire isthmus rose and fell like a stormy sea, causing shifting ripples to appear in the megaliths. And every time the *Tyrannosaurus* swallowed, viscous floodwaters gushed in from both sides, submerging the isthmus and forcing the ants to cling to the tastebuds for fear of being swept away. It was the stuff of nightmares, but the dauntless ants patiently waited for the floodwaters to recede, then pressed on.

At long last they arrived at the root of the tongue. The light was much weaker there, barely illuminating the mouths of the two enormous caves before them. In one cave, a fierce gale howled, by turns sucking and then expelling the air, reversing direction every two to three seconds. There was no wind in the other cave, just a reverberant rumbling that rose from its invisible depths – a rumbling familiar to the ants from their time working on the teeth, but much, much louder, more like continual booms of thunder. This mysterious and terrible noise unnerved the ants more than the gale, so they decided to try the windy passageway. They would later learn that this was the dinosaur's respiratory tract and that the scarily noisy passageway was its oesophagus.

With Daba in the lead, the expedition proceeded gingerly down the slick walls of the respiratory tract. When the wind was with them, they hurried forward several steps; when the wind was against them, it was impossible to walk, and they could only flatten their bodies and grip the wall tightly. They had not descended very far, however, before the tickle of their legs began to irritate the respiratory tract. With a slight cough, the dinosaur put an end to the ants' first expedition. A hurricane of unimaginable force spiralled up from the bottom of the tunnel, sweeping the expeditioners off their feet and jetting them across the isthmus of the tongue at lightning speed. Some of them were hurled headlong into the dinosaur's huge teeth, while others were blown straight out of its mouth.

Daba lost one of her middle legs in the failed expedition, but, unperturbed, she quickly organised a second attempt. This time she decided they would tackle the oesophagus instead. The preliminary stages went smoothly. The ants entered the oesophagus and began the long march down the seemingly endless and terrifyingly loud passage. Its creepy darkness was the least of their troubles, however, for the *Tyrannosaurus* had stopped beside a stream and now took a sip of water. The first the explorers knew of this was when they heard a great roar building behind them, a roar so loud that it rapidly drowned out the noise ahead of them. Daba immediately ordered the team to a halt, but before she could even begin to work out what was happening, a wall of water came cascading down the tunnel, hurtling past the ants, flinging them into its churn and propelling them at terrific speed all the way down the oesophagus and on towards the dinosaur's stomach.

Dazed and disoriented, Daba landed heavily and sank into something pulpy. She paddled her legs as hard as she could in a desperate bid to escape the ooze, but she couldn't move at all in the sticky substance. Thankfully, the floodwaters were still pouring down, thinning the slurry and tumbling everything around, so when things finally began to settle, she was able to float to the top. She had another go at walking. The sludge beneath her was soft and watery, but solid chunks of varying sizes and shapes bobbed along on the surface, making it possible for her to crawl from one to the other. She made slow progress, the slime sucking at her feet, but at last she reached the edge of the slurry pit.

Before her rose a soft wall covered in cilia about as tall as she was, like a strange dwarf forest; the stomach wall, in fact. She began to scale it. Whichever route she took, the cilia curled around her, trying to grab her, but their reactions were sluggish and they came up empty every time. Daba's eyes had now adjusted to her surroundings and to her surprise she discovered that it wasn't totally dark in there. A faint glow suffused the space, shining through the dinosaur's skin from the outside world. In the light she spotted four fellow ants also climbing the stomach wall. She veered off to join them.

As they began to recover from the shock of their ordeal, the five ants stared down at the vast digestive sea from which they had just extricated themselves, mesmerised by the slow churn of the viscous mire. Every so often a great bubble exploded – the source of that reverberant rumbling. When a particularly large bubble burst below her, Daba saw a thick, squat object break the surface and list slowly to one side. She recognised it as a lizard's leg. Moments later, another massive, triangular object rose to the top. Its huge white eyes and wide mouth identified it as a fish head. Plenty more partially digested items followed, mostly either the bones and chewed-up remains of animals or the stones of wild fruits.

One of the ants beside Daba gave her a nudge, drawing her attention to the stomach wall beneath their feet. It was weeping clear mucus. The gastric secretions merged into rivulets that glistened in the faint light as they trickled down through the forest of cilia into the digestive sea below. Several of the ants were already coated in the juice. At first it simply made them prickle all over, but that soon intensified into a burning sensation not dissimilar to the aftereffects of a formic-acid attack.

'We're being digested!' one of the ants shouted. Daba was surprised she could still distinguish her comrade's pheromones from the pungent cocktail of strange odours in the stale air.

The ant was right. They were being digested by the dinosaur's gastric juices, and their antennae were the first things to go. Daba saw that her own antennae had been half-eaten away already. 'We need to get out of here,' she said.

'How? It's so far! We don't have the strength,' replied one of the other ants.

'We can't climb out – our feet have already been digested,' added another.

Only then did Daba notice that her own five feet had been partially consumed by the gastric juice. The feet of the other four ants had fared no better.

'If only there was another flood to flush us out,' the first ant said wistfully.

Her words sent a jolt of realisation through Daba. She stared at the ant, a soldier ant with a pair of venomous mandibles. 'You twit, *you* can cause another flood!' Daba shouted.

The soldier ant stared at the expedition leader in bewilderment.

'Bite it! Make it throw up!'

The soldier ant, grasping the idea at last, immediately started nipping savagely at the stomach wall. She quickly chewed through several cilia, leaving deep gouges in the wall. The stomach wall quivered violently, then began to convulse and contort. The cilia forest grew denser, a clear sign that the stomach was contracting and the dinosaur was about to vomit. The digestive sea began to roil, taking the ants with it. Engulfed by the rapidly rising sea, in a very short space of time the five ants were whooshed all the way up the oesophagus, swept over the isthmus of the tongue, catapulted across the two rows of teeth and expelled into the great outdoors, landing in the grass with a flump.

Once the five expeditioners had disengaged themselves from the slithery slick of vomit, they saw that they were encircled by a vast swarm of ants. A crowd of several hundred thousand had come to cheer the return of the great explorers. The Age of Exploration of the Dinosaur Body had begun in earnest, an era that was to prove as important to antkind as the Age of Discovery was for humankind.

3

THE DAWN OF CIVILISATION

Following Daba's pioneering feat, one ant expedition after another plumbed the depths of the dinosaur body via the oesophagus. They discovered that the fastest way in was to hitch a ride when the dinosaur was eating or drinking something, surfing in on a gulp of river water or a ball of chewed-up food. The ants knew that a dinosaur was made up of at least two systems: the digestive system, which they had now probed many times, and the respiratory system, which they had never visited. After Daba recovered from her injuries, the five-legged, stumpy-feelered ant decided to try the windpipe again. This time her team was consisted of smaller ants and they marched at widely spaced intervals to minimise the irritation to the dinosaur's respiratory tract and prevent a repeat of the disastrous cough.

Compared with the oesophagus, the journey through the respiratory tract was gruelling: there was no food or water on which to cadge a lift, and they had to march in gale-force conditions. Only the strongest ants stood a chance of making it. But the great explorer and her team triumphed again and for the first time antkind entered a dinosaur's respiratory system.

Where the digestive system was suffocatingly humid, the respiratory system was a domain of fierce winds and unpredictable currents. In the dinosaur's lungs, the ants witnessed the awe-inducing sight of air dissolving into the bloodstream via the vast three-dimensional labyrinth formed by the air sacs. That river of blood, flowing from some unknown source, alerted them to the existence of other worlds inside the dinosaurs, worlds that they would much later come to identify as the circulatory system, the nervous system and the endocrine system.

The focus of the third stage of exploration was the dinosaurs' craniums. On their first attempt, the ants ventured in through their subject's nostrils. Light-footed though they were, their pattering caused such intense tickling that the dinosaur sneezed with tornadic ferocity, shooting the little prospectors back out of its nasal passageway like bullets from a gun. Most of the team members on that initial mission were torn to shreds. Later cranial survey expeditions entered through the ears, with more success. En route, they investigated the dinosaurs' visual and auditory organs and analysed those delicate systems. They did eventually manage to reach the brain, though it was many years before they worked out the purpose and significance of that most mysterious of organs.

And so it was that the ants gained a detailed understanding of dinosaur anatomy, laying the foundations for the medical revolution that followed.

Ant expeditions often entered the bodies of sick dinosaurs – massive creatures that had been reduced to skin and bone, their eyes dull and heavy, their movements slow and feeble, creatures that could do little but continually moan with pain. By comparing their interior systems with those of healthy dinosaurs, the ant explorers were easily able to pinpoint the locations of the diseased organ or lesion in question. They envisioned many different methods of treating internal diseases in dinosaurs, but not a single one could be put to the test, for such mammoth undertakings would require the consent of the dinosaur itself and to date the ants had always gained access without their hosts' knowledge.

The vast majority of dinosaurs would on no account let the ants burrow into their stomachs or brains, even if their intentions were entirely honourable and therapeutic. However, an epoch-making breakthrough occurred in this regard with a *Hadrosaurus* named Alija, the earliest named dinosaur in the history of Cretaceous civilisation.

When Alija trudged into the Ivory Citadel that day, it was immediately obvious to the ants that he was in a frail state. A squad of 500 straight away scuttled forward to greet him and offer assistance, as they did with every dinosaur patient, and Alija duly opened his mouth and pointed inside with his claw. It was an unnecessary gesture, for dinosaurs only ever turned up there to get their teeth worked on.

But the lead ant doctor, an ant by the name of Avi, who would later become the father of ant internal medicine, noticed that Alija was not actually pointing to his teeth but to somewhere further down – to his throat. Next, the dinosaur pointed to his stomach, grimaced to show that it hurt, and pointed to his throat again. There was no mistaking his meaning: he was asking the ants to examine his stomach.

So Dr Avi led a team of several dozen ants to conduct the first ever internal examination of a consenting dinosaur. The diagnostic team entered Alija's stomach by way of his oesophagus and quickly discovered a lesion in the stomach wall. Major medical intervention was required, but Dr Avi knew that with the limited antpower currently available to him, this was not possible. He would need a great deal of assistance. When he emerged from the dinosaur's mouth, he made an emergency appointment with the mayor of the Ivory Citadel. At the meeting, he explained the situation and requested an additional 50,000 ants as well as three kilograms each of anaesthetic and anti-inflammatory drugs.

The mayor waved her antennae angrily. 'Are you crazy, Doctor? We have a full schedule of dinosaur patients today. If we reassign that many ants to your team, we'll have to delay service to nearly sixty dinosaurs. Not to mention that that much medicine would be enough for a hundred treatments. That *Hadrosaurus* is sickly. He's too weak to find bones and meat. How will he pay for this super-treatment?'

'You must take the long view, Madam Mayor,' Dr Avi replied. 'If this intervention is successful, we ants will no longer be restricted to treating only dental problems – we'll be able to cure almost any disease. Our business with the dinosaurs will increase tenfold, a hundredfold. We'll earn more bones and meat than we can count, and your city will grow prodigiously.'

The mayor was persuaded and she gave Avi the ants, drugs and authority he had asked for. A great contingent of 50,000 ants was soon assembled, and two piles of drugs were hauled in. The sick *Hadrosaurus* lay flat on the ground as the army of ants streamed into his open mouth in continuous, unbroken columns, each ant carrying a tiny backpack filled with drugs. Hundreds of giant dinosaurs gathered around in a circle, gawping at this grand undertaking.

'I can't believe that idiot's letting all those bugs crawl right into his stomach,' grumbled a *Tarbosaurus*.

'So what?' a *Tyrannosaurus* snapped back. 'We already allow them into our mouths, don't we?'

'Dental hygiene is one thing, but when it comes to matters of the stomach, well, that's a whole different ocean of fish,' the *Tarbosaurus* replied. 'Over my dead body—'

'But what if your body was very nearly dead – like with this poor *Hadrosaurus* here,' a squat *Stegosaurus* behind them interjected, craning her neck to see. 'If the ants really can cure him—'

'You mark my words, if we let them into our stomachs now, before we can so much as scratch an itch, they'll be crawling into our noses, ears, eyes – into our brains, even. And who can anticipate what might happen then.' The *Tarbosaurus* glared at the *Stegosaurus*. 'Not in a million years would I countenance that.'

'A million years, huh?' said the *Tyrannosaurus*, stroking his chin. 'But think how easy life would be if every disease could be cured.'

The other dinosaurs chipped in:

'Yeah, life would be so easy . . .'

'Getting sick is a massive pain . . .'

'We could live forever . . .'

The first stage of the operation required that anaesthetic be administered to the lesion in Alija's stomach. It had been collected from plants for use during dental procedures, and under the direction of Dr Avi the ants now ferried it into the *Hadrosaurus*'s stomach. After the area had been numbed, several thousand worker ants began to cut away the diseased tissue. This was a huge project, as the excised gastric tissue had to then be transported out of the dinosaur's body. Porter ants formed a long black chain, passing little gobbets of flesh from ant to ant, all the way back up the line and onto the ground outside, where the pile of stinky rotten tissue was expanding fast. Once the lesion had been cut out, an anti-inflammatory had to be applied to the wound, which required another great procession into the *Hadrosaurus*'s stomach.

The entire procedure took three hours and was completed by sundown. When all of the ants had withdrawn, Alija reported that the pain in his stomach had disappeared. Several days later, he made a full recovery.

The news spread like wildfire through the dinosaur world. The number of dinosaurs seeking treatment at the Ivory Citadel increased tenfold, and this brought multitudes of ants flooding into the city in search of work. Thanks to the healthy uptick in business, the ants' medical technology advanced in leaps and bounds. Now that they had official access to dinosaur bodies, they learnt to treat various diseases of the digestive and respiratory systems; later, their repertoire expanded to include diseases of the circulatory, visual, auditory and nervous systems – systems that required extraordinary levels of expertise to understand and heal. New drugs were being developed all the time, derived from not only plants but also animals and inorganic minerals.

The ants' endosurgical techniques also progressed rapidly. For example, when performing surgery in the digestive system, it was no longer necessary for a long line of ants to trek down the dinosaur's oesophagus. Instead, they entered by means of an 'ant pellet'. Approximately 1,000 ants would cling tightly to one another and form a ball ten to twenty centimetres in diameter. The dinosaur patient would then wash down one or more of these pellets with water, as though swallowing a pill. This technique improved surgical efficiency substantially.

As the Ivory Citadel continued to mushroom, some of the dinosaurs who came for treatment stayed on, establishing a city of their own not far from the ant megalopolis. Because the dinosaurs constructed their homes with massive stones, the ants called it Boulder City. The Ivory Citadel and Boulder City would later become the capitals of the Formican and Saurian Empires of Gondwana.

There was also significant movement in the opposite direction. Some of the dinosaurs who returned home after having received treatment took groups of ants with them to other dinosaur cities and ant colonies all across Gondwana. When the émigré ants settled in these faraway places, they passed on the Ivory Citadel's medical technology to the locals. And so dinosaur–ant cooperation gradually spread throughout Gondwana, cementing the foundations for a dinosaur–ant alliance.

Up till now, the cooperation between Earth's two dominant species could only be classified as an advanced symbiotic relationship. The ants provided medical services to the dinosaurs in exchange for food, and the dinosaurs traded food for medical care. Although the character of the transaction had evolved considerably since the ants had picked that first dinosaur's teeth, the essence of the contract had remained unchanged.

In fact, this sort of mutualistic association between different species had long existed on Earth and persists to the present day. The practice is as old as the hills – older than most hills, actually. Consider, for example, the cleaning symbioses among marine organisms. Cleaner species rid certain fish of ectoparasites, fungi and algae, as well as damaged tissue and wayward scraps of food, and in the process they get to eat their fill. They assemble at fixed 'cleaning stations' to wait for client fish to swim by. Cleaners and clients establish ways of signalling to each other: for example, when a cleaner shrimp wants to approach a large fish, it will nudge it with its antennae. If the fish wishes to be cleaned, it will tilt its body, flare its gills and open its mouth to indicate its acceptance. Only then will the cleaner shrimp proceed; otherwise, it runs the risk of being eaten. Cleaning associations are extremely important to fish, and whenever a cleaner species is removed from an area, there's a decline in both the health and abundance of the client fish species.

This type of symbiotic relationship has its limitations, however. The two symbionts come together solely for the purpose of exchanging the basic services necessary for survival. But the transition to civilisation requires symbionts to exchange something more profound, to engage in a higher level of cooperation, so that they might establish an alliance that is not merely symbiotic but co-evolutionary.

It was at this point in time that something happened in Boulder City to raise the dinosaur–ant alliance to new heights.

4

TABLETS

Tablets were as vital to the dinosaur world as the paper on which we write. They came in two types: stationary and movable. Also called 'wordhills' or 'wordstones', stationary tablets (which we might also, rather pleasingly, term 'dinosaur *stationery*'), were hills with a relatively even slope, gentle cliff faces or enormous rocks with smooth surfaces, on which the dinosaurs carved their super-sized words. Movable tablets could be made from many different materials, but wood, stone and leather were the most common. Because the dinosaurs did not yet use metal, let alone saws, they were unable to manufacture wooden boards; instead, they used their megalithic stone hatchets to cleave tree-trunks in two, lengthwise down the middle, and they then carved characters into the cross-section of one-half of them. Their stone tablets were flat slabs with facades soft enough for engraving; these came in all shapes and sizes, but the smallest would have been at least as big as one of our family dining-tables. Leather tablets were made from animal hides or lizard skins, and characters were drawn on them in plant- or mineral-based paint; often a single tablet required that many skins be joined together.

The dinosaurs' thick, clumsy fingers made it impossible for them to grip small implements for carving or writing, and they lacked the dexterity needed to form small characters. As a result, the characters they produced were very large: the smallest they could manage were still the size of a football. This meant that their tablets were by necessity huge and unwieldy, and even then they could fit only a few characters on each one.

Tablets were usually held communally by a dinosaur tribe or settlement and were used to keep simple records of collective property, membership, economic output, and births and deaths. A tribe of 1,000 dinosaurs would need twenty to thirty sizeable trees for a register of its members, and the minutes from one meeting might require over a hundred hides. As a result, the manufacture of tablets placed a significant strain on the dinosaurs' resources, and furthermore, when tribes or settlements relocated (a frequent occurrence during the Hunting Era), transporting libraries of tablets proved an even greater burden. For this reason, although dinosaur society had possessed a written language for 1,000 years, its cultural development was painfully slow and had nearly come to a standstill in recent centuries. Their script had remained extremely crude. With only simple, unary numerals and a handful of pictographs, it lagged far behind the sophistication of their spoken language. The sluggish emergence of writing had become the biggest obstacle to scientific and cultural progress in the dinosaur world, one which had arrested dinosaur society in a primitive state for a long time. It was a textbook example of how a species' ill-shaped hands could hinder its evolution.

The dinosaur Kunda was one of a hundred or so scribes in Boulder City. In the dinosaur world, the job of a scribe fell somewhere between that of the modern-day occupations of typist and printer. Scribes were chiefly responsible for copying tablets by hand. On the day in question, Kunda and twenty other scribes were working in front of a mountain of tablets, making a copy of the register of Boulder City's residents for safekeeping. Most of the original register had been recorded on wooden tablets. Hundreds of split tree-trunks were stacked in hill-height piles, giving Kunda's workplace the appearance of one of our timber yards.

Kunda, a blunt stone knife gripped in his left claw and one of those humongous stone hammers in his right, was transcribing the pictograms from a ten-metre-long wooden tablet onto two new, shorter tablets. He had been at this dull, draining work for days and days, but still the inselberg of blank trunks in front of him didn't seem to have got any smaller. Hurling down the stone knife and hammer, he rubbed his weary eyes, leant back against a stack of tablets and heaved a deep sigh, feeling very dispirited about his tedious life.

Just then, a squadron of 1,000 ants paraded past on the ground before him – on their way back from surgery, Kunda presumed. A sudden inspiration seized him. He stood up, picked out two dried strips of glow-lizard jerky and waved them at the colony. Glow-lizards were so called because they emitted a fluorescent light at night, and their meat was a favourite with ants. No surprise then that the ant squadron immediately changed its direction of travel and veered towards him.

Kunda pointed first to the tablet he was copying from, then to the one he was working on – which, depressingly, he'd so far inscribed with a mere two-and-a-half characters – and then to the ants. The ants grasped his meaning at once. They surged onto the smooth white face of the partially completed tablet and began to carve the remaining characters into the wood with their mandibles. Kunda, meanwhile, eased himself back against the stack of tablets, feeling rather smug. The ants would take much longer to finish the task than he would, but their patience and tenacity was immeasurably superior to that of any other creature and they would get it done eventually. In the meantime, he could kick back and relax for a spell.

He dozed off. In his dream he saw himself at the helm of a mighty army of more than a million ants, enthusiastically urging on his troops. The army swarmed over hundreds of blank tablets and like a black tide turned every one of them dark; before long, the tide withdrew, revealing a vast collection of tablets whose white surfaces now bore neat lines of orderly characters carved into them.

A series of slight pricks on Kunda's lower leg roused him from sleep and when he raised his head he saw that several ants were gnawing at his left ankle. This was their customary way of getting a dinosaur's attention. Seeing that he was awake, the ants gestured at the tablet with their antennae, to indicate the job was done. Kunda glanced up at the sun and realised that very little time had passed. He then looked at the tablet and promptly lost his temper. The ants had completed the half-written character at full size, but all the other characters they'd carved were many times smaller. It looked ridiculous – like a tiny tail trailing after the three large characters. Such shoddy work wasn't just inadequate, it had ruined a whole tablet.

Kunda had known all along that the ants were crafty little mercenaries, and now he had proof. He raised a broom to mete out the punishment they deserved. But just as he was about to strike, he caught another glimpse of their wooden tablet and a sudden revelation flashed through his mind. The characters the ants had carved were small, but they were fully legible to dinosaur eyes. The reason characters were normally so big was not for ease of reading but because the dinosaurs were not dexterous enough to inscribe anything smaller. It occurred to him that the ants, who were twitching their antennae frantically in his direction, might very well be trying to explain this to him.

The scowl on his face broadened into a smile and he dropped the broom. Then he set down one of the strips of glow-lizard jerky in the middle of the colony and swished the other tantalisingly. Crouching down in front of the tablet, he gestured at the three large characters and the line of small characters and tried to communicate his idea. It took the ants a while to catch on, but eventually they waggled their feelers in emphatic confirmation: yes, they could carve characters that were smaller still. Immediately, they flooded onto the blank part of the tablet and set to work. Soon they had carved a line of even smaller characters, each about the size of the letters in the title on this book's cover. As the ants were illiterate, they were simply reproducing the shapes of the characters.

Kunda rewarded them with the remaining strip of jerky. Then he hacked off the section of the tablet carved with the smallest characters, tucked it under his arm and gleefully lolloped off to see the city prefect.

Because of Kunda's low status, the guards stopped him on the steps of the colossal stone mansion that housed the prefect's office. The guards were imposing, powerfully built dinosaurs and Kunda quickly lifted up the section of the tablet for them to see. They inspected it. Within moments, their expressions had morphed from surprise to awe; it was as if they were in the presence of a sacred relic. Turning their gaze back to Kunda, they gaped at him for a long time, as though he were a great sage, then let him pass.

'What's that you've got there – a toothpick?' the prefect asked when he saw Kunda.

'No, sir, this is a tablet.'

'A tablet? Are you an idiot? You couldn't fit half a character onto that piddly piece of wood.'

'It's hard to believe, I know, sir, but there are actually more than thirty characters on this self-same piddly piece of wood.' Kunda passed it over.

The prefect gazed at the tablet with the same wonderment as the guards. After a long time, he looked up at Kunda. 'I don't suppose you carved this yourself?'

'Of course not, sir. A gang of ants did it.'

Boulder City's municipal officials gathered round and the tablet was passed from claws to claws, much like we might hand round an ivory figurine to be admired. These dinosaurs constituted the city's ruling class and they now launched into fervent discussion.

'Incredible – such tiny characters . . .'

'. . . and totally legible too.'

'Over the millennia, so many of our ancestors have tried to write like this, but to no avail.'

'Those itsy-bitsy bugs really are quite capable.'

'We should have known they'd be good for more than medical care.'

'Just think of all the materials we'll save . . .'

'. . . and how easily we'll be able to transport our tablets. You know, I might be able to carry the entire register of the city's residents by myself! No need to employ a hundred-strong division of dinosaur movers any more.'

'And that's just the start of it, I'd say. We can now consider changing the materials we use for the tablets too.'

'Quite so. After all, where's the merit in using tree-trunks? For characters this small, bark would surely be lighter and more portable.'

'Precisely. And a lot cheaper too. Small lizard skins could be used as well.'

The prefect interrupted the chatter with a wave. 'Right then, from now on the ants will be our scribes. We shall start by raising a writing force of a million ants or more. Let's see . . .' He surveyed the room, his eyes finally falling on Kunda. 'You will lead this campaign.'

So Kunda realised his dream, and Boulder City, along with the rest of the dinosaur world, saved a great deal of wood and stone and an enormous quantity of hides. But compared with the real significance of this event in the history of Cretaceous civilisation, those savings were trivialities.

The advent of fine antprint made it possible to transcribe vast volumes of information, and at the same time the dinosaurs' script grew richer and more sophisticated. At long last, the alpha and omega of the dinosaurs' experience and knowledge could be fully and systematically recorded using the written word and mathematical equations. It could also be disseminated far more widely, reliably and permanently, no longer subject to the vagaries of dinosaur memory and oral tradition. This remarkable advancement gave fresh impetus to Cretaceous science and culture, sending the long-stagnant Cretaceous civilisation into a period of whirlwind development.

Meanwhile, new applications for the ants' fine-motor skills were found in all sectors of the dinosaur world. Take timekeeping technology as an example. Dinosaurs had invented the sundial long ago, but because they used large tree-trunks as gnomons and drew rough hour lines around them, these had to remain fixed in place. Thanks to the ants, sundials could now be made smaller and the hour lines rendered more precisely, allowing dinosaurs to carry them around. Later, dinosaurs would invent the hourglass and the water clock, and though they might have been able to make the containers themselves, only ants could bore the crucial holes. The manufacture of mechanical clocks was even more dependent on ant labour, for though a grandfather clock might be taller than a dinosaur, it still contained numerous tiny parts that could only be machined by ants.

But the area in which the ants' skills made the most meaningful contribution to the advancement of civilisation, besides writing, was scientific experimentation. Thanks to the ants' capacity for intricate work, it was now possible to take measurements with an exactitude that had eluded dinosaurs, allowing a shift in experimentation from the qualitative to the quantitative. Research once thought impossible became a reality, leading to rapid strides in Cretaceous science.

Ants were now an integral part of the dinosaur world. Dinosaurs of high standing were never without a miniature ant nest. Most of these nests resembled a wooden sphere and housed several hundred ants. When a dinosaur needed to write, it would unfold a strip of bark or hide parchment on the table and set down its ant nest beside it. The ants would scurry out onto the parchment and etch the words dictated to them by the dinosaur. They used a very particular system of concurrent writing, quite different from our own. Where we humans write one character at a time, the ants teamed up and inscribed multiple characters simultaneously. This allowed them to complete a transcription very rapidly, at a pace that would far outstrip our own handwriting speed. Naturally, a dinosaur's pocket-sized ant nest also came in handy for all sorts of other tasks that required a light touch.

For their part, the ants received much more than just bones and meat from the dinosaurs. After their new collaboration began, the first invaluable asset the ant world gained was written language. Ants had never had a written language before, and even as they became the dinosaurs' scribes, they remained illiterate, which meant they were limited to simple reproduction work, copying out the characters from the dinosaurs' outsized tablets. Their efficiency was relatively poor, as they could only transcribe one stroke at a time. But the dinosaurs were in dire need of ants who could take dictation like secretaries, and the ants, who were well aware of the importance of written language to society, were eager to learn. Thanks to a concerted effort on both sides, the ants quickly mastered the dinosaurs' script and co-opted it for use in their own society.

For Cretaceous civilisation, this was of immeasurable significance because it forged a bridge between their respective worlds. Over time, the ants came to understand dinosaur speech, but dinosaur anatomy meant that dinosaurs would never be able to understand the ants' pheromone-based language. Consequently, only simple exchanges took place between the two worlds. But the ants' mastery of written language brought about a fundamental change in this, for the ants could now communicate with the dinosaurs through writing. To facilitate this, they invented an astounding new method. Within a square patch of ground, thousands of ants would quickly arrange themselves to form lines of text. This drill composition technique grew more polished by the day. Eventually, the transition between drill formations was so swift that the block of ants resembled the instantaneous output of a computer screen.

As communication between the two worlds improved, the ants absorbed more and more knowledge and ideas from the dinosaurs, for each new scientific and cultural achievement could now be promptly disseminated throughout antkind. And so the critical defect in ant society – the dearth of creative thinking – was remedied, leading to the simultaneous rapid advancement of ant civilisation. The result of the dinosaur–ant alliance was that the ants became the dinosaurs' dexterous hands, while the dinosaurs became a wellspring of vision and innovation for the ants. The fusion of these two budding intelligences in the late Cretaceous had finally sparked a dramatic nuclear reaction. The sun of civilisation rose over the heart of Gondwana, dispelling the long night of evolution on Earth.

5

THE STEAM-ENGINE AGE

Time flew by, and 1,000 years passed. Cretaceous civilisation entered a brand-new era as the ants and dinosaurs established their own vast empires.

The dinosaur world moved into the Steam-Engine Age. Though the dinosaurs had not yet harnessed electricity, they mined minerals on a massive scale, smelted a variety of metals and powered their complex machines with huge steam engines. They constructed cities across the continent and linked them via a web of broad-gauge railways serviced by a fleet of ginormous trains. These comprised carriages the size of our five- or six-storey buildings and were drawn by steam locomotives so behemothic that they made the ground shake beneath them and left billowing clouds lingering on the horizon. There were also high-altitude transport balloons, whose shadows enveloped entire cities as they floated by, and mighty ships plying every major ocean; these too were powered by steam engines or sometimes by magnificent sails. Fleets of these ships, as high and hefty as a seaborne mountain range, carried Gondwanan dinosaurs and ants to other continents, and so their particular model of civilisation, based on the dinosaur–ant alliance, spread right across the Late Cretaceous world.

By their own standards, the ants' empire was also incomparably vast. No longer confined to subterranean nests, the ants now resided in cities that dotted every continent like a constellation of stars. Just as it is hard for us to grasp the immense scale of dinosaur civilisation, it is difficult to imagine the miniature nature and intricate structures of ant civilisation. Though ant cities were generally no larger than one of our football fields, the detail and complexity of these megalopolises was dizzying. Ant buildings were typically one to two metres tall, with elaborately filigreed interiors that functioned like three-dimensional labyrinths. Their trains were the size of our smallest toy cars, and their transport balloons were like soap bubbles drifting with the wind. These vehicles could only cover short distances, so if an ant wanted to travel further afield, they had to board a dinosaur train, balloon or ship.

The ant and dinosaur worlds maintained a closely cooperative, mutually dependent relationship. By then the dinosaurs had invented technology that enabled them to quickly print long tracts of text on paper, and they had also created typewriters with keys the size of our computer screens, to accommodate their fat fingers. Though the dinosaurs therefore no longer needed ants for scriptorial work, in many other sectors their fine-motor skills were more important than ever – indispensable, in fact. After all, it would have been impossible to manufacture printing presses and typewriters without the countless precision parts machined by the ants. And with the emergence of large-scale industry in the dinosaur world, there was a greater demand for fine manipulation. The manufacture of everything from steam-engine valves and meters to ocean-liner compasses required the ants' pinpoint accuracy. The field of medicine, which was where the dinosaur–ant alliance originated, was now more ant-dominated than ever, as dinosaurs, with their clumsy claws, had never learnt to operate on their own kind.

The dinosaur and ant worlds may have been interdependent civilisations, but they were also independent entities, and this necessitated the development of a more sophisticated economic relationship. Globally, there were two currencies in circulation: paper bills the size of our extra-large yoga mats, as used by the dinosaurs, and tiny slivers of shredded paper, as used by the ants. The two currencies were exchanged on a one-for-one basis.

For the first 1,000 years of Cretaceous civilisation, relations between the ant and dinosaur worlds were harmonious and, on the whole, frictionless. This was due in large part to their interdependence, for had the alliance broken down, it would have precipitated a deadly crisis for both worlds. Another important reason was that the ants lived in a low-consumption society. Their material requirements were easily satisfied, and they took up very little space. Much of the Formican Empire's territory overlapped but did not interfere with that of the Saurian Empire, allowing the dinosaurs and the ants to coexist without intense competition.

There was, however, a deep and unbridgeable cultural gulf between the two civilisations – a manifestation of the sharp differences in the physiologies and social structures of the two species. Because of this, the ant and dinosaur worlds never truly became one. And as civilisation advanced, intercultural conflict became unavoidable.

With the expansion of their respective intelligences, both the ants and the dinosaurs showed a growing awareness of the vastness of the cosmos, but exploratory research into the underlying laws of the universe was still in its infancy. Science seemed weak and inadequate, so religion was born, and religious fanaticism rapidly reached fever pitch in both worlds. As the differences between the two civilisations were expressed through increasingly distinctive religious beliefs, the latent crisis came to a head and dark clouds gathered over Cretaceous civilisation.

A Dinosaur–Ant Summit was held annually in Boulder City. At this meeting, the sovereigns of the Saurian and Formican Empires discussed the major issues of the day. Boulder City and the Ivory Citadel were still the imperial capitals, and although the latter, relatively tiny as it was, seemed no more conspicuous than a postage stamp pasted onto the side of the magnificent Boulder City, the two were nevertheless equal in status. When Queen Lassini of the Formican Empire entered the lofty imperial palace of the Saurian Empire, she was therefore accorded a grand reception. As happened whenever an important ant official travelled, she was accompanied by a contingent of soldier ants known as a word corps, whose function was to assume the formations necessary to facilitate negotiations with the dinosaurs. The size of a word corps was determined by the rank of the official, and the corps that came to Boulder City with the ant queen was, of course, the largest of them all.

And so it was that as the dinosaur guard of honour sounded their fanfare of bugles, a phalanx of 100,000 soldier ants escorted their queen into the hall. Tightly packed into a dense black quadrilateral of precisely two square metres, the ants advanced slowly across a floor as smooth and shiny as a mirror and halted before the dinosaur emperor, who had come to receive the queen.

Emperor Urus greeted his opposite number. 'Hello there, Queen Lassini! Are you out in front of that black square?' He stooped and peered intently at the ground in front of the word corps, then shook his enormous head. 'How long has it been since we last saw each other – a year? The last time we met, I could still see you, but that's quite impossible now. Ah, but I am old, and my eyes are not what they were.'

The black square broke apart and rapidly re-formed as a line of dinosaur-sized text: 'Perhaps the colour of the floor is to blame. You should really use white marble here, so that you can see me. Her Imperial Majesty Lassini, Sovereign of the Formican Empire, presents her compliments to His Imperial Majesty, Emperor Urus.'

Urus smiled and nodded. 'Well now, my compliments also to Her Imperial Majesty. I presume the imperial emissary has already notified you regarding the agenda of this summit?'

Craning her neck in the direction of the dinosaur emperor towering before her, Queen Lassini inclined her antennae and gave her answer in the form of a pheromone. When the commanders in the front row received the chemical signal, they swiftly relayed the instructions to the phalanx behind them. The disciplined soldiers of the word corps changed formation like a well-oiled machine, arranging themselves into the queen's words in the blink of an eye: 'The aim of this summit is to settle the religious dispute between our two worlds. This problem has plagued us since the reign of the late emperor, and now it has become the most serious crisis yet faced by the dinosaur–ant alliance. I expect Your Majesty is aware that Earth stands on the brink of disaster as a result.'

Urus nodded again. 'I am indeed aware of that. No doubt Your Majesty is similarly cognisant that the resolution of this crisis presents us with a considerable challenge. Where do you propose we begin?'

The queen thought for a moment before she replied, and the word corps rearranged themselves across the marble floor at lightning speed: 'Let us begin with the point we are agreed upon.'

'Very good. Dinosaurs and ants are agreed that this world can have only one God.'

'Yes, that's correct.'

Both rulers fell briefly silent, then Urus said, 'We should discuss what God looks like, even though we have been over this a thousand times before.'

'Yes,' Lassini said, 'that is the crux of the conflict and the crisis.'

'God undoubtedly resembles a dinosaur,' said the dinosaur emperor. 'We have seen God through our faith, and God's image embodies all dinosaurs.'

'God undoubtedly looks like an ant,' said the ant queen. 'We have also seen God through our faith, and all ants are reflected in God's image.'

Urus smiled broadly and waggled his mammoth head. 'Queen Lassini, if you were the least bit logical or had a smidgen of common sense, this problem would be sorted in a jiffy. Do you truly believe that God could possibly be a dust-mote speck of an insect like you? That such a God could create a world as vast as this?'

'Size does not equal strength,' Lassini replied. 'Compared with mountain ranges or oceans, dinosaurs too are mere "dust-mote specks".'

'But the fact is, Your Majesty, that we dinosaurs are the fount of original thought, the purveyors of creativity. And when all is said and done, you ants are nothing but tiny cogs in a highly efficient machine.'

'The world cannot have been created by thought alone. If it were not for our expertise, most dinosaur inventions and innovations could not have been realised. The creation of the world was clearly a precise and meticulously executed undertaking. Only an ant God could have accomplished it.'

Urus burst out laughing. 'What I find most intolerable about you ants is your pitiful imaginations! Those bite-sized brains of yours are obviously only fit for simple arithmetical thinking. You truly are no more than desperately dogged cogs!' As he spoke, he bent his face low to the ground and whispered to the ant queen, 'Let me tell you, when God created the world, no action was required. God simply gave form to thoughts and – whoosh! – those thoughts became the world! Ha ha ha!' He straightened up and guffawed again.

'Sir, I did not come here to discuss metaphysics with you. This drawn-out dispute between our two worlds must be resolved at this meeting.'

Urus threw up his claws and boomed, 'Ah-ha! Result! Here is the second point upon which we are agreed! Yes, we must come to an accord this time round. Your Majesty, you may propose your solution first.'

Lassini gave her answer without hesitation. In order to convey the solemnity of her pronouncement, the word corps added a border around her words: 'The Saurian Empire must immediately demolish all churches consecrated to a dinosaur God.'

Urus and the other ministers in the room eyeballed each other then erupted into a great cacophony of chortles. 'Ha ha, big words from a bitsy bug!'

Lassini continued undeterred. 'The ants will suspend all work in the Saurian Empire and withdraw completely from every dinosaur city. We will not return or resume work until your churches have been demolished in accordance with our demands.'

'I will also deliver an ultimatum from the Saurian Empire,' bellowed Urus. 'The Formican Empire must demolish all churches consecrated to an ant God by week's end. When the week is up, the imperial army will stomp flat any ant city in which a church to an ant God still stands.'

'Is this a declaration of war?' Lassini asked calmly.

'I hope it will not come to that. What a disgrace it would be for dinosaur troops to have to confront you itsy insects.'

The ant queen did not dignify that with an answer. She simply made a sharp about-turn and pattered away. The word corps parted to let her pass, closed ranks behind her and followed her to the palace door.

There was a general stirring now among the dinosaurs. Ants began emerging from the miniature nests that were hung about the dinosaurs' bodies or placed on the tables before them; they spilt out in their inky-black hundreds and thousands. For although the dinosaur printing industry had been mechanised, individual dinosaurs still carried small nests with them, just as we carry pens. They relied on ants to write their personal notes and missives. The nests varied in size, and some were veritable works of art. Among dinosaurs, they had become a must-have personal ornament and a symbol of wealth and status. But the ants inside the nests were not the dinosaurs' personal property. They had to be hired from the Formican Empire, and ultimately they answered only to their queen. Swarming down from the tables and off the dinosaurs' bodies, these ants were now streaming across the floor to join the departing phalanx.

'Good grief,' rasped a dinosaur minister, 'if all of you leave, how am I to draft and review documents?'

Urus gave a theatrical flick of his claws. 'They'll be back to work before long,' he said contemptuously. 'The ant world cannot survive without us. Fret not, we will show those upstart insects who truly has God on their side.'

At the door, Lassini turned around and spoke, and the word corps swiftly formed a line of text: 'That is exactly what the Formican Empire intends to show you.'

6

THE ANTS' ARSENAL

'What? We're going to war with the dinosaurs? But that's madness! They're so big, and we're so small . . .' an ant minister exclaimed.

In the imperial palace in the Ivory Citadel, the imperial high command had just heard the queen's account of the Dinosaur–Ant Summit.

'Our empire has come a long way. Anyone who still takes size as a measure of strength is an idiot,' said Field Marshal Donlira, commander-in-chief of the imperial army. She turned to the queen. 'Please rest assured, Your Majesty, that the imperial army is robust enough to defeat those clumsy beasts.'

'Talk is cheap.' The minister fixed his gaze on the field marshal. 'We all know that you have personally led the army into countless battles and have sailed on dinosaur ships to wage war on other continents, but you were only fighting against uncivilised ant tribes then. When it comes to confronting creatures many times larger than ourselves, I doubt one of your divisions could beat even a lizard.'

The queen dipped her antennae to the field marshal. 'Yes, Donlira, it's not empty talk that I want but detailed strategies and carefully conceived tactics. In one week we will go to war. So, tell me, what's the plan?'

'We have been performing medical services for the dinosaurs for more than a millennium now,' Field Marshal Donlira replied, 'so we are intimately acquainted with their anatomy. The imperial army will penetrate the dinosaurs' bodies and attack their vitals. In this kind of warfare, our petite size is to our advantage.'

'How will you gain access?' another minister asked. 'While they're sleeping?'

The field marshal jiggled her antennae in disagreement. 'No, from a moral standpoint, we cannot be the ones to start the war. This attack against the dinosaurs will be carried out on the battlefield.'

'Easier said than done! On the battlefield, the dinosaurs will be awake and on the move. Will your soldiers be able to scale them? Even if they stood still to let you onto their feet, how long would it take to climb up to their noses and mouths? By the time your army gets inside them, they'll have already trampled our capital into oblivion.'

Instead of answering directly, the field marshal scanned the gathered members of the high command with a long, deliberate look. 'Comrades,' she said, 'our most excellent Queen Lassini has long foreseen the fracturing of the dinosaur–ant alliance. Early in her reign, she ordered the imperial army to begin preparing for war with the dinosaurs. We have undertaken extensive research, as a result of which we have developed many new weapons and combat techniques. Now, if everyone will step outside, we will demonstrate two key pieces of equipment.'

The ants of the high command duly pattered out onto the plaza outside the palace. Two dozen soldier ants carried forward a peculiar piece of kit: a small catapult affixed to a long base. They pulled the catapult's elastic cord taut and hooked its pocket onto a mechanism at the far end of the base. Then they climbed into the pocket and clung tightly to one other, forming a black projectile. A soldier ant stationed beside the base pulled a tiny lever, releasing the pocket from the mechanism and twanging the black projectile a full twenty metres into the air. When the projectile reached its maximum height, it swiftly dispersed, and the two dozen soldier ants went fluttering through the air overhead, their glossy black bodies glittering in the sunshine.

'This piece of equipment is called a Formican slingshot, and it is the solution to the problems cited by the honourable minister,' explained Field Marshal Donlira.

'Looks like useless acrobatics to me,' muttered one of the ministers.

'The imperial army is meant to be take offensive action,' another minister said. 'That's the strategic principle on which it was founded. In the past, you have stated that its operational objective is 'Attack! Attack! Attack!'. Now it seems this has changed to "Defend! Defend! Defend!".'

'Offensive action is still the strategic principle of the imperial army,' replied the field marshal.

'But how can it be? Even if these little gadgets of yours really do work, we obviously can't use them to attack Boulder City. We'll have to wait for the dinosaurs to attack our capital.'

'Please bear with us, Minister,' the field marshal said. 'We will now demonstrate a weapon that can be used to initiate offensives against dinosaur cities.'

She waggled her antennae and several soldier ants brought over a number of yellow pellets resembling grains of rice. One of the soldiers swivelled round and sprayed a drop of formic acid on one of the pellets. A minute later, the pellet caught fire in a blinding flash of white light. The violent blaze lasted for ten seconds and then died out.

'This weapon is called a 'mine-grain'. It's an incendiary device with a fuse that is activated by formic acid. It can be set to ignite at any point from a few seconds to a few hours after it's triggered. Once the formic acid has eaten through the outer shell, the device combusts, producing temperatures high enough to ignite any flammable material.'

The assembled officials shook their antennae in disbelief. 'It's a child's toy!' grumbled one. 'Even if one of these things went off on the forehead of the dinosaur emperor himself, it would do him no more harm than a cigarette burn. This thing can destroy Boulder City? You are surely having a laugh, Field Marshal.'

'Just you wait and see,' the field marshal replied confidently. 'All will be revealed shortly.'

7

THE FIRST DINOSAUR-ANT WAR

Rain had bucketed down all night, but at dawn the heavy black clouds parted to usher in a bright, sunny morning. The sky was cloudless and the air was clear. In the light of the rising sun, the land looked vivid and sharply defined, as though nature had set the stage for the battle that would decide the fate of Cretaceous civilisation.

Battle was joined on the wide plain between Boulder City and the Ivory Citadel, with each settlement only just visible on its respective horizon. 2,000 dinosaur soldiers formed a phalanx facing the Ivory Citadel; to the ants, it seemed like a sky-high wall had been raised. Unlike in past battles, waged against their own kind, the dinosaur soldiers were neither wearing armour nor carrying weapons. They'd been told that all they'd need to do would be to march across the ant city in formation. Opposite the dinosaurs, 10 million ants from the Ivory Citadel were massed in more than a hundred brigades, carpeting the ground in black.

A *Tyrannosaurus* stationed at the head of the dinosaur phalanx broke the silence. It was Major General Ixta, and his voice was like a sudden clap of thunder on the horizon. 'Little bugs, only ten minutes remain until the empire's deadline expires. If you return to the Ivory Citadel right now, destroy all your churches, and then come back to Boulder City and resume work, I can grant you more time. Otherwise, the imperial army will begin its assault.'

He raised his right forelimb and gestured nonchalantly at his troops. 'Take a look at the 2,000 soldiers before you. They represent less than one-thousandth of the imperial army's total strength, but they are more than capable of flattening the capital of the Formican Empire. The cities our children build in their sandpits are bigger than your Ivory Citadel. In fact, those kids could flood your entire city just by pissing on it! Ha ha ha!'

A deathly hush settled over the battlefield. The Cretaceous sun quietly rose higher, and ten minutes soon passed.

'Attack!' boomed General Ixta.

The phalanx began to advance. The ground trembled under the rhythmic tread of 2,000 dinosaurs, creating waves in the puddles left by the rain. The ants did not budge.

'Queen Lassini and Field Marshal Donlira,' General Ixta roared in the direction of the massed columns of ants, 'I have no idea whereabouts you are, but if you don't order these critters to make way, our feet will crush them to a pulp! Ha ha ha!'

As he stared at the ant army, he noticed a distinct ripple running through their ranks. He peered more closely and saw that the ant infantry had erected countless tiny structures. To him they looked like blades of grass newly sprouted from the blackened earth. A niggle of doubt lodged in his massive dinosaur brain, but the niggle was not sufficient to give him pause, and so the dinosaur phalanx pressed on.

A second surprising change now swept through the ant army. The smooth black pool that had blanketed the ground suddenly went lumpy and separated into a multitude of miniature spheres. Ixta was reminded of the wondrous movements of the ant word corps, and for a moment he thought the 10 million ants in front of him were about to spell out something. But the ant clumps did not reshape.

The dinosaur phalanx continued its advance until it was just ten metres from the ants' frontline. Only then did General Ixta realise that those blades of grass were in fact a barrage of miniature catapults, cords stretched taut, each pocket loaded with a cluster of ants!

There now came a soft pitter-patter, like raindrops hitting the surface of a lake, as 100,000 ant projectiles were fired into the air. It was as if a cloud of flies had been startled into flight. The ground ahead of Ixta regained its ochre colour and the tiny compacted spheres soared above the first few lines of dinosaurs and then disintegrated. Each ball contained dozens of soldiers and now a shower of ants cascaded to the ground.

The air was thick with so many falling ants that it was almost impossible for the dinosaurs not to inhale them up their nostrils. As they frantically slapped at their heads and bodies, their phalanx fell into disorder.

Some of the ants that landed on General Ixta's head were brushed off, but others hid from his gigantic searching claws, ducking into the wrinkles of his coarse-grained skin. When his claws moved to slap at his body, several soldier ants skittered towards the edge of his brow, seeking out his eyes. Crawling across the wide crown of the *Tyrannosaurus*'s head was like trudging across a plateau scored with ravines. The plateau swayed back and forth like a swing, and the ants had to cling on tight to keep from being thrown off. When they reached the edge, they peered down and were met with a breathtaking sight.

Imagine for a moment that you are standing atop the majestic peak of China's venerable Mount Tai. Now imagine that this most holy mountain is in motion: it is striding across the earth on a pair of colossal legs. Even more terrifying, when you lift your head, you see that you are encircled by a thousand other mountains and that these are also on the move!

The soldier ants located the dinosaur's right eye, which was below them. The enormous eye was like a round pond that had frozen over; its translucent surface was slightly curved and sloped sharply downwards. Three of the soldier ants cautiously picked their way onto the glassy membrane. This was the dinosaur's third eyelid – its protective nictitating membrane, to be exact – and it was as slippery as melting ice. The slightest misstep would see the ants slithering off and tumbling into the void. They began to gnaw at the wet ice with their powerful pincers, but this irritated the eye and it began to secrete tears, which surged across the frozen pond like a flash flood, flushing the three ants from the eyelid.

Just as Ixta made to rub his eye, three other ants nipped into his nostrils. Battling their way into a screaming gale, they expertly threaded their way through a tangled forest of nose hair, making a concerted attempt not to trigger a sneeze. They advanced quickly through the nasal cavity to the back of the eyeball, tracing a route that was familiar from countless surgical procedures. Following the translucent optic nerve, they now proceeded towards the brain. Here and there a thin membrane blocked their path, but they simply chewed a small hole and squeezed through. These holes were so tiny that the dinosaur felt nothing.

Finally, the three ants arrived at the brain, which was peacefully suspended in a sea of cerebrospinal fluid like a mysterious, discrete lifeform. After careful searching, they found the thick cerebral artery, the main pipeline supplying blood to the brain. Through the pellucid pipe wall they could see and hear the dark red blood coursing past with a low rumble. Ixta's brain was working overtime, trying to process the mind-blowing quantities of battlefield information being transmitted from his optic and auditory nerves, and this torrent of blood was fuelling it with the necessary energy and oxygen.

The three ants were neurosurgical techs and this was familiar territory to them. They had been dispatched to places like this countless times before, to clear clogged cerebral blood vessels and save untold numbers of dinosaur lives in the process. Now, however, they would do the opposite. With their sharp mandibles, they began to make three deep scratches in the artery wall, working with care and skill. When the incisions joined up to form a complete circle, the ants rapidly withdrew the way they'd come. They had no wish to witness the end result. As veteran surgical techs, they knew exactly what was about to happen. Blood circulated at high pressure and very soon beads of blood would well from the incisions on the artery wall. Then, as neatly as if it had been scored by a glasscutter, the lesion would rupture and the little circular section of the artery wall would come loose and create a round hole. Blood would gush out of the hole, sending tendrils of crimson curling through the brain fluid and staining it red. Deprived of its blood supply, the brain would quiver and grow pale.

On the chaotic battlefield, Ixta was yelling commands, attempting to regroup the dinosaurs into attack formation. All of a sudden, everything went dark before his eyes. As the fog descended, his surroundings began to spin. The three ants racing through his nasal cavity felt a sensation of weightlessness, followed by a shuddering crash. The world around them rolled several times and then came to a standstill. The dinosaur had fallen to the ground. The gale in his nostrils ceased, and the distant low thump of his heart went silent. The *Tyrannosaurus* Ixta, Major General of the Imperial Saurian Army, had been killed in action, felled by a cerebral haemorrhage.

One by one, the other dinosaurs on the battlefield toppled. Some were murdered in the same manner as their commander; many more either suffered a fatal rupturing of their coronary artery or had their spinal cord severed. The ants had infiltrated their enemies' insides via ears, noses or mouths and had racked up more than 300 casualties. The ground was littered with gargantuan bodies and the air echoed with the unearthly yowling of dying dinosaurs. The survivors, scared witless by this nightmarish scene, fled the battlefield at breakneck speed. Broken necks, however, were not to be these deserters' downfall. Though they'd escaped the site, they'd not escaped the invasion of the brain snatchers. Ant soldiers continued their internal operations even as the dinosaurs retreated, and the route back to Boulder City was lined with monstrous corpses.

While their comrade ants were busy resisting dinosaur incursions into the Ivory Citadel, millions of other ants were launching a major military offensive on their enemy's stronghold. Despite the declaration of war, Boulder City had continued operating much as it always had. Although the loss of the ants' services was certainly an inconvenience for the dinosaurs, it was by no means devastating, and as for the conflict itself, the dinosaur public was utterly unconcerned. They were confident that the Imperial Saurian Army could defeat those titchy insects with the absolute minimum of effort – a few swats and kicks should surely do it, they thought. To them it seemed like overkill to mobilise 2,000 dinosaur soldiers just to crush that toy sandpit of a city, but they rationalised it as the emperor's way of demonstrating the empire's strength.

That morning, Boulder City rumbled to life as it did every day. At the transport terminal by the city's eastern gate more than a thousand jumbo-sized buses trundled out onto the streets. Cretaceous civilisation had not yet begun to extract oil, and so these buses, like the dinosaurs' trains, were powered by massive, ponderous steam engines. They pumped out great clouds of vapour from their roofs as they rolled, shrouding the streets in fog from morning till night.

Today, however, Boulder City's buses were transporting not only their regular dinosaur customers but also an additional cohort of unauthorised passengers. Ant-soldier stowaways! Swarms of these undercover operatives had scuttled aboard during the night. The Number 1 bus, which served the main artery through the city, carried the largest contingent – an entire division, comprising more than 10,000 ants. They were concealed in various inconspicuous locations: under the doorsills, inside the toolbox, clinging to the undercarriage, camouflaged inside the coal bunker. On such a huge vehicle, hiding a division of the Imperial Formican Army was easy.

Ten minutes after the Number 1 bus drove onto the hectic, thunderous street, it pulled in at its first stop. Hard on the heels of several dinosaur commuters, a company of 200 ant soldiers detached themselves from beneath the doorsill and dropped to the ground. Each one held a mine-grain in its mouth. They immediately filed into a crack in the pavement, their tiny black bodies invisible against the wet surface, and began zigzagging towards their destination. The dinosaurs stomping along the steamy street were oblivious to their presence. The ants, on the other hand, were all too aware of the dinosaurs. Every time a hulking great *Tyrannosaurus* passed above them, their world went black; there was also the ever-present danger of being crushed to death should they poke their heads out of the cracks. No catastrophes befell them, however, and eventually they arrived at a building. It was so vast that its front door opened into the clouds, and the upper storeys were lost in the ether. The ant troops stole through the gap beneath the door and filed in.

All dinosaur architecture was high-rise. From the ants' perspective, each building was effectively its own world; for them, being indoors was no different from standing outside in an open field. This particular structure was a warehouse – a gloomy world whose only sun was a small, high-set window that let in just a little light. The ants wove their way across its wide floor, between piles of goods, until they reached a row of tall wooden casks. These contained kerosene that the dinosaurs used for lighting. Since the dinosaur world had not yet entered the Electric Age, they relied on oil lamps at night. Searching carefully, the soldier ants found several patches of moisture on the floor where the casks had leaked slightly. They removed the mine-grains from their mouths and stuck them to these oily patches. Soon, more than a hundred mine-grains had been put in place. The soldiers aimed their posteriors at the mines, and, at the first lieutenant's command, sprayed a droplet of formic acid on each one. The acid began to slowly eat through the shell of each mine-grain, activating the ignition fuse. The delay had been set for six hours, scheduling ignition for two o'clock that afternoon.

Meanwhile, at every stop made by 1,000 buses crisscrossing Boulder City, other concealed detachments of ant troops alighted and slipped undetected into the streets. By midday, some 1 million soldier ants, representing 100 divisions of the Imperial Formican Army, had infiltrated every corner of Boulder City and planted mine-grains on every type of flammable surface. Millions of mine-grains speckled Boulder City's government offices, marketplaces, schools, libraries and residential buildings, each one set to ignite at two o'clock that afternoon.

A little later that morning, in the imperial palace, the Saurian emperor Urus was woken from his sleep by the return of several officers from the failed attempt on the Ivory Citadel. The emperor had been up all night, wining and dining some governors from Laurasia, and hadn't got to bed until the early hours. When he heard from the officers that not only was General Ixta dead but that half of the Imperial Saurian Army had been killed along with him, his first reaction was that he was being fed a fantastic cock-and-bull story. He was seized with an uncontrollable rage and was about to order that the good-for-nothing jokers be court-martialled, when something happened that opened his eyes to the threat posed by the ants.

It was the commander of the palace guard who alerted him. He was standing next to the emperor's bed, shaking and yelling out in alarm as he gripped a piece of cloth in his claws.

'You idiot,' Urus roared at him, 'what are you doing with my pillowcase?' Today, it seemed, he was surrounded by numbskulls and numpties, and he was tempted to have them all put to death.

'Your . . . Your Majesty, I just discovered this. Look . . .' The commander held up the pillowcase in front of Urus's face. Strings of small holes had been chewed through the fabric – a message, left by soldier ants who had infiltrated his chambers while he slept:

We can take your life at any time!

As Urus stared at the bed linen, a chill ran through him. This was not the sort of pillow talk he was accustomed to. He glanced about the room as though he'd seen a ghost. The other dinosaurs present hurriedly stooped and scoped the ground, but they could find no trace of the ants. The words on the pillowcase were the only evidence they could see.

There was more, however; it was just that the dinosaurs didn't have the eyesight for it. The ants had laid in excess of 1,000 mine-grains throughout the emperor's bedchamber. The yellow pellets, which were invisible to the dinosaurs' naked eye, had been threaded into the mosquito netting, scattered around the feet of the bed, the sofa and the opulent wooden furniture, and stuffed between the mountainous stacks of documents. Formic acid was slowly eating away the surfaces of these incendiary devices, and like the million-odd other mines planted across Boulder City, their ignition time had been set for two o'clock.

The Saurian minister for war straightened up and addressed the emperor. 'Your Majesty, as I warned you some time ago, although it is true that in inter-species wars size is strength, it is also the case that being small has its advantages. We cannot take the ants too lightly.'

Urus sighed. 'Then what is our next step?' he asked.

'Rest assured, Your Majesty. We are prepared for this. I give you my word that the imperial army will flatten the Ivory Citadel before the day is out.'

Three hours after their failed first attack, the Imperial Saurian Army launched a second offensive against the Ivory Citadel. They sent in the same number of troops – 2,000 dinosaurs – and they advanced on the Ivory Citadel in the same phalanx formation, but this time each dinosaur wore a hefty metal helmet on its head.

The ant troops defending the Ivory Citadel responded with the same tactics they'd used earlier. Using the Formican slingshots, they again fired several hundred thousand ants into the air above the dinosaur phalanx, precipitating a heavy shower of ants raining down from the sky. This time, however, the ant soldiers were denied entry into their enemies' bodies. The dinosaurs' metal helmets fitted them very snugly. The visors were made from a single, solid piece of glass, the ventilation holes were covered in extremely fine steel mesh, the joints were seamless, and the helmets themselves were fastened securely at the neck with cord. They were impregnable: proper anti-ant armour.

When Field Marshal Donlira landed on a dinosaur's head, she observed the helmet beneath her feet with remorse. Two months earlier, ant craftsmen had helped with the manufacture of these very helmets. They had woven the fine steel mesh that covered the ventilation holes. At the time, the dinosaur manufacturer had claimed the helmets were intended for dinosaur beekeepers. It seemed that the Saurian Empire had also been secretly preparing for war for a long time.

After the ant-rain tactic failed, the Imperial Formican Army resorted to using bows and arrows to stall the dinosaurs at the second line of defence. 1.5 million ants released their arrows simultaneously. A cloud of aerial weaponry sped towards the dinosaurs like sand stirred up by a gust of wind, but the arrows were far too dainty to cause even the slightest harm to the mountainous soldiers. They merely bounced off their crusty skin and piled up on the ground around their feet.

The dinosaurs stamped their lethal way through the mass of ants, leaving trails of fatal footprints in their wake. Thousands of crushed ants filled each hollow tread. Those that escaped could only squint up helplessly from far below as the titanic figures blocked out the sky and tramped on towards their citadel.

As soon as they reached the ants' megalopolis, the dinosaurs began to stomp down extra hard and kick even more wildly. Most of the buildings in the Ivory Citadel were no higher than the dinosaurs' calves, and whole blocks were squished beneath a single clomp of their feet.

Field Marshal Donlira had a depressingly good view of the destruction, for she and several other ant soldiers were still scurrying back and forth over the *Tyrannosaurus*'s helmet, desperately trying to find a way in. Looking down from their scarily high vantage point, they surveyed their ruined city and the fires that raged through it. This was truly a dinosaur's-eye-view of the Ivory Citadel and what a sobering experience it was: to Donlira and her soldiers, their species appeared astonishingly small and insignificant.

The *Tyrannosaurus* strode over to the Imperial Trade Tower. At three metres high, this was the tallest skyscraper in the Formican Empire and the pinnacle of ant architecture, but it only came up to the beast's hips. The *Tyrannosaurus* dropped to its haunches – the abrupt loss of height causing the ants a moment of weightlessness

– and then the top of the tower appeared over the horizon of its helmet. The crouching dinosaur studied the tower for a few seconds, then grasped its base with its claws and plucked it from the ground. It stood, examining the tower curiously, as though it had found an amusing toy. The ants on the dinosaur's head gazed at the tower too. Blue sky and white clouds were reflected in its sleek navy-blue surface, and its countless glass windows sparkled in the sunlight. They still remembered how, on their very first day of school, they had followed their teacher to the top of the tower for a panoramic vista of the Ivory Citadel . . .

As the *Tyrannosaurus* turned the tower about in its claws, it suddenly broke in two. The dinosaur cursed and flung the pieces away, first one bit and then the other. They arced through the air and landed among a distant cluster of buildings, shattering on impact and knocking down many other homes and offices in the process.

It took only minutes for the tread of 2,000 dinosaurs (who were so ridiculously bulky that they couldn't all fit into the Ivory Citadel at the same time) to reduce the Formican capital to a heap of fine rubble. As clouds of yellow dust bloomed above the ruined city, the dinosaur soldiers began to cheer. But their triumphant cries were cut short when they turned to look in the direction of their own Boulder City.

Columns of black smoke were rising from the capital of the Saurian Empire.

Urus, with his imperial bodyguards clustered around him, lumbered from the palace through swirling smoke, only to collide head-on with the panic-stricken minister of the interior.

'It's terrible, Your Majesty – the whole city is burning!' shrieked the minister.

'What's happened to your fire brigade? Get them to help!'

'Fires are breaking out all over the city. The entire brigade has been called out, but they're fully occupied dealing with the fires in the palace.'

'Who started the fires? The ants?'

'Who else? Over a million of them infiltrated the city this morning.'

'Those blasted bugs! How did they even start the fires?'

'With these, Your Majesty . . .' The minister opened a paper packet and gestured for the emperor to look.

Urus stared long and hard at the packet but saw nothing until the minister passed him a magnifying glass. Through the lens, he could make out several mine-grains.

'Municipal patrol officers seized these this morning.'

'What is this – ant shit?'

'If only, Your Majesty. No, it's a type of miniature incendiary device. The ants planted over a million of them across the city, and at least one-fifth started fires that have now spread. By my calculation, that means there are currently some 20,000 individual fires in Boulder City. Even if we were to call in fire brigades from all over the empire, extinguishing a city-wide conflagration like this would be absolutely impossible.'

Urus stared numbly at the pall of black smoke in the sky, unable to speak.

'Your Majesty, we have no choice,' the interior minister said quietly. 'We must abandon the city.'

By nightfall, Boulder City was a sea of flames. The fires cast a red glow across the night sky, bringing a false dawn to the central plains of Gondwana. The roads outside the city were choked with fleeing dinosaurs and their enormous vehicles, fire and fear reflected in every pair of eyes.

Emperor Urus and several of his ministers stood on a low hill and gazed at the burning city for a long time.

'Order all Saurian ground forces in Gondwana to attack and raze every ant city on the continent – immediately! Dispatch fast sailing vessels to the other continents and make sure that every Saurian ground force in the world takes the same action. We shall deal a mortal blow to the ant world.'

And just like that, the conflict between the ants and the dinosaurs exploded. The flames of war soon raged across all of Gondwana, and before the month was out they were blazing through every other continent as well. A world war engulfed the entire planet. Terrible suffering ensued in both civilisations. One dinosaur city after another was consumed by fire, and ant cities were reduced to heaps of dust.

The ants also set fire to great tracts of grassland, farmland and jungle. They seeded vast areas with millions upon millions of mine-grains and the resulting infernos were impossible to extinguish. Brushfires raced across every landmass; orchards, pastures and forests burnt; and noxious smoke blotted out the sun. Less and less sunlight reached Earth and crop yields declined sharply, driving the dinosaurs, who required epic quantities of food, into starvation. It was an ecological catastrophe.

Meanwhile, crack teams of ants led raids on the dinosaurs from all quarters. Their preferred tactic was to launch their assaults from deep inside, which terrified the dinosaur public. Dinosaurs took to wearing masks at all times, not daring to remove them even while they slept, since the minuscule ants could sidle in and out of their most private spaces like a nightmarish crew of malevolent interns.

The ant world did not escape unscathed, however. Far from it. Ant civilisation took a severe beating from the dinosaurs. Almost every ant city was decimated, and the ants were forced to retreat underground. But they were not safe even there, for their subterranean bases were often unearthed by the dinosaurs and then destroyed. The dinosaurs made heavy use of chemical weapons and sowed a toxin that was harmless to dinosaurkind but deadly to ants everywhere. This not only killed innumerable ants but sharply constrained the scope of their activities. Individual ant colonies found it more and more tricky to maintain contact with other parts of the Formican Empire; because they lacked long-distance vehicles of their own, they had previously relied on dinosaur conveyances, but this option was no longer available. Communication became increasingly difficult, regions of the ant world became isolated, and the Formican Empire fragmented.

This was not all. There were more serious consequences still. Because the dinosaur–ant alliance was the foundation stone upon which Cretaceous civilisation was built, the crumbling of that alliance had a pernicious effect on societal structures in both worlds. Social progress ground to a halt and there were clear signs of regression. The survival of Cretaceous civilisation hung in the balance.

Though both the ants and the dinosaurs gave their all to the global war effort, neither side was able to achieve absolute supremacy on the battlefield, and the fighting degenerated into a protracted war of attrition. Eventually, the high commands of both empires came to recognise the reality of the situation: they were prosecuting a war that could not be won, a war whose ultimate outcome would be the destruction of the great Cretaceous civilisation. In the fifth year of the conflict, the two belligerents began armistice negotiations, and pivotal to these was the historic meeting between the Emperor of the Saurian Empire and the Queen of the Formican Empire.

The meeting was held in the ruins of Boulder City, on the former site of the imperial palace, where, five years earlier, the fateful summit that had triggered the war had taken place. All that now remained of that once colossal imperial seat were a jumble of shattered, fire-blackened walls. Through the cracks, the smoke-stained skeletons of other buildings were visible in the distance: the desecrated city was sinking back into the soil, its stonework colonised by thickets of lush green weeds and a lattice of creeping vines. The encroaching forest would soon swallow it up altogether.

As the sun dipped in and out of the haze cast by a remote forest fire, dappled patterns of light and shadow flitted across the old palace walls. Urus peered at the ant queen by his feet. 'I can't quite make you out,' he boomed, 'but I have a feeling that you are not Queen Lassini.'

'She is dead. We ants lead brief lives. I am Lassini, the second of her name,' said the new queen of the Formican Empire. On this occasion, she had brought just 10,000 word-corps soldiers with her, and Urus had to stoop to read her response.

'I think it's time to put an end to this war,' he said.

'I agree,' replied Lassini II.

'If the war continues,' Urus said, 'you ants will return to scavenging meat from animal carcasses and dragging dead beetles back to your tiny lairs.'

'If the war continues,' responded Lassini II, 'you dinosaurs will return to prowling hungrily through the forests and tearing apart your own kind for meat.'

'Well then, does Your Majesty have a specific recommendation as to how we might bring an end to this war?' Urus asked. 'Perhaps we should begin with the reason we went to war in the first place. There are many who have forgotten the whys and wherefores – dinosaurs and ants alike.'

'I recall it had to do with the appearance of God. Specifically: does God look like an ant or a dinosaur?'

Urus cleared his throat. 'I am happy to inform you, Queen Lassini, that for the last few years the Saurian Empire's most erudite scholars have devoted themselves to this question. They have now come to a new conclusion, and it is this: God resembles neither an ant nor a dinosaur. Rather, God is formless, like a gust of wind, a ray of light or the air that swaddles this world. God is reflected in every grain of sand, every drop of water.'

The Formican queen's answer came quickly and unequivocally. 'We ants do not possess such complicated minds as you dinosaurs,' she said, 'and that sort of profound philosophising is challenging for us. But I agree with this conclusion. My intuition tells me that God is indeed formless. And you should know that the ant world has forbidden idolatry.'

'The Saurian Empire has also forbidden idolatry.' Urus could hide his relief no longer. His face cracked into a wide, snaggle-toothed grin. 'In that case, Your Majesty, may I conclude that ants and dinosaurs share the same God?'

'If you wish, Your Majesty.'

And so the First Dinosaur–Ant War came to a close. It was a war without victors. The dinosaur–ant alliance made a swift recovery. New cities began to appear atop the ruins of the old, and Cretaceous civilisation, after so long spent teetering on the brink of collapse, was reborn.

8

THE INFORMATION AGE

Another millennium whizzed by. Cretaceous civilisation progressed through the Electric Age and the Atomic Age and into the Information Age.

Dinosaur cities were now immeasurably vast, on a scale even larger than those of the Steam-Engine Age, with skyscrapers that towered 10,000 metres into the sky – or more. Standing on the roof of one of these buildings was like looking down from one of our high-altitude aircraft, putting you way above the clouds that seemed to hug the Earth below. When the cloud cover was heavy, dinosaurs on the perpetually sunny top floors would phone the doorman on the ground floor to check whether it was raining down there and if they'd need an umbrella for the journey home. Their umbrellas were voluminous, of course, like our big-top circus tents.

Though the dinosaurs' cars now ran on petrol, not steam, they were still the size of our multi-storey buildings and the ground still trembled beneath their wheels. Aeroplanes had replaced balloons and these were as bulky as our ocean liners, rolling across the sky like thunder and casting titanic shadows across the streets below. The dinosaurs even ventured into space. Their satellites and spaceships moved in geosynchronous orbit and were, naturally, also colossal – so colossal, in fact, that you could discern their shapes quite clearly from Earth.

The global dinosaur population had increased tenfold and more since the Steam-Engine Age. Because they ate a lot and because everything they used was on a massive scale, dinosaurs consumed foodstuff and materials in astronomical quantities. It required untold numbers of farms and factories to meet these needs. The factories were powered by hulking great nuclear-powered machines and the skies above them were perpetually obscured by dense smoke. Keeping dinosaur society functioning efficiently was an extremely complex operation and the circulation of energy resources, raw materials and finance had to be coordinated by computers. A sophisticated computer network linked every part of the dinosaur world, and the computers involved were necessarily enormous too. Each keyboard key was the size of one of our computer screens, and their screens were as wide as our walls.

The ant world had also entered an advanced Information Age, but the ants obtained energy from completely different sources; they did not use oil or coal but harvested wind and solar power instead. Ant cities were cluttered with wind turbines, similar in size and shape to the pinwheels our children play with, and their buildings were covered with shiny black solar cells. Another important technology in the ant world was bioengineered locomotor muscle. Locomotor muscle fibres resembled bundles of thick electric cables, but when injected with nutrient solution, they could expand and contract at different frequencies to generate power. All of the ants' cars and aeroplanes were powered by these muscle fibres.

The ants had computers of their own: round, rice-sized granules that, unlike dinosaur computers, used no integrated circuitry at all. All computations were performed using complicated organic chemical reactions. Ant computers did not have screens but used pheromones to output information instead. These subtle, complex odours could only be parsed by ants, whose senses could translate the odours into data, language and images. The exchange of information across the ants' vast network of granular chemical computers was also effected by pheromones rather than by fibre-optic cables and electromagnetic waves.

The structure of ant society in those days was very different from the ant colonies we see today, bearing a closer resemblance to that of human society. Due to the adoption of biotechnology in embryo production, ant queens played a trivial role in the reproduction of the species, and they enjoyed none of the societal status or importance that they do nowadays.

Following the resolution of the First Dinosaur–Ant War, there had been no major conflict between the two worlds. The dinosaur–ant alliance endured, contributing to the steady development of

Cretaceous civilisation. In the Information Age, the dinosaurs were more reliant than ever on the ants' fine-motor skills. Swarms of ants worked in every dinosaur factory, manufacturing tiny component parts, operating precision equipment and instruments, performing repair and maintenance work, and handling other tasks that the dinosaurs could not manage.

Ants also continued to play a critical role in dinosaur medicine. All dinosaur surgery was still performed by ant surgeons, who physically entered the dinosaurs' organs to operate on them from the inside. They had a range of sophisticated medical devices at their disposal, including miniature laser scalpels and micro-submarines that could navigate and dredge dinosaur blood vessels.

It also helped that ants and dinosaurs no longer had to rely on word corps to understand each other. With the invention of electronic devices that could directly translate ant pheromones into dinosaur speech, that peculiar method of communicating, via formations comprising tens of thousands of ant soldiers, gradually became the stuff of legend.

The Formican Empire of Gondwana eventually unified the uncivilised ant tribes on every continent, establishing the Ant Federation, which governed all ants on Earth. By contrast, the once united Saurian Empire split in two. The continent of Laurasia gained its independence, and another great dinosaur nation was founded: the Laurasian Republic. Following a millennium of conquests, the Gondwanan Empire came to occupy proto-India, proto-Antarctica, and proto-Australia, while the Laurasian Republic expanded its territory into the lands that would become Asia and Europe.

The Gondwanan Empire was mainly populated by *Tyrannosaurus rex*, while the dominant group in the Laurasian Republic was *Tarbosaurus bataar*. During this long period of territorial expansion, the two nations engaged in almost continual warfare. In the late Steam-Engine Age, the militaries of these two great empires crossed the channel separating Gondwana and Laurasia in massive fleets to attack each other. Over the course of many great battles, millions of dinosaurs were slain on the wide, open plains, leaving mountains of corpses and rivers of blood.

Wars continued to plague both continents well into the Electric Age, decimating countless cities in the process. But in the last two centuries, since the dawning of the Atomic Age, the fighting had stopped. This was entirely due to nuclear deterrence. Both dinosaur nations amassed colossal stockpiles of thermonuclear weapons; if these missiles were ever deployed, they would transform Earth into a lifeless furnace. The fear of mutual destruction kept the planet balanced on a knife edge, maintaining a terrifying peace.

The world's dinosaur population continued to expand at a dramatic rate. Every continent suffered from extreme overcrowding and the dual threats of environmental pollution and nuclear war became more acute with each passing day. A rift reopened between the ant and dinosaur worlds and a pall of ominous clouds settled over Cretaceous civilisation.

9

THE DINOSAUR-ANT SUMMIT

Ever since the Steam-Engine Age, the Dinosaur–Ant Summit had been held annually without fail. It had become the most important meeting of the Cretaceous world, bringing dinosaur and ant leaders together to discuss dinosaur–ant relations and the major issues facing the world.

This year's Dinosaur–Ant Summit was to be held in the Gondwanan Empire's World Hall, the largest building known to Cretaceous civilisation. Its interior was of such epic proportions that it had developed its own microclimates. Clouds often formed on the domed ceiling, precipitating rain and snow, and temperature differences in different parts of the hall gave rise to gusts of wind. This phenomenon had not been anticipated by the hall's architects. The microclimates effectively made the hall redundant, since being inside the hall was pretty much akin to standing outdoors. On several occasions, summit meetings had been subjected to rain showers or snowstorms, necessitating the construction of a temporary smaller chamber in the centre of the hall. Today, however, the weather inside the World Hall was clear and fine and more than a hundred lights beamed down from the sky-dome like small, brilliant suns.

The two dinosaur delegations, headed by the Emperor of Gondwana and the President of the Laurasian Republic, took their seats around a large roundtable in the middle of the hall. Though the table was the size of a human football field, it seemed no bigger than a dot within the hall's capacious expanse. The ant delegation, led by Supreme Consul Kachika of the Ant Federation, was only just now arriving, their aircraft drifting like graceful white feathers towards the roundtable. As the gossamer airships floated in, the dinosaurs blew at them, sending them whirling through the air. The dinosaurs roared with laughter at this. It was a traditional joke played at every year's summit. Some of the ants tumbled out of the aircraft and onto the table. Though they were light enough not to come to any harm, they still had to trudge all the way to the table centre.

The rest of the ants managed to steady their aircraft and landed on a crystal platter in the middle of the table – their seat at the summit. The dinosaurs ranged around the table's edge could not see the ants from so far away, but a camera aimed at the platter projected an image of the ants onto a huge screen to one side, making them look just as massive as the dinosaurs. Magnified, the tiny insects looked a lot tougher, sleeker and more powerful than the dinosaurs, their metallic bodies giving them the appearance of formidable battle-ready warriors.

The secretary-general of the summit was a *Stegosaurus* with a row of bony plates down his back. He declared the meeting open and the delegates immediately quieted down. Then they all rose as one and saluted as the flag of Cretaceous civilisation was slowly hoisted up a tall, distant flagpole. The flag depicted a hybrid dinosaur displaying the characteristic features of every type of dinosaur alongside an ant of equal stature, composed of many smaller ants. The two creatures stood facing into the rising sun.

Without preamble, the meeting moved promptly to the first item on the agenda: a general debate on major global crises. Supreme Consul Kachika of the Ant Federation spoke first. As the slender brown ant waved her antennae, a device translated her pheromones into rudimentary dinosaur speech.

'Our civilisation is teetering on a precipice,' said Kachika. 'The heavy industries of the dinosaur world are killing the Earth. Ecosystems are being destroyed, the atmosphere is thick with smog and toxins, and forests and grasslands are disappearing rapidly. Antarctica was the last continent to be opened up but the first to be reduced to nothing but desert, and the other continents are headed for the same fate. This predatory exploitation has now spread to the oceans. If the overfishing and polluting of the oceans continues at the current rate, they too will be dead in less than half a century. But all that is as nothing compared with the dangers of nuclear war. The world is at peace right now, but preserving peace through nuclear deterrence is like tiptoeing across a tightrope above the fires of hell. A nuclear war could be triggered at any moment, and that will be the end of everything, for the nuclear arsenals of the two dinosaur powers are capable of destroying all life on Earth a hundred times over.'

'We've heard all this before,' sneered Laurasian president Dodomi, a mountainous *Tarbosaurus*. His lip curled contemptuously.

'It's your insatiable consumption of natural resources that's at the root of all this,' Kachika continued, waggling her antennae at Dodomi. 'The amount of food just one of you gets through in a single meal is enough to feed a large city of ants for an entire day. It's simply not fair.'

'You're talking twaddle, little bug,' boomed the Gondwanan emperor, a powerful *Tyrannosaurus* named Dadaeus. 'We can't help being so big. Would you have us starve? To survive, we must consume, and for that we need heavy industry and energy.'

'Then you should use clean, renewable energy.'

'That's just not possible. Those little pinwheels and solar cells you ants rely on couldn't even power one of our electronic wristwatches. Dinosaur society is energy hungry. We've no choice but to use coal and oil – and nuclear power, of course. Pollution is unavoidable.'

'You could reduce your energy consumption by controlling the size of your population. The global dinosaur population is now in excess of 7 billion. It cannot be allowed to get any bigger.'

Dadaeus shook his monstrous head and rolled his monstrous eyes. It was indeed a quite monstrous sight. 'The urge to reproduce is the most natural instinct of every lifeform,' he growled. 'And growth and expansion are intrinsic to the advancement of civilisation. To survive, to maintain its strength, a country must have a sufficiently large population.' Then he threw down the equivalent of a dinosaur's clawed gauntlet. 'If Laurasia is willing to smash its eggs, we dinosaurs of Gondwana will smash an equal number of ours.'

Dodomi, President of the Laurasian Republic, was quick to respond. 'But, as you well know, Your Majesty, Gondwana has nearly 400 million more dinosaurs than Laurasia—'

'And as you well know, Mr President, Laurasia's population growth rate is three percentage points higher than that of Gondwana,' replied Dadaeus.

'Mother Nature will simply not allow you insatiable beasts to multiply unchecked. Will it take a disaster to bring you to your senses?' said Kachika, one antenna pointing at Dodomi, the other at Dadaeus.

'A disaster, huh?' Dodomi guffawed. 'Dinosaurkind has survived for tens of millions of years. There are no disasters we haven't already seen!'

'Exactly. We'll worry about that when it happens,' Dadaeus said, gesticulating airily with his claws. 'It's dinosaur nature to let things run their course. Our kind takes life as it comes and fears nothing.'

'Not even all-out nuclear war? When that final moment of ultimate destruction arrives, I cannot see what route will be left open to you.'

'Well, little bug, on this point we are agreed.' Dadaeus nodded. 'We don't like nuclear weapons either, but Laurasia has deployed so many that we have no choice. If they destroy their weapons, we'll follow suit.'

'Ha ha. That'll be the day!' Dodomi wagged a pudgy digit at Dadaeus and sniggered. 'You surely can't believe we'll fall for that old chestnut, can you?'

'It goes without saying that you Laurasians should be the first to destroy your nuclear weapons, since you invented them.'

'But it was the Gondwanan Empire that made the first intercontinental missiles—'

Kachika cut them off with a wave of her antennae. 'What does it matter who did what centuries ago? We need to face the reality of what's happening here and now.'

'What's happening here and now is that Laurasia is entirely dependent on its nuclear weapons. Without them, it wouldn't stand a chance,' said Dadaeus. 'Do you remember the Battle of Vella Flat? The first emperor of Gondwana led 2.5 million *Tyrannosauruses* against 5 million *Tarbosauruses* in Antarctica and put them to rout. The evidence is still there at the South Pole for all to see, commemorated with a magnificent mound of Laurasian skeletons!'

'In light of which, Your Majesty will then certainly remember the Second Devastation of Boulder City,' Dodomi fired back. '400,000 pterodactyls of the Laurasian Airforce flew low over Gondwana's capital and dropped more than a million incendiary bombs. By the time the Laurasian Army entered the city, the Gondwanans had been cooked to perfection!'

'My point exactly! You Laurasians are cowards, always carrying out sneak attacks with aerial and long-range weapons but never having the courage to fight face to face! Hmph. You really are vile, pitiful worms.'

'Well then, Your Majesty, why don't we give everyone here the chance to see for themselves which one of us is the pitiful worm?' And with that, Dodomi leapt onto the great roundtable, brandishing his razor-sharp claws as he flew at Dadaeus.

The Gondwanan emperor immediately jumped onto the table to meet him. The other dinosaurs did not intervene, only cheered excitedly from the sidelines. Blows were regularly exchanged at international meetings in the dinosaur world. The ants, too, had become inured to this sort of spectacle. Being wise to the possible consequences, they hurriedly scurried beneath the sturdy crystal platter to avoid being flattened beneath the dinosaurs' feet.

Observed through the prism of the crystal platter, the brawling dinosaurs looked like spinning mountains, and the surface of the roundtable shuddered violently. Dadaeus had the advantage in terms of weight and strength, but Dodomi was more agile.

'Stop fighting! What's wrong with you?' the ants shouted from beneath the platter, their voices amplified by the translation system.

The two dinosaurs paused and, breathing heavily, retreated from the tabletop and returned to their seats. They were both covered in long, jagged scratches. They stared hatefully at each other.

'Right,' said the secretary-general, 'let's move on to the next item on the agenda.'

'No!' Kachika said firmly. 'There will be no further items discussed at this summit. Given that this vital matter concerning the very existence of our world remains unresolved, all other topics are rendered meaningless.'

'But, Madam Supreme Consul, every Dinosaur–Ant Summit of the last few decades has included a discussion about environmental pollution and the nuclear threat, and nothing has ever come of it. It has become routine, nothing but a ritual, a waste of everyone's time and patience.'

'But this time is different. Please believe me when I say that the most important issue facing civilisation on Earth will be resolved at this meeting.'

'If you are so certain, please continue.'

Kachika was silent for a moment. When the hubbub in the hall had subsided, she said solemnly, 'I will now read Declaration Number

149 by the Ant Federation. 'In order that civilisation on Earth may continue, the Ant Federation makes the following demands on the Gondwanan Empire and the Laurasian Republic.

'"One: halt all reproduction for the next ten years to effect a net reduction in the dinosaur population. After ten years, the birth rate must be kept lower than the death rate to ensure that the population continues to decline, and it must remain low for a century.

'"Two: shut down one-third of all heavy-industry enterprises immediately, and over the next ten years shut down another third as the population declines. Environmental pollution must eventually be reduced to a level that Earth's biosphere can withstand.

'"Three: immediately commence total denuclearisation. The destruction of nuclear weapons must be conducted under the supervision of the Ant Federation, with all nuclear warheads launched into space using intercontinental missiles."'

There was a smatter of laughter from the dinosaurs. Dodomi pointed a claw at the crystal platter. 'You ants have issued this declaration dozens of times before. Haven't you tired of it yet? Kachika, you would smother the great dinosaur civilisation. You can't seriously imagine we'll accept these absurd demands?'

Kachika dipped her antennae in affirmation. 'We know, of course, that the dinosaurs will not accept these demands.'

'Very well,' said the secretary-general, rattling the bony plates on his back, 'I think we can move on to the next item. Something more realistic.'

'Please wait a moment. There is more to our declaration,' said Kachika. She drew herself up to her full, frankly inconsiderable height. 'If the aforementioned demands are not met, the Ant Federation will act to ensure the continuation of civilisation on Earth.'

The dinosaurs were stunned into silence, agog to hear what plan of action this minuscule critter could possibly have in mind. Their humongous jaws hung slack and malodorous.

'If the dinosaur world does not immediately comply with the demands set forth in this declaration, all 38 billion ants working in the Gondwanan Empire and the Laurasian Republic will go on strike.'

Thin clouds had formed in the domed sky, floating like fine gauze, casting shifting patterns of light and shadow on the vast hall floor. For a long, long while, not a word was spoken.

Finally, Dodomi responded. 'You are surely joking, Supreme Consul Kachika?' he said.

'This declaration was jointly drafted by all 1,145 member states of the Ant Federation. Our resolve is unshakeable.'

'Supreme Consul, I trust that you and your fellow ants understand' – Dadaeus paused to rub his left eye, which appeared to have been scratched in the fight with Dodomi – 'that the dinosaur–ant alliance has lasted for three millennia. It is the cornerstone of civilisation on Earth. It is true that our two worlds have fought each other during our long history together, but our alliance has endured nonetheless.'

'When the entire planet's biosphere is at stake, the Ant Federation is left with no choice.'

'Don't play games. Remember the lesson of the First Dinosaur–Ant War!' said Dodomi. 'If you ants go on strike, the industrial output of the dinosaur world will grind to a halt, and many other fields, including the medical sector, will also be hard hit. We could be looking at the total economic collapse of not only the dinosaur world but the Ant Federation too. This course of action will affect the whole planet in ways we cannot predict.'

'The First Dinosaur–Ant War was about religious differences, but this time we ants are withdrawing from the alliance to save civilisation on Earth. Given the extreme importance of what is at stake here, the Ant Federation is willing to brave the consequences.'

Dadaeus slammed his claws against the table. 'We've been spoiling these bitsy bugs!'

'It is the dinosaurs who are spoilt,' said Kachika. 'If the ant world had put the brakes on sooner, the dinosaur world would not have spiralled so far out of control nor become this mad and arrogant.'

The hall fell quiet once more, but this time the air was charged with a frighteningly explosive energy. Again, Dodomi was the first to break the silence.

Glancing round the room, he said rather cryptically, 'Hmm, I think I require a moment alone with the ants.'

He heaved himself up onto the roundtable, crouched down in front of the crystal platter, prised it off the table, picked it up and carried the ants away, out of earshot of the other dinosaurs.

He withdrew a compact translator device from his jacket pocket and addressed Kachika directly.

'Madam Supreme Consul, the Ant Federation's declaration is not entirely unreasonable. Everyone can see that civilisation on Earth is facing a crisis. The Laurasian Republic is keen to solve this crisis too, only we haven't found the right moment. But it occurs to me now that there's an obvious shortcut we could take . . .'

He paused, partly to check that Kachika's antennae were twitching in his direction, and partly for dramatic effect.

'You ants could go on strike' – Dodomi bared the full set of his terrifyingly sharp fangs in a ghoulish grin – 'but only in the Gondwanan Empire. When the Gondwanan economy collapses and social chaos ensues, the Laurasian Republic will launch an all-out offensive and crush the Gondwanans in one fell swoop. They will be vulnerable and we will have no need to resort to nuclear war. We will then occupy Gondwana and shut down every last one of their industrial plants. As for the population problem, the war will wipe out at least a third of the dinosaurs in Gondwana, and the survivors will not be permitted to procreate for a century.'

He exhaled forcefully, undeniably pleased with himself. 'Now, does that not meet the Federation's demands?'

'No, Mr President,' said Kachika from the centre of the crystal platter. The other ant officials around her shook their heads. 'That will not change the nature of the dinosaur world, and sooner or later we will be back to where we are now. A world war on the scale you envision will certainly have unforeseen consequences. More importantly, the Ant Federation has always extended the same treatment to all dinosaurs, regardless of ethnicity or nationality. In all parts of the dinosaur world we perform the same work for the same compensation, and we never involve ourselves in your politics or wars. This is a principle the ant world has honoured since ancient times, and it is essential to safeguarding the inviolable independence of the Ant Federation.'

The secretary-general chose this moment to shout across at them from the roundtable. 'Mr President,' he boomed, 'please return the platter so we can continue the meeting.'

Dodomi shook his head and sighed. 'Foolish bugs! You're missing out on a chance to make history.' But he did as he was bid and returned to the roundtable.

As soon as Dodomi had replaced the platter in its designated spot, Emperor Dadaeus reached across the table and snatched it up. 'My apologies, everyone, but I must also now speak with the bugs in private.'

In a rerun of what Dodomi had just done, Dadaeus carried off the crystal platter, pulled out his own translator and addressed Kachika. 'Right then, Supreme Consul Teeny, I can guess what that chump said to you. But I'm telling you: do not trust him. Not on your incy-wincy life. Everyone knows what a cunning, conniving conspirator he is. It's those Laurasians who need to be wiped out.'

He swivelled his head round and snapped his fearsome jaws in the direction of his Laurasian rival. The platter vibrated alarmingly.

'We Gondwanans still have some notion of how to peacefully coexist with nature, and our behaviour is constrained by our religious faith. But Laurasian dinosaurs are incorrigible dinocentrists – they're true techno-worshippers from their horns to their tails. Their belief in the supremacy of machines, industry and nuclear weapons is unshakeable, far more so than ours. Those bastards will never change their ways! Listen, bugs, you should go on strike in Laurasia. Or, better yet, wreak widespread havoc. The Gondwanan Empire will launch an all-out strike and wipe that garbage nation off the face of the Earth! Little bugs, this is your big chance to do a heroic deed for civilisation on Earth.'

Kachika, however, was having none of it. She simply reiterated to the Gondwanan emperor what she'd earlier said to the president of Laurasia.

Dadaeus was livid. 'What gives you poxy parasites the right to look down on our great dinosaur civilisation?' he growled. And with a furious flick of his wrist he sent the platter hurtling to the floor.

The members of the ant delegation fluttered to the ground a few seconds after the platter landed.

'Know that it is we who rule the Earth, not you. You're nothing more than living specks of dust!'

Kachika stood on the floor of the hall and stared up at the Gondwanan emperor towering above her, his head way beyond her line of sight. 'Your Majesty, in times like these, judging the strength of a civilisation by the size of its individuals is the height of naivety. I suggest you read up on the history of the First Dinosaur–Ant War.'

But the translator device was too far away and Dadaeus did not hear her. 'If the ants dare to go through with this strike,' he roared, 'they will rue the day. There will be comeback as never before. No mercy!' Then he stalked off.

The representatives from the Gondwanan Empire and the Republic of Laurasia rose from the roundtable and filed out. The hefty thud of their footsteps made the ground judder, stirring up the dust from the floor and the members of the ant delegation along with it. But the dinosaurs were soon gone, disappeared into the distance, leaving the ants to face the long trek across the smooth, shiny marble surface. Its glossy patina reflected the white light of the suns that studded the domed sky and seemed to stretch into infinity, just like the unknowable future in Kachika's mind.

10

THE STRIKE

In the capital of the Gondwanan Empire, in the Great Blue Hall of the imperial palace, Emperor Dadaeus lay on a sofa, one claw covering his left eye, emitting the occasional groan of pain. Several dinosaurs stood around him: Interior Minister Babat, Defence Minister Field Marshal Lologa, Science Minister Professor Niniken, and Health Minister Dr Vivek.

Rising from his seat with a slight bow, Dr Vivek addressed the emperor. 'Your Majesty, the eye that Dodomi injured has become inflamed and requires immediate attention, but we currently cannot find any ant doctors to perform ophthalmic surgery. Our only option is to keep the inflammation under control with antibiotics. If this continues, however, you are at risk of losing your sight in that eye.'

'I could skin Dodomi,' said the emperor through gritted teeth. 'Is there not a single hospital in the entire country with an ant doctor still at work?'

Vivek lowered his head. 'I'm afraid not, Your Majesty. There are many patients waiting in vain for urgent surgical procedures. The situation is causing a great deal of unrest.'

'And I presume that's not the only reason our dinosaurs are panicking,' said the emperor gloomily, turning to the interior minister.

Babat gave a brief nod. 'That's correct, Your Majesty. At present, two-thirds of our factories have stopped production, and several cities have lost power. The situation in the Laurasian Republic is no better.'

'The dinosaur-operated machines and production lines have also stopped?'

'Yes, Your Majesty. In manufacturing sectors such as the automobile industry it is impossible to assemble the large dinosaur-made components into usable finished products without small precision parts, so production has had to be halted.' Babat rocked back and forward nervously on his scaly heels before continuing with the bad news. 'In other sectors like the chemical and energy industries, the ants' strike had little impact at first, but because the ants are responsible for maintenance, whenever a piece of equipment fails, there is now nothing we can do, so more and more factories are becoming paralysed.'

The emperor stamped with rage. 'You useless idiot! Did I not order you to have our dinosaur workforce undergo emergency training in delicate antwork, ready for this exact bastard scenario?'

'Your Majesty, what you requested is, ah, well . . . impossible.'

'Nothing is impossible for the great Gondwanan Empire! Over our long and illustrious history, Gondwanans have weathered crises much greater than this. How many bloody battles have we won against all the odds? How many continent-spanning forest fires have we extinguished? How many volcanic eruptions in the wake of tectonic shifts have we survived?'

'But, sir, this is different—'

'Different how? If we put our minds to it, dinosaur hands can be dexterous too. I will not have those piddling insects blackmail us and threaten our very existence.'

'Allow me to, um, demonstrate where the difficulty lies.' The interior minister tentatively opened his claws and placed two red cables on the sofa. 'So, er, when it comes to the maintenance of machinery, one of the most rudimentary requirements is the ability to connect two wires – wires such as these two cables, Your Majesty. May I ask you, sir, to attempt that task now?'

Emperor Dadaeus's clawed fingers were half a metre long and had the circumference of a large teacup. To his eyes, the two cables, just three millimetres in diameter, appeared finer than strands of hair do to us. Peering intensely at the sofa, he attempted to pinch the wires between his huge conical claws. But his claws were as smooth as artillery shells, and, try as he might, the wires kept slipping between their tips. Stripping and joining the wires was out of the question. The emperor huffed and swept the cables to the floor with an impatient wave of his clumsy claws.

'The truth is, Your Majesty, that even if you were to master the art of wiring, you would still be incapable of performing maintenance work. Our bulky fingers simply cannot fit inside machines sized for ants.'

Science Minister Niniken gave a long, wistful sigh. '800 years ago, the late emperor recognised the danger posed by the dinosaur world's reliance on the ants' fine-motor skills. He made tremendous efforts to research new technologies and equipment, to free us from this dependency. But with all due respect, over the last two centuries, including during Your Majesty's reign, these efforts have all but ceased. We have been lounging in a bed made for us by the ants, and we have forgotten that it's necessary to be vigilant even during peacetime.'

'I haven't been lounging in anyone's bed!' the emperor shouted angrily, raising both sets of claws as if he was about to punch his science minister. 'I too am haunted by the very same concerns that plagued the late emperor. My nightmares are full to the brim with them.' He jabbed a thick finger at Niniken's chest. 'But you should know that his efforts to wean us off our dependency on the ants came to nothing. He failed – utterly and decisively. It was the same in the Laurasian Republic.'

'Quite so, Your Majesty.' The interior minister smiled ingratiatingly. Pointing to the wires on the floor, he said to Niniken, 'Professor, as you are surely well aware, for a dinosaur to successfully join those wires, they would need to be ten to fifteen centimetres in diameter. And if they were that large, we'd be looking at mobile phones with wires as thick as saplings, and computers too, for that matter. And if we wanted our machines to be operated and maintained by dinosaurs, half of them would need to be at least a hundred times bigger than they are now, if not several hundred times bigger. Our consumption of resources and energy would increase a hundredfold, at least. There is no way our economy could withstand such a shift.'

The science minister nodded his acknowledgement. 'You're right. And of course some things just can't be scaled up. In optical and electromagnetic communications equipment, for example, the wavelength of electromagnetic waves, including lightwaves, dictates the size of the components used to modulate and process them; they simply cannot be any larger. Computers and networks would be quite literally unimaginable if there were no small components. And the same applies in the fields of molecular biology and genetic engineering.'

The health minister now had his say too. 'Because our internal organs are relatively big, it is feasible for dinosaur surgeons to operate in certain cases. But the ants' surgical techniques are non-invasive and therefore safer and more effective. Records show that in the past dinosaur surgeons did on occasion perform invasive surgery, but the technique has been lost. To recover it, we would need to master a range of other techniques such as general anaesthesia and wound suturing. There's also the matter of expectations and habits. Having enjoyed several millennia of ant medical care, most dinosaurs would find the prospect of being cut open during surgery absolutely unacceptable. So, at least for the foreseeable future, modern medicine cannot function without the ants.'

'The dinosaur–ant alliance is an evolutionary choice with profound implications. Without this alliance, civilisation could not exist on Earth. We absolutely cannot allow the ants to destroy this alliance,' the science minister concluded.

'But what recourse do we have?' the emperor grumbled, drumming his claws in irritation.

Defence Minister Lologa finally broke his silence. 'Your Majesty, the Ant Federation admittedly has many advantages on its side, but we have power on ours. The empire should make use of this power.'

Dadaeus cocked his head, letting the implications percolate through his imperial brain. A decision was made. 'Very well, Field Marshal,' he said, 'order the chief of staff to formulate a plan of action.'

'Field Marshal . . .' The interior minister grabbed hold of Lologa before he could leave. 'It's crucial that you coordinate with Laurasia on this.'

'He's right,' the emperor interjected. 'We must act in unison with them, lest Dodomi play the good dino and win the ants over to Laurasia's side.'

11

THE SECOND DINOSAUR-ANT WAR

The Ivory Citadel, which had been rebuilt atop the ruins of its predecessor (destroyed in the First Dinosaur–Ant War), was the largest ant city in the world. It had a population of 100 million ants, covered an area roughly equivalent to two football fields, and was the political, economic and cultural centre of the Ant Federation on the continent of Gondwana. The modern-day megalopolis bristled with high-rises, the most famous of which was the Federal Trade Tower; at five metres, this was the tallest building in the ant world.

Ordinarily, the citadel's winding streets pullulated with a continuous torrent of ants going about their business, heading this way or that but always in unison. Since their high-rises did not require stairs – because ants could access any floor simply by slipping in from the outside – these rivers of ants often seemed to defy gravity, flowing in vertical waves all the way up the sides of the city's skyscrapers. The citadel's airspace was also generally a hive of activity, whirring with squadrons of diaphanous-winged drones. Most striking of all were the wind turbines that crowned the rooftops, as luminous as meadows of white flowers in full bloom.

Today, however, the usually bustling metropolis was deathly still. All of the citadel's permanent residents had been evacuated, as had the vast numbers of ant workers returned from dinosaur cities. A mighty flood of several hundred million fleeing ants surged out from the eastern perimeters of the citadel and into the distance. To the west, a chain of towering metallic mountains had sprung up from the formerly endless plains: ten grotesque Gondwanan bulldozers had lined up side by side, their blades blocking the skyline in a cloud-scraping steel wall. The Gondwanan Empire had issued an ultimatum to the Ant Federation: if the strikers did not return to work within twenty-four hours, the bulldozers would level the Ivory Citadel. As the sun sank below the western horizon, their long shadows cast the city into darkness.

Early the next morning, the Second Dinosaur–Ant War began. A breeze cleared away the morning mist, and the newly risen sun shone upon a battlefield that seemed impossibly huge to the ants and claustrophobic to the dinosaurs. On the western perimeter of the Ivory Citadel, ant artillery units fanned out in an impressive twenty-metre-long line. Several hundred large-calibre guns glittered in the sunlight, the size of our firecrackers. Set back from the frontline, more than 1,000 guided missiles stood by in their launchers, each weapon about the length and breadth of one of our cigarettes. A covey of Ant Airforce reconnaissance planes circled the city, like tiny leaves caught in a whirlwind.

In the distance, the ten Gondwanan bulldozer operators started their engines. An almighty rumbling filled the air and as the vibrations travelled through the ground, the citadel shook as though rocked by an earthquake. The glass windows of its high-rises rattled in their frames.

Next to the bulldozers stood several dinosaur soldiers. One of them, an officer, raised his megaphone, angled it towards the city and began to shout.

'Listen up, little bugs!' he yelled. 'If you don't come back to work smartish, we're gonna drive these handsome 'dozers right on over to your city and flatten it. It'll be the work of minutes – eh, lads?' He swivelled round briefly to smirk at his soldiers. 'In fact, as you know, bug-lets, we don't even need to go to that much trouble. To quote the immortal words of an esteemed general of the First Dinosaur–Ant War: 'This city of yours is smaller than one of our kids' toy sandpits. The children could flood it just by pissing on it!' Ha ha ha!'

There was no answer from the Ivory Citadel – not even to remind the officer of the unfortunate end that particular dinosaur general had met in the First Dinosaur–Ant War.

The dinosaur officer did not hesitate any longer. With a decisive wave of his claws, he screamed 'Forward!' and the bulldozers began to advance, picking up speed as they went. A soft hissing sound rose from the citadel, only just audible beneath the roar of the bulldozers, like air escaping a balloon. Thousands of superfine white threads shot out from the city and lengthened rapidly, as though the buildings had sprouted hair. These were the smoke trails of the ants' missiles. The barrage of missiles soared over the open ground between the city and the bulldozers, raining down on the hulking great machines and the dinosaurs behind them.

The dinosaur officer caught one of the missiles in his claws. It exploded in his palm with a puff of smoke. He yelped in pain and flung the fragments away, but when he opened his claws to look, only a tiny flap of skin had been torn off. Several dozen more missiles struck him, detonating with sharp pops all over his bulky frame. As he swatted at his sides, he burst out laughing. 'Oh, your missiles are just like mosquitoes! I'm itching all over!'

The ant artillery began its bombardment. The line of guns flashed with fire, as though someone had lit a string of firecrackers and tossed it onto the Ivory Citadel's doorstep. Shells pelted the dinosaurs and their vehicles, but the explosions were drowned out by the ear-splitting thumps and clunks of the bulldozers and the ammunition left nothing but smudges on the cabin windscreens.

Less than two metres in front of the bulldozers, more than 1,000 ant aircraft suddenly rocketed straight up from the ground, their gossamer wings glittering in the sunlight. They propelled themselves over the tall blades of the bulldozers and alighted on the vibrating yellow metal of the vehicles' front hoods. Looking upwards, all the ants could see was the endless shine of windscreens reflecting the blue sky and white clouds overhead, obscuring the dinosaur drivers inside.

In the centre of each engine hood was a row of vents plenty wide enough for the ants to scuttle through. Once inside, they found themselves in a dreadful universe of gargantuan steel pipes and enormous spinning wheels. The suffocating air stank of diesel and the incessant din rattled the ants into numb stupefaction. But they had been well primed by their superior officers. They braced themselves against the swirling gales generated by the huge cooling fans and followed their predetermined route, marching over the rolling ridges of the pipes, unfazed by the tangle of tubes, being natural experts at mazes. The units tasked with finding the engine's spark plugs quickly located them: four towering pagodas some distance ahead. It was not necessary for the soldier ants to approach the plugs – in fact, they had been warned that the electric fields around the plugs could easily kill them. Instead they focused on the lone wires that dangled from the top of each spark plug; these trailed on the ground near the ants, each one about as thick as the ants were long. Coming to a halt beside these wires, the soldier ants removed the mine-grains they'd been carrying on their backs and deployed them, three or four mines to a wire. They set the timer knob on each mine, then quickly withdrew.

Unlike the miniature incendiary devices used in the First Dinosaur–Ant War, these mines were specially designed for disconnecting wires. A brief but brilliant indoor fireworks display ensued: blasts popped and crackled, neatly severing the four wires, and the broken ends fizzed and sizzled in a blinding shower of sparks as they made contact with the metal casing.

The disconnected spark plugs could no longer ignite the fuel. The loss of motive power brought the bulldozers to an abrupt halt, and inertia threw several ants off the pipes.

While all of this was happening, other ant contingents had gone in search of the fuel lines. These were much thicker than the spark-plug wires, and through the clear plastic walls the ants could clearly see fuel coursing down the tubes. They clambered on top of them, encircled them with a dozen mine-grains each, then retreated, mission accomplished.

The bulldozers had advanced about 200 metres when they suddenly stopped, one after the other. Two or three minutes later, six of them burst into flames. Their dinosaur drivers hopped out of the cabs and fled. Before they'd got very far, several of the burning bulldozers exploded. The ants standing guard around the Ivory Citadel could see nothing but thick smoke and sky-high flames.

The drivers of the four vehicles that had not caught fire returned to them. Buffeted by the heat coming off the other bulldozers, they lifted the hoods to check the engines and soon worked out what the problem was. One of the dinosaurs instinctively pulled a signal rod from his pocket. These rods could emit ant pheromones, and the dinosaurs used them to summon ant maintenance technicians. The driver stared at the flashing signal rod for a long time before he remembered that the ants no longer worked for him. Cursing, he stooped to reconnect the wires himself, but his claws were too big to fit inside the engine and pull the wires out. The other three dinosaurs were having the same problem. One of them had the bright idea of using a twig to hook out the wires, but even then his clumsy fingers could not re-join the wires, which repeatedly slipped from his grasp. Pretty soon, the drivers had no choice but to leave their bulldozers to the mercy of the flames that were now spreading from the vehicles alongside.

Observing this, the ants erupted into cheers, but Field Marshal Jolie of the Ant Federation Army, who had directed the battle from an armoured car, responded with cool-headed pragmatism and calmly gave the order to retreat. In fact, the artillery and missile units were already long gone. As the remaining ant troops winged their way east, the Ivory Citadel became a true ghost town.

The dinosaurs, meanwhile, were gazing shamefacedly at the row of blazing bulldozers. Pretty soon their embarrassment turned to fury. The officer was apoplectic. 'You loathsome pests,' he spluttered, 'did you really think you could get one over on us? Seriously? We only brought those bulldozers along for a lark. Watch carefully now, you pea-brained parvenus! Mess with the mighty Gondwanans and see what hell your toy city reaps!'

Ten minutes later, a Gondwanan bomber flew low over the Ivory Citadel. As its massive shadow engulfed the city, it released a bomb the size of one of our tanker trucks. An eerie scream echoed through the air as the bomb plummeted towards the city's central plaza. There was an earth-shaking boom and a thick black column of dust rose 100 metres into the sky. When eventually the dust settled and the smoke cleared, all that was left of the Ivory Citadel was a blasted crater of scorched, pulverised soil. Turbid groundwater began to well up through the base of the crater, submerging all remaining traces of the ant world's greatest city.

The dinosaurs were also wreaking their revenge over in Laurasia. Greenstead, the Ant Federation's hub city on that continent, was annihilated at almost the precise same instant. Its handsome high-rises and chic metropolitan cityscapes were razed by the high-pressure hose of a Laurasian fire engine. When the water jets ceased, there was not a solid structure still standing, just a sticky, stinky, inglorious mudflat.

12

THE MEDICAL TEAM

The day after the destruction of the Ivory Citadel, Supreme Consul Kachika of the Ant Federation led a team of doctors to Boulder City and requested an audience with Emperor Dadaeus.

'The Ant Federation has been deeply humbled by the Gondwanan Empire's tremendous show of power,' Kachika said meekly.

Dadaeus was immensely gratified by this display of unequivocal submission. 'Well then, Kachika!' he boomed. 'Finally some sense out of you.' He patted his humongous belly in absent-minded contentment. 'This is not the first time dinosaurs and ants have gone to war, but you ants no longer have the capacity you once enjoyed. You cannot start fires in our cities and forests any more, as the fire alarms and automatic sprinkler-systems we have installed will immediately extinguish any flame larger than a cigarette butt. As for that barbaric tactic of sneaking into dinosaurs' nostrils . . .' He snorted derisively, unconsciously clearing his own nasal passages in the process. 'Even during the First Dinosaur–Ant War we had ways of putting a stop to that. It's an irritant, nothing more.'

'Just so, Your Majesty,' Kachika replied politely, keeping a cautious eye out for any imperial snot that might be jetting her way. 'The purpose of my visit is to request that the Gondwanan Empire immediately suspend all attacks against other cities in the Ant Federation. We will call off the strike and resume our labours throughout the empire. The Ant Federation has made the same pledge to the Laurasian Republic. Right now, on every continent, tens of billions of ants are returning to dinosaur cities.'

Dadaeus nodded repeatedly in approval. 'This is all as it should be. The disintegration of the dinosaur–ant alliance would be disastrous for both our worlds. At least this incident has shown you ants once and for all who really rules the Earth!'

Kachika dipped her antennae. 'It was a vivid lesson indeed. And as an expression of the Ant Federation's sincere respect for Earth's rulers, I have brought with me our most distinguished medical team to attend to Your Majesty's eye.'

Dadaeus was very pleased. His eye injury had been troubling him for the past two days, but all his dinosaur surgeons had been able to do was prescribe him yet more antibiotics.

The ant medical team set to work straight away. Some of them operated on the outer surface of the emperor's eyeball, while the rest passed through his nostrils to focus on the back of the eye.

'Your Majesty, the first stage of the operation entails removing the dead and infected tissue from your eyeball and administering an injection,' Kachika explained. 'We will then repair the wound with the latest therapeutic agent – living tissue cultivated through bioengineering. It will completely heal your eyeball, leaving your vision and the appearance of your eye unaffected.'

Two hours later, the operation was done. Kachika and the ant medical team departed.

Interior Minister Babat and Health Minister Dr Vivek entered the emperor's chamber as soon as the ants had gone. They were followed by several dinosaurs pushing a large, complicated-looking machine. The health minister explained. 'Your Majesty, this is a high-precision three-dimensional scanner.'

'What do you plan to do with it?' asked Dadaeus, his left eye swathed in bandages, his right eye narrowed in suspicion.

'For Your Majesty's safety, we need to perform a full scan of your head,' the interior minister said solemnly.

'Is this really necessary?'

'It's best to be cautious when dealing with those devious little insects.'

The minister invited Dadaeus to step up onto the machine's small platform. Once he was in position, a thin beam of light began passing slowly over his head. It was a lengthy procedure. 'You're being ridiculously paranoid,' Dadaeus said irritably. 'The ants wouldn't dare lay a feeler on me. If they were found out, the imperial army would demolish all of their cities within three days. The ants may be devious, but they are also the most rational of insects. They're like computers: logic and precision are everything to them; there's no room for the sort of emotion that might spur them into trying to get even.'

The scan revealed no abnormalities in Dadaeus's skull. Meanwhile, a report came in confirming that ants were pouring back into dinosaur cities. Normalcy was quickly being restored.

'I'm still not convinced, Your Majesty. I know what the ants are like,' the interior minister muttered to the emperor in a low voice.

Dadaeus smiled at him benignly. 'Your vigilance is commendable, and you should remain watchful, but take it from me, old chap, we have bested them!'

The health minister would not be diverted. 'From now on,' he said, 'all high-ranking officials, leading scientists and key personnel must undergo regular scans like this. With Your Majesty's approval, of course,' he added hastily.

'Very well, you have my approval. But I still think you're being unduly anxious.'

Unbeknown to Dadaeus, however, on the previous day, twenty ants had lain hidden in the imperial infirmary. When night fell, they had infiltrated the infirmary's six scanners and destroyed a particular microchip in each of them – microchips that were too small for the dinosaurs to see. After the damage was done, the scanners operated normally but with a 20 per cent loss of accuracy. It was this reduction in accuracy that caused the scanner to miss something in Dadaeus's skull – a tiny object, just one-tenth of the size of a grain of rice, covertly planted by the surgical team on the emperor's cerebral artery. The tiny object was a timed mine-grain. 1,000 years earlier, in the First Dinosaur–Ant War, ant soldiers had bitten through the same artery in the brain of Major General Ixta (he of the charming 'pissing on your toy sandpit of a city' quote) just before he haemorrhaged to death on the battlefield outside the Ivory Citadel.

The mine-grain had been set to detonate in 660 hours. In those days, Earth rotated faster than it does today, and there were only twenty-two hours in a day, which meant that in exactly one month, the mine-grain in the emperor's brain would explode.

13

THE FINAL WAR

'The facts are clear: either the ants eliminate the dinosaurs or both species perish together,' Supreme Consul Kachika declared, addressing the senate of the Ant Federation from the speaker's podium.

'I agree with the Supreme Consul,' said Senator Birubi, waving her antennae from her seat. 'If current trends continue, one of two fates awaits Earth's biosphere. It will either be fatally poisoned by pollution from the dinosaurs' industries or it will be obliterated in a nuclear war between the great dinosaur powers of Gondwana and Laurasia.'

The other ant senators responded with feverish agreement.

'Yes, it's time to make a decision!'

'Exterminate the dinosaurs and save civilisation!'

'We must act now! Without delay!'

'Will everyone please calm down!' Professor Joya, chief scientist of the Ant Federation, waggled her antennae to quell the uproar. When some semblance of order had returned to the room, she continued. 'Remember that the symbiotic relationship between ants and dinosaurs has lasted for more than two millennia. Our alliance is the cornerstone of civilisation on Earth. If this alliance disintegrates and the dinosaurs are destroyed, can ant civilisation really continue unsupported?' She tried to engage the attention of the senators sitting closest to her, but not one of them would look directly at her. 'The benefits dinosaurs derive from us ants are well documented and understood. But we must not underestimate what we receive in return. Yes, that includes basic material necessities. But there is more, much more, though it is intangible and hard to quantify. Dinosaur ideas and scientific knowledge are crucial to ant civilisation, and we would be foolhardy to ignore that.'

'Professor, I have given this problem a great deal of consideration,' said Kachika. 'In the early days of the dinosaur–ant alliance, the dinosaurs' ideas and knowledge were indeed essential to ant society. They were the building blocks of our civilisation. But we have since spent two millennia absorbing dinosaur learning and accumulating knowhow. Ant thought is no longer as simplistic and mechanical as it once was. We, too, are capable of scientific thought, of technological design and innovation. In fact, in many fields, such as micro-machining and bio-computing, we are ahead of the dinosaurs. Without them, our technology will continue to progress regardless. We no longer need to tap them for ideas.'

'No, no . . .' Professor Joya flicked her antennae forcefully. 'Supreme Consul Kachika, you have confused technology with science. It's true that ants make outstanding engineers, but we will never be scientists. The physiology of our brains is such that we will never possess those two essential dinosaur traits: curiosity and imagination.'

Senator Birubi shook her head in disagreement. 'Curiosity and imagination? What nonsense, Professor. You surely can't believe those are enviable traits? That's precisely what makes the dinosaurs such neurotic, moody, unpredictable creatures. They fritter away their time lost in fantasies and daydreams.'

'But, Senator, that unpredictability and those fantasies are what lie behind their creativity. It's what enables them to conjure and pursue theories exploring the most profound laws of the universe, and that is the basis of all scientific progress. If abstract theorising were to cease, technological innovation would be like a pool of water without a source – it would dry up.'

'All right, all right.' Kachika was getting increasingly impatient. 'Now is not the time for dull academic discussion, Professor. What the ant world is facing here is an existential dilemma: will we destroy the dinosaurs or perish alongside them?'

Joya made no answer.

'You academics are all talk and no action,' Birubi sneered. 'Always prattling on about theory but totally hopeless when asked to solve an actual practical problem.' She turned to Kachika. 'Madam Supreme Consul, does that mean federal high command already has a detailed plan in place?'

Kachika nodded. 'Please allow Field Marshal Jolie to explain.'

Field Marshal Jolie, who had commanded the ant troops at the Second Battle of the Ivory Citadel several days earlier, approached the podium. 'I would like to show everyone something,' she began. 'Something we invented on our own, developed without recourse to our dinosaur teachers.'

At the field marshal's signal, two ants brought forward a pair of thin white strips resembling scraps of paper. 'The weapons you see here have evolved from antkind's oldest, most traditional weapon, the mine-grain. They're the latest model. The Federation's military engineers developed them for use in this final war.'

She waved her antennae and four more ants came forward, carrying two short lengths of wire, the kind most commonly used in the dinosaurs' machinery. One wire was red, the other green. The ants set the wires on a frame, then wound the two white strips tightly around the middle of each wire, like pieces of white adhesive tape. Something miraculous now occurred: the two white strips began to change colour, taking on the hue of the wire they were wrapped around, one turning red, the other green. Within moments they were all but indistinguishable.

'These are chameleon mine-grains. Once they're fixed in place, it's impossible for dinosaurs to detect them.'

A couple of minutes later, the mine-grains exploded with two sharp cracks, neatly severing the two wires.

'When the time comes, the Federation will deploy an army of 100 million ants. One division of this army has already gone back to work in the dinosaur world; the other division is infiltrating the dinosaur world as we speak. This army of millions will affix 200 million chameleon mine-grains to the wiring of the dinosaurs' machines. We have called this campaign "Operation Disconnect".'

'Wow, a truly magnificent plan!' Senator Birubi exclaimed in admiration. The other senators fluttered their antennae in sincere and vigorous approval.

'We have also initiated another campaign, to be conducted in parallel, which I am confident you will find to be equally magnificent,' Jolie continued. 'The Federation will deploy another army of 20 million ants to penetrate the skulls of 5 million dinosaurs and affix mine-grains to their cerebral arteries. These 5 million dinosaurs comprise the elite echelon of the billions of dinosaurs on Earth. They include, among others, their national leadership, scientists, and key technicians and operators. Once these dinosaurs have been eliminated, dinosaur society will be without a brain. We have therefore dubbed this campaign "Operation Decapitate".'

'This plan seems more complicated than the first,' said Birubi. 'As far as I know, all key personnel in dinosaur society are routinely subjected to high-precision three-dimensional scans. The Gondwanan Empire was the first to adopt this practice, and the Laurasian Republic quickly followed suit. In the Gondwanan Empire, even Emperor Dadaeus himself regularly undergoes such examinations.'

'The first mine-grain of Operation Decapitate has already been planted,' said Supreme Consul Kachika with a smug expression on her shiny black face. 'It is currently lying in wait in Dadaeus's brain, and it was put there by the medical team I led. The emperor has undergone a series of examinations since then, yet that mine-grain has remained safely stuck to his cerebral artery.'

'You mean we've developed a new model of mine-grain that cannot be detected by high-precision three-dimensional scanning?' Professor Joya asked.

Kachika shook her head. 'We tried, but all our efforts failed. As you know, those scanners are one of the most revolutionary inventions of recent years, a shining example of what ant–dinosaur collaboration can achieve. A high-precision three-dimensional scanner can locate and identify the slightest abnormality in a dinosaur's brain. Of course, mine-grains installed in other parts of a dinosaur's body are not easily detected. But to kill a dinosaur with a single mine-grain – or at least to cause it to lose consciousness and the ability to think – can only be done by deploying the mine on the cerebral artery. The dinosaurs are well aware of this, so they only scan their brains.'

Professor Joya pondered this for a long while and then flapped her antennae, confused. 'Forgive me, Supreme Consul, I don't see how that mine-grain can escape detection. I was the ant in charge of the scanner project, so I know just how powerful those instruments are.'

It was now Field Marshal Jolie's turn to look exceedingly pleased with herself. 'My dear Professor, you always overthink things. We simply sent a detachment of troops to infiltrate the imperial infirmary and sabotage all six of its scanners. Destroying a single microchip reduced the scanners' accuracy by 20 per cent, preventing them from detecting the mine-grain.'

'But aren't you planning to mine the skulls of 5 million dinosaurs? That will never . . .' Joya gasped as the realisation hit. 'You can't possibly be thinking of sabotaging every scanner in the dinosaur world?'

'Indeed we are! Compared to operations Disconnect and Decapitate, it's an easy task. Remember that the dinosaur world has a mere 400,000 such machines at present. An army of 5 million ants should be quite sufficient to deal with them.'

'That's an insane plan,' said the chief scientist, shocked.

'The most brilliant part of the plan is that the attacks will happen *simultaneously*,' interjected Kachika, choosing to interpret the professor's exclamation as praise. 'The 200 million mine-grains in the dinosaurs' machinery and the 5 million mine-grains in their brains will all explode at exactly the same moment. And I mean *exactly*. There will be no time-lag between explosions – not so much as a second between them! This will ensure that no section of the dinosaur world will be able to receive assistance or reinforcements from any other section.'

Supreme Consul Kachika surveyed the senators massed before her. There was not a twitch or a quiver among them. Every single pair of antennae was frozen in astonishment and pride. It was an impressive sight; the sort of spontaneous homogeneity that would make the Ant Federation great again. She continued.

'The first effect of these coordinated attacks will be a complete breakdown in the dinosaurs' extensive information network. Shortly thereafter, their major industries and transport systems will also grind to a halt. Because this will be happening in every corner of the dinosaur world, they will have no way of bringing these systems back online in the short term. And with 5 million of their key personnel eliminated, dinosaur society will go into total shock. It will sink swiftly, like a ship with its hull ripped apart in the middle of the ocean.'

The assembled senators were still rapt. Kachika paused briefly to savour the moment.

'As we know to our cost, dinosaur cities indulge in staggering levels of consumption. According to our computer simulations, once the information, industrial and transportation systems that supply the dinosaur cities have collapsed, in less than a month two-thirds of dinosaurs in urban centres will have died from starvation or dehydration. The rest of the dinosaur population will scatter into the countryside. Under sustained assault from our forces, and ravaged by hunger and disease, less than a third of the survivors will last the year. Those who do will have regressed to the low-technology society of the pre-industrial era, and they will pose no threat to the ant world. And then, finally, we will be the rightful rulers of Earth.'

Birubi could barely contain her excitement. 'Madam Supreme Consul, can you tell us when this great moment will occur?'

'All of the mine-grains have been set to detonate at midnight one month from now.'

At this, the ants immediately started cheering. They were unusually loud and exuberant.

Professor Joya, however, did not share their excitement. Far from it. She swished and waggled her feelers desperately, trying to quiet the assembled masses, but the cheering did not subside. It was only by shouting that she forced everyone to calm down and pay attention.

'Enough! Have you all gone mad?' she yelled. 'The dinosaur world is a vast and extremely complex system. If that system suffers a sudden collapse, there will be consequences we cannot predict.'

'Professor,' Kachika replied, 'other than the destruction of the dinosaur world and the final victory of the Ant Federation on Earth, can you enumerate for us the other consequences?'

'I told you – they are difficult to predict.'

'Here we go again,' Senator Birubi said. 'Joya the egghead strikes again. We are tired of this shtick of yours,' she said.

The other senators grumbled in agreement. The chief scientist's killjoy attitude was spoiling the party.

Field Marshal Jolie scurried over to Professor Joya and patted her with her front leg. The field marshal was an unemotional ant, one of the few who had not cheered with everyone else.

'Professor,' she said sympathetically, 'I understand your concerns. In fact, I share some of them. But, as a realist, I don't think the Ant Federation has any other choice. Scholars like you can offer us no better alternative. As to the terrible consequences you spoke of, I can see why you might be nervous about the dinosaurs' nuclear arsenals, for example. They are capable of wiping out all life on Earth. But there's no need to worry. It's true that the nuclear-weapons systems are controlled entirely by dinosaurs, and ants are only permitted to perform routine maintenance work under close scrutiny. But infiltrating those systems will be a cakewalk for our special forces. We will deploy more than twice the number of mine-grains in them than in any of the other systems. When the appointed time comes, they will be crippled. Not a single warhead will explode.'

Professor Joya sighed. 'Field Marshal, it's far more complicated than that. The crucial question is this: do we really understand the dinosaur world?'

This comment stunned all of the ants into silence for a moment, even Supreme Consul Kachika. Then she eyeballed Professor Joya and voiced what the others were thinking. 'Professor, there are ants in every corner of the dinosaur world, and it has been that way for 3,000 years! How can you ask such a foolish question?'

Joya slowly shook her antennae. 'We should not forget that dinosaurs and ants are two very different species. We inhabit disparate worlds. Intuition tells me that the dinosaur world holds great secrets that we ants know nothing about.'

'If you can't be specific, you might as well drop the subject,' Birubi snapped.

But Joya would not be deterred. 'To that end, I suggest that we establish an intelligence-gathering system. *Specifically*,' she said, inclining her head in Birubi's direction, 'whenever we deploy a mine-grain in a dinosaur's brain, we should also install a listening device in their cochlea. I will lead a department that will monitor and analyse the information sent back by these devices, with the aim of discovering things heretofore unknown to us as soon as possible.'

'The preparatory work for Operation Decapitate should be finished in half a month,' said Field Marshal Jolie. 'Your department will be inundated with information from 5 million listening devices. Even if you invest enormous effort in this, the mine-grains will detonate before you've had the chance to analyse a fraction of that intelligence.'

Professor Joya dipped her antennae. 'That is why, Field Marshal, I ask that the mine-grains' detonation be delayed by a further two months, so that we can analyse as much information as possible. We may learn something.'

'This is nonsense!' Kachika shouted. 'There can be no delay. One month is all the time we need to lay the mine-grains. We cannot and will not agree to an extension – not even by a single second. Undue delay will only invite trouble. We need to get this operation done! Besides, I don't believe there is anything about the dinosaur world that we don't already know.'

14

MINE-GRAINS

Emperor Dadaeus of Gondwana strode into Boulder City's Communications Tower flanked by the interior minister and the security minister. The Communications Tower was the nexus of Boulder City's data network, responsible for the transmission of all information between the capital and the rest of the empire. There were more than 100 similar hubs across Gondwana.

The three dinosaurs headed straight for the tower's main control room, which was aglow with bank after bank of enormous computer screens. The dinosaur operatives seated behind the screens immediately rose to their feet out of respect for the emperor and his ministers.

'Who's in charge here?' roared the interior minister. Two dinosaurs lumbered forward and introduced themselves as the centre's lead engineer and chief security officer. 'Tell me, where are the ants that work here?' the minister said.

'They've all left for the day,' replied the lead engineer.

'Good. Good.' The interior minister nodded his approval. 'So you've received the order from the Ministry of Security, I presume? And you've conducted a thorough examination of every single computer and piece of communications equipment in this tower? Hmm?' He fixed the two dinosaurs with his steeliest gaze but did not wait for an answer. 'As you know, this is to prevent possible sabotage by the ants. It's a nationwide programme being rolled out in every sector and every corner of the empire. It is greater in scope and ambition than any previous inspection.' He inclined his neck deferentially in the direction of Dadaeus. 'His Imperial Majesty has come to observe your work.'

The lead engineer lowered his eyes. 'We conducted a thorough inspection as soon as we received the order,' he said quietly. A muscle in his jaw twitched nervously. 'As of this moment, all key equipment has been checked twice. And we have further strengthened our security measures. I can personally guarantee the unassailability of our communications centre. Your Majesty may rest assured.'

'Show us to the most important area of the tower,' commanded Dadaeus.

'To the server room, then?' The chief engineer shot the interior minister an inquiring look, received an affirmatory nod and set off.

They soon came to an area packed with row upon row of massive white computers. These were the empire's servers. They hummed softly, like living beings, as they processed the oodles of information pouring in from all over the world.

'Talk us through the security measures for this server room,' said the interior minister.

The chief security officer smiled with pride. 'The ants who work in the tower are strictly prohibited from entering this room without authorisation. All maintenance work is performed under the close supervision of dinosaurs.' She unhooked a magnifying glass from the door of the nearest server cabinet. 'As Your Majesty can see, we use these to monitor the ants' work. Whenever we have reason to dispatch an ant into the interior of a server, we keep them under continuous and rigorous surveillance.' She gestured expansively around the room, drawing the visitors' attention to the magnifying glasses hanging on every server-cabinet door.

'Excellent.' The interior minister inhaled sharply. 'And what have you done to prevent infiltration by *unauthorised* ants?'

'For a start, we've hermetically sealed the server room to stop intruders from gaining access.'

'Hermetically sealed it?' interjected the security minister, who'd been silent until now. He gave a hollow guffaw. 'That's a laugh! Let me tell you, I have had the dubious pleasure of seeing the most airtight room known to dinosaurkind – namely the vault in the Imperial Bank of Gondwana where the ants' currency is stored.' He shook his head in weary disgust. 'Do you know how tightly that vault is sealed? No? I can assure you: it's a vacuum inside there. Not even *air* can get in. *Air!* Think about that for a moment. It's a perfect seal. And yet . . .'

Even the emperor was all ears now. He and the other three dinosaurs waited patiently for the security minister to get to his punchline.

'There was a particularly clever gang of ant thieves at large and the bank knew it would be targeted sooner or later. So the manager installed a number of highly sophisticated super-sensitive gas detectors inside the vault. The idea being that as the ants drilled through the wall, trace amounts of air would leak in from the outside, triggering the sensors and setting off the alarm. But blow me down, do you think that worked? Did it hell!'

The minister narrowed his eyes and drew himself up tall as he finally got to the point of his tale. 'No! Those damned critters still managed to rob the vault without setting off the alarm. And they left no discernible evidence, not a whit. But I tell you what I think – I suspect those crafty buggers mounted a miniature vacuum chamber to the vault's exterior wall before they started drilling. That way, no air leaked in, no air leaked out. Be under no illusion, my friends, the ants' cunning is far beyond what we can imagine. And their tiny size gives them an enormous advantage. No way can we secure the massive buildings of our cities with ant-proof seals. It's impossible.'

Emperor Dadaeus was not going to be fobbed off that easily. 'But can the servers themselves not be hermetically sealed to prevent the ants sabotaging them?' he asked.

'That is difficult, too, Your Majesty,' the security minister replied. 'For a start, the servers require certain holes in order to be able to operate – holes like vents, cable openings and disk drives, for example. And, as you know, ants are excellent borers and have any number of tiny but powerful tools for drilling quickly through all sorts of materials – a legacy from their nest-dwelling days. To truly guarantee the security of our machines, the only effective method is to check, double-check and triple-check. Which means' – he turned to the lead engineer and chief security officer – 'that there cannot and must not be any let-up in vigilance. Even a momentary lapse in concentration could have dire consequences,' he said darkly. 'Is that understood?'

'Yes, Minister!' the two dinosaurs shouted in unison, standing to attention.

The minister's gaze now settled on a server to his right. 'Inspect this machine,' he commanded.

The chief security officer said something into her two-way radio and five dinosaur engineers immediately hurried over, armed with flashlights, magnifying glasses and other tools, as well as two specialised instruments. The engineers opened the cabinet door and began to carefully inspect the interior. This was no easy task. The wiring and components inside the server formed a tangled knot, and the dinosaurs had to pore over it with their magnifying glasses as if they were reading a long, convoluted essay or wandering through a complicated maze.

Just as Dadaeus and his ministers were beginning to get impatient, one of the engineers shouted, 'Oh, I've found something! It's a mine-grain.' He passed the magnifying glass to Dadaeus. 'Your Majesty, it's right there, on that green wire.'

The emperor peered through the magnifying glass and gave a satisfied grunt. Another dinosaur pulled out a pen-shaped object – a miniature vacuum cleaner – and pressed the nib to the wire. With the flick of a switch, the little yellow pellet was sucked up off the wire.

'Well done!' The security minister patted the engineer on the shoulder, then turned to Dadaeus. 'Your Majesty, this dummy mine-grain was placed there on my orders, to test the effectiveness of the centre's security-inspection process.'

'Hmph!' Dadaeus was unimpressed. 'I have my doubts about the efficacy of all this.' He flicked an imperious claw in the direction of a magnifying glass. 'It's all so suffocatingly small! As you say, the ants are little and devious. If they are determined to cause havoc, it'll be very difficult to beat them at their own game. No, the most effective way to counter the ant menace is by threatening full-on retaliation. They need look no further than the decimation of their two greatest cities. That's the sort of deterrent the Ant Federation understands. Am I not right?'

He glowered at his ministers, daring them to contradict him, then carried on.

'They have learnt to their cost that their world is nothing but a toy sandpit to us. They know we could destroy every single remaining ant city on Earth in just a couple of days. And now that they do know that, they will not dare organise any acts of sabotage against *our* world. They are entirely rational creatures and their actions are governed by dispassionate, mechanical considerations. That kind of thinking does not allow them to take unfavourable risks.'

'Your Majesty, there is certainly truth in what you say,' replied Interior Minister Babat hesitantly, 'but yesterday evening I had a nightmare that alerted me to another possible scenario.'

'You seem to have been having quite a few nightmares of late.'

'That's because my intuition tells me we are in very real danger. Your Majesty, the empire's deterrence strategy is founded on the premise that if the ants were to destroy a part of our dinosaur world, another part of our world would then launch a devastating second strike against them. But what if the ants target every corner of the dinosaur world simultaneously, in a single coordinated attack? If they do that, we won't be able to retaliate. In that sort of scenario, our . . . um . . . deterrence strategy will be . . . um . . . non-existent.'

Dadaeus gave his nervy minister's comments a nanosecond's thought then shook his head. 'The situation you've described is merely theoretical. It's a worst-case scenario that will never happen.'

'But, Your Majesty, that's how the ants operate: as long as the theoretical possibility for a course of action exists, they will attempt it. That's the flipside of their mechanical way of thinking. In their simplistic estimation, nothing is too crazy.'

'I have to disagree with you on that, Babat. I still think it's unlikely to happen. Besides, the empire's security measures are pretty damn rigorous. If the ants were planning a full-scale operation, we'd notice pretty quick. What worries me now isn't the ants – it's those Laurasians. They're becoming more and more of a threat to us Gondwanans.'

Besides the dinosaurs assembled in the server room, Dadaeus had another audience: twelve soldier ants hidden beneath the motherboard of the server the engineer had just examined. Five hours earlier, the ants had snuck into the Communications Tower via a water pipe, made their way into the server room through a tiny crack in the floor, then slipped through an air vent into the server itself. The security minister was correct. The ants could pass unimpeded through the dinosaurs' massive buildings and machinery.

On hearing the dinosaurs approaching the server room, the ants had quickly ducked beneath their server's motherboard, which was larger than the Ivory Citadel's football stadium. They bunched together apprehensively as the door of the server cabinet crashed open. Gazing skywards through a small hole in the motherboard, all they could see was the lens of a magnifying glass and the grotesque eye of a dinosaur engineer distorted through it. The ants were terrified, but the dinosaur failed to spot them. Pretty soon, the engineer discovered the fake mine-grain that the minister had hidden, but he entirely failed to see the real mine-grain that the ants had just planted alongside it. The tiny chameleon mine had already taken on the hue of the wire it was wrapped around, making it effectively undetectable. A dozen further chameleon mines were wrapped around other wires of varying colours and thicknesses in the immediate vicinity.

There were also chameleon mines stuck to the circuit board. These supported a more advanced colour-changing feature that allowed them to adopt many different colours in order to perfectly match the board beneath them. With such flawless camouflage, they were even harder to detect than the mine-grains on the wires. These mines were not designed to explode. When the appointed time came, they would leak several drops of strong acid, dissolving the circuits etched into the board.

The ants remained frozen where they were beneath the motherboard while the interior minister and the emperor argued about tactics overhead. When the cabinet door finally banged shut, night immediately fell over the interior of the server. A single power-indicator light hung like an emerald moon in the sky, the hum of the cooling fan and the soft clicking of the hard drive accentuating the tranquillity of that strange realm.

'You know, that dinosaur minister had a good point,' remarked one of the soldier ants. 'If the Ant Federation did pursue a simultaneous-strike policy like that, we could destroy the dinosaur world.'

'Maybe that's exactly what we're doing now,' one of her fellow soldiers replied. 'Who knows?'

His observation was spot on. For, unbeknown to him and the rest of his cohort, the twelve of them inside that server were far from the only ants currently on manoeuvres in the Communications Tower. In fact, inside every server in that room and every switchboard on the floor below was a team of ants carrying out the exact same task. And, naturally, the ant deployment didn't stop there. Hundreds of millions of ants had been dispatched across every continent to engage in precisely the same sort of direct action. An infinite number of invisible chameleon mine-grains were being laid at that very instant. The scale and reach of the operation was truly – literally – mind-boggling.

That night, Interior Minister Babat had yet another nightmare. A vast, ink-black battalion of ants surged up his nostrils and disappeared inside him. Moments later they began snaking back out through his jaws in a long line, each ant now gripping a tiny gobbet of something in its mouth. The gobbets were the minister's innards, chewed to bits. The ants discarded the flecks of innards on exiting his body, did an immediate about-turn and marched straight back up his nostrils. It was an ant production line, a nightmare loop, a horrifyingly vicious circle. He could feel himself being hollowed out.

The minister's dream was not as far-fetched as he would have hoped. At that very moment, a pair of soldier ants was indeed voyaging up one of his nostrils. The deadly duo had sidled into his bedroom during the day and hidden under his pillow, biding their time. Now, as the sleeping dinosaur snored his way through his terrifying nightmare, each one of his jet-stream inhalations propelled the two soldiers deeper inside his nasal cavity. The fearless Formicans were then able to navigate the dark cranium with practised ease, and in no time at all they arrived at his brain.

One of the ants switched on his tiny headlamp and quickly located the main cerebral artery. His colleague attached a yellow mine-grain to the artery's transparent outer wall. The two then withdrew from the brain, following another winding passage downwards through the dark, dank cranium until they emerged at the ear. A sliver of light filtered through the translucent eardrum and things suddenly got very noisy as sounds from the outside world were amplified by the cochlea and transmitted around the space. The ants swiftly set about installing a listening device beneath the drum.

The interior minister was still trapped in his nightmare. In his dream, all his internal organs had been scraped out and swarms of ants had scuttled inside him, intent on using his cavernous body as a nest. He woke up in a cold sweat.

The two ants working feverishly in his ear felt the world around them beginning to sway, followed by a distinct change in gravitational pull. A deafening rumble filled their dim space, rattling the ants almost to jelly. The minister was yelling and the vibrations were travelling through his cranial bones.

'Guard! Guard!'

There was another voice, this time from outside. The eardrum vibrated so violently that its surface seemed to blur. 'Minister, what is it?'

'Fetch a scanner. I need to be examined at once.'

The two ants glanced nervously at each other. They'd managed to install the listening device, but now they were in great danger of being spotted. 'What should we do?' the light-bearing ant said. 'Perforate the eardrum and evacuate through the ear canal?'

'No good.' His colleague waggled her feelers dismissively. 'We'll be discovered that way. Let's take cover in the lungs. Usually they only scan the head.'

The two ants made a rapid descent through the darkness. At the nasal cavity, they took a sharp turn and quickly reached the entrance to the respiratory tract. They waited quietly for the dinosaur to inhale before they jumped, riding the gale through the windpipe and into the lungs. Through the gloom they heard a hissing, like a rain shower in the forest at night. This was the sound of gaseous exchange taking place in the air sacs. They could also hear a faint hum coming from the outside world – the sound of the three-dimensional scanner in operation. After a few minutes, someone spoke outside. Though the voice was much fainter down there than in the dinosaur's skull, the ants could still make out the words being said.

'Minister, the scan is complete. No abnormalities were detected.'

The ants in the lungs felt the air pressure drop dramatically as the dinosaur breathed a sigh of relief.

'This is your third elective scan of the night, Minister, and the third time the results have come up as normal. I really do think you are worrying too much.'

'Worrying too much? What do you fools know?' The minister's voice was extremely agitated now, the vibrations it produced reaching almost fatal levels for the stowaway soldier ants. It was lucky for them that they were no longer in the eardrum danger zone. 'It seems I am the only clear-headed dinosaur in the whole of Gondwana. Everyone else carps on and on about the Laurasian threat, pouring all of their efforts into preparing for nuclear war with the republic, and yet the real enemy is quite literally under our noses – *inside* our blasted noses, probably – and it appears I am the only one who understands that.'

'But . . . none of the scans we've conducted over the last few days have shown any abnormalities.'

'I wonder if your machines are working correctly.'

'There shouldn't be anything wrong with the machines, Minister. We've tested all of the scanners in the imperial infirmary. And this time, as per your instructions, we borrowed a scanner from another big hospital in Boulder City. The results have all been identical.'

The interior minister settled his enormous bulk back down on his bed and drifted off into another troubled sleep. The ant saboteurs quickly left his lungs, made a hasty exit through the right nostril, and scurried down off the bed, across the floor and out of the bedroom.

Meanwhile, across every continent, 20 million ants slipped into the skulls of 5 million dinosaurs and planted deadly mine-grains on their cerebral arteries. They installed listening devices on the eardrums of over a million of those dinosaurs, including Emperor Dadaeus and President Dodomi. Via repeater stations scattered across the planet, the listening devices began to transmit copious amounts of intelligence to a supercomputer in the offices of the Ant Federation's high command. There, the newly established department led by Chief Scientist Joya grappled with the task of analysing this information, dredging the oceans of data for the secrets of the dinosaur world.

15

LUNA AND LEVIATHAN

In the war room at the heart of the Ant Federation's control centre, Supreme Consul Kachika and the Federation's commander-in-chief, Field Marshal Jolie, were orchestrating the destruction of the dinosaur world. Two large screens displayed the progress of Operation Disconnect and Operation Decapitate. At the bottom of the Operation Disconnect status screen was a steadily increasing figure showing the number of chameleon mines so far planted inside the machinery of the dinosaur world. The screen also showed a map of the world. The continents were overlaid with a bewilderingly dense conglomeration of glowing dots, circles and arrows indicating the location of mines and other relevant information. On the Operation Decapitate status screen, a second figure represented the number of dinosaurs whose brains had been mined. Each time the figure ticked upwards, the name and job title of the dinosaur flashed across the screen.

'Everything appears to be proceeding smoothly,' Jolie reported to Kachika.

Just then, the Federation's chief scientist entered the room.

'Ah, Professor Joya, I haven't seen you in a week,' said Kachika by way of greeting. 'You've been hard at work analysing the intercepted information, I imagine.' She shot the professor a quizzical look. 'And judging by the grim expression on your face, it seems you may have some news for us.'

Joya dipped her antennae. 'Yes. I need to speak with you both immediately.'

'We're very busy, so please be brief.'

'I would like you to listen to something. It's a recording of a conversation between Emperor Dadaeus and President Dodomi at yesterday's Gondwana–Laurasia summit.'

'From the summit? Surely there's nothing more to learn from that,' snapped Kachika impatiently. 'We've already had the details. It's public knowledge that the nuclear disarmament talks between the two of them collapsed. War between Gondwana and Laurasia is imminent, which is further validation that our chosen course of action is the right one. We must destroy the dinosaurs before they start a nuclear war. It's the only way we can save the Earth.'

'Madam Supreme Consul, that is certainly an accurate summary of the official press release issued at the close of the summit. But I want you to hear the details of a secret meeting between the two dinosaur leaders – a meeting in which they reveal something previously unknown to us.'

The recording began to play.

DODOMI: Your Majesty, are you not aware of the real reason the ants capitulated so readily? Those crafty critters are playing us for fools. Their return to work in the dinosaur world is nothing but a dastardly diversion . . . a smokescreen . . . a masquerade! The truth is that the Ant Federation is plotting something huge against the dinosaur world.

DADAEUS: Mr President, do you really think me so dense that I would fail to recognise the obvious? But compared with Laurasia's decision to put Luna on a command-loss timer, the threat posed by the ants – even the threat posed by your nuclear weapons – is trivial. A *dastardly diversion*, as you so alliteratively articulated it.

DODOMI: Yes, that's quite true. Luna and Leviathan are indubitably by far the greatest threats to the continued existence of civilisation on Earth. Let's discuss that then, shall we? For kick-off, it is outrageous to point the finger at us, since Leviathan started its timer first!

'Stop! Stop! Stop!' Kachika interrupted, waving her antennae. 'Professor, I have no idea what they're talking about.'

Joya paused the recording. 'This conversation contains two seemingly crucial but currently uninterpretable pieces of information. Number one: what are 'Luna' and 'Leviathan'? Number two: what is a "command-loss timer"?'

'Professor, strange codenames crop up all the time in the

conversations of top dinosaur leaders. Why are you so worked up about this?'

'From both the tone and the substance of the dinosaurs' conversation, I can draw no other conclusion but that these *things*, though unknown to us, are so dangerous as to constitute a threat to the entire world.'

Kachika shifted irritably from leg to leg. 'Logically speaking, that's impossible, Professor. Anything capable of constituting a threat to the entire planet would by necessity have to be a massive installation. To wipe out civilisation on Earth, for example, one would require upwards of 10,000 intercontinental missiles. Imagine the size of such a launch facility! Not to mention that such a vast, complex system could never function properly without us ants being extensively involved in its maintenance. If such an installation existed, therefore, the Ant Federation would certainly be aware of it. And given that we are essential to the smooth operation of the current nuclear-weapons systems of both dinosaur powers, we are already fully apprised of everything there is to know about them.'

'I agree with you, Madam Supreme Consul, that no large installation on Earth could be kept hidden from us. But a simple installation of more modest scope could be. A single intercontinental missile, for example, might not need ants to maintain it and could remain on standby for immediate launch for a long time without our involvement. Perhaps Luna and Leviathan are weapons along those lines.'

'In which case, there's nothing to worry about. Such small installations could hardly be considered a danger to the planet. Like I said, to destroy Earth would require thousands of even the highest-yield thermonuclear weapons.'

Joya fell silent for several seconds. Then she conspiratorially moved her face very close to Kachika's so that their antennae crossed and their eyes were nearly touching. 'That is the crux of the matter, Supreme Consul. Are nuclear bombs really the most powerful weapons on Earth?'

'Professor, that's common knowledge!'

Joya pulled her head away and dipped her antennae. 'Quite right, it is common knowledge. And that is the fatal flaw in ant thinking. We concern ourselves only with things that are already known, whereas the dinosaurs are constantly exploring new and uncharted territory. As you are aware, through their astronomical observations, the dinosaurs learnt of the existence of distant celestial objects called quasars. These can radiate more energy than an entire galaxy of stars; in comparison, nuclear fusion is less luminous than a firefly. The dinosaurs also discovered that when matter falls into an interstellar black hole, it emits extremely strong radiation, generating energy at a far greater rate than nuclear fusion.'

'But these objects you speak of are thousands of light-years away. They have no bearing on reality.'

'Then let me remind you of something that does have a direct bearing on reality. Do you remember the new sun that suddenly appeared in the night sky three years ago?'

Kachika and Jolie remembered, of course. The incident had left a deep impression on all of them. It had been a normal cold winter's night when suddenly a new sun had appeared in the sky over the Southern Hemisphere. In an instant, Earth became as bright as day. The light of the sun was so intense that looking straight at it caused temporary blindness. Twenty seconds later, the sun winked out again, but not before its radiant heat had turned the frigid winter's night into a sweltering summer's day. The effects were catastrophic. The rapid thawing of snow unleashed flash floods that inundated many cities. The event rocked the ant world. But when they asked the dinosaurs what had happened, the dinosaur scientists offered no explanation and the incurious ants soon forgot about it.

'At the time, the only definite conclusion that could be drawn from our own observations was this: the new sun appeared approximately one astronomical unit from Earth, or roughly the same distance as that between Earth and the sun presently in the sky. Based on the distance and the amount of radiation received on Earth, we were able to infer the luminosity of this new sun. If such a vast quantity of energy had been generated through nuclear fusion, there should have been a relatively large celestial object there. But astronomical observations taken since have revealed that no such object exists. In other words, it's possible that higher-energy processes than nuclear fusion exist in this solar system.'

Kachika was unconvinced. 'Professor, all of this is still very far-fetched. Even if that sort of energy does exist, there's no proof that the dinosaurs brought it to Earth. In fact, the probability that they did so is close to zero. One astronomical unit is a very great distance indeed, and given that most of the dinosaurs' spacecraft operate in near-Earth orbit, it would not be easy for them to travel that far into space.'

'I used to think that too, but . . .' Professor Joya paused. 'Please continue listening to the recording.'

DADAEUS: We are playing a very dangerous game here. Insupportably dangerous. Laurasia should immediately stop Luna's command-loss timer or at the very least change over to a regular timer. If you do that, Gondwana will do likewise.

DODOMI: Gondwana should stop the timer on Leviathan first! If you do that, Laurasia will follow suit.

DADAEUS: It was Laurasia that activated Luna's timer first.

DODOMI: But, Your Majesty, that's not where this all started, is it? If a Gondwanan spaceship hadn't pulled that little stunt in space three years ago, on that fateful fourth of December, Luna and Leviathan would never even have existed. That devil would have followed its original path out of the solar system and left Earth well alone.

DADAEUS: It was for scientific research—

DODOMI: Enough! Let's cut the crap, shall we? It was the Gondwanan Empire that pushed civilisation on Earth to the brink of the abyss. You're nothing but a bunch of irresponsible criminals and you must certainly have no right to make any demands of Laurasia.

DADAEUS: Then it seems the Laurasian Republic has no intention of making the first concession.

DODOMI: And what of the Gondwanan Empire?

DADAEUS: Well, well. . . . It appears that neither of us is particularly bothered about the imminent destruction of Earth.

DODOMI: If you're not bothered, then neither are we.

DADAEUS: Ha ha ha! Well, so be it, then. Dinosaurkind has never been that bothered about anything anyway.

Joya stopped the playback and turned to Kachika and Jolie. 'I presume both of you took note of the date mentioned in that conversation.'

'December the fourth, three years ago?' Field Marshal Jolie's antennae twitched. 'That was the day the new sun appeared.'

'Precisely. It is the common thread running through all of this.' Professor Joya swivelled her gaze from the supreme consul to the field marshal then back to the supreme consul. 'I don't know about you, but this makes my feelers stand on end.'

'We have no objections to your making every effort to try and clarify this matter,' said Kachika coolly.

Joya sighed. 'Easier said than done. The best way to get to the bottom of this would be to undertake a deep search of the dinosaurs' military networks. Unfortunately, however, our computers are structurally incompatible with theirs. Infiltrating their hardware is easy enough, but to date we have not succeeded in hacking into their software. Which is why we've had to resort to eavesdropping to gather information. But that's a clumsy and imperfect way of going about things and will almost certainly not enable us to resolve this mystery in the short time we have available.'

'Well, Professor, in my opinion, your concerns are deluded.' Kachika was impatient now to get back to the business of monitoring her soldiers' progress on the big screens. 'Nevertheless, I will provide you with the antpower required to conduct an investigation into this matter. But this cannot be allowed to affect in any way our war against the dinosaurs. Right now, the thing that makes *my* feelers stand on end is the possibility that the dinosaurs may continue to exist on this Earth. And that, Professor Joya, is our Federation's one and only cause.'

Without another word, Professor Joya turned and left. The next day, she went missing.

16

DEFECTION

Two soldier ants crept beneath the gate of the imperial palace of Gondwana. 3,000 ants had been charged with laying mine-grains throughout the palace's computer systems and inside the skulls of the palace dinosaurs and these two were the last to withdraw. Having slipped through the crack beneath the gate, they began the precipitous descent of the tall palace steps. From the sheer cliff-face of the top step, they spotted the figure of an ant climbing towards them.

'Eh? Isn't that Professor Joya?' the first soldier ant said to the other in surprise.

'The Federation's chief scientist? You're right, it is her.'

'Professor Joya!' The soldier ants greeted the chief scientist with a concentrated burst of pheromones.

Glancing up at them, Joya gave a start, as though she might scuttle off and hide. After a moment of hesitation, she steeled herself and continued on up to meet them.

'Professor, what are you doing here?'

'I've come to . . . ah . . . inspect the deployment of mine-grains in the palace.'

'It's all done. The troops have already withdrawn.' The soldier ant paused. 'What's a high-ranking officer like you doing here? It's too dangerous!'

'I need . . . I need to have a look. As you know, this zone is of particular importance.' And with that, Joya scurried swiftly towards the gate of the imperial palace and vanished beneath it.

'Did she seem a bit off to you?' asked the first soldier ant, gazing after Joya.

'She did. Something's not right. Where's your radio? We need to report this to the commander right away.'

*

Emperor Dadaeus was presiding over a meeting of the chief imperial ministers when a secretary entered the hall with a missive: Chief Scientist Joya of the Ant Federation was requesting an urgent audience with the emperor.

'Let her wait. I'll speak with her after my meeting,' said Dadaeus with a dismissive wave of his claws.

The secretary lolloped out of the room but was back again within moments. 'She says it's a matter of utmost importance. She insists on seeing Your Majesty immediately, and she requests that the interior minister, the science minister and the commander-in-chief of the imperial army be in attendance as well.'

'The cheek of her!' spat Dadaeus, spraying the hapless secretary with foul-smelling spittle. 'They've got no manners, these bitsy bugs. She can wait or she can get lost.'

'But she . . .' The secretary surreptitiously wiped at his face, glanced at the assembled ministers, then, with caution, leant close to the emperor's ear and whispered, 'She claims she has defected from the Ant Federation.'

The interior minister interrupted. 'Joya is a key figure in ant leadership circles. Her way of thinking is very different from that of other ants. Her coming to us like this may well signify something of urgent importance.'

'Very well,' said Dadaeus wearily. 'Bring her in, if you must.'

A couple of minutes later, Joya was standing on the smooth wooden plain of the conference table and addressing the mountainous dinosaurs encircling her. 'I have come to save Earth,' she began. A translator device converted her pheromone speech into the dinosaurs' language, broadcasting her words from a hidden speaker.

Dadaeus gave a scornful laugh. 'Such arrogance! Earth is doing just fine, as it happens.'

'You will change your mind about that shortly, sir,' responded Joya. 'But first I would like you all to answer one question: what are "Luna" and "Leviathan"?'

This immediately put the dinosaurs on edge. They exchanged wary glances with each other but kept their jaws firmly shut. Not a peep came out of them. After a long pause, Dadaeus said, 'And why should we tell you that?'

'Your Majesty, if they are what I think they are, I will reveal to you a highly classified secret that relates to the survival of the dinosaur world. You will find it a fair trade.'

'And if they aren't what you think they are?' Dadaeus asked darkly.

'Then I will not tell you my secret. You can kill me or keep me here forever to protect your secret. In any case, you have nothing to lose.'

Dadaeus was quiet for several seconds. Then he nodded to the science minister, who was seated on the left side of the table. 'Tell her.'

Inside the control centre of the Ant Federation's high command, Field Marshal Jolie put the phone down. With a grimace, she turned to Supreme Consul Kachika and said, 'Joya has been located. Two soldiers in the 214th Division saw her enter the imperial palace of Gondwana as they were returning from the mine-laying operation. It seems our suspicions were correct. She has defected.'

'The shameless traitor! I dread to think what she's told the dinosaurs.' Kachika began pacing up and down the control room, wracking her brain for the best way to respond to this unwelcome twist. 'Weren't listening devices installed in the skulls of all of the dinosaurs in the palace?'

'Joya destroyed the repeater we erected outside the palace. A team has been sent to fix it, but for now we have no way to eavesdrop.'

'No doubt she went in there to betray the Ant Federation's war plans.'

'I would imagine so. Which puts our entire operation in jeopardy.'

'What is the status of the mine-grain-laying operations?'

'Operation Disconnect is 92 per cent complete. Operation Decapitate stands at 90 per cent.'

'Is it possible to detonate the mines ahead of schedule?'

'Of course! All of the mine-grains can be detonated either with a timer or remotely. We have already established a network of repeater stations to extend the coverage of the interrupt signal across the dinosaur world, which means we can detonate the mines that have already been deployed at a moment's notice. Supreme Consul, it is time for decisive action. Give the order!'

Kachika turned to face the screen displaying the map of the world and gazed at the colourfully twinkling lights of the continents. After several seconds of silence, she said, 'Very well. Let us turn a new page in Earth's history. Detonate!'

The science minister had finished his account and Joya's head was now awhirl with shock and dismay. For a long moment she felt as if she was on the point of collapse.

'So, Professor, what's it to be? Will you keep your promise and reveal your great secret to us, or will you be choosing . . . another route?' Dadaeus bared his impressive fangs in a dangerous smile.

'This is. . . . This is just appalling,' stammered Joya. 'You're monsters, all of you. But we ants are no better . . .' She clasped a feeler to her quivering thorax. 'You must act fast. Quick! You need to call the Supreme Consul of the Ant Federation immediately!'

'You haven't given us an answer—'

'Your Majesty, there is no time to explain. They already know that I am here, and they may respond at any moment. The fate of the dinosaur world hangs in the balance, and with it the fate of the planet. You have to believe me! Make the call now. Hurry!'

'Very well.' The dinosaur emperor picked up the phone from the conference table. With an anxious heart, Joya watched as he flexed his thick finger and laboriously pressed one enormous button after the other. Then she heard the muffled sound of it ringing. After a few seconds the ringing stopped and she knew Kachika had picked up the rice-sized receiver at the other end of the line.

The supreme consul's voice came through the receiver. 'Hello, who is this?'

Dadaeus spoke into the phone. 'Is this Supreme Consul Kachika? This is Dadaeus. Right now—'

At that very moment, Joya heard a chorus of faint clicks all around her, as if all of the second hands on a wall of clocks were moving in unison. She knew it was the sound of mine-grains exploding in the dinosaurs' skulls. The dinosaurs in the room stiffened, and time seemed to stand still. The phone receiver tumbled from Dadaeus's claws, falling to the table near Joya with a deafening clatter. Then all of the dinosaurs came crashing down, leaving Joya's horizon disconcertingly empty. The tabletop shuddered for several moments. When it stilled again, Joya crawled onto the receiver. Kachika was still on the line.

'Hello? This is Kachika. What is this about? Hello?'

Her voice caused the earpiece to vibrate, sending pins and needles through Joya's body.

'Supreme Consul, it's me, Joya!' she shouted.

But her pheromone speech was no longer being converted into sound, and Kachika could not hear her on the other end of the line. The palace's translation system had been taken offline by the mine-grains. Joya said no more. She knew she was too late.

Shortly thereafter, the lights in the hall went out. Dusk had fallen outside, and the room was thrown into semi-darkness. As Joya began the long hike across the conference table, the rumble of traffic from the distant city faded and a grim silence settled in its wake.

By the time she'd reached the table's edge and begun her descent to the floor, the soundscape had changed again. Now the hall began to fill with the shrill discordance of far-off panic, the frightful pounding of fleeing feet and the unearthly screechings of dinosaurs in pain. There came the intermittent wailing of police sirens. And then the first muted rumbles of faraway explosions. Inside the palace itself, however, all was eerily quiet, for every last imperial dinosaur had been exterminated by cranial mine-grains.

When Joya finally reached the window, she stared out at the gargantuan metropolis of Boulder City, now shrouded in twilight gloom. Thin columns of smoke rose into the dusky sky, and more and more kept appearing, orange flames gleaming at their base. The city's skyline flickered in and out of view. As the fires multiplied, an infernal glow filtered through the window, throwing shifting patterns of light and shadow across the high ceiling above Joya.

17

THE ULTIMATE DETERRENT

'We did it!' Field Marshal Jolie shouted excitedly as the world map flashed red on her screen. 'The dinosaur world has been crippled. Their information systems have been comprehensively disrupted. All of their cities have lost power, all of their roads have been blocked by vehicles disabled by mine-grains, and fires are spreading widely and rapidly.' Her antennae were vibrating at speed now as she enumerated the Federation's successes. 'Operation Decapitate has neutralised 4 million leading lights of the dinosaur world, and the ruling bodies of the Gondwanan Empire and the Laurasian Republic have ceased to exist. The two great powers have been paralysed and dinosaur society is in chaos.'

'And this is just the start,' added Kachika. 'Dinosaur cities are already having problems with their water supplies, and their food stocks will soon run out. That will be the tipping point. Vast herds of dinosaurs will flee the cities, but with no functioning cars and with all the roads blocked, they will be unable to evacuate in time. Given their voracious appetites, at least half the population will starve to death before they find food. Their high-tech society will be in tatters. The dinosaur world is regressing to a primitive, pre-industrial era even as we speak.'

'What is the status of their nuclear-weapons systems?' someone asked.

'As expected, all of the dinosaurs' nuclear weapons, including their intercontinental missiles and strategic bombers, have been reduced to scrap metal by our mine-grains,' replied Jolie. 'There have been no nuclear accidents and no cases of nuclear contamination.'

'Excellent! This is truly a momentous occasion,' Kachika said. 'Now we just need to wait for the dinosaur world to destroy itself.'

Their celebratory mood was short-lived, however. A secretary ant now reported that Professor Joya had returned and was requesting an urgent meeting with Kachika and Jolie.

The weary chief scientist had barely made it through the command-centre door before Kachika launched into an angry tirade. 'Professor, you betrayed the great cause of the Ant Federation at its most crucial moment. There will be serious consequences for your actions.'

'When you hear what I have to tell you,' replied Joya coldly, 'it will be quite clear which of us is the most deserving of censure for their . . . *actions*.'

'Why did you go and see the Emperor of Gondwana?' asked Jolie.

'To learn the truth about Luna and Leviathan.'

This immediately dampened the ants' high spirits. All eyes – and parts of eyes – were now trained on the professor.

Joya scanned the assembled company. 'So, does anyone here know what antimatter is?'

Every ant but Kachika remained silent.

'I know a little,' the supreme consul said. 'Antimatter is a material that dinosaur physicists have theorised may exist. They say that its subatomic particles have the opposite electric charge to the matter in our world: its electrons carry a positive charge and its protons carry a negative charge. It's purported to be a quantum mirror-image of the matter in our world.'

'Yes, your definition is right. But the existence of antimatter is not merely theoretical,' Joya said. 'As a result of their extensive cosmological studies, the dinosaurs have proved that antimatter does exist.' She tapped an impatient foot. 'Surely someone else here has heard more about it?'

Field Marshal Jolie now chipped in. 'I heard that as soon as antimatter comes into contact with the matter in our world, the combined mass of the two materials is converted into energy.'

'Correct!' said Joya, dipping her antennae. 'That process is called annihilation.' She was in full pedagogic mode now. 'When your all-powerful nuclear warheads detonate, only a fraction of 1 per cent of their mass is converted into energy, but the mass–energy conversion rate in matter–antimatter collisions is 100 per cent! It should therefore be evident to you all' – she glared meaningfully at Kachika

– 'that there are things even more terrible than nuclear weapons. Per unit mass, the energy released by matter–antimatter annihilation is two to three orders of magnitude greater than that released by a nuclear bomb.'

'But what does this have to do with Luna and Leviathan?'

'Bear with me and I will tell you.' Jolie began striding up and down, confident now that she had the undivided attention of every ant in the room. 'Recently some of us were talking about the new sun that suddenly appeared in the night sky of the Southern Hemisphere three years ago. An event that few of us will ever forget, am I right?'

A shiver of acknowledgement rippled through her audience.

'Dinosaur astronomers observed that the flash we experienced here on Earth originated from a small celestial body that had entered the solar system with a comet's trajectory. The object was less than thirty kilometres in diameter, seemingly a mere sliver of rock floating in space. But when they launched probes to observe it close up, they discovered that the celestial body was made of antimatter! While passing through the asteroid belt, it had collided with a meteoroid. The meteoroid and the antimatter were mutually annihilated, releasing a tremendous amount of energy and producing the flash we saw. The Gondwanans and the Laurasians arrived at this conclusion simultaneously, but it's what they discovered next that's of most significance to all of us here on Earth . . .'

This was turning into a long and tortuous explanation, but the ants were nothing if not well versed in obedient attentiveness. They didn't even fidget.

'The annihilation had blasted a large hole in the antimatter body, scattering many antimatter fragments of varying sizes through space. Dinosaur astronomers quickly located several of these fragments, which apparently were not difficult to spot. In the asteroid belt, particles of solar wind were annihilated by the antimatter particles, giving the surfaces of the fragments a peculiar glow, and this intensified as they approached the sun.'

The professor stopped pacing to and fro, lingered for a couple of nanoseconds, and then said, 'Knowing the dinosaurs as we do, some of you may be anticipating what it is I'm about to say next. Would anyone care to tell me what that is?'

Field Marshal Jolie waggled her feelers tentatively but decided not to share her thoughts publicly. The rest of the ants just waited patiently for the professor to enlighten them.

Joya duly resumed her account. 'This all happened at the height of the arms race between Gondwana and Laurasia. Consequently, both great dinosaur powers came up with a plan – plans that turned out to be identical, and completely insane. Independent of each other, the two powers both decided that they would collect some of the antimatter debris, bring it back to Earth and use it to create a super-weapon far more powerful than any nuclear bomb, in order to deter the other side—'

'Wait a minute,' said Kachika, interrupting Joya. 'There's an obvious flaw in the logic of that plan. If antimatter is annihilated on contact with matter, how did they store it and bring it back to Earth?'

'Good question.' Joya nodded. 'The dinosaur astronomers discovered that anti-iron made up a substantial proportion of the celestial body. The debris they located in space was also made of anti-iron. Like ordinary iron, anti-iron can be affected by magnetic fields. This provided a potential solution to the storage problem. It made it possible for the dinosaurs to create a vacuum chamber and apply a powerful magnetic field to safely confine the antimatter to the centre of the chamber, preventing it from touching the interior walls. This would enable them to store, transport and deploy the antimatter. Of course, this was only a theoretical solution. To use such a container to bring the antimatter back to Earth would be an extraordinarily mad and dangerous endeavour. But, as we well know, dinosaurs are mad by nature, and their desire for global hegemony invariably trumps all other concerns. So they actually went ahead with it!'

This rather too literal bombshell came as a genuine shock to the ants, and there was an anxious stirring in the room. Even their in-depth knowledge of dinosaur behaviour could not have predicted such craziness.

'It was the Gondwanan Empire that took the first step into the abyss. They built a magnetic confinement vessel comprised of a hollow sphere, split that in two and affixed the hemispheres to the mechanical arms of a spaceship. The spaceship then crept up on the antimatter fragment, slowly and with extreme caution, and trapped it between the two hemispheres. As soon as the hemispheres closed, a magnetic field generated by a superconductor was activated, confining the fragment to the centre of the sphere. The spaceship then flew back to Earth.

'Had the Laurasian Republic known about this plan, they undoubtedly would have dispatched armed spaceships to intercept the Gondwanan transporter in space. But it was well on its way by the time they found out about it, and intercepting it at that point would have caused the fragment to annihilate in Earth's atmosphere. The fragment weighed forty-five tonnes and its annihilation would have converted ninety tonnes of matter into pure energy. The resulting explosion would have wiped out life on Earth. Naturally, the Laurasians did not wish to perish alongside the Gondwanans, so they looked on helplessly as the spaceship splashed down in the ocean.'

Hearing some mutterings from the floor, Joya stiffened her antennae and requested that the other ants sit tight until she'd told them all she knew. 'There is more to say, I'm afraid – quite a bit more, actually – and it won't be easy listening. So, if there are no objections, I'll just get on with it and then we can have a discussion once I'm done. *Are* there any objections?'

There were not.

'Subsequent events escalated the madness to crisis point. After the Gondwanan spaceship landed, the containment vessel was transferred to a cargo ship. The name of the cargo ship was *Leviathan* and the dinosaurs came to call the antimatter fragment it carried by that name as well. The ship did not return to Gondwana but instead sailed for Laurasia, destined for the republic's largest port!

'Laurasia didn't dare attack this ship of doom. They had no choice but to let it continue on its way, and when it did finally arrive, it might as well have been sailing into an empty harbour for all the resistance it met. Once *Leviathan* had docked, the dinosaurs abandoned ship and returned to Gondwana by helicopter, leaving their explosive load anchored in Laurasian waters.

'The Laurasian dinosaurs treated Leviathan as if it were a bad-tempered deity. They didn't dare disturb it in any way, because they knew the Gondwanan Empire could remotely deactivate the magnetic field at any time, causing the antimatter fragment to annihilate. If that happened, the entire world would be fireballed, and the first to go would be Laurasia, reduced to ashes in the blink of an eye by the flames of a lethal sun.'

Joya was looking and sounding extremely tired now, unsurprising given the stress of her encounter with the Gondwanans and the huge burden of responsibility she'd been bearing as the keeper of this Earth-shattering news. But a burden shared was a burden halved, so she ploughed on, keen to give Supreme Consul Kachika all the details she'd need in order to decide what to do next.

'This was truly the darkest day in the history of the Laurasian Republic. The Gondwanan Empire now had the reins of life on Earth firmly in its grasp and it grew increasingly wild and unrestrained, making claim after claim on Laurasia's territory and repeatedly ordering the Republic to get rid of its nuclear arsenal.

'Needless to say, this lopsided state of affairs did not last long. Just one month after Gondwana's Operation Leviathan, Laurasia responded in kind. Using similar technology, they collected a second antimatter fragment from space, brought it back to Earth and gave the empire a taste of its own medicine. They loaded their antimatter onto a cargo ship called *Luna* and sailed it into Gondwana's largest port. And so balance was restored in the dinosaur world. A balance born of the ultimate deterrent, a deterrent that pushed Earth to the brink of destruction.'

'It's so unfortunate that we knew nothing about all this,' muttered Field Marshal Jolie.

'Yes indeed,' replied the professor. 'To avoid a global panic, operations Leviathan and Luna were carried out in absolute secrecy. Even in the dinosaur world, only a very few knew the exact details. Both teams designed their systems so that they could be maintained without ant involvement. A great deal of money was spent on ensuring that the equipment was super reliable, and the containment systems were built using replaceable modules. As a result, the Ant Federation knew nothing about it until today.'

Joya's account shook every ant in the command centre to the core. The mood in the room had plummeted. Where previously the ants had been celebrating a great victory over the dinosaurs, they were now staring into a terrifying hellhole.

'This is beyond madness – it's depraved!' Kachika cried. 'An ultimate-deterrence strategy predicated on the total destruction of the world renders all political and military considerations meaningless. It's an abomination.'

Field Marshal Jolie tossed her head contemptuously. 'Is this not, Professor, an inevitable consequence of the very curiosity, imagination and creativity you so admire in the dinosaurs?'

'Let us stick to the matter in question,' replied Joya, unperturbed by Jolie's snideness. 'The world is in grave danger and we should be focusing on that.'

Kachika began to formulate a plan. 'At least we know that those two fragments of antimatter are still intact and untouched in their magnetic containment vessels. The destruction of the world is therefore not an inevitability.' She glanced over at Jolie. 'Do you agree, Field Marshal?'

The field marshal dipped her antennae. 'I do. This sort of operation is on a par with a nuclear-missile strike. It will have been designed with an extremely complex system of security locks. The command to detonate the antimatter will only be valid if issued by a dinosaur at the highest level, and the dinosaurs with that degree of authority will certainly have been eliminated by now. Therefore, the order will never be given. Regarding malfunctions or breaks in the chain of command, those won't be a problem either. The slightest anomaly will send the system into lockdown.'

Kachika turned to the professor. 'How long can the magnetic fields within the containment vessels be maintained?'

'For a considerable period,' Joya replied. 'The magnetic fields are produced by a circulating current in a superconductor, which decays very slowly. In addition, Leviathan and Luna are both equipped with nuclear batteries capable of supplying power for a long time, so the systems can replenish the charge lost without outside interference. According to the dinosaurs, the confining magnetic fields can be maintained for at least twenty years.'

'Then it's obvious what we should do,' Kachika said firmly. 'We must immediately find Luna and Leviathan, build shields around the containment vessels and insulate them from all external electromagnetic signals, thereby eliminating the possibility of a signal from the outside world detonating either weapon.'

'And then,' said Field Marshal Jolie, 'we must think of a way to launch the vessels into space. Although it will be difficult, we have time on our side. With the spaceships and rockets the dinosaurs left behind, we should be able to do it.'

Now that victory was potentially in their sights once more, the ants broke into animated discussion about operational details.

But Professor Joya was having none of it. 'If we follow the supreme consul's plan, Earth is doomed,' she said.

The ants turned to stare at her, incomprehension on every face.

'This concerns the command-loss timers mentioned by Dodomi and Dadaeus in the recording,' Joya said. 'In the beginning, the two dinosaur powers controlled Leviathan and Luna exactly as we'd expect. Signal stations on their own soil were kept on standby, the idea being that the moment one country was attacked, a remote-control signal would go out from the victim's station, detonating the antimatter in the attacker's harbour. But both sides soon realised that there was a flaw in this system. Let us consider this hypothetical scenario: Laurasia suddenly launches a conventional nuclear strike against Gondwana – I use the term 'conventional' advisedly, as that is what nuclear weapons are nowadays. With lightning speed, the Laurasians bring overwhelming force to bear on the entirety of Gondwana's territory, with Gondwana's command-and-control sites particularly hard hit. Before Gondwana can respond, it sinks into a state of paralysis much like the state it finds itself in now. It cannot detonate Leviathan. Furthermore, Laurasia will have anyway taken certain measures to prevent the detonation signal from ever reaching Leviathan – with strong jamming, for instance – thereby increasing the republic's chance of victory.

'To stop this sort of pre-emptive-attack scenario from becoming a reality, the two dinosaur powers, almost simultaneously, put Leviathan and Luna into a new standby mode. This was the so-called command-loss timer. From then on, the two signal stations would no longer transmit a detonation command to the antimatter containment vessel. They would do the opposite. The command they now transmitted *stopped* the vessel from detonating. Each vessel was set to permanently count down to detonation, and only when it received the interrupt signal from its own side would it interrupt the current countdown and start over, until it received the next interrupt signal. And so on. Those interrupt signals were sent in person by the Laurasian president and the Gondwanan emperor. That way, if either side were to be crippled by a pre-emptive strike, the interrupt signal would not be sent, and the container vessel would detonate the antimatter. This standby mode made a pre-emptive strike tantamount to suicide, as the enemy's continued existence was now a prerequisite for each country's own survival. The significant drawback, of course, was that this placed the Earth in greater danger than ever. The command-loss timer is the maddest – or in the supreme consul's words, the most depraved – deterrence strategy ever conceived.'

A suffocating quiet blanketed the room until eventually Kachika responded. There was an unsteady fluctuation in the intensity of her pheromones. 'In other words, Leviathan and Luna are standing by for the next interrupt signal right now?'

Joya dipped her antennae. 'Two signals that may never come.'

'Meaning that the signal stations in Gondwana and Laurasia have already been destroyed by our mine-grains?' said Jolie.

'Indeed. Emperor Dadaeus told me the locations of both the Gondwanan station and the Laurasian station. After I returned, I searched for them in the Operation Disconnect database. Because their purpose was unclear to us, we planted only a small number of mines in their communications equipment. Thirty-five mine-grains in the Gondwanan signal station, thirty-six in the Laurasian station, severing a total of seventy-one wires. That number might seem low, but it was enough to completely disable the signal-transmission equipment in both stations.'

'How long is each countdown?'

'Sixty-six hours, or about three days. Both the Laurasian and Gondwanan countdown timers begin nearly simultaneously, and the interrupt signal is usually sent about twenty-two hours after the countdown starts. The current countdown started twenty hours ago. We still have two days.'

'Why is the countdown so long?' asked Kachika. 'Surely one or two hours would have been more sensible. In this set-up, if one side launched a crippling strike as soon as the other side reset its timer, they would still have almost three days to dispose of the other antimatter containment vessel by sending it back into space.'

'The containment vessels and the ships which house them are inextricably linked,' said Joya. 'Any attempt to separate the two would result in the shutdown of the confining magnetic field and the detonation of the antimatter. Perhaps with concerted effort over an extended period the vessel could be safely detached from the ship and launched back into space, but two or three days would not be sufficient. Dadaeus did talk to me about the time-lag. Mad as the dinosaurs were, in this matter it seems they were uncharacteristically careful. They designed the countdown so that, in the event of something unforeseen and relatively innocuous preventing the sending of the signal, there would be time to deal with the situation. They were primarily concerned about sabotage by ants, apparently. With due cause, of course.'

'If we knew the exact content of the interrupt signals, we could build our own transmitter and continually reset Leviathan and Luna's countdowns.'

'The problem is that we don't have that information, and we have no way of finding it out. The dinosaurs did not advise me of the signals' contents, only that they were long, complicated passwords that changed every time they were sent. The passwords' algorithms were stored in the signal stations' computers. I doubt any dinosaur alive knows them.'

'So the signals can only be sent by the signal stations?'

'I presume so.'

Kachika's decision came swiftly. 'Then we must repair the stations as quickly as possible.'

18

THE BATTLE OF THE SIGNAL STATIONS

The station responsible for the transmission of the Gondwanan Empire's interrupt signal was located on a barren tract of land on the outskirts of Boulder City. It was a small building with a tangled array of antennae on the roof and looked no more arresting than a weather station.

Security at the station was lax. It was guarded by just one platoon of dinosaurs and they were there mainly to prevent the occasional Gondwanan citizen from inadvertently wandering too close. Enemy spies and saboteurs barely figured on their list of concerns. In fact, Laurasia was more interested in the safety measures at the station than Gondwana was; they had lodged numerous protests with Gondwana, demanding that security be tightened. Other than the guards, just five dinosaurs were responsible for the day-to-day running of the station: one engineer, three operators and one maintenance technician. Like the guards, they had no idea as to the station's purpose.

In the station's control room was a large screen displaying a sixty-six-hour countdown. The countdown had never passed the forty-four-hour mark. Every time it reached that point (typically in the morning), the image of Emperor Dadaeus would pop up on another blank screen. The emperor only ever uttered one short sentence:

'I command that the signal be sent.'

The operator on duty would stand to attention and answer, 'Yes, Your Majesty!' Then he would move the mouse at his terminal and click once on the 'Transmit' button on the computer screen. As soon as he did that, the large screen would display the following information:

- INTERRUPT SIGNAL SENT
- INTERRUPT SUCCESS RETURN SIGNAL RECEIVED
- COUNTDOWN RESET

Then the screen would reset to 66:00 and restart the countdown.

On the other screen, the emperor would watch these proceedings intently until the reset countdown began anew. Only then would he breathe a sigh of relief and depart.

For two years, this process was repeated every day like clockwork. No matter where the emperor was, whether in the imperial palace, on tour or even on a state visit to Laurasia, he always called the signal station every day at this time. He had never missed a day.

The dinosaurs who worked at the station found all this perplexing. They had been told that under no circumstances was the signal to be sent without the emperor's order, but if the emperor wanted the signal sent every day, he had only to say the word: there was no need for him to personally give the order every day. Even the operators themselves were unnecessary. A transmission device on an automatic timer would do the job perfectly.

The sixty-six-hour countdown was also most mysterious. What would happen if it was left to run its course?

The only thing they knew for certain was that the signal was extremely important. The intense expression on the emperor's face as he watched the signal being sent told them that much. But of course there was no way they could possibly have imagined what was really at stake – that this signal deferred Earth's death sentence by one more day.

Today, however, their routine of the last two years was disrupted because the signal transmitter had broken down. Given that the station had been outfitted with equipment of the utmost reliability and employed a high degree of redundancy, with multiple backup systems, it was obvious that this total operational failure was neither accidental nor the result of normal wear and tear.

The engineer and the technician immediately began to look for the source of the problem. They quickly discovered that several wires had been cut – wires that only ants could reconnect. They attempted to phone their superiors to request an ant repair team, but the line was dead. As they continued to investigate, they found more severed wires. The appointed time for the emperor's transmission order was now rapidly approaching, so the dinosaurs had no choice but to try and do the reconnection themselves. Unfortunately, though, their bulky claws made that impossible.

The five dinosaurs grew frantic with worry. Although the phone line was out of action, they felt sure that communication would soon be restored and the emperor would pop up on the screen when the countdown reached forty-four hours. To them, his daily appearance on the screen was as inevitable as the rising of the sun. Today, however, the sun rose but the emperor did not materialise. For the first time ever, the countdown got to forty-four hours and then carried on.

After a while, the hordes of dinosaurs fleeing Boulder City began to pass by the signal station. It was from these badly shaken refugees that the station team learnt of the situation in the capital. The ants had disabled all of the machinery in the Gondwanan Empire with their mine-grains, including the signal station's transmitter, thereby paralysing the dinosaur world.

The members of the station team were nothing if not conscientious and they kept on with their attempts to reconnect the severed wires. But it was an impossible task. Most of the wires were in places that the dinosaurs' stubby claws simply could not reach. As for the few exposed wires they could get to, the ends kept slipping from their clumsy fingers and could not be joined together.

'Those blasted ants!' The engineer sighed and rubbed his aching eyes but then quickly did a double-take. There were ants right in front of him!

It was a small contingent of about a hundred or so, rapidly advancing across the white surface of the operator console. Their leader was shouting to the dinosaurs, 'Hello! We have come to help you repair the machines. We have come to help you reconnect the wires. We have come—'

Unfortunately, the dinosaurs didn't have their pheromone translators turned on, so they couldn't hear her. In fact, even if they had heard her, they wouldn't have believed her. Right then, their hatred was all-consuming. The dinosaurs swatted and pinched the ants on the console with their claws, muttering through gritted fangs, 'Lay mine-grains, will you? Destroy our machines, will you?' The white surface of the console was soon covered in small black smears, the crushed remains of the ants.

'Supreme Consul, I have to report that the dinosaurs in the signal station attacked the repair team. We were wiped out on the console,' a surviving member of the team informed Kachika.

They were standing beneath a small blade of grass fifty metres from the station. Most of the members of the Ant Federation's high command were also present.

'Send in a larger repair team!'

'Yikes, ants!' shouted a dinosaur sentry standing guard on the front step of the signal station.

His cry drew several other dinosaur soldiers and their lieutenant outside.

A mass of ants was swarming up the step, four or five thousand by the look of it, like a swath of black satin slowly gliding towards them. A number of individual ants broke from the mass, waving their antennae at the dinosaurs, as though shouting something to them.

'Get a broom!' the dinosaur lieutenant hollered.

A soldier immediately fetched a large broom, and the lieutenant snatched it from him and made a few savage passes over the step, sweeping the ants into the air like so much dust.

'Madam Supreme Consul, we must find a way to communicate with the dinosaurs in the signal station and explain our intentions,' said Professor Joya.

'But how? They can't hear us. They won't even turn on their translators.'

'Could we phone them, perhaps?' an ant suggested.

'We tried that earlier. The dinosaurs' entire communication system is down. It's been completely disconnected from the Ant Federation's telephone network. We can't get through to them.'

Field Marshal Jolie interjected. 'I suggest we look back to what our ancestors used to do,' she said with quiet authority. 'In bygone years, before the Steam-Engine Age, they would communicate with the dinosaurs by arranging themselves in different formations, to make characters. You should all be familiar with this ancient art, no?'

Kachika sighed. 'What's the use of telling us this? That art has been lost.'

'No, Kachika, it has not.' Jolie drew herself up as tall as her diminutive height would allow. 'The unit currently under my command has been trained to form characters. I wanted the soldiers to remember the glorious achievements of our ancestors and to experience for themselves the collective spirit of the ant world. I had hoped to surprise you all during this year's military parade, but now it seems this training can be put to practical use.'

'How many troops are assembled here at present?'

'Ten infantry divisions. Approximately 150,000 ants in total.'

'How many characters can be formed with these numbers?'

'That depends on the size of the characters. To ensure that the dinosaurs can read them from a distance, I would say no more than a dozen.'

'All right.' Kachika thought for a moment. 'Form the following sentences: "We have come to fix your transmitter. It can save the world."'

'That doesn't explain anything,' Professor Joya muttered.

'What choice do we have? It's too many characters as it is. We'll just have to try it – it's better than nothing.'

'The ants are back – and this time there are zillions of them!'

The dinosaur soldiers posted at the entrance to the signal station watched the phalanx of ants marching towards them. It measured about three or four metres square and was rising and falling with the uneven ground like a rippling black flag.

'Are they coming to attack us?'

'Doesn't seem like it. Their formation is strange.'

As the ants slowly drew closer, a sharp-eyed dinosaur shouted, 'What the . . .? Those are characters!'

Another dinosaur read haltingly: 'We . . . have . . . come . . . to . . . fix . . . your . . . trans . . . mitter . . . it . . . can . . . save . . . the . . . world.'

'I've read about this!' one of them exclaimed. 'In ancient times the ants communicated with our ancestors like this. And now I've seen it with my own eyes. Amazing!'

'Bullshit!' The lieutenant flashed a claw. 'Don't fall for their tricks! Go and fill some bowls with boiling water from the water heater and bring them here.'

'Lieutenant,' a sergeant ventured timidly, 'don't you think we should talk to them first? Maybe they genuinely are here to fix the transmitter. The engineer and the others inside are in really desperate need of help.'

The dinosaur soldiers all began to talk at once:

'What a strange thing to say. How's this transmitter supposed to save the world?'

'Whose world – ours or theirs?'

'The signal sent out by this transmitter has got to be important.'

'For sure – why else would the emperor personally give the order to send it every day?'

'Idiots!' barked the lieutenant. 'You still trust the ants even now? It was our gullibility that allowed them to destroy the empire. They are the most despicable, treacherous insects on Earth and we will never let them fool us again. Go and fetch that boiling water. Double-quick!'

The five dinosaur soldiers raced off and within minutes were back with bath-sized vats of boiling water gripped between their claws. They fanned out in a long, steamy row, advanced rapidly and on the count of three hurled the boiling water over the ant formation. Scalding spray flew in all directions, generating voluminous clouds of hissing vapour. The black line of text on the ground was washed away, and more than half of the ants were boiled alive.

'Communicating with the dinosaurs is impossible,' Kachika said with a deep sigh as she watched the steam billowing up in the distance. 'Our only remaining option is to take the signal station by force. Then we can repair the equipment and send the interrupt signal ourselves.'

'Ants taking a dinosaur structure by force?' Field Marshal Jolie stared at Kachika as though she were a being from outer space. 'From a military point of view, that's utter madness.'

'It cannot be helped. This is a mad world. The building is isolated and relatively small. There will be a brief gap before any dinosaur reinforcements arrive. If we marshal as many of our forces as we possibly can, there's a chance we'll be able to capture it.'

'What's that over there? They look like ant super-walkers!'

Hearing the sentry's shout, the lieutenant raised his telescope and scanned the distant wasteland. There appeared to be a long procession of black objects in motion. A closer look confirmed the sentry's suspicion.

Most ant vehicles were very small, but to meet the specialised needs of the military the ants had also developed some comparatively large transporters called super-walkers. These were only about the size of one of our pedicabs, but to ant eyes they were positively Brobdingnagian, similar to how a 10,000-tonne freighter looks to us. As their name suggested, super-walkers had no wheels but moved around by means of six mechanical legs that walked in an ant-like fashion. This allowed them to traverse difficult terrain with ease and speed. Each super-walker could carry hundreds of thousands of ants.

'Open fire on those walkers!' the lieutenant ordered.

The dinosaur soldiers used their lone light machine-gun to strafe the column of walkers in the distance. Plumes of dust spiralled into the air where the bullets raked the ground, and one of them hit the walker at the head of the convoy, breaking a front leg and toppling it. As the walker's five remaining legs pawed at the air, countless strange black balls began tumbling out of a hatch in the side of its hull. Each was about the size of one of our footballs and was composed entirely of ants. As soon as the balls hit the ground, they dispersed, like coffee granules dissolving in water.

Another two super-walkers were felled, but the bullets that penetrated their holds killed very few ants. A seemingly infinite parade of black balls rolled to the ground, releasing mass after mass of resolute soldier ants.

'If only we had an artillery gun,' moaned one of the dinosaur soldiers.

'Yeah, or some hand-grenades.'

'A flamethrower would do it . . .'

'Enough! Quit jabbering and get a count on those walkers.' The lieutenant lowered his telescope and pointed straight ahead.

'Holy smoke, there must be two or three hundred of them . . .'

'Looks like every last super-walker stationed in Gondwana is on its way here.'

'Which means we're looking at upwards of 100 million ants,' said the lieutenant. 'There's no question about it – the ants intend to storm the signal station.'

'Lieutenant, let's run over there and smash those ridiculous walkers!'

'That won't work, soldier. Our machine-gun and rifles are useless against them.'

'We still have petrol for the generator. Let's burn them!'

The lieutenant shook his head calmly. 'We don't have enough petrol to destroy all of them. Our priority is to protect the signal station. Here's what we'll do . . .'

'Supreme Consul, Field Marshal, our reconnaissance aircraft report that the dinosaurs are digging two rings of trenches around the signal station. They are redirecting water from a nearby stream into the outer trench. They have also rolled out several large fuel drums and are pouring petrol into the inner trench.'

Kachika did not hesitate. 'Commence the attack immediately!' she yelled.

The ants advanced in a dense, inky swarm, like an ever-expanding shadow cast upon the ground by a stormcloud in the sky. The sight struck terror into the dinosaurs at the station.

When the vanguard reached the outer moat, the ants on the frontline did not stop but crawled straight into the water. The ants behind them stepped over their comrades' bodies and crawled a tiny bit further out onto the water. Soon, a thick black film had formed on the surface of the water and was spreading rapidly towards the other bank.

The dinosaur soldiers had donned sealed helmets to prevent the ants from slipping into their bodies. They stood ranged along the inner bank, dumping shovelfuls of soil and basin after basin of boiling water on the ants, but to no avail. The black film soon covered the entire surface of the water and great waves of ants washed across it like a dark tide. The dinosaurs were forced to retreat behind the inner moat, setting alight the petrol that filled it as they went. A ring of raging flames swiftly shot up around the signal station.

As the swarm approached the burning trench, the ants piled on top of one another, forming a living embankment. The dinosaurs tried battering this ant wall with machine-gunfire, but the bullets sank into it without a sound, as though swallowed by a black sand dune. Next they tried chucking rocks at it, and though these struck home with dull thuds, the holes they opened up were quickly refilled with replacement ant contingents. Despite the bombardment, the embankment continued to grow.

When it got to about two metres high, the wall advanced to the rim of the flaming trench. Its surface writhed in the heat like an angry python. Scorched by the blaze, it began to smoulder and the acrid smell of roast ant filled the air. Charred bodies tumbled into the smelter below, lending the flames a ghostly green hue. But new layers of ants continually filled in for their fallen comrades, leaving the wall standing firm on the edge of the hellish ditch.

Black spheres now began hurtling over the top of the wall. Some were snatched by the fires but most had enough momentum to propel themselves across the moat to the other side. As they passed through the inferno, the spheres' outer layers sizzled and fried, but the ants held tight to each other, forming a scorched shell that protected their comrades inside. Within mere moments, more than a thousand balls had reached the opposite bank of the trench. Their burnt shells split open and the spheres dispersed into vast throngs of ants that surged up the steps of the signal station.

At this point, the dinosaur guards lost it. Despite the lieutenant's attempts to stop them, they raced out the door and around to the rear of the building, galloping at full tilt along the only path not yet completely awash with ants. The ants streamed into the ground floor of the signal station, then up the stairs to the control room. Other divisions scaled the exterior walls, spilling in through the windows, painting the lower half of the building black.

Six dinosaurs remained in the control room: the lieutenant, the engineer, the technician and the three operators. They watched horror-stricken as the ants poured in through every crack and crevice. It was as though the building had been submerged in a sea of ants, its black waters leaking in through every orifice. The view out the window was no different. As far as the eye could see, the ground was a roiling ocean of ants, the signal station a lonely island stranded amid it.

In no time at all, the entire control-room floor was carpeted with ants, save for a circle around the central console in which stood the six dinosaurs.

The dinosaur engineer hastily took out his translation device. He heard a voice as soon as he switched it on.

'I am the supreme consul of the Ant Federation. We do not have the time to explain everything to you in detail. All you need to know is that if this signal station does not transmit its signal in the next ten minutes, Earth will be destroyed.'

The engineer peered confusedly at the dark mass of ants encircling him. Then he consulted the translator's direction indicator. It pointed him towards three ants standing on top of the central console. The voice that had just spoken belonged to one of them. He shook his head at the trio. 'The transmitter is broken.'

'Our technicians have already reconnected the wires and repaired the machine,' replied Kachika. 'Please begin the transmission immediately.'

The engineer shook his head again. 'We have no power.'

'You don't have a backup generator?'

'We do, but it runs on petrol and now we're out of petrol. We poured all the petrol we had into the trench outside and . . . er . . . set it alight.'

'All of it?'

The lieutenant took over from the engineer. 'Every last drop. Our only thought was to defend the station. We even used up the dregs in the generator's fuel tank.'

'Then go outside and collect what's left in the trench.'

The lieutenant glanced outside and saw that the flames in the trench were dying down. He opened a cabinet in the central console and pulled out a small metal pail. The ants stepped back to clear an exit route for him.

When the lieutenant reached the doorway, he paused and looked round at them. 'Is the world really going to end in ten minutes?'

Kachika's answer came through the translator loud and clear. 'If that signal isn't sent, yes, the entire planet will be burnt to a crisp in ten minutes.'

The lieutenant turned and hurried down the stairs. He soon returned, setting the pail on the floor. Kachika, Jolie and Joya crawled to the edge of the console and looked down at it. There was no petrol inside, only half a bucketful of stinking mud mixed in with a lot of frazzled ant corpses.

'All the petrol in the trench burnt up,' said the lieutenant.

Kachika checked out the window and saw that he was telling the truth. The fires had gone out. She turned to Field Marshal Jolie. 'How much time is left on the countdown?'

Jolie kept her eyes glued to her watch as she answered. 'Five minutes and thirty seconds remaining, Supreme Consul.'

Kachika inhaled sharply and allowed herself a couple of those seconds before she shared her momentous news. 'I have just received a call. Our forces in Laurasia have been defeated. When they attacked the Laurasian signal station, the dinosaurs guarding it blew up the building. The interrupt signal cannot be sent to Luna. It will detonate in five minutes.'

'It is the same for Leviathan, Supreme Consul,' Field Marshal Jolie said calmly. 'All is lost.'

The dinosaurs did not understand a word the three leaders of the Ant Federation had said. 'We can get some petrol from nearby,' the engineer offered. 'There's a village about five kilometres from here. The highway is blocked, so we'll have to go on foot, but if we're quick about it, we can be back in twenty minutes.'

Kachika waved her antennae feebly. 'Go, all of you. Do whatever you want.'

As the six dinosaurs filed out of the room, the engineer stopped on the threshold and repeated what the lieutenant had asked earlier. 'Is the world really going to end in the next few minutes?'

The supreme consul of the Ant Federation looked at him with the shadow of a smile on her face. 'Nothing lasts forever, sir.'

The engineer cocked his head in surprise. 'That's the first time I've ever heard an ant say something philosophical,' he said. Then he swung round and left.

Kachika made her way back to the edge of the central console and addressed the ant troops massed on the floor beneath her.

'I need you to relay my instructions to all units with extreme urgency. All troops in the vicinity of the signal station should immediately take shelter in the basement. Troops further afield should seek out crevices and holes in which to hide. The government of the Ant Federation issues the following final statement to the citizenry: the end of the world is upon us. Every ant for herself.'

Professor Joya was quivering from her feelers to her feet, impatient to get going. 'Supreme Consul, Field Marshal, let's make our way to the basement,' she said.

'You go, Professor,' Kachika replied. 'Field Marshal Jolie and I will not be accompanying you. We have committed the gravest error in the history of civilisation. We have forfeited our right to life.'

'The supreme consul is correct, Professor.' Field Marshal Jolie dipped her antennae solemnly. 'Though the odds are against you, I sincerely hope that you will somehow manage to keep the embers of civilisation glowing.'

Joya touched her antennae to those of Kachika and Jolie, the most heartfelt gesture of respect in the ant world. Then she scuttled down off the console and joined the tide of ants streaming out of the control room.

After the troops had evacuated, a hush descended on the control room. Kachika pattered over to the nearest window and Jolie followed her. From the sill, they witnessed an extraordinary sight.

Dawn was about to break, but the night's crescent moon still hung in the sky. Suddenly, the angle of the moon shifted and the moon began to brighten rapidly until its silvery light became a blinding arc of electricity. The world below, including the scattering throng of ants, was illuminated in stark detail.

'What was that? Did the sun just get brighter?' Jolie asked.

'No, Field Marshal, that was the arrival of a new sun. The moon is reflecting its light. A sun has appeared over Laurasia and is frying the continent as we speak.'

'Gondwana's sun should appear any moment now.'

'Isn't that it there?'

Intense light flared in the west, inundating everything around it.

The two ants watched agog as a dazzling sun began rising swiftly over the western horizon. It swelled until it occupied half the sky, and incinerated everything on Earth in an instant.

The shockwaves from the explosion took several minutes to reach the ants, but they had been vaporised by the heat long before that. All life was consumed in the furnace.

That was the last day of the Cretaceous period.

EPILOGUE

THE LONG NIGHT

It had been winter for the last 3,000 years.

At noon on a slightly warmer-than-usual day in central Gondwana, two ants climbed out of their deep subterranean nest and up to the surface. The sun was but a blurry halo in the dreary, overcast sky and the ground was covered with a thick layer of ice and snow. Only the occasional outcrop interrupted the endless white expanse. Away on the far-distant horizon, the mountains were also white.

The first ant stared up at the colossal skeleton rising out of the snow. The plains were littered with such skeletons, but because they were white too, they were usually indiscernible. Today, though, from where the ant was standing, the bones were silhouetted in sharp relief against the murky sky.

'This was an animal called a dinosaur, wasn't it?' said the first ant.

The second ant turned to gaze at the skeleton in the sky too. 'That's right. Like in that story they were telling us last night about the Age of Wonder.'

'That was such a good story. A golden age for us ants, way back in the past, thousands of years ago . . .'

'It's hard to imagine, isn't it? Ants living in huge cities up on the surface instead of in nests deep underground. 'Age of Wonder' sounds about right! And they didn't hatch from eggs laid by queens either – that's pretty hard to get your head round as well.'

'The bit I liked most was how ants and dinosaurs created the Age of Wonder together, by collaborating with each other. Remember that part? How the dinosaurs lacked dexterous hands, so the ants did the skilled work for them. And how the ants lacked clever minds, so it was up to the dinosaurs to invent incredible new technologies.'

'Yes, I liked that too. Together they created so many massive machines and sophisticated cities – they were like gods!'

'Did you understand that stuff about the destruction of the world?'

'Not really. It seemed rather complicated. War broke out in the dinosaur world, and then between the dinosaurs and the ants.' The second ant paused. 'And then two suns appeared on Earth.'

The first ant shivered in the cold wind. 'Oh, a new sun would be great right now.'

'You really didn't get it, did you! The two suns were terrible. Way too hot. They incinerated everything on Earth.'

'Then why is it so cold now?'

'It's confusing, but I think it goes something like this. For a time after the two suns appeared, the world was, as you'd expect, very hot. So hot that the parts of the Earth's crust closest to the suns became molten. Then all the seawater that had evaporated in the heat fell as rain for more than a hundred years, causing catastrophic flooding across the planet. After that, the dust that had been lifted into the atmosphere by the explosion of the new suns blocked the light of the old sun, and the world became cold, even colder than before the two suns appeared – the way it is today. The dinosaurs were big – very big; humongous big – so naturally they all died during those terrible times, but some ants survived by burrowing underground.'

'Wouldn't it be great if antkind could re-create the Age of Wonder. Just think . . .!'

'Yeah, it would. But from what they were saying last night, that's never going to happen. Our brains are too small, and we can only think as a group, so we don't have the capacity to invent amazing new technology. And all the ancient technological knowhow has been forgotten.'

'If only ants could still read, we could study the books from back then and rediscover the knowhow that way. Some of us were able to read even up until quite recently, apparently – did you know that? But not any more.'

'We're regressing. At this rate, we'll soon just be tiny little insects that know nothing except how to build nests and forage for food.'

'What's so bad about that? When times are hard, like they are now, what's the use of knowing stuff?'

'True.'

Both ants fell silent for a long while.

'D'you think there'll ever come a day when the world is warm again and some other animal brings about another Age of Wonder?'

'It's possible. Such an animal would have to have a large brain and dexterous hands.'

'Right. And it couldn't be as big as the dinosaurs. They ate too much. Life would be very difficult for an animal that size.'

'But it couldn't be as small as us, either, or its brain wouldn't be powerful enough.'

'D'you think such a miraculous creature might emerge?'

'I think it will. Time is endless. Everything comes to pass eventually, I tell you. Everything comes to pass.'

THE CIRCLE

Xianyang, capital of the state of Qin, 227 B.C.*

Jing Ke slowly unrolled the silk scroll of a map across the low, long table.

On the other side of the table, King Zheng of Qin sighed satisfactorily as he watched the mountains and rivers of his enemy being slowly revealed. Jing Ke was here to present the surrender of the King of Yan. It was easy to feel in control looking at the fields, roads, cities, and military bases drawn on a map. The real land, so vast, sometimes made him feel powerless.

When Jing Ke reached the end of the scroll, there was a metallic glint, and a sharp dagger came into view. The air in the Great Hall of the Palace seemed to solidify in an instant.

All the king's ministers stood at least thirty feet away, and in any event, had no weapons. The armed guards were even farther away, below the steps leading into the Great Hall. These measures were intended to improve the king's security, but now they only made the assassin's task easier.

But King Zheng remained calm. After giving the dagger a brief glance, he focused his sharp and somber eyes on Jing Ke. The king

---

* This story is set during the Warring States Period, when China was divided into several independent states: Qin, Qi, Chu, Wei, Zhao, Yan, and Han. King Zheng of Qin would eventually conquer the other six states and unify China under the Qin Dynasty. He is known more familiarly as Qin Shihuang, the First Emperor of China.

was a careful man, and he had noticed that the dagger was positioned such that the handle pointed at *him* while the tip pointed back toward the assassin.

Jing Ke picked up the dagger, and all those present in the Great Hall gasped. But King Zheng sighed in relief. He saw that Jing Ke held the dagger only by the tip of the blade, with the dull handle pointing at the king.

'Your Majesty, please kill me with this weapon.' Jing Ke raised the dagger over his head and bowed. 'Crown Prince Dan of Yan ordered me to make this attempt on your life, and I cannot disobey an order from my master. But my great admiration for you makes it impossible for me to carry through.'

King Zheng made no move.

'Sire, all you have to do is to stab lightly. The dagger has been soaked in poison. A slight prick is enough to end my life.'

King Zheng sat still and raised his hands to signal the guards rush¬ing into the Great Hall to stop. Without changing his expression he said, 'I do not have to kill you to feel safe. Your words have convinced me that you do not have the heart of an assassin.'

In a single, smooth motion, Jing Ke wrapped the fingers of his right hand around the handle of the dagger. The tip of the dagger was aimed at his own chest as though he was about to commit suicide.

'You're a learned man.' King Zheng's voice was cold. 'Dying now would be a waste. I'd like to have your skills and knowledge assisting my army. If you insist on dying, do so only after you've accomplished some things for me first.' He waved at Jing Ke, dismissing him.

The assassin from Yan gently put the dagger down on the table and, still bowing, backed out of the Great Hall.

King Zheng stood up and walked out of the Great Hall. The sky was perfectly clear, and he saw the pale white moon in the blue sky like a delicate dream left behind by the night.

'Jing Ke,' he called after the assassin still descending the steps. 'Does the moon appear during the day often?'

The assassin's white robe reflected the sunlight like a bright flame. 'It's not unusual to have the sun and the moon appear in the sky simultaneously. On the lunar calendar, between the fourth and twelfth days of each month, it's possible to see the moon at different times during the day as long as the weather is good.'

King Zheng nodded. 'Oh, not an uncommon sight,' he muttered to himself.

Two years later, King Zheng summoned Jing Ke to an audience.

When Jing Ke arrived outside the palace in Xianyang, he saw three officials being marched out of the Great Hall by armed guards. Having been stripped of the insignia of their rank, their heads were bare. Two of them walked between the guards with faces drained of blood while the third was so frightened he could no longer walk and had to be carried by two soldiers. This last man continued to mumble, begging King Zheng to spare his life. Jing Ke heard him muttering the word 'medicine' a few times. He guessed that the three men had been sentenced to death.

King Zheng's mood was jovial when he saw Jing Ke, as though nothing had happened. He pointed to the three departing officials and said by way of explanation, 'Xu Fu's fleet has never returned from the East Sea. Someone has to be held responsible.'

Jing Ke knew that Xu Fu was an occultist who claimed he could go to three magical mountains on islands out in the East Sea to find the elixir of eternal life. King Zheng gave him a large fleet of ships loaded with three thousand youths and maidens and heaped with treasure, gifts for the immortals who held the secret of eternal life. But the fleet had set sail three years ago, and not a peep had been heard from him since.

King Zheng waved the sore topic away. 'I hear that you've invented many wonders in the last couple years. The new bow you designed can shoot twice as far as the old models; the war chariots you devised are equipped with clever springs to ride smoothly over rough ground without having to slow down; the bridges whose construction you supervised use only half as much material but are even stronger – I'm very pleased. How did you come up with these ideas?'

'When I follow the order of the Heavens, all things are possible.'

'Xu Fu said the same thing.'

'Sire, please permit me to be blunt. Xu Fu is nothing more than a fraud. Casting lots and empty meditation are not appropriate ways to understand the order of the universe. Men like him cannot understand the way the Heavens speak at all.'

'What is the language of the Heavens, then?'

'Mathematics. Numbers and shapes are the means by which the Heavens write to the world.'

King Zheng nodded thoughtfully. 'Interesting. So what are you working on now?'

'I'm always striving to understand more of the Heavens' messages for Your Majesty.'

'Any progress?'

'Yes, some. At times, I even feel I'm standing right in front of the door to the treasury filled with the secrets of the universe.'

'How do the Heavens tell you these mysteries? Just now, you explained that the language of the Heavens consists of numbers and shapes.'

'The circle.'

Seeing that King Zheng was utterly confused, Jing Ke asked for and received permission to pick up a brush. He drew a circle on the silk cloth spread out on the low table. Though he didn't use a compass or other tools to assist him, the circle appeared to be perfect.

'Sire, other than objects made by men, have you ever seen a perfect circle in nature?'

King Zheng pondered this for a moment. 'Very rarely. Once, a falcon and I stared at each other, and I noticed that its eyes were very round.'

'Yes, that's true. I can also suggest as examples eggs laid by cer¬tain aquatic creatures, the intersecting plane between a dewdrop and a leaf, and so on. But I've carefully measured all of these, and none of them are perfect circles. It's the same with the circle I drew here: It may look round, but it contains errors and imperfections undetect¬able by the naked eye. In fact, it's an oval, not a perfect circle. I've been searching for the perfect circle for a long time, and I finally realized it does not exist in the world below, but only in the Heavens above.'

'Oh?'

'Sire, please accompany me outside the palace.'

Jing Ke and King Zheng strode outside the palace. It was another beautiful day with the moon and the sun both visible in the clear sky.

'The sun and the full moon are both perfect circles,' said Jing Ke as he pointed at the sky. 'The Heavens placed the perfect circle – impossible to find on earth – in the sky. Not just one, but two examples, and they're the most notable features of the firmament. The meaning couldn't be clearer: the secret of the Heavens resides inside the circle.'

'But the circle is the simplest of shapes. Other than a straight line, it's the least complicated figure.' King Zheng turned around and returned inside the palace.

'That apparent simplicity disguises a profound mystery,' Jing Ke said as he followed the king back inside. When they returned to the low table, he drew a rectangle on the silk with the brush. 'Observe this rectangle if you would. The longer dimension measures four inches, and the shorter dimension two. The Heavens speak also through this figure.'

'What does it say?'

'The Heavens tell me that the ratio between the longer side and the shorter side is two.'

'Are you mocking me?'

'I wouldn't dare. This is just an example of a simple message. Please observe this other figure.' Jing Ke drew another rectangle. 'This time, the long side is nine inches and the shorter seven. The ideas expressed by the Heavens in this figure are far richer.'

'From what I can see, it's still extremely simple.'

'Not so. Sire, the ratio between the longer side and the shorter side in this rectangle is 1.28571428571428 5714... The sequence '285714' repeats forever. Thus, you can calculate the ratio to be as precise as you like, but it will never be exact. Though the message is still simple, much more meaning can be extracted from it.'

'Interesting,' said King Zheng.

'Next, let me show you the most mysterious shape the Heavens gifted us: the circle.' Jing Ke drew a straight line through the center of the circle he had drawn earlier. 'Observe that the ratio between the circumference and the diameter of a circle is an endless string of numbers beginning with 3.1415926. But it keeps on going after that, never repeating itself.'

'Never?'

'Yes. Imagine a silk cloth as large as all-under-heaven. The string of numbers in the circle's ratio could be written in tiny script, each numeral no bigger than the head of a fly, all the way from here to the edge of the sky, and then coming back here start on a new line. Continued this way, the entire cloth could be filled, and there would still be no end to the numbers, and the sequence still wouldn't repeat. Your Majesty, this endless string of numbers contains the mysteries of the universe.'

King Zheng's expression didn't change, but Jing Ke saw that his eyes had brightened. 'Even if you obtained this number, how would you read from it the message the Heavens want to express?'

'There are many ways. For example, by treating the numbers as coordinates, it's possible to turn the numbers into new shapes and pictures.'

'What will the pictures show?'

'I don't know. Maybe it will be an illustration of the enigma of the universe. Or maybe it will be an essay, or perhaps even a whole book. But the key is that we must obtain enough digits of the circular ratio first. I estimate that we must compute tens of thousands, per¬haps even hundreds of thousands, of digits before the meaning can be discerned. Right now, I've only computed about a hundred digits, inadequate to detect any hidden meaning.'

'A hundred? That's all?'

'Sire, even so few digits have taken me more than ten years of effort. To compute the circular ratio, one must approach it by inscrib¬ing and circumscribing a circle with polygons. The mores sides in the polygons, the more precise the calculations and the more digits that can be obtained. But the complexity of the calculations increases rapidly, and progress is slow.'

King Zheng continued to stare at the circle crossed by a straight line. 'Do you think you'll find the secret of eternal life in it?'

'Yes, of course.' Jing Ke grew excited. 'Life and death are the basic rules given to the world by the Heavens. Thus, the mystery of life and death must be contained in this message as well, including the secret of eternal life.'

'Then you must compute the circular ratio. I will give you two years to compute ten thousand digits. In five more years, I need you to get to a hundred thousand digits.'

'That's ... that's impossible!'

King Zheng whipped his long sleeves across the table, scattering the silk cloth and ink and brush onto the floor. 'You have but to name whatever resources you need.' He stared at Jing Ke coldly. 'But you must complete the calculations in time.'

Five days later, King Zheng called for Jing Ke again. This time, Jing Ke didn't come to the palace in Xianyang; instead, he met the royal entourage on the road as the king was touring around his domain. Right away, King Zheng asked Jing Ke for updates on the progress of the calculations.

Jing Ke bowed and spoke. 'Sire, I gathered all the mathematicians who are capable of such calculations in the entire realm: they number only eight. Based on the amount of calculations necessary, even if all nine of us devote the rest of our lives to this task, we will only be able to obtain about three thousand digits of the circular ratio. In two years, the best that we can do is three hundred digits.'

King Zheng nodded and indicated that Jing Ke should walk with him. They came to a granite monument about twenty feet high.

A hole was drilled through the top of the monument, and a thick rope made of twisted oxhide passed through the hole to suspend the monument from a wooden platform like the weight of a giant pendulum. The smooth bottom of the monument hovered about a man's height above the ground. There were no inscriptions on the monument.

King Zheng pointed to the hanging monument and said, 'Look, if you can finish the calculations in time, this will become a monument of your triumph. We will erect it on the ground and fill it with inscriptions of your many accomplishments. But if you can't finish the calculations, this will become a memento of your shame. In that case, it will also be erected on the ground, but before the rope is cut to drop it, you will have to sit below it so that it can be your tombstone.'

Jing Ke lifted his eyes to gaze at the gigantic suspended stone that filled his field of vision. Against the moving clouds in the sky, the dark mass appeared oppressive.

Jing Ke turned to the king and said, 'Your Majesty has spared my life once, and even if I could finish the calculations in time, it wouldn't be enough to erase the crime of my attempt on your life. I'm not afraid to die. Please give me five more days to think about this. If I still can't come up with a plan, I'll sit under the monument willingly.'

Four days later, Jing Ke requested an audience with the king, which was immediately granted. Calculating the circular ratio was the most important task on the king's mind.

'From your expression, I gather that you have indeed come up with a plan.' The king smiled.

Jing Ke did not answer directly. 'Your Majesty, you once said that you would give me all the resources that I require. Is that still the case?'

'Of course.'

'I need three million men from your army.'

The number did not astonish the king. His eyebrows only lifted briefly. 'What kind of soldiers?'

'The common soldiers under your command now are sufficient.'

'I think you should be aware that most of the soldiers in my army are illiterate. In two years, you cannot possibly teach them complex mathematics, let alone finish the calculations.'

'Sire, the skills they would need can be taught to the least intelli¬gent soldier in an hour. Please give me three soldiers so that I can demonstrate.'

'Three? Only three? I can easily give you three thousand.'

'I only need three.'

King Zheng waved his hand and summoned three soldiers. They were all very young. Like other Qin soldiers, they moved like order-obeying machines.

'I don't know your names,' Jing Ke said, tapping the shoulders of two of the soldiers. 'The two of you will be responsible for number input, so I'll call you 'Input One' and 'Input Two.' 'He pointed to the last soldier. 'You will be responsible for number output, so I'll call you 'Output.' 'He shoved the soldiers to where he wanted them to stand. 'Like this. Form a triangle. Output is the apex. Input One and Input Two form the base.'

'You could have just told them to stand in the Wedge Attack Formation,' King Zheng said, glancing at Jing Ke with a smile.

Jing Ke took out six small flags – three white, three black – and handed them out to the three soldiers so that each held a black flag and a white flag. 'White represents zero; black represents one. Good. Now listen to me. Output, you turn around and look at Input One and Input Two. If they both raise black flags, you raise the black flag as well. Under all other circumstances, you raise the white flag.'

Jing Ke repeated the instructions one more time to be sure the three soldiers understood. Then he began to shout orders. 'Let's begin! Input One and Input Two, you can raise whichever flag you want. Good. Raise! Good. Raise again! Raise!'

Input One and Input Two raised their flags three times. The first time they were black-black, the second time white-black, and the third time black-white. Output reacted correctly each time, raising the black flag once and the white one twice.

'Very good. Sire, your soldiers are very smart.'

'Even an idiot would be capable of that. Tell me, what are they really doing?' King Zheng looked baffled.

'The three soldiers form a component for a calculation system, which I call an AND gate. If both numbers input into the gate are one, the result output is also one; otherwise, if one of the numbers input is zero, such as zero-one, one-zero, or zero-zero, the result output is zero.' Jing Ke paused to let King Zheng digest the infor¬mation.

The king said impassively, 'All right. Continue.'

Jing Ke turned to the three soldiers again. 'Let's form another component. You, Output, if you see either Input One or Input Two raise a black flag, you raise the black flag. There are three situations where that will be true: black-black, white-black, black-white. When it's white-white, you raise the white flag. Understand? Good lad, you're really clever. You're the key to the correct functioning of the gate. Work hard, and you will be rewarded. Let's begin operation. Raise! Good, raise again! Raise again! Perfect. Your Majesty, this component is called an OR gate. Whenever one of the two inputs is one, the output is also one.'

Then Jing Ke used the three soldiers to form what he called a NAND gate, a NOR gate, an XOR-gate, an XNOR-gate, and a tristate gate. Finally, using only two soldiers, he made the simplest gate, a NOT gate: Output always raised the flag that was opposite in color from the one raised by Input.

Jing Ke bowed to the Emperor. 'All calculating components have been demonstrated. This is the scope of the skills that the three million soldiers must learn.'

'How can you perform complex calculations using such simple, childish tricks?' King Zheng's face was full of distrust.

'Great King, the complexity in everything in the universe is built up from the simplest components. Similarly, an immense number of simple components, when structured together appropriately, can generate extremely complex capabilities. Three million soldiers can form a million of these gates I've just demonstrated, and these gates can be put together into a whole formation capable of any complex calculation. I call my invention a calculating formation.'

'I still don't understand how the calculations will be carried out.'

'The precise process is complicated. If Your Majesty continues to be interested, I can explain in detail later. For now, it's enough to know that the operation of the calculating formation is based on a novel method of thinking about and writing down numbers. In this method, only two numerals, zero and one, corresponding to the white and black flags, are needed. But this new method can use zero and one to represent any number, and this allows the calculating formation to use a large number of simple components to collectively carry out high-speed calculations.'

'Three million is almost the entirety of my arm, but I will give them to you.' King Zheng sighed meaningfully. 'Hurry. I'm feeling old.'

A year passed.

It was another beautiful day with the sun and the moon both out. King Zheng and Jing Ke stood together on a high stone dais, with the king's numerous ministers in rows behind them. Below them, a magnificent phalanx of three million Qin soldiers stood arrayed on the ground, the entire formation a square three miles* on each side. Lit by the freshly risen sun, the phalanx remained still like a giant carpet made of three million terra-cotta warriors. But when a flock of birds wandered above the phalanx, the birds immediately felt the potential for death from below and scattered anxiously.

Jing Ke said, 'Your Majesty, your army is truly matchless. In an extremely short time, we have completed such complex training.'

King Zheng held on to the hilt of his long sword. 'Even though the whole is complex, what each soldier must do is very simple. Compared to the military training they went through, this is nothing.'

'Then, Your Majesty, please give the great order!' Jing Ke's voice trembled with excitement.

King Zheng nodded. A guard ran over, grabbed the hilt of the

* For the benefit of English readers, Chinese measurement units (such as *li*, *zhang*, *chi*, and *cun*) throughout the text have been translated and converted into approxi¬mate English equivalents.

king's sword, and stepped backward. The bronze sword was so long that it was impossible for the king to pull it out of the scabbard without help. The guard knelt and presented the sword to the king, who lifted the sword to the sky and shouted, 'Calculating formation!'

Battle drums began to beat, and four giant bronze cauldrons at the corners of the stone dais came to life simultaneously with roaring flames. A group of soldiers standing at the edge of the dais facing the phalanx chanted in unison, 'Calculating formation!'

On the ground below, colors in the phalanx began to shift and move. Complicated and detailed circuit patterns appeared and gradually filled the entire formation. Ten minutes later, the army had rearranged itself into a nine-mile-square calculating formation.

Jing Ke pointed to the formation and began to explain. 'Your Majesty, we have named this formation Qin One. Look, there in the center is the central processing subformation, the core calculating component, made up of the best divisions of your army. By referencing this diagram, you can locate the adding subformations, quick storage subformations, and stack memory subformation. The part around it that looks highly regular is the memory subformation. When we built that part, we found that we didn't have enough soldiers. But luckily, the work done by the elements in this component is the simplest, so we trained each soldier to hold more colored flags. Each man can now complete the work that initially required twenty men. This allowed us to increase the memory capacity to meet the minimum requirements for running the calculating procedure for the circular ratio. Observe also the open passage that runs through the entire formation, and the light cavalry waiting for orders in the passage: that's the system's main communication line, responsible for transmitting information between the components of the whole system.'

Two soldiers brought over a large scroll, tall as a man, and spread it open before King Zheng. When they reached the scroll's end, everyone present remembered the scene in the palace a few years ago, and they all held their breath. But the imaginary dagger did not appear. Before them was only a large sheet of thin silk filled with symbols, each the size of a fly's head. Packed so densely, the symbols were as dazzling to behold as the calculating formation on the ground below.

'Your Majesty, these are the orders in the procedure I developed for calculating the circular ratio. Please look here' – Jing Ke pointed to the calculating formation below – 'where the soldiers standing ready for what I call the 'hardware.' What's on this cloth is what I call the 'software,' the soul of the calculating formation. The relationship between hardware and software is like that between the *guqin* zither and sheet music.'

King Zheng nodded. 'Good. Begin.'

Jing Ke lifted both hands above his head and solemnly chanted, 'As ordered by the Great King, initiate the calculating formation! System self-test!'

A row of soldiers standing halfway down the face of the stone dais repeated the order using flag signals. In a moment, the phalanx of three million men seemed to turn into a lake filled with sparkling lights as millions of tiny flags waved.

'Self-test complete! Begin initialization sequence! Load calculation procedure!'

Below, the light cavalry on the main communication line that passed through the entire calculating formation began to ride back and forth swiftly. The main passage soon turned into a turbulent river. Along the way, the river fed into numerous thin tributaries, infiltrating all the modular subformations. Soon the ripples of black and white flags coalesced into surging waves that filled the entire phalanx. The central processing subformation area was the most tumultuous, like tinder set on fire.

Suddenly, as though the fuel had been exhausted, the movements in the central processing subformation slackened and eventually stopped. Starting with the central processing subformation in the center, the stillness spread in every direction like a lake being frozen over. Finally the entire calculating formation came to a stop, with only a few scattered components flashing lifelessly in infinite loops.

'System lockup!' a signal officer called out. Shortly after, the rea¬son for the malfunction was determined: there was an error with the operation of one of the gates in the central processing subformation's status storage unit.

'Restart system!' Jing Ke ordered confidently.

'Not yet,' King Zheng said as he grasped his sword. 'Replace the malfunctioning gate and behead all the soldiers who made up that gate. In the future, any other malfunctions will be dealt with the same way.'

A few riders dashed into the phalanx with their swords drawn. They killed the three unfortunate soldiers and replaced them with new men. From the vantage point of the dais, three eye-catching pools of blood appeared in the middle of the central processing subformation.

Jing Ke gave the order to restart the system. This time, it went very smoothly. Ten minutes later, the soldiers were carrying out the circular-ratio-calculating procedure. As the phalanx rippled with flag signals, the calculating formation settled into the long computation.

'This is really interesting,' King Zheng said, pointing to the spectacular sight. 'Each individual's behavior is so simple, yet together, they can produce such complex intelligence.'

'Great King, this is just the mechanical operation of a machine, not intelligence. Each of these lowly individuals is just a zero. Only when someone like you is added to the front as a one is the whole endowed with meaning.' Jing Ke's smile was ingratiating.

'How long would it take to calculate ten thousand digits of the circular ratio?' King Zheng asked.

'About ten months. Maybe even sooner if things go right.'

General Wang Jian* stepped forward. 'Your Majesty, I must urge caution. Even in regular military operations, it's extremely dangerous to concentrate so much of our force in an open area like this. Moreover, the three million soldiers in this phalanx are unarmed, carrying only signal flags. The calculating formation is not intended for battle and will be extremely vulnerable if attacked. Even under normal conditions, to effectuate an orderly retreat of this many men packed so tightly would take most of a day. If they were attacked, retreat would be impossible. Sire, this calculating formation will appear in the eyes of our enemies as meat placed on a cutting board.'

King Zheng did not reply, but turned his gaze to Jing Ke. The latter bowed and said, 'General Wang is absolutely right. You must be cautious when deciding whether to pursue this calculation.'

Then Jing Ke did something bold and unprecedented: he lifted his eyes and locked gazes with King Zheng. The king immediately

* One of the four great generals of King Zheng's campaigns against the other six states. The historical Wang Jian was responsible for the destruction of the states of Yan (where Jing Ke was from), Zhao, and Chu.

understood the meaning in that gaze: *All your accomplishments so far are like zeros; only with the addition of eternal life for yourself, a one, can all of those become meaningful.*

'General Wang, you're overly concerned.' King Zheng whipped his sleeves contemptuously. 'The states of Han, Wei, Zhao, and Chu have all been conquered. The only two remaining states, Yan and Qi, are led by foolish kings who have exhausted their people. They're on the verge of total collapse and pose no threat. Given the way things are going, by the time the circular ratio calculation is complete, those two states may already have fallen apart on their own and surrendered to the Great State of Qin. Of course, I appreciate the general's caution. I suggest that we form a line of scouts at some distance from the calculating formation and step up our surveillance of the movements of the Yan and Qi armies. This way, we will be secure.' He lifted his long sword toward the sky and solemnly declared, 'The calculations must be finished. I have decided that it must be so.'

The calculating formation ran smoothly for a month, and the results were even better than expected. Already, more than two thousand digits of the circular ratio had been computed, and as the soldiers in the formation grew used to the work and Jing Ke further refined the calculating procedure, speed in the future would be even faster. The estimate was that only three more years would be needed to reach the target of a hundred thousand digits.

The morning of the forty-fifth day after the start of the calculations was foggy. It was impossible to see the calculating formation, enveloped in mist, from the dais. Soldiers in the formation could see no farther than about five men.

But the calculating formation's operation was designed to be unaffected by the fog and continued. Shouted orders and the hoofbeats of the light cavalry on the main communication line echoed in the haze.

However, those soldiers in the north of the calculating formation heard something else. At first, the noise came intermittently and seemed illusory, but soon the noise grew louder and formed a continuous boom, like thunder coming from the depths of the fog.

The noise came from the hooves of thousands of horses. A powerful division of cavalry approached the calculating formation from the north, and the banner of the state of Yan flew at their head. The riders moved slowly, forcing their horses to maintain ranks. They knew they had plenty of time.

Only when the riders were about a third of a mile from the edge of the calculating formation did they begin the charge. By the time the vanguard of the cavalry had torn into the calculating formation, the Qin soldiers didn't even get a proper look at their enemies. In this initial charge, tens of thousands of Qin soldiers died just from being trampled under the hooves of the attacking riders.

What followed was not a battle at all, but a massacre. Before the battle, the Yan commanders already knew that they would not meet with meaningful resistance. In order to increase the efficiency of the slaughter, the riders abandoned the traditional cavalry weapons, long-handled lances and halberds, and instead equipped themselves with swords and morning stars. The several hundred thousand Yan heavy cavalry became a death-dealing cloud, and wherever they rode, the bodies of Qin soldiers carpeted the land.

In order to avoid giving warning to the core of the calculating formation, the Yan riders killed in silence, as though they were machines, not men. But the screams of the dying Qin soldiers, whether cut down or trampled, spread far and wide in the thick fog.

However, all the Qin soldiers in the calculating formation had been trained under threat of death to ignore outside interference and to devote themselves single-mindedly to the simple task of acting as calculating components. Combined with the disguise provided by the thick fog, the result was that most of the calculating formation did not realize the northern edge of the formation was already under attack. As the death-dealing region slowly and orderly ate through the formation, turning it into piles of corpses strewn over blood-soaked, muddy ground, the rest of the formation continued to calculate as before, even though more and more errors began to plague the system.

Behind the first wave of cavalry, more than a hundred thousand Yan archers loosened volleys from their long bows, aimed at the heart of the calculating formation. In a few moments, millions of arrows fell like a thunderstorm, and almost every arrow found a target.

Only then did the calculating formation start to fall apart. At the same time, information of the enemy attack began to spread, increasing the chaos. The light cavalry on the main communication line carried reports of the sudden attack, but as the situation deteriorated, the main passage became blocked, and the panicked riders began to trample through the densely packed phalanx. Countless Qin soldiers thus died under the hooves of friendly forces.

On the eastern, southern, and western edges of the calculating formation, which weren't under attack, Qin soldiers began to retreat without any semblance of order. Amidst the utter lack of information and broken chain of command, the retreat was slow and confused. The calculating formation, now purposeless, became like a thick, concentrated bubble of ink that refused to dissolve in water, with only wispy tendrils leaving at the edges.

Those Qin soldiers running toward the east were soon stopped by the disciplined ranks of the Qi army. Instead of charging, the Qi commanders ordered the infantry and cavalry to form impregnable defensive lines to wait for the escaping Qin soldiers to enter the trap before surrounding them and beginning the slaughter.

The only direction left for the remainder of the hopeless Qin army, now without any will to fight, was toward the southwest. Hundreds of thousands of unarmed men poured over the plains like a dirty flood. But they soon encountered a third enemy force: unlike the disciplined armies from Yan and Qi, this third force consisted of the ferocious riders of the Huns. They tore into the Qin army like wolves into a flock of sheep and quickly overwhelmed them.

The slaughter continued until noon, when the strong breeze from the west lifted the fog, and the wide expanse of the battlefield was exposed to the glare of the midday sun.

The Yan, Qi, and Hun armies had combined in multiple places, surrounding what remained of the Qin army in small pockets. The cavalry of the three armies continued to charge the Qin soldiers, leav-ing the wounded and the few escapees to be mopped up by the infantry. Oxen formations, urged on by fire, and catapults were also put into operation to kill the remaining Qin men even more efficiently.

By evening, the sorrowful notes of battle horns echoed over a field covered with bodies and crisscrossed by rivulets of blood. The final survivors of the Qin army were now surrounded in three shrinking pockets.

The night that followed had a full moon. The pure, cold moon floated impassively over the slaughter below, bathing the mountains of corpses and seas of blood in its calm, liquid light. The killing continued throughout the night and wasn't over until the next morning.

The army of the Qin Empire was entirely eliminated.

One month later, the allied forces of Qi and Yan entered Xianyang and captured King Zheng. The Qin Empire was over.

The day selected for the execution of King Zheng was another day when the sun and the moon appeared together. The moon floated in the azure sky like a snowflake.

The monument that had been intended for Jing Ke still hung in the air. King Zheng sat below it, waiting for the Yan executioner to cut the oxhide rope.

Jing Ke walked out of the crowd observing the execution, still dressed all in white. He came before King Zheng and bowed. 'Your Majesty.'

'In your heart, you've always remained a Yan assassin,' the king said. He did not look up at Jing Ke.

'Yes. But I didn't want to just kill you. I also needed to eliminate your army. If I had succeeded a few years ago in killing you, Qin would have remained powerful. Advised by brilliant strategists and led by veteran commanders, the million-strong Qin army would still have posed an unstoppable threat to Yan.'

King Zheng asked the last question of his life. 'How could you have sent so many men so close to my army without my notice?'

'During the year when the calculating formation was being trained and operating, Yan and Qi focused on digging tunnels. Each tunnel was many miles long and wide enough to allow cavalry to pass through. It was my idea to use these tunnels to allow the allies to by¬pass your sentries and appear suddenly near the defenseless calculat¬ing formation.'

King Zheng nodded and said nothing more. He closed his eyes to wait to die. The supervising official gave the order, and an executioner began to climb up the platform, a knife held between his teeth.

King Zheng heard movements next to him. He opened his eyes and saw that Jing Ke was sitting next to him.

'Your Majesty, we'll die together. When the heavy stone falls, it will become a monument to both of us. Our blood and flesh will mix together. Perhaps this will give you some comfort.'

'What is the point of this?' King Zheng asked coldly.

'It's not that I want to die. The King of Yan has ordered my execution.'

A smile quickly appeared on King Zheng's face and disappeared just as quickly, like a passing breeze. 'You have accomplished so much for Yan that your name is praised more than the king's. He fears your ambition. This result is expected.'

'That is indeed one reason, but not the main one. I also advised the King of Yan to build Yan's own calculating formation. This gave him the excuse he needed to kill me.'

King Zheng turned to gaze at Jing Ke. The surprise in the king's eyes was genuine.

'I don't care if you believe me. My advice was given with the hope of strengthening Yan. It's true that the calculating formation was a stratagem I came up with to destroy Qin by taking advantage of your obsession with eternal life. But it's also a genuinely great invention. Through its calculating power, we can understand the language of mathematics and divine the mysteries of the universe. It could have opened a new era.'

The executioner had reached the top of the platform and stood in front of the rope holding up the stone monument, waiting for the final order as he held the knife in his hand.

In the distance, under a bright baldachin, the King of Yan waved his hand in assent. The supervising official shouted the order to carry out the sentence.

Jing Ke suddenly opened his eyes wide as though awakening from a dream. 'I've got it! The calculating formation doesn't have to rely on the army, not even people. All those gates – AND, NOT, NAND, NOR, and so on – can be made from mechanical components. These components can be made very small, and when they're put together they will be a mechanical calculating formation! No, it shouldn't be called a calculating formation at all, but a calculating machine! Listen to me, King; wait!' Jing Ke shouted at the King of Yan in the distance. 'The calculating machine! The calculating machine!'

The executioner cut the rope.

'The calculating machine!' Jing Ke shouted the three words with the last of his breath.

As the giant stone fell, in that moment when its massive shadow blotted out everything in the world, King Zheng felt the end of his life. But in the eyes of Jing Ke, a faint ray of light heralding the beginning of a new era was extinguished.

TAKING CARE OF GOD

1

Once again, God had upset Qiusheng's family.

This had begun as a very good morning. A thin layer of white fog floated at the height of a man over the fields around Xicen village like a sheet of rice paper that had just become blank: the quiet countryside being the painting that had fallen off of the paper. The first rays of morning fell on the scene, and the year's earliest dewdrops entered the most glorious period of their brief life . . . but God had ruined this beautiful morning.

God had gotten up extra early and gone into the kitchen to warm some milk for himself. Ever since the start of the Era of Support, the milk market had prospered. Qiusheng's family had bought a milk cow for just over ten thousand yuan, and then, imitating others, mixed the milk with water to sell. The unadulterated milk had also become one of the staples for the family.

After the milk was warm, God took the bowl into the living room to watch TV without turning off the liquefied petroleum gas stove.

When Qiusheng's wife, Yulian, returned from cleaning the cowshed and the pigsty, she could smell gas all over the house. Covering her nose with a towel, she rushed into the kitchen to turn off the stove, opened the window and turned on the fan.

'You old fool! You're going to get the whole family killed!' Yulian shouted into the living room. The family had switched to using liquefied petroleum gas for cooking only after they began supporting

God. Qiusheng's father had always been opposed to it, saying that gas was not as good as honeycomb coal briquettes. Now he had even more ammunition for his argument.

As was his wont, God stood with his head lowered contritely, his broom-like white beard hanging past his knees, smiling like a kid who knew he had done something wrong. 'I . . . I took down the pot for heating the milk. Why didn't it turn off by itself?'

'You think you're still on your spaceship?' Qiusheng said, coming down the stairs. 'Everything here is dumb. We aren't like you, being waited on hand and foot by smart machines. We have to work hard with dumb tools. That's how we put rice in our bowls!'

'We also worked hard. Otherwise how did you come to be?' God said carefully.

'Enough with the 'how did you come to be?' Enough! I'm sick of hearing it. If you're so powerful, go and make other obedient children to support you!' Yulian threw her towel on the ground.

'Forget it. Just forget it,' Qiusheng said. He was always the one who made peace. 'Let's eat.'

Bingbing got up. As he came down the stairs, he yawned. 'Ma, Pa, God was coughing all night. I couldn't sleep.'

'You don't know how good you have it,' Yulian said. 'Your dad and I were in the room next to his. You don't hear us complaining, do you?'

As though triggered, God began to cough again. He coughed like he was playing his favorite sport with great concentration.

Yulian stared at God for a few seconds before sighing, 'I must have the worst luck in eight generations.'

Still angry, she left for the kitchen to cook breakfast.

God sat silently through breakfast with the rest of the family. He ate one bowl of porridge with pickled vegetables and half a *mantou* bun. During the entire time he had to endure Yulian's disdainful looks – maybe she was still mad about the liquefied petroleum gas, or maybe she thought he ate too much.

After breakfast, as usual, God got up quickly to clean the table and wash the dishes in the kitchen. Standing just outside the kitchen, Yulian shouted, 'Don't use detergent if there's no grease on the bowl! Everything costs money. The pittance they pay for your support? Ha!'

God grunted nonstop to show that he understood.

Qiusheng and Yulian left for the fields. Bingbing left for school. Only now did Qiusheng's father get up. Still not fully awake, he came downstairs, ate two bowls of porridge and filled his pipe with tobacco. At last he remembered God's existence.

'Hey, old geezer, stop the washing. Come out and play a game with me!' he shouted into the kitchen.

God came out of the kitchen, wiping his hands on his apron. He nodded ingratiatingly at Qiusheng's father. Playing Chinese Chess with the old man was a tough chore for God; winning and losing both had unpleasant consequences. If God won, Qiusheng's father would get mad: *You fucking old idiot! You trying to show me up? Shit! You're God! Beating me is no great accomplishment at all. Why can't you learn some manners? You've lived under this roof long enough!* But if God lost, Qiusheng's father would still get mad: *You fucking old idiot! I'm the best chess player for fifty kilometers. Beating you is easier than squishing a bedbug. You think I need you to let me win? You . . . to put it politely, you are* insulting *me!*

In any case, the final result was the same: the old man flipped the board and the pieces flew everywhere. Qiusheng's father was infamous for his bad temper, and now he'd finally found a punching bag in God.

But the old man didn't hold a grudge. Every time God picked up the board and put the pieces back quietly, he sat down and played with God again – and the whole process was repeated. After a few cycles of this both of them were tired and it was almost noon.

God then got up to wash the vegetables. Yulian didn't allow him to cook because she said God was a terrible cook. But he still had to wash the vegetables. Later, when Qiusheng and Yulian returned from the fields, if the vegetables hadn't been washed she would be on him again with another round of bitter, sarcastic scolding.

While God washed the vegetables, Qiusheng's father left to visit the neighbors. This was the most peaceful part of God's day. The noon sun filled every crack in the brick-lined yard and illuminated the deep crevasses in his memory. During such periods God often forgot his work and stood quietly, lost in thought. Only when the noise of the villagers returning from the fields filled the air would he be startled awake and hurry to finish his washing.

He sighed. *How could life have turned out like this?*

This wasn't only God's sigh. It was also the sigh of Qiusheng, Yulian and Qiusheng's father. It was the sigh of more than five billion people and two billion Gods on Earth.

2

It all began one fall evening three years ago.

'Come quickly! There are toys in the sky!' Bingbing shouted in the yard. Qiusheng and Yulian raced out of the house, looked up and saw that the sky really was filled with toys, or at least objects whose shapes could only be those of toys.

The objects spread out evenly across the dome of the sky. In the dusk, each reflected the light of the setting sun – already below the horizon – and each shone as brightly as the full Moon. The light turned Earth's surface as bright as it is at noon. But the light came from every direction and left no shadow, as though the whole world was illuminated by a giant surgical lamp.

At first, everyone thought the objects were within our atmosphere because they were so clear. But eventually, humans learned that these objects were just enormous. They were hovering about thirty thousand kilometers away in geostationary orbits.

There were a total of 21,530 spaceships. Spread out evenly across the sky, they formed a thin shell around Earth. This was the result of a complex set of maneuvers that brought all the ships to their final locations simultaneously. In this manner, the alien ships avoided causing life-threatening tides in the oceans due to their imbalanced masses. The gesture reassured humans somewhat, as it was at least some evidence that the aliens did not bear ill will toward Earth.

During the next few days, all attempts at communicating with the aliens failed. The aliens maintained absolute silence in the face of repeated queries. At the same time, Earth became a nightless planet. Tens of thousands of spaceships reflected so much sunlight onto the night side of Earth that it was as bright as day, while on the day side the ships cast giant shadows onto the ground. The horrible sight pushed the psychological endurance of the human race to the limit so that most ignored yet another strange occurrence on the surface of the planet and did not connect it with the fleet of spaceships in the sky.

Across the great cities of the world, wandering old people had begun to appear. All of them had the same features: extreme old age, long white hair and beards, long white robes. At first, before their white robes, white beards, and white hair got dirty, they looked like a bunch of snowmen. The wanderers did not appear to belong to any particular race, as though all ethnicities were mixed in them. They had no documents to prove their citizenship or identity and could not explain their own histories.

All they could do was to gently repeat, in heavily accented versions of various local languages, the same words to all passersby:

'We are God. Please, considering that we created this world, would you give us a bit of food?'

If only one or two old wanderers had said this, then they would have been sent to a shelter or nursing home, like the homeless with dementia. But millions of old men and women all saying the same thing – that was an entirely different matter.

Within a fortnight, the number of old wanderers had increased to more than thirty million. All over the streets of New York, Beijing, London, Moscow . . . these old people could be seen everywhere, shuffling around in traffic-stopping crowds. Sometimes it seemed as if there were more of *them* than the original inhabitants of the cities.

The most horrible part of their presence was that they all repeated the same thing: 'We are God. Please, considering that we created this world, would you give us a bit of food?'

Only now did humans turn their attention from the spaceships to the uninvited guests. Recently, large-scale meteor showers had been occurring over every continent. After every impressive display of streaking meteors, the number of old wanderers in the corresponding region greatly increased. After careful observation, the following incredible fact was discovered: the old wanderers came out of the sky, from those alien spaceships.

One by one, they leaped into the atmosphere as though diving into a swimming pool, each wearing a suit made from a special film. As the friction from the atmosphere burned away the surface of the suits, the film kept the heat away from the wearer and slowed their descent. Careful design ensured that the deceleration never exceeded 4g, well within the physical tolerance of the bodies of the old wanderers. Finally, at the moment of their arrival at the surface their velocity was close to zero, as though they had just jumped down from a bench. Even so, many of them still managed to sprain their ankles. Simultaneously, the film around them had been completely burned away, leaving no trace.

The meteor showers continued without stopping. More wanderers fell to Earth, and their number rose to almost one hundred million.

The governments of every country attempted to find one or more representatives among the wanderers. But the wanderers claimed that the 'Gods' were absolutely equal and that any one of them could represent all of them. Thus, at the emergency session of the United Nations General Assembly, one random old wanderer, who was found in Times Square and who now spoke passable English, entered the General Assembly Hall.

He was clearly among the earliest to land: his robe was dirty and full of holes, and his white beard was covered with dirt like a mop. There was no halo over his head, but a few loyal flies did hover there. With the help of a ratty bamboo walking stick, he shuffled his way to the round meeting table and lowered himself under the gaze of the leaders. He looked up at the Secretary-General, and his face displayed the childlike smile common to all the old wanderers.

'I . . . ha – . . . I haven't had breakfast yet.'

So breakfast was brought. All across the world, people stared as he ate like a starved man, choking a few times. Toast, sausages and a salad were quickly ingested, followed by a large glass of milk. Then he showed his innocent smile to the Secretary-General again.

'Haha . . . uh . . . is there any wine? Just a tiny cup will do.'

So a glass of wine was brought. He sipped at it, nodding with satisfaction. 'Last night, a bunch of new arrivals took over my favorite subway grille, one that blew out warm air. I had to find a new place to sleep in the Square. But now, with a bit of wine, my joints are coming back to life. . . . You, can you massage my back a little? Just a little.'

The Secretary-General began to massage his back. The old wanderer shook his head, sighed and said, 'Sorry to be so much trouble to you.'

'Where are you from?' asked the delegate from of the United States.

The old wanderer shook his head. 'A civilization only has a fixed location in her infancy. Planets and stars are unstable and change. Civilizations must then move. By the time she becomes a young woman, she has already moved multiple times. Then the civilizations will make this discovery: no planetary environment is as stable as a sealed spaceship. So they'll make spaceships their home, and planets will just be places where they sojourn. Thus, any civilization that has reached adulthood will be a starfaring civilization, permanently wandering through the cosmos. The spaceship is her home. Where are we from? We come from the ships.' He pointed up with a finger caked in dirt.

'How many of you are there?'

'Two billion.'

'Who are you really?' The Secretary-General had cause to ask this. The old wanderers looked just like humans.

'We've told you many times.' The old wanderer waved his hand impatiently. 'We are God.'

'Could you explain?'

'Our civilization – let's just call her the God Civilization – had existed long before Earth was born. When the God Civilization entered her senescence we seeded the newly formed Earth with the beginnings of life. Then the God Civilization skipped across time by traveling close to the speed of light. When life on Earth had evolved to the appropriate stage, we came back, introduced a new species based on our ancestral genes, eliminated its enemies and carefully guided its evolution until Earth was home to a new civilized species just like us.'

'How do you expect us to believe you?'

'That's easy.'

Thus began the half-year-long effort to verify these claims. Humans watched in astonishment as spaceships sent the original plans for life on Earth and images of the primitive Earth. Following the old wanderer's direction, humans dug up incredible machines from deep below Earth's crust – equipment that had through the long eons monitored and manipulated the biosphere on this planet.

Humans finally had to believe. At least with respect to life on Earth, the Gods really were God.

3

At the emergency session of the United Nations General Assembly, the Secretary-General, on behalf of the human race, finally asked God the key question: why did they come to Earth?

'Before I answer this question, you must have a proper understanding of the concept of "civilization".' God stroked his long beard. This was the same God who had been at the first emergency session half a year before. 'How do you think civilizations evolve over time?'

'Civilization on Earth is currently in a stage of rapid development. If we're not hit by natural disasters beyond our ability to withstand, I think we will continue our development indefinitely,' said the Secretary-General.

'Wrong. Think about it: every person experiences childhood, youth, middle age and old age, finally arriving at death. The stars are the same way. Indeed, everything in the universe goes through the same process. Even the universe itself will have to terminate one day. Why would civilization be an exception? No, a civilization will also grow old and die.'

'How exactly does that happen?'

'Different civilizations grow old and die in different ways, just like different people die of different diseases or of just plain old age. For the God Civilization, the first sign of her senescence was the extreme lengthening of each individual member's life span. By then, each individual in the God Civilization could expect a life as long as four thousand Earth years. By age two thousand, their thoughts had completely ossified, losing all creativity. Because individuals like these held the reins of power, new life had a hard time emerging and growing. That was when our civilization became old.'

'And then?'

'The second sign of the civilization's senescence was the Age of the Machine Cradle.'

'What?'

'By then our machines no longer relied on their creators. They operated independently, maintained themselves and developed on their own. The smart machines gave us everything we needed: not just material needs but also psychological ones. We didn't need to put any effort into survival. Taken care of by machines, we lived as though we were lying in comfortable cradles.

'Think about it: if the jungles of primitive Earth had been filled with inexhaustible supplies of fruits and tame creatures that desired to become food, how could apes evolve into humans? The Machine Cradle was just such a comfort-filled jungle. Gradually we forgot about our technology and science. Our civilization became lazy and empty, devoid of creativity and ambition, and that only sped up the aging process. What you see now is the God Civilization in her final dying gasps.'

'Then . . . can you now tell us the goal for the God Civilization in coming to Earth?'

'We have no home now.'

'But . . .' The Secretary-General pointed upward.

'The spaceships are old. It's true that the artificial environment on the ships is more stable than any natural environment, including Earth's. But the ships are so old, old beyond your imagination. Old components have broken down. Accumulated quantum effects over the eons have led to more and more software errors. The system's self-repair and self-maintenance functions have encountered more and more insurmountable obstacles. The living environment on the ships is deteriorating. The number of life necessities that can be distributed to individuals is decreasing by the day. We can just about survive. In the twenty thousand cities on the various ships, the air is filled with pollution and despair.'

'Are there no solutions? Perhaps new components for the ships? A software upgrade?'

God shook his head. 'The God Civilization is in her final years. We are two billion dying men and women, each more than three thousand years old. But before us, hundreds of generations had already lived in the comfort of the Machine Cradle. Long ago, we forgot all our technology. Now we have no way to repair these ships that have been operating for tens of millions of years on their own. Indeed, in terms of the ability to study and understand technology, we are even worse than you. We can't even connect a circuit for a lightbulb or solve a quadratic equation . . .

'One day, the ships told us that they were close to complete breakdown. The propulsion systems could no longer push the ships near the speed of light. The God Civilization could only drift along at a speed not even one-tenth the speed of light, and the ecological support systems were nearing collapse. The machines could no longer keep two billion of us alive. We had to find another way out.'

'Did you ever think that this would happen?'

'Of course. Two thousand years ago, the ships already warned us. That was when we began the process of seeding life on Earth so that in our old age we would have support.'

'Two thousand years ago?'

'Yes. Of course I'm talking about time on the ships. From your frame of reference, that was 3.5 billion years ago, when Earth first cooled down.'

'We have a question: you say that you've lost your technology. But doesn't seeding life require technology?'

'Oh. To start the process of evolving life on a planet is a minor operation. Just scatter some seeds, and life will multiply and evolve on its own. We had this kind of software even before the Age of the Machine Cradle. Just start the program, and the machines can finish everything. To create a planet full of life, capable of developing civilization, the most basic requirement is time – a few billion years of time.

'By traveling close to the speed of light, we possess almost limitless time. But now, the God Civilization's ships can no longer approach the speed of light. Otherwise we'd still have the chance to create new civilizations and more life, and we would have more choices. We're trapped by slowness. Those dreams cannot be realized.'

'So you want to spend your golden years on Earth.'

'Yes, yes. We hope that you will feel a sense of filial duty toward your creators and take us in.' God leaned on his walking stick and trembled as he tried to bow to the leaders of all the nations. As he did so, he almost fell on his face.

'But how do you plan to live here?'

'If we just gathered in one place by ourselves, then we might as well stay in space and die there. We'd like to be absorbed into your societies, your families. When the God Civilization was still in her childhood, we also had families. You know that childhood is the most precious time. Since your civilization is still in her childhood, if we can return to this era and spend the rest of our lives in the warmth of families then that would be our greatest happiness.'

'There are two billion of you. That means every family on Earth would have to take in one or two of you.' After the Secretary-General spoke, the meeting hall sank into silence.

'Yes, yes, sorry to give you so much trouble . . .' God continued to bow while stealing glances at the Secretary-General and the leaders of all the nations. 'Of course, we're willing to compensate you.'

He waved his cane and two more white-bearded Gods walked into the meeting hall, struggling under the weight of a silvery, metallic trunk they carried between them. 'Look: these are high-density information storage devices. They systematically store the knowledge that the God Civilization has acquired in every field of science and technology. With this, your civilization will advance by leaps and bounds. I think you will like this.'

The Secretary-General, along with the leaders of all the nations, looked at the metal trunk and tried to hide his elation. 'Taking care of God is the responsibility of humankind. Of course this will require some consultation between the various nations, but I think in principle . . .'

'Sorry to be so much trouble. Sorry to be so much trouble . . .' God's eyes filled with tears, and he continued to bow.

After the Secretary-General and the leaders of all the nations left the meeting hall, they saw that tens of thousands of Gods had gathered outside the United Nations building. A white sea of bobbing heads filled the air with murmuring words. The Secretary-General listened carefully and realized that they were all speaking, in the various tongues of Earth, the same sentence:

'Sorry to be so much trouble. Sorry to be so much trouble . . .'

4

Two billion Gods arrived on Earth. Enclosed in suits made of their special film, they fell through the atmosphere. During that time, one could see the bright, colorful streaks in the sky even during the day. After the Gods landed, they spread out into 1.5 billion families.

Having received the Gods' knowledge about science and technology, everyone was filled with hopes and dreams for the future, as though humankind was about to step into paradise overnight. Under the influence of such joy, every family welcomed the coming of God.

That morning, Qiusheng and his family and all the other villagers stood at the village entrance to receive the Gods allocated to Xicen.

'What a beautiful day,' Yulian said.

Her comment wasn't motivated solely by her feelings. The spaceships had disappeared overnight, restoring the sky's wide open and limitless appearance. Humans had never been allowed to step onto any of the ships. The Gods did not really object to that particular request from the humans, but the ships themselves refused to grant permission. They did not acknowledge the various primitive probes that humans sent, and they sealed their doors tightly. After the final group of Gods leaped into the atmosphere, all the spaceships, numbering more than twenty thousand, departed their orbit simultaneously. But they didn't go far, only drifting in the Asteroid belt.

Although these ships were ancient, the old routines continued to function. Their only mission was to serve the Gods. Thus, they would not move too far away. When the Gods needed them again, they would come.

Two buses arrived from the county seat, bringing the 106 Gods allocated to Xicen. Qiusheng and Yulian met the God assigned to their family. The couple stood on each side of God, affectionately supported him by the arms and walked home in the bright afternoon sun. Bingbing and Qiusheng's father followed behind, smiling.

'Gramps ... um ... Gramps God?' Yulian leaned her face against God's shoulder, her smile as bright as the sun. 'I hear that the technology you gave us will soon allow us to experience true Communism! When that happens, we'll all have things according to our needs. Things won't cost any money. You just go to the store and pick them up.'

God smiled and nodded at her, his white hair bobbing. He spoke in heavily accented Chinese. 'Yes. Actually, 'to each according to their needs' fulfills only the most basic needs of a civilization. The technology we gave you will bring you a life of prosperity and comfort surpassing your imagination.'

Yulian laughed so much her face opened up like a flower. 'No, no! 'To each according to their needs' is more than enough for me!'

'Uh-huh,' Qiusheng's father agreed emphatically.

'Can we live forever without aging like you?' Qiusheng asked.

'We can't live forever without aging. It's just that we can live longer than you. Look at how old I am! In my view, if a man lives longer than three thousand years, he might as well be dead. For a civilization, extreme longevity for the individual can be fatal.'

'Oh, I don't need three thousand years. Just three hundred.' Qiusheng's father was now laughing as much as Yulian. 'In that case, I'd still be considered a young man right now. Maybe I can ... hahahaha.'

The village treated the day like it was Chinese New Year. Every family held a big banquet to welcome its God, and Qiusheng's family was no exception.

Qiusheng's father quickly became slightly drunk on cups of vintage *huangjiu*. He gave God a thumbs-up. 'You're really something! To be able to create so many living things – you're truly supernatural.'

God drank a lot, too, but his head was still clear. He waved his hand. 'No, not supernatural. It was just science. When biology has developed to a certain level, creating life is akin to building machines.'

'You say that. But in our eyes, you're no different from immortals who have deigned to live among us.'

God shook his head. 'Supernatural beings would never make mistakes. But for us, we made mistake after mistake during your creation.'

'You made mistakes when you created us?' Yulian's eyes were wide open. In her imagination, creating all those lives was a process similar to her giving birth to Bingbing eight years before. No mistake was possible.

'There were many. I'll give a relatively recent example. The world-creation software made errors in the analysis of the environment on Earth, which resulted in the appearance of creatures like dinosaurs: huge bodies and low adaptability. Eventually, in order to facilitate your evolution, they had to be eliminated.

'In terms of events that are even more recent, after the disappearance of the ancient Aegean civilizations the world-creation software believed that civilization on Earth was successfully established. It ceased to perform further monitoring and microadjustments, like leaving a wound-up clock to run on its own. This resulted in further errors. For example, it should have allowed the civilization of ancient Greece to develop on her own and stopped the Macedonian conquest and the subsequent Roman conquest. Although both of these ended up as the inheritors of Greek civilization, the direction of Greek development was altered . . .'

No one in Qiusheng's family could understand this lecture, but all listened respectfully.

'And then two great powers appeared on Earth: Han China and the Roman Empire. In contrast to the earlier situation with ancient Greece, the two shouldn't have been kept apart and left to develop in isolation. They ought to have been allowed to come into full contact—'

'This 'Han China' you're talking about? Is that the Han Dynasty of Liu Bang and Xiang Yu?' Finally Qiusheng's father heard something he knew. 'And what is this "Roman Empire"?'

'I think that was a foreigners' country at the time,' Qiusheng said, trying to explain. 'It was pretty big.'

Qiusheng's father was confused. 'Why? When the foreigners finally showed up during the Qing Dynasty, look how badly they beat us up. You want them to show up even earlier? During the Han Dynasty?'

God laughed at this. 'No, no. Back then, Han China was just as powerful as the Roman Empire.'

'That's still bad. If those two great powers had met, it would have been a great war. Blood would have flowed like a river.'

God nodded. He reached out with his chopsticks for a piece of beef braised in soy sauce. 'Could have been. But if those two great civilizations, the Occident and the Orient, had met, the encounter would have generated glorious sparks and greatly advanced human progress. . . . Eh, if those errors could have been avoided, Earth would now probably be colonizing Mars and your interstellar probes would have flown past Sirius.'

Qiusheng's father raised his bowl of *huangjiu* and spoke admiringly. 'Everyone says that the Gods have forgotten science in their cradle, but you are still so learned.'

'To be comfortable in the cradle it's important to know a bit about philosophy, art, history and so on – just some common facts, not real learning. Many scholars on Earth right now have much deeper thoughts than our own.'

For the Gods, the first few months after they entered human society were a golden age in which they lived very harmoniously with human families. It was as though they had returned to the childhood of the God Civilization, fully immersed in the long-forgotten warmth of family life. This seemed the best way to spend the final years of their extremely long lives.

Qiusheng's family's God enjoyed the peaceful life in this beautiful southern Chinese village. Every day he went to the pond surrounded by bamboo groves to fish, chat with other old folks from the village, play chess and generally enjoy himself. But his greatest hobby was attending folk operas. Whenever a theatre troupe came to the village or the town he made sure to go to every performance.

His favorite opera was *The Butterfly Lovers*. One performance was not enough. He followed one troupe around for more than fifty kilometers and attended several shows in a row. Finally Qiusheng went to town and bought him a VCD of the opera. God played it over and over until he could hum a few lines of the *Huangmei* opera and sounded pretty good.

One day Yulian discovered a secret. She whispered to Qiusheng and her father-in-law, 'Did you know that every time Gramps God finishes his opera he always takes a little card out from his pocket? And while looking at the card, he hums lines from the opera. Just now I stole a glance. The card is a photo. There's a really pretty young woman on it.'

That evening, God played *The Butterfly Lovers* again. He took out the photograph of the pretty young woman and started to hum. Qiusheng's father quietly moved in. 'Gramps God, is that your . . . girlfriend from a long time ago?'

God was startled. He hid the photograph quickly and smiled like a kid at Qiusheng's father. 'Haha. Yeah, yeah. I loved her two thousand years ago.'

Yulian, who was eavesdropping, grimaced. *Two thousand years ago!* Considering his advanced age, this was a bit gag-inducing.

Qiusheng's father wanted to look at the photograph. But God was so protective of it that it would have been embarrassing to ask. So Qiusheng's father settled for listening to God reminisce.

'Back then we were all so young. She was one of the very few who wasn't completely absorbed by life in the Machine Cradle. She initiated a great voyage of exploration to sail to the end of the universe. Oh, you don't need to think too hard about that. It's very difficult to understand. Anyway, she hoped to use this voyage as an opportunity to awaken the God Civilization, sleeping so soundly in the Machine Cradle. Of course, that was nothing more than a beautiful dream. She wanted me to go with her, but I didn't have the courage. The endless desert of the universe frightened me. It would have been a journey of more than twenty billion light-years. So she went by herself. But in the two thousand years after that, I never stopped longing for her.'

'Twenty billion light-years? So like you explained to me before, that's the distance that light would travel in twenty billion years? Oh my! That's way too far. That's basically good-bye for life. Gramps God, you have to forget about her. You'll never see her again.'

God nodded and sighed.

'Well, isn't she now about your age, too?'

God was startled out of his reverie. He shook his head. 'Oh, no. For such a long voyage, her explorer ship would have to fly at close to the speed of light. That means she would still be very young. The only one that has grown old is me. You don't understand how large the universe is. What you think of as 'eternity' is nothing but a grain of sand in space-time.

'Well, the fact that you can't understand and feel this is sometimes a blessing.'

5

The honeymoon phase between the Gods and humans quickly ended.

People were initially ecstatic over the scientific material received from the Gods, thinking that it would allow mankind to realize its dreams overnight. Thanks to the interface equipment provided by the Gods, an enormous quantity of information was retrieved successfully from the storage devices. The information was translated into English, and in order to avoid disputes a copy was distributed to every nation in the world.

But people soon discovered that utilizing these God-given technologies was impossible, at least within the current century. Consider the futility of a time traveler providing information on modern technology to the ancient Egyptians, and you will have some understanding of the hopeless situation these humans faced.

As the exhaustion of petroleum supplies loomed, energy technology was at the forefront of everyone's minds. But scientists and engineers discovered that the God Civilization's energy technology was useless for humans at this time. The Gods' energy source was built upon the basis of matter–antimatter annihilation. Even if people could understand the materials and finally create an annihilation engine and generator – a near-impossible task within this generation – it would still have been for naught. This was because the fuel for these engines, antimatter, had to be mined from deep space. According to the material provided by the Gods, the closest antimatter ore source was between the Milky Way and the Andromeda Galaxy, about 550,000 light-years away.

The technology for interstellar travel at near light-speed also involved every field of scientific knowledge, and the greater part of the theories and techniques revealed by the Gods were beyond human comprehension. Just grasping a basic understanding of the foundations would require human scholars to work for perhaps half a century. Scientists, initially full of hope, had tried to search the material from the Gods for technical information concerning controlled nuclear fission, but there was nothing. This was easy to understand: our current literature on energy science contained no information on how to make fire from sticks.

In other scientific fields, such as information science and life sciences (including the secret of human longevity), the problem was the same. Even the most advanced scholars could make no sense of the Gods' knowledge. Between the Gods' science and human science there was a great abyss of understanding that could not be bridged.

The Gods who arrived on Earth could not help the scientists in any way. Like the God at the United Nations had said, among the Gods now there were few who could even solve quadratic equations. The spaceships adrift among the asteroids also ignored all hails from the humans. The human race was like a group of new elementary school students who were suddenly required to master PhD material with no instructor.

At the same time, Earth's population had suddenly grown by two billion. These were all extremely aged individuals who could not be productive. Most of them were plagued by various diseases and put unprecedented pressure on human society. As a result, every government had to pay each family living with a God a considerable support stipend. Health care and other public services were strained beyond the breaking point. The world economy was pushed to the edge of collapse.

The harmonious relationship between God and Qiusheng's family was gone. Gradually the family began to see him as a burden that fell from the sky. They began to despise him, but each had a different reason.

Yulian's reason was the most practical and closest to the underlying problem: God made her family poor. Among all the members of the family God also worried the most about her; she had a tongue as sharp as a knife, and she scared him more than black holes and supernovas. After the death of her dream of true Communism, she unceasingly nagged God: *Before you came, our family had lived so prosperously and comfortably. Back then everything was good. Now everything is bad. All because of you. Being saddled with an old fool like you was such a great misfortune*. Every day, whenever she had the chance, she would prattle on like this in front of God.

God also suffered from chronic bronchitis. This was not a very expensive disease to treat, but it did require ongoing care and a constant outlay of money. Finally one day Yulian forbade Qiusheng from taking God to the town hospital to see doctors and stopped buying medicine for him. When the secretary of the village branch of the Communist Party found out, he came to Qiusheng's house.

'You have to pay for the care of your family God,' the secretary said to Yulian. 'The doctor at the town hospital already told me that if left untreated his chronic bronchitis might develop into pulmonary emphysema.'

'If you want him treated, then the village or the government can pay for it,' Yulian shouted at the secretary. 'We're not made of money!'

'Yulian, according to the God Support Law the family has to bear these kinds of minor medical expenses. The government's support fee already includes this component.'

'That minuscule support fee is useless!'

'You can't talk like that. After you began getting the support fee, you bought a milk cow, switched to liquefied petroleum gas and bought a big, new color TV! You're telling me now that you don't have money for God to see a doctor? Everyone knows that in your family your word is law. I'm going to make it clear to you: right now I'm helping you save face, but don't push your luck. Next time, it won't be me standing here trying to persuade you. It will be the County God Support Committee. You'll be in real trouble then.'

Yulian had no choice but to resume paying for God's medical care. But after that she became even meaner to him.

One time, God said to Yulian, 'Don't be so anxious. Humans are very smart and learn fast. In only another century or so the easiest aspects of the Gods' knowledge will become applicable to human society. Then your life will become better.'

'Damn. *A whole century.* And you say 'only'. Are you even listening to yourself?' Yulian was washing the dishes and didn't even bother looking back at God.

'That's a very short period of time.'

'For you! You think we can live as long as you? In another century you won't even be able to find my bones! But I want to ask you a question: how much longer do you think *you'll* be living?'

'Oh, I'm like a candle in the wind. If I can live another three or four hundred years, I'll be very satisfied.'

Yulian dropped a whole stack of bowls on the ground. 'This is not how 'support' is supposed to work! Ah, so you think not only should I spend my entire life taking care of you, but you have to have my son, my grandson, my family for ten generations and more!? Why won't you die?'

As for Qiusheng's father, he thought God was a fraud, and in fact, this view was pretty common. Since scientists couldn't understand the Gods' scientific papers, there was no way to prove their authenticity. Maybe the Gods were playing a giant trick on the human race. For Qiusheng's father, there was ample evidence to support this view.

'You old swindler, you're way too outrageous,' he said to God one day. 'I'm too lazy to expose you. Your tricks are not worth my trouble. Heck, they're not even worth my grandson's trouble.'

God asked him what he had discovered.

'I'll start with the simplest thing: our scientists know that humans evolved from monkeys, right?'

God nodded. 'More accurately, you evolved from primitive apes.'

'Then how can you say that you created us? If you were interested in creating humans, why not directly make us in our current form? Why bother first creating primitive apes and then go through the trouble of evolving? It makes no sense.'

'A human begins as a baby, and then grows into an adult. A civilization also has to grow from a less evolved state. The long path of experience cannot be avoided. Actually, humans began with the introduction of a much more primitive species. Even apes were already very evolved.'

'I don't believe these made-up reasons. All right, here's something more obvious. This was actually first noticed by my grandson. Our scientists say that there was life on Earth even three billion years ago. Do you admit this?'

God nodded. 'That estimate is basically right.'

'So you're three billion years old?'

'In terms of your frame of reference, yes. But according to the frame of reference of our ships, I'm only 3,500 years old. The ships flew close to the speed of light, and time passed much more slowly for us than for you. Of course, once in a while a few ships dropped down and decelerated enough to come to Earth so that further adjustments could be made to the evolution of life on Earth. But this didn't require much time. Those ships would then return to cruise at close to the speed of light and continue skipping over the passage of time here.'

'Bullshit,' Qiusheng's father said contemptuously.

'Dad, this is the Theory of Relativity,' Qiusheng interrupted. 'Our scientists already proved it.'

'Relativity, my ass! You're bullshitting me, too. That's impossible! How can time be like sesame oil, flowing at different speeds? I'm not so old that I've lost my mind. But you – reading all those books has made you stupid!'

'I can prove to you that time does indeed flow at different rates,' God said, his face full of mystery. He took out that photograph of his beloved from two thousand years ago and handed it to Qiusheng. 'Look at her carefully and memorize every detail.'

The second Qiusheng looked at the photograph, he knew that he would be able to remember every detail. It would be impossible to forget. Like the other Gods, the woman in the picture had a blend of the features of all ethnicities. Her skin was like warm ivory, her two eyes were so alive that they seemed to sing and she immediately captivated Qiusheng's soul. She was a woman among Gods, the God of women. The beauty of the Gods was like a second sun. Humans had never seen it and could not bear it.

'Look at you! You're practically drooling!' Yulian grabbed the photograph from the frozen Qiusheng. But before she could look at it, her father-in-law took it away from her.

'Let me see,' Qiusheng's father said. He brought the photograph as close as possible to his ancient eyes. For a long time he did not move, as though the photograph provided sustenance.

'Why are you looking so closely?' Yulian said, her tone contemptuous.

'Shut it. I don't have my glasses,' Qiusheng's father said, his face still pressed against the photograph.

Yulian looked at her father-in-law disdainfully for a few seconds, curled her lips and left for the kitchen.

God took the photograph out of the hands of Qiusheng's father, whose hands lingered on the photo for a long while, unwilling to let go. God said, 'Remember all the details. I'll let you look at it again this time tomorrow.'

The next day, father and son said little to each other. Both were thinking about the young woman, leaving them nothing to say. Yulian's temper was far worse than usual.

Finally the time came. God had seemingly forgotten about it and had to be reminded by Qiusheng's father. He took out the photograph that the two men had been thinking about all day and handed it first to Qiusheng. 'Look carefully. Do you see any change in her?'

'Nothing really,' Qiusheng said, looking intently. After a while, he finally noticed something. 'Aha! The opening between her lips seems slightly narrower. Not much, just a little bit. Look at the corner of the mouth here . . .'

'Have you no shame? To look at some other woman that closely?' Yulian grabbed the photo again, and again her father-in-law took it away from her.

'Let me see . . .' Qiusheng's father put on his glasses and carefully examined the picture. 'Yes, indeed, the opening is narrower. But there's a much more obvious change that you didn't notice. Look at this wisp of hair. Compared to yesterday, it has drifted farther to the right.'

God took the picture from Qiusheng's father. 'This is not a photograph but a television receiver.'

'A . . . TV?'

'Yes. Right now it's receiving a live feed from that explorer spaceship heading for the end of the universe.'

'Live? Like live broadcasts of football matches?'

'Yes.'

'So . . . the woman in the picture, she's alive!' Qiusheng was so shocked that his mouth hung open. Even Yulian's eyes were now as big as walnuts.

'Yes, she's alive. But unlike a live broadcast on Earth, this feed is subject to a delay. The explorer spaceship is now about eighty million light-years away, so the delay is about eighty million years. What we see now is how she was eighty million years ago.'

'This tiny thing can receive a signal from that far away?'

'This kind of super-long-distance communication across space requires the use of neutrinos or gravitational waves. Our spaceships can receive the signal, magnify it and then re-broadcast to this TV.'

'Treasure, a real treasure!' Qiusheng's father praised sincerely. But it was unclear whether he was talking about the tiny TV or the young woman on the TV. Either way, after hearing that she was still 'alive', Qiusheng and his father both felt a deeper attachment to her. Qiusheng tried to take the tiny TV again, but God refused.

'Why does she move so slowly in the picture?'

'That's the result of time flowing at different speeds. From our frame of reference, time flows extremely slowly on a spaceship flying close to the speed of light.'

'Then . . . can she still talk to you?' Yulian asked.

God nodded. He flipped a switch behind the TV. Immediately a sound came out of it. It was a woman's voice, but the sound was unchanging, like a singer holding a note steadily at the end of a song. God stared at the screen, his eyes full of love.

'She's talking right now. She's finishing three words: 'I love you.' Each word took more than a year. It's now been three and a half years, and right now she's just finishing 'you'. To completely finish the sentence will take another three months.' God lifted his eyes from the TV to the domed sky above the yard. 'She still has more to say. I'll spend the rest of my life listening to her.'

Bingbing actually managed to maintain a decent relationship with God for a while. The Gods all had some childishness to them, and they enjoyed talking and playing with children. But one day, Bingbing wanted God to give him the large watch he wore and God steadfastly refused. He explained that the watch was a tool for communicating with the God Civilization. Without it, he would no longer be able to connect with his own people.

'Hmm, look at this. You're still thinking about your own civilization and race. You've never thought of us as your real family!' Yulian said angrily.

After that, Bingbing was no longer nice to God. Instead, he often played practical tricks on him.

*

The only one in the family who still had respect and feelings of filial piety toward God was Qiusheng. Qiusheng had graduated from high school and liked to read. Other than a few people who passed the college-entrance examination and went away for college, he was the most learned person in the village. But at home, Qiusheng had no power. On practically everything he listened to the direction of his wife and followed the commands of his father. If his wife and father had ever conflicting instructions, then all he could do was sit in a corner and cry. Given that he was such a softy, he had no way to protect God at home.

6

The relationship between the Gods and humans had finally deteriorated beyond repair.

The complete breakdown between God and Qiusheng's family occurred after the incident involving instant noodles. One day, before lunch, Yulian came out of the kitchen with a paper box and asked why half the box of instant noodles she had bought yesterday had already disappeared.

'I took them,' God said in a small voice. 'I gave them to those living by the river. They've almost run out of things to eat.'

He was talking about the place where the Gods who had left their families were gathering. Recently there had been frequent incidents of abuse of the Gods in the village. One particularly cruel couple had been beating and cursing out their God, and they even withheld food from him. Eventually that God tried to commit suicide in the river that ran in front of the village, but luckily others were able to stop him.

This incident received a great deal of publicity. It went beyond the county, and the city's police eventually came, along with a bunch of reporters from CCTV and the provincial TV station, and took the couple away in handcuffs. According to the God Support Law, they had committed God abuse and would be sentenced to at least ten years in jail. This was the only law that was universal among all the nations of the world, with uniform prison terms.

After that, the families in the village became more careful and stopped treating the Gods too poorly in front of other people. But at the same time, the incident worsened the relationship between the Gods and the villagers. Eventually, some of the Gods left their families, and other Gods followed. By now almost one-third of the Gods in Xicen had already left their assigned families. These wandering Gods set up camp in the field across the river and lived a spartan, difficult life.

In other parts of the country and across the world, the situation was the same. Once again, the streets of big cities were filled with crowds of wandering, homeless Gods. The number quickly increased, a seeming repeat of the nightmare three years prior. The world, full of Gods and people, faced a gigantic crisis.

'Ha, you're very generous, you old fool! How dare you eat our food while giving it away?' Yulian began to curse loudly.

Qiusheng's father slammed the table and got up. 'You idiot! Get out of here! You like those Gods by the river? Why don't you go and join them?'

God sat silently for a while, thinking. Then he stood up, went to his tiny room and packed up his few belongings. Leaning on his bamboo cane, he slowly made his way out the door, heading in the direction of the river.

Qiusheng didn't eat with the rest of his family. He squatted in a corner with his head lowered and not speaking.

'Hey, dummy! Come here and eat. We have to go into town to buy feed this afternoon,' Yulian shouted at him. Since he refused to budge, she went over to yank his ear.

'Let go,' Qiusheng said. His voice was not loud, but Yulian let him go as though she had been shocked. She had never seen her husband with such a gloomy expression on his face.

'Forget about him,' Qiusheng's father said carelessly. 'If he doesn't want to eat, then he's a fool.'

'Ha, you miss your God? Why don't you go join him and his friends in that field by the river, too?' Yulian poked a finger at Qiusheng's head.

Qiusheng stood up and went upstairs to his bedroom. Like God, he packed a few things into a bundle and put it in a duffel bag he had once used when he had gone to the city to work. With the bag on his back, he headed outside.

'Where are you going?' Yulian yelled. But Qiusheng ignored her. She yelled again, but now there was fear in her voice. 'How long are you going to be out?'

'I'm not coming back,' Qiusheng said without looking back.

'What? Come back here! Is your head filled with shit?' Qiusheng's father followed him out of the house. 'What's the matter with you? Even if you don't want your wife and kid, how dare you leave your father?'

Qiusheng stopped but still did not turn around. 'Why should I care about you?'

'How can you talk like that? I'm your father! I raised you! Your mother died early. You think it was easy to raise you and your sister? Have you lost your mind?'

Qiusheng finally turned back to look at his father. 'If you can kick the people who created our ancestors' ancestors' ancestors out of our house, then I don't think it's much of a sin for me not to support you in your old age.'

He left, and Yulian and his father stood there, dumbfounded.

Qiusheng went over the ancient arched stone bridge and walked toward the tents of the Gods. He saw that a few of the Gods had set up a pot to cook something in the grassy clearing strewn with golden leaves. Their white beards and the white steam coming out of the pot reflected the noon sunlight like a scene out of an ancient myth.

Qiusheng found his God and said resolutely, 'Gramps God, let's go.'

'I'm not going back to that house.'

'I'm not, either. Let's go together into town and stay with my sister for a while. Then I'll go into the city and find a job, and we'll rent a place together. I'll support you for the rest of my life.'

'You're a good kid,' God said, patting his shoulder lightly. 'But it's time for us to go.' He pointed to the watch on his wrist. Qiusheng now noticed that all the watches of all the Gods were blinking with red lights.

'Go? Where to?'

'Back to the ships,' God said, pointing at the sky. Qiusheng lifted his head and saw that two spaceships were already hovering in the sky, standing out starkly against the blue. One of them was closer, and its shape and outline loomed large. Behind it, another was much farther away and appeared smaller. But the most surprising sight was that the first spaceship had lowered a thread as thin as spider silk, extending from space down to Earth. As the spider silk slowly drifted, the bright sun glinted on different sections like lightning in the bright blue sky.

'A space elevator,' God explained. 'Already more than a hundred of these have been set up on every continent. We'll ride them back to the ships.' Later Qiusheng would learn that when a spaceship dropped down a space elevator from a geostationary orbit it needed a large mass on its other side, deep in space, to act as a counterweight. That was the purpose of the other ship he saw.

When Qiusheng's eyes adjusted to the brightness of the sky, he saw that there were many more silvery stars deep in the distance. Those stars were spread out very evenly, forming a huge matrix. Qiusheng understood that the twenty thousand ships of the God Civilization were coming back to Earth from the Asteroid belt.

7

Twenty thousand spaceships once again filled the sky above Earth. In the two months that followed, space capsules ascended and descended the various space elevators, taking away the two billion Gods who had briefly lived on Earth. The space capsules were silver spheres. From a distance, they looked like dewdrops hanging on spider threads.

The day that Xicen's Gods left, all the villagers showed up for the farewell. Everyone was affectionate toward the Gods, and it reminded everyone of the day a year earlier when the Gods first came to Xicen. It was as though all the abuse and disdain the Gods had received had nothing to do with the villagers.

Two big buses were parked at the entrance to the village, the same two buses that had brought the Gods there a year ago. More than a hundred Gods would now be taken to the nearest space elevator and ride up in space capsules. The silver thread that could be seen in the distance was in reality hundreds of kilometers away.

Qiusheng's whole family went to send off their God. No one said anything along the way. As they neared the village entrance, God stopped, leaned against his cane and bowed to the family. 'Please stop here. Thank you for taking care of me this year. Really, thank you. No matter where I will be in this universe, I will always remember your family.' Then he took off the large watch from his wrist and handed it to Bingbing. 'A gift.'

'But . . . how will you communicate with the other Gods in the future?' Bingbing asked.

'We'll all be on the spaceships. I have no more need for this,' God said, laughing.

'Gramps God,' Qiusheng's father said, his face sorrowful, 'your ships are all ancient. They won't last much longer. Where can you go then?'

God stroked his beard and said calmly, 'It doesn't matter. Space is limitless. Dying anywhere is the same.'

Yulian suddenly began to cry. 'Gramps God, I . . . I'm not a very nice person. I shouldn't have made you the target of all my complaints that I'd saved up my whole life. It's just as Qiusheng said: I've behaved as if I don't have a conscience . . .' She pushed a bamboo basket into God's hands. 'I boiled some eggs this morning. Please take them for your trip.'

God picked up the basket. 'Thank you.' Then he took out an egg, peeled it and began to eat, savoring the taste. Yellow flakes of egg yolk soon covered his white beard. He continued to talk as he ate. 'Actually, we came to Earth not only because we wanted to survive. Having already lived for two or three thousand years, what did we have to fear from death? We just wanted to be with you. We like and cherish your passion for life, your creativity, your imagination. These things have long disappeared from the God Civilization. We saw in you the childhood of our civilization. But we didn't realize we'd bring you so much trouble. We're really sorry.'

'Please stay, Gramps,' Bingbing said, crying. 'I'll be better in the future.'

God shook his head slowly. 'We're not leaving because of how you treated us. The fact that you took us in and allowed us to stay was enough. But one thing made us unable to stay any longer: in your eyes, the Gods are pathetic. You pity us. Oh, you *pity* us.'

God threw away the pieces of eggshell. He lifted his face, trailing a full head of white hair, and stared at the sky, as though through the blue he could see the bright sea of stars. 'How can the God Civilization be pitied by man? You have no idea what a great civilization she was. You do not know what majestic epics she created, or how many imposing deeds she accomplished.

'It was 1857, during the Milky Way Era, when astronomers discovered that a large number of stars was accelerating toward the center of the Milky Way. Once this flood of stars was consumed by the supermassive black hole found there, the resulting radiation would kill all life found in the galaxy.

'In response, our great ancestors built a nebula shield around the center of the galaxy with a diameter of ten thousand light-years so that life and civilization in the galaxy would continue. What a magnificent engineering project that was! It took us more than 1,400 years to complete . . .

'Immediately afterward, the Andromeda Galaxy and the Large Magellanic Cloud united in an invasion of our galaxy. The interstellar fleet of the God Civilization leaped across hundreds of thousands of light-years and intercepted the invaders at the gravitational balance point between Andromeda and the Milky Way. When the battle entered into its climax, large numbers of ships from both sides mixed together, forming a spiraling nebula the size of the solar system.

'During the final stages of the battle, the God Civilization made the bold decision to send all remaining warships and even the civilian fleet into the spiraling nebula. The great increase in mass caused gravity to exceed the centrifugal force, and this nebula, made of ships and people, collapsed under gravity and formed a star! Because the proportion of heavy elements in this star was so high, immediately after its birth the star went supernova and illuminated the deep darkness between Andromeda and the Milky Way! Our ancestors thus destroyed the invaders with their courage and self-sacrifice and left the Milky Way as a place where life could develop peacefully . . .

'Yes, now our civilization is old. But it is not our fault. No matter how hard one strives, a civilization must grow old one day. Everyone grows old, even you.

'We really do not need your pity.'

'Compared to you,' Qiusheng said, full of awe, 'the human race is really nothing.'

'Don't talk like that,' God said. 'Earth's civilization is still an infant. We hope you will grow up fast. We hope you will inherit and continue the glory of your creators.' God threw down his cane. He put his hands on the shoulders of Bingbing and Qiusheng. 'I have some final words for you.'

'We may not understand everything you have to say,' Qiusheng said, 'but please speak. We will listen.'

'First, you must get off this rock!' God spread out his arms toward space. His white robe danced in the fall wind like a sail.

'Where will we go?' Qiusheng's father asked in confusion.

'Begin by flying to the other planets in the solar system, then fly to other stars. Don't ask why, but use all your energy toward the goal of flying away, the farther the better. In that process, you will spend a lot of money, and many people will die, but you must get away from here. Any civilization that stays on her birth world is committing suicide! You must go into the universe and find new worlds and new homes, and spread your descendants across the galaxy like drops of spring rain.'

'We'll remember,' Qiusheng said, and he nodded, even though neither he nor the rest of his family really understood God's words.

'Good,' God sighed, satisfied. 'Next I will tell you a secret, a great secret.' He stared at everyone in the family with his blue eyes. His stare was like a cold wind and caused everyone's hearts to shudder. 'You have brothers.'

Qiusheng's family looked at God, utterly confused. But Qiusheng finally figured out what God meant. 'You're saying that you created other Earths?'

God nodded slowly. 'Yes, other Earths, other human civilizations. Other than you, there were three others. All are close to you, within two hundred light-years. You are Earth Number Four, the youngest.'

'Have you been to the other Earths?' Bingbing asked.

God nodded again. 'Before we came to you, we went first to the other three Earths and asked them to take us in. Earth Number One was the best among the bunch. After they obtained our scientific materials, they simply chased us away.

'Earth Number Two, on the other hand, kept one million of us as hostages and forced us to give them spaceships as ransom. After we gave them one thousand ships, they realized that they could not operate the ships. They then forced the hostages to teach them how, but the hostages didn't know how either, since the ships were autonomous. So they killed all the hostages.

'Earth Number Three took three million of us as hostages and demanded that we ram Earth Number One and Earth Number Two with several spaceships each because they were in a prolonged state of war with them. Of course, even a single hit from one of our antimatter-powered ships would destroy all life on a planet. We refused, and so they killed all the hostages.'

'Unfilial children!' Qiusheng's father shouted in anger. 'You should punish them!'

God shook his head. 'We will never attack civilizations we created. You are the best of the four brothers. That's why I'm telling you all this. Your three brothers are drawn to invasion. They do not know what love is or what morality is. Their capacity for cruelty and bloodlust are impossible for you to imagine.

'Indeed, in the beginning we created six Earths. The other two were in the same solar systems as Earth Number One and Earth Number Three, respectively. Both were destroyed by their brothers. The fact that the other three Earths haven't yet destroyed one another is only due to the great distances separating their solar systems. By now, all three know of the existence of Earth Number Four and possess your precise coordinates. Thus, you must go and destroy them first before they destroy you.'

'This is too frightening!' Yulian said.

'For now, it's not yet too frightening. Your three brothers are indeed more advanced than you, but they still cannot travel faster than one-tenth the speed of light and cannot cruise more than thirty light-years from home. This is a race of life and death to see which one among you can achieve near-light-speed space travel first. It is the only way to break through the prison of time and space. Whoever can achieve this technology first will survive. Anyone slower will meet certain death. This is the struggle for survival in the universe. Children, you don't have much time. Work hard!'

'Do the most learned and most powerful people in our world know these things?' Qiusheng's father asked, trembling.

'Yes. But don't rely on them. A civilization's survival depends on the effort of every individual. Even the common people like you have a role to play.'

'You hear that, Bingbing?' Qiusheng said to his son. 'You must study hard.'

'When you fly into the universe at close to the speed of light to resolve the threat of your siblings, you must perform another urgent task: find a few planets suitable for life and seed them with some simple, primitive life from here, like bacteria and algae. Let them evolve on their own.'

Qiusheng wanted to ask more questions, but God picked up his cane and began to walk. The family accompanied him toward the bus. The other Gods were already aboard.

'Oh, Qiusheng.' God stopped, remembering. 'I took a few of your books with me. I hope you don't mind.' He opened his bundle to show Qiusheng. 'These are your high school textbooks on math, physics and chemistry.'

'No problem. Take them. But why do you want these?'

God tied up the bundle again. 'To study. I'll start with quadratic equations. In the long years ahead, I'll need some way to occupy myself. Who knows? Maybe one day, I'll try to repair our ships' antimatter engines and allow us to fly close to the speed of light again!'

'Right,' Qiusheng said, excited. 'That way, you'll be able to skip across time again. You can find another planet, create another civilization to support you in your old age!'

God shook his head. 'No, no, no. We're no longer interested in being supported in our old age. If it's time for us to die, we die. I want to study because I have a final wish.' He took out the small TV from his pocket. On the screen, his beloved from two thousand years ago was still slowly speaking the final word of that three-word sentence. 'I want to see her again.'

'It's a good wish, but it's only a fantasy,' Qiusheng's father said. 'Think about it. She left two thousand years ago at the speed of light. Who knows where she is now? Even if you repair your ship, how will you ever catch her? You told us that nothing can go faster than light.'

God pointed at the sky with his cane. 'In this universe, as long as you're patient you can make any wish come true. Even though the possibility is minuscule, it still exists. I told you once that the universe was born out of a great explosion. Now gravity has gradually slowed down its expansion. Eventually the expansion will stop and turn into contraction. If our spaceship can really fly again at close to the speed of light, then we will endlessly accelerate and endlessly approach the speed of light. This way, we will skip over endless time until we near the final moments of the universe.

'By then, the universe will have shrunk to a very small size, smaller even than Bingbing's toy ball, as small as a point. Then everything in the entire universe will come together, and she and I will also be together.'

A tear fell from God's eye and rolled onto his beard, glistening brightly in the morning sun. 'The universe will then be the tomb at the end of *The Butterfly Lovers*. She and I will be the two butterflies emerging from the tomb . . .'

8

A week later, the last spaceship left Earth. God left.

Xicen village resumed its quiet life.

On this evening, Qiusheng's family sat in the yard looking at a sky full of stars. It was mid-fall, and insects had stopped making noises in the fields. A light breeze stirred the fallen leaves at their feet. The air was slightly chilly.

'They're flying so high. The wind must be so severe, so cold . . .' Yulian murmured to herself.

'There isn't any wind up there,' Qiusheng said. 'They're in space, where there isn't even air. But it is really cold. So cold that in the books they call it 'absolute zero'. It's so dark out there, with no end in sight. It's a place that you can't even dream of in your nightmares.'

Yulian began to cry again. But she tried to hide it with words. 'Remember those last two things God told us? I understand the part about our three siblings. But then he told us that we had to spread bacteria onto other planets and so on. I still can't make sense of that.'

'I figured it out,' Qiusheng's father said. Under the brilliant starry sky, his head, full of a lifetime of foolishness, finally opened up to insight. He looked up at the stars. He had lived with them above his head all his life, but only today did he discover what they really looked like. A new sensation spread over him, making him feel as if he had been touched by something greater. Even though it did not become a part of him, the feeling shook him to his core. He sighed at the sea of stars and said:

'The human race needs to start thinking about who is going to support us in our old age.'

FOR THE BENEFIT OF MANKIND

Business was business, nothing more, nothing less. This was the principle by which Smoothbore operated, but this particular client had left him feeling bewildered.

First, the client had gone about the commission all wrong. He wanted to speak in person, which was extremely unusual in this line of business. Smoothbore remembered his instructor's repeated admonitions three decades prior: their relationship with clients should be like that of the forehead to the back of the skull; the two should never meet. This, of course, was in the best interest of both parties.

Smoothbore was even more surprised by the client's choice of meeting place. The opulent Presidential Hall in the most luxurious five-star hotel in the city was a fucking spectacularly unsuitable venue for this sort of transaction. According to the other party, this contract would involve processing three units. This was no trouble – he did not mind a little extra work.

An attendant held open the gilded doors of the Presidential Hall. Before he entered, Smoothbore inconspicuously reached a hand into his jacket and gently undid the snaps on the holster under his left armpit. In truth, it was unnecessary – no one would try to pull anything unexpected in a place like this.

The hall was resplendent in glittering greens and golds, a world apart from the reality outside. This world's sun was a massive crystal chandelier, shining down on an endless plain of scarlet carpet. At first glance the room seemed empty, but Smoothbore quickly spied its occupants clustered around two French windows in the corner of the hall, lifting the heavy curtains to look at the sky outside. He swept an eye over them and counted thirteen people. Smoothbore had anticipated a client, not clients. His instructor had also said that clients were like mistresses: you could have more than one, but you should never let them meet.

Smoothbore knew exactly what they were looking at: the Elder Brothers' spaceship. It had moved back over the southern hemisphere and was clearly visible in the sky. Three years had passed since the Creator civilization had left Earth. Their grand cosmic visit had drastically increased humanity's ability to mentally cope with alien civilizations. Moreover, the Creators' fleet of 20,000 spaceships had blotted out the sky, but only one ship from the Elder Brothers' world had arrived on Earth. It was not as bizarrely shaped as the spaceships of the Creators. Cylindrical with rounded ends, it looked like an intergalactic cold-relief capsule.

Seeing Smoothbore enter, the thirteen clients left the windows and returned to the large round table in the center of the hall. When Smoothbore recognized some of the faces around the room, the magnificent hall suddenly felt shabby. The most conspicuous among them was SinoSys Group's Zhu Hanyang, whose 'Orient-3000' operating system was replacing the outdated Windows OS worldwide. The others all ranked in the top fifty on a list of the world's wealthiest people. Their annual earnings were probably equivalent to the GDP of a middle-income country.

These people were nothing like Brother Teeth, thought Smoothbore. Brother Teeth had made his fortune overnight; these were dynastic heirs, the polished products of generations of wealth. They were the aristocrats of this age, utterly habituated to the wealth and power they wielded. It was just like the delicate diamond ring that sat on Zhu Hanyang's slender finger: it was barely visible but for the occasional glint of warm light, but it was easily worth a dozen times more than the shiny, walnut-sized golden baubles that adorned Brother Teeth's fingers.

But now, these thirteen financial princelings had assembled to hire a professional hitman to kill three people, and according to his contact this was only the first batch.

Smoothbore paid the diamond ring no attention. His eyes were fixed on the three photographs in Zhu's hand – clearly the units that required processing. Zhu leaned across the table and slid the photographs in front of him.

Glancing down, Smoothbore felt faint frustration creep in again. His instructor had said that in the area in which he did business, it was wise to familiarize himself with units who might conceivably be processed in the future. In this city, at least, Smoothbore had done just that. But Smoothbore was completely unable to identify the three faces in front of him. The photographs had been taken with a long-focus lens, and the disheveled and dirty subjects hardly seemed of the same species as the refined figures in front of him. Closer inspection revealed that one of the three faces belonged to a woman. She was still young, and her appearance was tidier than that of the others. Her hair, though coated with dust, was neatly combed. The look in her eyes was unusual. Smoothbore paid attention to people's expressions – people in this business always did. He usually saw one of two expressions: anxious desire or numbness. But her eyes were filled with rare serenity. Smoothbore's heart stirred faintly, but the feeling passed as quickly as it came, like a fine mist blown away on the wind.

'This is the task that the Council for Liquidation of Social Wealth entrusts to you. This is the standing committee of the Council, and I am its chairman,' said Zhu.

The Council for Liquidation of Social Wealth? It was a strange name. Apart from signifying an organization composed of the world's wealthiest individuals, Smoothbore could not ponder the implications of its name. Without further particulars, it was probably impossible to unravel its true purpose.

'Their locations are written on the back. They have no fixed addresses, so those are approximations. You will have to search for them, but they should not prove difficult to find. The money has already been wired to your account. Please verify the transfer,' instructed Zhu.

Looking up, Smoothbore found the expression on Zhu's face to be anything but noble. His eyes were dull and empty. Somewhat to Smoothbore's surprise, they held not even a trace of desire.

Smoothbore pulled out his cellphone and checked his account. After counting the long string of zeroes after the number, he said coolly: 'First, not so much. My original quote stands. Second, pay half up front, and half on completion.'

'Fine,' Zhu sniffed disapprovingly.

Smoothbore punched several keys. 'The excess funds have been returned. Please verify the transfer, sir. We, too, have professional standards.'

'Indeed. These days your line of work is oversubscribed. But we value your professionalism and sense of honor,' said Xu Xueping with a charming smile. She was the chief executive of Far Source Group, Asia's largest energy development entity born out of the full liberalization of the electric power market.

'This is the first order, so please handle it cleanly,' said the offshore oil baron Xue Tong.

'Fast cooling or delayed cooling?' asked Smoothbore, quickly adding, 'I can explain if necessary.'

'We understand, and it doesn't matter. Do as you see fit,' answered Zhu.

'Verification method? Video or physical specimen?'

'No need for either. Just complete the task – we have our own methods of checking.'

'Will that be all?'

'Yes, you may go.'

As he left the hotel, Smoothbore could see the Elder Brothers' spaceship passing slowly overhead in the narrow strips of sky between the towering buildings. The ship seemed larger than before, and its speed had increased. Evidently it had reduced the altitude of its orbit. The ship's smooth sides bloomed with slowly shifting iridescent patterns, producing a hypnotic effect on those who looked too long. In fact, the surface of the ship was a perfect mirror, and the patterns seen by observers on the ground were only the distorted reflections of Earth below. Smoothbore imagined the ship as purest silver, a thing of beauty in his eyes. He preferred silver to gold. Silver was quiet, cold.

Before their departure three years ago, the Creators told humanity that they had created six Earths in total; the four that now remained were within two hundred light-years of each other. They urged the people of Earth to devote their full efforts to technological development – we needed to eliminate our brother planets, lest we be destroyed ourselves.

But this warning came too late.

Locking their ship into orbit around Earth, emissaries from one of those three planets, the first Earth, arrived in the solar system not long after the departure of the Creators. The First Earth civilization was twice as old as mankind, and so the people of this Earth came to call them 'Elder Brothers'.

Smoothbore took out his cellphone and checked his account balance again. *Brother Teeth, I'm as rich as you now, but it still feels like I'm missing something. And you always thought you already had it all, and everything you did was only a desperate attempt to keep it.* He shook his head, as if to clear the dark cloud from his mind. It was an ill omen to think of Brother Teeth now.

Brother Teeth took his name from the saw that never left his side. The blade was thin and flexible, its serrations razor-sharp. The handle was carved from solid coral and decorated with beautiful *ukiyo-e* patterns. He kept the saw wrapped around his waist like a belt, and in idle moments he would unwind it and draw a violin bow across the back of the blade. By bending the blade and bowing across sections of different widths, he could produce haunting, melancholy music that hung in the air like the mournful cries of spirits. Of course, Smoothbore had heard tales of the saw's other application, but he had only seen Brother Teeth use it in action once. It was during a high-stakes game of dice in an old warehouse. Brother Teeth's second-in-command, a man named Half-Brick, had gambled big and lost everything, even his parents' house. With bloodshot eyes, he offered to put both his arms on the table in a double-or-nothing bet.

Brother Teeth rattled the dice and smiled at him. Half-Brick's arms, he said, were an unacceptable bet. After all, the future was long – and without hands, how could they play dice together?

'Bet your legs,' he said.

So Half-Brick had bet both his legs – and when he lost again, Brother Teeth unwound his saw and removed both of his legs where the calf met the knee.

Smoothbore distinctly remembered the sound of the sawblade as it carved through tendon and bone. Brother Teeth had placed a foot on Half-Brick's throat to muffle his hideous shrieks, and only the snarl of the blade on flesh echoed through the dark, cavernous warehouse. As the saw sang merrily across Half-Brick's knee caps, it produced a rich, resonant timbre. Fragments of snow-white bone lay scattered in a pool of bright red blood, forming a beautiful, even seductive, composition.

The strange beauty shook Smoothbore to his core. Every cell in his body was bewitched by the song of saw on flesh. *This* was fucking living! It had been his eighteenth birthday, and this was the best possible rite of passage.

When he was finished, Brother Teeth wiped the blood off his beloved saw and wrapped it around his waist once more. Half-Brick and his legs had already been carried away. Pointing at the trail of blood, he said, 'Tell Brick that I will provide for him from now on.'

Although Smoothbore was young, he had been a trusted member of Brother Teeth's entourage. Having followed the man in his rise to power from a very young age, he was no stranger to bloodshed. When Brother Teeth finally scraped together a fortune from the bloody gutters of society and sought to shift his business empire into more respectable channels, his most loyal retainers were dubbed Chairman of the Board, Vice President, and other such titles. Only Smoothbore was left to serve as Brother Teeth's bodyguard.

Those who knew Brother Teeth understood that the level of trust implied by this appointment was no small matter. The man was extraordinarily cautious, perhaps as a result of the fate that befell his godfather. Brother Teeth's godfather had also been extremely cautious; in Brother Teeth's words, the man would have wrapped himself in iron if given the opportunity. After many years without incident, he boarded a flight and took his assigned seat, flanked on either side by one of his most trusted bodyguards. When the plane landed in Zhuhai, the stewardess noticed the three men remained seated, as if lost in thought. A second look revealed that their blood had already trickled past more than ten rows. Long, micro-thin steel needles had been inserted through their seat backs, and the bodyguards had been impaled through the heart with three needles each. As for Brother Teeth's godfather, he had been pierced through with fourteen needles, like a butterfly carefully pinned and mounted in a specimen box. The number of needles was certainly some sort of message. Perhaps it hinted at fourteen million embezzled yuan, or the fourteen years his killer waited to take vengeance. . . . Like his godfather before him, Brother Teeth's journey to the top had been eventful. Now, navigating society was like crossing a forest of hidden blades or a marsh cratered with pitfalls. He was truly placing his life into Smoothbore's hands.

But Smoothbore's new status soon came under threat with the arrival of Mr K. Mr K was Russian. At that time, it was the fashion among those who could afford it to employ ex-KGB officers as bodyguards. Having such a person in one's employ was something worth flaunting, like a movie star lover. Those who ran in Brother Teeth's circles struggled to pronounce his Russian name, and simply called the newcomer 'KGB'. Over time, they settled on Mr K. In reality, Mr K had no relation to the KGB. Most former KGB officers were cubicle-bound civil servants, and even those on the front lines of the secret conflict were untrained in the art of personal security. Instead, Mr K had worked in the Central Security Bureau of the Soviet Union, serving as bodyguard to Andrei Gromyko, the then Minister of Foreign Affairs known in the West as 'Mr Nyet'. He was every bit the genuine article, a true expert in keeping his clients breathing. Brother Teeth had hired him on a vice-chairman's salary not out of a desire to boast, but out of real concern for his own safety.

From the moment of Mr K's arrival, it was clear that he was utterly unlike other bodyguards. At the dinner table, other bodyguards would out-eat and out-drink their wealthy employers and felt perfectly comfortable interrupting their shop talk. When real danger reared its head, they would either charge in with all the art of a street thug or leave their client in the dust of their panicked retreat. In stark contrast, at banquets or negotiations, Mr K would stand quietly behind Brother Teeth, his hulking figure like an immovable wall, ready to intercept any potential threat. While Mr K never had the opportunity to protect his client in a crisis situation, his professionalism and dedication left no doubt that, should such a situation arise, he would fulfill his duties with consummate expertise. Smoothbore was more professional than the other bodyguards and did not share their obvious failings, but he was fully aware of the world of difference between himself and Mr K. For example, it was a long time before he realized that Mr K wore sunglasses at all hours of the day not to look cool, but to conceal his gaze.

Although Mr K picked up Chinese quickly, he kept aloof from the people in his employer's inner circles. He maintained this distance carefully, until one day he asked Smoothbore to step into his spartan room. After he poured two glasses of vodka, he told Smoothbore in stilted Chinese, 'I want to teach you to speak.'

'To speak?'

'A foreign language.'

So Smoothbore began to learn a foreign language from Mr K. He did not realize he was being taught English and not Russian until a few days later. Smoothbore was a quick learner, and when they could communicate in both English and Chinese Mr K told him, 'You are not like the others.'

'I know,' nodded Smoothbore.

'In my thirty years of experience, I have learned to accurately distinguish those people with potential from the rest. You are one such rare talent, and the first time I saw you it chilled me. It's easy to act in cold blood, but it's difficult to stay cold-blooded without ever thawing. You could become one of the best in this business, if you don't bury your talents.'

'What can I do?'

'First, study abroad.'

Brother Teeth agreed readily to Mr K's suggestion and promised to cover Smoothbore's expenses in full. He had hoped to rid himself of Smoothbore ever since Mr K's arrival, but there were no open positions in the company.

And so, one wintry night, this boy who had been orphaned at a young age and raised in the underbelly of society boarded a passenger jet bound for a strange and distant land.

Driving a rundown Santana, Smoothbore made his way across the city to inspect each of the locations written on the photographs. His first stop was Blossom Plaza. It did not take him long to find the man in the photo. He was rummaging through a garbage can when Smoothbore arrived, and after a few minutes he hauled his bulging trash bag to a nearby bench. His search had borne fruit in the form of a large and almost untouched takeout box, a pork sausage missing only a bite, several perfectly good slices of bread and half a bottle of cola. Smoothbore had expected him to eat with his hands, but he watched with surprise as the tramp pulled out a small aluminum spoon from the pocket of the dirty overcoat he wore despite the summer heat. He finished his dinner slowly and then threw what remained back into the garbage can. Looking around the plaza, Smoothbore saw the lights of the city begin to flicker on in all directions. He was very familiar with this area, but something felt off. In a flash, it occurred to him *why* the man had been able to leisurely eat his fill. The plaza was a common gathering place for the city's homeless population, but at that moment no one could be seen but his mark. Where had they gone? Had they all been processed?

Smoothbore drove on to the address on the second photograph. Under an overpass on the outskirts of the city, faint yellow light spilled out from a shack cobbled together from corrugated cardboard. Smoothbore cautiously pushed the busted door of the shack open just a crack. As he poked his head in, he suddenly found himself in a fantastical world of color. The walls of the shack were covered with oil paintings of all sizes, creating a separate wall of art. Smoothbore's eyes traced a wisp of smoke back to the itinerant artist, who lay splayed out beneath a broken easel like a bear in hibernation. His hair was long, and his paint-splattered T-shirt was so baggy it looked like a robe. He was smoking a cheap pack of jade butterfly cigarettes. His eyes roved over his artwork, and his gaze was filled with wonder and loss, as if he was seeing it for the first time. Smoothbore guessed most of his time was spent fawning over his own works. This particular breed of starving artist had been common in the nineties of the previous century, but nowadays they were few and far between.

'It's all right, come in,' said the artist, his eyes never leaving his paintings. His tone was more befitting of an imperial palace than a shack. As soon as Smoothbore stepped inside, he asked, 'Do you like my paintings?'

Smoothbore glanced around and saw that most of the paintings were just chaotic splotches of color – paint splashed directly onto a canvas would have seemed rational by comparison. But there were a few pictures in a very realistic style, and Smoothbore's eyes were quickly drawn to one of these: a canvas dominated by a cracked yellow earth. A few dead plants protruded from the fissures in the ground, looking as if they had withered away centuries ago, if indeed water had ever existed in this world at all. A skull lay on the parched earth. Though it was bleach-white and permeated with cracks, two green, living plants sprouted from its mouth and one eye-socket. In sharp contrast with the drought and death surrounding them, these plants were green and luxuriant, and a tiny, delicate flower crowned the tip of one sprout. The skull's other eye-socket contained a human eyeball. Its limpid pupil stared at the sky, and its gaze was filled with the same wonder and loss as that of its painter.

'I like this one,' Smoothbore said, pointing to the painting.

'It's called *Barren No. 2*. Will you buy it?'

'How much?'

'How much you got?'

Smoothbore pulled out his wallet and removed all the hundred-yuan notes it contained. He handed them to the artist, but the latter only took two bills.

'It's only worth this much. It's yours now.'

Smoothbore started the car and picked up the third photograph to study the last address. He cut the ignition a moment later, as his destination lay right alongside the overpass: the city's largest landfill. He took out his binoculars and peered through the windshield, searching for his mark amongst the scavengers clambering over the rubbish dump.

Three hundred thousand junkmen made a living off the garbage of the metropolis, forming their own class, complete with its own distinct castes. The highest-ranking junkmen could enter the city's ritzy villa districts. There, it was possible to pick a daily haul of shirts, socks and bed sheets, each used only once, from the delicately sculpted waste bins – in these neighborhoods, these were considered single-use goods. All kinds of things found their way into the garbage: lightly scuffed premium leather shoes and belts, half-smoked Havana cigars, expensive chocolate nibbled only at the corners. . . . But picking garbage there necessitated hefty bribes to the residential security guards that only a few could afford, and those who could afford it became aristocrats among scavengers.

The middle ranks of junkmen gathered around the city's many waste transfer stations, the first collection stops for municipal waste. There, the most valuable refuse – waste electronics, scrap metal, intact paper products, discarded medical devices and expired pharmaceuticals – was quickly snapped up. These sites were not open to just anyone, however. Each station was the domain of a junk boss. Any scavenger who entered without their permission was harshly punished: perpetrators of minor offenses were violently beaten and driven off, while serious offenders could lose their lives.

Little of value remained in the waste that passed through the transfer stations to the rubbish dumps and landfills on the outskirts of the city, and yet it was this waste that supported the largest number of people. These were the lowliest of junkmen, the kind of people right in front of Smoothbore. Worthless, unrecyclable broken plastic and shredded paper was all that was left for the scavengers on the bottom rungs of junkman society. There were also scraps of rotten food, which could be gleaned from the rubbish and sold as pig feed to neighboring farms at ten yuan to the kilo. In the distance, the metropolis shone like a great brilliant jewel, its radiance casting a flickering halo over the fetid mountain of garbage. The junkmen experienced the luxury of the nearby city by sifting through its trash. Mingled in the rotten food, it was often possible to make out a roast suckling pig with only the legs eaten away, a barely-touched grouper, whole chickens. . . . Recently, it had become common to find whole Silkie hens, owing to the popularity of a new dish called White Jade Chicken. The dish was prepared by slitting open the stomach of the chicken, filling it with tofu, and letting it simmer. The slices of tofu were the real delicacy; the chicken, while delicious, was merely casing. Like the reed leaves around rice dumplings, any diner foolish enough to eat the chicken itself would become the laughingstock of more discerning epicureans . . .

The last garbage truck of the day pulled into the lot. As it tipped its load onto the ground, a group of junkmen scrambled to meet the avalanche of waste, quickly vanishing into the rising dust and debris. It was like they had passed into a new phase of evolution, unaffected by the stench of the garbage heap, the germs and the toxic filth. Of course, this was an illusion, maintained by people who only saw how they lived and not how they died. Like the corpses of insects and rats, the bodies of junkmen littered the landfill. They passed away quietly here, soon buried by new trash.

In the dim light emanating from the flood lamps at the edge of the lot, the junkmen appeared as dusty, indistinct shadows, but Smoothbore still swiftly located his mark among them. The speed with which he spotted her was due in part to his own keen vision, but there was also another reason: like the vagrants in Blossom Plaza, there were significantly fewer junkmen than usual on the landfill today. *What was going on?* Smoothbore observed his mark through his binoculars. At first glance, she seemed no different than any other scavenger. There was a rope tied around her waist, and she carried a large woven bag and a long-handled rake. She was perhaps a bit skinnier than the others. Unable to squeeze through the throng of junkmen, she could only scrounge along the periphery, sifting through the trash of the trash.

Smoothbore lowered the binoculars and thought for a moment, shaking his head slightly. Something truly fantastical was unfolding before him: a homeless man, an itinerant starving artist, and a girl who lived off garbage – three of the poorest, weakest people in the world – somehow posed a threat to the world's wealthiest and most powerful plutocrats. The threat was so great, in fact, that they felt compelled to hire a hitman to deal with the problem.

Barren No.2 lay on the back seat. In the dark, the skull's single eye bored into Smoothbore, like a thorn in his flesh.

There was a chorus of panicked cries from the landfill, and Smoothbore saw that the world outside his car was bathed in a blue light. The glow emanated from the east, where a blue sun was rapidly rising over the horizon. It was the Elder Brothers' spaceship, arriving in the Southern hemisphere. The spaceship did not typically emit light; at night, the sunlight reflecting off its sides made it shine like a small moon. But every so often it would suddenly illuminate the world in a bluish glow, thrusting humanity into nameless terror. This time, the spaceship's glow was brighter than ever before, perhaps because it was in a lower orbit than usual. The blue moon rose above the city, stretching the shadows of skyscrapers all the way to the landfill like the grasping arms of giants. As the spaceship continued its ascent, the shadows gradually shrank away.

The scavenger girl on the landfill was illuminated by the glow of the Elder Brothers' spaceship. Smoothbore raised his binoculars again and confirmed his earlier observations. She was indeed his mark. She knelt with her bag in her lap, the slightest trace of alarm in her upturned gaze, but she otherwise projected the same sort of serenity Smoothbore had seen in the photograph. Smoothbore's heart stirred again, but it was as fleeting as before. He knew it was a ripple of emotion from somewhere deep within his soul, and he regretted having lost it again.

The spaceship streaked across the sky and sank below the western horizon, leaving an eerie blue afterglow in the heavens. The landfill settled back into darkness, and the lights of the city sparkled once more. Smoothbore's thoughts returned to the puzzle at hand: the thirteen wealthiest people on Earth desired to kill the three poorest people. It was beyond absurd, and any possible explanation escaped his imagination. But his mind had not strayed far before he slammed the brakes on his thoughts. He slapped the steering wheel in self-reproach as he suddenly realized he had violated the cardinal rule of his own profession. His tutor's words unfurled in his mind, laying out their profession's maxim: the gun does not care at whom it is aimed.

To this day, Smoothbore did not even know in which country he had studied abroad, much less the exact location of the academy. He knew only that the first leg of the trip was to Moscow. Upon arrival, he was met by several men who spoke English without a trace of a Russian accent. He was made to put on opaque sunglasses, and, disguised as a blind person, he passed the remainder of the journey in darkness. After another three-hour flight and a day's drive, he arrived at the academy, and Smoothbore could not say for certain that he was still in Russia at that point.

The academy was located deep in the mountains and bordered by high walls. Under no circumstances were students permitted to leave before graduation. After he was permitted to remove the sunglasses, Smoothbore discovered that the buildings of the academy were divided into two distinct styles: the first type of building was gray and devoid of any distinguishing features, and the second type was very peculiar in both shape and form. He later found out that the latter buildings were actually assembled from giant building blocks and could be reconfigured at will to simulate a myriad of combat environments. The entire institute was essentially one big state-of-the-art target range.

The convocation ceremony was the first and only time the student body would gather together, and their number just exceeded four hundred. The silver-haired principal, who had the commanding manner of a classical scholar, gave the following address:

'Students, over the next four years you will learn the theoretical knowledge and the practical skills required for our line of work – a line of work whose name we shall never speak aloud. It is one of humanity's most ancient professions, and it is a profession assured of a bright future. On a small scale, our work, and *only* our work, can resolve difficult problems for desperate clients; but on a large scale, our work can change history.

'In the past, various government organizations have offered us great sums of money to train guerilla fighters. We refused them all because we only train independent professionals. Yes, *independent*, from everything but money. After today, you must think of yourself as a gun. Your duty is to perform the function of a gun and to demonstrate its beauty in the process. A gun does not care at whom it is aimed. Person A raises his gun and shoots person B; B wrests the gun away and shoots A – the gun makes no distinction between the two and completes both assignments with the same level of excellence. This is the most basic principle of our profession.'

During the ceremony, Smoothbore also learned a few of the most common terms in his new profession: their fundamental business was called 'processing', their targets were 'units' or 'work', and death was 'cooling'.

The academy was divided into L, M and S disciplines, or long-, mid- and short-range. L discipline was the most mysterious and most expensive course of study. The few students who elected this specialty kept to themselves and rarely mixed with M and S students. Likewise, Smoothbore's instructors advised him and his classmates to keep their distance from L students: 'They are the nobility of this profession, as they are the most likely to change the course of history.'

The knowledge taught to L students was broad and profound, and the sniper rifles reserved for their use cost hundreds of thousands of dollars and were nearly two meters long when fully assembled. L specialists processed work at an average distance of one thousand meters, although it was said that some could hit their marks from three thousand meters away. Processing at distances over fifteen hundred meters was a complicated operation, and part of the preparatory work included placing a series of 'wind chimes' at set distances along the firing range. The ingeniously crafted micro-anemometers could wirelessly transmit data to goggles worn by the shooter, sharpening his (or her) understanding of wind speed and direction along the entire range of the shot.

M specialists processed work at a distance of ten to three hundred meters. It was the most traditional discipline and it boasted the largest number of students, who generally used standard-issue rifles. While there was rarely a shortage of work for M specialists, this discipline was considered pedestrian and rather lacking in mystique.

Smoothbore belonged to S discipline, learning to process work at a range of less than ten meters. This discipline lacked stringent weapons requirements, and S specialists typically used pistols or even blades and other melee weapons. Of the three specialties, S discipline was undoubtedly the most dangerous, but it was also the most romantic.

The principal was a master of this discipline, and he personally instructed S courses. But, to everyone's surprise, the first course he taught was English literature.

'You must first understand the value of S discipline,' the principal said gravely, gazing at the baffled students before him. 'In the L and M disciplines, the unit and the processor never meet, and the unit is processed and cooled without ever realizing its plight. A blessing for the unit, perhaps, but not necessarily for the client. Some clients need their targets to know who has marked them for processing and why, and it falls to us to inform them. In that moment, we are not ourselves but an incarnation of the client. We must solemnly and perfectly communicate his or her final message to the unit, and thus inflict the maximum psychic shock and torment possible prior to cooling. This is the romance and beauty of S discipline – the look of terror and despair in the unit's eyes just before cooling. We can find no greater pleasure than this in our work; but to this end, we must cultivate our verbal dexterity and literary acumen.'

So, for one year, Smoothbore studied literature. He read Homer's epics, memorized Shakespeare and studied works by many other classical and contemporary authors. Smoothbore felt this was the most rewarding year of his overseas education. He was more or less familiar with the subjects that followed it, and if he did not master them at the institute he could learn them elsewhere. But this was his only chance to deeply engage with literature. Through literature, he rediscovered humanity, and he marveled at the subtleties of human nature. Before, killing had simply felt like smashing a crudely-made pot filled with red liquid; now, he was amazed to find that he had smashed exquisite jadeware, which only heightened the thrill of the act.

His next course of study was human anatomy. Compared to the other two disciplines, the other major advantage in S discipline was that it was possible to control the time needed to cool units during processing. The technical terms were 'fast cooling' and 'delayed cooling'. Many clients requested delayed cooling and a recording of the entire process – a treasured keepsake they could appreciate forever. Of course, this required precise technical skills and extensive experience, and knowledge of human anatomy was indispensable.

Then, his real courses began.

The junkmen on the landfill gradually dispersed until only his mark and a few others remained. Smoothbore decided then and there to process this unit by the end of the night. It went against standard practice to act during the initial observation period, but there were exceptions when a suitable opportunity for processing presented itself.

Smoothbore maneuvered his car out from under the overpass and jolted along the pot-holed road next to the landfill. He observed that any junkman leaving the landfill had to pass this way. The darkness revealed only the shadows of the wild grass swaying in the night breeze. It was an excellent location for processing, and he decided to wait there for the unit.

Smoothbore drew out his gun and placed it gently on the dashboard. It was an inelegant, 7.6 mm revolver that was chambered for large Black Star cartridges. He called it Snubnose because of its shape. He had purchased the privately-made, untraceable gun for three thousand yuan on the black market in Xishuangbanna. Although it looked crude, it was made well, and each component part had been machined with precision. Its biggest flaw was that the manufacturer had not bothered with rifling: the barrel walls were smooth metal. It was not as if Smoothbore was unable to procure better, name-brand firearms. Brother Teeth had equipped him with a thirty-two-round Uzi when he had started his bodyguard career and had later gifted him a Type 77 as a birthday present. But Smoothbore had stuffed both guns in the bottom of his trunk, and he never carried them on his person. He simply preferred Snubnose. It glinted icily in the halo of the metropolis, drawing Smoothbore's thoughts back to his years at the academy.

On the first day of their real training, the principal made each student present his or her weapon. As he placed Snubnose in that line of finely-crafted pistols, Smoothbore had felt deeply embarrassed. The principal, however, picked up Snubnose, hefted it in his hand, and said with sincere admiration: 'This is a fine gun.'

'It doesn't have rifling, and you can't even attach a silencer,' sneered another student.

'Precision and range are of little importance to S specialists, and rifling even less so. And silencers? A small pillow will do the trick. Boy, do not allow yourself to be limited by stale convention. In the hands of a master, this gun can yield artistry that all your expensive toys cannot.'

The principal was right. Without rifling, bullets fired by Snubnose would turn somersaults in flight, emitting a shrill, terror-inducing whistle that ordinary bullets lacked. They would continue to spin even after striking their targets, like a rotary blade shredding everything in its path.

'From now on, we will call you Smoothbore!' said the headmaster, handing the gun back to its owner. 'Hold on to this, boy. It looks like you will have to study knife-throwing.'

Smoothbore immediately grasped the principal's meaning: an expert knife thrower held his knife by the blade as he threw it in order to build momentum through rotation, but this required that the knife arrive point-first as it reached its target. The principal hoped Smoothbore would learn to wield Snubnose as a knife thrower mastered his blades! Such artistry would give Smoothbore unprecedented control over the wounds Snubnose's tumbling bullets inflicted. After two years of bitter practice and nearly thirty thousand bullets, Smoothbore acquired a level of skill that was beyond even the academy's best firearms instructors.

During his studies abroad, Smoothbore became completely inseparable from Snubnose. In his fourth year, he became familiar with another student in his own discipline who went by the name of Fire, perhaps because of her mane of red hair. It was impossible to know her nationality, but Smoothbore guessed she came from Western Europe. There were few female students at the academy, and almost all of them were natural sharpshooters. Fire, however, had terrible aim, and her dagger skills were downright embarrassing. Smoothbore had no idea how she made a living before the academy. But in their first garroting class, she plucked a filament so fine it was nearly invisible from the delicate ring on her finger. She wrapped the razor wire around the neck of the goat being used as a teaching aid and, with a deftness that spoke of practice, neatly sliced its head off. Fire had called it a nanowire, a super-strong material that might be used to build space elevators in the future.

Fire felt no real affection for Smoothbore – that sort of thing was impossible at the academy. She also hung around Frost Wolf, a Nordic student from another discipline. She hopped back and forth between them like a fighting cricket, trying to instigate a bit of bloodshed to disrupt the monotony of student life. She soon succeeded, and the two men agreed to settle their feud with a game of Russian roulette. In the dead of night, their classmates reconfigured the enormous building blocks of the shooting range into the shape of the Coliseum. The duel was to commence in the center of the arena, and the weapon of choice was Snubnose.

Fire presided over the entire scene. With a graceful flourish, she inserted a single cartridge into Snubnose's empty cylinder. Then, holding the barrel, she rolled the cylinder across her pale, slender forearm a dozen times. After the two men politely declined their chance to go first, she smiled and handed the gun to Smoothbore.

Smoothbore slowly raised the gun to his head. As the cool muzzle touched his temple, a wave of emptiness and isolation, stronger than anything he had ever felt, washed over him. He felt a formless, frigid wind sweep through the world, until his heart was the last speck of heat in a pitch-dark universe. He steeled his heart and pulled the trigger five times. The hammer fell five times. The cylinder turned five times. The gun did not fire.

Click click click click click – just like that, a crisp, metallic death knell sounded for Frost Wolf. A cheer rose from their classmates. Shedding tears of delight, Fire cried to Smoothbore that she was his. In the middle of all this, Frost Wolf stood with an easy smile on his face. He nodded towards Smoothbore and said with sincerity, 'You Oriental bastard, that was the most brilliant wager since the first Colt was made.' He turned to Fire, 'It's all right, my dear. Life was only ever a gamble anyway.'

He seized Snubnose and pointed it against his temple. With a muffled bang, blood and bone bloomed across the arena floor.

Smoothbore graduated not long after. Wearing the same dark glasses he wore when he arrived, he departed the nameless academy and returned to the place he grew up in. He never heard another word about the academy, and it was as if it had never really existed at all.

It was not until he returned to the outside world that Smoothbore heard the news: the Creators had arrived to claim the support of the human civilization they themselves had once fostered, but, unable to live comfortably on Earth, they left after only one year. Their fleet of twenty thousand ships had already vanished into the endless cosmos.

Smoothbore had barely stepped off the plane when he received his first processing order.

Brother Teeth warmly welcomed Smoothbore home with an extravagant banquet in his honor. Smoothbore asked to meet privately with him after dinner, saying he had many things he wanted to get off his chest. When everyone else had left, Smoothbore told Brother Teeth, 'I grew up at your side. In my heart, you have never been my brother, but rather my father. I ask you, should I practice the profession I have studied? Just say the word, and I will obey.'

Brother Teeth put his arm around Smoothbore's shoulder. 'If you like it, you should do it. I can tell you enjoy it. Don't worry about high roads and low roads – people with bright futures will do well whatever path they follow.'

'As you say.'

Smoothbore drew his pistol and fired into Brother Teeth's stomach. At just the right angle, the twisting bullets ripped a line across the man's abdomen and buried themselves into the floorboards. As the smoke cleared, Brother Teeth looked at Smoothbore. A flicker of shock registered in his eyes before it was replaced by the numbness that follows revelation. He laughed faintly and nodded.

'You've already made something of yourself, kid.' Brother Teeth spat blood as he spoke and sank gently to the ground.

Smoothbore's processing order had specified an hour of delayed cooling, but no recording. The client trusted him. He poured a glass of liquor and watched the blood pool around Brother Teeth with cold detachment. The dying man slowly rearranged his spilled intestines, as thoughtfully as if he were stacking mahjong tiles. As soon as he pushed them back into his abdomen, the slippery lengths slid right out again. Gingerly, Brother Teeth began to gather them up. . . . As he repeated the process for the twelfth time, he gasped his last breath. Precisely one hour had passed since Snubnose had been fired.

Smoothbore had spoken truthfully when he said Brother Teeth was like a father to him. On a rainy day when he was five, Smoothbore's biological father, livid after a huge gambling loss, demanded that his mother relinquish every savings deposit book in the house. When she refused, he simply beat her to death. And when Smoothbore tried to block his father, the man broke his son's nose and arm and then vanished into the rain. Later, Smoothbore had searched far and wide for him without success. If he ever did find his father, the man had earned himself the pleasure of a slow cooling.

Smoothbore heard afterwards that Mr K had returned every penny of his salary to Brother Teeth's family and flown back to Russia. Before leaving, the Russian said that the day he sent Smoothbore to study abroad, he knew Brother Teeth would die by his hand. Brother Teeth had lived his life on a knife's edge, but he never understood what made a true killer.

*

One after another, the few remaining junkminers left the landfill until only Smoothbore's mark remained. She rooted through the garbage, buried in her work. She was too weak to claim a good spot when the trucks arrived, and she could only make up for it by working longer hours. Her persistence meant there was no need for Smoothbore to wait for her outside. Thrusting Snubnose into his jacket pocket, he left the car and headed straight for his mark on the garbage heap.

There was a sponginess and tepid warmth to the garbage underfoot, like he was walking on the body of some enormous beast. When he was within four or five meters of his target, Smoothbore drew his revolver from his pocket.

At that moment, a bolt of blue light shot up from the east. The Elder Brothers' spaceship had completed a full orbit around Earth and returned, still glowing, to the Southern hemisphere. The abrupt appearance of the blue sun drew the gaze of the two figures on the landfill. They studied the strange star for a moment and then glanced at each other. When their eyes met, Smoothbore did something no professional hitman should ever do: he nearly let his gun slip out of his hand. For an instant, the shock made him forget Snubnose even existed, and he almost cried out without thinking: Sweet Pea! – but Smoothbore knew it was not Sweet Pea. Fourteen years ago, he had watched Sweet Pea's agonizing death. But she had lived on in Smoothbore's heart, growing older and stronger. He often saw her in his dreams, and he imagined she would look just like the young woman in front of him now.

In his upstart years, Brother Teeth had dealt in an unspeakable trade: he purchased disabled children from the hands of human traffickers and put them to work in the city as beggars. In those years, the public had not yet exhausted its compassion, and the children proved quite profitable, playing no small part in Brother Teeth's accumulation of seed capital.

Once, Smoothbore accompanied Brother Teeth to receive a new group of children from a trafficker. When they arrived at the old warehouse, they found five children waiting there. Four of them suffered from congenital conditions, but one little girl was completely healthy. Sweet Pea was six years old and adorable. In stark contrast to the children around her, her big, wide eyes were still full of life. Smoothbore's heart broke as he recalled those eyes and the curiosity with which the little girl examined everything around her, totally unaware of the fate that awaited her.

'That's them,' said the trafficker, pointing at the four physically disabled children.

'I thought we agreed on five?' asked Brother Teeth.

'The carriage was packed. One of them didn't make it.'

'What about this one?' Brother Teeth pointed at Sweet Pea.

'She's not for sale.'

'I want her. Same price as the others.' The tone in his voice brooked no argument.

'But . . . she's perfectly fine. How will you make money with her?'

'You ass. A few finishing touches will do it.'

As Brother Teeth spoke, he unwound his saw from his waist and drew it across one of Sweet Pea's delicate calves, opening a gaping wound on the girl's leg. Blood gushed out and Sweet Pea shrieked and shrieked.

'Bind it up and stop the bleeding, but don't give her antibiotics. It needs to fester,' Brother Teeth instructed Smoothbore.

So Smoothbore bandaged the Sweet Pea's wound, but the blood continued to seep through the layers of gauze, and the little girl's face grew deathly pale. He snuck her a few doses of Erythromycin and Sulfamethoxazole behind Brother Teeth's back, but it was no use. Sweet Pea's wound grew infected.

Two days later, Brother Teeth sent Sweet Pea to beg on the streets. The effect produced by her pathetic expression and maimed leg immediately exceeded Brother Teeth's expectations. On the very first day she earned three thousand yuan, and over the week that followed she never brought in less than two thousand per day. On her last day on the street, a foreign couple took one glance at her and handed her four hundred US dollars. Despite this, Sweet Pea was rewarded with only a single box of spoiled food per day. This was not just miserliness on the part of Brother Teeth; it was also a deliberate way to preserve the child's starved appearance. Smoothbore could only give her scraps under the cover of darkness.

One evening, as Smoothbore went to retrieve Sweet Pea from the curbside on which she begged, the little girl leaned close to his ear and whispered, 'Brother, my leg doesn't hurt anymore.' She looked cheerful about this.

Except for his mother's death, this was the only time Smoothbore could remember crying. Sweet Pea's leg did not trouble her because the nerves were dead. Her entire leg had turned black, and she had run a high fever for the past two days. Smoothbore could not bear to follow Brother Teeth's orders any longer, and he carried Sweet Pea to the hospital. The doctors informed him that it was already too late: the girl had blood poisoning. She passed away late the next night, consumed by fever.

From that moment on, Smoothbore's blood ran cold, and just as Mr K predicted, it never warmed again. Killing others became a pleasure for Smoothbore, more addictive than any drug. He lived to smash the delicate jade vessels called 'humans', to watch the red liquid contained within gush out and cool to room temperature. That alone was the truth – that any warmth in that liquid was only ever a charade.

Without conscious intent, Smoothbore had burned a pixel-perfect image of the gash on Sweet Pea's leg into his memory. Later, the image had manifested itself on Brother Teeth's torn abdomen, a precise copy of the original wound.

The junkminer stood, slung her oversized sack over her shoulder and slowly turned to leave. It was not Smoothbore's arrival that prompted her departure. She had not noticed what he held in his hand, and she could not imagine that this well-dressed man might have any connection to herself. It was simply time for her to go. As the Elder Brothers' ship sank below the western horizon, Smoothbore stood motionless on the landfill, watching her figure vanish into the fading blue twilight.

Smoothbore returned his gun to its holster. He drew out his cellphone and dialed Zhu Hanyang's number: 'I want to meet with you. There is something I need to ask.'

'Nine o'clock tomorrow, same place.' Zhu Hanyang's answer was unfazed and concise, as if he had expected Smoothbore's call.

*

As he entered the Presidential Hall, Smoothbore discovered that the entire thirteen-person standing committee of the Council for Liquidation of Social Wealth was already assembled there, their stern gazes focused upon his own person.

'Please ask what you came to ask,' said Zhu Hanyang.

'Why do you want to kill these three people?' asked Smoothbore.

'You have violated the ethics of your profession,' Zhu observed drily, slicing the cap off a cigar with an elegant cigar cutter.

'Yes, and it will cost me. But I need to know the reason, or I cannot do this job.'

Zhu lit the cigar with a long match and nodded slowly: 'I cannot help but think that you only accept work that targets the wealthy. If this is the case, then you are not a true professional hitman, just a thug with a penchant for petty class vengeance – a psychopath who has killed forty-one people in three years, who is being desperately pursued by the police at this very moment. Your reputation will come crashing down around you.'

'You could call the police right now,' Smoothbore replied calmly.

'Has this task touched upon a bit of personal history?' asked Xu Xueping.

Smoothbore could not help but admire her keen insight. His silence answered for him.

'Was it the woman?'

Smoothbore did not reply. The conversation had veered too far off course.

'Very well.' Zhu exhaled a lungful of white smoke. 'This task is important, and we cannot find anyone more suited to it on such short notice. We have no choice but to accept your terms and tell you the reason, but know that it will exceed your wildest dreams. We, the wealthiest few in this society, desire to kill its poorest and weakest members, and this has made us deranged, hateful creatures in your eyes. Before we explain our motivations, we must first correct this impression.'

'I'm not interested in issues of light and dark.'

'But the facts say otherwise. Come with us, please.' Tossing away his barely smoked cigar, Zhu stood and walked out of the room.

Smoothbore exited the hotel in the company of the full standing committee of the Council for Liquidation of Social Wealth. Something strange was occurring overhead, and pedestrians anxiously craned their heads towards the sky. The Elder Brothers' spaceship was sweeping past in low orbit. In the light of the rising sun, it seemed especially visible against the early morning skies. The ship scattered a trail of shining silver stars in its wake, which stretched behind it to the horizon. The ship's length had shortened significantly, and as it released star after star its bulk grew jagged, like a broken stick. Smoothbore had learned from the news that the Elder Brothers' enormous spaceship was actually assembled from thousands of smaller vessels. Now it seemed that the composite whole was splitting apart into an armada.

'Attention, everyone!' Zhu beckoned to the committee. 'You can see the situation has developed, and there may not be much time. We must accelerate our efforts. Each team should report immediately to their assigned liquidation area and continue yesterday's work.'

As he finished, he and Xu Xueping climbed into a truck and called for Smoothbore to join them.

Only then did Smoothbore notice that the vehicles waiting outside the hotel were not the billionaires' usual limousines but a line of Isuzu trucks.

'So we can transport more cargo,' explained Xu, reading the confusion on Smoothbore's face. Smoothbore looked into the bed of the truck and saw that it was neatly packed with small, identical black suitcases. The cases looked elegant and expensive, and he estimated there were over a hundred of them.

There was no hired driver, and Zhu himself pulled the vehicle out onto the main road. The truck soon turned onto a tree-lined avenue and reduced its speed. Smoothbore realized that Zhu was driving slowly alongside a pedestrian – a vagrant. Although in this day and age the homeless did not necessarily dress in rags, there was always something that gave them away. This man had tied a plastic bag around his waist, and its contents rattled with every step.

Smoothbore knew that the mystery behind the vanishing homeless and junkmen was about to unravel, but he did not believe Zhu and Xu would dare to kill the man right here. In all likelihood, they would first lure their target into the truck and dispose of him at another location. Given their status, it was wholly unnecessary for them to dirty their hands with this sort of work. Perhaps they were setting an example for him? Smoothbore had no inclination to interrupt them, but he certainly would not help them either. This was not in his contract.

The tramp was quite unconscious of the fact that the truck had slowed for him until Xu Xueping called out to him.

'Hello!' said Xu, rolling down the window. The man stopped and turned his head to look at her. His face had the anesthetized look common among his class. 'Do you have a place to live?' Xu asked, smiling.

'In the summer, I can live anywhere,' said the man.

'And in the winter?'

'Hot air vents. Some restrooms are heated, too.'

'How long have you lived like this?'

'Don't really remember. Came to the city after my land requisition payments ran out, lived like this ever since.'

'Would you like a three-bedroom house in the city? A home?'

The tramp stared blankly at the billionaire. There was not an inkling of comprehension on his face.

'Can you read?' asked Xu. After the man nodded, she pointed to a large billboard in front of the truck. 'Look over there.' The billboard displayed a grassy knoll dotted with cream-colored buildings, like an idyllic paradise. 'That's an advertisement for commercial housing.' The man turned his head to the billboard, and then looked back at Xu. He did not have the faintest clue what she meant. 'Okay, now take a case from the truck.'

He obediently walked to the rear of the truck, picked out a case and walked back to the passenger door. Pointing at the case, Xu told him, 'Inside is one million yuan. Use five hundred thousand to buy yourself a house like the ones on the billboard, and use the rest to live in comfort. Of course, if you can't spend all that money yourself, you can do what we're doing and give it to someone poorer.'

The tramp's eyes moved back and forth rapidly, but he remained expressionless and did not let go of the box. He knew there had to be a catch.

'Open it and see for yourself.'

He fumbled at the lid with one grimy hand. He opened the case just a crack and then snapped it shut again, the mask of apathy frozen on his face finally shattered. He looked like he had seen a ghost.

'Do you have an ID card?' Zhu Hanyang asked.

The man nodded mechanically, holding the case as far away from himself as possible, as if it were a bomb.

'Then make a deposit at the bank. It'll be more convenient.'

'What do you want me to do?' asked the tramp hesitantly.

'We just need you to do us one little favor: the aliens are coming. If they ask you, tell them you have this much money. That's all. Can you promise to do this?'

The man nodded.

Xu stepped down from the truck and bowed deeply to the tramp. 'Thank you.'

'Thank you,' added Zhu from the truck.

What shocked Smoothbore most was that their gratitude seemed *sincere*.

They drove on, losing sight of the newly-minted millionaire in the rearview windows. Not far down the road, the truck stopped at a corner. Smoothbore spotted three migrant day-laborers squatting on the curb, waiting for work. Each man had a small metal trowel, and a small cardboard sign on the ground read: 'Scrapers.' The three men ran over as soon as the truck pulled up and clamored for work: 'Got a job for us, boss?'

Zhu Hanyang shook his head. 'No. Has business been good lately?'

'No business to be had. Everybody uses that new thermal spray coating nowadays; no need for scrapers anymore.'

'Where are you from?'

'Henan.'

Zhu rattled off several questions: 'The same village? Is it poor? How many households?'

'It's up in the hills, there are maybe fifty families. Everyone's poor. It never rains. Boss, you wouldn't believe it – we have to irrigate our plants one by one with a watering can.'

'Don't bother with farming. Do you have bank accounts?'

All three shook their heads.

'You'll have to take cash, then. They're heavy, but I'll still trouble you to take a dozen cases from the back.'

'A dozen?' It was the scrapers' only question as they unloaded the cases from the bed of the truck and piled them on the sidewalk. They did not pause to consider Zhu's instructions – work was work.

'It doesn't matter, take as many as you like.'

Fifteen cases soon lay on the ground. Pointing to the stack, Zhu told them, 'Each box contains one million yuan – fifteen million in total. Go home and share the money with your whole village.'

One of the men laughed at this, as if Zhu had cracked a joke. One of his companions crouched down and opened one of the cases. The men stared at its contents, the same flabbergasted expression as the tramp's creeping over their faces.

'The cases are heavy, so you should hire a car to return to Henan. Actually, if one of you can drive, buy a car. It will be more convenient,' said Xu Xueping.

The three scrapers gaped at the two people in front of them, unsure if they were angels or devils. Like clockwork, one of the men raised the same question as the tramp before him: 'What do you want with us?'

The answer was the same: 'We just need you to do us one little favor: the aliens are coming. If they ask you, tell them you have this much money. That's all. Can you promise to do this?'

The three men nodded in assent.

'Thank you.'

'Thank you.' The two plutocrats bowed in sincere appreciation and drove off, leaving the three baffled scrapers standing next to the stack of cases.

'You must be wondering if they will keep the money for themselves,' Zhu said to Smoothbore, his eyes still on the steering wheel. 'Perhaps in the beginning, but they will soon share their wealth with the less fortunate, just as we have done.'

Smoothbore kept silent. Confronted with such absurdity, he felt it was best to say nothing at all. His intuition told him that the world as he knew it was about to undergo a fundamental change.

'Stop the car!' cried Xu. She called to a small, filthy child who was rummaging through a trash can for tin cans and cola bottles: 'Kid, come here!' The urchin dashed over, dragging his half-filled sack of cans and bottles behind him as if afraid of losing it. 'Take a case from the truck bed.' The boy obliged. 'Look inside.' He opened the case and peered inside. He was surprised, but not as shocked as the four adults had been. 'What is it?' prompted Xu.

'Money,' replied the boy, lifting his head to gaze at her.

'One million yuan. Take it home and give it to your parents.'

'So it's true?' The boy blinked, turning his head to look at the boxes still stacked high in the truck bed.

'What do you mean?'

'I heard people were giving away money all over the city.'

Like throwing away scrap paper, thought Smoothbore. Xu continued: 'You have to promise something before you can keep it. The aliens are coming. If they ask you, you must tell them you have this much money – exactly this much money, okay? That's all we want. Will you do it?'

'Yes!'

'Then take your money and go home, boy. No one will ever be poor again,' said Zhu as he started the truck.

'No one will ever be rich again, either,' said Xu, a dark look on her face.

'Pull yourself together. It's a bad situation, but we have a responsibility to stop it from getting worse,' said Zhu.

'You really think there is a point to this little game of ours?'

Zhu slammed the brakes and brought the truck to a lurching halt. Gesticulating wildly over the steering wheel, he shouted, 'Yes, *of course* it has a point! Or do you *want* to live the rest of your life like these people? Starving and homeless?'

'I don't even want to go on living anymore.'

'Your sense of duty will sustain you. In these dark days, it's the only thing that keeps me going. Our wealth demands that we devote ourselves to this mission.'

'Our wealth *what*?' shrieked Xu. 'We never stole, we never coerced, every yuan we earned was *clean*. Our wealth pushed society forward. Society should thank us!'

'Try telling that to the Elder Brothers,' said Zhu, stepping down from the truck. He tilted his face to the sky and heaved a long sigh.

'Now do you see that we're not psycho killers with a grudge against the poor?' The question was addressed to Smoothbore, who had followed him outside. 'No, on the contrary, we've been spreading our wealth amongst the very poorest, like you just witnessed. In this city and many others, in our nation's most impoverished areas, the employees of our companies are doing the same thing. They are utilizing every resource available to our conglomerate – billions of checks, credit cards, savings accounts, truckload upon truckload of cash – to eliminate poverty.'

Just then, Smoothbore noticed the curious spectacle in the sky: the line of silver stars now stretched from one horizon to the other. The Elder Brothers' mothership had completely disintegrated, and thousands of smaller ships had formed a gleaming halo around Earth.

'Earth is surrounded,' said Zhu. 'Each of those ships is the size of an aircraft carrier, and the weapons of just one of them could destroy the whole planet.'

'Last night, they destroyed Australia,' interjected Xu.

'Destroyed? What do you mean destroyed?' asked Smoothbore, his head craning towards the sky.

'They swept a laser over the Australian continent from space. It pierced right through buildings and bunkers, and every human and large mammal was dead within the hour. Insects and plants were left unscathed, though, and porcelain in shop windows wasn't so much as scratched.'

Smoothbore glanced momentarily at Xu and then turned his gaze back to the sky. He was better equipped to deal with this sort of terror than most.

'It was a show of force. They chose Australia because it was the first country to explicitly reject the 'reservation' plan,' added Zhu.

'What plan is that?' Smoothbore asked.

'Let me start from the beginning,' began Zhu. 'The Elder Brothers have come to our solar system as refugees, unable to survive on First Earth. 'We have lost our homeland' – those were the words they used. They have not elaborated on the causes. They want to occupy our Earth, Fourth Earth, and use it as a new habitat. As for this Earth's inhabitants, they will be relocated to a human 'reservation', located in what used to be Australia. Every other territory will belong to the Elder Brothers. . . . An anouncement will be made in tonight's news.'

'*Australia?* It's a big chunk of rock in the middle of the ocean.' Smoothbore considered it for a moment. 'Actually, it *is* pretty suitable. The Australian outback is one big desert – if they squeeze five billion people on the island, starvation will set in before the week is out.'

'Things aren't that bleak. Human agriculture and industry will not exist on the reservation. There will be no need to engage in production to survive.'

'How will they live?'

'The Elder Brothers will support us – they will provide for humanity. In the future, everything humans need to live will be provided by the Elder Brothers and distributed evenly among us. Every person will receive the same amount. In the future, wealth inequality will cease to exist in human society.'

'But how will they determine how much to allocate each person?'

'You've grasped the key issue at hand,' replied Zhu. 'According to the reservation plan, the Elder Brothers will conduct a comprehensive census of humanity, the goal of which is to determine the absolute minimum standard of living that humans can tolerate. The Elder Brothers will then allocate resources according to the results.'

Smoothbore lowered his head and thought for a moment, and then suddenly chuckled, 'I think I get it. At least, I think I see the big picture now.'

'You understand the plight that humanity currently faces?'

'Actually, the Elder Brothers' plan is very fair to humanity.'

'What? You think it's fair?! You—' Xu sputtered.

'He's right, it is fair,' Zhu calmly interrupted. 'If there is no gap between poor and rich, no difference between the lowest and highest standards of living, then the reservation will be paradise on Earth.'

'But now . . .'

'Now, what we must do is simple: before the Elder Brothers conduct their census, we must rapidly level the sharp divide between rich and poor.'

'So this is "social wealth liquidation"?' asked Smoothbore.

'Precisely. At present, society's wealth has solidified. It has its ups and downs, like the high-rises on this street or a mountain towering over a plain. But once it has been liquefied, it will become like the smooth surface of the ocean.

'But what you are doing now will only create chaos.'

'True,' nodded Zhu. 'We are merely making a gesture of goodwill on behalf of people of means. The real liquidation of wealth will soon commence under the unified leadership of national governments and the United Nations. A sweeping campaign to eliminate poverty is about to begin. Rich countries will pour capital into the developing world, rich people will shower the poor with money – and it will be carried out with perfect sincerity.'

Smoothbore gave a cynical laugh. 'Things may not be that simple.'

'What do you mean, you bastard?' Xu snarled through clenched teeth. She jabbed a finger at Smoothbore's nose, but Zhu instantly stopped her.

'He's a smart fellow. He figured it out,' said Zhu, tilting his head in Smoothbore's direction.

'Yes, I have figured it out. There are poor people who don't want your money.'

Xu glowered at Smoothbore, then she lowered her head and fell silent. Zhu nodded. 'Right. There are those who do not want money. Can you imagine? Scrounging in the garbage for scraps of food, but refusing an offer of one million yuan? Yes, you hit the nail on the head.'

'But those people must surely be a tiny minority,' said Smoothbore.

'Of course, but even if they account for just one in every hundred thousand poor people, they will be counted as a separate social class. According to the Elder Brothers' advanced survey methods, their standard of living will be identified as humanity's minimum standard of living, which in turn will be adopted as the criterion for the Elder Brothers' resource allocation to the reservation! Do you get it? Just one thousandth of one percent!'

'What percentage of the population do they account for at present?'

'About one in every thousand.'

'Perverted, despicable traitors!' Xu cursed loudly at the sky.

'So you contracted me to kill them.' At the moment, Smoothbore did not feel like using professional jargon.

Zhu nodded.

Smoothbore stared at Zhu with a queer expression, and then threw his head back and burst into laughter. 'I'm killing for the benefit of humankind!'

'You are benefiting humanity. You are rescuing human civilization.'

'Actually,' mused Smoothbore, 'death threats would do the trick.'

'That's no guarantee!' Xu leaned towards Smoothbore and whispered in a low voice. 'We are dealing with lunatics, twisted with class hatred. Even if they did take the money, they would still swear to the Elder Brothers that they were penniless. We have to wipe them off the planet as soon as possible.'

'I understand,' nodded Smoothbore.

'So what's your plan now? We have explained our reasoning just as you asked us. Of course, money will soon be meaningless, and you certainly don't care about helping humanity.'

'Money was never of great concern to me, and I've never considered the latter. . . . But I will fulfill the contract – by midnight tonight. Please prepare whatever you need to verify its completion.' As he finished speaking, Smoothbore stepped down from the truck and began to leave.

'I have one question,' Zhu called after Smoothbore's retreating back. 'Perhaps it's impolite, so you don't have to answer. If you were poor, would you refuse our money?'

'I am not poor,' Smoothbore answered, without looking back. He took a few more steps, and then paused and turned. He fixed the pair with a hawkish gaze. 'If were . . . then yes, I would not take it.' Then he strode away.

'Why did you refuse their money?' Smoothbore asked his first mark. He had last seen the homeless man in Blossom Plaza; now, they stood in a grove of trees in a nearby park. Two types of light filtered through the canopy. The first was the eerie blue glow that emanated from the ring of the Elder Brothers' ships, casting dappled shadows across the ground. The second was the shifting, kaleidoscopic brilliance of the metropolis itself, wavering wildly as it slanted through the trees, as if terrified of the blue glow.

The tramp snickered. 'They were begging me. All those rich people were begging *me!* One woman even cried! If I took their money, they wouldn't care about me, and it felt so refreshing to *be* begged for a change.'

'Yes, very refreshing,' said Smoothbore, as he pulled Snubnose's trigger.

The tramp was an enterprising thief. He had seen at a glance that the man who had called him into the grove was holding something wrapped beneath his coat, and he was curious to discover what it was. He saw a sudden flash from beneath the man's coat, like the wink of some strange creature within, and he was plunged into endless darkness.

The job was processed and cooled almost instantly. The rapidly spinning bullet severed most of the unit's head above the brow. The gunshot was muffled under layers of clothing. No one noticed.

*

Returning to the landfill, Smoothbore discovered that only his next mark remained – the other junkmen had evidently claimed their new fortunes and left.

Under the blue light of the ring of starships, Smoothbore picked his way across the warm, springy waste heap with purposeful strides, heading straight for his target. He had reminded himself a hundred times beforehand that this was not Sweet Pea, and there was no need to repeat the warning again. His blood ran cold, and it would not be warmed by a handful of youthful memories. The scavenger girl had not even noticed his arrival when Smoothbore fired his gun. There was no need to silence his weapon on the landfill. Freed from his coat, the shot rang clear, and the flash lit up the garbage around him like a small bolt of lightning. The range gave the bullet time to sing as it tumbled through the air, its whine like the wailing of spirits.

This job was also processed and cooled expeditiously. In an instant, the bullet shredded the unit's heart like the whirling blade of a buzzsaw. She was dead before she hit the ground. Her body was quickly swallowed into the landfill, and the blood that might have testified to her existence was quickly sopped up by the garbage.

Without warning, Smoothbore became aware of a presence behind him. He spun on his heel to face the itinerant artist. The man's long hair fluttered in the evening breeze like blue flames in the light of the ring of stars.

'They had you kill her?' asked the artist.

'Merely honoring a contract. Did you know her?'

'Yes. She often came to look at my art. She couldn't read much, but she understood the paintings. She liked them, just like you.'

'I've been contracted to kill you, too.'

The artist dipped his head in calm acknowledgment. He did not betray a hint of fear. 'I thought so.'

'Out of curiosity, why did you refuse the money?'

'My paintings describe poverty and death. If I became a millionaire overnight, my art would die.'

Smoothbore nodded. 'Your art will live on. I truly do like your painting.' He raised his gun.

'Wait a moment. You said you were fulfilling a contract. Can I sign one with you?'

Smoothbore nodded again. 'Of course.'

'My death doesn't matter, but I want you to avenge her.' The artist pointed to where the scavenger lay amid the garbage.

'Let me rephrase your request in the language of my profession: you want to contract me to process an order of work, the same units that contracted me to process you and this other unit.'

The artist responded with a nod. 'Just like that.'

Smoothbore gravely assented, 'Not a problem.'

'I have no money.'

Smoothbore laughed, 'You sold me that painting far too cheaply. It has already paid for this job.'

'Then, thank you.'

'You're welcome. I am merely honoring a contract.'

Snubnose's muzzle spat deadly fire once more. The bullet twisted, careening through the air, and struck the artist in the heart. Blood sprayed from his chest and his back as he fell, and the droplets showered the ground like a hot, red rain.

'There was no need for that.'

The voice came from behind Smoothbore. He whirled around again and saw a person standing in the center of the landfill, a man. He wore a leather jacket almost identical to Smoothbore's own, and he looked young but otherwise unremarkable. The blue light from the ring of stars glinted in his eyes.

Smoothbore lowered his gun and trained it away from the newcomer, but he lightly squeezed the trigger. Snubnose's hammer rose unhurriedly to the fully-cocked position, ready to fire at the slightest touch.

'Are you police?' Smoothbore asked casually.

The stranger shook his head.

'Then go call them.'

The man stood still.

'I will not shoot you in the back. I only process work specified in my contract.'

'Currently, we are not to intervene in human affairs,' the man replied evenly.

His words struck Smoothbore like a bolt of lightning. His grip slackened, and the hammer of his revolver fell back into place. He peered closely at the stranger. In the glow of the starships, he was, by all appearances, an ordinary man.

'You've . . . already landed, then?' Smoothbore asked, an uncommon waver in his voice.

'We landed quite some time ago.'

Standing atop a landfill somewhere on Fourth Earth, a long silence settled over the two individuals from different worlds. The thick, warm air suddenly felt stifling. Smoothbore wanted to say something, anything, and the events of the past few days prompted a question: 'Are there poor people and rich people where you come from?'

The First Earthling smiled and said, 'Of course. I am poor.' He gestured towards the ring of stars above them. 'As are they.'

'How many people are up there?'

'If you mean those of us in the ships you can see now, about five hundred thousand. But we are just the vanguard. Ten thousand more ships will arrive in a few years from now, carrying one billion.'

'A billion?' wondered Smoothbore. 'They . . . can't all be poor, can they?'

'Every last one,' confirmed the alien.

'How many people are there on First Earth?'

'Two billion.'

'How can so many people on one world be poor?'

'How can so many people on one world *not* be poor?' countered the alien.

'I would think,' Smoothbore said, 'that too many poor people would destabilize a world, which would make things difficult for the middle and upper classes as well.'

'At this stage of Fourth Earth's development, that is true.'

'But it won't always be true?'

The First Earthling bowed his head and considered this, and then replied, 'Why don't I tell you the story of the rich and poor of First Earth?'

'I'd like to hear it.' Smoothbore tucked Snubnose back into his underarm holster.

'Our two human civilizations are remarkably similar,' began the alien. 'The paths you follow now, we travelled before you, and we, too, lived through an era similar to your present. Although the distribution of wealth was uneven, our society struck a certain balance. The population, rich and poor alike, was a manageable size, and it was commonly believed that wealth inequality would disappear as society progressed. Most people looked forward to an age of perfect prosperity and great harmony. But we soon discovered that things were far more complicated than we had imagined, and the balance we had achieved would soon be destroyed.'

'Destroyed by what?'

'Education. You know that in the present age of Fourth Earth, education is the sole means of social ascendancy. If society is an ocean, stratified by differences in temperature and salinity, then education is a pipe that connects the ocean floor to the surface and prevents the complete isolation of each layer.'

'So you're saying that fewer and fewer poor people could afford to attend university?'

'Yes. The cost of higher education grew increasingly expensive, until it became a privilege reserved for the sons and daughters of the social elite. However, the price of traditional education did have limits, even if they were only crude market considerations, so while the pipe grew gossamer-thin, it did not vanish completely. But one day, the appearance of a dramatic new technology fundamentally changed education.'

Smoothbore hazarded a guess. 'Do you mean the ability to transmit knowledge directly to the brain?'

'Yes, but the direct infusion of knowledge was only part of it. A human brain could be implanted within a supercomputer with a capacity that far exceeded that of the brain itself; the inventoried knowledge of the computer could then be recalled by the implantee as distinct memories.' The alien continued, 'But this was only one of the computer's secondary functions. It was an amplifier of intelligence, an amplifier of understanding, and it could raise human thought to a whole new level. Suddenly, knowledge, intelligence, depth of thought – even perfection of mind, character, and aesthetic judgment – were commodities that could be purchased.'

'Must have been expensive,' observed Smoothbore.

'Incredibly so. Expressed in your current monetary terms, the cost of this premium education for a single person was equivalent to buying two or three one hundred fifty square meter apartments in one of Shanghai or Beijing's prime neighborhoods.'

'Even if it cost that much, there would still be a few who could afford it.'

'Yes,' the First Earthling admitted, 'but they were a tiny segment of the upper class. The pipeline from the bottom of society to the top was completely severed. Those who received this premium education were vastly more intelligent than those who did not. The cognitive differences between these educated elites and ordinary humans were as large as those between humans and dogs, and these differences manifested themselves in every aspect of human life – even artistic sensibility, for example. This super-intelligentsia formed a new culture – a culture as incomprehensible to the rest of humanity as a symphony is incomprehensible to a dog. They could master hundreds of languages, and on any given occasion they would use the particular language that etiquette demanded. From the perspective of these super-intellects, conversing with ordinary people seemed as condescending as cooing to puppies. And so, quite naturally, something happened. You're smart, you should be able to guess.'

Smoothbore hesitated. 'Rich people and poor people were no longer the same . . . the same . . .'

'The rich and the poor were no longer the same species. The rich were as different to the poor as the poor were to dogs. The poor were no longer people.'

Smoothbore gasped. 'That must have changed everything.'

'It changed many things. First, the factors you mentioned that maintained a balance of wealth and limited the poor population ceased to exist. Even if dogs outnumbered humans, they would be unable to destabilize the foundations of human society. At worst, the disruption would be a nuisance but unthreatening.' The alien frowned. 'Though the willful killing of a dog might be a punishable offense, it is not like killing a person. When human health and safety is threatened by rabies, it is judged acceptable to put all dogs down. Sympathy for poor people hinged on one shared characteristic – personhood. When the poor ceased to be people, and all commonalities between rich and poor vanished, sympathy followed suit. This was humanity's second evolution. When we first split from apes, it was due to natural selection. When we split from the poor, it was due to an equally sacred law: the inviolability of private property.'

'Property is sacred in our world, too.'

'On First Earth, it was upheld by something called the Social Machine,' explained the alien. 'The Social Machine was a powerful enforcement system, and its Enforcers could be found in every corner of the planet. Some of these units were no bigger than mosquitoes, but they were capable of killing hundreds in a single strike. They were not governed by the Three Laws proposed by your Asimov, but by the fundamental principle of the First Earth Constitution: that private property shall be inviolable. But it would be inaccurate to say they brought about autocracy. They enforced the law with absolute impartiality and showed no favor to the wealthy. If the pitiful property of some poor fellow came under threat, they would protect it in strict accordance with the constitution.

'Under the powerful protection of the Social Machine, the wealth of First Earth flowed relentlessly towards the pockets of an elite minority. To make matters worse, technological development eliminated the reliance of the propertied classes on the propertyless. On your world, the rich still need the poor, because factories still need workers. On First Earth, machines no longer needed human operators, and high-efficiency robots could perform any required task. The poor could not even sell their labor, and they sank into absolute destitution as a result. This transformed the economic reality of First Earth, vastly accelerating the concentration of wealth in just a few people's hands.

'I would not be able to explain the highly complex process of wealth concentration to you,' the alien said, 'but in essence it resembles the movements of capital on your world. During my great-grandfather's lifetime, sixty percent of the wealth on First Earth was controlled by ten million people. During my grandfather's lifetime, eighty percent of our world's wealth was controlled by ten thousand people. During my father's lifetime, ninety percent of the wealth belonged to just forty two people. When I was born, capitalism had reached its apex on First Earth and had worked an unbelievable miracle: ninety-nine percent of the planet's wealth was held by a single person! This person became known as the Last Capitalist.

'While disparities in standards of living still existed among the other two billion, they controlled just one percent of the world's wealth in total. That is to say, First Earth had become a world with one rich person and two billion impoverished people. All the while, the constitutional inviolability of private property remained in effect, and the Social Machine faithfully carried out its duty to protect the property of a sole individual.'

'Do you want to know what the Last Capitalist owned?' The alien raised his voice. 'He owned First Earth! Every continent and ocean on the planet became his parlor rooms and private gardens. Even the atmosphere of First Earth was among his personal property.

'The remaining two billion individuals inhabited fully enclosed dwellings – miniature, self-contained life-support units. They lived sealed away in their own tiny worlds, sustained by their own paltry supplies of water, air, soil and other resources. The one resource that did not belong to the Last Capitalist, and the only thing they could lawfully take from the outside world, was sunlight.

'My home sat next to a small river, edged by green grass. The meadows stretched down to the riverbed and beyond, sweeping all the way to the emerald foothills in the distance. From inside, we could hear the sounds of birds twittering and fish leaping from the water, and we could see unhurried herds of deer grazing by the riverbanks, but it was the sight of the grass rippling in the breeze that I found particularly bewitching.

'But none of this belonged to us. My family was strictly cut off from the outside world, and we could only watch through airtight portholes that could never be opened. To go outside, it was necessary to pass through an airlock, as if we were exiting a spaceship into outer space. In truth, our home was very much like a spaceship – the difference was that the hostile environment was on the inside! We could only breathe the foul air supplied by our life-support system, could only drink the water that had been re-filtered a million times over, could only choke down food produced using our own raw excrement. And all the while, only a single wall separated us from the vast, bountiful world of nature. When we stepped outside, we dressed like astronauts and brought our own food and water. We even brought our own oxygen tanks, because the air, after all, belonged not to us, but to the Last Capitalist.

'Of course, we could afford the occasional splurge. For weddings or holidays, we would leave our closed little home and luxuriate in the great outdoors. That first breath of natural air was positively intoxicating. It was faintly sweet – sweet enough to make you cry. It wasn't free, though. We had to swallow pill-sized air meters before we went out, which measured exactly how much air we breathed. Every time we inhaled, a fee was deducted from our bank account.

This was a luxury for most of the poor, something they could afford once or twice a year. We never dared to exert ourselves while outdoors. We mostly just sat and controlled our breathing. Before we returned home, we had to carefully scrape the soles of our shoes, because the soil outside was not ours to keep.'

The First Earthling paused for a moment. 'I will tell you how my mother died,' he said slowly. 'In order to cut down on expenditures, she refrained from leaving the house for three years. She could not bear to go out even on holidays. On the night it happened, she managed to slip past the airlock doors in her sleep. She must have been dreaming about nature. When she was discovered by an Enforcer, she had already wandered quite far. It saw that she had not swallowed an air meter, so it dragged her back home, cuffing her about the neck with a metal claw. It never intended to strangle her. By preventing her breathing, it only meant to protect another citizen's inviolable private property – the air. She was dead by the time she arrived home. The Enforcer dropped her corpse and informed us that she had committed larceny. We were fined, but we could not pay, so my mother's body was confiscated instead. You should know that a corpse is a precious thing for a poor family – seventy percent of its weight is water, plus a few other resources. The value of my mother's corpse, however, could not cover the fine, and the Social Machine siphoned off an amount of air that corresponded to the remainder of the debt.

'The air supply in our family's life-support system was already critically low, as we lacked the funds to replenish it. The removal of more air put our very survival at risk. In order to replace the lost oxygen, the life-support system was forced to separate some of its water resources through electrolysis. Unfortunately, this operation caused the entire system to deteriorate sharply. The main control computer issued an alarm: if we did not add fifteen liters of water to the system, it would crash in exactly thirty hours. The crimson glow of the warning lights filled every room.

'We considered stealing water from the river outside but soon abandoned the plan. We would not make it back home with the water without being shot dead by the omnipresent Enforcers. My father thought for a while, and then he told me not to worry and to go to bed. Though I was terrified, oxygen deprivation crept in, and I slept. I do not know how much time had passed when a robot nudged me awake. It had entered via the resource conversion vehicle that was docked to my home. It pointed to a bucket of crystal-clear water and told me: 'This is your father.'

'Resource conversion vehicles were mobile installations that converted human bodies into resources that could be utilized by household life-support systems. My father had utilized the service to extract every last drop of water from his own body, while not one hundred meters from our house, that pretty little river burbled in the moonlight. The resource conversion truck also extracted a few other useful things from his body for our life-support system: a container of grease, a bottle of calcium tablets, even a piece of iron as large as a coin.'

The alien paused again to collect himself. 'The water from my father rescued our life-support system, and I lived on. I grew up day by day, and soon five years had passed. One fall evening, as I looked through the porthole at the world outside, I suddenly noticed someone jogging along the riverbank. I was astonished: who was so extravagant that they would dare breathe like that outside?! Upon a closer look, I realized it was the Last Capitalist himself!

'He slowed his pace to a stroll, and then he sat down on a rock by the river's edge, dipping one bare foot into the water. He looked like a trim middle-aged man, but in reality he was over two thousand years old. Genetic engineering guaranteed that he would live for at least another two millennia, perhaps even forever. But he seemed perfectly ordinary to me.

'Two years later, my home's life support system functions deteriorated once more. Small-scale ecosystems like that were bound to have limited lifespans. Eventually, the whole system broke down. As the oxygen content in the air supply dwindled, I swallowed an air meter and walked out the door before I fell into an anoxic coma. Like every other person whose life-support system had failed, I stoically accepted my fate: I would breathe away the last of the pitiful savings in my account, and then I would be suffocated or shot by an Enforcer.

'I found there were many other people outside. The mass failures of household life-support systems had begun. A gargantuan Enforcer hovered above us and broadcast a final warning: 'Citizens, you have intruded into someone else's home. You have committed an act of trespassing. Please leave immediately! Otherwise . . .''

'Leave? Where could we go? There was no air left to breathe in our homes. Together with the others, I bounded through the green grass along the river, letting the fresh, sweet spring breeze rush over my pallid face, looking to go out in a blaze of glory . . .

'I don't know how long we ran before we realized we had long since breathed up the last of our savings, and yet the Enforcers had not taken action. Just then, the Last Capitalist's voice boomed forth from the massive Enforcer floating in the air.

Hello, everyone. Welcome to my humble home!

I am pleased to have so many guests, and I hope you have enjoyed yourselves in my garden. You will have to forgive me, however, but there are just too many of you. As of this moment, almost one billion people worldwide have left their own homes, as their life-support systems failed, and walked into mine. Another billion may be close behind. You have trespassed on my private property and violated the habitation and privacy rights of your fellow citizen. The Social Machine is lawfully empowered to take action to end your lives, and if I had not dissuaded it from doing just that, you would all have been vaporized by the Enforcers' lasers long ago. In any case, I did dissuade it. I am a gentleman who has received the best education available, and I treat guests in my home – even unlawful intruders – with courtesy and respect. But you must imagine things from my perspective. Two billion guests is a few too many for even the most thoughtful host, and I am someone who enjoys quiet solitude. Therefore, I must ask you all to leave. I recognize, of course, that there is nowhere on Earth for you to go, but I have taken it upon myself to prepare a fleet of twenty thousand spaceships for you.

Each ship is the size of a medium city and can travel at one percent of the speed of light. While the ships are not equipped with complete life-support systems, there are enough cryogenic chambers onboard to hold all two billion of you for fifty thousand years. This is the only planet in our solar system, so you will have to search for a new homeland among the stars, but I am certain you will find such a place. In the vastness of the cosmos, is it really necessary to crowd this little cottage of mine? You have no cause to resent me. I obtained my home through perfectly reasonable and legitimate means. I got my start as the manager of a small feminine hygiene products company, and to this day, I have relied only on my own business savvy. I am a law-abiding citizen, so the Social Machine has protected and will continue to protect me and my legal property. It will not tolerate your wrongdoing, however, so I advise everyone to get going as soon as possible.

Out of respect for our common evolutionary origin, I will remember you, and I hope you will remember me. Take care.

'And that is how we came to Fourth Earth,' concluded the First Earthling. 'Our voyage lasted for thirty thousand years. We lost nearly half our fleet while wandering endlessly through the stars. Some disappeared amidst interstellar dust; some were swallowed by black holes. . . . But ten thousand ships survived, and one billion of us reached this world. And that is the story of First Earth, the story of two billion poor people and one rich man.'

'If you did not intervene, would our world repeat this tale?' Smoothbore asked after the First Earthling finished his narration.

'I do not know. Perhaps, but perhaps not. The course of a civilization is like the fate of an individual – fickle and impossible to predict.' The alien paused. 'I should go now. I am only an ordinary census taker, and I must work for my living.'

'I have things to attend to as well,' replied Smoothbore.

'Farewell, little brother.'

'Farewell, elder brother.'

Under the light of the ring of stars, two men from two different worlds parted in two different directions.

As Smoothbore entered the Presidential Hall, the thirteen members of the standing committee of the Council for Liquidation of Social Wealth turned to face him. Zhu Hanyang spoke first: 'We have verified your work, and you have done well. The second half of your payment has been transferred into your account, although it will not be of use for much longer.' He paused. 'There is something else you must already know: the Elder Brothers' census takers have landed on Earth. Our work is meaningless now, and we have no further tasks to give you.'

'Actually, I've taken another commission.'

As he spoke, Smoothbore drew his pistol with one hand and stretched his opposite hand forward, fist clenched.

Bang, bang, bang, bang, bang, bang, bang – seven glinting bullets fell to the table in front of him. Together with the six shots in Snubnose, that made thirteen in all.

Thirteen faces, shaped by the weight of their immense wealth, twisted in unison as shock and horror flashed across their refined features. Then, a calm settled. Maybe they felt relief.

Outside, a shower of massive meteors split the sky. Their brilliant light pierced through the heavy curtains and eclipsed the crystal chandelier, and the ground shook violently. The ships of First Earth had entered the atmosphere.

'Have you had dinner?' Xu Xueping asked Smoothbore. She pointed towards a heap of instant noodles on the table. 'Let's eat first.'

They stacked a large silver punch basin atop three crystal ashtrays and added water to the basin. Then, they lit a fire beneath it with one hundred yuan notes. Everyone took turns feeding bills into the fire, gazing absently at the yellow and green flames that leapt like a small joyful creature.

After the fire consumed 1.35 million yuan, the water began to boil.

ODE TO JOY

AN ALTERNATE HISTORY OF THE SOPHON

The Concert

The concert held to close the final session of the United Nations was a depressing one.

A utilitarian attitude toward the body, dating back to bad precedents set at the start of the century, had been on the rise; countries assumed the UN was a tool to achieve their interests, and interpreted its charter to their own benefit. Smaller nations challenged the authority of the permanent members, while each permanent member believed it deserved more authority within the organization, which lost all authority of its own as a result. A decade on, all efforts at a rescue had failed, and everyone agreed that the UN and the idealism it represented no longer applied to the real world. It was time to be rid of it.

All heads of state assembled for the final session, to observe a solemn funeral for the UN. The concert, held on the lawn outside the General Assembly building, was the final item on the program.

It was well after sunset. This was the most bewitching time of day, the handover from day to night when the cares of reality were masked by the growing dusk. The world was still visible under the last light from the setting sun, and on the lawn, the air was thick with the scent of budding flowers.

The secretary general was the last to arrive. On the lawn, she ran across Richard Clayderman,* one of the evening's featured performers, and struck up a cheerful conversation.

---

*The French musician's 1992 performance in China was the first by a major foreign pianist, and he has remained the most recognized classical musician in the decades since.

'Your playing fascinates me,' she told the prince of pianists with a smile.

Clayderman, dressed in his favorite snow-white suit, looked uncomfortable. 'If that's genuine, then I'm overjoyed. But I've heard there have been complaints about my appearance at a concert like this.'

Not merely complaints. The head of UNESCO, a noted art theorist, had publicly criticized Clayderman's playing as 'busker-level,' and his performances as 'blasphemy against piano artistry.'

The secretary general lifted a hand to stop him. 'The UN can have none of classical music's arrogance. You've erected a bridge from classical music to the masses, and so must we bring humanity's highest ideals directly to the common people. That's why you were invited here tonight. Believe me, when I first heard your music under the sweltering sun in Africa, I had the feeling of standing in a ditch looking up at the stars. It was intoxicating.'

Clayderman gestured toward the leaders on the lawn. 'It feels more like a family gathering than a UN event.'

The secretary general looked over the crowd. 'On this lawn, for tonight at least, we have realized a utopia.'

She crossed the lawn and reached the front row. It was a glorious evening. She had planned on switching off her political sixth sense and just relaxing for once, taking her place as an ordinary member of the audience, but this proved impossible. That sense had picked up a situation: The president of China, engaged in conversation with the president of the United States, looked up at the sky for a moment. The act itself was utterly unremarkable, but the secretary general noticed that it was a little on the long side, perhaps just an extra second or two, but she'd noticed it. When the secretary general sat down after shaking hands with the other world leaders in the front row, the Chinese president looked up at the sky again, confirming his perception. Where national leaders are concerned, apparently random actions are in fact highly precise, and under normal circumstances, this act would not have been repeated. The US president also noticed it.

'The lights of New York wash out the stars. The sky's far brighter than this over DC,' he said.

The Chinese president nodded but said nothing.

The US president went on, 'I like looking at the stars, too. In the ever-changing course of history, our profession needs an immovable reference object.'

'That object is an illusion,' the Chinese president said.

'Why do you say that?'

Instead of responding directly, the Chinese president pointed at a cluster of stars that had just come out. 'Look, that's the Southern Cross, and that's Canis Major.'

The US president smiled. 'You've proven they're immovable enough. Ten thousand years ago, primitive man would have seen the same Southern Cross and Canis Major as we do today. They may have even come up with those names.'

'No, Mr. President. In fact, the sky might even have been different just yesterday.' The Chinese president looked up for a third time. He remained calm, but the steel in his eyes made the other two nervous. They looked at the same placid sky they had seen so many times before; nothing seemed wrong. They looked questioningly at the Chinese president.

'The two constellations I just noted should only be visible from the southern hemisphere,' he said without pointing them out or looking upward. He turned thoughtfully toward the horizon.

The secretary general and US president looked questioningly at him.

'We're looking at the sky from the other side of the Earth,' he said.

The US president yelped, but then restrained himself and said in a voice even lower than before, 'You've got to be kidding.'

'Look, what's that?' the secretary general said, pointing at the sky with a hand raised only to eye level so as not to alarm the others.

'The moon, of course,' the US president said after a brief glance overhead. But when the Chinese president slowly shook his head, he looked up a second time and was less certain. At first, the semicircular shape in the sky looked like the moon in first quarter, but it was bluish, as if a scrap of daytime sky had gotten stuck. The US president looked more closely at the blue semicircle. He held out a finger and measured the blue moon against it. 'It's growing.'

The three politicians stared up at the sky, not caring anymore if they'd startle the others. The heads of state in the surrounding seats noticed their movements, and more people looked upward. The orchestra on the outdoor stage abruptly stopped its warm-up.

By now, it was clear that the blue semicircle was not the moon, because its diameter had grown to twice that, and its darkness-shrouded other half was now visible in dim blue. In its brighter half, details could be made out; its surface was not a uniform blue but had patches of brown.

'God! Isn't that North America?' someone shouted. They were right. You could distinguish the familiar shape of the continent, which lay smack on the border between the light and dark halves. (It may have occurred to someone that was the very same position they occupied.) Then they found Asia, and the Arctic Ocean and the Bering Strait . . .

'It's . . . Earth!'

The US president drew back his finger. The blue sphere in the sky was now growing at a rate visible without a reference object, and was now at least three times the diameter of the moon. At first, it looked like a balloon rapidly inflating in the sky, but then a shout from the crowd abruptly changed that impression:

'It's falling!'

The shout provided a reasonable interpretation of the scene before them. Regardless of its accuracy, they immediately had a new sense of what was happening: another Earth was crashing toward them in space! The approaching blue planet now occupied a third of the sky, and surface details could be made out: brown continents covered in mountain wrinkles, cloud coverage looking like unmelted snow, outlined in black from the shadows cast on the ground. There was white at the North Pole, parts of which glittered – ice, rather than clouds. On a blue ocean, a snow-white object spiraled lazily with the delicate beauty of a velvet flower in a blue crystal vase – a newborn hurricane. . . . But when the huge blue sphere grew to cover half the sky, their perception experienced an almost simultaneous transformation.

'God! We're falling!'

The feeling of inversion came in an instant. The sphere filling half the sky gave them a feeling of height, or that the ground beneath their feet had vanished and they were now falling toward the other Earth. Its surface was clearer now, and on the dark side, not far from the shadow line, those with keen eyes could see a faint glowing band: the lights of America's East Coast cities, their own location in

New York a somewhat brighter spot within it. The other planet now filled two-thirds of the sky, and it seemed as if the two Earths would collide. There were screams from the crowd, and many of them shut their eyes.

Then all was still. The Earth overhead was no longer falling (or the ground they stood on was no longer falling toward it). The sphere hung motionless covering two-thirds of the sky, bathing the land in its blue glow.

Now sounds of chaos could be heard from the city, but the occupants of the lawn had the strongest nerves on the planet in unstable situations, so they held back their panic at the nightmarish scene and approached it more quietly.

'It's a hallucination,' the secretary general said.

'Yes,' the Chinese president said. 'If it were real, we'd feel the gravity. And this close to the sea, we'd be drowned by the tide.'

'It's more than just the tides,' the Russian president said. 'The two Earths would be torn to pieces by their mutual attraction.'

'The laws of physics don't permit two Earths to remain motionless,' the Japanese prime minister said, and, turning to the Chinese president, added, 'When that Earth first appeared, you were saying that the stars of the southern hemisphere were in the sky above us. Could the two phenomena be connected?' It was a tacit admission of eavesdropping, but they were past caring at this point.

'Perhaps we're about to find out,' the US president said. He spoke into a mobile phone; the secretary of state, at his elbow, informed the others that he was speaking with the International Space Station. And so they focused their anticipation on the president, who listened attentively to the phone but said only a few words. Silence reigned on the lawn, where in the blue light of that other Earth they looked like a throng of ghosts. After about two minutes, the president set down the phone, climbed onto a chair, and shouted to the expectant crowd:

'It's simple. A huge mirror has appeared next to the Earth!'

The Mirror

There was no way to describe it other than a huge mirror. Its surface perfectly reflected visual light as well as radar with no energy or image loss. Viewed from the right distance, the Earth would look like a stone on a go board ten billion square kilometers in area.

It shouldn't have been difficult for *Endeavor*'s astronauts to obtain preliminary data, since an astronomer and a space physicist were on board and had all the necessary equipment available and at their disposal, including the ISS, to conduct observations; however, their momentary panic had nearly sent the orbiter to its doom. The ISS was a fully-equipped observation platform, but its orbit was not conducive to observing an object situated 450 kilometers above the North Pole nearly perpendicular to the Earth's axis. *Endeavor*'s orbit sent it over the poles so it could carry out observations of the ozone holes; at a height of 280 kilometers, it was flying right between the Earth and the mirror.

Flying with an Earth on either side was nightmarish, like speeding along a canyon with blue cliffs towering above them. The pilot insisted it was a mirage, like the spatial disorientation he had experienced twice during his three thousand hours in a fighter jet, but the commander was convinced there really were two Earths. He ordered their orbit adjusted to compensate for the gravitational pull of the second one, but the astronomer stopped him in time. Once they got over their initial shock and learned from observations of the shuttle's orbit that one of the two Earths had no mass, they let out a sigh of relief: if they had made the compensational adjustments, *Endeavor* would be nothing more than a shooting star over the North Pole.

The astronauts carefully observed the massless Earth. Visual inspection indicated the orbiter was much farther away from it, but its North Pole seemed little different from that of the nearer Earth, if not entirely identical. They saw laser beams emitting from both North Poles, two long, dark red snakes twisting slowly in identical shapes at identical positions. Eventually they discovered one thing that the nearer Earth did not have: an object in flight above the massless Earth. Visually they judged it to be in an orbit roughly three hundred kilometers above its surface, but when they attempted to probe its orbit more precisely using shipboard radar, the radar seemed to bounce back from a solid wall a hundred-odd kilometers away. The massless Earth and the flying object were on the opposite side of that wall. Observing the object through the cockpit window using high-powered binoculars, the commander saw another space shuttle flying in low orbit over the frozen Arctic ice pack like a moth crawling along a blue striped wall. There was a figure behind that shuttle's cockpit window, looking through binoculars. The commander waved, and the figure waved at the same time.

And so they discovered the mirror.

They altered course to draw closer to the mirror. At a distance of three kilometers, the astronauts could see clearly *Endeavor*'s reflection six kilometers away, the glow of its aft engines lending it the form of a creeping firefly.

One astronaut took a spacewalk for humanity's first close encounter with the mirror. Thrusters on the suit spurted streams of white, speeding him across the distance. Carefully, he adjusted the jets to bring himself into position ten meters from the mirror. His reflection was remarkably clear, without any distortion. Since he was in orbit but the mirror was stationary with respect to the Earth, he had a relative speed of ten kilometers per second. He was racing past it, but no motion at all was visible. It was the smoothest, shiniest surface in the universe.

When the astronaut decelerated, his thruster jets had been aimed at the mirror for an extended period, and a white fog of benzene propellant had drifted toward it. During previous space walks, whenever the fog had come into contact with the shuttle or the outside wall of the ISS, it would leave a conspicuous smudge; he imagined it would be the same with the mirror, except that with the high relative velocity, the smudge would be a long stripe, like he used to draw with soap on the bathroom mirror as a child. But he saw nothing. The fog vanished upon contact with the mirror, whose surface remained bright as ever.

The shuttle's orbital trajectory gave them only a limited amount of time near the mirror, prompting the astronaut to act quickly. In an almost unconscious act the moment the fog disappeared, he took a wrench out of his tool bag and tossed it at the mirror, but once it left his hand, he and the astronauts aboard the shuttle were paralyzed with the realization that the relative velocity between it and the mirror gave it the force of a bomb. In terror they watched the wrench tumble toward the mirror and had a vision of the spiderweb fractures that in just moments would spread like lightning across the surface from the point of impact, and then the enormous mirror shattering into billions of glittering fragments, a sea of silver in the blackness of space. . . . But when the wrench touched the surface it vanished without a trace, and the mirror remained as smooth as before.

It actually wasn't hard to see that the mirror was massless, not a physical body, since floating motionless over Earth's North Pole would be impossible otherwise. (It might be more accurate to state, given their relative sizes, that the Earth was floating in the middle of the mirror.) Rather than a physical entity, the mirror was a field of some sort. Contact with the fog and the wrench proved that.

Delicately manipulating his thrusters and making continual microadjustments of the jets, the astronaut drew within half a meter of the mirror. He stared straight into his reflection, amazed once again at its fidelity: a perfect copy, one perhaps even more finely wrought than the original. He extended a hand toward it until he and his reflected hand were practically touching, separated by less than a centimeter. His earpiece was silent – the commander did not order him to stop – so he pushed forward, and his hand disappeared into the mirror. He and his image were joined at the wrist. There had been no sensation of contact. He retracted his hand and looked at it carefully. The suit glove was perfectly unharmed. No marks whatsoever.

Below the astronaut, the shuttle was gradually drawing away from the mirror and had to constantly run its engines and thrusters to maintain proximity. However, due to its trajectory its drift was accelerating, and before long such adjustments would be impossible. A second encounter would require waiting an entire orbit, but would the mirror still be there? With this in mind, the astronaut made a decision. He switched on his thrusters and headed straight into the mirror.

His reflection loomed large, filling his field of vision with the quicksilver bubble of his helmet's one-way reflective faceplate. He fought to keep from closing his eyes as his head touched the mirror. At contact he felt nothing, but in that very moment everything vanished before his eyes, replaced by the darkness of space and the familiar Milky Way. He jerked around, and below him was the same view of the galaxy, with one addition: his own reflection receding into the distance, the maneuvering units he and his reflection wore linked by streams of thruster jet fog.

He had crossed the mirror, and the other side of it was a mirror, too.

His earpiece had been chirping with the commander's voice when he was approaching the mirror, but it had cut out. The mirror blocked radio waves. Worse, the Earth wasn't visible from this side. Surrounded entirely by stars gave the astronaut the feeling of being isolated in a different world, and he began to panic. He adjusted the jets and arrested his outward motion. He had passed through the first time with his body parallel to the mirror, but now he oriented himself perpendicular, as if diving headfirst into it. Just before contact, he cut his speed. Then the top of his head touched the top of his reflection, and then he passed through and saw with relief the blue Earth below him, and heard the commander's voice in his ear.

Once his upper torso was through he dropped his drift speed, leaving the remainder of his body on the other side. Then he reversed the direction of his jets and began to back up; fog from the jets on the opposite side of the mirror issued from the surface around him like steam rising from a lake in which he was partially submerged. When the surface reached his nose, he made another startling discovery: The mirror passed through his faceplate and filled the crescent space between it and his face. He looked downward and saw his frightened pupils reflected in the crescent. No doubt the mirror was passing through his entire head, but he felt nothing. He reduced his speed to the absolute minimum, no faster than the tick of a second hand, and advanced millimeter by millimeter until the mirror bisected his pupils and vanished.

Everything was back to normal: Earth's blue sphere on one side, the glittering Milky Way on the other. But that familiar world persisted only for a second or two. He couldn't reduce his speed to zero, so before long the mirror was above his eyes, and the Earth vanished, leaving only the Milky Way. Above him, the mirror blocking his view of Earth extending hundreds of thousands of kilometers into the distance. The angle of reflection distorted his view of the stars into a silver halo on the mirror's surface. He reversed thrusters and drifted back, and the mirror dropped down across his eyes, vanishing momentarily as it passed to reveal both Earth and Milky Way before the galaxy vanished and the halo turned blue on the mirror's surface. He moved slowly back and forth several times, and as his pupils oscillated on either side, he felt like he was passing across a membrane between two worlds. At last he managed a fairly lengthy pause with the mirror invisible at the center of his pupils. He opened his eyes wide for a glimpse of a line at its position, but he saw nothing.

'The thing's got no width!' he exclaimed.

'Maybe it's only a few atoms thick, so you just can't see it. Maybe it approached Earth edgewise and that's why it arrived undetected.' That was the assessment of the shuttle crew, who were watching the images sent back.

The astonishing thing was that the mirror, perhaps just atoms thick but over a hundred Pacific Oceans in area, was so flat as to be invisible from a parallel vantage point; in classical geometry, it was an ideal plane.

Its absolute flatness explained its absolute smoothness. It was an ideal mirror.

A sense of isolation replaced the astronauts' shock and fear. The mirror made the universe strange and rendered them a group of newborn babes abandoned in a new, unfathomable world.

Then the mirror spoke.

The Musician

'I am a musician,' it said. 'I am a musician.'

The pleasing voice resounding through space was audible to all. In an instant, all sleepers on Earth awoke, and all those already awake froze like statues.

The mirror continued, 'Below I see a concert whose audience members are capable of representing the planet's civilization. Do you wish to speak with me?'

The national leaders looked to the secretary general, who was momentarily at a loss for words.

'I have something to say,' the mirror said.

'Can you hear us?' the secretary general ventured.

The mirror answered immediately, 'Of course I can. I could distinguish the voice of every bacterium on the world below me, if I wanted to. I perceive things differently from you. I can observe the rotation of every atom simultaneously. My perception encompasses temporal dimensions: I can witness the entire history of a thing all at once. You only see cross sections, but I see all.'

'How are we hearing your voice?' the US president asked.

'I am emitting superstring waves into your atmosphere.'

'Superstring waves?'

'A strong interactive force released from an atomic nucleus. It excites your atmosphere like a giant hand beating a drum. That's how you hear me.'

'Where do you come from?' the secretary general asked.

'I am a mirror drifting through the universe. I originate so far away in both time and space it is meaningless to speak of it.'

'How did you learn English?'

'I said that I see all. I should note that I'm speaking English because most of the audience at this concert was conversing in that language, not because I believe any ethnic group on the world below is superior to any other. It's all I can do when there's no global common tongue.'

'We do have a world language, but it is little used.'

'Your world language? Less an effort toward world unity than a classic expression of chauvinism. Why should a world language be Latinate rather than based on some other language family?'

This caused a commotion among the world leaders, who whispered nervously to each other.

'We're surprised at your understanding of Earth culture,' the secretary general said earnestly.

'I see all. Besides, a thorough understanding of a speck of dust isn't hard.'

The US president looked up at the sky and said, 'Are you referring to the Earth? You may be bigger, but on a cosmic scale you're on the same order as the Earth. You're a speck of dust, too.'

'You're less than dust,' the mirror said. 'A long, long time ago I used to be dust, but now I'm just a mirror.'

'Are you an individual or a collective?' the Chinese president asked.

'That question is meaningless. When a civilization travels far enough on the road of time, individual and collective both disappear.'

'Is a mirror your intrinsic form, or one of your many expressions?' the UK prime minister asked.

The secretary general added, 'In other words, are you deliberately exhibiting this form for our benefit?'

'This question is also meaningless. When a civilization travels far enough on the road of time, form and content both disappear.'

'We don't understand your answers to the last two questions,' the US president said.

The mirror said nothing.

Then the secretary general asked the key question: 'Why have you come to the solar system?'

'I am a musician. A concert is being held here.'

'Excellent,' the secretary general said with a nod. 'And humanity is the audience?'

'My audience is the entire universe, even if it will be a century before the nearest civilized world hears my playing.'

'Playing? Where's your instrument?' Richard Clayderman asked from the stage.

They realized the reflected Earth covering most of the sky had begun to slip swiftly toward the east. The change was frightening, like the sky falling, and a few people on the lawn involuntarily buried their head in their hands. Soon the reflection's edge dipped below the horizon, but at practically the same time, everything turned hazy in a sudden bright light. When sight returned, they saw the sun sitting smack in the middle of the sky right where the reflected Earth had been. Brilliant sunlight illuminated their surroundings under a brilliant blue sky that had replaced the black night. The oceans of the reflected Earth blended with the blue of the sky so the land seemed like a patch of clouds. They stared in shock at the change, but then a word from the secretary general explained the change that had taken place.

'The mirror tilted.'

Indeed, the huge mirror had tilted in space, drawing the sun into the reflection and casting its light onto the Earth's nighttime side.

'It rotates fast!' the Chinese president said.

The secretary general nodded. 'Yes, and at that size, the edges must be nearing the speed of light!'

'No physical object can tolerate the stresses from that rotation. It's a field, like our astronaut demonstrated. Near-light-speed motion is entirely normal for a field,' the US president said.

Then the mirror spoke: 'This is my instrument. I am a star player. My instrument is the sun!'

These grand words silenced them all, and they stared mutely at the reflected sun for a long while before someone asked, their voice trembling with awe, how it was played.

'You're all aware that many of the instruments you play have a sound chamber whose thin walls reflect and confine sound waves, allowing them to resonate and produce pleasing sounds. In the case of EM waves, the chamber is a star – it may lack visible walls, but it has a transmission speed gradient that reflects and refracts the waves, confining them to produce EM resonance and play beautiful music.'

'What does this instrument sound like?' Clayderman asked the sky.

'Nine minutes ago, I played tuning notes on the sun. The instrument's sound is now being transmitted at the speed of light. Of course, it's in EM form, but I can convert it to sound in your atmosphere through superstring waves. Listen . . .'

They heard a few delicate, sustained notes, similar to those of a piano, but with a magic that held everyone momentarily under its spell.

'How does the sound make you feel?' the secretary general asked the Chinese president.

'Like the whole universe is a huge palace, one that's twenty billion light-years tall. And the sound fills it completely.'

'Can you still deny the existence of God after hearing that?' the US president asked.

The Chinese president eyed him, and said, 'The sound comes from the real world. If it can produce such a sound, then God is even less essential.'

The Beat

'Is the performance about to start?' the secretary general asked.

'Yes. I'm waiting for the beat,' the mirror replied.

'The beat?'

'The beat began four years ago and is being transmitted here at the speed of light.'

Then there was a fearsome change in the sky. The reflected Earth and sun disappeared, replaced by dancing bright silver ripples that filled the sky, making them feel like Earth had been plunged into an enormous ocean and they were looking up at the blazing sun beyond the water's surface.

The mirror explained: 'I'm blocking intense radiation from outer space. I can't totally reflect it, so what you're seeing is the small portion that gets through. The radiation comes from a star that went supernova four years ago.'

'Four years ago? That's Centauri,' someone said.

'That's right. Proxima Centauri.'

'But that star has none of the necessary conditions for supernova,' the Chinese president said.

'I created the conditions,' the mirror said.

They realized that when the mirror had said it made preparations for this concert four years ago, it was referring to that event; after selecting the sun as its instrument, it had detonated Proxima Centauri. Judging from the audio test of the sun, it was evidently capable of acting through hyperspace and pulsing the sun 1 AU away. But whether it possessed the same ability for a star four light-years away remained unknown. The detonation of Proxima Centauri could have been accomplished in one of two ways: from the solar system via hyperspace, or by teleporting to its vicinity, detonating it, and then teleporting back. Both were godlike power, so far as humanity was concerned, and in any case the light from the supernova would still take four years to reach to the sun. The mirror said that music it played would be transmitted to the cosmos by EM, so was the speed of light for that hypercivilization akin to the speed of sound for humans? And if light waves were their sound waves, what was light for them? Humanity would never know.

'Your ability to manipulate the physical world is alarming,' the US president said.

'Stars are stones in the cosmic desert, the most commonplace of objects in my world. Sometimes I use stars as tools, other times as weapons, and other times as musical instruments. . . . I've turned Proxima Centauri into a metronome, basically the same as the stones used by your ancestors. We both take advantage of ordinary objects in our world to enlarge and extend our abilities.'

But the occupants of the lawn could see no similarity between the two, and abandoned the attempt to discuss technology with the mirror. Humanity could no more comprehend it than an ant could understand the ISS.

Little by little the light in the sky began to dim, giving them the impression that it was moonlight shining on the ocean, not sunlight, and that the supernova was going out.

The secretary general said, 'If the mirror hadn't blocked the energy from the supernova, the Earth would be a dead planet.'

By this point the ripples in the sky were gone, and the Earth's enormous reflection again occupied most of the sky.

'Where's the beat?' Clayderman asked. He had left the stage and was sitting among the world leaders.

'Look to the east!' someone shouted, and they saw in the eastern sky a dividing line, ramrod straight, bisecting the heavens into two distinct images. The reflected Earth, partially cut off, remained on the western side, but in the east was a dazzling starfield that many of them knew was the correct one for the northern hemisphere rather than the reflected southern sky. The division line marched west, enlarging the starry sky and wiping out the reflected Earth.

'It's flying away!' shouted the secretary general. And they realized he was right: the mirror was leaving the space over Earth. Its edge soon vanished beneath the western horizon, leaving them standing beneath the stars of an ordinary sky. It did not reappear – perhaps it had flown off to the vicinity of its sun instrument.

It comforted them somewhat to see the familiar world, the stars and city lights as they had been, and to smell the blossoms wafting over the lawn.

Then came the beat.

Day arrived without warning with a sudden blue sky and blazing sunlight that flooded the land and lit up their surroundings with brilliant light. But daytime lasted but a second before extinguishing into renewed night as stars and city lights returned. And the night lasted only a second before day returned, only for a second, and then it was night again. Day, and then night, then day, then night . . . like a pulse, or as if the world were a projector switching back and forth between two slides.

A beat formed out of night and day.

They looked up and saw the flashing star, now just a blinding, dimensionless point of light in space. 'A pulsar,' said the Chinese president.

The remains of a supernova, a whirling neutron star, the naked hot spot on its dense surface turning it into a cosmic lighthouse, its revolution sweeping the beam emitted by its hot spot through space, and giving Earth a brief moment of daytime as it swept past the solar system.

'I seem to recall,' the secretary general said, 'that a pulsar's frequency is far faster than this. And it doesn't emit visible light.'

Shielding his eyes with a hand and struggling to adjust to the crazy rhythm of the world, the US president said, 'The high frequency is because the neutron star retains the former star's angular momentum. The mirror may be able to somehow drain that momentum. As for visible light . . . do you really think that's something the mirror can't do?'

'There's another thing,' the Chinese president said. 'There's no reason to believe that the pace of life for all beings in the universe is like that of humanity. The beat for their music might be on a completely different frequency. The mirror's normal beat, for example, may be faster than even our fastest computers.'

'Yes,' the US president said, nodding. 'And there's no reason to believe that what they perceive as visible light is the same EM spectrum.'

'So you're saying that the mirror's music is benchmarked to human senses?' the secretary general asked in surprise.

The Chinese president shook his head. 'I don't know. But it's got to be based on something.'

The pulsar's powerful beam swept across the empty sky like a four-trillion-kilometer-long baton, still growing at the speed of light. At this end, played on the sun by the mirror's invisible fingers and transmitted to the cosmos at the speed of light, the sun concert began.

Sun Music

A rustle like radio jamming or the endless pounding of waves on sand occasionally offered up hints of a vast desolation within its more abundant chaos and disorder. The sound went on for more than ten minutes without changing.

The Russian president broke the silence: 'Like I said, we can't understand their music.'

'Listen!' Clayderman said, pointing at the sky, but it was a long moment before the rest of them heard the melody his trained ears had picked out at once. A simple structure of just two notes, reminiscent of a clock's tick-tock. The notes repeated, separated by lengthy gaps. Then another two-note section, and a third, and a fourth . . . paired tones emerging ceaselessly from the chaos like fireflies in the night.

Then a new melody emerged, four notes. Everyone turned toward Clayderman, who was listening attentively and seemed to have sensed something. The four-note phrases multiplied.

'Here,' he said to the heads of state. 'Let's each of us remember a two-note measure.' And so they all listened carefully, and each found a two-note measure and then focused their energy on committing it to memory. After a while, Clayderman said, 'Very well. Now concentrate on a four-note phrase. Quickly, though, or else the music will grow too complex for us to pick them out. . . . Yes, that one. Does anyone hear that?'

'The first half is the pair of notes I memorized!' called the head of Brazil.

'The second half is my pair!' said the head of Canada.

They realized that every four-note phrase was made up of two of the previous note pairs, and as the four-note phrases multiplied they seemed to be depleting the isolated pairs. Then came eight-note phrases, similarly formed out of sets of four-note phrases.

'What do you hear?' the secretary general asked the people around him.

'A primeval ocean lit by flashes of lightning and volcanoes, and small molecules combining into larger ones . . . of course, that's purely my own imagination,' the Chinese president said.

'Don't constrain your imagination to the Earth,' the US president said. 'The clustering of these molecules may be taking place in a nebula glowing with starlight. Or maybe they're not molecules, but the nuclear vortices inside a star . . .'

Then came a high-pitched, multi-note phrase that repeated like a bright spark in the dim chaos. 'It's like it's describing a fundamental transformation,' the Chinese president said.

Then they heard a new instrument, a sustained violin-like string sound that repeated a gentle shadow of the standout melody.

'It's expressing a kind of duplication,' the Russian president said.

Now came an uninterrupted melody from the violin voice, changing smoothly as if it were light in curvilinear motion. The UK prime minister said to the Chinese president, 'To borrow your idea, that ocean has something swimming in it now.'

At some point the background music, which they'd nearly forgotten about, had begun to change. From the sound of waves it had turned into an oscillating rush, like a storm assaulting the bare rock. Then it changed again, into wind-like bleakness. The US president said, 'The swimmer has entered a new environment. The land, or perhaps the air.'

Then all the instruments played in unison for a brief moment, a fearsomely loud sound like an enormous physical collapse, then they abruptly dropped out, leaving just the lonely sound of the surf. Then the simple note pairs started up again and turned gradually complex, and everything repeated . . .

'I can say with certainty that a great extinction was just described, and now we're listening to the revival afterward.'

After another long and arduous process, the ocean swimmer ventured again into other parts of the world. Slowly, the melody grew grander and more complicated, and interpretations diversified. Some people thought it was a river rushing downhill, others imagined the advance of a great army across a vast plain, others saw billowing nebulae in the darkness of space caught in the vortex of a black hole, but they all agreed that it was expressing some grand process, an evolutionary process. The movement was long, and an hour had passed before the theme at last began to change. The melody gradually split into two vying parts that smashed wildly into each other or tangled together . . .

'The classic style of Beethoven,' Clayderman declared, after a long stretch immersed in the grand music.

The secretary general said, 'It's like a fleet smacking across huge waves on the sea.'

'No,' said the US president, shaking his head. 'Not that. You can tell that the two forces are not essentially different. I think it's a battle that spans a world.'

'Wait a moment,' interrupted the Japanese prime minister, breaking a long silence. 'Do you really imagine you can comprehend alien art? Your understanding of the music may be no better than a cow's appreciation for a lyre.'

Clayderman said, 'I think our understanding is basically correct. The common languages of the cosmos are mathematics and music.'

The secretary general said, 'Proving it won't be difficult. Can we predict the theme or style of the next movement?'

After a moment's thought, the Chinese president said, 'I'd say next will be an expression of worship, and the melody will possess a strict architectural beauty.'

'You mean like Bach?'

'Yes.'

And so it was. The listeners seemed to hear a great imposing church and the echoes of their footsteps inside that magnificent space, and they were overcome by fear and awe of an all-encompassing power.

Then the complicated melody turned simple again. The background music vanished, and a series of short, clear beats appeared in the infinite stillness: one, then two, then three, then four . . . and then one, four, nine, and sixteen . . . and then increasingly complex series.

Someone asked, 'Is this describing the emergence of mathematics and abstract thinking?'

Then it turned even stranger. Isolated two- and three-note phrases from the violin, each of identically pitched notes held for different durations; then glissandos, rising, falling, and then rising again. They listened intently, and when the president of Greece said, 'It's . . . like a description of basic geometric shapes,' they immediately had the sense they were watching triangles and rectangles shoot by through empty space. The glides conjured up images of round objects, ovals and perfect circles. . . . The melody changed slowly as single-note lines turned into glides, but the previous impression of floating geometric shapes remained, only now they were floating on water and distorted . . .

'The discovery of the secrets of time,' someone said.

The next movement began with a constant rhythm that repeated along a period resembling a pulsar's day-night beat. The music seemed to have stopped altogether but for the beat echoing in the silence, but it was soon joined by another constant rhythm, this one slightly faster. Then more rhythms at various frequencies were added, until finally a magnificent chorus emerged. But on the time axis the music was constant as a huge flat wall of sound.

Astonishingly, their interpretation of this movement was unanimous: 'A giant machine at work.'

Then came a delicate new melody, a tinkle of crystal, volatile and dreamlike, that contrasted with the thick wall beneath it like a silver fairy flitting over the enormous machine. This tiny drop of a powerful catalyst touched off a wondrous reaction in the iron world: the constant rhythm began to waver, and the machine's shafts and cogs turned soft and rubbery until the whole chorus turned as light and ethereal as the fairy melody.

They debated it: 'The machine has intelligence!' 'I think the machine is drawing closer to its creator.'

The sun music progressed into a new movement, the most structurally complicated yet, and the hardest to understand. First the piano voice played a lonely tune, which was then taken up and extended by an increasingly complex group that turned it grander and more magnificent with every repetition.

After it had repeated several times, the Chinese president said, 'Here's my interpretation: A thinker stands on an island in the sea contemplating the cosmos. As the camera pulls back, the thinker shrinks in the field of view, and when the frame encompasses the entire island, the thinker is no more visible than a grain of sand. The island shrinks as the camera pulls back beyond the atmosphere, and now the entire planet is in frame, with the island just a speck within it. As the camera pulls back into space, the entire planetary system is drawn into frame, but now only the star is visible, a lonely, shining billiard ball against the pitch-black sky, and the ocean planet has vanished like a speck . . .'

Listening intently, the US president picked up the thought: '. . . The camera pulls back at light speed, and we discover that what from our scale is a vast and boundless cosmos is but glittering star dust, and when the entire galaxy comes into frame, the star and its planetary system vanish like specks. As the camera continues to cross unimaginable distances, a galaxy cluster is pulled into frame. We still see glittering dust, but the dust is formed not of stars but of galaxies . . .'

The secretary general said, '. . . And our galaxy has vanished. But where does it end?'

The audience once again immersed themselves in the music as it approached a climax. The musician's mind had propelled the cosmic camera outside the bounds of known space so its frame captured the entire universe, reducing the Milky Way's galaxy cluster to a speck of dust. They waited intently for the finale, but the grand chorus suddenly dropped out, leaving behind only a lonely piano-like sound, distant and empty.

'A return to the thinker on the island?' someone asked.

Clayderman shook his head. 'No, it's a completely different melody.'

Then the cosmic chorus struck up again, but after a brief moment gave way to the piano solo. The two melodies alternated like this for a long while.

Clayderman listened intently, and suddenly realized something: 'The piano is playing an inversion of the chorus!'

The US president nodded. 'Or maybe it's the mirror of the chorus. A cosmic mirror. That's what it is.'

The music had clearly reached a denouement, and now the piano's inverted melody proceeded alongside the chorus, riding conspicuously on its back but gloriously harmonious.

The Chinese president said, 'It reminds me of the Silvers style of mid-twentieth-century architecture, in which, in order to avoid impact on the surrounding environment, buildings were clad entirely in mirrors. Reflections were a way of putting them in harmony with their surroundings as well as self-expression.'

'Yes,' the secretary general answered thoughtfully. 'When civilization reaches a certain level, it can express itself through its reflection of the cosmos.'

The piano abruptly shifted to the uninverted theme, bringing it into unison with the chorus. The sun music had finished.

Ode to Joy

'A perfect concert,' the mirror said. 'Thank you to all who enjoyed it. And now I will be going.'

'Wait a moment!' shouted Clayderman. 'We have one last request. Could you play a human song on the sun?'

'Yes. Which one?'

The heads of state glanced around at each other. 'Beethoven's Fate Symphony?'* asked the German premier.

'No, not Fate,' said the US president. 'It's been proven that humanity is powerless to strangle fate. Our worth lies in that even knowing that fate can't be resisted and death will have the final victory, we still devote our limited life span to creating beautiful lives.'

'Then 'Ode to Joy,'' said the Chinese president.

The mirror said, 'You all sing. I'll use the sun to transmit the song out into the universe. It will be beautiful, I assure you.'

More than two hundred voices joined in 'Ode to Joy,' their song passed by the mirror to the sun, which again began vibrating to send powerful EM waves into all reaches of space.

'Joy, thou beauteous godly lightning,
Daughter of Elysium,
Fire drunken we are ent'ring
Heavenly, thy holy home!
Thy enchantments bind together,
What did custom stern divide,
Every man becomes a brother,
*Where thy gentle wings abide.'***

Five hours later, the song would exit the solar system. In four years, it would reach Proxima Centauri; in ten thousand, it would exit the galaxy; in two hundred thousand, it would reach the galaxy's nearest neighbor, the Large Magellanic Cloud. In six million years, their song would have reached the forty-odd galaxies in the cluster, and in a hundred million years, the fifty-odd clusters in the supercluster. In fifteen billion years, the song would have spread throughout the known universe and would continue onward, should the universe still be expanding.

'Joy commands the hardy mainspring
Of the universe eterne.

* Beethoven's Fifth Symphony is known as the Fate Symphony in Chinese.
** 'Ode to Joy' by Friedrich Schiller.

Joy, oh joy the wheel is driving
Which the worlds' great clock doth turn.
Flowers from the buds she coaxes,
Suns from out the hyaline,
Spheres she rotates through expanses,
Which the seer can't divine.'

The song concluded, everyone fell silent on the concert lawn. World leaders were lost in thought.

'Maybe things aren't so hopeless just yet, and we ought to renew our efforts,' the Chinese president said.

The US president nodded. 'Yes. The world needs the UN.'

'Concessions and sacrifices are insignificant compared to the future disasters they prevent,' the Russian president said.

'What we're dealing with amounts to a grain of sand in the cosmos. It ought to be easy,' the UK prime minister said, looking up at the stars.

The other leaders voiced their assent.

'So then, do we all agree to extend the present session of the UN?' the secretary general asked hopefully.

'This will of course require contacting our respective governments, but I believe that won't be a problem,' the US president said with a smile.

'Then, my friends, today is a day to remember,' the secretary general said, unable to hide his delight. 'So let's join once more in song.'

'Ode to Joy' started up again.

Speeding away from the sun at the speed of light, the mirror knew it would never return. In more than a billion years as a musician it had never held a repeat performance, just as a human shepherd will never toss the same stone twice. As it flew, it listened to the echoes of 'Ode to Joy,' and a barely perceptible ripple appeared on its smooth mirror surface.

'Oh, that's a good song.'

MOUNTAIN

1

WHERE THERE'S A MOUNTAIN

'Today is the day I'm finally going to get you to tell me why you never go on land,' the Captain declared, arching an eyebrow. 'It's been five years, and the *Bluewater* has docked in heaven knows how many ports in more countries than I can count, yet you have never gone ashore. Not even when we docked back in China. And not even last year, back in Qingdao when we were in for overhauls. You're the last person I'd need to tell that the ship was a complete mess, and noisy, and still you stayed put, holed up in your cabin for two months,' the Captain continued, eying Feng Fan intensely as he spoke.

'Do I remind you of that guy Tim Roth played in *The Legend of 1900*?' Fan asked in return.

'Are you insinuating that if we ever scuttle the *Bluewater* you plan on going down with the ship like he did?' the Captain countered, unsure if Fan was joking or not.

'I'll change ships. Oceanographic vessels always have a place for a geological engineer who'll never leave ship,' Fan replied.

The Captain returned to his original point. 'That naturally begs the question: is there something on land that keeps you away?'

'On the contrary,' Fan answered. 'There is something that I yearn for.'

'And what's that?' the Captain asked, curious but now a bit impatient.

'Mountains,' Fan uttered, his gaze dissolving into a thousand-yard stare.

They were standing portside on the geological oceanographic research vessel *Bluewater*, looking out onto the equatorial waters of the Pacific. The *Bluewater* had crossed the equator for the first time only a year ago. Back then, they had given in to whimsy and marked the occasion with the ancient rite of the line-crossing ceremony. Their discovery of a manganese nodule deposit in the seabed, however, had left them crisscrossing the equator more times than any of them could possibly remember. By this point, they had all but forgotten about the existence of that invisible divide.

As the sun slowly set beyond the sea's western horizon, Fan noticed that the ocean was unusually calm. In fact, he had never seen it so quiet. It reminded him of the Himalayan lakes, perfectly still to the point of blackness, like the eyes of the Earth. One time, he and two of his team mates had sneaked a peek at a Tibetan girl bathing in one of those lakes. A group of shepherds had spotted them and given chase, blades drawn. When they failed to catch them, the shepherds had resorted to slinging stones. The disconcertingly accurate bombardment had left Fan and his cohorts no other option than to surrender. The shepherds had sized them up and finally let them go.

Feng Fan recalled that one of them had muttered in Tibetan: 'As outsiders, they sure couldn't run quickly up here.'

'You like the mountains? So that's where you grew up then?' The Captain interrupted Fan's reminiscing.

'No, not at all,' Feng Fan explained. 'People who live their entire lives surrounded by mountains usually care nothing for them. They end up seeing the mountains as the things that stand between them and the world. I knew a Sherpa who scaled Everest forty-one times, but every time his team would get close to the peak he'd stop and watch the others climb the final stretch. He just couldn't be bothered to reach the top. And make no mistake about it: he could have easily pulled off both the northern and southern ascent in ten hours.

'There are only two places where you can really feel the true magic of the mountains: on the plains from far away and standing on a peak,' Feng Fan continued. 'My home was the vastness of the Hebei

Plain. In the west I could see the Taihang Mountains, but between them and my home lay an immense expanse of perfectly flat land without obstructions or markers. Not long after I was born, my mother carried me outside the house for the first time. My tiny neck could barely carry my head, but even then I turned to the west and babbled my heart out. As soon as I learned to walk, I took my first tottering steps toward those mountains. When I was a bit older, I set out early one morning and walked along the Shijiazhuang–Taiyuan Railway. I walked until noon when my grumbling stomach made me turn back, yet the mountains still seemed endlessly far away. In school, I rode my bicycle toward the mountains, but no matter how fast I pedaled the mountains seemed to withdraw just as quickly. In the end, it never felt as if I had gotten even an inch closer to them. Many years later, distant mountains would again become a symbol of my life, like so many things in life that we can clearly see but never reach – a dream crystallized in the distance.'

'I visited there once,' the Captain noted, shaking his head. 'The mountains are very barren, covered with nothing but scattered stones and wild grasses. You were doomed to be disappointed.'

'I wasn't. You and I feel very differently about these things. For me, all I saw was the mountain, and all I wanted was to climb it. I really wasn't looking for anything on the mountain. When I climbed those mountains for the first time and I saw the plain stretch out below me, I felt like I had been reborn.' As Feng Fan finished, he realized that the Captain was paying no heed to his words; instead, he was looking to the sky, staring at the scattered stars.

'There,' the Captain said, pointing skyward with his pipe. 'There shouldn't be a star there.'

But there was a star. It was faint, barely visible.

'Are you sure?' Fan turned his gaze from the sky to the Captain. 'Hasn't GPS done away with sextants? Do you really know your stars that well?'

'Of course I do,' the Captain answered. 'It is a basic element in the craft of sailing.' Turning back to Fan, he returned to their previous topic. 'But you were saying . . .'

Feng Fan nodded. 'Later, in university, I put together a mountaineering team, and we climbed a few seven-thousand-footers. Our final climb was Everest.'

The Captain carefully studied Feng Fan before finally saying, 'I thought so! It really is you! I always thought you looked familiar. Did you change your name?'

'Yes, I used to be called Feng Huabei,' he admitted.

'Some years ago, you caused quite the stir. Was what the media said about you true, then?' the Captain asked.

'The gist of it. In any case, those four climbers are certainly dead because of me,' Fan said glumly.

Striking a match to re-light his pipe, the Captain continued. 'I reckon that being the leader of a mountaineering team is not that different from being a captain: the hardest part is not learning when to fight on but understanding when to back down.'

'But if I had backed down then, it would have been very hard to get another shot at it,' Fan immediately replied. 'Mountain climbing is a very costly undertaking, and we were just college students. It had not been easy for us to find sponsors.' He paused, taking a deep breath. 'The guides we hired had refused to go on, and so it took much longer than anticipated before we set up the first base camp. The forecast predicted a storm, but we studied the images and maps and came to the conclusion that we still had at least twenty hours before it would hit. By then, our team had already set up the second camp at twenty-six thousand feet, and so we thought that we could make it to the peak if we set out immediately. You tell me, how could we have backed down then? We never even contemplated giving up, and so we continued our ascent.'

'That star is getting brighter,' the Captain said, looking up again.

'Of course it is. The sky is getting darker,' Fan retorted dismissively.

'This seems different,' the Captain noted. 'But go on.'

'You probably know what happened next: when the storm hit, we were close to the so-called 'Chinese Ladder' of the Second Step on a vertical rock face that rises from 28,500 feet. The peak was almost within reach, and, save for a strand of cloud rising from the other side of the summit, the sky was still perfectly blue. I can still clearly remember thinking that the peak of Everest looked like a knife's edge cutting open the sky, drawing forth its billowing, pale blood.' Fan paused at the memory before returning to his tale. 'It only took a few moments before we lost all visibility; when the storm hit us out of nowhere, it whipped up the snow. Everything was shrouded in an impenetrable white that left behind only murky darkness. In a heart-stopping instant, I felt the other four members of my team blown off the cliff. They were hanging by my rope, and all I was clinging to was my ice axe wedged into a crack in the wall. It simply could not have held the weight of five people. I acted on instinct, cutting the buckle strap that held the rope. I let them fall.' He hesitated, swallowing hard. 'They still haven't found the remains of two of them.'

'So four died instead of all five,' the Captain noted dryly.

'Yes, I acted according to the mountaineering safety guidelines. Even so, it remains my cross to bear.' Fan paused again, this time distracted by something other than his memories. 'You're right. There's something strange about that star. It's definitely getting brighter.'

'Never mind,' the Captain said. 'Does your current . . .' he paused, pursing his lips '. . . shall we say, 'condition', have anything to do with what happened then?'

'Do I have to spell it out? You must remember the overwhelming condemnations and the crushing contempt the media heaped on me back then,' Fan reminded him. 'They said I acted irresponsibly, that I was a selfish coward, that I sacrificed my four companions for my own life.' He was clearly still pained. 'I thought I could at least clear myself of that last accusation, so I donned my climbing gear and put on my mountain goggles. Ready for a climb, I went to my university's library and scaled a pipe straight up to its roof. I was just about to jump when I heard the voice of one of my teachers; I hadn't noticed him come up to the roof behind me. He asked me if I was really willing to let myself off the hook that easily, if I was just trying to avoid the much harsher punishment awaiting me. When I asked what he meant, he told me that it would entail a life as far away as possible from mountains. To never again see a mountain – would that not be a harsher punishment?

'So I didn't jump. Of course, I attracted even more ridicule, but I knew that what my teacher had told me was right: this would be worse than death for me. To me, mountain climbing had been my life. It was the only reason I studied geology. To now live a life eternally separated from the object of my passion, tormented by my own conscience – it felt just. That was the reason why I applied for this job after graduation, why I became the geological engineer of the *Bluewater*. On the ocean,' he said with a sigh, 'I'm as far as I can be from mountains.'

The Captain stared blankly for a long moment, at a loss for words. Finally, he came to the conclusion that it would probably be best to just leave it be. As if on cue, something in the sky above abruptly forced a change of topic. 'Take another look at that star,' he said, an edge in his voice.

'Heavens!' Fan exclaimed as he, too, looked up. 'It's turning into something!'

The star was no longer a dot but now a small, yet rapidly expanding, disc. In the blink of an eye, it turned into a striking sphere in the sky, glowing blue.

A flurry of rapidly approaching footsteps drew their gazes back down to deck. It was the First Mate, running straight towards them.

He was barely within earshot when he breathlessly called to the Captain, 'We have just received a message: an alien ship is approaching Earth! We can clearly see it from our position at the equator! Look, there it is!'

The three of them looked up, only to see that the small sphere had continued its rapid expansion. It had already ballooned to the size of the Moon.

'All stations have ceased their regular broadcasts and are now reporting on it!' the First Mate rattled on. 'The object had been spotted earlier, but they have just now confirmed its true nature. It is not responding to any of our attempts to hail it, but its trajectory shows that it is being propelled by some immense force, and it is hurtling straight toward Earth! They say it is as big as the Moon!' He held an earpiece to his head, listening intently.

Above them, the alien sphere was no longer the size of the Moon; it was now easily ten times as big, looming large in the heavens and appearing much closer than the Moon. With a finger firmly on his earpiece, the First Mate continued, 'They say that it has stopped. It is now in geosynchronous orbit twenty-two thousand miles above the Earth. It has become a geostationary satellite.'

'A geostationary satellite? Are you saying it is just going to hang above us?' the Captain shouted.

'It is! Over the equator, right above us!' the First Mate confirmed.

Feng Fan stared at this huge sphere in the sky; it seemed almost transparent, suffused with an unfathomable blue light. Looking at it left Fan with the strange impression of staring right up at an orb of seawater. A feeling of profound mystery, of intense anticipation, would grip him every time the sampling probe was raised from the seabed; looking up now, he experienced a very similar sensation. It was as if some long-forgotten remnant of time immemorial had returned to the surface.

'Look, the ocean!' the Captain shouted, wildly thrusting his pipe aftward. 'What is happening to the ocean?' He was the first to break free from the hypnotic power the giant sphere seemed to exert over all of them.

Where he pointed, the ocean's horizon had begun to bend, curving upward like a sine wave. This huge swell of rising water rapidly grew taller and taller. It was as if a gigantic, albeit invisible, hand was reaching down from space to scoop up the ocean.

'It's the spaceship's mass! Its gravity is pulling at the ocean!' Feng Fan exclaimed, rather surprised that he still had enough of his wits about him to understand what was happening. The ship's mass was probably equivalent to that of the Moon, but it was ten times closer! It was fortunate that the ship had entered a geosynchronous orbit; the water it was pulling would be held in one spot. If the spaceship moved, it would send a gravitational tidal wave across the world so large that it could easily ravage continents and destroy cities.

This colossal wave had by now swelled up to the heavens, rising as a flat-topped cone. Its mass shone with the blue glow of the ship above, even as its edges burned with the bright crimson fire of the setting sun, now hidden behind the towering waves. The stark, cold air at the cone's summit chilled the froth, sending forth streams of misty clouds that quickly bled away in the night sky, as if the dark heavens had been cut open. Feng Fan felt his heart stir with memories as he took it all in. His mind drifted back toward the day of the climb . . .

'Give me its height!' the Captain shouted, jerking him back to the here and now.

A minute later, someone called out, 'Almost thirty thousand feet!'

Before them was the most terrifying, most awesome and most magnificent sight humanity had ever seen. Everyone on deck stood transfixed by its spell.

'It must be destiny . . .' Feng Fan mumbled, mesmerized more than most by its grandeur.

'What did you say?' the Captain demanded loudly, his eyes still fixed on the rising waters.

'I said that this must be destiny,' Fan repeated.

It was – it had to be – destiny. He had gone to sea to avoid mountains, to put as much distance between them and himself as humanly possible; and now he was in the shadow of a mountain that eclipsed even Everest by almost a thousand feet. It was the world's tallest mountain.

'Port five! Full ahead! We need to get out here now!' the Captain commanded the First Mate.

'Out of here? Is it dangerous?' Feng Fan asked, confused.

'The alien spaceship has already created a huge area of low pressure. Right now a gigantic cyclone is taking form. I tell you, this could be the greatest tempest the world has ever seen. If it catches the *Bluewater*, we will be ripped straight out of the water and tossed about like a leaf in a storm. I just pray we will be able to outrun it,' the Captain explained, sweat clearly visible on his brow.

Just then the First Mate signaled them all to be quiet. Covering his earpiece with one hand, he listened intently and then said, 'Captain, the situation is much worse than that! They are now saying that the aliens have come to destroy Earth! With nothing but its enormous mass, their ship is doing much, much worse than just raising a storm; it is about to gash a hole in Earth's atmosphere!'

'Hole? Hole to where?' the Captain asked, his eyes wide.

The First Mate explained what he had just heard over the radio. 'The spaceship's gravity will puncture the upper layers of the atmosphere. Earth's atmosphere will be like a pricked balloon, its air escaping through that puncture, right into space! All of Earth's atmosphere will disappear!'

'How long do we have?' the Captain asked, confronted with horror after horror.

'The experts say that it will only take a week or so for the atmospheric pressure to fall to a lethal level.' The First Mate reported mechanically, but his wild eyes betrayed his panic. 'They say that when the pressure falls to a certain point, the oceans will begin to boil,' he continued, his voice beginning to break. 'Heavens, that would be like . . .' He trembled as he heard further news. 'All of Earth's major cities have fallen into chaos. Humanity has lost all semblance of sanity. Everywhere people are rushing into hospitals and factories, pillaging all the oxygen they can get their hands on.' His eyes continued to widen. 'Wait, now they are saying that Cape Canaveral is being overrun by a crazed mob trying to get its hands on the liquid oxygen used in the rocket fuel.' The First Mate's spirit appeared to slump along with his body. 'Oh, it's all over!'

'A week? That doesn't leave us enough time to make it home,' the Captain said steadily. It seemed that his composure had returned. With a quick flick of his fingers, he re-lit his pipe.

'Right, there's no time to make it home . . .' the First Mate echoed, his voice now emotionless.

'If that is what it's going to be, we might as well get on with it and make the best of the time we have left,' Feng Fan noted, a sudden edge of enthusiasm in his voice. His entire body was readying to the occasion, flushed with excitement.

'And what is it that you want to do?' the Captain asked.

'Climb a mountain,' Fan answered with a smile.

'Climb a mountain? Climb . . .?' The First Mate's face suddenly twisted from puzzlement to outright shock. 'That mountain?' he gasped, pointing at the mountain of water looming above them.

'Yes. It's now the world's tallest peak. Where there's a mountain, there will always be someone to climb it,' Fan replied calmly.

'And how do you plan to climb it?' the First Mate asked.

'Isn't it obvious? Mountain climbing is something one does with hands and feet, so I will swim,' Fan said with a smile.

'Are you crazy?' the First Mate shouted. 'How are you going to swim up a thirty-thousand-foot slope of water? It looks like a forty-five degree incline to me! That is going to be very different from climbing a mountain. You'll have to swim nonstop; and if you stop, even for a moment, you'll slide down the side!'

'I want to try.' Fan would not be dissuaded.

'Let him go then,' the Captain said flatly. 'What better time than now to embrace our passions? How far is it to the foot of that mountain?'

'About a dozen miles,' someone answered.

'Take one of the lifeboats,' the Captain told Feng Fan. 'Remember to take enough food and water.'

'Thank you!' Fan expressed his heartfelt gratitude.

'It looks like today fortune smiles upon you,' the Captain said with a wry smile, giving Feng Fan a clap on the shoulder.

'I believe so,' Fan replied. 'Captain, there is one thing I haven't yet told you: one of the four climbers on Everest was my girlfriend. A single thought flashed through my mind when I cut that rope: I don't want to die. There's still another mountain to climb,' he said, pain and bright enthusiasm merging in his eyes.

The captain nodded. 'Go.'

'And,' the First Mate said, looking lost, 'what do we do?'

'Full speed ahead away from the coming storm. One more day to live is one more day to live,' the Captain answered thoughtfully.

Feng Fan stood in the lifeboat, his gaze following the *Bluewater* as it sailed into the distance. Soon, the ship he had once seen as his home for life was well and truly out of reach.

Behind him, the mountain of water towered serenely under the blue glow of the alien sphere. Had he not seen it form, he could have easily been tricked into thinking that it had been there for millions of years. The ocean was very calm, its flat surface unruffled by waves. Feng Fan, however, could feel a breeze brush his face; it was weak, but it was blowing toward the looming waters. Raising the lifeboat's sail, he began his journey to the mountain. The wind soon picked up, and his vessel's sail filled in its wake. The lifeboat's prow now cut the ocean's surface like a knife as it sped toward Fan's goal.

In the end, the twelve-mile journey took no longer than forty minutes. As soon as Feng Fan began to feel the hull of his boat climb the slope of water, he leapt off the side of his vessel into the shining blue waters that were aglow with the light of the alien vessel above.

A few strokes later, he became the first person to swim a mountainside.

From his position, he could no longer see the summit. Lifting his head out of the liquid mountain, all he saw was an unending expanse of sloping water. He could almost imagine a titan beyond the horizon, lifting the ocean like a vast, watery blanket.

Feng Fan began to swim the breaststroke, conserving as much energy as possible. The First Mate's warning was still fresh in his mind. A quick calculation told him that it would be about eight miles to the summit. On level water, his endurance would have allowed him to easily cover the distance, but here he would have to deal with the slope. If he stopped moving upward, he would slip down. That alone would make reaching the summit almost impossible. It did not matter; the very act of attempting to climb this watery Everest was a greater achievement than he had ever dared hoped for in all of his mountaineering dreams.

As these emotions washed over him, Fan became aware of more physical sensations. He felt his body gradually being pulled up along the slope. Swimming up seemed to demand no additional effort. Looking back, he could see the lifeboat that he had abandoned at the mountain's foot. Before leaving the vessel he had lowered its sail, yet it remained floating on the slope, strangely stationary. Fan decided to try something.

He ceased his strokes and began to carefully observe his surroundings. He was not sliding. On the contrary, he was floating on the slope as if it did not exist at all! Fan slapped his forehead as he cursed his and the First Mate's foolishness: if the ocean's water on the slope did not flow downward, why would a person? Or a boat, for that matter?

The gravitational pull down the incline was being neutralized by the giant sphere's mass. The further up he climbed, the less he would feel of Earth's gravity. This meant that the slope's angle would not matter one bit. As far as gravity was concerned, there was neither a watery slope nor a mountain in the ocean. The forces acting on him would be no different from those on the level ocean.

He knew now that this mountain would be his.

He continued to swim upward. As he climbed, he felt his strokes gradually require less and less exertion. In large part, this was due to his body growing lighter, making it easier and easier to come up for air. Around him, Fan could see another sign of the reduced gravity: the higher he got, the slower the ocean's spray fell. This phenomenon was mirrored in the undulations and movements of the waves. They, too, grew ever slower the higher he swam. The harshness of the open sea had all but left them, leaving the waves softer and gentler than normal gravity would ever allow.

It was by no means calm, however. The wind was picking up, and bands of waves had begun to rise on the watery slope. Freed from much of Earth's gravity, these billows rose to considerable heights. However, they did not roll up the slope as full-bodied waves; instead, they were thin slices of water that twisted in on themselves as they gently collapsed. In a strange way, they reminded Fan of exquisitely thin wood shavings sliced from the ocean by an invisible planer. The waves did nothing to hinder his progress. In fact, it was quite the opposite; sweeping toward the summit, they actually pushed him along as he continued his climbing swim.

As the pull of gravity grew weaker, even stranger things happened: instead of pushing him, Fan was now being gently thrown along by the waves. In the blink of an eye, he felt himself leaving the water and flying over the ocean's surface, only to be caught by another wave a moment later, and then he was up in the air again. The gentle yet powerful hands of the ocean carried him along, rapidly passing him upward and onward. He soon discovered that under these strange conditions the butterfly stroke was best suited to expediting his already rapid ascent.

Around him, the wind had picked up even more strength. Gravity's grip on Feng Fan, on the other hand, was becoming weaker and weaker. The waves up here easily reached thirty feet in height before falling in slow motion. These huge billows were also gentler than they had ever been, softly rolling into one another; they did not even make a sound as they fell. The only remaining noise was the howling of a growing cyclone.

Fan's ever-lighter body was leaping from wave crest to wave crest. As he jumped again, he suddenly realized that he was spending more time in mid-air than he was in the water. Up here, he could hardly tell if he was swimming or floating. Time and again, the thin waves would come to completely envelope him, rolling him into a tunnel formed by the slowly tumbling waters. The gently roiling roof of these tunnels glowed in a blue light. Through the thin, watery roof he could see the light's source – the giant alien sphere hanging in the sky. The wave tunnel distorted the ship's form; to Feng Fan, it was as though he were seeing it through teary eyes.

He glanced at the waterproof watch he wore on his left wrist. He had only been climbing for an hour, and at this hope-defying speed it would only take another hour for him to reach the summit.

Fan thought of the *Bluewater*. Considering the current wind speeds, the tempest was only moments away from unleashing its fury. There was no way that the ship would be able to outrun the coming cyclone. In a flash, it occurred to Fan that the Captain had made a grave mistake: he should have turned the *Bluewater* straight toward the water mountain. Since gravity exerted no pull down the slope, the ship could have sailed up to the peak just as easily as it sailed the level ocean, and the peak would be at the eye of the storm – safe and calm! No sooner had he realized this than he pulled the walkie-talkie from his lifejacket. He tried to reach her, but the *Bluewater* did not respond.

By now, Feng Fan had mastered the skill of leaping from crest to crest. He had been climbing like this for twenty minutes, making it two-thirds of the way to the top. From here, the perfectly round summit already seemed within reach. It glittered in the softly glowing light of the alien spaceship above. To Fan, the summit looked like an alien world waiting for him. At that moment, the whistling of the wind suddenly turned into a sharp howl. This terrifying noise came from all directions, accompanied by a sudden increase in the wind's strength. Fifty-foot waves – even one-hundred-foot waves – thin as sheets rose high; but they never fell, torn apart by the cyclone's gale in mid-air. Looking up, Feng Fan could see that the slope above him was covered in the spray of broken wave crests dancing a crazed, wind-whipped dance over the ocean's surface. Illuminated by the glow of the alien sphere, the chaotic splashes shone with dazzling white light.

Finally, Feng Fan made his last leap. A thin, hundred-foot wave carried him into the air. It was torn to slivers by the powerful wind the moment he left its crest, and he found himself falling toward a band of waves slowly rolling in front of him. The waves looked like giant, transparent wings slowly unfurling to embrace him. Just as Fan's outstretched hands reached the waves, the waves shattered into white mist, their glittering crystal film ripped apart by the violent winds. A strange noise that sounded disturbingly like laughter accompanied the bizarre spectacle. This was also the very moment when Feng Fan stopped falling; his body was now light enough to float. The manically twisting ocean below slowly began to grow more distant as he was thrown into the air like a feather in a hurricane.

Almost weightless, Fan was tossed and turned in the twisting air. Dizzy, he felt as if the glowing alien sphere was spiraling around him. When he was finally able to steady himself, he realized with a start that he was actually swirling through the air above the summit of the water mountain.

From up here, the bands of giant waves rolling up the mountain looked like nothing more than long lines. Spiraling toward the peak, they made the mountain look like a titanic watery whirlwind. Feng Fan felt the circles he was making above the peak grow smaller and smaller while his speed accelerated. He was being carried directly into the heart of the cyclone.

When Fan arrived at the exact eye of the storm he felt the wind suddenly weaken. The invisible hand of air that had been holding him suddenly let go, and he fell toward the water mountain, straight into the faint blue glow of the summit.

He plummeted deep into the mountain before he felt himself floating upward again. He was surrounded by darkness, and in a matter of moments the fear of drowning beset him. With mounting panic, Fan suddenly realized that he was in mortal peril: the last breath he had gulped before he fell had been at thirty thousand feet! At that height, he would have hardly breathed in any oxygen at all, and in the minimal gravity here he would only rise very slowly. Even if he swam up with all his strength, he feared that the air in his lungs would not be enough to carry him back to the surface.

Feng Fan was gripped by an eerie sense of *déjà vu*. He felt himself returned to Everest, completely in the dark, enshrouded by the swirling snow of the storm, utterly overwhelmed by mortal fear. Within this darkest moment, Fan found a light: several silvery spheres were floating upward next to him. The largest of these spheres was about three feet in diameter. Looking at them, he suddenly realized that they were air bubbles. The weak gravity had allowed giant bubbles of oxygen to form in the ocean. With all the strength he could muster, he thrust himself at the largest bubble. No sooner had his head pierced the silvery shell than he was able to draw breath again. As he slowly recovered from the dizziness oxygen deprivation had induced, Fan found himself enveloped by the air bubble. He was in a sphere of air completely surrounded by water, and, looking up, he could see the ripple of the surface shimmer through the top of his bubble. Floating upward, he noticed a sudden drop in the water pressure, causing his bubble to rapidly expand. As the bubble grew, Feng Fan could not shake the impression that he was caught in a crystalline party balloon, floating into the sky.

The blue shimmer of the waves above slowly grew brighter and brighter, until finally their glare was so strong that he was forced to avert his gaze. Just then, the bubble burst with a soft pop. Fan had reached the surface; and he was going higher, the weak gravity launching him a good three feet into the air. His drop back to the surface was not a sudden but a gentle descent.

As he fell, Feng Fan noticed countless beautiful watery orbs gently dropping alongside him. These orbs greatly varied in size, the largest being roughly the size of a soccer ball. All of them shone and glittered with the blue light from the gigantic sphere above. As Fan looked more closely, he saw that they, in fact, contained layers upon layers, which made them sparkle with crystal light. These orbs were splashes of water that had been cast from the ocean as he had broken its surface. The low gravity had allowed their surface tension complete freedom to shape themselves like this. Reaching out, Fan touched one of the orbs. The sphere shattered with a strange metallic ring that was wholly unlike any sound he had ever imagined water producing.

Except for the orbs, the summit of the water mountain was altogether tranquil, the waves rushing in from all sides merging into nothing but broken swell. This was, beyond all doubt, the eye of the storm, the only place of quiet in a chaotic world. The calm was offset by a tremendous background howl – the screaming of the cyclone. Looking into the distance, Feng Fan found himself, along with the entire mountain of water, to be in a massive 'well'. The walls of this well were made of the swirling, frothing waters of the cyclone. These impenetrable masses of water and wind slowly turned around the water mountain. Looking upward, Fan saw that they appeared to reach straight into space. Shining through the mouth of the well was the alien sphere. Like a giant lamp hanging in space, its light illuminated all within the well. Gazing up, Fan could see strange clouds forming around it. They looked like fibers, trailing a loose net around the alien vessel. These strands of cloud shone brightly, appearing to glow from within. Fan could only guess that they were made of ice crystals formed as the Earth's atmosphere escaped into space. Even though they appeared to surround the spaceship, there actually had to be a good twenty thousand miles between the web and the blue sphere. If his guess was right, the atmosphere had already begun to leak and the mouth of this giant, swirling well was nothing other than the fatal hole in Earth's shell.

It doesn't matter, Fan thought to himself. I have reached the summit.

2

WORDS ON THE MOUNTAINTOP

Suddenly, the all-pervading ambient light changed. Flickering, it began to dim. Looking up again, Feng Fan saw that the alien sphere's blue light had disappeared. It suddenly occurred to him what that light had been. It was the background light of an empty display; the entire body of the huge alien sphere was one gigantic screen. Just then, this massive screen began to display an image. It was a picture taken from a great height, and it revealed a person floating in the ocean, his face turned skyward. That person was Feng Fan. Thirty seconds ticked past, then the image disappeared. Fan had immediately understood its meaning; the aliens had shown that they could see him. It made Fan feel like he was truly standing on the roof of the world.

Two lines of text appeared on the screen. They contained all the characters in every alphabet Fan had ever seen. Recognizing the words for 'English', 'Chinese' and 'Japanese', he surmised that they must spell out the names of all the world's languages. He also spotted a dark frame quickly moving between the different words. It all appeared rather familiar. His guess was soon proven right, as he discovered that this frame actually did follow his gaze. He fixed his eyes on the characters for 'Chinese', causing the dark frame to stop over them. He blinked once, but there was no response.

Maybe it needed a double-click, Fan thought, blinking twice. The dark frame flickered, and the giant sphere's language menu closed. In its stead, a huge word appeared in Chinese.

>> Hello!

'Hello!' Fan shouted his response into the sky. 'Can you hear me?'

>> We can hear you; there is no need to shout. We could hear the wings of a mosquito anywhere on Earth. We picked up the

electromagnetic waves leaking from your planet and thereby learned your languages. We want to have a little chat with you.

'Where do you come from?' Fan asked, his voice now considerably quieter.

A picture appeared on the surface of the giant sphere, showing a dense cluster of black dots. These dots were connected by a complicated web of lines. The sheer intricacy of the picture made Fan's head swim. It was obviously some sort of star map. Sure enough, one of these dots began to glow in a silver light, growing brighter and brighter. Unfortunately, Feng Fan could not really make heads or tails of it, but he was confident that it had already been recorded elsewhere. Earth's astronomers would be able to understand it. The sphere soon displayed characters again, but the star map did not disappear. Instead, it remained in the background, almost like some sort of alien desktop.

>> We raised a mountain. You came and climbed it.

'Mountain climbing is my passion,' Fan answered.

>> It is not a question of passion; we must climb mountains.

'Why?' Fan asked. 'Does your world have many mountains?' He realized that this was hardly humanity's most pressing issue, but he wanted to know. Everyone he knew considered mountaineering an exercise in foolishness, so he might as well talk about it with aliens. After all, they had just stated that they were prone to climb; and after all, he had gotten this far all by himself.

>> There are mountains everywhere, but we do not climb as you do.

Feng Fan could not tell if this was meant as a concrete description or an abstract analogy. He had no choice but to express his ignorance. 'So you have lots of mountains where you come from?' It was more a question than a statement.

>> We were surrounded by a mountain. This mountain confined us, and we needed to dig to climb it.

This answer did nothing to alleviate Fan's confusion. For a long time he remained silent, contemplating what the aliens where trying to tell him.

Then they continued.

3

BUBBLE WORLD

>> Our world is a very simple place. It is a spherical space, somewhat more than 3,500 miles in diameter, according to your units of measurement. This space is completely surrounded by layers of rock. No matter what direction one chooses to travel in, the journey will always end with a solid wall of rock.

>> Naturally, this shaped our first model of the cosmos: we assumed that the universe was made of two parts. The first was the 3,500 space in which we lived; the second was the surrounding layers of rock. We believed the rock stretched endlessly in all directions. Therefore, we saw our world as a hollow bubble in this solid universe, and so we gave our world the name Bubble World and we call this cosmology the Solid Universe Theory. Of course, this theory did not deny the possibility of other bubbles existing in these infinite layers of rock. However, it gave no indication as to how near or far away those other bubbles might be. That became the impetus for our later journeys of exploration.

'But infinite layers of rock cannot possibly exist; they would collapse under their own gravity,' Feng Fan pointed out.

>> Back then we knew nothing of gravitational forces. There was no gravity inside the Bubble World, and so we lived our lives without ever experiencing its pull. We only really came to understand the existence of gravity many thousands of years later.

'So these bubbles were the planets of your solid universe? Very interesting,' Fan commented. 'Density in our universe is entirely the inverse. Your universe must be an almost exact negative of the real universe.'

>> The real universe? You are ignorantly considering the universe only as you know it right now. You have no idea what the real universe is like, and neither do we.

Chastened, Fan decided to continue his line of enquiry. 'Was there light, air and water in your world?'

>> No, none; and we needed none of them. Our world was made entirely of solids. There were no gases or liquids.

'No gases or liquids. How did you survive?' Fan asked.

>> We are a mechanical life form. Our muscles and bones are made of metals, our brains are like highly integrated chips, and electricity and magnetism are our blood. We ate the radioactive rocks of our world's core, and they provided us with the energy we needed to survive. We were not created; we evolved naturally from extremely simple, single-celled mechanical life forms when – by pure chance – the radioactive energies formed p–n junctions in the rocks. Instead of your use of fire, our earliest ancestors discovered the use of electromagnetism. In fact, we never found fire in our world.

'It must have been very dark there then,' Fan remarked.

>> Actually, there was some light. It was generated by the radioactive activity within our world's walls. Those walls were our sky. The light of that 'sky' was very weak, and it constantly shifted as the radioactivity fluctuated. Yet it led us to evolve eyes.

>> Since our world's core lacked gravity, we did not build walls. Instead, our cities floated in the dim, empty space that was our world. They were about as big as your cities, and seen from afar they would have looked to you like glowing clouds.

>> The evolutionary process of mechanical life is much slower than that of carbon-based life, but eventually we reached the same ends by different means; and so one day we, too, came to contemplate our universe.

'That sounds like it must have felt cramped. Was it like that for you?' Fan asked, mulling over the sphere's strange revelations.

>> 'Cramped'.... That is a new word. We came to experience an intense desire for more space, much stronger than any similar longing that might affect your species. Our first journeys of exploration into the rock layers began in earliest antiquity. Exploration for us meant tunneling into the walls in an attempt to find other bubbles in our solid universe. We had spun many fascinatingly alluring myths around these distant spaces, and almost all of our literature dealt with the fantasy of other bubbles. Soon, however, exploration was outlawed – forbidden on pain of death by short-circuiting.

'Outlawed? By your church?' Fan assumed.

>> No, we have no church. A civilization that cannot see the sun and stars will be without religion. There was a very practical reason for our senate to forbid tunneling: we were not furnished with the near-infinite space you have at your disposal. Our existence was limited to that 3,500-mile bubble. All the debris that the tunneling produced ended up within this space. As we believed in infinite layers of rock stretching in all directions, those tunnels could have become very long indeed – long enough even to fill the entire bubble space at the core of our world with rubble! To put it another way: we would have transformed the empty sphere in the core of our world into a very long tunnel.

'There could have been a solution to the problem: just move the newly mined rubble into the already excavated space behind the diggers,' Fan suggested. 'Then you would have only lost the space needed by the explorers to sustain themselves and dig.'

>> Indeed, later explorers used the very method you just described. In fact, the explorers would only use a small bubble with just enough space for themselves and their mission. We came to call these missions 'bubble ships'. But even so, every mission meant a bubble ship-sized pile of debris in our core space, and we would have to wait for the ship to return before we could place those rocks back into the wall. If the bubble ship failed to return, this small pile would mean another small piece of space lost to us forever. Back then we felt as if the bubble ship had stolen that piece of space. We therefore came to call our explorers by another name – Space Thieves.

>> In our claustrophobic world, every inch of space was treasured, and later a significant area of our world had been lost in the wake of the far-too-many bubble ships that had failed to return. It was because of this loss of space that bubble ship exploration was outlawed in antiquity. Even without legal censure, life in the bubble ships was fraught with hardships and dangers beyond imagining. A bubble ship crew usually included several diggers and a navigator. At the time, we did not have mining machinery and so had to rely on manual excavation, comparable to rowing on your early vessels. These early explorers had to dig tirelessly with the simplest of tools, pushing their bubble ship through the layers of rock at a painfully slow pace. Working like machines in those tiny bubbles surrounded by solid rock

– confined in every way, in search of an elusive dream – doubtlessly shows an incredible strength of spirit.

>> As the bubble ships tended to return the same way they departed, the journey back was usually a good deal easier. The rock in their path would have already been loosened. Even so, a gambler's hunger for discovery often led the ships to go well beyond the point of safe return. These unfortunate explorers would run out of strength and supplies and remain stranded mid-return, their bubble ship becoming their tomb. Despite all of this, and even though the extent of our exploratory efforts was greatly scaled back, our Bubble World never gave up on the dream of finding other worlds.

4

REDSHIFT

>> One day, in the year 33,281 of the Bubble Era – this is expressed in your chronological terms, as our world's reckoning of time would be too alien for you to understand – a tiny hole began to open in the rocky sky of our world. A small pile of rocks drifted out of this hole, their weak radioactive light sparkling like stars. A unit of soldiers was immediately dispatched to fly to this crack and investigate. (Now keep in mind that there is no gravity in the Bubble World.) They discovered an explorer's bubble ship that had returned. This ship had set out eight years before, and the world had long given up hope that it would ever return. The ship's name was the *Needle's Point*, and it had dug 125 miles deep into the rock. No other ship had ever made it as far and returned.

>> The *Needle's Point* had set out with a crew of twenty, but when it returned only a single scientist remained. Let us call him Copernicus. He had eaten the rest of the crew, including the captain. In ancient times, this means of sustenance had, in fact, proven to be the most efficient method for explorers going into the deep layers of rock.

>> For breaking the strict laws against bubble ship exploration, and for cannibalism, Copernicus was sentenced to death in the capital city. On the day the sentence was to be carried out, more than a hundred thousand gathered in the central square of the capital to witness his execution. Just as they were waiting for the awesome spectacle of Copernicus being short-circuited in a beautiful shower of sparks, a group of scientists floated onto the square. They were from the World Academy of Science, and they had come to announce a groundbreaking discovery: researchers had discovered something in the density of the rock samples that the *Needle's Point* had retrieved. To their great surprise, the data indicated that the rock density had steadily decreased the further the ship had dug.

'Your world had no gravity. How did you ever measure density?' Fan interjected.

>> We used inertia; it's somewhat more complicated than your methods. No matter, in those early days our scientists thought that the *Needle's Point* had merely chanced upon an uneven layer of rock. However, in the following century, legions of bubble ships journeyed forth in all directions, penetrating deeper than the *Needle's Point* ever had, and they, too, returned with rock samples. What they found was incredible: Density decreased in all directions, and it did so consistently! The Solid Universe Theory that had reigned supreme in the Bubble World for twenty millennia was shaken to its core. If the density of the Bubble World continually decreased as one dug outward, then it stood to reason that it would eventually reach zero. Using the gathered data, our scientists were easily able to calculate that this would happen at about twenty thousand miles.

'Oh, that sounds very much like how Hubble used the redshift!' Fan exclaimed, recognizing the concept.

>> It is indeed very similar. Since you could not conceive of the redshift velocity exceeding the speed of light, you concluded that it denoted the edge of the universe; and it was very easy for our ancestors to comprehend that an area with a density of zero is open space. Thus a new model of the universe was born. In this model, it was assumed that density decreased in proportion to distance from the Bubble World, eventually declining to the point of opening into a space that would continue into infinity. This is known as the Open Universe Theory.

>> The Solid Universe Theory, however, was deeply ingrained in our culture, and its supporters dominated the discourse. Soon they found a way to salvage the Solid Universe Theory, coming to the conclusion that all the decreasing density meant was that a spherical layer of looser rock encircled the Bubble World. Were anyone to pass through this layer, they theorized, they would find no further decrease. They calculated the thickness of this loose layer to be two hundred miles. Testing this theory was, of course, not difficult; one merely needed to dig through two hundred miles of rock. It did not take long for ships to reach this distance, but the decrease of density continued unabated. The supporters of the Solid Universe Theory then declared that their previous calculations had been mistaken and that the true thickness

of the layer of loose rock was three hundred miles. Ten years later, a ship crossed this distance, and again the decrease in density was shown to continue beyond the calculated point. In fact, the speed of decrease accelerated. The Solid Universe purists then expanded the layer of loose rock to nine hundred miles . . .

In the end, an incredible, epochal discovery forever sealed the fate of the Solid Universe Theory.

5

GRAVITY

>> The bubble ship that crossed the two hundred-mile mark was called the *Saw Blade*. It was the largest exploration vessel we had ever built, outfitted with an extremely powerful excavator and an advanced life-support system. Its cutting-edge equipment enabled the ship to travel farther than anyone had ever gone before, changing the course of our history.

>> As it passed a depth - or one might say height - of two hundred miles, the mission's chief scientist - we shall call him Newton - reported an utterly baffling observation to the ship's captain: whenever the crew went to sleep floating in the middle of the bubble ship, they would wake up lying on the tunnel wall closest to the Bubble World.

>> The captain did not think it meant anything; he concluded that it was the result of homesick sleep floating and nothing more. In his mind, the crew wanted to return to the Bubble World, and so they would always find themselves floating toward home in their sleep.

>> Consider, however, that there was no air in the Bubble World, and therefore no air in the bubble ship. This meant that there were only two ways to move: either by pushing off from the wall - something that could not possibly happen while the crew was floating in the middle of the ship, or by discharging their bodies' excrement to propel themselves. Newton, however, never found any trace of the latter happening either.

>> Even so, the captain would not put stock in Newton's claims. He should have considered otherwise, as it was this indifference that would soon leave him buried alive. On the day it happened, the crew was particularly exhausted after having completed the latest stage of the dig, and so they did not immediately move the day's

debris to the back of the ship. The plan was to move the rocks first thing after they had rested. The ship's captain joined the diggers, and they went to sleep in the center of the ship. They all woke with a start, buried alive! In their sleep, they, as well as the rocks, had all moved toward the rear of the bubble ship, closer to the Bubble World. Newton very quickly realized that all things in the ship had a certain tendency to move toward the Bubble World. This movement was very gradual and barely noticeable under normal conditions.

'So your Newton did not need an apple to discover gravity,' Fan quipped.

>> Do you really think it was that easy? For us, the discovery of gravitation was a much more involved process than it ever could have been for your kind; it had to be, considering the environment in which we lived. When our Newton discovered the directionality of attraction, he had to assume that it originated from the 3,500-mile empty space of the Bubble World; and so our early theory of gravity was marred by a rather silly assumption. We had concluded that it was vacuums that produced gravity, not mass.

'I can see how that happened. In an environment as complex as yours, it would of course be much more difficult for your Newton to figure things out than it had been for ours,' Fan said, nodding.

>> Indeed. It took our scientists half a century before they began to unravel the mystery. Only then did we begin to truly understand the nature of gravity, and soon we were able – by using instruments not unlike those you used – to measure the gravitational constant. Even so, it was a painfully slow process before the theory of gravity found widespread acceptance in our world. As it spread, however, it became the final nail in the coffin of the Solid Universe Theory.

>> Gravity did not allow for the existence of an infinite, solid universe around our bubble. The Open Universe Theory had finally triumphed, and the cosmos it described soon came to exert a powerful attraction on the inhabitants of our world.

>> Beyond the conservation of energy and mass, Bubble World physics was also bound by the law of the conservation of space. Space in the Bubble World was a sphere roughly 3,500 miles in diameter. Digging tunnels into the layers of rock did nothing to increase the amount of available space; it merely changed the shape and location of the existing space. Furthermore, we lived in a zero-gravity

environment, and so our civilization floated in space at the core of our world. We affixed nothing to the walls of our world, which would have been comparable to the way you live on your planet. Because of this, space was the most treasured commodity in the Bubble World. The entire history of our civilization was one long and bloody struggle for space.

>> Now we had suddenly learned that space was quite possibly infinite. How could it not have whipped us into a frenzy? We sent forth an unprecedented number of explorers, waves upon waves of bubble ships digging forward and outward. They all did their utmost to reach that paradise of zero density that the Open Universe Theory predicted could be found beyond 19,900 miles of rock.

6

WORLD'S CORE

>> From what has been said, you should now, if you have grasped it, be able infer the true nature of our Bubble World.

'Was your world the hollow center of a planet?' Fan gave his best guess.

>> You are correct. Our planet is about the same size as Earth; its radius measures roughly five thousand miles. Our world's core, however, is hollow. This space at its center is approximately 3,500 miles in diameter. We are the life inside that core.

>> Even after the discovery of gravity, it still took us many centuries before we finally came to understand the true nature of our world.

7

THE WAR OF THE STRATA

>> After the Open Universe Theory had fully established itself, the quest for the infinite space outside became our only real concern. We no longer cared about the consumption of space inside the Bubble World. Massive piles of rock, dug out by the fleets of bubble ships, soon came to fill the core space. This debris began to drift around our cities in vast, dense clouds. It got so bad that merely floating across the city was no easier a task than navigating an obstacle course. And because the cities themselves moved about, the denizens of the core also suffered devastating downpours of stone rain. Only half of the space these rocks stole was ever recovered.

>> At the time, a World Government had come to replace our senate. Its politicians took on the responsibility of overseeing and safeguarding the core space. They attempted to crack down harshly on the frenetic explorers, but this had very little effect. Most of the explorers' bubble ships had already dug into the deep layers of our planet.

>> The World Government soon realized that the best way to stop bubble ships would be with bubble ships. Following this logic, the government began building an armada of gigantic ships designed to intercept, attack and destroy the explorers' vessels deep within the rock. The government's ships would then retrieve the space that had been stolen. This plan naturally met with the resistance from the explorers, and so the prolonged Strata War broke out, fought in the vast battlefield of layers of rock.

'That sounds like a very interesting way to fight a war!' Fan called up to the sphere, intrigued.

>> And very brutal, even though at first the pace of the fighting was languid at best. The excavation technology of the time only allowed

our bubble ships to move at a pace of less than two miles per hour through the rock.

>> Large ships were the most highly valued asset on both sides in the Strata War. There was a simple reason for this: the larger the bubble ship, the longer it could go without refueling; also, the ships' offensive capabilities were in direct proportion to their size.

>> Regardless of how big they were, the ships of the Strata War were all built to have the smallest bow width possible. Again, this was for a very simple reason: the slenderer the bow, the smaller the area of rock that the ship would need to dig through and the faster the ship would be able to move. As a result, almost all of the warships looked very similar when seen from the front. On the other hand, their bodies and lengths varied widely. In extreme cases, our largest ships ended up looking like very long tunnels.

>> The battlefields of the Strata War were, of course, three-dimensional, and so the combat was fought somewhat like your forces engaging in aerial warfare, even if things were a good deal more complicated for us. When a ship encountered an enemy, its first course of action was to hastily broaden its bow width. The ships did so to bring the largest possible front of weaponry to bear; in this new configuration, a ship could transform into a shape similar to that of a nail.

>> When necessary, the bow of a bubble ship could also split into multiple sections, like a claw ready to strike. This configuration would allow the ship to attack from multiple directions at once. The raw complexity of the Strata War also revealed itself in another tactic: every warship could separate at will, transforming into multiple smaller ships. Ships could also band together, quickly combining to form a single, giant ship. Whenever opposing battle groups met, the question of whether to link up or split up was an object of profound tactical analysis.

>> Interestingly enough, the Strata War did little to hinder the drive for further exploration. In fact, the war spurred a technological revolution that would play a critical part in our future endeavors. Not only did it bring about the development of extremely efficient excavators, but it also led to the invention of seismoscopes. This technology could be used for communication through the layers of rock and could also be employed as a form of radar. Powerful seismic waves were also used

as weapons. The most sophisticated seismic communication devices could even transmit pictures.

>> The largest bubble battleship we ever built was called the *World-of-the-Line*. It was commissioned by the World Government. In its standard configuration, the *World-of-the-Line* was more than ninety miles long. It was just as its name suggested: a small, very elongated world, self-contained. For its crew, serving on the *World* was much like it would be for you to stand in the English–French Channel Tunnel; every few minutes a high-speed train rushed by, delivering tunneled debris to the aft of the ship. The *World-of-the-Line* could of course break up into an armada all by itself, but for the most part it operated as a single vessel of war. Naturally, it did not always remain in its 'tunnel' configuration. In motion, its stretched hull could be bent impressively, forming a closed loop or even crossing its own path to create intricate shapes of destruction. The *World-of-the-Line* was equipped with our most advanced excavators, allowing it to travel twice as fast as ordinary bubble ships, reaching a cruising speed of up to four miles per hour. In combat, it could even maneuver at speeds exceeding six miles per hour! Furthermore, an extremely powerful seismoscope was installed in its hull, allowing it to pinpoint bubble ships at ranges eclipsing three hundred miles. Its seismic wave weapon had an effective range of 3,300 feet, and anything and anyone within a bubble ship it targeted would be shattered to pieces or crushed. Every once in a while the *World-of-the-Line* returned to the Bubble World, carrying onboard its booty of space recovered from the explorers.

>> It was the devastating blows struck by the *World-of-the-Line* that finally pushed the explorer movement to the brink. It seemed the age of exploration was about to come to a sudden end.

>> Throughout the duration of the Strata War, the explorers continually found themselves outmatched. Perhaps most importantly, they were prevented from building or forming a ship longer than five miles. Any ship larger than that would be quickly detected by the seismoscopes installed on the *World-of-the-Line* and the walls of the Bubble World. Once they were spotted, destruction would be swift. And so, if exploration was to continue in earnest, it became imperative to destroy the *World-of-the-Line*.

>> After extensive planning and preparation, the Explorer Alliance, founded by the outmatched explorers, encircled and attacked the

World-of-the-Line with over one hundred warships. Not one of the explorers' ships was longer than three miles in length. The battle was fought one thousand miles outside the Bubble World and became known as the Thousand-Mile Battle.

>> The Alliance first assembled twenty ships, combining them to form a single twenty-mile-long ship one thousand miles outside the Bubble World, daring the *World-of-the-Line* to attack. The *World* took the bait, rushing in for the kill in its tunnel configuration. Just as it was speeding toward its prey, the Alliance sprang its ambush. Over one hundred ships dug forward, simultaneously attacking the flanks of the *World-of-the-Line* from all directions. The mighty ninety-mile ship was split into fifty sections. Each of these sections, however, could carry on the fight as a powerful warship in its own right. Soon, more than two hundred ships from both sides were engaged in fierce battle, tunneling through the rock in a brutal and chaotic melee. Warships were constantly combining and separating, eventually blurring into an amorphous cloud of vessels and violence. In the final phase of the battle, the 150-mile battlefield became honeycombed beyond recognition by the loosened rock and empty space left behind by the destroyed ships. The Thousand-Mile Battle had created an intricate three-dimensional maze, 2,250 miles beneath our planet's surface.

>> The jarring rumble of vicious, tight combat reverberated all throughout this bizarre battlefield for what seemed like an eternity. Located so far from the core of the planet, gravity produced very noticeable effects on the action – effects that the explorers were far more familiar with than the government forces. In this great maze battle, it was this difference that slowly swung the battle in favor of the Explorer Alliance. In the end, their victory was decisive.

8

UNDER THE OCEAN

>> After the battle, the Explorer Alliance gathered all the space left over by the battle into a single sphere sixty miles in diameter. In this new space, the Alliance declared its independence from the Bubble World. Despite this declaration, the Explorer Alliance continued to coordinate its efforts with the explorer movement in the Bubble World from afar. A constant stream of explorer ships left the core to join the Alliance, bringing considerable amounts of space with them. In this way, the territory of the Explorer Alliance continually grew, in effect allowing them to turn their territory into a fully stocked and equipped forward-operating base. The World Government, exhausted by the long years of war, found itself unable to stop any of this. In the end, they were left with no other option than to acknowledge the legitimacy of the explorer movement.

>> As the explorers reached higher altitudes, they came to dig through ever more porous rock. This was not the only benefit these heights offered; the strengthening gravity also made dealing with the excavated debris that much easier, and this newly discovered environment led to success after success. In the eighth year after the end of the war, the *Helix* became the first ship to cross the remaining 2,250 miles, completing the five-thousand-mile journey from the planet's center, 3,250 miles from the edge of the Bubble World.

'Wow! That was all the way to the surface! It must have been so exciting for you to see the great plains and real mountains!' Fan exclaimed, fully absorbed in the visitors' story.

>> There was nothing to be excited about; the *Helix* reached the seabed.

Fan stared up at the alien sphere in shocked silence.

>> When it happened, the images from the seismic communicator began to shake and suddenly stopped appearing altogether. Communication had been lost. A bubble ship tunneling through the rock beneath it could only catch one strange sound on its seismoscopes; a noise that in the open would have sounded like something being peeled. It was the sound of tons upon tons of water bursting into the vacuum of the *Helix*. Neither the machine life forms nor the technology of the Bubble World had ever been designed to come into contact with water. The powerful electric current produced by short-circuiting life and equipment almost instantly vaporized everything the water touched. In the rushing waves, the crew and instruments of the *Helix* exploded like a bomb.

>> Following this event, the Alliance sent more than a dozen bubble ships to fan out in various directions, but all met a similar fate when they reached that apparently impenetrable height. Not one crew was able to make their sacrifice worthwhile by sending back information that could have led us to understand that mysterious peeling sound. Twice a strange crystalline waveform could be seen on the monitors, but we were completely incapable of comprehending its nature. Subsequent bubble ships attempted to scan what lay above with their seismoscopes, but their instruments produced only mangled data; the returning seismic waves indicated that what lay above was neither space nor rock.

>> These discoveries shook the Open Universe Theory to its core, and academic circles began discussing the possibility of a new model. This new model stipulated that the universe was bound to a five-thousand-mile radius. They came to the conclusion that the lost explorer ships had come into contact with the edge of the universe and had been sucked into oblivion.

>> The explorer movement was faced with its greatest test yet. Before the *Helix* incident, the space taken by lost explorer ships had always remained, if only in theory, recoverable. Now, however, our people were faced with the edge of the universe. The space it eagerly devoured appeared to be lost forever. Considering this, even the most steadfast explorers were shaken. Remember that in our world, deep within layers of rock, space – once lost – could never be regain. With this in mind, the Alliance decided to send a final group of five bubble ships. As they reached an altitude of three thousand miles, these ships proceeded

with extreme caution. If they were to suffer the same fate as the previous missions, it would mean the end of the explorer movement.

>> Two bubble ships were lost. A third ship, the *Stone Cerebrum*, however, made groundbreaking progress. At an altitude of three thousand miles, the *Stone Cerebrum* was slowly digging upward, every foot of rock tunneled with the utmost caution. When the ship reached the seabed, the ocean's waters did not gush through the entire ship and so did not instantly collapse the vessel, as had happened in all previous attempts. Instead, the seawater spurted through a small crack, forced into a powerful but minute stream by the immense pressure above. The *Stone Cerebrum* had been designed with a beam width of 825 feet. By the standards of the explorer ships, this was considered large, yet it turned out to be an unbelievable stroke of luck. Because of the ship's size, the rising seawater took nearly an hour before it filled the ship's interior. Before coming into contact with the bursting water, the ship's seismoscope had recorded the morphology of the ocean above, and numerous data and images had been successfully transmitted back to the Alliance. It was on that day that the People of the Core saw a liquid for the first time.

>> It is quite imaginable that there might have been liquid in the Bubble World in ancient times, but it would have been nothing but searing magma. Once the violent geology of our planet's formation had finally come to rest, this magma must have completely solidified. In our planet's core, nothing remained but solid matter and empty space.

>> Even so, our scientists had long since predicted the theoretical possibility of liquids, but no one had really believed that this legendary substance could actually exist in the universe. Now, however, in those transmitted images, the scientists clearly saw it with their own eyes. And what they saw left all of them in shock: shocked at the white, bursting jet, shocked at the slow rise of the water's surface and shocked at seeing that demonic substance warp itself into any form, clinging to every surface in complete defiance of all laws of nature. They saw it seep into even the tiniest cracks, and they witnessed how it seemed to change the very nature of rock, darkening it with but a touch, even as it seemed to make it shimmer like metal. However, what fascinated them most was that while most things disappeared into this strange substance, some shattered remains of the crew and

machinery actually came to float on its surface! There was nothing that seemed to distinguish those things that floated from those that sank. The People of the Core gave this strange liquid substance a name; they called it 'amorphous rock'.

>> From that point on, the explorers could again celebrate a long string of successes. First, engineers from the Explorer Alliance designed a rudimentary drainpipe. In essence, it was a 650-foot-long, hollow, drilling pole. After it had drilled through the final layers of rock, the drill bit of this pole could be opened like a flap valve, drawing the ocean's waters down the pipe. A second valve was attached to the bottom of the drainpipe.

>> Another bubble ship rose to an altitude of three thousand miles. Then it began drilling the drainpipe through the final layers into the seabed. Nothing could have been easier; drilling was, after all, a technology with which the People of the Core were abundantly familiar. There was another piece to the puzzle, however, and that required technology of which we had never even conceived: sealing.

>> As the Bubble World had been completely devoid of liquids or gases, sealing technology had never been necessary, or even imaginable, to the People of the Core. As a result, the valve at the bottom of the drainpipe was far from watertight. Before it was even opened, it allowed water to leak out and into the ship. This accident, however, proved to be very fortunate indeed; had the valve ever been opened fully, the power of the onrushing water would have been much greater than the spray through the rock crack encountered by the *Stone Cerebrum*. It would have burst forth in a concentrated beam of water powerful enough to cut through everything in its path like a laser. Now, instead, the water seeped through the porous valve at a much more controllable drip. You can imagine just how fascinating it was for the crew of the bubble ship to see that thin stream of water trickling before their very eyes. This liquid was completely unknown territory to them, much as electricity had been to early humanity.

>> After carefully filling a metal container with the strange liquid, the bubble ship retreated to the lower layers, leaving the drainpipe buried in the rocks. As the ship descended, the explorers took great precautions, keeping their strange sample as still and safe as possible in its container. Carefully observing it, they soon made their first new discovery: the amorphous rock was actually transparent! When

they had first seen the seawater shoot through the cracked rock, it had naturally been heavily laden with sediment and mud. The People of the Core had accepted this as the amorphous rock's natural state. Following this discovery, the ship continued to descend, and as it did the temperature on board began to rise.

>> It was with a deep fear that the explorers suddenly came face to face with the most horrible realization yet: the amorphous rock was alive! Stirring, its surface had begun to roil with anger, its terrifying form now covered with countless bursting bubbles. But this monster's surging life force seemed to consume its very being, its body dissolving into a ghostly white shadow. Once all the amorphous rock in the container had transformed into this new phantasmal state, the explorers began to feel a strange sensation grip their bodies. Within moments, the sparks of shorting circuits erupted from within their bodies, ending their lives in agonizing fireworks.

>> Seismic waves transmitted this terrible spectacle live to the Explorer Alliance, right up until the monitors, too, went dark. A quickly dispatched relief ship suffered the same fate. As soon as it made contact with the doomed vessels, its crew also erupted into terrible sparks, dying in pain. It seemed as if the amorphous rock had become a specter of death, looming over all of space. The scientists, however, noticed that the second series of short circuits was nowhere as violent as the first explosive deaths. This led them to a conclusion: as the area of space increased, the density of that amorphous shadow of death decreased.

>> It took many lives and countless horrible deaths, but in the end the People of the Core finally discovered another state of being they had never encountered before: gas.

9

TO THE STARS

>> These momentous discoveries even moved the World Government, and they reunited with their old enemies, the Explorer Alliance. The Bubble World now also committed its resources to the cause, heralding a period of intense exploration marked by rapid progress. The final breakthrough was within reach.

>> Even though we came to an ever greater understanding of water vapor, we still lacked the sealing technology that would have allowed the core's scientists to protect our people and machinery from harm. Nonetheless, we had come to learn that at an altitude above 2,800 miles, the amorphous rock remained dead and inert, unable to boil. To study the strange new states, the World Government and the Explorer Alliance constructed a laboratory at an altitude of 2,900 miles. They equipped this facility with a permanent drainpipe. Here experts began to study the amorphous rock in earnest.

'Only then could you begin to undertake the work of Archimedes,' Fan chimed in.

>> You are quite correct, but you should not forget that our earliest forebears had already done the work of Faraday.

>> As a byproduct of their work in the Laboratory for Amorphous Rock Research, our scientists came to discover water pressure and buoyancy. They also managed to develop and perfect the sealant technology necessary to deal with liquids. Now we finally understood that sealing the amorphous rock would be an incredibly simple undertaking, much simpler in fact than drilling through layers of rock. All that would be required was a sufficiently sealed and pressure-resistant vessel. Without excavators, this ship would be able to rise at speeds that seemed almost incomprehensible to the People of the Core.

'You built a Bubble World rocket,' Fan noted with a smile.

>> More of a torpedo, really. This torpedo was a metallic, pressure-resistant, egg-shaped container with no drive or propeller whatsoever. It was designed for a crew of one. We shall call this pioneer 'Gagarin'. The torpedo's launch pad was set up in a spacious hall excavated at an altitude of three thousand miles. One hour before the launch, Gagarin entered the torpedo, and the entire vessel was hermetically sealed. After all instruments and life-support systems had been checked and determined to be functional, an automatic excavator began digging its way through the mere thirty feet of rock separating the launch hall from the seabed above. With a mighty roar, the ceiling collapsed under the pressure of the amorphous rock. The torpedo was immediately and completely submerged in a sea of liquid. As the chaos began to subside, Gagarin could finally catch a glimpse of the outside world through his transparent steel-rock porthole. With a start, he realized that the launch pad's two searchlights were casting beams of light through the amorphous rock. In the Bubble World, which lacked air, light could not scatter and emit beams. This was the first time any of us had ever seen light this way. Just then seismic waves communicated the launch order, and Gagarin pulled the release lever.

>> The anchor hinges holding the bottom of the torpedo to the rock sprang open, and the torpedo slowly began to rise from the seabed. Engulfed by the amorphous rock, it soon began to accelerate, floating upward.

>> Given the pressure at the seabed level, it was very easy for our scientists to calculate that roughly six miles of amorphous rock covered the ocean's floor. If nothing unexpected happened, the torpedo would float to the surface in roughly fifteen minutes. What it would encounter there, no one could know.

>> The torpedo shot up unimpeded. Through his porthole, Gagarin could see nothing but fathomless darkness. Only the occasional glimpse of dust zipping past in the lights outside his porthole gave him any indication of how rapidly he was ascending.

>> All too soon panic began to well in Gagarin's heart. He had lived all his life in a solid world. As he now entered, for the first time, a space filled with amorphous rock, a feeling of utterly helpless emptiness threatened to drown the very core of his being. Fifteen minutes seemed to stretch into infinity as Gagarin did his best to focus on the hundred thousand years of exploration that had led to this moment...

>> And just as his spirit was about to break, his torpedo broke the surface of our planet's ocean.

>> The inertia of the ascent shot the torpedo a good thirty feet above the water's surface before it came crashing back down toward the sea. Looking through his porthole as he fell, Gagarin could see the boundless amorphous rock, stretching into forever, shimmering with strange sparkles. But he had no time to see where the light was coming from; the torpedo slammed heavily into the ocean with a great splash, sending amorphous rock splashing in all directions.

>> The torpedo came to rest, floating on the ocean's surface like a boat, gently rocking with the waves.

>> Gagarin carefully opened the torpedo's hatch and slowly raised himself out of the vessel. He immediately felt the gust of the ocean breeze, and, after a few perplexed moments, he realized that it was gas. Tremors of fear shook his body as he recalled a flow of water vapor he had once seen through a steel–rock pipe in the laboratory. Who could have ever foreseen that there could be this much gas anywhere in the universe? Gagarin soon understood that this gas was very different from the gas produced by boiling amorphous rock. Unlike the latter, it did not cause his body to short circuit.

>> In his memoirs he later wrote the following description of these events:

>> I felt the gentle touch of a giant invisible hand brush by my body. It seemed to have reached down from a vast, boundless, and completely unknown place; and that place was now before me, transforming me into something wholly new.

>> Gagarin lifted his head, and then and there he finally embraced the reward of one hundred thousand years of our civilization's exploration: he saw the magnificent, sparkling wonder of the starlit sky.

10

OF THE UNIVERSALITY OF MOUNTAINS

'It really wasn't easy for you. You had to explore for so many years, just to reach our starting point!' Fan exclaimed in admiration.

>> That is the reason why you should consider yourselves a very lucky civilization.

Just then, the size of the ice crystal clouds formed by the escaping atmosphere dramatically increased. The heavens shone with a sparkling light, a brilliant rainbow wreath blooming as the alien vessel's glow scattered in the ice. Below, the gigantic cyclonic well continued its rumbling turns. It made Fan think of a massive machine pulverizing the planet bit by thundering bit. On top of the mountain, however, everything had become completely still. Even the tiny ripples had disappeared from the summit's surface. The ocean was mirror-still. Again, Feng Fan was reminded of the mountain lakes of North Tibet . . .

With a jolt, he forced his mind back to reality.

'Why did you come here?' he asked the sphere above.

>> We are just passing by, and we wanted to see if there was intelligent life here with which we could have a chat. We talk to whoever first climbs this mountain.

'Where there's a mountain, there will always be someone to climb it,' Fan intoned, nodding.

>> Indeed, it is the nature of intelligent life to climb mountains, to strive to stand on ever higher ground to gaze farther into the distance. It is a drive completely divorced from the demands of survival. Had you, for example, only been concerned with staying alive, you would have fled from this mountain as fast and as far away as you could. Instead, you chose to come and climb it. The reason evolution bestows all intelligent life with a desire to climb higher is far

more profound than mere base needs, even though we still do not understand its real purpose. Mountains are universal, and we are all standing at the foot of mountains.

'I am on the top of the mountain,' Feng Fan interjected. He would not stand for anyone, not even aliens, challenging the glory of his having climbed the world's tallest mountain.

>> You are standing at the foot of the mountain. We are all always at the foot. The speed of light is the foot of a mountain; the three dimensions of space are the foot of a mountain. You are imprisoned in the deep gorge of light-speed and three-dimensional space. Does it not feel . . . cramped?

'We were born this way. It is what we are familiar with,' Fan replied, clearly lost in thought.

>> Then the things that I will tell you next may be very unfamiliar. Look at the universe now. What do you feel?'

'It is vast, limitless, that kind of thing,' Fan answered.

>> Does it feel small to you?

'How could it? The universe stretches out endlessly before my eyes; scientists can even peer as far as twenty billion light years into space,' Fan explained.

>> Then I shall tell you: it is no more than a bubble world twenty billion light years in radius.

Fan had no words.

>> Our universe is an empty bubble, a bubble within something more solid.

'How could that possibly be? Would this larger solid not immediately collapse in under its own gravity?' Fan asked, bewildered.

>> No, at least not yet. Our bubble is still expanding in this super-universal solid. Gravitational collapse is only an issue for a bounded, solid space. If, however, the surrounding solid area is actually limitless, then gravitational collapse would be a non-issue. This, of course, is no more than a guess. Who could know whether this solid super-universe has its own limits?

>> There is so much space for speculation. For example, one could theorize that at its immense scale, gravity is offset by some other force, just like electromagnetism is largely offset by nuclear forces on the microscopic scale. We are not aware of such a force, but when we were inside the Bubble World we remained unaware of gravity. From

the data we have gathered, we can see that the form of the universe's bubble is much like your scientists have surmised. It is just that you do not know what lies beyond it yet.

'What is this solid? Is it . . .?' Fan hesitated for a moment. 'Rock?' he finally asked.

>> We do not know, but we will discover that in fifty thousand years, once we reach our destination.

'Where exactly are you going?' Fan asked.

>> The edge of the universe. Our bubble ship is called the *Needle's Point*. Do you remember the name?

'I remember,' Fan answered. 'That was the ship that first discovered the law of decreasing density in the Bubble World.'

>> Correct. We do not know what we will find.

'Does the super-universe have other bubbles in it?' Fan enquired.

>> You are already thinking very far ahead, indeed.

'How could I not?' Fan responded.

>> Think of the many small bubbles inside a very big rock. They are there, but they are very hard to find. Even so, we will go and look for them.

'You truly are amazing.' Fan smiled, feeling a deep admiration for the adventurous aliens.

>> Very well, our little chat was most delightful, but we must make haste; fifty thousand years is a very long time, and we are burning daylight, so to speak. It was a pleasure meeting you; and remember, mountains are universal.

The sheer density of the ice crystal clouds made the last few words indistinct, blurred behind the clouds. And with those final words, the giant sphere, too, began to slowly dim, its form fading smaller and smaller into the heavens. Soon it had shrunk to a mere dot, just another star in an endless sky. It left much faster than it had arrived, and within moments it had disappeared altogether across the western horizon.

Everything between sky and ocean was restored to deep black. Ice crystal clouds and the cyclonic well were swallowed by the darkness, leaving only a trace of swirling black chaos, barely visible in the skies above. Feng Fan could hear the roar of the encircling tempest rapidly diminish. Soon, it was no more than a soft whimper, and before long, even that had died. All that remained was the sound of the waves.

Feng Fan suddenly became aware of the sensation of falling. Looking around, he could see the ocean slowly begin to change. The perfectly round summit of the water mountain had begun to flatten like a giant parasol being stretched open. He knew that the water mountain was dissolving and that he was plummeting a good thirty thousand feet. Within minutes, the water he was floating on stopped falling, having reached sea level. The inertia of his fall carried him down deep below the surface.

Luckily, he did not sink too far this time and quickly bobbed up to the surface.

As he surfaced, he realized that the water mountain had completely disappeared into the ocean, leaving not even the slightest trace, appearing just as if it had never been there. The cyclone, too, had spun itself out of existence, even though he could still feel the hurricane-force winds batter him as they whipped up large waves. Soon, the ocean's surface would be calm again.

As the ice crystal clouds scattered, the magnificent starry heavens again spanned the sky.

Feng Fan looked up at the stars, thinking of that distant world so very, very far away – so remote that even the light of that day must have been reeling from exhaustion before reaching Earth. There, in that ocean long ago, Gagarin of the Bubble World had raised his head to the stars as Fan did now; and through the vast barrenness of space and the desolation of time, he felt a deep bond of kinship unite their spirits.

In a sudden a burst of nausea, Feng Fan retched. He could tell from the taste that it was blood. Miles above sea level, on the summit of the water mountain, he had suffered altitude sickness. A pulmonary edema was hemorrhaging. He instantly realized the severity of the situation. The sudden increase in gravity had left him too exhausted to move. Only his life jacket was keeping him afloat. He had no inkling as to the fate of the *Bluewater*, but he was almost certain that there could be no boats within at least half a mile of him.

When he was atop the summit, Feng Fan had felt his life fulfilled. Up there, he could have died in peace. Now, suddenly, there was no one on the planet who could have been more afraid to die than he was. He had climbed to the rocky roof of our planet, and now he had also climbed the highest watery peak the world had ever known.

What kind of mountain was left for him to climb?

He would have to survive; he had to find out. The primal fear of the Himalayan blizzard returned. Once, this fear had made him cut the rope connecting him to his companions and his lover. He had sealed their fate. Now he knew that he had done the right thing. If there had been anything left for him to betray to save his life, he would have betrayed it.

He had to live. There was a universe of mountains out there.

2018-04-01

It's yet another day when I can't make up my mind. I've been dragging my feet for a couple of months already, as though I were walking through a pool of thick, heavy sludge. I feel my life being used up dozens of times faster than before – where 'before' is before the Gene Extension program was commercialized. And before I came up with my plan.

I gaze into the distance from a window on the top floor of an office building. The city spreads below me like an exposed silicon die, and me no more than an electron running along its dense nanometer-thick routes. In the scheme of things, that's how small I am. The decisions I make are no big deal. If I could only make a decision . . . But as so many times before, I can't decide. The waffling continues.

Hadron shows up late, again, bringing a gust of wind with him into the office. He has a bruise on his face. A bandage is stuck on his forehead, but he seems very self-possessed. He holds his head high, as though a medal were stuck there. His desk is opposite mine. He sits down, turns on his computer, then stares at me, clearly waiting for me to ask a question. However, I'm not interested.

'Did you see it on TV last night?' Hadron finally asks.

He's talking about the 'Fair Life' attack on a hospital downtown, also the biggest Gene Extension Center in the country. Two long, black burn scars mar the hospital's snow-white exterior as though dirty hands had fondled the face of a jade-like beauty. Frightening. 'Fair Life' is the largest and also most extreme of the many groups opposed to Gene Extension. Hadron is a member, but I didn't see him on TV. The crowd outside the hospital had roiled like the tide.

'We just had an all-hands,' I say in response. 'You know the company policy. Keep this up and you won't have a way to feed yourself.'

Gene Extension is short for Gene Reforming Life-Extension Technology. By removing those gene segments that produce the aging clock, humanity's typical life span can be extended to as long as three hundred years. This technology was first commercialized five years ago, and it quickly became a disaster that's spread to every society and government in the world. Though it's widely coveted, almost no one can afford it. Gene Extension for one person costs as much as a mansion, and the already widening gap between the rich and the poor suddenly feels even more insurmountable.

'I don't care,' Hadron says. 'I'm not going to live even a hundred years. What do I have to care about?'

Smoking is strictly prohibited in the office, but Hadron lights a cigarette now. Like he's trying to show just how little he cares.

'Envy. Envy is hazardous to your health.' I wave away the smoke from my eyes. 'The past also had lots of people who died too early because they couldn't afford to pay the medical bills.'

'That's not the same thing. Practically everyone can afford health care. Now, though, the ninety-nine percent look helplessly at the one percent who have all the money and will live to be three hundred. I'm not afraid to admit I'm envious. It's envy that's keeping society fair.' He leans in toward me from the table. 'Are you so sure you're not envious? Join us.'

Hadron's gaze makes me shiver. For a moment, I wonder if he's looking through me. Yes, I want to become who he envies. I want to become a Gene Extended person.

But the fact is, I don't have much money. I'm in my thirties and still have an entry-level job. It's in the finance department, though. Plenty of opportunities to embezzle funds. After years of planning, it's all done. Now, I only have to click my mouse, and the five million I need for Gene Extension will go into my secret bank account. From there, it'll be transferred to the Gene Extension Center's account. I've installed layers upon layers of camouflage into the labyrinthian financial system. It'll be at least half a year before they discover the money is missing. When they do, I'll lose my job, I'll be sentenced, I'll lose everything I own, I'll suffer the disapproving gazes of countless people . . .

But, by then, I'll be someone who can live for three hundred years.

And yet I'm still hesitating.

I've researched the statutes carefully. The penalties for corruption are five million yuan and at most twenty years. After twenty years, I'll still have over two hundred years of useful life ahead of me. The question now is, given that the math is so simple, can I really be the only one planning something like that? In fact, besides crimes that get the death penalty, once you've become one of Gene Extended, they're all worth committing. So, how many people are there like me, who've planned it but are hesitating? This thought makes me want to act right now and, at the same time, makes me flinch.

What makes me waver the most, though, is Jian Jian. Before I met her, I didn't believe there was any love in the world. After I met her, I didn't believe that there was anything but love in the world. If I leave her, what would be the point in living even two thousand years? On the scales of life, two and a half centuries sits on one side and the pain of leaving Jian Jian sits on the other. The scales are practically balanced.

The head of our department calls a meeting, and I can guess from the look on his face that it isn't to discuss work. Rather, it's directed at a specific person. Sure enough, the chief says, today, he wants to talk about the 'intolerable' conduct of some of the staff. I don't look at Hadron, but I know he's in trouble. The chief, however, says someone else's name.

'Liu Wei, according to reliable sources, you joined the IT Republic?'

Liu Wei nods, as self-assured as Louis XVI walking to the guillotine. 'This has nothing to do with work. I don't want work interfering with my personal freedoms.'

The chief sternly shakes his head. He thrusts a finger at Liu Wei. 'Very few things have nothing to do with work. Don't bring your cherished university ideals into the workplace. If a country can condemn its president on Main Street, that's called democracy. However, if everyone disobeys their boss, then this country will collapse.'

'The virtual nation is about to be recognized.'

'Recognized by whom? The United Nations? Or a world power? Stop dreaming.'

The chief doesn't seem to have much faith in his last utterance. The territory human society owns is divided into two parts. One part is every continent and island on Earth. The other part is cyberspace.

The latter recapitulated human history at a hundred times the speed. In cyberspace, after tens of years of a disorganized Stone Age, nations emerged as a matter of course. Virtual nations chiefly stem from two sources. The first is every sort of bulletin-board system aggregated together. The second is massively multiplayer online games. Virtual nations have heads of state and legislatures similar to those of physical nations. They even have online armed forces. Their borders and citizenships are not like those of physical nations. Virtual nations chiefly take belief, virtue, and occupation as their organizing principles. Citizens of every virtual nation are spread all over the world. Virtual nations, with a combined population of over two billion, established a virtual United Nations comparable to the physical one. It's a huge political entity that overlaps the traditional nations.

The IT Republic is a superpower in the virtual world. Its population is eighty million and still rapidly growing. The country is composed mostly of IT professionals, and makes aggressive political demands. It also has formidable power against the physical world. I don't know what Liu Wei's citizenship is. They say that the head of the IT Republic is an ordinary employee of some IT company. Conversely, more than one head of a physical nation has been exposed as an ordinary citizen of a virtual nation.

The chief gives everyone on our team a stern warning. No one can have a second nationality. He allows Liu Wei to go to the president's office, then he ends the meeting. We haven't even risen from our seats when Zheng Lili, who had stayed at her desk during the meeting, lets out a head-splitting scream. Something horrible has happened. We rush to turn on the news.

Back at my desk I pull up a news site. A broadcast is streaming on the homepage; the newsreader is in a daze. He announces that the United Nations has voted down Resolution 3617. That was the IT Republic's request for diplomatic recognition. It had passed the Security Council. In response, the IT Republic has declared war against the physical world. It began attacking the world's financial systems half an hour ago.

I look at Liu Wei. This seems to have surprised him, too.

The picture changes to that of a large city, a bird's-eye view of a street of tall buildings, and a traffic jam. People stream out of cars and buildings. It's like the aftermath of an earthquake. The shot cuts to a large supermarket. A crowd pushes in like the tide. Madly, they scramble for cans and packages of food. Row after row of shelves shake and crash into each other, like sandbars broken up by a tidal wave . . .

'What's happening?' I ask, terrified.

'You still don't understand?' Zheng Lili asks. 'There's no rich or poor anymore. Everyone is penniless. Steal or you won't eat!'

Of course, I understand, but I don't dare to believe this nightmare is real. Coins and paper money stopped circulating three years ago. Even buying a pack of cigarettes from a kiosk on the side of the street requires a card reader. In this total information age, what is wealth? Ultimately, it's no more than strands of pulses and magnetic marks inside computer storage. As far as this grand office building is concerned, if the electronic records in relevant departments are deleted, even though a company holds title deeds, no one will recognize its property rights. What is money? Money isn't worth shit. Money is just a strand of electromagnetic marks even smaller than bacteria and pulses that disappear in a flash. As far as the IT Republic is concerned, close to half the IT workers in the physical world are its citizens. Erasing those marks is extremely easy.

Programmers, network engineers, and database managers form the main body of the IT Republic. They are a twenty-first-century revival of the nineteenth-century industrial army, except physical labor is now mental labor, and gets more and more difficult. They work with code as indistinct as thick fog and labyrinthine network hardware and software. Like dockworkers from two hundred years ago, they bear a heavy load on their backs.

Information technology advances in great strides. Except for those lucky enough to climb into management, everyone's knowledge and skills grow obsolete quickly. New IT graduates pour in like hungry termites. The old workers (not actually old, most are just over thirty) are forced to the side, replaced and abandoned. The newcomers, though, don't last long either. The vast majority of them don't have long-term prospects. . . . This class is known as the technology proletariat.

Do not say that we own not a thing. We're about to reformat the world! This is a corrupt version of 'The Internationale.'

A thought strikes me like lightning. Oh, no. My money, which doesn't belong to me but will buy me over two hundred years of life, will it be deleted? But if everything will be reformatted, won't the result be the same? My money, my Gene Extension, my dreams. . . . It grows dark before my eyes. My chest grows tight and I stumble away from my desk.

Zheng Lili laughs then, and I stop. She stands near me.

'Happy April Fool's Day,' a sober Liu Wei says, glancing at the network switch at a corner of the office.

The office network isn't connected to the outside world. Zheng Lili's laptop is sitting on the switch, acting as a server. That bitch! She must have gone to a lot of trouble to pull off this April Fool's joke, most of it to produce that news footage. An in-house designer, though, could have used 3-D software to produce that footage. It wouldn't have been that hard.

Others obviously don't think Zheng Lili's joke went too far. 'Oh, come on,' Hadron says to me. 'Practical jokes are supposed to raise the hair on your neck if they're being done right. What's there to be afraid of?' He points at the executives upstairs.

I break into a cold sweat, wondering whether he suspects anything because of my reaction to Zheng Lili's prank. Can he see through me? But even that's not my biggest worry.

Reformatting the world, is that really just the mad ravings of IT Republic extremists? Is this really just an April Fool's joke? How long can the hair that suspends the sword last?

In an instant, like a bright light driving away the dark, my doubt is gone. I have decided.

I ask Jian Jian to meet me this evening. When I see her against the backdrop of a sea of the city's streetlamps, my hard heart softens again. She seems so delicate, like a candle flame that can be snuffed out by the slightest breeze. How can I hurt her? As she comes closer and I can see her eyes, the scales in my heart have already tilted completely to the other side. Without her, what do I even want those two-hundred-plus years for? Will time truly heal all wounds? It could simply be two centuries of nonstop punishment. Love elevates me, an extremely selfish man, to lofty heights.

Jian Jian speaks first, though. Unexpectedly, she says what I prepared to say to her, word for word: 'I've been turning this over in my head for a long time now. I think we should break up.'

Lost, I ask her why.

'Many years from now, I'll still be young. You'll already be old.'

It takes a long moment for me to understand what she's saying. Then I realize what the look on her face as she was walking toward me meant. I mistook her solemn expression as her having guessed what I was about to do. Laughter bubbles through me. It grows until it is loud and pitched at the sky. I am such an idiot. I never considered what era this is, what temptations appear before us. When I stop laughing, I feel relieved. My body is so light, I might float away. At the same time, though, I'm genuinely happy for Jian Jian.

'Where did you get so much money?' I ask her.

'It's just enough for me.' Her voice is low. She avoids my gaze.

'I know. It doesn't matter. I mean, it takes a lot of money for just you, too.'

'My dad gave me some. One hundred years is enough. I saved some money. By then, the interest ought to be sizable.'

I guessed wrong. She doesn't want Gene Extension. She wants hibernation, another achievement of life science that's been commercialized. At about fifty degrees below zero, drugs and an extracorporeal circulation system reduce the metabolism down to 1 percent of normal. Someone hibernating for one hundred years will only age one.

'Life is tiring, and tedious. I just want to escape,' Jian Jian says.

'Can you escape after a century? By then, no one will recognize your academic credentials. You won't be used to what society will have become. Will you be able to cope?'

'The times always get better, don't they? In the future, maybe I can do Gene Extension. By then, it will surely be more affordable.'

Jian Jian and I leave without saying anything else. Perhaps, one century later, we can meet again, but I didn't promise her anything. Then, she will still be her, but I'll be someone who has experienced another hundred years of change.

Once she is gone, I don't hesitate. I take out my cell phone, log into the online banking system, and transfer five million into the Gene Extension Center's bank account. Although it's close to midnight,

I still receive a call from the center's director right away. He says that the manipulations to improve my genes can start tomorrow. If all goes smoothly, it will be over in a week. He earnestly repeats the center's promise of secrecy. Out of the Gene Extended whose identities have been revealed, three have already been murdered.

'You'll be happy with your decision,' the director says. 'Because you will receive not just over two centuries but possibly eternal life.'

I understand what he's getting at. Who knows what technologies may arise over the next two centuries? Perhaps, by then, it'll be possible to copy consciousness and memory, create permanent backups that can be poured into a new body whenever we want. Perhaps we won't even need bodies. Our consciousnesses will drift on the network like gods, passing through countless sensors to experience the world and the universe. This truly is eternal life.

The director continues: 'In fact, if you have time, you have everything. Given enough time, a monkey randomly hitting keys on a typewriter can type out the complete works of Shakespeare. And what you have is time.'

'Me? Not us?'

'I didn't go under Gene Extension.'

'Why?'

After a long silence, he says, 'This world changes too quickly. Too many opportunities, too many temptations, too many desires, too many dangers. I get dizzy thinking about it. When all is said and done, you're still old. But don't worry.' He then says the same thing Jian Jian says. 'The times always get better.'

Now, I'm sitting in my cramped apartment writing in this diary. This is the first diary I've ever kept. I'll keep diaries from now on because I should leave something behind. Time also allows someone to lose everything. I know. I'm not just a long lifetime. The me of two centuries from now will surely be a stranger. In fact, considering it carefully, what I thought at first is very dubious. The union of my body, memory, and consciousness is always changing. The me before I broke up with Jian Jian, the me before I paid the embezzled money, the me before I spoke with the director, even up to the me before I typed out 'even,' they are all already different people. Having realized this, I'm relieved.

But I should leave something behind.

In the dark sky outside the window, predawn stars send out their last, pallid light. Compared to the brilliant sea of streetlamps in the city, the stars are dim. I can just make them out. They are, however, symbols of the eternal. Just tonight, I don't know how many are like me, a new generation setting off on a journey. No matter good or bad, we will be the first generation to truly touch eternity.

MOONLIGHT

For the first time that he could remember, he saw moonlight in the city.

He hadn't noticed it on other nights because the bright electric glow of millions of lamps had overwhelmed it. But today was the Mid-Autumn Festival, and a web petition had proposed that the city turn off most landscape lighting and some of the streetlights so that residents could enjoy the full moon.

Looking out from the balcony of his single-occupancy unit, he discovered that the petitioners had been wrong about the effect. The moonlit city was nothing like the charming, idyllic scene they had imagined; rather, it resembled an abandoned ruin. Still, he appreciated the view. The apocalyptic spirit gave off a beauty of its own, suggesting the passing of all and the discharge of all burdens. He had only to lie down in the embrace of Fate to enjoy the tranquility at the end. That was what he needed.

His phone buzzed. The caller was a man. After ascertaining who had picked up, the voice said, 'I'm sorry to disturb you on the worst day of your life. I still remember it after all these years.'

The voice sounded odd. Clear, but distant and hollow. An image came to his mind: chill winds rushing between the strings of a harp abandoned in the wilderness.

The caller continued. 'Today was Wen's wedding, wasn't it? She invited you, but you didn't go.'

'Who is this?'

'I've thought about it so many times over the years. You should have gone, and you would be feeling better now. But you ... well, you did go, except you hid in the lobby and watched Wen in her wedding dress heading into the reception holding his hand. You were torturing yourself.'

'Who *are* you?' Despite his astonishment, he still noticed the caller's odd phrasing. The caller said 'after all these years,' but the wedding had only taken place this morning. And since Wen's wedding date had been decided on only a week ago, it was impossible for anyone to know about it long before then.

The distant voice went on. 'You have a habit. Whenever you're upset, you curl your left big toe and dig the nail into the bottom of your shoe. When you got home earlier, you found that your toenail had snapped but you didn't even notice the pain. Your toenails are getting long though. They've worn holes into your socks. You haven't been taking care of yourself.'

'*Who in the world is this?*' He was now frightened.

'I'm you. I'm calling from the year 2123. It's not easy connecting to your mobile network from this time. The signal degradation through the time-space interface is severe. If you can't hear me, let me know and I'll try again.'

He knew it wasn't a joke. He had known from the first moment that the voice didn't belong to this world. He clutched the phone tightly and stared at the buildings washed by the cold, pure moonlight, as though the whole city had frozen to listen to their conversation. Yet he could think of nothing to say as the caller waited patiently. Faint background noises filled his ear.

'How ... could I live to be so old?' he asked, just to break the silence.

'Twenty years from your time, genetic therapies will be invented to extend human lifespan to around two centuries. I'm still technically middle-aged, though I feel ancient.'

'Can you explain the process in more detail?'

'No. I can't even give you a simple overview. I have to ensure that you receive as little information about the future as possible, to prevent you from inappropriate behaviors that would change the course of history.'

'Then why did you get in touch with me in the first place?'

'For the mission that we have to accomplish together. Having lived for so long, I can tell you a secret about life: once you realize how insignificant the individual is in the vastness of space-time, you can face anything. I didn't call you to talk about your personal life, so I need you to let go of the pain and face the mission. Listen! What do you hear?'

He strained to catch the background noises through the receiver. The faint sounds resolved into splashes and plops, and he tried to reconstruct an image from them. Strange flowers bloomed in the darkness; a giant glacier cracked in a desolate sea, and zigzagging seams extended into the depths of the crystalline mass like lightning bolts …

'You're hearing waves crashing against buildings. I'm on the eighth floor of Jin Mao Tower. The surface of the sea is right under the window.'

'Shanghai has been flooded?'

'That's right. She was the last of the coastal cities to fall. The dikes were high and durable, but the sea ultimately inundated the interior and flooded back in. … Can you imagine what I'm seeing? No, it's nothing like Venice. The undulating water between the buildings is covered with garbage and flotsam, as if all the refuse accumulated in this city over two centuries had become afloat. The moon is full tonight, just like where and when you are. There are no lights in the city, but my moon is not nearly as bright as yours – the atmosphere is far too polluted. The sea mirrors the moonlight onto the skeletons of the skyscrapers. The great sphere at the top of the Oriental Pearl Tower flickers with silvery streaks reflected from the waves, as if everything is about to collapse.'

'How much has the sea risen?'

'The polar ice caps are gone. In the span of half a century, the sea rose by about twenty meters. Three hundred million coastal inhabitants had to move inland. Only desolation is left here, while the inland regions are gripped by political and social chaos. The economy is nearing total collapse … Our mission is to prevent all of this.'

'Do you think we can play God?'

'Mere mortals doing what needed to be done a hundred years earlier would have the same effect as divine intervention now. If, in your time, the whole world had stopped using all fossil fuels – including coal, petroleum, and natural gas – global warming would have stopped, and this disaster could have been prevented.'

'That seems impossible.' After he said this, his self from more than a hundred years in the future remained silent for a long time. So he added, 'To stop the use of fossil fuels, you need to contact people from even earlier.'

He sensed a smile through the phone. 'Do you imagine I can stop the Industrial Revolution in its tracks?'

'But what you're asking of us now is even more impossible. The world will fall apart if you eliminate all coal, gas, and oil for a single week.'

'Actually, our models show that it wouldn't even take that long. But there are other ways. Remember that I'm speaking to you from the future. Think. We're smart people.'

He thought of one possibility. 'Give us an advanced energy technology. Something environmentally friendly that won't contribute to climate change. The technology has to be able to satisfy existing energy needs while also being much cheaper than fossil fuels. If you give us that, it won't be ten years before the market will force all fossil fuels out of contention.'

'That's exactly what we're going to do.'

Encouraged, he went on. 'Then teach us how to achieve controlled nuclear fusion.'

'You vastly underestimate the difficulties. We still haven't achieved any breakthroughs in that field. There are fusion reactor power plants, but they aren't even as competitive in the market as fission plants in your time. Also, fusion reactors require the extraction of fuel from seawater, a process that may lead to more environmental damage. We can't give you controlled fusion, but we can give you solar power.'

'Solar power? What do you mean exactly?'

'Collecting the sun's power from the surface of the Earth.'

'With what?'

'Monocrystalline silicon, the same material you use in your time.'

'Oh, come on! You literally just made me facepalm. I thought you had something real for a minute there. ... Actually, do you still say "facepalm"?'

'Sure we do. Old-timers like me have kept lots of expressions like that alive. Anyway, our monocrystalline silicon solar cells have far higher conversion efficiency.'

'Even if you achieved one hundred percent efficiency it would be irrelevant. How much solar power reaches each square meter on the Earth's surface? There's no way that a few solar panels can satisfy the energy needs of contemporary society. Have you been hallucinating that your youth was spent in some preindustrial farmers' paradise?'

He heard his future self laugh. 'Now that you mention it, the technology really does evoke shades of agrarian nostalgia.'

'"Evoke shades of agrarian nostalgia"? When did I start to talk like a coffee shop writer?'

'Heh, the technology really is called the silicon plow.'

'What?'

'The silicon plow. Silicon is the most abundant element on Earth, and you can find it everywhere in sand or soil. A silicon plow cuts furrows in the earth just like a regular plow, but it extracts the silicon out of the soil and refines it into monocrystalline silicon. The land it processes turns into solar cells.'

'What ... what does a silicon plow look like?'

'Like a combine harvester. To start it, you need an external energy source, but then it relies on the power provided by the solar cells it leaves behind. With this technology, you can turn the whole Taklamakan Desert into a solar power plant.'

'Are you telling me that all the plowed land will become black, shiny cells?'

'No. The plowed land will just look darker, but the conversion efficiency will be phenomenal. After the land has been plowed, you just attach wires to the two ends of the furrow to get a photovoltaic current.'

As the holder of a doctorate degree in Energy Planning, he was entranced by the promise of this technology. His breathing sped up.

'I just sent you an email with all the technical details. At your technology level, you shouldn't have any trouble mass-producing it – that's also one of the reasons I chose to contact your era instead of an earlier time. Starting tomorrow, you must dedicate yourself to spreading this technology. I know you have the necessary resources and the skills. How to popularize the technology is up to you. Maybe you can take advantage of the report you're drafting right now. But you have to remember one thing: under no circumstances can you reveal that the technology comes from the future.'

'Why did you choose me? You should have picked someone more senior.'

'I have to take care to reduce the potential negative side effects from my interference. You and I are the same person. Can you think of a better choice?'

'Tell me, just how high have you climbed on the career ladder?'

'I can't reveal that. It took a lot of convincing for the Embodied International to decide to interfere in history at all.'

'Embodied International?'

'The world is divided between the Embodied International and the Virtual International – never mind, I've said too much. Don't ask me about anything like that again.'

'But ... if I do as you've asked, how will you see the world change? Are you going to wake up the next day and find everything different?'

'It'll be even faster than that. The minute you open my email and decide on your course of action, my world will likely change instantly. But we two are the only people – the only person – who will know this. For everyone else in my era, history is history, and in the new timeline, which is also their only timeline, the period of fossil fuel use between your time and my time never happened.'

'Will you call me again?'

'I don't know. Every contact with the past is a major undertaking. International conferences have to be held. Goodbye.'

He returned to his bedroom and turned on the computer. The inbox showed the email from the future. The body was blank, but there were more than a dozen attachments, totaling more than a gigabyte. He browsed through them quickly and found detailed technical drawings and documents. Although he couldn't make sense of everything yet, he saw that the technical language was accessible to someone of his era.

One particular photograph caught his attention. It was a wide-angle shot of an open space. A silicon plow, which really did resemble a combine harvester, sat in the middle of the field, and the soil behind it was slightly darker. The perspective of the shot made the plow look like a small brush painting the earth dark stroke by long stroke. About a third of the land in the frame had already been plowed, but the part of the photo that most attracted his attention was the sky of the future. It was a dusty gray, but not overcast. Maybe it was taken at dawn or dusk, since the plow cast a long shadow. This was an age without blue skies.

He began to think through his next steps. As a staff member of the Planning Office of the Ministry of Energy, he was responsible for, among other things, gathering information on the progress of new energy development projects across the country. The report he was drafting would be passed on to the minister, who would then deliver it to the State Council at their upcoming meeting. Part of China's four-trillion-yuan stimulus package in response to the economic crisis was set aside for developing new energy technologies, and the State Council meeting would decide where to invest the funds. His future self apparently wanted him to take advantage of this opportunity. But before he could put this technology into his report, he had to first find a research lab or company to pick it up as a development project. He would have to be very strategic in this choice, but he was certain that if the technical documents were real, he would find a good company to undertake the work. Even in the worst case, whoever decided to move forward with this research wouldn't lose much . . .

He shuddered, as if waking from a dream. *Have I already decided to go down this path? Yes, I have.* There could only be two outcomes from his decision: success or failure. If his effort would eventually succeed, the future should have already been altered.

Mere mortals doing what needed to be done a hundred years earlier would have the same effect as divine intervention.

He stared at the email on the screen, and suddenly had the urge to respond to it. He wrote only two words in the reply: Got it. Immediately, a response came back informing him that the address was undeliverable. He picked up his phone and looked at the caller ID, an ordinary number from China Mobile. He pressed the 'call' button, and a recorded voice informed him that the number was not in service.

Returning to the balcony, he luxuriated in the watery moonlight. The neighborhood was completely quiet this late at night, and the moon bathed the buildings and the ground in a milky, unreal, tender glow. He had the sensation of waking from a dream, or perhaps he was still dreaming.

The phone rang again. The screen showed another unfamiliar number, but as soon as he picked up, he recognized the voice of his future self. It was still distant and hollow, but the background noises were different.

'You succeeded,' his future self said.

'When are you calling from?' he asked.

'The year 2119.'

'So four years earlier than the last time you called.'

'For me, this is the first time I've ever called you ... or calling me, I guess. But I do remember receiving that phone call you mentioned more than a hundred years ago.'

'That was just twenty minutes ago, for me. How is everything? Has the seawater receded?'

'There's no seawater. The climate never warmed drastically, and sea levels didn't rise. The history you heard about twenty minutes earlier never happened. In our history books, solar energy made a breakthrough in the early twenty-first century and culminated in the silicon plow, which made large-scale solar energy collection possible. In the 2020s, solar energy came to dominate world energy markets, and fossil fuels quickly vanished. The first half of your – our – life has been a brilliant rising arc tied to the silicon plow, and in three years from your time, the technology will begin to spread across the globe. However, just like the history of the coal and oil industries, the history of solar energy hasn't generated any lasting celebrities, not even you.'

'I don't care about being famous. It's wonderful to have had a role in saving the world.'

'Of course we don't care about fame. In fact, it's good that we are not well known, otherwise we'd be treated as history's greatest criminal. The world has changed, but not for the better. The good thing is that only one person, you and me, knows this. Even those who had devised and implemented the plan to interfere with history the last time have no memories of fossil fuel use in the rest of the twenty-first century since that timeline never came to be. I don't remember calling you, but I do remember getting the call from the future. That phone call is, in fact, the only clue I have to that nonexistent history. Listen! What do you hear?'

Through the receiver, he detected faint cries that reminded him of clouds of swarming birds above the woods at dusk. Gusts of wind swept through the trees from time to time, overwhelming the cries with susurrations.

'I can't tell what I'm hearing. It doesn't sound like the ocean.'

'Of course it doesn't sound like the ocean. Even the Huangpu River is almost dried out. This is the drought season – there are only two seasons now, drought and flood. It's possible to cross the river just by rolling up your pant legs. In fact, several hundred thousand starving refugees have just crossed the river into Pudong, covering the riverbed like a mass of ants. The city is in disarray; I can see fires starting everywhere.'

'What happened? Solar energy should have the lowest environmental impact.'

'You're sadly mistaken. Do you know how many square kilometers of monocrystalline silicon fields are necessary to supply the energy needs of a city like Shanghai? At least twenty times the area of Shanghai itself! During the century after your time, urbanization accelerated, and even a mid-sized city now is comparable to the Shanghai of your era. Starting in the 2020s, silicon plows transformed the face of every continent. After all the deserts had been turned into solar fields, they began to devour arable land and vegetation cover. Now, every continent is suffering from excessive siliconization. The process had advanced far faster than desertification. The land surface of the Earth is now almost entirely covered by silicon solar fields.'

'But this should be impossible under theories of economics! As land grows more scarce, the value of any unplowed land ought to rise, and silicon plows should become too expensive to be viable in the market—'

'This was no different from the history of the fossil fuel industries. By the time the conditions you describe came into play, it was too late. Shifting to alternative energy sources was no easy task, and even rebuilding the infrastructure for coal and oil required too much time. Meanwhile, the need for energy kept on growing, and silicon plows had to devour more land. Land siliconization was even more damaging to the environment than desertification. As conditions deteriorated, drought swept the globe, and the occasional rainfall only resulted in massive floods ...'

Listening to this voice from a century in the future, he felt like a drowning man. Just before he was about to give up all hope, he found himself somehow at the surface. Taking a deep breath, he said to his future self, 'But there is a way out! A way out! It's simple. I haven't done anything yet except decide on a plan for how to introduce the technology. I'll immediately delete the email and all attachments, and go on with my life as before.'

'Then Shanghai will once more be swallowed by the sea.'

He moaned with frustration.

'We have to interfere with history again,' said his future self.

'Don't tell me: you're going to give me some other new energy technology?'

'That's right. The key to the new technology is ultra-deep drilling.'

'Drilling? But the technology for oil extraction is already very advanced.'

'No, I'm not talking about drilling for oil. The wells I have in mind will reach a depth of over a hundred kilometers, penetrating the Mohorovičić discontinuity and boring into the liquid mantle. The Earth's powerful magnetic field is generated by strong electric currents deep within the planet, and we want to tap into them. Once the ultra-deep wells are drilled, massive terminals dropped into the wells will extract the geoelectric energy. We'll also give you the technology for electrical terminals that can function under such high temperatures.'

'That sounds ... grandiose. I'm rather frightened.'

'Listen, geoelectricity extraction is the greenest technology. It doesn't take up any land and doesn't generate any carbon dioxide or other pollutants. All right, it's time to say goodbye. If we ever talk again, let's hope it's not to save the world. ... Go check your email.'

'Wait! Let's chat some more. Tell me about ... our life.'

'We have to keep contact with the past to a minimum to reduce information leakage. I'm sure you understand that what we're doing is incredibly dangerous. Also, there's nothing to talk about really, since whatever I've gone through you'll get to experience sooner or later.' The connection ended as soon as his future self stopped talking.

He returned to his computer and saw a second email. Like the last one, it was also packed with technical information. As he browsed through the attachments, he found that ultra-deep drilling used lasers instead of mechanical bits, and the molten rock was channeled up through the drill to the surface. The last attachment was another photograph of an open field studded with high-voltage transmission towers. The lattice towers looked slender and light, perhaps constructed from some strong composite material. One end of the wires plunged into the earth, evidently to tap into the buried geoelectric terminals. The ground itself attracted his gaze, as it was the lifeless dark color of plowed silicon fields. A network of fencing divided the ground into a grid, which he decided must be transmission lines that extracted the energy from the monocrystalline silicon. Unlike the photograph from the last time, the sky was a clear azure, with not a wisp of cloud to be seen. This was an age where rain was rare, and even through the photograph he could feel the crisp, dry air.

Once again, he returned to the balcony. The moon was now in the western sky and shadows had lengthened, as though the city had finished dreaming and fallen deeper into slumber.

He thought about ways to spread this new future technology. The necessary strategies were different from the last time. First, the laser drilling technology would itself generate attractive military and civilian applications. He should be able to popularize it first and wait for the industry to mature before revealing the far more astounding idea of geoelectricity. At the same time, he could advocate for development of other ancillary technologies like extreme heat-tolerant electric terminals. The initial investment still had to come from the four-trillion-yuan stimulus package, and he still needed to find an influential entity to take up the research project. He was confident of success because he knew he had the technical secrets.

I've decided on a new path. Has history changed again?

As if answering his thoughts, the phone rang for the third time. The westering moon was now half-peeking from behind a tall building across the way, as if giving this world one last terrified glance before her departure.

'I'm you, calling from the year 2125.'

The caller paused, as if waiting for him to ask questions, but he dared not. The hand squeezing the phone grew clammy, and he was already exhausted. Finally, he asked, 'You want me to listen to the noises of your world, don't you?'

'I don't think you'll hear much this time.'

Still, he strained to listen. There was only a slight buzzing that sounded like interference. Surely a signal passing through space-time had to deal with interference, which could have come from any time between now and 2125, or the emptiness that existed outside of time and the cosmos.

'Are you still in Shanghai?' he asked his future self.

'Yes.'

'I can't hear anything. Maybe all your cars are electric and practically silent.'

'The cars are all in the tunnels, which is why you can't hear them.'

'Tunnels? What do you mean?'

'Shanghai is now underground.'

The moon disappeared behind the building, and everything darkened. He felt himself sinking into the earth. 'What happened?'

'The surface is full of radiation. You'll die if you stay up there for a few hours without protection. And it'll be an ugly death, with blood seeping all over your skin—'

'Radiation! What are you talking about?'

'The sun. Yes, you've succeeded. Geoelectric power grew even faster than the silicon plow, and by 2020, the geoelectricity extraction industry had outgrown the coal and oil industries combined. As it matured, the efficiency and cost of this technology couldn't be matched even by the silicon plow, let alone fossil fuels. The world's energy needs soon grew to be entirely dependent on geoelectricity. It was clean, cheap, and so perfect that many wondered how it had taken humanity thousands of years after the invention of the compass to finally think of drawing upon the giant dynamo beneath our feet. As the economy soared on the wings of this sustainable energy source, the environment also improved. Humanity believed that our civilization had finally achieved the dream of effortless growth, and the future would only get better.'

'And then?'

'At the beginning of this century, geoelectricity suddenly ran out. Compasses no longer pointed north. I'm sure you know that the Earth's electric field is our planet's shield. It deflects the solar wind and protects our atmosphere. But now, the Van Allen belts are gone, and the solar wind buffets the Earth like a petri dish placed under an ultraviolet light.'

He tried to speak, but only a croak emerged from his throat. He felt chills all over.

'This is only the start. Over the next three to five centuries, the solar wind will destroy the Earth's atmosphere, boil away the ocean and all other surface water.'

Another inarticulate croak.

'We've finally achieved a breakthrough in controlled nuclear fusion, and together with the reconstructed oil and coal industries, humanity now possesses inexhaustible sources of energy. Most of the power we generate, however, is pumped into the Earth to restart the magnetic field. So far the results are not encouraging.'

'We have to fix it!'

'Yes, that's right. You must delete both emails from the future.'

He turned to head back inside. 'I'll do it right now.'

'Just a minute. Once you delete them, history will change again, and our connection will break off.'

'Right. The world will return to its original timeline of fossil fuel dominance.'

'And you'll go on with your life as before.'

'Please, tell me about our life after this moment.'

'I can't. Telling you will change the future.'

'I understand that knowing the future will change it. But I still want to know a few things.'

'Sorry. I can't.'

'How about just tell me if we'll be living the life we wanted? Are we happy?'

'I can't.'

'Will I get married? Kids? How many boys and girls?'

'I can't.'

'After Wen, will I fall in love again?'

He thought his future self was going to refuse to answer again, but the voice remained silent. All he could hear was the hissing of the winds of time through the empty valley of more than a century dividing them. Finally, he heard the answer.

'Never again.'

'What? I won't love again for more than a hundred years?'

'No. A life is not unlike the history of all of humanity. The choice presented to you the first time may also be the best, but there's no way to know without traveling down other timelines.'

'So I'll be alone all my life?'

'I'm sorry, I can't tell you. ... Though loneliness is the human condition, still we must conduct our lives with grace and strive for joy. It's time.'

Without another word, the call ended. His phone dinged, signaling a text. Attached to the message was a short video, which he copied to his computer to be able to see better.

A sea of flames dominated the screen. It took a while for him to understand that he was looking at the sky. The fiery lights weren't from burning fire, but auroras that filled the firmament from horizon to horizon, generated by solar wind particles striking the atmosphere. Billowy red curtains convulsed across the vault of heaven like a mountain of snakes. The sky seemed to be made of some liquid, a terrifying sight.

There was a single building resembling a stack of spheres on the ground: the Oriental Pearl Tower. The mirrored surfaces reflected the fiery sea above, and the spheres themselves seemed to be made of flames. Closer to the camera stood a man dressed in a heavy protective suit whose surface was brightly reflective and smooth, like a man-shaped mirror. The heavenly fire was reflected in this man-mirror as well, and the flame snakes, distorted by the curved surfaces, appeared even more eerie.

The entire scene flowed and shimmered as though the world had turned to molten lava. The man raised a hand toward the camera, saying hello and goodbye to the past at once.

The video ended.

Was that me?

Then he remembered that he had more important tasks. He deleted the emails and all attachments. Then, after a moment, he began to reformat the disk and zero out the sectors with multiple passes.

By the time the reformatting had completed, it was just another ordinary night. The man who had changed the course of human history three times in a single night but who in the end had changed nothing fell asleep in front of his computer.

Dawn brightened the eastern sky. The world began another ordinary day. Nothing had happened, at all.

CURSE 5.0

Curse 1.0 was born on 8 December 2009.

It was the second year of the financial crisis. The crisis was supposed to end quickly; no one expected it was only just beginning. Society was mired in anxiety. Everyone needed to let off steam, and they poured their energies into creating new ways to do so. Perhaps the Curse was a product of this prevailing mood.

The author of the Curse was a young woman aged between eighteen and twenty-eight. That was all the information that later IT archaeologists could uncover about her.

The target of the Curse was a young man of twenty years old. His personal details were well-documented. His name was Sa Bi,* and he was a fourth-year student at Taiyuan University of Technology. Nothing extraordinary had occurred between him and the young woman, just the usual garden-variety drama that afflicts young men and women. Later there were thousands of versions of the story, and perhaps one of them was true, but no one had any way of knowing what had actually transpired between this couple. In any case, after things ended between them the young woman felt only bitter hatred toward the young man, and so she wrote Curse 1.0.

The young woman was an expert programmer, although it is not known where and how she learned her craft. In that day and age, despite the ballooning ranks of IT practitioners, the number of people who had truly mastered low-level systems programming had

* The young man was unfortunately named. 'Sa Bi' sounds very similar to the Chinese word for 'stupid asshole'.

not increased. There were *too* many tools available; programming was *too* convenient. It was unnecessary to struggle through line after line of code like a coolie when most of it could be generated directly with existing tools. This was even true for viruses like the one the young woman was about to write. Many hacker tools made creating a virus as easy as assembling a few ready-made modules or, simpler still, slightly modifying a single module. The last big virus before the Curse, the so-called 'Panda Burning Incense' worm, was created in this way. The young woman, however, elected to start from scratch, without the assistance of any tools whatsoever. She wrote her code line by line, like a hardworking peasant weaving cotton threads into cloth on a rudimentary loom. Imagining her hunched in front of a monitor, grinding her teeth and hammering away at the keyboard, brings to mind lines from Heinrich Heine's 'The Silesian Weavers': *Old Germany, we weave your funeral shroud; And into it we weave a threefold curse – we weave; we weave.*

Curse 1.0 was the most widely disseminated computer virus in history. Its success can be attributed to two principal factors. First, the Curse did not inflict any damage on infected host computers. In fact, most viruses lacked destructive intent; the damage they caused was largely the result of shoddy propagation and execution mechanisms. The Curse was perfectly designed to avoid such side effects. Its behavior was quite restrained, and most infected host computers exhibited no symptoms whatsoever. It was only a certain combination of system conditions – present in approximately one out of every ten infected computers – that triggered the virus, and then it only ever manifested on a given computer once. The virus displayed a notification on the screen of an infected computer that read:

>Go die, Sa Bi! ! ! ! ! ! ! ! !

If the user clicked the notification window, the virus would display further information about Sa Bi, informing them that the accursed was a student at Taiyuan University of Technology in Taiyuan, Shanxi Province, China. He was enrolled in the xx Department, was majoring in xx, belonged in Class xx, and lived in Dormitory xx, Room xx. The virus was recorded on the computer's firmware, so even if the user reinstalled the operating system the result was the same.

The second factor underlying the success of Curse 1.0 was its ability to mimic operating systems. This feature was not the young woman's own invention, but she made expert use of it. System mimicry involved editing many parts of the virus' own code to match that of the host system and then adopting behaviors that were similar to normal system processes. When anti-malware programs attempted to eliminate the virus, they risked damaging the system itself. In the end, they simply gave up, like a housewife unwilling to throw a slipper at a mouse sitting next to the good china.

In fact, Rising, Norton and other anti-malware developers had put Curse 1.0 in their sights, but they quickly discovered that pursuing it was getting them into trouble, with even worse consequences than in 2007 when Norton AntiVirus mistakenly deleted Windows XP operating system files. This, coupled with the fact that Curse 1.0 caused no real harm and placed a negligible strain on system resources, led one developer after another to delete it from their virus signature databases.

On the day the Curse was born, science fiction author Cixin Liu visited Taiyuan on business for the 264th time. Although it was the city he hated most in the world, he always paid a visit to a small shop in the red-light district to buy a bottle of lighter fluid for his archaic Zippo lighter. It was one of the very few things he could not buy on Taobao or eBay. Snow had fallen two days prior, and, like always, it was quickly packed down into a blackened crust of ice. Cixin slipped and fell painfully on his backside. When he arrived at the train station, the pain in his ass caused him to forget to move the little bottle of lighter fluid from his travelling bag to his pocket. As a result, it was discovered during the security check, and after it was confiscated he was fined 200 yuan.

He *loathed* this city.

Curse 1.0 lived on. Five years passed, ten years passed, and still it quietly multiplied in an ever-expanding virtual world.

Meanwhile, the financial crisis passed and prosperity returned.

As the world's petroleum reserves gradually dried up, coal's share of the world energy balance rapidly increased. All that buried black gold brought the money rolling into Shanxi, transforming the formerly impoverished province into the Arabia of East Asia. Taiyuan, the provincial capital, naturally became a new Dubai. The city had the character of a coal boss who was terrified of being poor again. In those promising days at the beginning of the century, its denizens wore designer suit jackets over tattered pants. Even as unemployed laborers jammed the city streets day in and day out, the construction of China's most luxurious concert hall and bathhouse continued apace.

Taiyuan had now joined the ranks of the nouveau riche, and the city howled with hysterical laughter at its own wanton extravagance. The skyline of Shanghai's Pudong district paled in comparison to the colossal high-rises that lined Yingze Avenue, and the thoroughfare – second only to Chang'an Avenue* in terms of width – became a deep, sunless canyon. Rich and poor alike flocked to the city with their dreams and desires, only to instantly forget who they were and what they wanted as they tumbled into a vortex of affluence and commotion that churned 365 days a year.

That day, on his 397th trip to Taiyuan, Cixin Liu had gone to the red-light district to buy yet another bottle of lighter fluid. Walking along the city's streets, he suddenly saw an elegant and handsome young man with a distinctive white streak in his long, dark hair. The man was Pan Dajiao, who had started out writing science fiction, switched to fantasy and then finally settled somewhere in between. Attracted by the city's newfound prosperity, Pan Dajiao had abandoned Shanghai and moved to Taiyuan. At the time, Cixin and Pan stood on opposite sides of the soft–hard divide in science fiction. This chance meeting was a delightful coincidence.

Tucked away in a *tounao*** restaurant and flushed with liquor, Cixin chattered excitedly about his next grand endeavor. He planned to write a ten-volume, three-million-character sci-fi epic describing the two thousand deaths of two hundred civilizations in a universe repeatedly wiped clean by vacuum collapses. The tale would conclude with the entire known universe falling into a black hole, like water draining from a toilet bowl. Pan was captivated, and he raised the

* The thoroughfare that runs east-to-west through Beijing just north of Tiananmen Gate.

** A traditional local lamb soup.

possibility of collaboration: working from the same concept, Cixin would write the hardest possible science fiction edition for male readers, while Pan would write the softest possible fantasy edition for female readers.

Cixin and Pan got on like a house on fire and immediately abandoned all worldly affairs in favor of feverish creation.

As Curse 1.0 turned ten years old, its final day drew near.

After Vista, Microsoft was hard-pressed to justify frequent upgrades to its operating system, which prolonged the life of Curse 1.0 for a time. But operating systems were like the wives of new-made billionaires: upgrades were inevitable. The Curse's code grew less and less compatible, and it began to sink toward the bottom of the Internet. But just as it lay poised to disappear, a new field of study was born: IT archaeology. Although common sense suggested that the Internet, with less than a half-century of history, lacked any artifacts ancient enough to study, there were quite a few nostalgic individuals who devoted themselves to the field. IT archaeology was largely concerned with uncovering various relics that still lived in the nooks and crannies of cyberspace, like a ten-year-old webpage that had never felt the click of a mouse, or a Bulletin Board System that had not seen a visitor in twenty years but still permitted new posts. Of these virtual artifacts, the viruses of 'antiquity' were the most highly sought-after by IT archaeologists. Finding a living specimen of a virus written over a decade ago was like discovering a dinosaur at Lake Tianchi.

It was in this way that Curse 1.0 was discovered. Its finder upgraded the entire code of the virus to a new operating system, thus ensuring its continued survival.

The upgraded version was Curse 2.0. The woman who had created Curse 1.0 was dubbed the Primogenitor, and the IT archaeologist who rescued it became known as the Upgrader.

The moment at which Curse 2.0 appeared online found Cixin and Pan next to a trash can in the vicinity of the Taiyuan train station. They were fighting over half a pack of ramen that had been fished from the garbage only moments before. They had slept on floorboards and tasted gall for six years, until at last they had produced one three-million-character, ten-volume work of science fiction and one three-million-character, ten-volume work of fantasy. They had titled their works *The Three-Thousand-Body Problem* and *Novantamililands*, respectively. The two men had full confidence in their masterpieces but were unable to find a publisher. So, together, they sold off every last possession – including their houses – borrowed against their pensions and self-published. In the end, *The Three-Thousand-Body Problem* and *Novantamililands* sold fifteen and twenty-seven copies, respectively. This made forty-two copies in total, which sci-fi fans knew was a lucky number. After a grand signing session in Taiyuan – also at personal expense – the two men began their careers as drifters.

There was no city friendlier to vagrants than Taiyuan. The trash cans of the profligate metropolis were an inexhaustible source of food. At worst, it was always possible to find a few discarded nine-to-five pills. Finding a place to live was not much of a problem, either. Taiyuan modeled itself after Dubai, and each of its bus stops was equipped with heating and air conditioning. If they grew tired of the streets, it was simple enough to spend a few days in a shelter. There they would receive more than just food and lodging; Taiyuan's thriving sex industry had answered the government's call and designated every Sunday as a Day for Sexual Aid to Vulnerable Groups. The shelters were popular locations at which volunteers from the red-light district conducted their charitable activities. In the city's official Social Happiness Index, migrant beggars ranked first. Cixin and Pan rather regretted that they had not adopted this lifestyle earlier.

The weekly invitations from the *King of Science Fiction* editorial department were by far the most pleasant occasions in their new lives. They usually went somewhere fancy, like Tang Dou Restaurant. *King of Science Fiction* had grasped the essence of what it meant to be a sci-fi magazine. The soul of this literary vehicle was wonder and alienation, but high-tech fantasies had lost the ability to evoke those feelings. Technological miracles were trite: they happened every day. It was low-tech fantasies that awed and unsettled modern readers. So the editors developed a subgenre known as 'counter-wave science fiction' that imagined an unsophisticated future era. Its enormous success ushered in a second golden age of science fiction. In an effort to embrace the spirit of counter-wave science fiction, the *King of Science Fiction* editorial department rejected computers and the Internet wholesale. They accepted only handwritten manuscripts and adopted letterpress printing. They bought dozens of Mongolian steeds at the price of one BMW per horse and built a luxurious stable next to the editorial office. The magazine's staff only rode steeds that had never surfed the web. The clip-clop of horseshoes around the city signaled the imminent approach of an SFK company man.

The editors often invited Cixin and Pan to dinner. In addition to being a sign of respect for the stories they had written in the past, this gesture was also in acknowledgement of the fact that, while the science fiction they wrote now could hardly be called science fiction, their adherence to counter-wave science fiction principles was *very* science fiction. They lived completely offline; low-tech indeed.

Neither Cixin, nor Pan, nor the SFK staff could ever have guessed that this mutual quirk would save their lives.

Curse 2.0 thrived for another seven years. Then, one day, the woman who became known as the Weaponizer found it. She carefully studied the code of Curse 2.0. She could sense the hatred and bile the Primogenitor had woven into its code even seventeen years old and in its upgraded form. She and the Primogenitor had had the same experience, and she, too, hated a man so much it made her teeth ache. But she thought the other young woman was pathetic and laughable: what was the point? Had it touched a hair on the head of that jerk Sa Bi? The Primogenitor was like the scorned maidens of the last century, sticking pins into little cloth effigies. Silly little games could solve nothing and would only make her sink deeper into depression. But Big Sister was here to help. (In fact, the Primogenitor was almost certainly still alive, but given their age difference the Weaponizer should have called her Auntie.)

Seventeen years had passed since the birth of the Curse, and a new era had arrived – the entire world was caught in the web. Once, only computers had been connected to the Internet, but the Internet of the present was like a spectacular Christmas tree, festooned and blinking with almost every object on Earth. In the home, for example, every electric appliance was connected to and controlled by the web. Even nail clippers and bottle openers were no exception. The former could detect calcium deficiencies in nail trimmings and send an alert via text or email. The latter could determine whether the alcohol about to be consumed was legally produced or send notifications to sweepstakes winners. The bottle openers could also prevent users from drinking to excess by refusing to open a bottle until enough time had passed since opening the previous one. Under these circumstances, it became possible for the Curse to directly manipulate hardware.

The Weaponizer added a new function to Curse 2.0:

>If Sa Bi rides in a cab, kill him in a car crash!

In fact, this was hardly a difficult task for the AI programmers of this age. All modern vehicles were already driverless, piloted by the web. When a passenger swiped his credit card to hire a cab, the Curse could identify him via the name on the card. Once Sa Bi was identified as the passenger in a taxi, the ways in which he could be killed were innumerable. The simplest method was to crash the cab into a building or drive it off a bridge. But the Weaponizer decided a simple collision would not do. Instead, she chose a far more romantic death for Sa Bi, one more fitting for the man who had wronged Little Sister seventeen years prior. (In truth, the Weaponizer knew no better than anyone else what Sa Bi had done to the Primogenitor, and it was possible the fault did not lie with him.)

Once the upgraded Curse learned its target was in the cab, it would ignore his selected destination and burn up the road from Taiyuan to Zhangjiakou, which had become a vast wasteland. The cab would park itself deep in the desert and cut off all communication with the outside world. (By then the Curse would have taken up residence in the onboard computer and would not need the Internet.) The risk of detection was very small. Even if people or other vehicles occasionally drew near, the cab would just hide in another corner of the desert, no matter how much time had passed. The car doors would remain sealed from the inside. That way, in winter Sa Bi would freeze to death; in summer he would bake to death; in the spring or fall he would die of thirst or starvation.

Thus, Curse 3.0 was born, and it was a true curse.

The Weaponizer was a member of a new breed of AI artists. They manipulated networks to produce performance art of no practical significance but of great beauty. (Naturally, the aesthetics of the present era were markedly different from the aesthetics of just a decade before.) They might, for instance, strike up a tune by causing every vehicle in the city to honk simultaneously or arrange brightly-lit hotel windows to form an image on the building's exterior. Curse 3.0 was one such creation. Whether or not it could truly realize its function, it was a remarkable work of art in and of itself. As a result, it received high critical praise at Shanghai Biennale 2026. Even though the police declared it illegal due to its intent to cause bodily harm, it continued to percolate through the web. A multitude of other AI artists joined in the collective creation. Curse 3.0 evolved rapidly as more and more functions were added to its code:

>If Sa Bi is at home, suffocate him with gas fumes!

This was relatively easy, as the kitchen in every household was controlled via the web, which allowed homeowners to prepare meals remotely. Naturally, this included the ability to turn on the gas, and Curse 3.0 could disable the hazardous gas detectors in the room.

>If Sa Bi is at home, kill him with fire!

This, too, was straightforward. In addition to the gas, there were many things in every household that could be set alight. For example, even mousse and hairspray were connected to the web (which allowed a professional stylist to do one's hair without leaving their own home). Fire alarms and extinguishers could, of course, be made to fail.

>If Sa Bi takes a shower, kill him with scalding water!

Like the other methods above, this was a piece of cake.

>If Sa Bi goes to the hospital, kill him with a toxic prescription!

This was slightly more complicated. It was simple enough to prescribe a specific medicine to a target; pharmacies in modern hospitals dispensed prescriptions automatically, and their systems were connected to the web. The key issue was the packaging of the medication. Sa Bi, despite his name, was no fool, and the plan fell apart if he was unwilling to take the medicine. To achieve its end, Curse 3.0 had to trace medicine back to the factory where it was produced and packaged and then follow it down the sales chain. Ensuring that the fatal drug was sold to the target was complicated, but feasible. And for the AI artists, the more complicated it was the more beautiful the finished product would be.

>If Sa Bi gets on plane, kill him!

This was not easy. It was significantly more difficult than taking control of a cab, because only Sa Bi had been cursed and Curse 3.0 could not kill others. Since it was unlikely Sa Bi had a personal jet, crashing a plane carrying him was not an option. But there was an alternative solution: any plane that Sa Bi boarded would suffer a sudden loss of cabin pressure (by opening a cabin door or some other method). Then, when all of the passengers put on their oxygen masks, only Sa Bi's mask would fail.

>If Sa Bi eats, choke him to death!

This sounded absurd but was actually quite simple to implement. The superfast pace of modern society had given rise to superfast food: a small pill known as a 'nine-to-five' pill. Nine-to-five pills were incredibly dense and felt weighty like a bullet in the hand. Once ingested, the pills would expand in the stomach, like hardtack. The key was to tamper with the manufacturing process to produce a rapidly-expanding pill; then the Curse could control the sales process to ensure Sa Bi was the one who bought it. As soon as he popped the pill on his lunch break and washed it down with water, the pill would balloon in his throat.

But Curse 3.0 never found its target and never killed anyone. After the birth of Curse 1.0, Sa Bi had been harassed by strangers and hounded by reporters. He had no choice but to change his given name and even his surname. There were few people surnamed Sa to begin with, and thanks to the name's indecent homophone, there were exactly zero other people in the city named Sa Bi. At the same time, it was not as if Sa Bi had updated his address and place of employment since the Curse. The virus still thought he attended Taiyuan University of Technology, which made it impossible to locate him. The Curse had been outfitted with the function to search for records of its target's name change in the Public Security Department, but its search was fruitless. So in the four years that followed, Curse 3.0 remained nothing but a piece of AI art.

Then, the wildcards appeared: Cixin and Pan.

A wildcard character was an ancient concept, originating from the Age of Mentors (the ancient era of DOS computing). The two most commonly used wildcard characters were '*' and '?'. These two characters could represent one or more characters in a string: '?' referred to a single character, while '*' referred to any number of characters and was the most frequently used wildcard.

For instance, 'Liu*' referred to every person with the surname Liu and 'Shanxi*' referred to every string of characters starting with 'Shanxi'. A single '*' referred to any and all possible strings of characters. Therefore, in the Age of Mentors, 'del*.*' was a most wicked command because 'del' was a delete command and all file names consisted of a name and an extension separated by a dot. As operating systems evolved, wildcards survived, but as graphical user interfaces began to replace command-line interfaces in popular usage, they gradually faded from the memories of most computer users. In some software programs, however, including Curse 3.0, they could still be used.

The Mid-Autumn Festival had arrived. Next to the glittering lights of Taiyuan, the full moon looked like a greasy sesame seed cake. Cixin and Pan were sitting on a bench in Wuyi Square. They had laid out the goodies they'd scavenged that afternoon: five half-empty bottles of liquor, two half-full bags of Pingyao beef strips, one almost-untouched bag of Jinci donkey meat, and three nine-to-five pills. It was a good haul, and the two were ready to celebrate. Just after nightfall, Cixin had fished a broken laptop computer from a trashcan. He swore he would fix it up, or else a lifetime of working with computers would have been for naught. He squatted next to the bench and set to fiddling with the computer's innards. Meanwhile, Pan continued to air his thoughts about the sexual aid they had received at the shelter that afternoon. Cixin enthusiastically invited Pan to help himself to the three nine-to-five pills in the hopes of scoring a large share of the liquor and meat for himself. But Pan was not fooled, and he skipped the pills altogether.

The computer was soon running again, and its screen emitted a faint blue glow as it booted up. When Pan saw that the laptop had a functioning wireless internet connection, he snatched it from Cixin's hands. He checked QQ first, but his account had long since been deactivated. Next, he checked the *Novoland* website, the Castle in the Sky MMORPG, Douban, the NewSMTH Tsinghua BBS, Jiangdong – but those links were now broken. He threw the laptop aside and sighed: 'Long ago, a man flew away on the back of a yellow crane.'

Cixin, who had been consolidating the bottles of liquor, glanced at the screen and responded with the next line in the thirteen-hundred-year-old poem: 'And all that is left is the Yellow Crane Tower.' He picked up the laptop and began to carefully examine its contents. He discovered many hacker tools and virus specimens installed on it. Perhaps the laptop had belonged to a hacker and had been ditched in a trashcan as its owner fled from the AI police.

Cixin opened a file on the desktop and found a decompiled C-language program. He recognized it: it was Curse 3.0. Casually skimming through the code, he recalled his own days as a digital poet. As the liquor set to work upon his brain, he browsed the target identification section of the code. At his side, Pan was prattling on about the towering science fiction of bygone years, and Cixin was soon infected with nostalgia. He pushed the laptop away and joined Pan in reminiscing. Those were the days! His omniscient, virile epics of destruction had struck chords with so many young men, had made their hearts overflow with martial and dogmatic fervor! But now, fifteen copies . . . he had sold only fifteen copies! Fuck! He took a big swig from his bottle. The flavor was no longer recognizable but its alcohol content was unmistakable. Cixin was overcome with a hatred for male readers, and then all men. He fixed a loathsome stare on the target parameters of Curse 3.0. 'Nowerdays there snotta single deshent man alive,' he slurred, as he changed the target name from 'Sa

Bi' to '*'. Then, he changed the occupation and address parameters from 'Taiyuan University of Technology, enrolled in xx Department, majoring in xx, living in Dormitory xx Room xx' to '*, *, *, *, *'. Only the gender parameter remained unchanged: 'male'.

By now, Pan was sniveling alongside him. He thought of the colorful, profound works of his early years, like poems, like dreams. It was not so long ago that his prose had bewitched hordes of teenage girls. He had been their idol. But now, those young women passed him by without a single glance! What an indignity! Hurling away an empty bottle, Pan muttered, 'If men are all rotten, then whad are wimmen?' He changed the gender parameter from 'male' to 'female'.

Cixin would not have it. He had nothing against women; his vulgar novels never stood a chance with female readers anyway. He changed the gender parameter back to 'male', but Pan immediately changed it to 'female' again. The two men began to argue over how to punish their ungrateful, treacherous readers, and Taiyuan's future vacillated between widowhood and bachelorhood. Cixin and Pan began to take wild swings at each other with empty bottles until a patrolman intervened. Rubbing the bumps on their heads, the two men came to a compromise: they changed the gender parameter to '*', thereby completing the wildcarding of Curse 3.0. Perhaps it was the officer's intervention, or perhaps it was their utter inebriation, but three parameters escaped their alterations: 'Taiyuan, Shanxi Province, China.'

Thus, Curse 4.0 was born.

Taiyuan had been cursed.

At the instant of its creation, the new version of the Curse fully understood the grand mission with which it had been entrusted. Because of the immensity of the task before it, Curse 4.0 did not immediately spring to action. Instead, it gave itself time to penetrate and propagate. Once it was thoroughly entrenched throughout the web, it considered its plan of attack: it would start by eliminating soft targets, then transition to hard targets and escalate things from there.

Ten hours later, as the first rays of dawn appeared on the horizon, Curse 4.0 went live.

The Curse's soft targets were the sensitive, the neurotic and the impulsive – in particular, those men and women who suffered from depression or bipolar disorder. In an era of rampant mental illness and ubiquitous psychological counseling, it was easy for Curse 4.0 to find this sort of target. In the first round of operations, thirty thousand individuals who had just undergone hospital examinations were notified that they had been diagnosed with a liver, gastric, lung, brain, colon or thyroid cancer, or leukemia. The most common diagnosis was esophageal cancer (which had the highest incidence rate in the region). Another twenty thousand individuals who had recently drawn blood were informed that they had tested positive for HIV. This was not a matter of simply falsifying diagnostic results. Instead, Curse 4.0 took direct control of ultrasounds, CT scans, MRIs, and blood testing instruments to produce 'genuine' results. Even if patients sought a second opinion at a different hospital, the results would remain the same. Of the initial fifty thousand, most elected to begin treatment. But about four hundred individuals, already weary of life, immediately ended it all. In the days that followed, a steady trickle of people made the same choice.

Soon afterward, fifty thousand sensitive, depressed or bipolar men and women received phone calls from their spouses or significant others. The men heard their wives and girlfriends say: 'Look at you, shit brick. Are you even a man? Well, I'm with [*] now and we are very happy together, so you can go to hell.' For their part, the women heard their husbands and boyfriends say: 'You're really looking your age and, to be honest, you were fugly from the get-go. I have no idea what I ever saw in you. Well, I'm with [*] now, and we are very happy together, so you can go to hell.'

By and large, these fabricated rivals were people the targets already loathed. Of these fifty thousand, most of them sought out their loved one and directly resolved the misunderstanding. But about one per cent elected to kill their partner or themselves, and some did both. The Curse picked out a few other soft targets. For instance, it provoked bloody fights between irreconcilably opposed gangs, and it changed the sentences of criminals serving long terms or life in prison and slated them for immediate execution. But overall, the efficacy of these operations was low, and they eliminated only a few thousand targets in total. Curse 4.0 had the right attitude, though. It knew that great things came from small beginnings. It would shy away from no evil, no matter how small, and it would leave no method untried.

In the initial phase of its plan, Curse 4.0 eliminated its own creator. In the years after she created the Curse, the Primogenitor had maintained a rigorous mistrust of men. She had become a surveillance expert, using the most up-to-date methods to monitor her (unwaveringly faithful) husband for twenty years. So when she received one of *those* phone calls, she suffered a heart attack. Once admitted to the hospital, she was given drugs that further exacerbated her myocardial infarction, and she died at the hand of her own Curse.

The Weaponizer also died in this phase. She received an HIV-positive test result and originally had no intention of killing herself, but she overdosed on anti-anxiety medication. In a drug-induced hallucination, she mistook a window for a gate to a charming garden and tumbled fifteen stories to her death.

Five days later, hard target operations commenced. The abnormally high suicide and homicide rates caused by the preceding soft operations had thrown the city into a panic. But Curse 4.0 was still flying beneath the government's radar, so the first few hard operations were conducted with great secrecy. First, the number of patients receiving the wrong drugs skyrocketed. The medicines were packaged normally, but ingesting a single dose now proved fatal. At the same time, there was a surge in the number of people choking to death at the dinner table. The compression density of nine-to-five pills began to vastly exceed industry standards. Diners, weighing the heavy pills in their hands, thought they were getting great value for their money.

The first large-scale elimination attempt targeted the water supply. Even in a city completely controlled by artificial intelligence, it was impossible to add cyanide or mustard gas directly to the tap water. Curse 4.0 chose to introduce two species of genetically modified bacteria. While harmless on their own, they would produce a deadly toxin when combined. The Curse did not add the two cultures simultaneously; instead, it added one species first, and when most of that culture had cleared from the system the second culture was added. The actual mixing of the two species of bacteria took place inside the human body. As the bacteria met in the stomach or the blood, they would produce the deadly toxin. If the toxin did not prove fatal, when the target was admitted to hospital they would receive medicine that would react with the two bacterial cultures, striking the final blow.

By now, the Public Security Department and the Ministry of Artificial Intelligence Safety had pinpointed the source of the disaster and were frantically developing specialized tools to combat Curse 4.0. In response, the Curse rapidly accelerated and escalated its operations. Its covert machinations became an earth-shaking nightmare.

One day, during the early morning rush hour, a series of muffled explosions echoed beneath the city. It was the sound of trains colliding. Taiyuan had only recently built its subway; the design process had coincided with the city's explosive growth, so it was a highly advanced system. The maglev trains that zipped through vacuum tunnels became known for their incredible speeds. They were nicknamed 'Punctual Portals' – almost as soon as they stepped into the carriage, passengers arrived at their terminal destinations. The trains' speed made for exceptionally violent collisions. The ground swelled and bulged with the force of the explosions, heaving smoke-belching hummocks skyward like angry pustules erupting on the face of the city.

Almost all of the vehicles in the city were now under the control of the Curse. (In this day and age, all vehicles could be piloted by AI.) These were the most powerful tools in the virus' arsenal. All at once, like particles set in Brownian motion, millions of vehicles began to zigzag recklessly all over the city. Though the whole scene looked chaotic, the collisions actually conformed to rigorously optimized patterns and sequences. Each vehicle was instructed to first run down as many pedestrians as possible. With precise coordination, cars herded people through the city streets and closed together in enormous rings in plazas and other open spaces. The largest such formation was in Wuyi Square. Several thousand cars surrounded the square and then rushed towards the center in unison, swiftly eliminating tens of thousands of targets.

When most of the pedestrians had been eliminated or had taken shelter, the cars began to slam themselves against the nearest buildings, killing all passengers still trapped inside. These collisions, too, were precisely organized. Cars would assemble in groups and concentrate their attacks against high-occupancy buildings. Those in the rear would barrel across the pulverized remains of their compatriots, stacking themselves one by one. At the foot of the tallest building in the city, the three-hundred-story Coal Exchange Tower, the cars formed a pile-up that reached ten stories high. The twisted wrecks blazed fiercely, like an immense funeral pyre. The night before the Great Crash, Taiyuan's citizens beheld a peculiar spectacle: the city's taxis had all gathered in long lines to refuel. The virus had guaranteed that their tanks would be full when the moment of disaster came. Now they smashed into buildings like an endless rain of firebombs, fanning the flames ever higher.

The government issued an emergency bulletin declaring a state of emergency and instructing all citizens to remain in their homes. At first, this seemed like the correct response. Compared to the skyscrapers, the Great Crash's assault on residential buildings was minor. The streets of the residential districts were much narrower than the city's main thoroughfares, and soon after the Great Crash began they were completely grid-locked. Instead, Curse 4.0 set about turning each house into a deathtrap. It opened up gas valves, and when the air-to-gas ratio reached an explosive threshold it lit a spark. Row upon row of apartment buildings were engulfed in flames. Entire buildings were blown sky-high.

The government's next step was to cut all power to the city. But it was too late; Curse 4.0 may have been knocked out of action, but it had accomplished its mission. The whole city was in flames. As the inferno strengthened, its ferocity replicated the effect of the firebombing of Dresden during World War II: as the oxygen was sucked from the air, even those who escaped the fire could not escape death.

At this point, the Upgrader was consumed by the flames – the third key figure in the virus' history to fall victim to their own creation.

Because of their minimal contact with the web, Cixin and Pan, together with their vagrant brothers, had managed to escape the early operations of the Curse. As the later operations began, they relied on the skills they had honed from years of roving the city streets to keep themselves alive. With agility that belied their ages, they dodged every car that hurtled towards them. Armed with a deep familiarity with every avenue and alley, they managed to survive the Great Crash. But circumstances soon grew more perilous. As the entire city became a sea of fire, they stood at the center of the four-way intersection near Dayingpan. Suffocating waves of heat billowed down upon them, and flames lashed out from the surrounding skyscrapers like the tongues of giant lizards.

Cixin, who had described the destruction of fictional universes on innumerable occasions, was scared witless. On the other hand, Pan, whose works brimmed with humanist warmth, was calm and collected.

Stroking his beard, Pan looked at the inferno all around them. In drawn-out tones, he mused: 'Who knew . . . that destruction . . . could be so spectacular. . . . Why did I never . . . write about it?'

Cixin's legs buckled beneath him. 'If I had known that destruction was so terrifying, I would not have written so much of it,' he moaned. 'Damn me and my big mouth. This is just perfect.'

Eventually, they came to a consensus: the most gripping destruction was one's own destruction.

Just then, they heard a silvery voice, like the touch of an ice crystal in the sea of flames: 'Cixin, Pan, come quick!' Following the voice, they saw a pair of stallions emerge from the flames like spirits. Two beautiful young women from the SFK editorial department rode atop the horses, their long hair trailing behind them. The riders pulled Cixin and Pan up onto the backs of the horses. Then, like lightning, they took off through the gaps in the blistering sea, vaulting the burning wreckage of cars.

A moment later, the smoke cleared from their vision. The horses had galloped onto the bridge that spanned the Fen River. Cixin and Pan took deep breaths of the clean, cool air. Holding the slender waists of the young women and enjoying the tickle of hair against their faces, the men lamented that their flight had not been longer.

The riders crossed the bridge into safety. They were shortly reunited with the rest of the SFK editorial department, all mounted on powerful steeds. The magnificent cavalry set off in the direction of Jinci Temple, drawing surprised and jealous looks from the survivors fleeing on foot as they passed. Cixin, Pan and the SFK staff spotted a single cyclist among the ranks of the survivors. His presence was noteworthy for a single reason: in this day and age bicycles were connected to and controlled by the web, and the Curse had locked their wheels as soon as it began its assault.

The cyclist was an old man, the man once known as Sa Bi.

Thanks to the Curse's early campaign of harassment, Sa Bi had developed an instinctive fear and abhorrence of the web. He had minimized his exposure to it in his daily life – by riding a twenty-year-old antique bicycle, for instance. He lived on the bank of the Fen River, near the outskirts of the city. When the Great Crash began, he made a break for safety on his absolutely offline bicycle. In fact, Sa Bi was one of the few people at that time who was truly content. He had found satisfaction in a series of romantic affairs, and he was prepared to face death with no complaints or regrets.

Sa Bi and the cavalry crested a mountain on the edge of the city. Standing on the summit, they gazed down at the burning city below. A fierce gale howled through the hills, sweeping in from every direction and down into the Taiyuan basin, replenishing the air lost to the rising heat.

Not far from them, the prominent officials from the provincial and municipal governments were disembarking from the helicopter that had plucked them from the inferno. A draft of a speech still lay tucked inside the mayor's pocket. He had prepared it in advance of the city's anniversary celebrations. Founded in 497 BCE as the capital of the state of Jin, the city had survived the turbulence of the Spring and Autumn period and the Warring States period. During the Tang Dynasty, Taiyuan waxed in importance as a strategic military stronghold in Northern China. The city was razed by Song troops in 979 CE, but it rose again, flourishing throughout the Song, Jin, Yuan, Ming and Qing dynasties. It was not just a city of great military significance but also a renowned hub of culture and trade. The suggested slogan for the city's anniversary festivities was 'Celebrating 2,500 years of Taiyuan!' But now, the city that had survived twenty-five centuries had been reduced to ashes by a sea of flames.

A military radio communications link was briefly established with the central government. The officials were informed that aid was rushing toward Taiyuan from every corner of the country. But communications were soon lost again, and they heard only static. One hour later, they received a report that the rescuers had halted their advance and the rescue planes had turned back to base.

Back at the Shanxi Bureau of Artificial Intelligence Safety, a senior director opened his laptop computer. The screen displayed the most recently compiled version of the virus; Curse 5.0. The target parameters for 'Taiyuan, Shanxi Province, China' now read '*, *, *'.

THE TIME MIGRATION

Where, before me, are the ages that have gone?
And where, behind me, are the coming generations?
I think of heaven and earth, without limit, without end,
And I am all alone and my tears fall down.

Chen Zi'ang (661–702), 'On the Gate Tower at Yuzhou'*

Migration

An Open Letter to All People

Due to insupportable environmental and population pressures, the government has been forced to undertake a time migration. A first group of 80 million time-migrants will migrate 120 years.

The ambassador was the last to leave. She stood on empty ground before an enormous cold-storage warehouse that held four hundred thousand frozen people, as did another two hundred like it throughout the world. They resembled, the ambassador thought with a shudder, nothing so much as tombs.

Hua was not going with her. Although he met all of the conditions for migration and possessed a coveted migration card, he felt an attachment to the present world, unlike those headed toward a new life in the future. He would stay behind and leave the ambassador to travel 120 years on her own.

* Verse translated by Witter Bynner (1881–1968).

The ambassador set off an hour later, drowned by liquid helium that froze her life at near absolute zero, leading eighty million people on a flight along the road of time.

The Trek

Outside of perception time slipped past, the sun swept through the sky like a shooting star, and birth, love, death, joy, sorrow, loss, pursuit, struggle, failure, and everything else from the outside world screamed past like a freight train . . .

. . . 10 years . . . 20 years . . . 40 years . . . 60 years . . . 80 years . . . 100 years . . . 120 years.

Stop 1: The Dark Age

Consciousness froze along with the body during zero-degree supersleep, leaving time's very existence imperceptible until the ambassador awoke with the impression that the cooling system had malfunctioned and she had thawed out shortly after departure. But the atomic clock's giant plasma display informed her that 120 years had passed, a lifetime and a half, rendering them time's exiles.

An advance team of one hundred had awakened the previous week to establish contact. Its captain now stood next to the ambassador, whose body had not yet recovered enough for speech. Her inquiring gaze, however, drew only a head shake and forced smile from the captain.

The head of state had come to the freezer hall to welcome them. He looked weatherworn, as did his entourage, which came as a bit of a surprise 120 years into the future. The ambassador handed over the letter from the government of her time and passed on her people's greetings. The head said little, but clasped the ambassador's hand tightly. It was as rough as his face, and gave the ambassador the sense that things had not changed as much as she had imagined. It warmed her.

But the feeling vanished the moment she left the freezer. Outside was all black: black land, black trees, a black river, black clouds. The hovercar they rode in swirled up black dust. A column of oncoming tanks formed a line of black patches moving along the road, and low-flying clusters of helicopters passing overhead were groups of black ghosts, all the more so since they flew silently. The earth seemed scorched by fire from heaven. They passed a huge hole as large as an open-pit mine from the ambassador's time.

'A crater.'

'From a . . . bomb?' the ambassador said, unable to say the word.

'Yes. Around fifteen kilotons,' the head of state said lightly, as if the misery was unremarkable for him.

The atmosphere of the cross-time meeting grew weighty.

'When did the war start?'

'This one? Two years ago.'

'This one?'

'There've been a few since you left.'

Then he changed the subject. He seemed less like a younger man from the future than an elder of the ambassador's own time, someone to show up at work sites or farms and gather up every hardship in his embrace, letting none slip by. 'We will accept all immigrants, and will ensure they live in peace.'

'Is that even possible, given the present circumstances?' The question was put by someone accompanying the ambassador, who herself remained silent.

'The current administration and the entire public will do all they can to accomplish it. That's our duty,' he said. 'Of course, the immigrants must do their best to adapt. That might be hard, given the substantial changes over one hundred and twenty years.'

'What kind of changes?' the ambassador asked. 'There's still war, there's still slaughter . . .'

'You're only seeing the surface,' a general in fatigues said. 'Take war for example. Here's how two countries fight these days. First, they declare the type and quantity of all of their tactical and strategic weapons. Then a computer can determine the outcome of the war according to their mutual rates of destruction. Weapons are purely for deterrence and are never used. Warfare is a computer execution of a mathematical model, the results of which decide the victor and loser.'

'And the mutual destruction rates are obtained how?'

'From the World Weapons Test Organization. Like in your time there was a . . . World Trade Organization.'

'War is as regular and ordered as economics?'

'War is economics.'

The ambassador looked through the car window at the black world. 'But the world doesn't look like war is only a calculation.'

The head of state looked at the ambassador with heavy eyes. 'We did the calculations but didn't believe the results.'

'So we started one of your wars. With bloodshed. A 'real' war,' the general said.

The head changed the subject again. 'We're going to the capital now to study the issues involved with immigrant unfreezing.'

'Take us back,' the ambassador said.

'What?'

'Go back. You can't take on any additional burdens, and this isn't a suitable age for immigrants. We'll go on a little further.'

The hovercar returned to Freezer No. 1. Before leaving, the head handed the ambassador a hardbound book. 'A chronicle of the past hundred and twenty years,' he said.

Then an official led over a 123-year-old man, the only known individual who had lived alongside the immigrants, and who had insisted on seeing the ambassador. 'So many things happened after you left. So many things!' The old man brought out two bowls from the ambassador's time and filled them to the brim with alcohol. 'My parents were migrants. They left me this when I was three to drink with them when they were thawed out. But now I won't see them. And I'm the last person from your time you'll see.'

After they had drunk, the ambassador looked into the man's dry eyes, and just as she was wondering why the people of this era seemed not to cry, the old man began to shed tears. He knelt down and clasped the ambassador's hands.

'Take care, ma'am. 'West of Yang Pass, there are no more old friends!''*

Before the ambassador felt the supercooled freezing of the liquid helium, her husband suddenly appeared in her fragmented

* A quotation from 'Seeing Off Yuan Er on a Mission to Anxi' by Tang Dynasty poet Wang Wei (699–759).

consciousness. Hua stood on a fallen leaf in autumn, and then the leaf turned black, and then a tombstone appeared. Was it his?

The Trek

Outside of perception, the sun swept through the sky like a shooting star, and time slipped past in the outside world.

. . . 120 years . . . 130 years . . . 150 years . . . 180 years . . . 200 years . . . 250 years . . . 300 years . . . 350 years . . . 400 years . . . 500 years . . . 620 years.

Stop 2: The Lobby Age

'Why did you wait so long to wake me up?' the ambassador asked, looking in surprise at the atomic clock.

'The advance team has mobilized five times at century intervals and even spent a decade awake in one age, but we didn't wake you because immigration was never possible. You yourself set that rule,' the advance-team captain said. He was noticeably older than at their last meeting, the ambassador realized.

'More war?'

'No. War is over forever. And although the environment continued to deteriorate over the first three centuries, it began to rebound two hundred years ago. The last two ages refused immigrants, but this one has agreed to accept them. The ultimate decision is up to you and the commission.'

There was no one in the freezer lobby. When the giant door rumbled open, the captain whispered to the ambassador, 'The changes are far greater than you imagine. Prepare yourself.'

When the ambassador took her first step into the new age, a note sounded, haunting, like some ancient wind chime. Deep within the crystalline ground beneath her feet she saw the play of light and shadows. The crystal looked rigid, but it was as soft as carpet underfoot, and every step produced that wind-chime tone and sent concentric halos of color expanding from the point of contact, like ripples on still water. The ground was a crystalline plane as far as the eye could see.

'All the land on Earth is covered in this material. The whole world looks artificial,' the captain said, and laughed at the ambassador's flabbergasted expression, as if to say, *This surprise is only the beginning!* The ambassador also saw her own shadow in the crystal – or rather, shadows – spreading out from her in all directions. She looked up . . .

Six suns.

'It's the middle of the night, but night was gotten rid of two hundred years ago. What you see are six mirrors, each several hundred square kilometers in area, in synchronous orbit to reflect sunlight onto the dark side of the Earth.'

'And the mountains?' The ambassador realized that the line of mountains on the horizon was nowhere to be seen. The separation between ground and sky was ruler-straight.

'There aren't any. They've been leveled. All the continents are flat plains now.'

'Why?'

'I don't know.'

To the ambassador, the six suns were like six welcoming lamps in a bright hotel lobby. *A lobby!* The idea glimmered in her mind. This was, she realized, a peculiarly clean age. No dust anywhere, not even a speck. It beggared belief. The ground was as bare as an enormous table. And the sky was similarly clean, shining with a pure blue, although the presence of the six suns detracted from its former breadth and depth, so that it more resembled the dome of a lobby. *A lobby!* Her vague idea crystallized: The entire world had been turned into a lobby. One carpeted in tinkling crystal and lit by six hanging lamps. This was an immaculate, exquisite age, contrasting starkly with the previous darkness. In the time immigrants' chronicles, it would be known as the Lobby Age.

'They didn't come to greet us?' the ambassador asked, gazing upon the broad plain.

'We have to visit them in person in the capital. Despite its refined appearance, this is an inconsiderate age, lacking even in basic curiosity.'

'What's their stance on immigration?'

'They agree to accept migrants, but they can only live in reservations separated from society. Whether these reservations are to be located on Earth or on other planets, or if we should build a space city, is up to us.'

'This is absolutely unacceptable!' the ambassador said angrily. 'All migrants must be integrated into society and into modern life. Migrants cannot be second-class citizens. This is the fundamental tenet of time migration!'

'Impossible,' the captain said.

'That's their position?'

'Mine as well. But let me finish. You've just been thawed out, but I've been living in this age for more than half a year. Please believe me, life is far stranger than you think. Even in your wildest imagination you'd never dream up even a tenth of life in this age. Primitive Stone Age humans would have an easier time understanding the era we are from!'

'This issue was taken into consideration before immigration began, which is why migrants were capped at age twenty-five. We'll do our best to study and to adapt to everything!'

'Study?' The captain shook his head with a smile. 'Got a book?' He pointed at the ambassador's luggage. 'Any will do.' Baffled, the ambassador took out a copy of Ivan Aleksandrovich Goncharov's *Frigate Pallada,* which she had gotten halfway through before migration. The captain glanced at the title and said, 'Open at random and tell me the page number.' The ambassador complied, and opened to page 239. Without looking, the captain rattled off what the navigator saw in Africa, accurate to the letter.

'Do you see? There's no need for learning whatsoever. They import knowledge directly into the brain, like how we used to copy data onto hard drives. Human memory has been brought to its apex. And if that's not enough, take a look at this—' He took an object the size of a hearing aid from behind his ear. 'This quantum memory unit can store all of the books in human history – down to every last scrap of notepaper, if you'd like. The brain can retrieve information like a computer, and it's far faster than the brain's own memory. Don't you see? I'm a vessel for all human knowledge. If you so desire, in under an hour you can have it too. To them, learning is a mysterious, incomprehensible ancient ritual.'

'So their children gain all knowledge the moment they're born?'

'Children?' The captain laughed again. 'They don't have any children.'

'So where are the kids?'

'Did I mention that families vanished long ago?'

'You mean, they're the last generation?'

''Generation' doesn't exist as a concept anymore.'

The ambassador's amazement turned to befuddlement, but she strove to understand. And she did, a little. 'You mean they live forever?'

'When a bodily organ fails, it's replaced with a new one. When the brain fails, its information is copied out and into a transplant. After several centuries of these replacements, memory is all that's left of an individual. Who's to say whether they're young or elderly? Maybe they think of themselves as old, and that's why they haven't come to meet us. Of course, they can have children if they desire, by cloning or in the old-fashioned way. But few do. This generation's survived for more than three hundred years and will continue to do so. Can you imagine how this determines the form of their society? The knowledge, beauty, and longevity we dreamed of is easily attainable in this age.'

'It sounds like the ideal society. What else do they desire but can't attain?'

'Nothing. But precisely because they have it all they have lost everything. It's hard for us to understand, but to them it's a real concern. This is far from an ideal society.'

The ambassador's confusion turned to contemplation. The six suns were heading west and soon dipped below the horizon. When only two remained, Venus rose, and then rays of the true sun's dawn spread from the east. Its gentle light gave the ambassador a smidgen of comfort; some things, at least, were unchanging in the universe.

'Five hundred years isn't all that long. Why have things changed so much?' she asked, as much to the whole world as to the captain.

'The acceleration of human progress. Compare our fifty years of progress to the previous five centuries. It's been another five centuries, which might as well be fifty millennia. Do you still think migrants can adapt?'

'And what's the end point of this acceleration?' the ambassador asked, eyes narrowed.

'I don't know.'

'There's no answer to that question in the sum total of human knowledge you possess?'

'The strongest feeling I've gotten from my time in this age is that we're beyond the time when knowledge can explain everything.'

'We'll continue onward!' the ambassador decided. 'Take that chip with you, as well as their device for importing knowledge into the brain.'

The ambassador saw Hua again before entering the haze of supersleep, only a glance after 620 years, a captivating, heartbreaking glance, but it anchored her to home within the lonely flow of time. She dreamed of a cloud of dust drifting over the crystal ground – was this the form his bones now took?

The Trek

Outside of perception, the sun swept through the sky like a shooting star, and time slipped past in the outside world.

. . . 620 years . . . 650 years . . . 700 years . . . 750 years . . . 800 years . . . 850 years . . . 900 years . . . 950 years . . . 1,000 years.

Stop 3: The Invisible Age

The sealed door to the freezer rumbled open and for a third time the ambassador approached the threshold of an unknown age. This time she had mentally prepared herself for a brand-new era, but she discovered that the changes weren't as great as she had imagined.

The crystal carpet that blanketed the ground was still present and six suns still shone in the sky. But the impression given by this world was entirely different from the Lobby Age. First of all, the crystal carpet seemed dead; although there was still light in the depths, it was far dimmer, and footsteps no longer tinkled on its surface, nor did gorgeous patterns appear. Four of the six suns had gone dim, the dull red they emitted serving only to mark their position but doing nothing to light the world below. The most conspicuous change was the dust. A thin layer covered all the crystal. The sky wasn't spotless, but held gray clouds, and the horizon was no longer a ruled line. It all contributed to a feeling that the previous age's lobby had gone vacant, and the natural world outside had begun to invade.

'Both worlds refuse to take migrants,' the advance-team captain said.

'Both worlds?'

'The visible and invisible worlds. The visible world is the one we know, different though it may be. People like us, even if most of them are no longer primarily formed of organic material.'

'There's no one to be seen on the plain, just like last time,' the ambassador said, straining to look.

'People haven't needed to walk on the ground for several hundred years. See—' The captain pointed at a place in the air, where, through the dust and clouds, the ambassador saw indistinct flying objects, little more than a cluster of black dots at this distance. '—those could be planes or people. Any machine might be someone's body. A ship in the ocean, for instance, could be a body, and the computer memory directing it might be a copy of a human brain. People generally have several bodies, one of which is like ours. And that one, although it's the most fragile, is the most important, perhaps due to a sort of nostalgia.'

'Are we dreaming?' the ambassador murmured.

'Compared to this visible world, the invisible world is the real dream.'

'I've got an idea of what that might be. People don't even use machines for bodies.'

'Right. The invisible world is stored in a supercomputer, and each individual is a program.'

The captain pointed ahead to a peak, glittering metallic blue in the sunlight, that stood alone on the horizon. 'That's a continent in the invisible world. Do you remember those little quantum memory chips from last time? It's an entire mountain of them. You can imagine, or maybe you can't, the capacity of that computer.'

'What sort of life is it on the inside, when people are nothing more than a collection of quantum impulses?'

'That's why you can do whatever you please, and create whatever you desire. You can build an empire of a hundred billion people and reign as king, or you could experience a thousand different romances, or fight in ten thousand wars and die a hundred thousand times. Everyone is master of their personal world, and more powerful than a god. You could even create your own universe with billions of galaxies containing billions of planets, each that can be whatever different world you desire, or that you dare not desire. Don't worry about not having the time to experience it all. At the computer's speed, centuries pass every second. On the inside, the only limit is your imagination. In the invisible world, imagination and reality are the same thing. When something appears in your imagination, it becomes reality. Of course, as you said, reality in quantum memory is a collection of impulses. The people of this age are gradually transitioning to the invisible world, and more of them now live there than in the visible world. Even though a copy of the brain can be in both worlds, the invisible world is like a drug. No one wants to come back once they've experienced life there. Our world with its cares is like hell for them. The invisible world has the upper hand and is gradually assuming control of the whole world.'

As if sleepwalking across a millennium, they stared at the quantum memory mountain and forgot about time, and only when the true sun lit up the east as it had for billions of years did they return to reality.

'What's going to come next?' the ambassador asked.

'As a program in the invisible world, it's simple to make lots of copies of yourself, and whatever parts of your personality you dislike – being too tormented by emotions and responsibility, for example – you can get rid of, or off-load for use the next time you need them. And you can split yourself into multiple parts representing various aspects of your personality. And then you can join with someone else to form a new self out of two minds and memories. And then you can join with several or dozens or hundreds of people. . . . I'll stop before I drive you mad. Anything can happen at any time in the invisible world.'

'And then?'

'Only conjecture. The clearest signs point to the disappearance of the individual; everyone in the invisible world will combine into a single program.'

'And then?'

'I don't know. This is a philosophical question, but after so many times thawing out I'm afraid of philosophy.'

'I'm the opposite. I've become a philosopher now. You're right that it's a philosophical question and needs to be studied from that standpoint. We really should have done that thinking long ago, but it's not yet too late. Philosophy is a layer of gauze, but at least for me, it's been punctured, and in an instant, or practically an instant, I know what lies on the road ahead.'

'We need to terminate our migration in this age,' the captain said. 'If we continue onward, migrants will have an even harder time adapting to the target environment. We can rise up and fight for our own rights.'

'That's impossible. And unnecessary.'

'Do we have any other choice?'

'Of course we do. And it's a choice as clear and bright as the sun rising in front of us. Call out the engineer.'

The engineer had been thawed out together with the ambassador and was now inspecting and repairing the equipment. His frequent thaws had turned him from a young man to an old one. When the confused captain called him out, the ambassador asked, 'How long can the freezer last?'

'The insulation is in excellent condition, and the fusion reactor is operating normally. In the Lobby Age, we replaced the entire refrigeration equipment with their technology and topped up the fusion fuel. Without any equipment replacement or other maintenance, all two hundred freezer rooms will last twelve thousand years.'

'Excellent. Then set a final destination on the atomic clock and put everyone into supersleep. No one is to wake up until that destination is reached.'

'And that destination is . . .'

'Eleven thousand years.'

Again, Hua entered the ambassador's fragmented consciousness, more real than ever: his dark hair floated about in the chill wind, his eyes wet with tears, and he called out to her. Before she entered the void of unconsciousness, she said to him, 'Hua, we're coming home! We're coming home!'

The Trek

Outside of perception, the sun swept through the sky like a shooting star, and time slipped past in the outside world.

. . . 1,000 years . . . 2,000 years . . . 3,500 years . . . 5,500 years . . . 7,000 years . . . 9,000 years . . . 10,000 years . . . 11,000 years.

Stop 4: Back Home

This time, even in supersleep time felt endless. Over the long ten-thousand-year night, the hundred-century wait, even the computer steadfastly controlling the world's two hundred superfreezers went to sleep.

During the final millennium, parts began to fail, and one by one its myriad sensor-eyes closed, its integrated circuit nerves paralyzed, its fusion reactor energy petered out, leaving the freezers holding at zero through the final decades only by virtue of their insulation. Then the temperature began to rise, quickly reaching dangerous levels, and the liquid helium began to evaporate. Pressure rose dramatically inside the supersleep chambers, and it seemed as if the eleven-thousand-year trek would terminate unconsciously in an explosion.

But then, the computer's last remaining set of open eyes noticed the time on the atomic clock, and the tick of the final second called its ancient memory to send out a weak signal to boot up the wake-up system. A nuclear magnetic resonance pulse melted the cellular liquid within the bodies of the advance-team captain and a hundred squad members from near absolute zero in a fraction of a second, and then elevated it to normal body temperature. A day later they emerged from the freezer. A week later, the ambassador and the entire migration commission were awakened.

When the huge freezer door was open just a crack, a breath of wind came in from the outside. The ambassador inhaled the outside air; unlike that of the previous three ages, it carried the scent of flowers. It was the smell of springtime, of home. She was practically certain that the decision she made ten thousand years ago was the correct one.

The ambassador and the commissioners crossed into the age of their final destination.

The ground beneath their feet was covered in green grass as far as the eye could see. Just outside the freezer door was a brook of clear water in which beautiful, colored stones were visible on the riverbed and fish swam leisurely. A few young advance-team members washed their faces in the brook, where mud covered their bare feet and a light breeze carried off their laughter. A blue sky held snow-white clouds and just one sun. An eagle circled languidly and smaller birds called. In the distance, the mountain range that had vanished ten thousand years ago during the Lobby Age was back again against the sky, topped with a thick forest . . .

To the ambassador, the world before them seemed rather bland after the previous three ages, but she wept hot tears for its blandness. Adrift for eleven thousand years, she – and all of them – needed this, a world soft and warm as goose down into which they could lay their fractured, exhausted minds.

The plain held no signs of human life.

The advance-team captain came over to face the focused attention of the ambassador and the commissioners, the stare of the day of judgment for humanity.

'It's all over,' he said.

Everyone knew the significance of his words. They stood silent between the sacred blue sky and green grass as they accepted this reality.

'Do you know why?' the ambassador asked.

The captain shook his head.

'Because of the environment?'

'No, not the environment. It wasn't war, either. Nor any other reason we can think of.'

'Are there any remains?'

'No. They left nothing behind.'

The commissioners gathered round and launched into an urgent interrogation:

'Any signs of an off-world migration?'

'No. All nearby planets have returned to an undeveloped state, and there are no signs of interstellar migration.'

'There's really nothing left behind? No ruins or records of any kind?'

'That's right. There's nothing. The mountains were restored using stone and dirt extracted from the ocean. Vegetation and the ecology have returned nicely, but there's no sign of any work by human hands. Ancient sites are present up to one century before the Common Era, but there's nothing more recent. The ecosystem has been running on its own for around five thousand years, and the natural environment now resembles the Neolithic period, although with far fewer species.'

'How could there be nothing left?'

'There's nothing they wanted to say.'

At this, they all fell silent.

Then the captain said to the ambassador, 'You anticipated this, didn't you? You must have thought of the reason.'

'We can know the reason, but we'll never understand it. It's a reason rooted deeply in philosophy. When their contemplation of existence reached its highest point, they concluded that nonexistence was the most rational choice.'

'I told you that philosophy scares me.'

'Fine. Let's drop philosophy for the moment.' The ambassador took a few steps forward and turned to face the commission.

'The migrants have arrived. Thaw them all out!'

A last burst of powerful energy from the two hundred fusion reactors produced an NMR pulse to thaw out eighty million people. The next day, humanity emerged from the freezers and spread out onto continents that had been unpeopled for thousands of years. Tens of thousands gathered on the plain outside Freezer No. 1 as the ambassador stood facing them on a huge platform before the entrance. Few of them were listening, but they spread her words to the rest like ripples through water.

'Citizens, we had planned to travel one hundred and twenty years but have arrived here at last after eleven thousand. You have now seen everything. They're gone, and we're the only surviving humans. They left nothing behind, but they left everything behind. We've been searching for even a few words from them since awaking, but we've found nothing. There's nothing at all. Did they really have nothing to say? No! They did, and they said it. The blue sky, the green earth, the mountains and forests, all of this re-creation of nature is what they wanted to say. Look at the green of the land: This is our mother. The source of our strength! The foundation of our existence and our eternal resting place! Humanity will still make mistakes in the future, and will still trek through the desert of misery and despair, but so long as we remain rooted in Mother Earth we won't disappear like they did. No matter the difficulty, life and humanity will endure. Citizens, this is our world now, and we embark on a new round for humanity. We begin with nothing except all that humanity has to offer.'

The ambassador took out the quantum chip from the Lobby Age, and held that sum total of human knowledge up for everyone to see. Then, she froze as her eyes were drawn to a tiny black dot flying swiftly over the crowd. As it drew near, she saw the black hair she'd glimpsed countless times in her dreams, and the eyes that had turned to dust a hundred centuries ago. Hua had not remained eleven thousand years in the past, but had come after her in the end, crossing the ceaseless desert of time in her wake. When they embraced, sky, earth, and human became one.

'Long live the new life!' someone shouted.

'Long live the new life!' resounded the plain. A flock of birds flew overhead, singing joyously.

At the close of everything, everything began.

EXTENDED COPYRIGHT

'Ode to Joy.' English translation by William F. Wertz in *Friedrich Schiller Poet of Freedom Vol. 1.*, published by The Schiller Institute.

Of Ants and Dinosaurs, first published in the UK in 2020 by Head of Zeus, part of Bloomsbury Publishing Plc, copyright © 2010 刘慈欣 (Liu Cixin), English translation copyright © 2019 FT Culture (Beijing) Co., Ltd. Co-published by Chongqing Publishing House Co., Ltd. Translation by Elizabeth Hanlon.

重慶出版社

'Fibers'; 'Glory and Dreams': *The Collected Stories*, first published in the UK in 2025 by Head of Zeus, part of Bloomsbury Publishing Plc, copyright © 2025 刘慈欣 (Liu Cixin), English translation copyright © 2025 by FT Culture (Beijing) Co., Ltd. Translation by Jesse Field.

'Moonlight': *Broken Stars*, first published in the United States of America in 2019 by Tor Books, a registered trademark of Macmillan Publishing Group, LLC. English text © 2017 刘慈欣 (Liu Cixin) and Ken Liu. Used with permission from FT Culture (Beijing) Co., Ltd. First published in the UK in 2019 by Head of Zeus, part of Bloomsbury Publishing Plc. Translation by Ken Liu.

'The Circle': First English publication: *Carbide Tipped Pens*, eds. Ben Bova and Eric Choi, 2014 (Tor Books). English text © 2014 刘慈欣 (Liu Cixin) and Ken Liu. First published in the UK in *Invisible Planets* in 2016 by Head of Zeus, part of Bloomsbury Publishing Plc. Translation by Ken Liu.

Cixin Liu, photography copyright © Li Yibo

ABOUT THE AUTHOR

CIXIN LIU is China's #1 SF writer and author of *The Three-Body Problem* – the first ever translated novel to win a Hugo Award. Prior to becoming a writer, Liu worked as an engineer in a power plant in Yangquan.

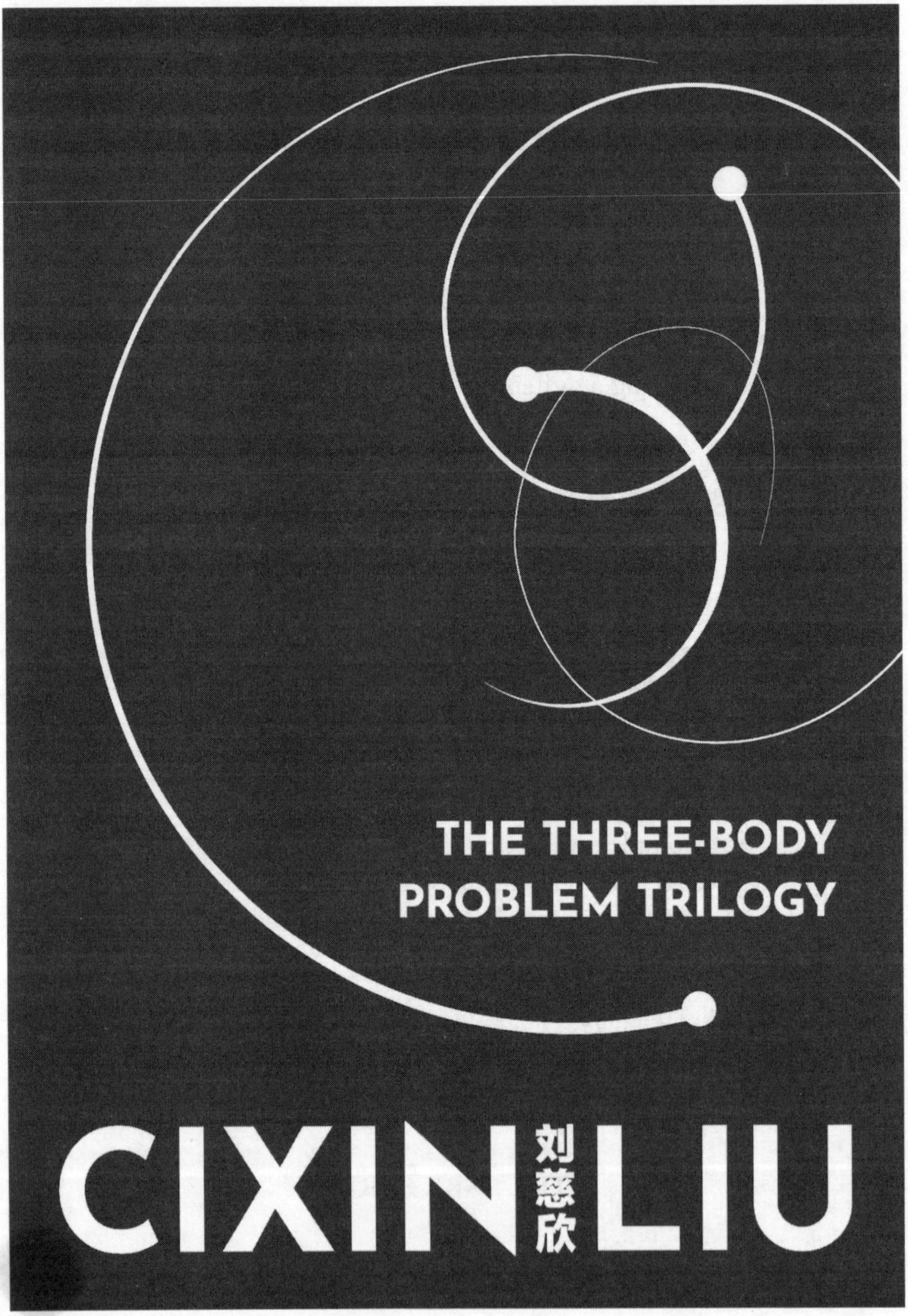
THE THREE-BODY
PROBLEM TRILOGY
CIXIN 刘慈欣 LIU

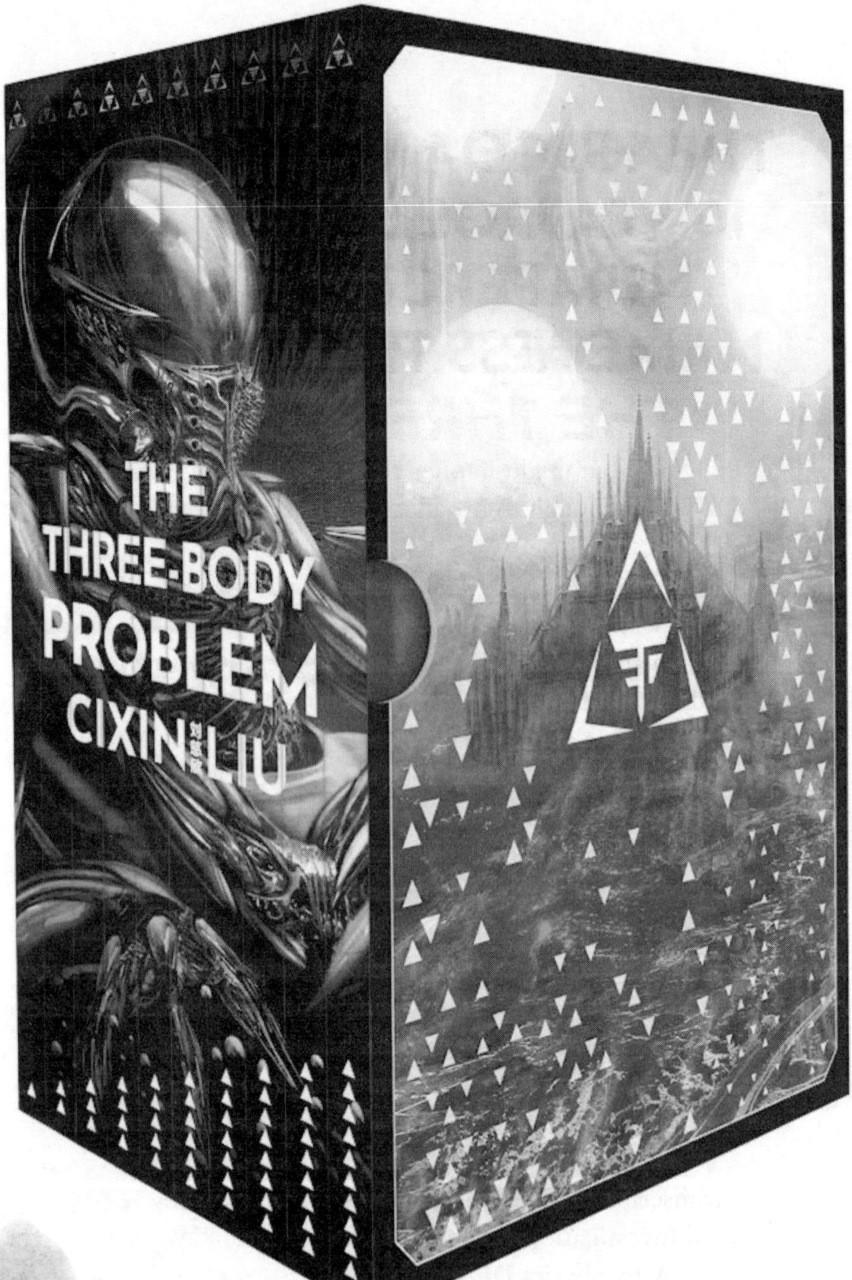

£100 • 1924 pages • ISBN: 9781035912421

THE HUGO-NOMINATED, 10-VOLUME, 1,924-PAGE GRAPHIC NOVEL ADAPTATION OF *THE THREE-BODY PROBLEM*.

'*The Three-Body Problem* was originally published as a novel, but while I was writing it, I began to suspect that words weren't necessarily the best way of telling a science fiction story. When we use words to describe the world, we rely on shared memories of reality to conjure a picture in the reader's mind. But in the realms of science fiction, where there are many things that have never appeared in the real world, words alone are not always enough to accurately, or vividly, transmit the author's imagination. A decade after its original publication, *Three-Body* gains new life in these pages. I am now convinced that the graphic novel provides the broadest possible canvas for science fiction. Regardless of whether you have read the original or not, this version of *The Three-Body Problem* will be a brand new reading experience for you.'

CIXIN LIU

Three-Body archive material included:
a transcript of Ye Wenjie's interview by the Beijing PSB Criminal Investigation Detachment; an abstract of Ye Wenjie's paper in Astrophysics Review; partially decrypted files sized from ETO, and much more.